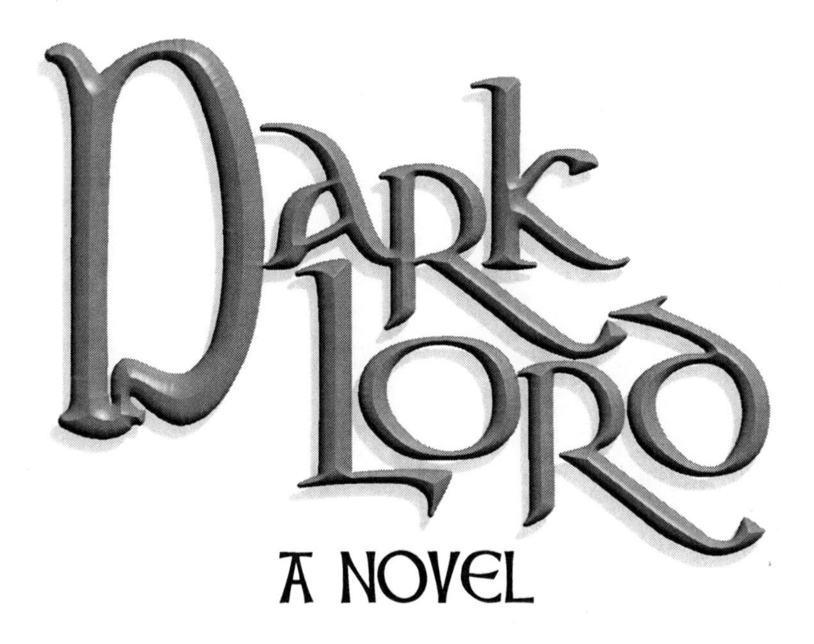

A NOVEL

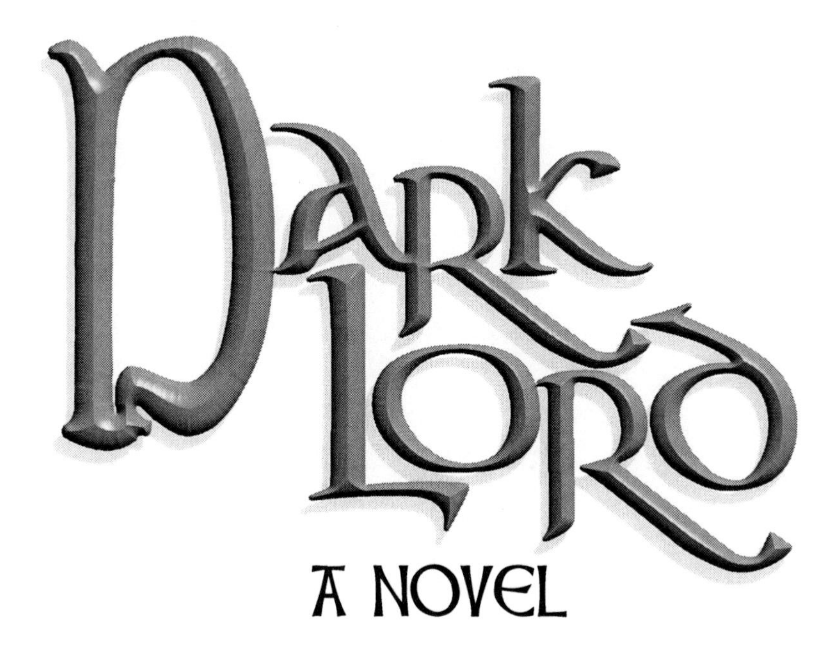

A NOVEL

JEANNE TREAT

AN
AHEAD OF THE HANGMAN PRESS
BOOK
PUBLISHED BY
TREAT ENTERPRISES, INC.

www.darklordthenovel.com

SECOND EDITION
CREATE SPACE

ISBN 978-1466460256

Manufactured in the United States of America

This work is fictional. Some characters' names and the events depicted in this novel have been extracted from historical records, however, neither these characters nor the descriptions of events are held to accurately represent real people or their conduct. Every effort has been made to present readers an exciting, interesting story set in a reasonably authentic environment. No other purpose than entertainment was intended or should be implied.

Cover design by Charles Randolph Bruce- rebelking.com

Interior character drawings by Jane Starr Weils- www.janestarrweils.com

This book is dedicated to my husband, who helped me to realize a dream, to my mother, who told everyone I was an author before it was true, and to dozens of seventeenth century Scots who lived in my head, guiding my pen.

SYNOPSIS

Dark Lord is the sequel to Dark Birthright. It opens less than six months after the conclusion of Dark Birthright, with all your favorite characters. Set during a time of political and religious strife, it features action, magic, romance, and politics. The author recommends that you reread book one. It lays the groundwork for this novel.

It's 1637 in Scotland. Dughall is settling into his new role when the King imposes an Anglican liturgy book on the Scottish church. Protests and riots plague the realm, forcing lords and commoners to take a stand. Dughall and Gilbert are placed in precarious positions, torn between loyalty to the crown, their families, and zealous subjects. To complicate matters, Dughall claims the sword of Red Conan and inherits the curse that comes with it. Challenged by real and supernatural enemies, he must fight to continue his line. Conflicts pit brother against brother and father against son. The National Covenant is signed and war breaks out. Tempers run hot and actions are rash. To maintain order, one brother must take Blackheart's place. Which raises the question… Who shall become the Dark Lord?

SCOTLAND
ENGLAND
WALES
L
G
C
J
D
E
F
A
B
I
H
R
S
K
N
M
O
P
T
Q
A- Peterhead
B- Whinnyfold
C- Drake Castle
D- Huntly Castle
E- Forest of Deer
F- Abbey
G- Forres
H- Aberdeen
I- Inverurie
J- Turriff
K- Dundee
L- Moray Firth
M- Edinburgh
N- Glasgow
O- Dunglass Castle
P- Kelso
Q- Dunse Law
R- Stonehaven
S- Dunnottar Castle
T- Jedburgh

SCOTLAND
BERWICK
BIRKS
NEWCASTLE
YORK
WALES
LONDON
ENGLAND

Many people contributed knowledge of their respective fields of expertise and interest to make this a better and more interesting book. I wholeheartedly thank those who gave their time and energies to improve my writing and those who allowed me to use them as models for the character drawings. Among those who went 'the extra mile' are:

Gregory Gumkowski, Heidi Schinas, Robert Davis, Robin Schulmeister, Anne Simon, Phoenix Hunter, and Bertamae Ives – who spent hours proofing the manuscript.

Greg Thrun, who provided me with information about cannons, muskets, artillery, and what it was like to participate in a battle.

Charles Randolph Bruce, Jane Starr Weils, and Susan Treat – artists.

Cecilia "Bunty" Penny - my historian friend from Scotland.

My character models –

Allen Casler (Fang)
Tom Caffarella (Brother Lazarus)
AJ (Lord Montrose)
Jason D. (Alex Hay)
Jillian Davis (Bridget)
Robert Davis (Lord Balmerino)
Sophia Guarrasi-Burns (Sara)
John Grimaldi (Juggler)
Kevin H. (Murdock)
Frank K. (Lord Drake - Dughall)
Doris K. (Jenny Geddes)
Gordon M. (General Alexander Leslie)
Ashley T. (Keira)
Kyle T. (Lord Aboyne)
Valerie Zaprzal (Mary Hay)

Lord Dughall
on Black Lightning

Chapter 1
Return to Huntly

June 16th 1637

TWO MILES FROM HUNTLY CASTLE
ABERDEENSHIRE SCOTLAND

It was a perfect summer day in the Highlands. Trees and wildflowers were in bloom and heather covered the hills and moors. A gentle breeze rustled leaves and rippled the surface of a stream.

Seventeen-year-old Dughall Gordon, newly recognized Duke of Seaford, rode with a party of three men and one woman through a forest that was familiar. The last time he traveled this path on foot, trying to escape the wrath of his cruel father. Now his father was dead, slain by his own hand, and he was returning to Huntly to attend the wedding of his brother Gilbert. Dughall's senses heightened as he heard the rush of the river Deveron and spotted the tower of the castle. He spurred on his beloved stallion and galloped ahead of his party.

"My Lord!" Jamison cried. "Allow me to accompany ye to the gate." The tall, muscular servant was pledged to defend him to the death. He rarely let him out of his sight.

Dughall pulled on the reins and came to a stop. He longed for simpler times when he was unfettered by so many protectors. "It's all right, friend. Father is dead and my brother is Earl. There's no danger here."

Jamison frowned. "Some blame ye for the Earl's death. The story of the battle spread far and wide and picked up supernatural elements."

Ian Hay brought his mare alongside. "He's right, brother. In a tavern, I heard that ye breathed fire. I nearly choked on my ale."

Dughall's eyes widened. "Well, it's not true. I didn't want to kill him. He gave me no choice."

"We know that," Ian said with a smile. "But some of these folks might not. Murdock says that yer wife needs ye."

Dughall's heart soared as he glanced at his wife, a raven-haired lass with eyes as green as a peacock's feather. She was riding a red mare alongside his faithful servant Murdock, who was driving a cart filled with wedding gifts. "What does she want?"

"I don't know, brother." Ian smirked. "Maybe she wants ye to drop yer breeks and do her right here."

"Ian!"

"The Earl's mistress claims that ye're hung like a horse."

"Oh God."

"Enough, lad!" Jamison said. "Show some respect."

Ian reddened.

Dughall guided his horse to a clearing where Murdock and Keira had stopped.

Murdock was bent over, checking her mare's shoe. He used a stick to clean debris from the hoof and put down the leg. "My Lord. We must ask the blacksmith to shoe this mare. A stone got stuck in there and loosened it up."

Dughall nodded. "Should we walk her the rest of the way?"

Murdock scratched his head. "Aye. The lass can ride in the cart."

"Nay. She can sit on the saddle in front of me. Come on, wife." He dismounted and helped the lass onto Lightning's back, then mounted behind her. The lavender in her hair made him smile.

"Oh husband," she sighed. "I see the castle in the distance. Are we welcome here?"

"Aye, lass. My brother wouldn't have invited us if it wasn't safe." He turned the horse and headed toward Jamison, gripping the reins with one hand.

Keira steadied herself against him. "I wish that Mary could have come along."

"Mother didn't think it wise for her to ride a horse in her condition. She's big for five months. It may be twins."

Keira smiled. "We'll have our hands full delivering those bairnies."

He used the pretense of pulling on the reins to snuggle close to her. In the last few months she'd gained weight, a welcome thing as she'd been too thin when he found her. Perhaps when she gained more her cycles would be regular and they'd be blessed with a bairn of their own.

"Will ye visit the woman who bears yer child?" she asked meekly. "Kate?"

Dughall kissed the back of her head. "I must." He felt her stiffen. "Remember my promise. I will stay faithful to the end of my days."

Keira relaxed in his arms. "Thank ye, husband."

"I need to check on her condition and make plans for her after the birth."

"Will ye send her away?"

"Aye. Gilbert has an idea. Paris, I think."

They reached Jamison and Ian as they were about to negotiate a wooden bridge which crossed the river. Murdock and the cart weren't far behind.

"I'm so excited!" Dughall cried. "I haven't seen Gilbert in months."

"Stay behind us my Lord," Jamison said as he guided his horse onto the narrow bridge. The clopping of hooves on planks snapped in the air. He got to the other side and signaled to Ian, who took his mare across. "*Now* m'Lord," Jamison directed. "Murdock, stay back until he gets across. I don't trust this bridge."

Dughall held his wife close as they crossed the swaying bridge. He remembered the time when he pondered throwing himself into the rushing water and was glad that he changed his mind. Lightning brought them to the other side safely and stepped off the bridge. They waited for Murdock and proceeded along a well-worn path to the gate at Huntly Castle. The imposing granite tower loomed before them as they waited to be recognized. A piercing whistle went up when they were spotted and the gate slowly opened.

***

Dughall recognized the face of Troup, a stocky fellow with large hands who attended the main gate. They'd played chess together on more than one occasion. The man opened the gate wide and bowed deeply.

"Welcome, my Lord. The Earl has been told of yer arrival." He refused to look him in the face.

Dughall detected fear in the man's demeanor. He couldn't understand why he would be afraid. "Troup? Don't ye recognize me?"

The man kept his head low. "Aye, my Lord. Ye're the Duke of Seaford."

"Hmmphh..." Jamison growled. "Let's bring our party through." He fingered his sword, took the first position, and led the procession through the gate.

Dughall glanced back to see a terror-stricken Troup making the sign of the cross in his direction. He swallowed hard, his throat burning with the realization that others saw him differently.

"What's wrong, husband?" Keira asked.

Dughall forced himself to relax. "Nothing, lass."

Stable hands met them to take their horses. They dismounted and unloaded the cart, directing the help to transport the trunks to their quarters. Dughall brushed off his breeks and looked up to see Gilbert walking across the courtyard to meet him. His brother looked well and was wearing a cape with the official brooch of the Earl of Huntly. Connor was at his side, armed and ready to protect his master.

"Gilbert!"

"Little brother! Or should I say the Duke of Seaford?" He took his hand and shook it vigorously, then embraced the young man.

"Little brother is just fine," Dughall said, his heart swelling with the love and respect he had for this man. "Ye look happy."

Gilbert smiled. "Radiantly happy! Tomorrow I marry the woman I love, thanks to ye."

Dughall watched Connor for a reaction, but saw none. "Let's not spread that around," he whispered. "I think there are a few who don't want me here."

Gilbert chuckled. "They're afraid of ye, lad! No one's ever defeated Father in a swordfight. From what I hear ye're quite famous."

The young Lord blushed. "Oh God. I know about the stories."

"All of them?"

Dughall's eyes widened. "Don't tell me. I'd rather not know." He introduced his wife. "Brother. This is Keira."

Gilbert took her hand and kissed it. "My Lady the Duchess. So this is the bonny lass ye waited for." He bowed slightly and released her hand.

Dughall smiled. "'Tis."

"I've situated ye in the guest quarters. Freshen up and meet me in an hour for dinner. Afterwards, we will retire to the study. We have important business to discuss."

Dughall watched him walk away. Jamison, Ian, and Murdock closed ranks around him as they crossed the courtyard, entered the castle, and took the stairs to the wing that housed the guest quarters. The young Lord and his wife entered a bed chamber to freshen up, while Murdock and Ian unpacked the trunks. Jamison stood guard outside his master's chamber to make sure they weren't disturbed.

***

Dinner was a somber affair. Soft candlelight and the tunes of a dulcimer made Dughall relax. He couldn't understand why his men were so jumpy, insisting on carrying weapons and guarding him at all times. Jamison noted that the inhabitants of the castle were fearful and close-mouthed at a time when they should be excited. After all, there was a wedding tomorrow, to be attended by nobles and common folk. Gilbert, Dughall, and Keira ate dinner together, making small talk. Gilbert explained that Bridget would not join them as it was bad luck to see the bride on the eve of the wedding.

The Duke was worried about his brother. In addition to ale, Gilbert drank from a flask of whisky just like their father had. He seemed nervous at times and anxious to finish dinner so they could talk alone. After the meal, Dughall accompanied his wife to their bed chamber and tucked her in. She was exhausted from the ride and needed sleep if she was to attend the wedding. He left Murdock outside the door and walked the long corridor to the study. Fully armed, Jamison and Ian followed and waited outside as he entered.

***

The study was a masculine place, dimly lit with wall sconces. Heavy curtains masked the windows and overstuffed chairs formed a circle. Dughall crossed the room, taking in the scents of spirits and tobacco. As his eyes adjusted to the light, he saw Gilbert sitting in a chair, sipping whisky. His brother opened a crystal decanter and began to pour another glass. "None for me, brother," Dughall said, holding up a hand.

"Why not, lad?"

Dughall sat opposite him. "I promised not to touch the stuff, for the sake of my sons." He watched his brother fill the glass and belt it down. The young Lord hoped that he wasn't sinking into madness like their father.

Gilbert frowned. "Hmmphhh... Have a cigar with me?"

Dughall nodded. "Aye."

Gilbert opened a mahogany humidor and removed two fine cigars. He cut the ends, handed one to his brother, and lit the end of his own with a burning taper.

Dughall accepted the taper and inhaled as he lit the cigar. The taste was rich, and reminded him of cherries and wood smoke. "Not bad. Is this from that island in the Caribbean Sea?"

"Aye."

"What do ye want to talk about?"

Gilbert's hand shook as he poured another glass. He was lifting it to his lips when Dughall reached out and held his wrist.

"Stop, brother." The young Lord took the glass and put it on a side table. "That's yer third in less than a few minutes. What's wrong?"

His brow furrowed. "There's been so much to do. Running the castle and dealing with my subjects."

"I know. Jamison and I have been struggling with the ledgers and keeping the nobles in line. That's part of being a Lord. What's really botherin' ye?"

Gilbert sighed. "I never thought about the unpleasant things I'd have to do as Earl. Father made it look easy."

"What did ye do?"

"I put a man to death yesterday."

Dughall's heart sank. "What did he do?"

"He planned an attempt on yer life." Gilbert balled his fists. "Oh, God. I did something that I thought I'd never do. I let Fang loose on him until I got a confession. I wanted to be sure he was operating alone."

"Oh."

"I was angry. I made a spectacle of him! Hanged him in public in front of his family…" He stared at the glass of whisky like he wanted to drown in it. "At least I didn't kill them. We took the gallows down this morning. God forgive me."

Dughall moved his chair closer and took Gilbert's hands. He understood now why everyone feared him. "I'm sorry, brother. It's not easy to kill a man." His voice was tight. "In spite of what they say, do ye think that I wanted to kill Father?"

Gilbert shook his head. "Nay, lad."

"God won't condemn ye for protecting yer family. But there's something we can do. Let's pray for the man's soul. What's his name?"

"James Adieson. He was one of Father's closest servants."

Dughall bowed his head and took a breath. He felt sorry for the man and worse that it happened on his account. "Heavenly Father, accept the soul of James Adieson into yer kingdom, regardless of what he meant to do. Forgive us for what we had to do to stop him. Perhaps someday we'll understand it. Amen."

Gilbert sniffled. "Amen."

Dughall released his hands. "Now, put away the whisky and get some sleep. Ye're getting married tomorrow."

Gilbert poured the whisky into the decanter and replaced the stopper.

Dughall stared. "Consider giving that up. It's easy to fall into madness when ye see life through a glass of whisky. We both bear the stripes and the tendency to be like him."

Gilbert's eyes widened as they stood and faced each other. "Keep yer men about ye, armed to the teeth. I don't know if I got them all."

Dughall embraced him. "I will. Is there anything else?"

Gilbert sighed. "Aye. Kate wants to talk to ye."

***

Dughall headed to his bed chamber with his mind a jumble of emotions. Jamison and Ian followed close behind, armed with dirks and swords. When they were alone, he told his protectors about the threat on his life and locked himself in his room so the men could plan a defense. It took him a long time to fall asleep. He was tired to the bone, worried about their safety, and anxious about what Kate had to say.

Kate Gunn

CHAPTER 2

KATE

THE NORTHERN FOREST BORDERING HUNTLY CASTLE

It was close to midnight in the well-appointed cottage of the mistress of the former Earl of Huntly. The hearth fire burned steadily, having been recently stoked by a servant. The air was warm and moist and bore the aroma of fresh baked scones.

Kate Gunn relaxed in a comfortable chair, dressed in an imported silk nightgown and a tartan robe. She was deep in thought, contemplating her situation. Since the discovery of her pregnancy, she'd been a prisoner in the cottage. At first, the Earl had allowed her to visit the town, but when he learned that she was seeking to end her pregnancy, he confined her to this place with a dimwitted maid. When word came that the Earl had been killed by his son, her heart soared. She was carrying the young Lord's child and there was nothing to stop them from being together. The next morning, her joy had been tempered by a rumor that he married a peasant lass. She'd gone into a rage and broken every dish in the cottage.

Kate burned with jealousy, yet she knew that she must be practical. *I don't need marriage or this bastard child. When he tires of his wife, I will be his mistress.* She glanced at her belly and smiled. *Perhaps I can do something to hurry that along.*

Kate put her feet up on a stool, exposing her slender legs. She'd gained weight as her pregnancy progressed, but not like most women. Her face was softer and her complexion was good. Some said that she was more beautiful than ever. Her breasts were swollen and her belly was round, but the rest was unaffected. Earlier that day after a bath, she'd examined herself in a full length mirror. "From the back, I don't even look pregnant."

"M'Lady?" The maid servant's ruddy face peeked up from her cot. "Can I get ye anything?" She yawned, presenting a mouthful of cracked yellow teeth.

"Nay, Mary!" Kate made no effort to hide the irritation in her voice. She would be glad when the child was born so that she could lose this stupid woman. "I'm not about to kill myself. Go to sleep!"

The servant rolled over and farted, emitting an odor of stale cabbage.

Kate wrinkled her nose and resumed her thoughts. Lord Gilbert had stopped by to announce that Dughall would be arriving for the wedding. He'd assured her that they'd make plans for her that would be to her liking. That was when she'd made her move, demanding to see the young Lord. She'd begged and cajoled and threatened to deny him the child, until Gilbert finally agreed. He would pass a message to his brother.

I shall see him, she thought, as her cheeks flushed with desire. *I will send Mary on an impossible errand, so that we can be alone. I'm carrying his precious child! He has to listen.* She reached inside her gown and stroked her breast, recalling the times they had together. The man could read her desires. Her hand moved lower, to her place of pleasure. It had been far too long. "I will do what ye want, my Lord," she whispered. "Command me."

As the candles dimmed, she allowed herself to think about her family. Eleven years had passed since she saw them last. At fifteen her father had promised her in marriage to a blacksmith, a cruel man with a scar that disfigured his eye. When she protested, he'd beaten her into submission as her mother looked on. The next day, she knelt before the Earl of Huntly and begged for a position at the castle. House maid, cook, anything would do. Her rare beauty earned her a special place, in the man's bed and at his side. *I showed them, and I arranged for their demise.* Within days, he'd banished her family from Huntly in spite of severe winter weather. For all she knew, they were dead.

At first, the Earl protected her and avenged her brutal treatment. She was smitten by him and expressed her love. He never returned the sentiment, even on a trip to Paris, where he introduced her to his fantasies in a brothel. In a few weeks, she learned the art of bondage, the French practice, and to distinguish between love and desire. The young Lord was different from his father. Seemingly innocent yet sexually intuitive, he'd captured her heart and imagination. He was handsome and giving. How could she let him go? She longed to introduce him to his father's obsessions.

The fire waned and the room grew cooler. Kate could get up and stoke the fire or crawl into a comfy bed. In the end she decided that she needed her beauty sleep. As she stood the baby kicked, making a visible impression against her silk nightgown. She touched her belly and felt the life stir within her. "Wait 'til tomorrow, wee one," she whispered. "Do this for yer father." She had no love for this child and was willing to use it as a bargaining chip.

Bridget

Chapter 3
A Royal Wedding

June 17 1637

HUNTLY CASTLE

Gilbert Gordon woke at dawn with a terrible hangover. His mouth was as dry as a bone and the sheets were damp with sweat. He sat up and massaged his temples, trying to lessen the effects of the whisky. Then he turned and realized that Bridget wasn't there.

Where can she be? He threw back the covers and planted his feet on the cold flagstone floor. It brought him to his senses. "Ach! It's our wedding day."

His stomach twisted as he longed for a stiff drink. The urges were coming earlier in the day. *My brother is right. If this continues, I'll be like Father in no time. I can live without whisky on my wedding day.*

Gilbert's head pounded as he made his way to the chamber pot. He had trouble controlling his urine stream and missed the fancy vessel. "Thank God she's not here to see this." There was a sudden knock at the door, followed by another. The Earl wrapped a towel around his waist and called out in irritation. "Who is it?"

The voice was gruff. "Conner, my Lord."

"It's daybreak. What do ye want?"

"I have something important to tell ye."

Gilbert shuffled to the door and opened it a crack. Connor appeared with disheveled clothes and unkempt hair. He looked like he'd been roused from bed.

"My Lord. Something bad is afoot."

The Earl opened the door and let him in. He went to his chiffarobe, where he dropped his towel and started to get dressed. "God damn it! It's my wedding day. I'm expected at the church at ten. Can they not leave me alone?"

Connor's face was grim. "That's what I must talk to ye about. A tavern keeper came to the gate this morning. He overheard two men planning an ambush at the church after yer nuptials. The Duke is the target."

Gilbert's blood ran cold. "Are ye sure?"

"Aye. That's not all. He said that one of the men was a priest."

He scowled as he tried to pin his kilt. "A priest? That makes no sense. Ach! My fingers don't work."

"My Lord. Can I help ye?"

"Get me something for this bloody headache!"

"A dram of whisky?"

His voice was shrill. "Nay! Send for water laced with willow bark and then wake my brother and his men. Tell them to take up arms and meet us in the dining room."

"As ye wish, m'Lord."

"One more thing! Ask Fang to join us."

Connor's nose wrinkled in disgust. "Fang Adams?"

"Aye! I need to know if Adieson confessed anything about a priest."

"As ye wish."

"Go!"

Connor bowed slightly and left the room.

Gilbert's head throbbed as he sat on a chair and pulled on his socks. Wedding or not, his brother had to be protected. Unfortunately, he didn't know who to trust.

***

Dughall took long strides as he walked to the dining room. At Connor's request, he'd dressed quickly, arming himself with a sword. Jamison, Ian, and Murdock accompanied him, guarding his person with weapons visible. They'd frightened more than one chamber maid. The young Lord's heart pounded as he reached the door of the dining room. He was having misgivings about leaving his wife. "Oh God. I should go back for Keira."

"Nay my Lord," Jamison said, placing a firm hand on his shoulder. "Connor sent a man to guard her. Ye're the one at risk."

Ian agreed. "She'll be all right. Don't frighten her."

Murdock gripped his sword until his knuckles were white. "The lad's right. This is no place for a woman."

They entered the dining room and saw Gilbert at the head of the table. To his right were Connor, Hawthorne, and Morris, all master swordsmen. Fang Adams, the castle's torturer, sat alone at the end of the long table. He smelled like he hadn't bathed in a season. Gilbert motioned for them to sit, and they did. Weapons were brought to their sides or laid on the table.

Dughall was shocked by his brother's appearance. He had dark circles under his eyes. "Are ye all right, brother?"

Gilbert sipped a glass of water. "I'm suffering from a hangover. This bark tea will take care of that." He took another swallow and winced. "We have a situation on our hands. Adieson wasn't acting alone. They plan to assassinate ye at my wedding."

Jamison pounded the table. "I suspected as much! How do ye know?"

"A tavern keeper overheard two men discussing the layout of the church. There's something I don't understand. One of them was a priest."

Dughall swallowed hard. "With white hair?"

Gilbert's eyes widened. "Fang! What did Adieson say?"

Fang picked something off his shirt, dropped it on the table, and watched it crawl away. "He blamed an old priest, but he was half-dead when he said it. Men say all sorts of things with their thumbs in the screws."

"Looks like yer priest. How do ye know him?"

The young Lord reddened. "I had a wee bit of a falling out with the Church. We rescued a man about to be burned alive as a witch."

Gilbert frowned, "Why would ye do that?"

"He was a dear friend of my wife."

"It's a risky thing, interfering with local justice. What's that got to do with the priest?"

Dughall tried to present it in a reasonable light. "He wouldn't release the prisoner to me, even though it was in my jurisdiction. I threatened his person and when that failed, I called his honor into question."

"How so?"

They were quiet for a moment. Ian smirked. "Just a wee accusation about the man fathering his brother's child..."

Dughall rolled his eyes. "Well, it was true!"

Gilbert shook his head, "No wonder he wants ye dead."

Jamison gripped his knife. "My Lord. We should return to Drake."

Gilbert frowned. "That may be their plan, to flush ye out. How well do we know the tavern keeper?"

Connor grunted. "That man would sell himself to the highest bidder, and then sell himself again. We gave him a handful of coins."

"So it could be a trap."

"Aye."

"Hmmphh…" They sat in silence, contemplating their options. Gilbert's shoulders slumped. "Let's move the wedding to the chapel. We will marry in private and limit their opportunities."

Dughall sensed his disappointment. Hundreds of guests were expected at the church. "This is my fault. Allow me to stay here during the ceremony."

Gilbert reddened. "Nay. Best that we don't split our forces." He drummed his fingers on the table, much like his father would have done. "Listen carefully. There's less than three hours before the wedding and we don't know who to trust. Tell no one of the change of plans."

"What about Lady Bridget?"

"I will go to her and explain the situation."

Hawthorne spoke, "It's bad luck to see the bride before the wedding."

Gilbert stared. "Worse luck to see my brother killed on my wedding day."

Conner ran a thumb along the edge of his knife. "What about the guests?"

"Let them gather in town. At the last minute, we'll send for the Bishop and bring him here to marry us. God willing, the guests can join us later for a celebration feast."

"There could be others involved in this attempt," Connor noted, "inside these castle walls."

The Earl pounded the table. "I'm aware of that! My brother is to be protected at all costs. I hold each of ye responsible! Is that understood?"

"Aye, my Lord."

The door opened, admitting serving lasses carrying trays of ham, eggs, bread, and pastries. A lad brought a steaming pot of tea and a pitcher of cream. They placed the food on the table and left the room.

Gilbert made the sign of the cross and folded his hands in prayer. "Heavenly Father. Thank ye for providing this bounty unto us, yer humble servants. Grant us protection from our enemies and give us strength to face what awaits us. Amen."

"Amen."

Dughall looked around the table. His prior deeds cast a shadow on Gilbert's wedding day. He felt responsible for these men and worried about his wife, who would be at his side. *"Great Goddess Morrigan!"* he prayed silently. *"Protect us from harm."*

The men attacked the food with gusto, not knowing if they'd be granted the gift of another day.

***

Bridget Murray stood in the dressing room, enduring the final adjustments to her wedding gown. The tailor kneeled at her feet with a mouthful of pins, tacking the hem. A maidservant attended her, styling her long blonde hair.

Bridget's back was sore. "Are ye almost done? I've been standing here for an hour."

The tailor took the pins out of his mouth. "Forgive me, my Lady. Give me a few minutes more."

Bridget sighed. "All right." She shifted her weight to the other foot and glanced at the clock. In less than an hour she'd marry her beloved, Gilbert Gordon, the Earl of Huntly. Her heart ached as she remembered the last time she saw him. He'd been furious about the plot on his brother's life and acted like his father, torturing and executing the perpetrator. She'd watched from the sidelines as he mounted the platform, threatened his subjects, and ordered the execution. With the body swinging, he left the courtyard and escaped to their chamber, pursued by demons of guilt and shame. She followed at a distance and found him kneeling at the hearth, clutching a rosary and retching on the floor.

Bridget sighed. He'd refused her comfort and curled up in a chair with a bottle of whisky, drinking until he was senseless. Would her beloved fall into madness like his father? How could she tell him that she was with child?

The tailor cleared his throat. "Forgive me, m'Lady. Could ye straighten yer shoulders?"

Bridget brought a delicate hand to her forehead, being mindful of the artfully applied rouge. She stood straight and glanced at the clock. "It's getting late."

"This is the last pin, lass."

"Where is my sister?"

Her maidservant placed a mother-of-pearl comb in her hair. "Julianna is in the corridor. Shall I fetch her?"

"Aye. We need to get to the church."

The servant opened the door and asked Julianna to step inside. The bonny young lass rushed to her sister, bubbling with excitement. "Ye look beautiful in that dress! Oh, sister. Lord Gilbert will be pleased."

Bridget smiled. "Thank ye, lass. Has our carriage arrived?"

Julianna frowned. "I watched from the window, but there's no sign of it."

The tailor stood. "It's done, m'Lady. I'll take my leave now." He bowed slightly and left the room.

Julianna's eyes widened. "I saw the Duke and his men! Carrying knives and swords in the courtyard. It's like they say, he's strong and handsome and hung like a horse."

"Julianna! I'm sure that it wasn't evident."

The girl smiled wickedly. "I bathed him once! He blushed when I touched his member."

"Hush, now. Ye mustn't talk about the Duke that way. Besides, he's married."

Julianna pouted. "She's a skinny thing with hardly any breasts. She'll never bear him an heir."

"Nevertheless, I hear that he loves her."

There was a knock on the door and Gilbert entered. Bridget studied her beloved, trying to read his face. The man was dressed in a fine kilt, a sporran, and cape, but a dirk was visible in his sock. Something was amiss.

Her sister cried out, "Leave this place, my Lord! It's bad luck to see the bride before the wedding."

Bridget frowned. "Julianna. Go into the hallway. I must talk to my future husband alone."

"But, sister…"

Gilbert's voice was harsh. "Go, child!"

The girl pouted, but she obeyed the Earl.

Bridget's heart pounded. Gilbert looked haggard. She hoped he hadn't been drinking. His face softened as he moved closer.

Gilbert took her hand and held it to his heart. "God in heaven. Ye look like an angel."

She blushed. "Oh, Gilbert. What are ye doing here? It *is* bad luck."

He kissed her hand. "We have a situation. Adieson wasn't acting alone. They plan to assassinate my brother at the church."

"Dear God. What must we do?"

"I've sent for the Bishop and his entourage. We'll marry in the chapel."

Her disappointment was palpable. "Oh… I suppose it's the best thing."

He grasped her shoulders gently. "I knew ye would understand. Ye're such a comfort to me."

Bridget's eyes filled with tears. "Ye didn't think so the other night."

Gilbert's face fell. "I didn't mean to hurt ye, lass. It's hard to kill a man, especially one I knew so well."

"But the whisky! I feel like I'm living with yer father. What will become of our sons?"

Gilbert hung his head in shame. He took a ragged breath and

touched her face. "I promise I'll never drink whisky again. My sons will be free of the whip."

"Oh Gilbert. Thank God. I've been so worried."

"Help me with this! If I even look at whisky, remind me of my children."

Bridget saw her chance and held his hand to her belly. "I won't have to, love. Before the year is out, ye'll be a father." She held her breath as the idea sank in.

Gilbert's expression changed from shock, to amazement, and pure joy. "Come wife," he whispered, as he took her in his arms. "The Bishop is on the way."

***

In the west wing of the castle, Jamison, Ian, and Murdock closed ranks around the Duke and his wife as they hurried along the corridor to a door that opened on the courtyard. They burst into the sunlight and crossed the cobblestones to a charming stone building with a crucifix on the door. A piper stood outside, bearing his bagpipes. The wedding was about to begin.

***

Hawthorne and Morris watched from a distance, talking to an archer. They saw the Duke and his party entering the chapel and noted that they were carrying weapons.

Hawthorne groaned. "Bad luck! They're armed to the teeth." His stomach churned.

Morris frowned. "'Haps we should kill him later."

"Nay! We might not get another chance." He unsheathed his sword. "It has to be done. The man is an abomination in the eyes of the Church."

The archer held out his hand, "Religion matters not to me. I'll take my silver now."

Hawthorne's eyes narrowed. He would be glad to see this mercenary take the blame. He reached in his pocket and took out a handful of coins, given to him by an emissary of God.

The archer snatched the coins and tucked them in a pocket. He drew an arrow from his quiver and straightened the feathers. "What about the Earl?"

"No one else dies! Do ye understand? Just the Duke and his men if they get in the way."

"Aye."

"The Earl's misguided, under the spell of that warlock. He'll thank me for this when it's over."

Morris hesitated. "Did the Duke really breathe fire?"

"Aye." Hawthorne stared. "They say his eyes glow red when he's angry, paralyzing his opponent. How else do ye think a mere lad could have defeated the Earl?"

"Don't know."

"He said that he saved a witch. His wife's likely a witch, too!"

The archer frowned. "I have six arrows. That should be enough to bring him down. Keep his men busy long enough for me to make my mark. Then I'll run."

"Can ye hit him from here?"

"I can shave a pimple off yer bare arse from this distance."

"Good." Hawthorne pulled a woolen mask over his face, disguising his person. He kissed a crucifix that hung around his neck and gripped his sword. Morris followed suit.

***

The chapel had been transformed into a magical place, worthy of the wedding of a Lord. Servants nestled candles in nooks and crannies of the granite walls, casting soft light on the room. The stone floors were swathed in blue and green plaids and adorned with silver bowls holding fresh flowers. The altar was draped in tartans and decorated with a candelabrum. The Bishop and two priests waited by the altar as their secretary adjusted their vestments. The important man kissed the cross on his stole before draping the long strip of cloth around his neck.

Gilbert watched as Dughall and his men entered the chapel carrying weapons and glancing over their shoulders. It seemed out of place at a wedding, but he understood their caution. "Where are Hawthorne and Morris?"

Connor frowned. "My Lord. They're watching the chapel from a distance. I thought that ye knew."

"I never ordered it."

"Hmmphh... I don't like this. Allow me to go outside and question them."

Bridget approached and touched the Earl's shoulder. "The Bishop wants to begin, my love."

Gilbert's heart soared. She looked like a princess in that silk dress, embroidered with thousands of tiny pearls. Her sister had placed a sprig of heather in her hair, a sign of good luck and fertility. He longed to marry her and take her to bed.

"My Lord?" Connor insisted. "Shall I go?"

Gilbert waved his hand. "Nay. Perhaps it's best that we have two men outside. Stay in the back with the Duke's men and guard the door."

Connor turned and walked away.

Bridget led her beloved to the altar. His heart fluttered as she took his hands and kissed him gently on the lips. Behind them stood Dughall, his wife Keira, and Julianna, acting as witnesses. The couple parted and faced the altar.

The Bishop opened a prayer book. "Dearly beloved, ye have come together in this church so that the Lord may seal and strengthen yer love in the presence of the Church's minister and this community. Christ abundantly blesses this love. He has already consecrated ye in baptism and now he enriches and strengthens ye by a special sacrament so that ye may assume the duties of marriage in mutual and lasting fidelity. And so, in the presence of the Church, I ask ye to state yer intentions." He turned the page. "Have ye come here freely and without reservation to give yerself to each other in marriage?"

Gilbert was eager to answer. "Aye."

Bridget sighed. "Aye."

"Will ye love and honor each other as man and wife for the rest of yer lives?"

They answered in unison. "Aye."

"Will ye accept children lovingly from God and bring them up according to the law of Christ and his Church?"

They both blushed. "Aye."

"Since it is yer intention to enter into this marriage, join yer right hands, and declare yer consent before God and his Church."

Gilbert took her hand. "Get on with it," he commanded nervously. "Give us the short version."

The Bishop raised his eyebrows. "As ye wish. Lord Gilbert Gordon, will ye take Bridget Murray here present, for yer lawful wife according to the rite of our Holy Mother, the Church?"

"Indeed I will."

He turned to the lass. "Bridget Murray, will ye take Lord Gordon here present, for yer lawful husband according to the rite of our Holy Mother, the Church?"

Her voice was soft. "I will."

"Ye may recite the promise, my Lord."

They faced each other and held hands.

"I, Gilbert Gordon, take ye Bridget, for my wife, to have and to hold, from this day forward, for better, for worse, for richer, for poorer, in sickness and in health, until death do us part."

It was her turn. "I, Bridget Murray, take ye Gilbert, for my husband, to have and to hold, from this day forward, for better, for worse, for richer, for poorer, in sickness and in health, until death do us part."

Gilbert placed a golden band on her finger. "With this ring, I thee wed, in the name of the Father, Son and Holy Ghost. Amen."

The Bishop smiled. "I now pronounce ye man and wife."

Gilbert drew her close and kissed her. "My wife..." His heart swelled with love as he lifted her into his arms and headed for the door.

"My Lord," Connor said. "Remain here while we check the courtyard."

"Oh Gilbert, " Bridget whispered. "I love ye so. Take me to bed."

The Earl felt a fire in his belly and threw caution to the wind. "No one knows of the change of plans. They're all waiting at the church.

Let me pass."

"As ye wish, m'Lord." Connor opened the door and ushered the wedding party through. "Draw swords," he commanded his men. "Be watchful!"

Gilbert carried his bride into the sunlight and put her down gently. Dughall, his wife Keira, and Julianna followed. As they gathered around, the piper played a traditional tune.

***

Dughall's heart was light as he watched the happy couple. His brother was a lucky man. Words formed in his mind as he listened to the piper.

Keira looped her arm in his. "Oh husband. They look so happy."

Dughall smiled. "Aye." He took her slender hand and kissed it. "Do ye know the words to this tune?"

"Nay. What's it called?"

"Burnie Bouzle. It's in the old language." He began to sing in a quiet voice.

♩♬♩

"Gin ye'll mairy me lass, at the kirk o Burnie Bouzle
till the day ye dee lassie, ye will ne'er repent it
Ye will weir whan ye are wad, a kirtle an a Hieland plaid
An sleep upon a heather bed, sae couthy an sae canty

Ye will gang sae braw, lassie, tae the kirk o Burnie Bouzle
Little brogues an aw, lassie, vou, but ye'll be canty
Yer wee bit tocher is but smaw, but hodden gray will weir for aw
A'll sauf ma siller for tae mak ye braw an ye will ne'er repent it

We'll hae bonny bairns an aw, some lassies fair an laddies braw
Juist like thair mither ane an aw, an yer faither he's consentit
A'll hunt the otter an the broch, the hart, the hare an heather cock
A'll pou ye limpets frae the rock, tae mak ye dishes denty"

♩♬♩

Keira smiled. "Words of true love... Do ye think that he knows 'Mairi's Wedding'?"

"Stay here, wife. I'll ask the man." He headed for the piper, who was standing alone by a stone bench.

Murdock walked along side. "My Lord. Ye mustn't go off by yerself. It's too dangerous."

The young Lord gripped his sword in mock warning. "It's all right, friend. I'm armed and ready to fight."

"But my Lord..."

Dughall gasped as a feeling of dread washed over him. The last time this happened, he was attacked by his father. He stopped before the piper and shuddered. "Oh God. Something's amiss."

"What is it?"

"I can't shake a bad feeling."

Murdock glanced over his shoulder and spotted a man stepping out from behind a tree. He was drawing a bow. The servant acted quickly, pushing his master to the ground.

Shhhh....oop... An arrow whizzed past, grazing the servant's arm and hitting the piper square in the chest. Murdock threw himself on his master and rolled, just as another arrow hit the ground beside them.

A cry went up and Jamison ran towards the archer, drawing his sword. A masked man intercepted him and they engaged in deadly combat. Ian ushered the Earl and the women into the chapel, while Connor pursued the archer. A second masked man blocked his way and drew his sword.

Shhhh...oop... Shhhh...oop...

Dughall's heart pounded with fear as he scrambled along the ground towards the chapel. An arrow struck, missing him narrowly and pinning his cape to the ground. He dropped his sword and turned to see the archer reach into his quiver for another arrow. Surely, this one would find its mark. His bowels churned. He spotted his brother coming out of the chapel.

Murdock was on him, tearing his cape to get him free. "Ian, over here!" he shouted. "Are ye hurt, lad?"

"Nay."

"Run for the chapel!" They moved quickly, staying low to the ground.

"Where is my wife?"

"I don't see her."

His legs failed him and he sank to his knees. "I'll die without her."

"My Lord!"

Ian grabbed Dughall's arm, lifting him to a standing position. "Keira's safe. Get in the chapel. I'm going after that archer."

"Ye could be killed, brother."

Ian reddened. "I'm pledged to protect ye! Let me do my job."

Shhhh...oop... An arrow grazed Ian's arm, streaking it with blood. "Ach! That's the last straw. Get him to safety, Murdock." He gripped his sword and ran towards the stand of trees where the attacker hid.

Murdock pushed Dughall towards the chapel door. Shhhh...oop... An arrow missed them by inches and struck the chapel wall, chipping stone. "Get inside, lad. Now!"

Dughall stood in the doorway. "Nay, friend. The archer's running and Ian's almost got him. I want to watch."

There was an anguished scream as Jamison ran his opponent through and twisted the blade to render the wound fatal. As the man lay dying, the servant ripped off his mask. "It's Morris!"

"Who?" Breathing heavily, Connor grounded his opponent and held a sword to his throat. "Traitor! And who might ye be?"

As Ian walked the archer back, Connor pulled off the man's mask and scowled. "Hawthorne? Why would ye do this to the Earl?"

The man glared. "He serves that warlock and the forces of hell that sustain him."

"The tales aren't true!" Connor cried. "Ye've sacrificed yer life for a lie."

"Take my life if ye must. Ye'll burn in hell for this, old friend!"

"Get the Earl out here!"

Dughall fetched Gilbert from the chapel. With heavy hearts they approached the prisoners.

The Earl stared with disbelief. "Morris and Hawthorne?" He groaned. "Two of my closest servants."

"Aye, my Lord. Traitors both. Shall I give them to Fang and have the gallows erected?" Connor asked.

"God in heaven." Gilbert sank slowly to his knees. "Is there no one I can trust?"

"Ye can trust me 'til the day I die. Shall we take their heads?"

The Earl retched on the ground. "Let me be. Oh, why must this blacken my soul on my wedding day?"

Connor frowned. "A crowd is gathering. We have to act. There may be others involved in this attack."

The Duke felt his brother's agony. He placed a hand on his shoulder. "They attempted to kill a Lord. They killed the piper. We must execute them, brother."

Gilbert shuddered. "Aye, we must."

"I shall take responsibility," Dughall said. He directed Connor and Jamison. "Don't torture them. There's no need for a gruesome display on my brother's wedding day. Take them below and execute them."

Gilbert threw up his hands. "Then send out a search party to find that priest!"

Connor grunted. "We will do as ye wish." He pulled Hawthorne to his feet and pushed him towards the castle.

When they were out of sight, Dughall whispered. "May God have mercy on their souls."

The women and the Bishop's party stayed in the chapel, awaiting word that it was safe. Ian and Murdock guarded the Gordon brothers as the condemned men were led into the castle to meet their fate.

Dughall found consolation in the words of his grandfather. Lord Drake once said that when ye must kill something, think not of what must die but of what will live. He sank down beside his brother. In spite of this advice, his conscience was tearing him to pieces. At heart, he was a simple fisherman. What right did he have to order a man's death?

With his second sight, he saw the archer pleading for mercy in the dungeon. He trembled as the axe blade touched his neck. It took two strikes before the man lost consciousness. "God forgive me," he whispered. "What have I done?"

"Where is God?" Gilbert cried in despair. "Where is God now?"

Dughall sighed. "He's all around us, brother. In rocks and trees and every man, woman, and child. He's in the men I condemned to death."

"I wish I had yer faith, lad." Gilbert frowned. "It's been one hell of a wedding day. This is no time for abstinence! Shall we retire to the study and open a bottle of twenty-year-old whisky?"

Dughall rolled his tongue. He could almost taste the smoky nectar and knew it would numb the pain. It was tempting, but he remembered his promise. "Nay, brother. That's the last thing we need."

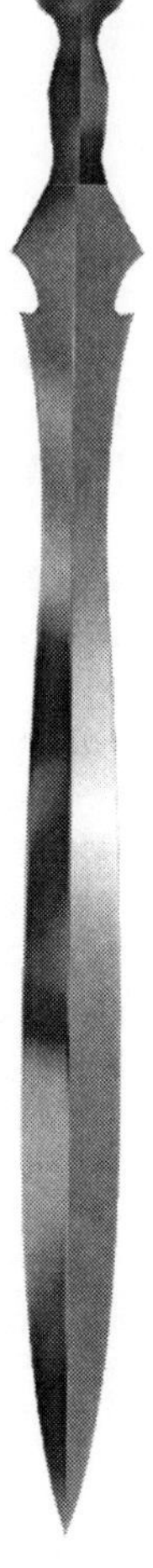

Chapter 4
Women Weapons and Recalling a Whipping

June 18th 1637

HUNTLY CASTLE THE SITTING ROOM

Morning light streamed through the lace curtains, casting intricate patterns on the stone floor. An uncomfortable silence pervaded the room.

Seventeen-year-old Keira Gordon sat in a brocade chair sipping a cup of raspberry tea. She wore a green silk gown and gilded slippers intended for a wedding reception that never happened. Deep in thought, her heart raced at the prospect of what her husband might be doing. Yesterday had been bewildering, with the attempt on his life and the cancellation of festivities. The young Lord was racked with guilt over the executions and spent the night on his knees begging his God for forgiveness.

Keira sighed. He was a man with a conscience, something she couldn't say about most in this strange new world. It wasn't like her woodland village where honor and loyalty were cheerfully given to each other and the Goddess.

"So," Julianna said. "Lord Gilbert and Bridget are married now. That makes us sisters-in-law."

The Duchess looked up. The yellow-haired lass in the opposite chair resembled her friend Mary. The girl *was* Bridget's little sister. "Aye, young one."

"So... Can we speak frankly?"

Keira was getting a bad feeling. "I suppose so, lass."

"Where is yer husband?" There was a sharpness to her question.

"He's gone to see Kate."

Julianna's eyes narrowed. "How can ye let him see her after all they've meant to each other?"

Keira's heart sank like a stone. Was her husband telling her the truth when he said it was over? "What do ye mean?"

"They were lovers! She's carrying his child."

Her cheeks flushed with shame. "I know that. We plan to raise it as our own."

"Kate plans to be his mistress. She says that he's hung like a horse. Is it true?"

"I don't know lass," she admitted. "I've never been with anyone else. He *is* skillful in bed. He knows what I want before I say it."

Julianna's eyes widened. "I knew it was true! What about the rest? Did he breathe fire when he ran the Earl through?"

"Nay, young one." Keira feared she'd said enough. "My husband is a good man. He didn't want to kill his father."

"Of course he did! The Earl nearly beat him to death. Kate says it was revenge."

Keira cringed at the mention of her rival's name. "Let's not talk about her anymore."

"But my Lady..."

She lost her temper. "Enough, lass! Let me be."

Julianna pouted as she stood and left the sitting room. Keira thought she heard a cry of frustration before the door fully shut. Could she trust this girl, even though she was family? She sipped the tea and considered her options. Should she seek him out to make sure that nothing was going on? If there was, would she want to see it? Thoughts of Dughall fondling the big-breasted lass cut her to the quick. Deep in her heart, she thought that she herself might be pregnant, but it was too early to tell. If she told him, would it tip the scales in her favor? Her mind was on fire with possibilities. What could she do? Back home she would go to the stones, invoke the presence of the Goddess, and pray. Here there were too many distractions, or were there?

Keira stood and smoothed her dress. She walked to the window and drew back the curtains. In the distance the forest was thick with foliage and the Deveron rushed along its banks. The sacred stones were to the east, nestled in a stand of pine trees. She only had to imagine them to receive their gift. Keira closed her eyes, held out her hands, and invoked the compassion of the Goddess. In the stillness, her voice was a whisper. "Blessed Mother. I surrender."

***

Dughall and Jamison walked briskly through the forest towards Kate's cottage. They were armed to the teeth with swords and dirks.

The Duke sensed his servant's anxiety. "What's wrong, friend?"

Jamison gripped his weapon. "My Lord. This is dangerous. Why did we not ride?"

Dughall reddened. "I need time to think about what to say."

"I thought that Lord Gilbert settled this matter."

"Somewhat. Kate agreed to give me the child when it's born, but there are conditions."

"Hmmphh..." Jamison growled. "A whore ought not dictate to a Duke."

Dughall was shocked at his choice of words. "She's not a whore. Kate is the mother of my child."

Jamison's eyes widened. "That she is, but I daresay that she's got a bad reputation."

"My wife says that we're all children of the Goddess, both saint and sinner alike."

"My Lord, saying such things will get ye killed. Hawthorne called ye a warlock, an abomination in the eyes of the church. He's not alone."

Dughall stopped and ran his fingers through his hair. Why couldn't they respect each other's beliefs? "God or Goddess, it's the same thing. When will we stop killing each other for it?"

Jamison looked around nervously. "We'll discuss this when we're safe at Drake. Let's go." They continued on the path until they came to the clearing where Kate's cottage stood. "My Lord. Please keep quiet about the witchcraft. Have mercy on me. It's hard to protect ye when so many are against it."

Dughall relented. "All right, friend. But I don't like it." They arrived at Kate's doorstep and hesitated. A short burly man stood guarding the door.

"Who are ye?" Jamison demanded.

"Gibbs, Sir. I've been assigned to guard Miss Kate, so that she won't run away." He bowed slightly. "His Lordship is expected."

Jamison frowned. "My Lord. Shall I accompany ye inside?"

"Nay. She wants to rut with me, not kill me. Stay outside with the guard and watch the door. I'll leave it unlatched." He knocked twice.

"Holler if ye need me, lad. Don't get into any more trouble."

The door opened a crack. Kate's bonny face appeared, lighting up with recognition. She opened it wide and motioned for him to come inside.

***

Dughall's heart pounded as he placed his sword on a table. He felt her standing behind him and smelled her lavender perfume. His senses heightened. This woman could play his body like a fine instrument. Was the madness returning?

Her voice was heavy with desire. "My Lord. Do ye not wish to see me?"

He turned and examined her from head to toe. She was as bonny as ever, with long chestnut hair and hazel eyes. The silk dressing gown covering her body failed to disguise her swollen breasts and belly. *She's carrying my child.*

Kate came closer and ran her fingers along his jaw. "I thought I'd never see ye again."

Dughall took her hand from his face. "I promised to come and here I am. What do ye want?"

Her eyes reflected hurt. "The Earl's dead now. He can't stand in our way."

The young Lord blushed. He couldn't believe that she thought it possible. "I'm married now. Surely, Gilbert told ye that."

She ran her slender hands up his chest. "That shouldn't stop us. All the Lords have mistresses."

He reached up and cupped her hands. "Not this Lord." He was about to move her hands away when she guided his to her underbelly.

"Can ye feel it?" she whispered. "Yer precious child kicked."

His eyes widened. "God in heaven."

"Forget God! I'm the mother of yer child! How can ye deny me?"

He stammered, "I'm married."

She flushed with anger. "Ye owe me this! He beat me to within an inch of my life! I almost lost the child."

He felt guilty that he didn't try to rescue her. "Forgive me, lass. I didn't know that ye were with child."

"Oh, the child!" Kate cried. "Is that all ye care about? What about me? I'd sell my soul to be with ye."

Dughall's head throbbed. "No man is worth that, lass. Least of all, me. I condemned two men to death yesterday. Find a decent man to marry ye."

Her expression hardened. "I don't want anyone else! I know what ye want. Tear off my gown! Take me to bed and command me."

The thought of what she wanted to do to him sent shivers up his spine. "Nay, lass."

Her eyes filled with tears. “Am I not pleasing to look at? Is it because I’m with child?”

Dughall couldn’t bear it. “It’s not that.” In truth, she was more beautiful than ever. Her tears were falling freely now. He held her close to comfort her.

“Then what?” she sobbed.

“I must stay faithful to my wife.”

Kate separated from him quickly. He sensed her anger and the betrayal she felt. For once, he was glad that he couldn’t read her thoughts. Would she change her mind? His heart pounded with fear. “Will ye keep my child from me?”

The lass looked surprised. “Now what would I want with a squalling bairn?”

His heartbeat slowed. “Ye’ll give her to me?”

“What will I get in return?”

“Gilbert and I will send ye to Paris and provide for all yer needs.”

“France?”

“Aye.”

“For how long?”

“Forever, if that’s what ye want.”

“A generous offer, I suppose.” Her voice was as cold as ice. “There’s one more thing.”

“What, lass?”

“I want ye to attend the birth.”

The young Lord nodded. “I’ll ask Gilbert to send a messenger when the time comes.” He touched her face gently. “Thank ye, Kate. I do care about ye.”

Her face softened. “Good, that’s a beginning. I’ve made some tea and scones with honey. Can ye stay a while and talk?”

“Nay, lass. It isn’t proper for us to be alone. I must take my leave now.”

“To go back to yer wife? That scrawny thing with hardly any breasts?”

Dughall reddened. “Why must ye judge others so harshly?”

Her eyes flashed. “Go! Before I change my mind about the child.”

She was silent as he picked up his sword and walked away. As he opened the door he heard her threaten under her breath. “If it’s the last thing I do, I will have ye in my bed.” His blood ran cold.

***

The young Lord burst through the door into the bright sunlight. He sheathed his sword and swore in frustration. “Ach!”

Jamison appeared at his side and they proceeded to move across the clearing out of earshot of the guard. “What’s wrong?”

Dughall clenched his fist. “I’ll never understand women.”

The servant smiled. “What did she want?”

"She demanded to be my mistress, as though we could pick up where we left off. She said that if it's the last thing she does, she'll have me in her bed."

Jamison's face darkened. "The harlot threatened ye?"

"Under her breath."

"Then our troubles are over. We will arrest her after the child's born. Threatening a Lord is a crime punishable by death."

"Nay! I can't bear another execution, especially a woman." They started walking through the forest. "Besides, what if my child found out that I killed its mother?"

"The child will never know."

"It would find out eventually. The rest of the world will know."

Jamison seemed frustrated. "Let's talk about it later. We leave this afternoon, m'Lord. Is there anything else ye need to do?"

Dughall nodded. "I mean to retrieve my Celtic sword."

Jamison frowned. "Lord Gilbert said that the blade's cursed. Are ye sure, lad?"

"Aye, it belongs to me. Will ye accompany me to the weapons chamber?"

"I will do as ye wish."

***

Mary MacQuattie trudged through the woods towards the cottage of her mistress, carrying an empty hand basket. Kate had sent her on an impossible mission. Her legs ached as she walked the last mile, fuming about the request. "She asked for frankincense and myrrh! Wasn't that somethin' from the Bible?" The woman at the apothecary had called her an idiot. The whole town would be mocking her by now.

Mary wasn't feeble-minded. Her lot in life had improved when she was assigned to her mistress as a companion. It was a step up from scullery maid, which involved endless days scrubbing floors, sinks, pots and dishes. Stringy red hair blew about her face. "I'm smart enough to stay alive! Mistress Kate will be lucky to survive beyond the birth."

Mary forced a smile as she approached the cottage. The guard outside had a sickly wife and three wee sons. She held no malice towards the wife, but considered him a prospect if she should die. The lass spoke sweetly. "Dear Donald. How are ye on this fine day?"

The man scratched his wiry beard. "Right as rain, miss. Did she send ye about on a mission again?"

"Aye." Mary reddened. "Determined to make a fool of me; that one is. Don't believe what they say. I'm on to her, but bound to do her bidding."

"We all are. I hauled a tub and water so her highness could have a bath." He wiped his nose with the back of his hand.

"No doubt she wanted to smell good for the Duke. That's all she talks about. Did he come by?"

"Not long ago with his man servant. But he went in alone."

Mary squeezed his arm and felt him tremble. She knew that he needed the comfort of a healthy woman. When his wife died, she would make her play to become the next Mrs. Gibbs. "It doesn't surprise me. Kate's carrying his child. What did the Duke do when he came out?" She would have a piece of gossip of her own to spread.

"He was swearin'... Throwin' his arms up in exasperation. His man servant threatened to punish the lass."

"What did the Duke say?"

"I was too far away to hear the words."

"Dinna fret. Kate can't keep her mouth shut. I'll find out." There was value in playing dumb, and this is what she would do to get the story. The lass opened the door and went inside. She couldn't wait to share the gossip.

***

The weapons chamber was a windowless torch-lit room in the ancient wing of the castle. Weapons lay in velvet-lined shelves and elaborate shields adorned the walls. Dughall spotted the sword of Red Conan, lying on the oak table where he'd left it on that fateful day. His father's practice sword lay next to it, as though they might have a rematch, but that would never happen. He picked up the bronze scabbard and unsheathed the old blade, admiring the etched designs on the base. There was a raven, a lion, and a shield knot honoring the triple Goddess. He felt himself slipping away.

His servant was red-faced. "That blade is cursed. Why must we retrieve it?"

Dughall ran a finger along the razor-sharp hammered edge. "If there's to be trouble, I want my sword."

"Then we must hurry," Jamison said. "The Earl expects ye for lunch."

Dughall picked up the leaf-shaped blade by the hilt and tested its balance. It was heavy, just like he remembered it. "It's good to have it back." Unable to resist, he closed his eyes and raised the sword to a defensive stance. Within moments, the room grew stifling hot and vibrated with the energy of one who came before him, wielding the magnificent weapon. The visions were overwhelming.

On a smoky moor swords clanged. Limbs were torn asunder and the smell of fresh blood flooded his senses. His soul belonged there along side his brother in a brave fight to the death. A raven glided to the ground beside him and morphed into an old crone dressed in black. She was carrying bloody garments. "Morrigan!" he cried, "Dinna take me yet! Aidan, help! Where are ye, brother?" He gasped as a blade thrust in his back and pierced him to the heart.

Jamison tugged his sleeve, shocking him back to reality. "Are ye all right, lad?"

Dughall opened his eyes. "What was I doing?"

"Wailing like a banshee." The servant was as pale as a ghost. "We must go."

The young Lord nodded. In a quick motion, he sheathed the blade and followed the servant to the door. Outside, they locked the chamber by touching a series of runic seals and walked the corridor to the sitting room.

***

Keira gazed out the window. Once again the love of the Goddess filled her being, leaving no room for suspicion. The door to the sitting room opened, admitting her handsome husband. A beautiful smile lit up his face. *How could I doubt him?*

Dughall closed the distance between them and embraced her tenderly. "Worried?"

She blushed furiously. With his Sight, it was impossible to hide anything. "Aye. But no more."

He stroked her hair as he delivered the news. "I saw Kate but nothing happened between us. The child will be mine when it's born."

"Thank the Goddess."

His voice tightened. "There's one condition. I must attend the birth."

Keira took a deep breath. Time and again, she'd experienced the peace of the Goddess, followed by a challenge. She stilled her heart and nodded. "It makes sense."

"She's quite far along, more so than Mary. I would guess early July."

Her practical nature took over. "Then we must find a wet nurse soon."

"Aye. I'll ask Gilbert to send for me when the time comes."

She spoke respectfully. "I want to attend the birth of our daughter. I'll stay outside with the wet nurse."

He hesitated for a moment. "All right, wife. Something tells me I might need yer help."

"Will Kate allow it?"

"I don't know. She's stubborn."

***

Lunch in the dining room was a formal affair. Velvet drapes were drawn for privacy and wall sconces provided soft light. The table was set with fine china and crystal water glasses.

The Earl sat at the head of the table with his wife Bridget at his right hand. Dughall and Keira sat to his left, partaking of roast fowl, vegetables, and a variety of breads.

Bridget picked absently at her food. She reached up and stroked her delicate throat. "What's wrong with me? I can't keep anything down."

Keira looked up. "Are ye with child, lass?"

Bridget flushed. "I could be."

"Try a bit of fennel seed tea, especially in the morning."

"Thank ye, sister." Bridget turned over a piece of squash on her plate and gagged. "Oh, dear. Forgive me." She stood and ran from the room.

Keira frowned. "Poor lass. Should I go after her?"

Gilbert shook his head. "Nay. She's been like this for days."

"I'll leave instructions for the tea and a decoction of herbs."

Dughall smiled. "So ye might be a father soon. What a blessing."

"Aye."

He tasted a piece of fowl. "A trip on horseback is always easier on a full stomach."

Gilbert looked haggard. "I'm concerned for yer safety, lad. Why not stay here and send for more men?"

Dughall was nervous about leaving, but masked it from his brother. The man seemed too stressed to burden him with suspicions. "Jamison thinks that we'll be safe. Besides, I have my Celtic sword."

Gilbert frowned. "Is that supposed to reassure me? Everyone knows that old blade's cursed. Do ye want to end up like Uncle George?"

Keira dropped her teaspoon. "What do ye mean?"

"There's no need to frighten her with stories."

"She should hear this. Except for a warrior named Red Conan, any man who claimed that sword died before the year was out."

Her eyes widened. "How *did* they die?"

"Various ways. Uncle George wasted away, clutching the ill-fated sword. Some died by fire or accident, others by sudden disease."

Dughall stared. "It's only a legend. Even Father thought so." In truth he believed the story, but couldn't say the rest. *The sword won't hurt me,* he thought. *I was Red Conan in a prior life.*

"Leave the blade here, brother."

The young Lord reddened. "Ye promised it to me."

"'Tis true."

"Then don't go back on yer word. The sword won't hurt me."

"Uncle George thought so, too. He had this daft idea that he was Red Conan in a prior life."

Dughall's skin crawled. Had the sword seduced him? Was he Red Conan or simply another victim of the powerful blade? His mind drifted in a sea of questions…

Suddenly, the young Lord found himself on horseback, crossing a river bed with a band of half-naked warriors. He was blood-soaked and the sword lay heavy in his hand. A familiar voice addressed him anxiously. "They're getting close, Red. What should we do?" The man's face was painted with a black mask and streaks of blue. This was Aidan, his brother. Somewhere in the distance, a woman begged him to return. But what woman? "Husband?" The voice was insistent now. His irritation grew. Was he married? Impossible! The vision faded...

Dughall found himself at Huntly, surrounded by his wife and brother.

Keira squeezed his arm. "Are ye all right?"

"I was in another time and place. Perhaps I was dreaming."

"That blade has ye under its spell," Gilbert said. "Leave it here."

Dughall's blood boiled at the thought of losing his sword. "The blade is mine!" He pounded the table, upsetting a water pitcher. "I will hear no more of this!"

Gilbert's eyes widened. "Then take it! But mark my words, no good will come of this. If ye fall ill before the year's end..."

Keira's voice was barely a whisper. "I will watch him."

"Silence, wife! Did I ask for help?"

She grasped her napkin and twisted it nervously, trying to stem her tears. They concluded lunch in silence, unsettled by his strange behavior. The three stood and said their goodbyes, with the men shaking hands.

Dughall was ashamed of his outburst. He embraced his brother, knowing the dangers they faced. "Forgive me, Gilbert. Whatever happens, remember that I love ye."

"All is forgiven, brother. Keep yer guard up, we never found the rogue priest."

They separated and Gilbert left the room to find his wife. Alone at last, Keira could no longer hold back her tears.

Dughall was pierced to the heart by her sobs. He drew her close and whispered in her ear. "Forgive me, lass." He was afraid of losing her and confused by his behavior.

"Leave the blade," she cried in desperation.

"I can't."

***

They left the room in silence and joined their servants in the hallway. Jamison, Ian, and Murdock closed ranks around them as they walked the corridor to the exit. The five entered the courtyard and kept a close watch as their wagon was loaded.

Murdock bowed slightly. "My Lord. Lightning is groomed and ready to ride. I will fetch him from the stables."

Dughall brightened at the thought of his beloved stallion. "I'll go with ye. He must miss me."

"I'm sure that he does."

The young Lord followed his servant to the stables, unlatched the door, and went inside. Murdock led the way past a crude fireplace to a stall and went inside.

"Lightning's in here."

Dughall grabbed a handful of hay for his favorite horse. As he approached the stall, he spotted an iron ring high up on a wall. It was four months since he left this place, but the memories of his whipping were raw. He dropped the feed and reached up to touch the ring.

Murdock emerged from the stall. "Ach! Don't look at it, lad."

Dark memories flooded back, of pain and strife and humiliation. "I must face this." Stripped of his shirt, the Earl had tied him to the ring and whipped him to within an inch of his life. Twenty-nine strokes with a three-tailed strap, eighty-seven lashes in all. He would bear the scars of that beating forever.

"M'Lord, please."

Dughall ran a hand along the stone wall and remembered how it felt against his bare chest. He'd thought it would go on forever. How could a father do this to his son? "He wouldn't let me speak or cry out."

"I know. I was there," Murdock said. "He's dead, lad. Gone from this earth forever. We have nothing to fear."

Dughall thought he was past this but here it was, digging its talons into his soul. He wasn't ready to forgive his father, so perhaps there was a lesson here. He looked into his servant's face and recalled that the man offered to bear his whipping. "Ye asked to take my punishment."

The servant's face flushed. "It was my duty as yer manservant!"

"Aye, but it was more than that. Tell the truth."

Murdock's lip trembled. "Forgive me for sayin' so. But I love ye like a brother."

Dughall's heart swelled. "Oh, Murdock." He wanted to embrace the man, but he knew it wasn't proper. "Come on, they're waiting for us." They entered the stall to get his beloved horse. It was time to leave Huntly Castle and all it represented.

King Charles I

Chapter 5
Divine Right

June 19th 1637
ONE DAY LATER

LONDON ENGLAND

King Charles I stood at an expansive window, overlooking the palatial gardens. Below, perfectly ordered hedges circled ornamental trees and flower beds were in bloom. The dwarf Jeffery Hudson was leading the royal dogs through the maze. For once he longed to walk among them, unfettered by the business of the crown and God's holy mandate. This morning he was dressed in a dark green doublet with a lace collar that fanned to his shoulders. As a complement, he wore brown velvet breeches and silk olive stockings. The monarch was awaiting the Archbishop of Canterbury and several foreign dignitaries.

Being King of England, Scotland, and Ireland was an awesome responsibility. Since his father's death, he'd been saddled with this obligation. He'd implemented the old man's policies and taken them to a new level. Charles stroked his neatly-trimmed beard as he recalled his father's words from a manual on Kingship he'd written for his sons...

"God gives not Kings the stile of Gods in vain
For on his throne his scepter do they sway:
And as their subjects ought them to obey
So kings should fear and serve their Gods again.
If then ye would enjoy a happy reign
Observe the statutes of your heavenly king,
And from his house make all your laws to spring,
Since his Lieutenant here you should receive
Reward the just; be steadfast, true and plain,
Repress the proud, maintaining aye the right
Walk always, as ever in his sight."

The manual outlined a doctrine of royal absolutism with the King as arbitrator in civil and religious matters, answerable to God alone. There could be no doubt about its meaning. The church was destined to become a tool of this doctrine, presided over by bishops, who would police the conscience and duty of the King's subjects.

Charles took these words to heart. His father conceived the concept of the Divine Right of Kings, but had been unwilling to implement it due to his tendency to negotiate with men and institutions. "Kings are not bound to give an account of their actions but to God alone," Charles said ominously, "and unlike my father, I mean to show what I speak in actions."

His brother Henry died after his eighteenth birthday, leaving Charles as the heir apparent. Shy, frail, and suffering from a speech impediment, he'd hidden behind a shield of protocol and became distant, cold, and formal.

Charles preferred the English church and was attracted to the beauty of its rituals. The reformation in England had been state-directed, allowing the new church to retain elements of the Catholic Church. He'd even married a Catholic, Princess Henrietta Maria of France, an attractive woman who'd born him six children, though the first was stillborn. It was a stormy relationship at best, but he remained committed to her. He hated to admit it, but she had influence over him in matters of church and state. Perhaps it was divine order.

The King sat at his desk to await the Archbishop of Canterbury, William Laud. His ankles were weak and bothered him whenever he stood for more than a half hour. The fact had been brought to light more than once, the last time when he posed for a portrait with the artist Antoon van Dyck. The painter had been warned not to speak of it upon the pain of death, and had been true to his word. The King of England, God's holy representative on earth, could never appear as physically weak.

Charles was frustrated by the lack of progress, so much so that bile rose in his throat. In his mind, the desires of the King should trump those of ordinary men. Since his father's death, with the help of the Archbishop, he'd managed to cow the Puritans, no small task even for a King. It was now time to turn his attention to the land of his birth, a wild and defiant place, Scotland.

Having left that land when he was a boy of four, he knew little of its people. His father had tried to force the Church of Scotland closer to Anglican ideals. Bit by bit, he'd gained ground as ministers accepted the power of bishops. In 1617, he'd proposed five new ceremonies, some of which involved kneeling at communion, private baptism, and observance of the principal Holy Days of the Church. Even though the reforms were approved by the General Assembly, many Scots refused to comply as the practices were contrary to Presbyterian ideals. The old King backed off and made no attempt to enforce them.

Charles couldn't understand why he retreated from this important matter. Was the Divine Right of Kings a principle to be ignored? How could he capitulate to a religion so plain and vulgar? He questioned his father in later years, but the man's senility made debate impossible. Thus the matter was left to him to resolve, a man who would rather that his brother had lived to rise to the challenge.

Last year, Charles had issued a royal warrant asserting royal supremacy over the Church of Scotland and authorizing a new set of clerical rules. Caring nothing for constitutional practice, he required the church to receive a new liturgy book to replace Knox's Book of Common Order. Every parish was ordered to obtain the book before Easter and use it in their services. The outcry had been great and the parishes refused, some daring to call the new book a 'Popish-English-Scottish-Mass-Service-Book'.

Charles' body trembled with anger. He was outraged by the audacity of his Scottish subjects. As he drummed his fingers on the ornate desk, he made an ill-fated decision. God's will was not to be denied! He would contact the Archbishop of Saint Andrews to require inaugural readings of the book in Edinburgh churches. They would begin on the third Sunday of July.

Drake Castle

Chapter 6
A Day at Drake

June 20th 1637
ONE DAY LATER

DRAKE CASTLE

The Duke woke in the dark to the sound of rain pelting the castle. The fire in the hearth was out and the room was unfamiliar. He ran a hand across the pillow to get his bearings. Silk bedding signified a Lord's chamber, but in which castle? Drake or Huntly? His wife lay next to him with raven hair spread upon her pillow. Her breathing was soft and regular, and gave him enormous comfort. At least they were together. Rising on one elbow, he rubbed his eyes and focused on a chair. The back splat bore a lion's head, the crest of Grandfather's clan. *Drake,* he thought with relief. *We're safe at last.*

Dughall pondered his confusion. This year he'd slept in many places, from a humble stone cottage to inns and castles. In dreams he slept under stars with skin clad warriors. "Who am I now?" he asked aloud. "Fisherman, Lord, or warrior?"

"My husband," Keira said, as she rolled to face him. "Are ye having black dreams again?" Gray dawn illuminated her face. She was gazing at him with soulful eyes as green as a peacock's feather.

"Nay, lass. Just dreams of another time and place."

"Good or bad?"

"Neither." He caressed her cheek. "I love ye more than life."

"I love ye, too." Keira sighed. "Give me a child! Nothing would please me more than to bear yer son."

It was a welcome invitation. Dughall's hand traveled her thigh, lifting her silky nightshirt. "Lay back, lass." He sensed that she was willing, but not yet ready. "Let me make love to ye."

His loins swelled as he kneeled above her, facing her flower and spreading her legs. He heard her gasp as he opened the patch of hair and blew softly on the bud. She loved poetry, so he described what he saw. "Like a rose, with petals like silk and a delicate center. And I am the bee who will feed on yer nectar." He bent his head to give her pleasure and felt her shiver. His Sight guided his tongue and encouraged him to linger.

Her hips rose slightly. "Dear Goddess!"

His mind raced as he teased her. The French practice was never far from his mind. Would she do the one thing he desired? Did he have to beg? Or command her as husband? His loins ached with expectation.

Keira clawed the bed sheet. "I can bear no more!" She grabbed his hair and pulled him back. "Give me a child."

His disappointment was palpable. But the act would only be worthwhile when it happened with her consent. It was his sacred duty to produce a male heir. With that in mind he changed position and mounted her.

***

Ian Hay lay in bed, adjusting his eyes to the darkness. Outside, a violent storm thrashed the castle walls. He sat up and swung his legs over the side of the bed, being careful not to wake Mary. When they arrived last night she'd been asleep, exhausted from the pregnancy. He'd kissed her cheek and joined Jamison in the kitchen to plan a protection strategy. The men talked until after midnight, drinking too much ale.

Ian went to the chamber pot which stood in a corner by the window. His urine stream was strong, but what was this? His erection would not go down. His skin flushed with anticipation. It was a situation all too familiar. He closed his eyes and connected to his brother. "Dughall!" he whispered. "Can ye not stop for one night? Maybe it *is* true what they say about ye."

His mind locked to his brother's passion. The raven-haired lass begged him to give her a child. His brother was sorely disappointed.

"What's wrong with ye? Take her!"

Ian dropped to his knees and held his breath as they coupled. The visions flooded him with sensations. "Ach! I can't bear it any longer!" In desperation, he grasped his manhood.

Ian stood on wobbly legs. Would they continue? He hurried to bed and nestled against his sleeping wife, sniffing her fragrant hair. How long had it been since they'd done the deed? Four weeks? Five? Could he ask her to accept him one more time? His frustration grew as he recalled his mother's advice. She might be carrying twins. It was too risky.

For a moment, he felt ashamed. The wives didn't know about their ability to 'eavesdrop' on each others act. For the brothers, it was a reminder of their connection. He held his breath. Nearby in the Lord's chamber, Dughall slipped his whang into her silky womanhood. This could last a long time. "Ach!"

***

The rain stopped at sunrise, leaving behind puddles of water and weeping foliage. Servants emerged from outbuildings to shake out bedding and start the new day.

Murdock hurried across the soggy courtyard, marveling at the scene around him. "This place is bigger than Huntly. I'll never get used to it."

Low buildings circled the castle, housing a cooper, a laundress, a blacksmith, a potter, and numerous tradesmen and servants. Behind them were horse barns and a kennel for breeding wolfhounds. Beyond that stood a chapel, an apothecary, an ale house, and a domicile for visiting nobles. This was all surrounded by impenetrable stone walls with guards at every entrance.

He'd risen early and haunted the bake house until the cook's apprentice offered him bread and tea. The widow had taken a shine to him in recent weeks, making him smile. This morning, she even dropped a hint about meeting her mother.

"A man could do worse than a woman who cooks," he mused. "Ah, sweet Sara." She was bonny too, with a shapely arse and ponderous breasts.

He reached the castle's entrance and waited to be acknowledged. The guard let him pass without incident. When he'd first arrived here no one knew him, but that soon changed. Within weeks he was known as the young Lord's personal servant, a title that gave him stature.

He took the stairs to the floor housing the Duke's bed chamber. Since the marriage, he'd been told to report no earlier than seven. The young Lord was trying to produce a male heir. The servant smiled. If the rumors were true, he'd have no problem. He arrived at the Duke's bed chamber and knocked. "My Lord?"

There was a muted sound within, and a voice called out.

"Murdock?"

"Aye. Would ye like me to come back?"

The door opened and Dughall appeared, clad in a blue robe and leather slippers. His hair was mussed and his neck bore bruises.

"My Lord," Murdock said, "Are ye ready for yer morning ablutions? Ahem. Perhaps we should wear something with a high collar today."

Dughall reddened. "Did she mark me again?"

"Aye. In more than one place."

"Oh God."

"Nay bother. Before long, these halls will be filled with the laughter of yer wee sons. After all, it is yer sacred duty."

"What a duty that is. Thank ye, friend."

"I've laid out yer clothes in the next room. Shall we let m'Lady sleep?"

Dughall stepped into the hallway. "That's a good idea." They entered the adjoining bed chamber.

Murdock asked the lad to sit and began to comb the knots out of his hair. He'd really made a mess of it this time.

"Ow!"

"Forgive me, m'Lord. Hair always gets tangled on a long ride."

Dughall blushed. "We both know what it's from. How embarrassing. I can't control myself."

Murdock loved this lad like a brother. "It's good to see ye so happy. She's yer wife! Ye don't have to control yerself."

"Thank God."

The servant put down the comb and picked up a washcloth. He soaked it in a porcelain bowl and warmed it between his hands before washing the young Lord's face. "There, ye look as good as new. Do ye want me to do yer privates?"

"Aye."

"Ahem... Are ye raw down there?"

Dughall sighed. "A bit."

"I'll be careful."

"Murdock?"

"What, m'Lord?"

"It was worth it."

***

Morning sunlight streamed through the open window, bathing the room in a wondrous light. Keira woke in an empty bed feeling secure in her husband's love. During their union, it was as if they merged body and soul. How could she have doubted him?

There was something he wanted, but was embarrassed to describe it. The lass didn't understand it. She wished that her mother was alive, so that she could ask her. Would he forget about it when she told him she was carrying his child? Nine weeks had passed since she had a cycle and she hoped that her prayers had been answered. If everything went well, she would tell him tonight.

Keira rolled over onto her stomach. The sheet was wet beneath her, fueling her fantasies. Would he take her this way tomorrow, forcefully from behind? The linens got wetter, but it didn't seem right. She jumped out of bed and looked at the sheet. Her heart sank; for a small amount of blood spotted the cloth, indicating the start of her cycle. The wee one she dreamed of was not to be. "Great Goddess!" she cried in desperation, "Why must ye test me this way?" Tears flowed down her cheeks. "Everyone else can have a child! Mary... Bridget... Kate... She doesn't want one! I saw the vision of my son... Oh Mother Goddess... When will he come?"

Feeling abandoned, she dressed in a shift and placed a woolen pad in her undergarment. As she slipped on her shoes, her mind obsessed on her inability to conceive a child. Perhaps it was time to visit the apothecary for chaste berry tea, which was known to aid conception. Feeling determined to try again; she splashed water on her face and left the chamber to join the family for breakfast.

***

Mary Hay

The formal breakfast room had tall windows that opened onto a large courtyard. A long table accommodated ten people in soft padded chairs and a sideboard graced one wall. The Duke sat at the head of the table with Keira and Jessie on his right and Ian and Mary on his left.

They were almost done with breakfast.

Ian's head reeled from the visions. He longed to question his brother, but not in present company. He poked absently at his eggs, forming a female breast with a nipple. Was he losing his sanity?

"What's wrong, brother?" Dughall asked.

Ian glared. "I woke with a strange vision. I'll tell ye about it later. When is Father returning?"

Jessie looked thoughtful. "We don't know. He left days ago for Moray Firth to co-captain a ship. If everything goes according to schedule, he'll return with his cargo in three weeks."

Dughall sipped his tea. "Was he happy about it?"

"Aye. He tried to help me in the surgery, but in truth he's missed the sea."

The young Lord studied his wife. "Have ye been crying, lass?"

Keira blushed. "Aye, but it's nothing."

Mary pushed away her plate and rubbed her temples. She'd been silent throughout the meal. "I can't keep my eyes open. Can I go back to my room?"

Ian was frightened by her sudden weakness. "What's wrong, lass? Ye seemed stronger this morning."

"My ankles are swollen. My middle has grown to twice its size. I can't wear the clothes I wore yesterday. Mother, is it usual?"

Jessie frowned. "Some women have no trouble, working the nets to the last day. Others need bed rest or they risk losing the child. Ye're bigger than most for a reason."

Keira nodded. "Mother and I agree that it doesn't feel like one child. But there's another possibility. Perhaps ye're farther along than ye think."

Mary reddened.

Jessie sighed. "This is no time for secrets. Is there a chance of that?"

Ian had a bad feeling. "There *was* that one time in the drying shed," he said. It was a secret he'd promised to keep.

Mary blushed furiously. "Ian!"

His head throbbed. "For God's sake, wife! Mother needs to know."

Dughall spoke softly. "Tell the truth, lass. No one here will judge ye."

Mary's eyes filled with tears. "Forgive me, m'Lord! It was just after yer abduction. Ian was upset so I gave myself to him to ease his pain. We didn't mean to make a child. I haven't had a cycle since."

"Dear God. That was late October."

Ian was ashen. "Mother. What does this mean?"

"She will deliver in four weeks, even less if it's twins." She turned to Mary. "No wonder ye're suffering, lass. It's bed rest from now on."

"Will I be all right? What about my child?"

Dughall smiled. "Don't worry. There will be two of the best midwives in Scotland at yer side." He clapped Ian on the back. "Congratulations, brother! Looks like ye beat me to fatherhood."

There were others who would have to be told. Mary's stern and moral parents, and worst of all, Alex. It was a prospect that Ian dreaded. His bowels churned. "Thank God that Father's not here."

They concluded breakfast and helped the pregnant lass to her bedroom. As they made her comfortable, an unspoken concern weighed heavily upon them. How could they handle a double delivery? Mary's new date was close to Kate's.

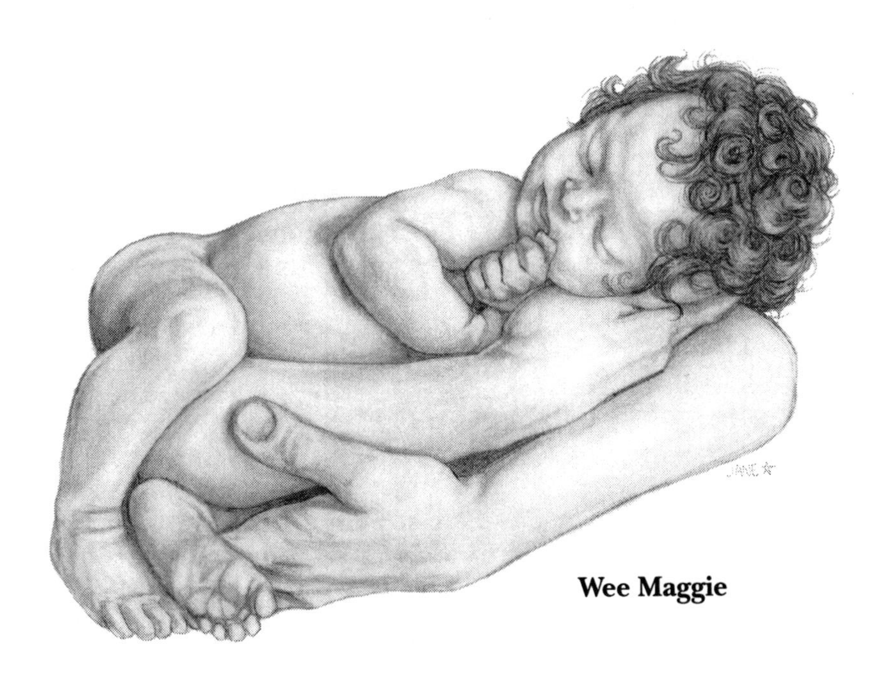
Wee Maggie

Chapter 7
Blessed Events

July 3 1637
TWO WEEKS LATER

DRAKE CASTLE

The library was an impressive room. A favorite space of the late Duke, it was graced with tall windows and rosewood furniture imported from Guiana. Glass-faced bookcases lined two walls, housing thousands of books, maps, and scrolls. To the delight of the new Duke, this library contained a world globe and a fine telescope.

The young Lord sat his desk, reviewing a provisions ledger with his servant, Jamison. He'd done this many times since the death of his grandfather and never failed to find discrepancies. He signed the bottom with a scrawl. "Question the steward about the casks of whisky. That's more than we need."

"Aye, m'Lord." The servant folded the list and tucked it into his jacket. "There will be a long list to review when Alex returns next week."

"Has anyone heard from him?"

"Nay, but that's usual. He might send a courier when they reach the harbor at Moray Firth."

Dughall sighed. "I miss him terribly and so does Mother."

"Ian is none too anxious to have him back."

The Duke smiled. "I don't blame him. He'll have to tell him about Mary's due date. There'll be hell to pay."

"Are ye sure? Alex seems a reasonable man."

"He is, except when it involves the honor of a lass. Ian must tell the truth. Father won't tolerate a lie."

They expected Mary to give birth today. She'd gone into labor just before midnight and was being attended upon by Keira. Nine hours had passed, but they weren't concerned. A first pregnancy often meant a lengthy delivery.

Jamison smirked. "Yer brother's a wreck. I've never seen him this nervous."

There was a knock on the door and Murdock entered. "My Lord. A messenger arrived at the gate, bearing a letter from Lord Gilbert." He handed him an envelope. "He says that it's important."

Dughall got a strange feeling. His daughter about to be born. He opened the sealed letter and read aloud. *"Dear brother… The day has finally come. This morning I was roused from bed with news that Kate had gone into labor. There is no need to worry. I provided her a good midwife and assigned additional guards to her cottage. Nevertheless, ye must come without delay. She says that ye must attend the birth if ye wish to retrieve the child. I have secured the castle for yer safety."*

Jamison stood. "We should leave now."

The Duke's heart was racing. "Aye. I don't want to miss the birth."

Murdock stared. "What about yer wife? She wanted to go with us."

Dughall was torn. It was true that he'd promised to take her. "Where is my mother?"

"Lady Jessie is in the surgery, attending to a woman who was burned. Beth just joined her."

There was no way that Keira could leave now. They suspected that Mary was carrying twins. It would be best to have more than one midwife.

Jamison stood. "I'll gather our weapons and ready the horses. We'd better get started. It will take four hours to get to Huntly."

Dughall turned to Murdock. "Fetch the wet nurse for the journey. She must bring the package of infant clothing."

"As ye wish, my Lord."

"Tell my mother about Kate. Then join us in the stables."

"What about the Duchess?"

He felt a pang of guilt. "My wife will understand."

***

47

MARY'S BED CHAMBER

Keira washed her hands in a porcelain bowl and dried them on a rough towel. She'd watched the clock on the mantle as the little hand went halfway around. It was time to check Mary's progress. *Clocks are strange things, but they can be useful.*

Mary clawed the sheets as a contraction seized her. "Ohhh... It's tearing me apart. Help me, husband."

Ian sat in a bedside chair, nervously chewing his thumbnail. He clutched her hand. "Forgive me, wife. I don't know what to do. Keira! Can ye stop the pain?"

"Nay. It's likely to get worse."

Mary shrieked. "Ach!"

Ian grimaced. "Can Mother stop the pain?"

"Nay. Childbirth is a painful thing, a rite of passage. So far everything's gone as expected. Men don't usually attend these things. Can ye stay the course?"

Mary cried out, "Don't leave me!"

Ian winced. "I'll stay."

Keira looked down at her friend on the bed. Until now, the pains had been far apart, but there were signs that they were coming faster. "I need to check ye again."

Sweat beaded on Mary's forehead. "That last one was so strong, I thought I'd die." She laid back and spread her knees apart.

Keira spoke softly as she slipped a hand into her opening. "I won't let ye die." She reached in and felt the cervix. "Good, it's opening up. Ian, find Mother and tell her the child is coming."

"Thank God!" Ian jumped up and headed for the door.

Keira pulled out her hand and wiped it on a towel. She spread oil on her hands and proceeded to knead Mary's enormous belly. "I think it's two. I feel a head here." She moved her hands skillfully. "And one here as well."

Mary smiled between grimaces. "Twins? What can I do to make them come faster?"

Keira thought for a moment. At home, she would use a birthing chair or get the lass on her knees. Was Mary strong enough to try it? Perhaps with something to lean on. She spotted two sturdy chairs and moved them to the bedside. Keira arranged them back to back, a few feet apart, and took Mary by the arm. "Can ye stand?"

Mary groaned. "What?"

"It's best to use the force of the earth to deliver the child. Can ye get on yer knees?"

"Aye. Ohhhh... Wait. There's another pain coming." She grasped

Keira's hand and squeezed until it was white.

"Breathe, lass!" The pain stopped, but it was clear that another was building. Keira helped her out of bed to her knees.

Mary kneeled between the two chairs and grasped the back splats. She panted as her body adjusted and spread her legs apart. "Something just happened. It feels like it dropped."

Keira laid down a blanket and rubbed her lower back. She reached under and entered her, feeling her open cervix. "I feel a head! That's good. It's not a breech."

Mary groaned. "Where's Mother?"

The door opened and in burst Ian and Jessie.

Ian's eyes widened. "What are ye doin' to her?"

Jessie came to Mary's side. "It's all right, son. This is the fastest way to birth a child if the lass can bear it."

Keira nodded. "The head's crowned." Indeed a wet hairy mass was peeking out from between her legs.

"Is it a lad?" Ian asked.

Jessie smiled. "We can't tell from the head." She kneeled and slipped her hands around the neck, slightly rotating the infant. The head fully appeared and then a shoulder popped out. Mary shrieked in agony.

Keira fetched her birthing kit and stood by. Her heart swelled with joy as the child glided into Jessie's hands and was placed on the floor. "It's a red-haired lad and a fine one at that." The child cried lustily.

Ian whooped. "I have a son!"

Keira wiped mucous from the child's face and head and tied the cord with deer sinew. She took out a sharp knife, cut the membrane, and swaddled the infant in a towel.

The new mother breathed heavily. "Is it over?"

Jessie gently kneaded Mary's belly. "Nay. There's another one in here." She reached between her legs and smiled. "The head has presented."

"I can't kneel any longer."

Keira remembered a time not so long ago, when she helped a friend through a difficult birth. She placed the wailing infant in a cradle. "Ian! Take the chairs away. We will kneel and support her." They moved the chairs and kneeled at her side, supporting her under each arm.

"Push hard, lass!" Jessie cried. "Bring the child into the world."

Mary groaned as she bore down. The infant's head appeared at once, and Jessie slipped her hands around the neck to rotate it. One gentle movement and a shoulder popped out, another push and the child's slender body slid into her hands.

"Another red-haired son. A bit small, but he looks good."

Ian sobbed with joy.

Jessie cleared the infant's nose and throat. This wee child was turning blue and needed gentle massage to start him breathing. He gasped as she rubbed him and started to cry. "Good laddie. Ian, get her on the bed." She worked quickly, attending to the cord.

They lifted Mary gently and laid her on the sheet. Her eyes were heavy with exhaustion. Ian leaned over and kissed her on the lips. "I love ye, lass. They're two fine sons."

Jessie cleaned and swaddled the tiny infant and placed him in Mary's arms. She picked up his brother and laid him in Ian's arms. "Two lads. What will ye name them?"

"Ye did the work, lass. Which one are ye holding?"

"Wee Andrew Thomas, named after my own dear Father."

Ian gazed at the robust infant in his arms. "Then this is Alexander Bruce. Perhaps Father will forgive me now that I've given him a namesake."

Mary's eyes filled with tears. "I'm so happy." She lowered her shift and offered her breast to the baby, who took it readily. "Oh... It feels wonderful."

Keira's heart was glad. The nursing infant would bring on the afterbirth in no time at all. She longed to bear a child as well, an heir for her beloved husband. "Where is Dughall?"

Jessie and Ian exchanged a furtive glance.

"Where is he, Mother?"

"He's on his way to Huntly Castle. Kate's in labor."

Keira felt like she'd been slapped. "We were supposed to go together. Did he leave word for me?"

"Nay."

The silence in the room spoke volumes.

***

NEARING HUNTLY CASTLE

It was starting to rain as the Duke approached Huntly on horseback. Jamison and Murdock rode at his side, followed by Gilroy and a wet nurse named Tarrah. Dughall's nerves were raw as he approached the wooden bridge that crossed the river Deveron. "Oh God. I'm going to be a Father."

Murdock smiled. "Indeed, m'Lord. Perhaps the child has already been born."

Dughall trusted his sixth sense. "Nay, friend. It doesn't feel right. My daughter will wait until I get there."

"Perhaps it will be a son," Jamison said, raising his eyebrows. "What makes ye think it's a lassie?"

"She spoke to me in a dream."

They were solemn as they crossed the bridge one by one, making sure that the ropes would hold. Tarrah was last. She hesitated, staring below at the rushing waters.

"Come on, lass! The water won't hurt ye." Murdock whistled for her mare.

The woman's horse shook its head and stepped onto the wooden planks. Tarrah closed her eyes and gripped the reins as the beast made its way to the other side.

"Gather 'round," Jamison commanded. "Last time we were here, there was an attempt on the Duke's life. We must stay alert and keep our weapons at hand."

Murdock and Gilroy nodded.

Dughall frowned. "Gilbert said that it was safe."

Jamison grunted. "I hope so. We're pledged to protect ye with our lives. Allow us to do our jobs."

"All right. When my child is born, we'll leave forthwith."

Gilroy took the lead as they closed ranks around their Lord. They waited for Tarrah and proceeded along a well-worn path to the gate at Huntly Castle. A piercing whistle went up when they were spotted and the gate slowly opened.

The gatekeeper recognized them and opened the door wide. He guided them in and bowed deeply. "M'Lord. The Earl left instructions to proceed to Kate's cottage."

Dughall shivered with anticipation. "When did he say this?"

He kept his head low. "Not long ago."

Jamison led the small party across the courtyard and past outbuildings until they reached a path that went through the forest. "Why did he not bring her to the castle? I don't like this. Stay alert!"

They reached the clearing where Kate's cottage stood. Next to it was a hastily erected shelter that housed Gilbert, Connor, and three swordsmen. The Earl left the structure and walked into the clearing, waving.

Dughall dismounted and approached his brother. "Gilbert!" They embraced roughly and parted.

"Welcome, little brother! It seems that ye're about to be a father. The midwife is with her, as well as her maid. She's had a hell of a time of it." Gilbert chuckled. "Kate's not one to bear pain and this brought out the worst in her. Better watch yer head."

"My head? What do ye mean?"

"Kate has a stack of dishes at her bedside. I hear that she's throwing them."

Jamison frowned. "Allow me to accompany ye inside. There's nothing worse than a scorned woman."

Dughall hesitated. "Nay, friend. I must face this alone."

"As ye wish. We'll secure the area. Holler if ye get into trouble."

Rain came down in torrents, sending them scrambling for the shed. Dughall waited for a break in the storm and ran to the cottage, bearing a bundle of clothing for the infant. With trepidation, he stood on the stoop and knocked.

***

The door opened a crack and a ruddy face appeared. Bowing slightly, Kate's personal maid admitted them and rushed to the bedside to tell her mistress.

Dughall stripped off his cape and gloves and laid them on a table. He saw a piece of broken glass on the floor and bent to retrieve it as a plate sailed past his head. Glass shattered against the wall.

"Ach!" He kept his head down. "She means to kill me!"

Kate shrieked. "Ye did this to me, worm!"

Dughall's heart raced as he stood to face her. This was his fault, after all. It was time to make peace. "Kate, be reasonable." He ducked a flying drinking glass as he walked to the bed. "Lass, please."

She was lying on the bed with her knees up, dressed in a white lace shift. Long chestnut hair covered the pillow. She was beautiful in spite of the painful ordeal.

An old midwife stood at the bed, examining her under the dress. "M'Lady, ye must help us. The child's head is crowning."

Kate clutched the bed sheets. "Damn ye! I don't want a child." A fresh contraction gripped her, breaking her will to pieces. "I would give anything to be rid of the wee bastard. Ohhhh... Don't let me die."

Dughall sat in a chair and took her hand. "Listen to me, lass." She struggled to get free, but he held it fast. "We won't let ye die. How close is she, mother?"

The midwife sighed. "She's been ready for a while, but keeps fighting it. The child will die if it goes on much longer."

"What should we do?"

"She must stay in a birthing position. Perhaps ye should wait outside with the men."

Kate's voice was childlike. "Don't leave me, m'Lord! Oh dear. Hold me!"

Dughall stood and crawled onto the bed. He sat behind her and cradled her in his arms. "Trust me, lass. Listen to the midwife."

Kate nestled against him and sighed. "Ye came back to me."

"I kept my promise."

The old woman lifted the lass' dress, grasped her knees, and moved them apart. "That's better. The head has presented. Tell her to bear down." She placed a hand on her belly to guide it.

"Do it, lass! Bear down."

Kate made a half-hearted effort and gasped in pain. "It hurts too much. I can't."

"Do it," Dughall insisted. "Or ye'll die with the child. Push against me and down. Bring our daughter into the world."

She shuddered violently. "Oh no. I can't bear it. The pain is coming again."

He held her tighter and insisted. "Push the child out! Do it for me. Now!"

She bore down until her face reddened and collapsed in his arms.

The old woman smiled, displaying toothless gums. "Good. The shoulders are out. It's a wee infant. I can guide it the rest of the way." She worked quickly, rotating the child's slender body. Another moment passed and the baby appeared in her hands. Her eyes widened with surprise. "God help us."

"What is it, old mother?"

"This child has a caul."

Indeed, a shimmering membrane covered the infant's face that made it appear like it was under water. The old woman removed it quickly with a piece of cheesecloth, cleared the child's nose and mouth, and slapped her bottom. The wee infant gasped and wailed as expected. "Forgive me for sayin' so, m'Lord. The caul is a sign of clairvoyance. This child may see the future or have dreams that will come to pass."

Dughall whispered, "No doubt."

She continued her inspection. "Great rulers come from the likes of these. What a shame that it's only a lassie."

"Wee Maggie." His eyes were glued to the tiny miracle and he longed to express gratitude. He hugged Kate and kissed the back of her head. "Thank ye, lass. This is the best gift."

The midwife tied the cord with a length of sinew and severed it. Finally, she wiped down the infant's body with a wet cloth. "She'll need a proper bath tomorrow. Ye're the father, m'Lord?"

"Aye. That I am."

"Would ye hold her while I deliver the afterbirth?"

Dughall nodded. He crawled off the bed, made Kate comfortable, and sat in the brocade chair. His heart swelled as the tiny infant was placed in his arms. Her flesh was against his flesh. "God in heaven. Wee Maggie… I'm a father at last."

"She's a beauty, m'Lord." She handed him a small blanket. "Keep her warm."

He cradled the child as though she might break and stroked her dark curls. Her right eye was swollen and the side of her face bruised, but otherwise she was perfect. The clan birthmark was on her hand, just like in his dream. "There's no doubt she's my daughter." It didn't seem possible, but he loved her already. He covered her nakedness with the blanket.

The midwife worked skillfully, kneading the lass' belly until the afterbirth delivered. She called for the maid and they proceeded to clean up the mess. Kate was strangely quiet.

Dughall felt guilty. "It's over, lass. Do ye want to hold her?"

"Nay."

"Are ye all right?"

Her eyes were full of tears. "Of course not! Will ye leave, now?"

"I have to go." His heart was a jumble of emotions.

Kate's voice was barely a whisper. "Back to yer wife?"

"Aye."

"Will ye kiss me goodbye?"

Dughall's heart was breaking. It was the least he could do, before he took her child. He stood and handed his daughter to the midwife, instructing her to bundle the baby for the trip home. He hesitated for a moment, torn by his morals, then leaned over and kissed Kate on the lips.

She gripped his dark curls and kissed him passionately; forcing her tongue between his lips. When he balked, she raked her sharp nails across his cheek. "Explain that to yer skinny wife!"

Shocked at her sudden aggression, he brushed his cheek and saw blood on his fingers. "I'm bleeding like a stuck pig. Why did ye do it, lass?"

"Something to remember me by." Her voice was cold and deliberate. "Mark my words, when yer marriage fails I will have ye in my bed."

Dughall was speechless. He walked to the table to retrieve his cape and gloves, shaking his head in disbelief. When he was dressed, he faced her and spoke softly. "It breaks my heart to say so, but we're finished. I'll never forget ye, Kate or the things that ye taught me. I wish ye all the happiness in the world."

She turned away and faced the wall, sobbing.

"Goodbye, lass."

As the young Lord accepted his child from the midwife, she spoke softly in his ear. "My Lord. The cloth that bears the caul is tucked in her blanket. 'Tis said that a man who owns one cannot drown."

Dughall acknowledged her gift with a smile and without further ado, left the cottage.

Alex Hay

Chapter 8
Fatherhood

July 10th 1637
ONE WEEK LATER

DRAKE CASTLE

Keira woke in the large featherbed to the sound of her husband whispering to his wee daughter. Since he'd brought her home a week ago, this ritual replaced their morning lovemaking. She rolled over and saw the child lying between them. He was on his side, stroking the baby's curls. "Ye got her from the wet nurse again?"

"Aye." Dughall looked up and smiled, melting her heart. "The wee lassie needed her Da. I felt it in my heart." He caressed the infant's cheek with his finger. "When I do this, she moves her mouth like she wants to tell me something."

Keira smiled. "Dear lad. She wants to nurse. That's all newborns think about."

"Not this child," he insisted. "I feel like I've known her forever."

She knew better than to question his Sight, so she changed the subject. "Such a bonny child. How could anyone give her up?"

"Lucky for me that Kate did."

"Oh..." Her stomach knotted at the mention of her name. "Are we done with that woman for good?"

He nodded. "I think so. She'll be leaving for Paris in a few weeks. In spite of what happened, I'm grateful to her."

"Grateful? She marked yer face with her nails! Mother said that it might scar."

"It was worth it, to get my daughter. When I think that she could have killed this little one, my blood runs cold. Even the Earl's death makes sense when I hold her in my arms."

"Grandmother used to say that everything happens for a reason. This child was meant to come to us."

"Grandmother was a wise woman."

Keira sat up and smoothed her silk nightshirt. "Can I hold her?" She needed to bond with this child if she was to be her mother.

He looked worried as he placed the child in her arms. "I guess I've kept her to myself. Be sure to hold her neck just so."

Keira never thought that he'd be a nervous father. "I'm a midwife, remember? I know how to hold a newborn." She kissed the baby's forehead and was rewarded with a contented gurgle.

"See, lass. She loves ye already."

Keira's heart warmed to their wee daughter. Suddenly, it didn't matter that she came from another woman. They were a family. The baby responded to her touch, snuggling against her chest and seeking a nipple. "I love ye too wee Maggie," she crooned. "But ye'll get no milk from these breasts."

Dughall frowned. "Don't fret, lass. Someday ye'll bear our child."

This was her chance. "There's only one way that can happen. Wee Maggie wants to nurse. Take her to Tarrah and come back to bed."

"But, lass..."

She handed him the child. "It's been a week since ye touched me. Do ye not want a son?"

He smiled broadly. "It would make my life complete."

"Then make love to me. Now, not later." Her body ached for his skillful touch.

Dughall ran a finger across the infant's rosy cheek. "What say ye, wee one? Da and Mum need time alone."

Maggie stiffened and let out a small cry. A dark wet spot appeared on her nappy, threatening to drip on the bed.

Keira giggled. Few men were willing to change a dirty nappy. Her husband was no exception.

"Ach!" Dughall stood and swaddled her in a towel. "How can one so small make such a stinky mess? Tarrah will know what to do." He started for the door. "Don't get up, lass. I'll come back to warm yer bed."

Keira smiled as she watched him leave the room. Perhaps the wee one knew what they needed. After all, she was *his* child and likely had the Sight.

***

Ian walked the hallway to the stairs. He'd just learned that Andrew and Morag McFarlein were at the gate, asking to see their daughter. Ian's heart pounded as he took the stairs to the ground floor. Would there be questions about Mary's due date, or would it cease to be an issue when Andrew saw his namesake? He was a man now and had no wish to incur his father-in-law's fiery wrath. Sweat beaded on his tired brow as he opened the door and stepped into the courtyard. The twins had kept them up half the night, crying, feeding, and messing their nappies.

"Ian Hay!" A familiar voice cried. "We're over here, lad."

He turned to see his in-laws, Andrew and Morag, crossing the courtyard with satchels. Suddenly, he was too tired for a confrontation. "God help me."

Andrew approached and shook his hand vigorously. "Prayin' to God, son? That's a good thing!" He looked around. "This place is magnificent."

Ian had forgotten that they'd never seen the castle. "Wait 'til ye see the inside. Andrew. Morag. Welcome to Drake." He took the satchel from his mother-in-law.

Morag smiled. "How is my daughter?"

Ian beamed with pride. "She's alive and well. Did the messenger reach ye?"

"Two days ago. Is it true?"

"Aye. Mary gave birth to twin boys last week. The lads are healthy, though one is small."

Morag nodded. "That's the nature of twins, that one outweighs the other."

"I thought she was due next month," Andrew said, frowning. "What happened?"

Ian's stomach churned. Would they fight over this? His mother-in-law stepped in and saved him.

"That's the other thing with twins," she said. "They always come early."

The young man offered no further explanation.

Andrew dropped the matter. "Can we see our daughter?"

"She's in the nursery with the bairns. Walk this way." They started across the busy courtyard.

"Did she have a rough time?"

Ian nodded. "Aye. The last weeks were difficult. She had to stay in bed. The birth was hard, but without complications. I was there."

Andrew raised a brow. "With the women?"

Ian reddened. "Mary begged me to stay. I wouldn't have missed it for the world." They reached the castle and gained entrance past the guard, who bowed slightly to Ian.

"Seems ye're respected here," Andrew said.

"There's an advantage to being the Duke's brother." They started up the stairs.

"Will we see his Lordship?"

Ian saw through his father-in-law's question. "Aye. We'll take some meals together and have a smoke in the study. Oh, and I asked him to speak to ye about trade."

Andrew clapped him on the back. "That's a good lad! I'm in yer debt."

Keep that in mind, Ian thought. *When ye learn that I got yer daughter with child in a shed.*

***

They arrived at the floor housing the bed chambers and walked the hallway towards the nursery. Andrew and Morag were awed by the portraits on the wall.

"Do ye live in this wing?" Andrew asked.

Ian recalled his first reaction. "We sleep here. I must stay near the Duke to protect him. The guest bed chambers are here as well."

"This is a big place. What's in the rest of the castle?"

"I'll take ye on a tour. There are areas for dining, entertaining, studying, and receiving guests. Servants occupy an entire wing. Mary never has to lift a finger and can devote all of her energy to raising our children. Mother has her own surgery."

Morag smiled. "How is my friend Jessie?"

"She misses Father terribly. He's at sea commanding one of the Duke's supply ships." They arrived at the nursery. "Father should return any day now. We're waiting for word."

They had arrived at the nursery. Ian opened the door and ushered his in-laws inside.

***

The nursery was a cheerful room. Brightly colored tapestries adorned the walls. Three cradles made of the finest mahogany sat in the center, surrounded by brocade chairs and two rockers. There was a faint odor of talcum powder.

Mary Hay sat in a rocker holding her tiniest son. Across from her, a wet nurse sat in a chair holding a newborn in a pink blanket.

Mary looked up and smiled. "Mother! Father!"

Morag hurried to her daughter. "I was worried about ye, child. But ye look well." She touched the infant's rosy cheek. "So precious. What's his name?"

Mary looked up her parents. "Mother. Father. I present to ye, wee Andrew Hay."

Andrew beamed with pride as he examined the tiny lad. "My namesake! No wonder, wife. He has my hair."

"Would ye like to hold him, Father?"

Andrew nodded and sat in a chair. "It's been a long time since I've held a bairnie this small." He accepted the boy into his arms and cradled him gently. "Wee red-haired laddie. We know who yer grandsire is."

Ian thought he saw tears in the man's eyes. He glanced at his wife, who was about to rise. "Don't get up, lass. Would ye like to hold one, Mother?"

Morag was all smiles as she took off her coat and sat in a chair. "Aye. I've waited for this for a long time."

Ian picked up his son from a cradle and placed him in her arms. He couldn't help correcting his father-in-law. "A robust lad, with crimson locks like mine. This is wee Alexander, named after my own dear father."

"Alex must be pleased." Andrew pointed to the wet nurse. "Whose child is the nurse holding?"

Ian reddened. "She's the daughter of the Duke, Margaret Christal Gordon, born on the same day as my own."

"And just how did that happen?"

"It's a long story and not widely discussed. If ye wish to trade with my brother, I wouldn't mention it."

Andrew agreed, "Wise advice, indeed."

They visited for an hour, grateful for the reunion and the offspring that signified the continuance of life. Mary needed to nurse, so Ian escorted his in-laws to their bed chamber to unpack.

***

Murdock left the bake house and hurried across the bustling courtyard. He'd reported for duty at seven, but was sent away. The Duke was back on track, trying to produce a male heir. *Lucky lad,* he thought. *A bonny wife, a new daughter, and an insatiable desire. What more could a man want?* His mind wandered to the lovely Sara Beth Ross, recently widowed cook's apprentice. He longed to ask for her hand in marriage but didn't know if he should. The young Lord had encouraged Jamison to marry, though he hadn't done so. Perhaps he would allow him to take a wife as well.

I'd move her into the married servants' quarters, he mused. Murdock reached the castle and was admitted past the armed guard. As he took the stairs, he heard a familiar voice behind him.

"Murdock, wait up!"

The servant turned and saw his friend, looking weather beaten and worn. Alex's hair was straggly from weeks at sea. His beard was full and there was a distinct odor of fish brine. "When did ye get back?"

"Just now. Have ye seen my wife?"

"Not since yesterday. Chances are she's with Mary and the bairns."

Alex's eyes widened. "Bairns?"

Murdock hesitated. "Perhaps yer wife should tell ye."

"Come on, friend."

"Much has happened since ye left. Ian's twin lads will be baptized today; as well as his Lordship's daughter."

"Glory to God!" Alex whooped. "I'm a grandfather at last. Are they healthy?"

"Aye."

"When were they born?"

"A week ago, I think. Have ye seen the Duke?"

"Nay."

"Good. That means I'm not late. Perhaps he's still ummm... indisposed."

"What do ye mean?"

"This is the first morning he's spent alone with his wife. He's been a bit of a nervous father with wee Maggie Christal."

"Maggie?" Alex's eyes filled with tears. "Oh God. He named his daughter after my aunt."

They reached the top of the stairs and saw Jessie running towards them, arms outstretched.

"Wife!"

"Oh Alex. They told me ye were back."

Murdock's heart was light as the couple united in a flurry of hugs and kisses. He could only hope to be as happy with the lovely Sara Beth. He took his leave and walked the hallway to deliver the good news to the Duke.

***

Dughall kissed his wife on the forehead and pulled the quilt up to her shoulders. Once again their passion had ignited, leaving them exhausted. "Sleep love," he whispered. "Duty calls." He ran his hand gently across her buttocks.

"Ummm... The baptism is this afternoon. I should get up."

"Nay, lass. There's plenty of time. I'll send a servant with yer breakfast."

There was a sudden knock on the door. The Duke closed his silk robe and ran his fingers through his hair. Perhaps there was something wrong with wee Maggie. He hurried to the door. "Who is it?"

"Murdock. I have important news for ye."

His fear blossomed. "About my daughter?"

"Nay, lad. It's not a bad thing. Are ye decent?"

The young Lord opened the door and stepped into the hallway. "Barely. I lost track of time. How late is it?"

Murdock seemed amused. "After nine. They told me to give ye some peace."

Dughall blushed. "Peace was the last thing on our minds! A week is far too long without the comfort of my wife. I'm afraid I lost control again."

"Come along, lad. There's business to attend to. Let's get ye dressed."

They entered the dressing room and went to the chiffarobe. He sat on a padded chair while Murdock soaked a cloth in a porcelain bowl. "What's the good news?"

The servant washed his face. "Andrew and Morag McFarlein arrived this morning to see their daughter and grandchildren."

"Just in time for the baptism. Ian must be nervous."

"Yer brother's a wreck." He picked up an ivory comb and started untangling his black locks.

"Ow!"

"Forgive me, m'Lord. I'll try to be more careful." He continued on, unraveling the strands one by one with his fingers. "There's more news. Alex has returned from the sea."

Dughall's heart swelled. "My father is back?"

"Aye."

"When I hold my daughter, I think of how he must have felt when we were born. Does he know about the bairns?"

"Aye. He's with yer mother now." Murdock chuckled. "I could scarcely tell them apart when they reunited, they were so entwined. I wouldn't be surprised if they were in their bed chamber." He put down the comb and motioned for him to stand. "Ahem... Shall I wash yer privates this morning?"

The young Lord stood. "Nay. Pour me a bath after breakfast. Something tells me my father needs one too." He cocked his head. "I sense that ye have something of a personal nature to ask me."

"Not on such an eventful day. I can wait."

"Go on, friend."

Murdock looked worried. "My Lord. I ask yer permission to marry. I'll continue to serve ye and..."

Dughall's heart was glad. His faithful servant deserved the comfort of a woman. "Murdock!"

"Please, my Lord!" He sank to his knees and clasped his hands. "I'm beggin' ye for this favor."

Dughall placed a hand on his shoulder. "Get up, old friend. Of course, it's all right. We'll talk about it after the baptism."

Murdock stood, looking relieved. "Thank ye, m'Lord. May the Almighty bless ye always! I'm in yer debt."

Dughall truly loved this man. He'd lost count of the times he saved his life. "We'll plan a wedding in the chapel and a dinner afterwards. Do I know the lass?"

The servant nodded. "Sara Beth Ross, the cook's apprentice. I'm lucky that she wants the likes of me."

He sensed that there was something else. "What's wrong?"

Murdock blushed furiously. "I grew up without a father. I've served Lords all my life."

"What are ye saying?"

"I'm ashamed to say it, but I've never been with a woman."

Silence hung between them like a curtain. Was the older man asking for advice? He didn't want to embarrass him.

"Help me, lad."

Dughall smiled. "Don't fret, my friend. We'll have a cigar in the study and I'll tell ye all about Kate."

"The Earl's mistress?"

"Aye," he said wistfully. "She taught me how to please a woman. There's just one condition."

"What's that?"

"Don't mention it to my wife."

***

Alex pulled his sweater over his head and tossed it on the floor of the bed chamber. His bonny wife stripped before him, dropping a stocking, then her tartan skirt. She was naked underneath. His loins swelled with desire. For weeks he'd imagined this moment as he tossed in the captain's bunk aboard the "Black Swan". The voyage had been long, taking him to ports in France, Ireland, and Spain, and testing his skill at every turn.

She removed her blouse, exposing ample breasts with pink nipples. She didn't look like a grandmother. "Husband?"

His heart burned with passion as he dropped his breeks on the floor. "Sweet lass. I'm afraid I smell like the sea."

Jessie closed the gap and snuggled against his naked body. "Just like old times."

It felt so good. "Ye... ah... don't want me to bathe first? And shave?"

"We never used to." She ran her hands up the muscles in his arms. "Hard as a rock, like when ye were young. It makes me want ye more. Pity a poor wench."

Alex groaned. "God in heaven." He picked her up, carried her to the bed, and laid her atop the quilt.

Her voice was soft. "I've waited so long." She gripped the spindles of the headboard, making her intentions clear. "Oh, Alex. Tease me like ye used to."

This was more than he could bear. The last time she'd asked for this was before the lads were born. With pounding heart, he straddled her and buried his tongue in her neck.

She trembled beneath him. "Oh… aye…"

Alex sealed her mouth with his lips and welcomed her passionate response. Moving on, he suckled each breast. Her body was so warm and silky.

"Oh… Alex…lower…"

The rest was unintelligible, but sent shivers through him. He started the slow descent to her navel and placed a hand between her open legs.

She stiffened and raised her hips to meet him. "Take me now, husband!"

His member throbbed in anticipation, begging for relief. Did she mean it, or should he continue their youthful game? He stroked the inside of her trembling thighs. "Are ye sure?"

"Oh, aye! I beg ye. There, I've said it!"

They coupled like young lovers, oblivious to their surroundings. Her soft moans inspired him and meant that she was close. Alex knew he was losing control as he went deeper still. In a moment of passion, fueled by love and desire, they cried out and found release.

He rolled off and lay at her side, stroking her long hair. Only then did he hear a knock on the door. He sat up and shouted "Who is it?"

The voice was familiar. "Dughall."

"Son?"

"Aye. The bairns are being baptized in three hours. I thought ye might join me for a bath."

His son, his Lord, and his master. They had much to discuss and he could use a bath and a shave. "I'll be there in a moment, my Lord."

***

The bath chamber was warmed by a fireplace that heated the room and provided soft light. Two copper tubs sat side by side and lavender scented steam hung in the air. The Duke rolled a bar of soap between his hands and lathered his chest. He was thinking about how good it was to have his father back.

Alex sat in a tub and blew his breath out slowly. "I'll never get used to this. The water's hot."

"I'll ask them to pour a warm bath next time."

"I don't wish to seem ungrateful m'Lord," Alex said. "Do ye want to talk about the voyage of the Black Swan?"

Dughall frowned. That was the second time he'd called him my Lord. Of course, he'd been to sea on official business where everyone referred to him as his Lordship. And he could be dead tired. "We can talk about the voyage after the baptism. We'll have a smoke in the study. Have ye seen the bairns?"

Alex soaped his feet. "Nay. When I arrived, yer mother whisked me away to our bed chamber." He blushed. "She needed me, smellin' like fish and all. Mary had twins?"

The young Lord smiled. "Aye. Ian's lads have red hair just like their father."

Alex frowned as he lathered his chest. "Hmmphhh... I thought they were due next month. I wonder if that lad violated her in the midst of all our troubles."

Dughall had seen this coming. "Now, Father. The good book says 'Let he who has no sin cast the first stone'. I certainly can't cast any and I won't allow it at the baptism."

Alex reddened. "Can I speak to him about it afterwards?"

"Nay, not ever. He named one of the lads after ye."

The older man brightened. "Alexander?"

"Aye, wee Alexander Bruce. A sturdy lad with a mind of his own."

"Did he name the other after McFarlein?"

"Aye. Andrew Thomas." He soaped his groin and winced. "Lad's a bit small, but healthy. Andrew and Morag are here for the baptism."

Alex smiled as he reached for a razor. "Then I'd better trim my beard for the ladies. I look like a vagabond." He gazed into a small attached mirror and started. "Murdock told me that ye have a daughter."

Dughall sighed. In a few short days, the child had become the apple of his eye. "I never thought that I could love someone so completely. From the first time I held her, my heart broke wide open. Now I know how ye felt when we were born."

His voice was barely a whisper. "It's so true."

"I named her Margaret Christal, after Aunt Maggie and my birth mother."

Alex's eyes filled with tears. "Wee Maggie... It's a fine name for a lassie. Yer aunt would be pleased." He completed his trim and put down the razor. Then he proceeded to wash his hair. "Ah... It's good to be clean. Are we done here?"

Dughall shook his head. "Nay. There's one more thing."

"What?"

"Ye don't have to call me my Lord."

Alex reddened. "I took a solemn oath. I'm pledged to serve ye as Lord and Master."

"Father..."

"By God! Ye're a man now with a difficult job to do. The people of Drake depend on ye and from what I've seen, hundreds more beyond."

"I'm the same man..."

"Nay, lad. It's yer birthright. Allow me to pay the respect ye deserve."

Deep in his heart, the young Lord understood. His brother Ian had expressed the same thing the other day. "In public ye can call me my Lord, but in private I'm yer son."

Alex hung his head. "I'm not yer real father. Everyone knows it."

So this was the problem. The young Lord reached out and touched his arm. "Ye may not have sired me, but ye are my true father. If not for ye, I'd be bitter about fatherhood."

The older man choked back a sob. "My son…"

Dughall longed to make it right. "I love ye, Father. Don't let anyone tell ye otherwise. Bloodlines don't matter. I'm proud to be yer son."

"Oh, lad. I love ye too."

Chapter 9
Ave Maria

July 10th 1637
LATER THAT AFTERNOON

DRAKE CASTLE

The chapel was a sight to behold. Red and blue tartans draped the altar and white lilies graced elaborate crystal vases. Pillar candles in marble bases provided light and filled the air with the scent of bayberry. Guests attending the baptisms sat in the first three pews, with guards and servants in the rear of the church.

Keira sat in the first row with her husband, the Duke of Seaford, holding their newborn daughter.

The Hays and the McFarleins sat in the second row, looking like proud grandparents. Gilbert and Bridget Gordon had just arrived and were taking their places behind them. Her husband turned and greeted them warmly.

Keira watched intently as Mary and Ian brought their bairns to the font to be baptized by a Protestant minister. The ceremony was lovely, with the proud father holding each infant as the minister sprinkled water on their foreheads and uttered sacred words. *Strange,* she thought. *They anoint with water.*

As if he heard her words, Dughall gave an explanation. "The water signifies being born again, into the Christian faith. It's always done this way."

She was beginning to understand, but had a question. "Why do we have a different priest for wee Maggie?" She smoothed the baby's curls from her damp forehead.

"Hmmm…" Dughall said. "Well, lass. There's the rub. The religion is split into two factions and each thinks it's the proper one. They argue about details."

"Like what?"

"The Blessed Virgin Mother. Catholics hold her in the highest regard."

The local priest, a lame old man named John Murray, approached and spoke in a soft voice. "My Lord and Lady. We're ready to baptize yer daughter." He had a worried look on his face. "Are ye sure that ye don't prefer the Bishop's blessing?"

The young Lord reddened. "Nay, Father John."

He bowed slightly. "As ye wish, Sire. Bring her forth to the font and into God's kingdom."

Dughall stood and accepted the child from her arms. Keira rose and fluffed the infant's long white dress, made of fine Irish lace. Her heart swelled as she stroked the child's rosy cheek. So sweet and innocent. How could she not love her? She recalled her mother's last words. "May ye have a daughter as good and true as ye." Momma and Grandmother would have adored her, but they were dead now. Her eyes filled with tears of regret.

"Are ye all right, lass?"

She sniffled. "Aye. I was thinking about my mother."

He smiled sympathetically. "Poor wife. It's been a hard life. Perhaps we can name a child after yer mother."

"Elspeth?"

"Aye, it's a good name." Soft flute music filled the air as they edged out of the pew and proceeded to the baptismal font. Gilbert and Bridget joined them and smiled. Keira stood by her husband as he held their wee daughter.

The priest opened his prayer book and began the ceremony. "My Lord and Lady. Grandparents, godparents, and honored guests. We gather today in this sacred place to welcome this child into the Christian community." He turned a page and addressed Dughall and Keira. "As parents, do ye want baptism for this child?"

The young Lord answered for both of them. "We do."

"What is the child's name?"

"Margaret Christal Gordon."

"Do ye promise to bring up this child, Margaret Christal, in the Catholic faith?"

"We do."

The priest turned to Gilbert and Bridget. "As godparents, do ye accept this duty and promise to raise this child in the faith if necessary?"

Gilbert nodded. "We do."

The priest made the sign of the cross on the baby's forehead. "M'Lords, m'Ladies. I ask ye to do the same."

Dughall and Keira complied, followed by Gilbert and Bridget. Indeed, Keira had practiced the symbol for days.

The priest unfastened the top button of the baby's gown and anointed her chest with sacred oil. "The Christian community welcomes this child with great joy! May she have a special friendship with Lord Jesus and the Blessed Virgin Mother." He droned on reading from the scriptures.

Keira's heart warmed as she thought of the Blessed Mother. Many a time had she come to this chapel and stood before the statue of the Virgin, holding her hands out in solemn prayer. Surely this was the Goddess, with her compassionate face and open arms. Mother of all, mistress of nature, and bearer of everlasting life. She knew it in her heart.

"Lass?" Dughall's voice was soft. "Are ye all right?"

She came to her senses and blushed. "Aye."

Dughall held the baby over the font while the priest blessed the water. The child gasped when the water poured on her forehead and the words were spoken.

"I baptize ye in the name of the Father and of the Son and of the Holy Ghost." He anointed her forehead with oil and was greeted with the child's plaintive cries.

"There, there..." Dughall crooned as he cradled her tiny body against his shoulder. "Yer Da loves ye, wee Maggie."

The priest cleared his throat and lit a special candle. Handing it to Keira, he prayed, "Receive the light of Christ".

"Thank ye Father John," Dughall said respectfully.

They left the font and returned to the pews to be greeted by friends and family.

Keira was glad to see Gilbert and Bridget, and warmed by the support of the Hays and McFarleins. She was in love with her husband and bonny wee daughter. There was only one problem. She was desperately homesick for her woodland village.

Luc

Chapter 10
Trouble

July 13th 1637
THREE DAYS LATER

DRAKE MILL NEAR DRAKE CASTLE

Nine-year-old Luc Deville ran for the mill with his dog at his heels. He'd lost track of time bow hunting rabbit and squirrel. Fear gripped him like an icy hand as he noted the sun's position in the sky. His stepfather would be angry he was late for work. He stopped at a tree and grasped his knees to catch his breath. Father wasn't outside splitting wood or tending the water wheel. If he could slip inside and grab a broom, he could say he'd been sweeping the floor.

"Run, Artus. Stay out of sight." The boy scratched the deerhound's ears and sent him on his way. The dog was a good friend and he couldn't bear to see him whipped.

Luc clutched his bow and walked the last yards to the millhouse door. There was no one in the window, but the door was unlatched. He hung up a string of dead squirrels on a nail, dropped his bow, and opened the door. So far so good. Father wasn't in the entrance room where he dealt with customers and kept his ledgers. The floor was lightly dusted with oat flour and there were footprints leading to the threshing chamber.

Thwack! The old man was beating oat stalks with a flail, two sturdy birch sticks joined by a leather band. Thwack! Thwack! His voice thundered with anger. "God damn it! Where is that wee bastard?"

Luc knew he was in for it now. He walked to the far wall and took an apron off a peg, trying to think of a good excuse.

"Don't ye dare put that on." The deep voice behind him struck terror in his heart. "Where the hell have ye been?"

"Umm… Hunting." Luc held his breath and awaited the inevitable beating. Behind him, the flail whistled through air and struck his shoulders. It would be a mistake to cry. "Forgive me, Sir. I won't be late again."

"Forgive ye?" His voice dripped with sarcasm. "Do I look like Jesus?" He doubled the rods and tapped his hand. "It's time ye learned a lesson. Take off yer shirt."

Luc's breath caught in his throat. *I can bear it like a man,* he thought. *It's only a flail.* He heard a belt slipping through loops and froze.

"Take it off!"

"Nay!" Did he say that out loud?

"What? Ye dare to defy me?"

Luc pulled the shirt over his head and threw it aside. Something was telling him to run from this place. He scanned the room and spotted the stairway to the tower. Perhaps he could get to the top and jump off.

"Don't run!"

The lad ducked and ran for the stairs, taking them two at a time. He was almost to the top when a hand grabbed his ankle and brought him to his knees. He turned to see the man's ruddy face.

"Ye'll be sorry ye were born."

Fingers pulled down his breeks, leaving him exposed. The man looped the belt and snapped it for effect.

Luc's heart thumped against his ribs. "Don't do this! I'm yer son." The belt cracked across his backside, taking his breath away.

"Ungrateful whelp!" He struck again, blistering skin and drawing blood. "How many times do I have to tell ye? I'm not yer sire."

The pain was unbearable. The belt snapped again and again, making its mark on backside and shoulders. Would the man ever stop? The boy cried out in pain and desperation. "Mercy!"

The beating stopped and the belt was thrown to the floor, but what was this? Father was opening his fly and bringing forth his swollen member.

"Don't ye dare scream." His hot breath stank of sour ale.

Luc groaned as fingers spread his cheeks and held his slender hips. Father's whang crowded his arse and gained painful entry. Would he die this time? How could God let this happen? In a moment of madness he threw the man off, scrambled to his feet, and climbed to the top of the stairs.

Strong hands pinned him to the floor so he couldn't move. Fingers locked in his hair, tearing the roots. Under his breath, he begged God to take his soul.

Father's boot crushed his outstretched hand, grinding it into a plank. "Tell and I'll kill ye."

Luc heard a sickening pop, screamed in agony, and passed out.

***

DRAKE CASTLE HOURS LATER

The library was unusually warm for this time of year, due to a heat wave. Drapes were drawn back from the windows, in hopes that a breeze would enter. The young Lord sat at his rosewood desk, reviewing the ledgers from the 'Black Swan' with his faithful servant.

Jamison ran his finger down a list. "Hmmphh… Nine dozen casks of wine and liquor from France. Gold and silver jewelry from Galway. Fine lace and china. Wood. Weapons. Dried fruit and spices. Not to mention the profit we realized from trade. Successful trip indeed, m'Lord."

"How does this compare to the last time these ships went out?"

Jamison looked up. "Better by far. It appears that Alex is keeping them honest."

Dughall smiled. "There's no better man for the job." He wiped a bead of sweat from his forehead. "God, it's hot."

"Yer Grandfather and Uncle spent weeks like these by the sea, on Moray Firth. There's a bonny estate with miles of rocky beach and fine Arabian horses."

"They belong to me?"

"Aye. Shall I arrange a trip to Seaford Shores?"

The young Lord sighed. "Nay." He longed to listen to sea birds, but wee Maggie was ill. "The child's down with a bit of colic."

"Poor wee lassie."

"My wife has been with her all morning."

The servant cleared his throat. "Forgive me for asking, but is m'Lady all right? She doesn't seem her usual self."

Guilt stabbed at his heart. He noticed it too, and it wasn't hard to guess why. "Keira misses her people. After the baptism, she begged me to take her home for a visit."

"I thought her family was dead."

"Aye. But she misses her friends and the stones as well."

"Hmmphh..." Jamison frowned. "I hoped that we could avoid that place after the witch burning incident. It could be dangerous. What did ye tell her?"

"I promised to make a decision soon. Perhaps we could go in the fall." The young Lord stood and signed the ledger with a scrawl. "This wraps it up. Arrange for the ships to be provisioned for the next run."

"As ye wish."

There was a knock on the door. Gilroy entered and presented his Lord with an envelope. "My Lord. A messenger from Huntly left this at the gate." The servant excused himself and left the room.

Dughall examined the envelope, which bore the wax seal of the Earl of Huntly, his brother Gilbert. He sliced it open with his dirk and saw that it had been hastily written. He began to read out loud.

"Brother - I received a disturbing communication from a friend in Edinburgh. The King is determined to impose his religion on the Protestants by way of a new liturgy book. On Sunday the twenty third of July, the book will be required to be read in Edinburgh churches. The Catholic faith is not threatened, but anything that causes unrest may influence the stability of this region. We should each send a servant to the reading to assess the situation. Dispatch yer best man as soon as possible and report to me when he returns. Trouble is brewing. Yer brother, Gilbert."

Jamison frowned. "Hmmphh... Lack of food or a work stoppage can be dealt with, but religious unrest is unpredictable. Would ye like me to go?"

Dughall nodded. "Aye, friend."

"There's ten days until the reading. I can make it on horseback in six, but we can't risk missing it. I will leave the day after tomorrow."

"Good."

There was a knock on the door. Murdock entered and placed a water goblet on the desk. "My Lord. The lady Jessie requests yer presence in the surgery."

Dughall took a sip of water. "What's wrong?"

"A young lad was brought in with a broken hand."

"How old is he?"

"Looks to be nine or ten."

Dughall dismissed Jamison and followed Murdock. It had been a while since he'd set a broken hand. "How did it happen?"

"Don't know. He won't speak."

"Did his parents bring him in?"

"Nay. A neighbor found him senseless on the floor of the mill."

"Senseless? How strange..."

They arrived at the door to the surgery as Jessie emerged with a basket on her arm. She looked worried and angry at the same time.

"Someone beat that child beyond reason. I got his clothes off, but he won't let me touch his hand."

"Where are ye going?'"

"To the apothecary for leopard's bane. The lad's a mass of breaks and bruises. A warm poultice might help."

"Who is he?"

"Luc Deville, the miller's stepson."

"Take Murdock with ye." Dughall sent them on their way and prepared to enter the surgery. Bowing his head slightly, he prayed for divine guidance. His last patient, a woman who'd been burned, succumbed to infection in spite of their efforts.

He entered the surgery and looked around. Flickering lanterns provided soft light in the windowless room. Per his request, the table had been moved to the center and padded with a soft quilt. The earthy smell of sweat and blood assaulted his nostrils. A young lad with straight brown hair lay on the table, facing the opposite wall. He was covered to his bare shoulders with a sheet.

Dughall made a quick assessment. The boy writhed in pain as he tried to get comfortable. His breathing was shallow and irregular, suggesting cracked ribs. He walked around the table and glanced down. There was blood in his hair and a vacant stare in his eyes. The hand had been crushed.

"Luc Deville? Do ye know who I am?"

The boy's eyes widened with recognition. His lips formed words, but he remained silent.

Dughall stroked his forehead gently, detecting a slight fever. He held a finger against the boy's throat and noted a rapid pulse. "There's no need to fear me. I'm a healer." He retrieved a flat board from the cupboard and laid it on the table. "Ye're a tough one from the looks of it. Lie face down and spread yer hand on the board."

The boy took a ragged breath and rolled onto his stomach.

Dughall saw pain in his eyes and sensed his desperation. He assisted him and splayed the hand to examine the bones. "This will hurt a bit." He grasped the hand, softened his eyes, and prodded the bones gently. There seemed to be more than usual, and that meant fractures. The child gasped in pain as he continued. "Two breaks, maybe three. We must set that hand if ye plan on using it."

The boy nodded his consent.

"Did someone hurt ye, son?" He released the hand and waited for an answer.

The lad's fine features betrayed his French heritage. Tears welled in his blue eyes, revealing a deep sadness. He didn't answer.

Dughall decided to ask questions later. He opened the cabinet door and searched through the supplies, selecting a hand brace with adjustable ties. Months ago he'd commissioned a leather smith to fashion a dozen such supports, in various shapes and sizes. Satisfied with his choice, he returned to the head of the table.

"Cry if ye must, Luc. I won't think less of ye." He grasped the injured hand and maneuvered the bones into place with his thumbs. The boy stoically bore the pain, gasping and gritting his teeth. At last, the brace was molded to the hand and laced on tight. He removed the flat board. "Does that feel better?"

Luc flexed his fingers slightly and managed a nod.

"No working in the mill until it's healed. Now lie still while I look at yer back." Dughall drew the sheet to the boy's knees, noting bruises and blistering from a belt. He used his fingers to trace a bruise and detected cracked ribs. There were signs he'd been birched and there were streaks of blood between his legs. He suspected the worse and needed to get a better look. "Take a deep breath. I won't hurt ye." He separated his cheeks to assess the damage.

"Nay!" Luc groaned. "Don't touch me there." He stiffened like a plank and held his breath.

Now they were getting somewhere. "So ye *can* talk."

"I'm not a dummy."

Dughall saw the boy shiver and drew the sheet to his shoulders. "Did yer father do this to ye?"

"Nay, my Lord. I fell down the stairs."

"I hope that's the truth, lad. Yer father will be here soon."

Luc's eyes widened. He attempted to rise on one hand, but fell back on the table. "He'll kill me!"

Dughall knelt and stroked his forehead. "Tell the truth and I won't let him take ye."

Luc sniffled. "Promise?"

"Aye."

The child took a ragged breath and began his heartbreaking story. "I made Father angry and he punished me."

"How?"

"He uhh... stripped off my clothes and beat me until I couldn't breathe. I begged him to stop but he wouldn't." Tears rolled down his dirty cheeks. "Then... Oh God... I can't say it."

"What, lad?"

"He buggered me. I wish I was dead."

Dughall recalled the abuse he suffered at the hands of the Earl. It was terrible, but this was worse. "What happened to yer hand?"

"When I ran, he held me down and crushed my hand with his boot. He said I deserved it."

"No man has a right to do that to his son."

"I'm not his son!" Luc sobbed. "My true father died years ago."

Dughall's heart ached with compassion. "Where's yer mother?"

"She died from the grippe last winter."

Poor wee orphan, Dughall thought.

The lad shuddered as he took a breath. “Why does my chest hurt?”

“Yer ribs are cracked. Let us treat yer wounds and keep ye here tonight.”

Luc sighed. “Thank ye.” He rested his head and closed his eyes. “My Lord?”

Dughall leaned closer. “What, lad?”

“Don’t send me home. Ever.”

He stroked his forehead. “Is there nothing there ye want?”

“Only my dog…” He started to drift. “Poor Artus…”

The door opened and Jessie entered, bearing a basket of supplies. They worked tirelessly on his wounds, applying poultices to bruises and salve to cuts. Two cracked ribs were bandaged as well. Thankfully he fell asleep before the last part, where they treated the sexual assault.

Jessie’s face was ashen. “How can a man do this to a child? Will he kill him next time?”

“Luc asked me to not send him home.”

“What will ye do? He’s not yer son.”

The question seemed outrageous. “Mother… God sent this child to us for safekeeping. Let the lad sleep, then move him to the guest bed chamber. I’ll check on him after I confront his stepfather.”

***

HOURS LATER

The Duke stood in his study, gazing out the window. He’d racked his brain thinking of ways to keep the child. His servants made inquiries and concluded that the miller would never give him up. From all accounts, Duff Aiken was a cruel and unreasonable man, wrapped up in drink and self-importance. There was only one way to handle this and he didn’t like it.

Dughall was about to give the performance of his life. He’d seen the Earl brutally interrogate a man, reducing him to a state of helplessness. Few men could bear the threat of torture and the miller was no exception. He placed a crystal decanter on the desk, removed the stopper, and poured a dram of whisky. Breaking his vow, he tipped the glass and took a long swallow. The amber nectar burned his throat and lessened his anxiety.

“Father always drank before he broke a man. I guess I’m no better.” Bile rose in his throat as he opened a drawer and took out a riding crop. His servants would return with the miller soon and he had to get ready. He ran his fingers through the leather strands and resolved to take the lad by force.

“Dear Jesus,” he prayed. “Grant me the wisdom to use this.” One by one, he reviewed the lad's injuries. The birch rods cut his shoulders and blistered his back. The belt was wielded with force, bruising the child's back and legs. Ribs were cracked and a hand crushed, not to mention the anguish from the sexual assault. The physical abuse was bad enough, but would he recover from the shame? Duff Aiken was a despicable man who deserved to be punished. The Earl would have taken his life in a cruel and unusual way. There was a knock on the door, interrupting his desperate thoughts.

Murdock entered and bowed slightly. "My Lord. The miller is outside. His hands are bound in front as ye requested." He stared at the whip and waited to be acknowledged.

Dughall sighed. "Ye're not going to like this. I despised the Earl for his methods, but it's the only way to keep the boy safe."

Murdock stared. "Aiken deserves to be punished. What would ye have us do?"

Dughall picked up the whip and cracked it on the desk. It was time to exert his authority as lord and master. "Drag him in here and throw him on his knees. We will do whatever it takes to get the child."

Murdock left the room.

Dughall stood tall as his servants entered the study, dragging the miller between them. He pointed to the floor and spoke in a cold deliberate voice. "On his knees, right there."

Jamison forced the prisoner to his knees and growled in his ear. Aiken shook with fear and tottered.

"Straighten him up!" He watched Murdock draw a knife and threaten the miller.

Dughall wondered how far he would have to go. He dragged the strands of the whip along the man's arm and watched him flinch. "Duff Aiken."

"Aye."

"Do ye know who I am?"

"Aye, m'Lord. The Duke of Seaford."

"That I am." He held up the whip and pretended to examine it. "My father called this an effective instrument of torture. I've never used it on a man before."

Aiken's eyes widened.

"Let's get down to business. This morning, I was summoned to the surgery to treat a lad who'd been brutalized. Yer stepson, Luc. His hand was fractured in three places and his ribs were cracked."

Aiken swallowed hard. "It was an accident, my Lord."

"Don't lie to me!" Dughall raised the crop and struck the man hard across the chest. The miller cried out in pain.

"Stupid man. We can do this the easy way or the hard way. Which will it be?" He paced back and forth. "The lad had been birched and beaten with a belt."

"Forgive me, m'Lord. But a man has the right to discipline his son."

Dughall's eyes widened. "Hmmphh... First it was an accident, now it's a matter of discipline. I suppose ye had the right to bugger him, too?"

Aiken stared. "He told ye that?"

"Aye."

"Lies!" The miller struggled to free his hands. "I assure ye that the lad will be punished for lying."

Dughall could barely control his anger. He threatened to strike and watched the man cower like a dog. "The child was buggered! I saw the evidence with my own eyes. This is a crime against God, as well as the Crown of Scotland."

The miller shook with fear. "What do ye want?"

"I want the boy. Luc will stay here from now on to serve as my page. We'll call it military conscription."

"Ye can't take a man's son. I need him in the mill. What if I don't agree?"

Dughall could hardly believe it. Obviously, the man thought he was in a position to bargain. He smiled coldly. "So ye won't give him up. All right. I'll return him after ye pay for yer crimes."

Aiken paled. "What do ye mean?"

"Ye'll suffer the same fate as the boy, no more, no less." He directed his servants. "Throw him in hole and send for Fang Adams. He's to be stripped naked and beaten, at least twenty hard strokes. Fang can bugger him while he's tied and break his hand in the thumb screws."

Murdock smirked. "With pleasure, m'Lord."

"I'm not through, yet. Hmmm... Since it's an eye for an eye, what shall we do about the cracked ribs?"

"Wait!" Aiken cried. "I'll give the lad up."

"What did ye say?"

"Keep him. He's nothin' but trouble."

Dughall sat at the desk and rubbed his hands together. "Excellent. I will compensate ye for the loss of his services. My barrister will draw up the papers in the morning. Oh, there's one more thing."

Aiken stared.

"I want yer dog as well."

Murdock smiled. "The beast is in the hallway, as ye requested."

The young Lord finished the whisky and pounded the glass on the desk. "Get him out of my sight before I change my mind and order an execution!"

Dughall watched as the miller was yanked to his feet and dragged out of the room. His conscience weighed heavily upon him. Who was he to command such a thing? A fisherman? Lord? Duke of Scotland? No wonder the Earl drank day and night. He felt numb as he replaced the stopper in the decanter. He was grateful that he didn't have to carry out his threat. "Must I sink to the tactics of my father? Does the end justify the means?" Seeking an answer, he left the study to head for a guest bed chamber. A young lad named Luc needed his care.

In the corridor a servant boy awaited him, sitting on the floor with a scruffy gray deerhound. He stood and bowed as he handed a rope to his master. "He's a fine hunting dog, my Lord."

Dughall smiled at the child's innocence. "That he is, lad. Now be off with ye." He accepted the leash and walked the hallway with the dog at his heels.

Chapter 11
Luc

Luc Deville woke in a large feather bed that was covered with silk sheets. He had a slight headache and his backside was on fire. The room was strange and he couldn't remember how he got there. *This isn't the mill or the surgery. Where am I?*

Dark memories flooded his senses. Father standing over him, lashing him with a flail... Beating him on the stairs with a belt until he couldn't breathe... Taking out his stiff whang and... The lad drew a breath in sharply. What was done to him was a sin in the eyes of God. How could he bear the shame?

He took stock of his aches and pains. The leather brace helped, but his hand throbbed when he moved his fingers. Deep breaths hurt in spite of a chest bandage and his nether parts were raw. He stared at the brace in wonder. Someone treated his wounds, but where were they now? Luc sat up and looked around. Where was this chamber with four poster bed, soft sheets, and iron-grated windows? It was bigger than his cottage.

Somewhere nearby angelic voices sang a hymn, accompanied by flute and harp. "Ave, ave, ave Maria..." It reminded him of the chapel on Christmas morning. Could it be that he was gone for good? He cleared his ears with his fingers, but the singing continued. *Oh God. Am I dead? Help me to remember.*

Memories danced at the edge of his consciousness. He was carried to the surgery, stripped of his clothes, and laid on the examination table. Praying for death, he'd resisted the healer and sent her away. His head throbbed with pain and anguish. Perhaps he was dead and in another place. Not heaven, because he wasn't good enough. Or hell, for he'd seen that in the eyes of his stepfather. This must be purgatory, the place that was in-between. Or was it?

Luc held up his hand and examined the brace. Now he remembered. An angel tended his wounds, heard his confession, and promised to keep him safe. He looked like the Duke, but that was a trick, for a Lord would never bother with a peasant lad. His stomach growled as he spotted a tray of cakes on a bedside table. Starved, he reached out and stuffed a sweet pastry into his mouth. It certainly tasted like heaven, and he was glad that there was food in the afterlife. The boy felt safe for the moment, but exhausted from his ordeal. He wrapped his arms around the soft pillow, got comfortable, and drifted into a fitful sleep.

***

Dughall arrived at the guest bed chamber and considered his options. He didn't want to frighten the lad, who was likely confused and in pain. He crouched beside the scraggly dog and stroked his large head, gaining his confidence. "Well, Artus. Ye know him best. What shall we do?" He scratched behind his ears.

The dog responded by licking his face. "Wuff..."

The young Lord smiled. "Good idea. I'll let ye make the introductions." He untied the animal and opened the door to the chamber a crack. "Go on. Find yer master."

Artus pushed the door and bolted into the chamber. Dughall saw him run around the bed to the other side and lick the sleeping boy's face. He entered the room as well.

Luc reached out to stroke the dog's head. His voice cracked with emotion. "Oh Artus. Did Father kill ye, too? Was it painful?"

Dughall watched intently. The child thought he was dead, and no wonder with what he endured. He allowed the reunion to continue until the dog took his paws off the bed and sat on the floor.

"Luc..."

The child rolled over and stared with eyes of wonder. "Have ye come to take me to heaven?"

"Nay, lad." Dughall sat on the side of the bed and felt his forehead. "Fever's gone. That's a good thing." He placed a finger against his wrist and took a pulse. "Yer life force is strong. I'd say ye're not dead after all."

Luc sat up. "I thought ye were my guardian angel."

"Nay, child. But I'll take that as a compliment." Dughall smiled as he took his hand and examined the brace. "Handy wee device. Does it feel better?"

"It throbs, but I can bear it. Are ye really the Duke?"

"That I am. And yer master now that I've settled things with Duff Aiken."

Luc cringed at the mention of his name. "I don't have to go back?"

"Nay. Ye'll stay here from now on as my servant."

"What about Artus?"

"The dog stays as well."

His eyes widened. "Oh bless ye, m'Lord. Was Father angry?"

There was no point in hiding the truth. "Aye. He argued and accused, so I threatened him to keep ye here."

Luc hung his head in shame. "Oh... Did he tell ye what happened?"

Dughall reddened. "He didn't have to, lad. I treated yer wounds."

The boy sniffled. “Then ye know that he…uhh…”

“Oh, Aye.”

Luc cried tears of frustration. “Why do ye want me, then?” They flowed freely down his dirty cheeks. “Why do ye care? What would a Lord know about it anyway?”

Dughall’s heart ached with compassion. He was ashamed of his scars, but they might help the child. “Can ye keep a wee secret?”

“I guess so.”

The young Lord unbuttoned his shirt slowly, dropped it to his waist, and turned away. He almost thought that he’d done the wrong thing, until he felt a small finger on his back.

The voice was a whisper. “Who did this to ye?”

Dughall turned slowly and faced him. “My birth father, the Earl of Huntly.” He pulled on his shirt and fastened a button. “With a three-tailed strap. The last time, he left me to die in a stable.”

The lad stared. “Oh…”

“I do understand. Can it be our secret?”

“I won’t tell a soul.”

Dughall sighed. “A few know about my trials, but not many. That’s the way it will be with ye. It doesn’t matter. We both have to go on.” He opened his arms and encouraged the child to come to him.

Luc melted into his embrace. “My Lord?”

Dughall’s heart swelled. “Aye?”

“Ye are an angel.”

Jenny Geddes

Chapter 12
Ominous News

August 8th 1637
THREE WEEKS LATER

DRAKE CASTLE THE LIBRARY

The Duke sat at his rosewood desk, pouring over an ancient manuscript. The book contained the writings of the Greek physician Galen. Rich in anatomical drawings and surgical commentary, it had become a mainstay in his library. Of particular interest were the dissections of live animals, which gave insight into how organs and blood vessels functioned. Years ago this would have bothered him, but now he understood the quest for knowledge.

This morning he was dressed in fine clothes; a kilt with sporran, a silver-buttoned waist coat, and a lace collared shirt. Earlier he'd attended a funeral for a noble, a popular man who served the community for years. The service had been somber as arthritis had plagued him for a decade. Many remarked that it was a blessing to return to God, while others mourned his passing. When the ceremony was done, he'd paid his respects and returned to the castle.

He ran a finger down a page, hoping to find a way to ease a woman's pain as they cut off her cancerous breast. Yesterday, he'd been called to the surgery to evaluate a desperate case. A sixty-year-old widow had come to his mother, complaining of a painful breast. After much cajoling, the woman had allowed him to examine her.

Dughall sighed. What he had seen affected him deeply. There was a thickness and swelling of the breast skin, which extended to the chest wall. The nipple was ulcerated and leaking malodorous pus. What was once so soft, so shapely, and gracious was now as hard as a stone. When he touched the breast, the woman complained of considerable pain. Her pale face, with grey lucid eyes, expressed the suffering she'd born for a year.

His thoughts were tormented. *Why did God choose this woman to bear such a terrible burden?* Her life was already difficult due to the loss of her husband. *Why did she wait so long to show us?* At this stage, the remedy was breast removal and even at that her life could be short. They'd told her what must be done and instructed her to return on the morrow.

He closed the book, disappointed with what he'd found. *The Greeks used laudanum for surgery as well. We are as much in the dark as they were.* Galen warned about the use of the opiate which was extracted from the pods of a poppy plant. The medicine muted pain, but caused death in high doses. The kill dose varied by patient; depending on weight and condition. It was a tricky thing to determine.

His mother was blending a batch of laudanum using a tincture of opium, camphor, anise oil, and whisky. When the woman returned, they would need it.

Dughall felt helpless in the matter. Keira lacked experience with this kind of surgery and his mother suffered from stiff fingers. Yet, he had to leave it in their hands. His advisors convinced him that it would be unwise for him to perform intimate surgery on a woman.

He stood and replaced the book in a glass-faced case and then gazed out the window. Several of his men were away on missions and were expected to return soon. His spirits brightened. In the courtyard, he saw Jamison dismount his steed and hand the reins to a stable boy. The servant helped an unfamiliar woman off a red mare and sent her in the direction of the bakehouse. Minutes passed as the man traversed the square and entered the castle.

Jamison had been sent to Edinburgh to investigate rumors of religious unrest. The King was imposing a new prayer book on his Protestant subjects, insisting that it be read in the capital.

The Duke was aware of the gravity of the situation. Weeks ago, Robert MacNeil paid them a visit, sailing the Bonnie Fay into the harbor. What he'd thought would be a cordial reunion with his uncle from Whinnyfold turned into an unpleasant confrontation. Furious at the prospect of religious persecution, Robert expected Alex to accompany him to Edinburgh. Dughall protested, but stopped short of forbidding his father from leaving. Worse yet, Robert had been angry that he'd become a Catholic.

The Duke sighed. Now Alex was gone on a potentially dangerous mission. Sailing to Edinburgh was risky in a fourteen foot scaffie, not to mention the trouble they might get into. Perhaps Jamison had news of him. As he waited, Dughall examined a world globe, tracing the countries of Scotland and England. He wondered how long the border would be accurate, given the rumors.

There was a knock on the door and his servant entered. His clothes were musty and his beard was unkempt.

Dughall sensed his concern. He sat at his desk and motioned for the man to join him. "Ye've been gone a long time."

Jamison grunted. "Aye, my Lord." He took a seat and cleared his throat. "Forgive my tardiness. I have much to tell ye."

The young Lord was glad to see him, but reserved his welcome for later. These were strange times when business and politics came before friendship. "What did ye find?"

Jamison scowled. "Edinburgh is in an uproar! I witnessed riots, a lynching, and open defiance of the King's edict. It looked like madness, but I can hardly blame them."

The servant had his attention. "Tell me about it to the smallest detail."

Jamison seemed tense. "When I arrived in the city, I learned that the liturgy book was to be read in churches on Sunday. The people were outraged and from what I saw, ministers were rousing the crowds."

"Which ministers?"

Jamison stroked his scraggly beard. "Henderson and Dickson... They claimed to have consulted Sir Thomas Hope and Lord Balmerino to get approval for their plans."

The Duke knew that this meant trouble. "Do we know this Lord Balmerino?"

Jamison nodded. "He was a friend of yer Grandfather. We received a letter from him when ye became Duke."

Dughall remembered dozens of letters, but he'd been too grief-stricken to pay attention. "What did the ministers say?"

Jamison took a flyer out of his pocket and leaned forward in his chair. "These pamphlets were scattered about the city." He began to read with passion. *"Beware of the new and strange leaven of man's inventions, against the word of God and the beliefs of the Kirk! The idolatry of kneeling at the moment of Communion, crossing in baptism, and the obeying of men's holy days shall not prevail!"*

"Hmmphh..."

"The new fatherless Service-Book is full of gross heresy, popish and superstitious, without warrant from Christ our savior! Obey not these bastard

canons that come from the Antichrist's foul womb..."

Dughall took a sharp breath. It was a serious matter indeed, if they were invoking the Antichrist. "What happened when the book was read?"

Jamison narrowed his eyes. "That Sunday, I stood in the back of St Giles, a grand cathedral with four massive pillars. I've never in my life seen such a church. By dawn, it was so packed that there was no way to get a seat. Serving women sat on three-legged stools, keeping places for their mistresses. I spoke with one, a lass named Jenny Geddes, who was determined to stop the blasphemy. Never before have I seen a woman with such fire in her belly." He reddened slightly. "When the time for services came, members of the King's Privy Council arrived to show support for the book. They brought armed guards."

"To the church?"

The servant frowned. "Aye."

"Go on..."

"Dean Hanna appeared carrying the leather-bound book and entered the grand pulpit. As he started to read the new service, the crowd protested, stamped their feet, and hissed to drown him out. It might have stopped there but for Jenny Geddes. She said, 'Villain! Dost thou say mass at my ear?'"

"What happened?"

"Jenny threw her stool, narrowly missing his head. Others joined in, tossing rotten cabbages."

"Did they injure the man?"

"Only his pride... Then the Bishop of Edinburgh entered the pulpit. He tried to quiet the crowd, but as he spoke things got worse."

Dughall's head ached. "How could they get worse?"

"They called him a beast, a false Christian wolf! The offspring of a devil and a witch..." Jamison coughed into his fist. "Pardon the words, my Lord. They're not mine. Some said that it was better that he be hanged as a thief than live to be such a pest to God's church."

"Strong words, indeed."

Jamison snorted. "I wish it had stopped at words... Guards forced the parishioners into the streets, where they rioted and threw stones at the cathedral's windows."

"They defaced a house of God?"

"Aye. When the Bishop left, a mob pursued his carriage, hurling stones and curses. They say that he shit himself." The servant's expression darkened. "Edinburgh is up in arms. Nearly a hundred were arrested and thrown in the Tollbooth."

Dughall's stomach turned. "Was my father there?"

"Alex?"

"Aye."

"Nay. Why did *he* go?"

The young Lord gritted his teeth. "It's a long story. My uncle insisted that he accompany him to the reading."

Jamison frowned. "He wasn't at St Giles on Sunday. Perhaps he was at Greyfriar's. Shall I go back for him?"

Dughall decided to trust his sight. "Nay. Let's wait a week to see if he returns. So, my friend... What's yer assessment of the situation?"

"The people are on fire with religious fervor. It won't be long before it reaches the Highlands."

Dughall reflected on this dangerous situation. Most of his subjects were Catholic, but more than three hundred were Protestant, including his father and mother. Given Alex's reaction, he wondered how it would affect them. Religious fervor was one thing, but acts of lawlessness would have to be punished. His main concern was about what the King would do. He had a reputation for stubbornness and cruelty. "We're a long way from Edinburgh. The unrest may not travel this far."

Jamison paled. "My Lord. I am afraid that I have rendered that impossible."

Dughall's stomach knotted. "How so?"

"After the riot, I sought out Jenny Geddes to inquire about the will of the people. We spent a week together visiting her contacts and discussing the rebellion. We ate, drank, and slept together. After that I married her."

This was too much to bear. "What!? Ye brought her here?" He recalled the lass in the courtyard.

Jamison hung his head. "Forgive me, my Lord. Ye did encourage me to marry."

"Aye, but to bring a rabble rouser in our midst..."

"I can control her."

Dughall was unsure about that. The women in his life were not easily controlled. "See that ye do."

Jamison looked stricken. "I've displeased ye, m'Lord. Do ye wish me to leave yer employ?"

Dughall clenched his teeth. It was an unthinkable prospect. "Nay, I need ye." Nonetheless, they needed to plan for the future. "Summon the scribe to meet with us. We must send word to Gilbert."

Jamison stood. "As ye wish, my Lord. Is there anything else?"

Dughall's expression was grim. "Bring yer wife to the library after supper. I must talk to her."

***

THE SURGERY

Jessie's stomach felt like it was full of butterflies. Beth had just informed her that Marjory was on the way to the surgery. The maid was sent to fetch her daughter-in-law and a bucket of coals for the cautery.

She examined her hands, which were swollen at the knuckles. Arthritis made it difficult to do fine work, but that couldn't stop her. As she waited, Jessie reviewed her preparations. She'd blended the laudanum and littered the floor with sawdust to catch blood. She'd cleaned the table and instruments with vinegar and doused them with witch hazel. When that was done, she'd prepared a spruce oil dressing and torn strips of cloth to restrain the woman. A good light would be needed to ensure a successful result. In spite of the heat, she'd positioned two oil lamps and set them ablaze.

Jessie massaged her temples. She'd been suffering from worry and a lack of sleep. Alex had promised her that he would return after the reading of the false book. It wasn't like him to break his word unless he was in mortal trouble. When Jamison arrived this morning without him, she feared for his very life.

Keira entered the room, carrying a small bucket of hot coals. She set it on the instrument table and stood back. "I'm here to assist, Mother."

Jessie placed the cautery iron into the bucket and buried the end in the coals. She hoped that they wouldn't need it. "Thank ye, daughter."

Keira's eyes widened. "Who shall have surgery today?"

"Marjory Fraser."

"Oh, the scullery maid... She reminds me of my grandmother. What's wrong with her?"

"Her breast is cancerous; beyond reasonable help."

"What do ye mean?"

"To save her life, we must remove the breast. I will do the surgery but ye must hold her still."

Keira winced. "Of course, Mother. What else can I do?"

"Ready the bandages on the sideboard."

As Keira worked, Jessie gazed at the surgery table. Eight feet in length, it had bars on each end which were used to restrain a patient. It seemed cruel, but a body had to be still as the knife was wielded.

Today we will cut off a woman's breast, she thought, unconsciously touching her own. It was such a part of her that she couldn't fathom losing it.

The door opened, admitting the kitchen maid. Marjory Fraser was an elderly woman with thick white hair and a wrinkled face. She was dressed in a long black skirt, woven blouse, and a simple shawl. Her voice quavered with fear. "I am ready, my ladies."

Jessie embraced her. "Try to be brave, friend. What we will do today will try us both."

Keira glanced over her shoulder and gave her a warm smile.

Marjory's eyes scanned the room and rested on the tray of sharp instruments. She turned away quickly, absently massaging her left breast. "Will it hurt when ye cut me?"

Jessie couldn't lie to this gentle soul. "I'm afraid so." She indicated the cup of laudanum on the tray. "But we've prepared a tonic to ease the suffering."

"Bless ye, m'Lady."

Keira spoke softly. "First ye must undress."

Marjory blushed. "Completely?"

"Aye. We don't want to ruin yer clothes."

The widow took off her shawl and placed it neatly on a chair. Then she pulled her blouse over her head and shimmied out of her skirt. After kicking off her shoes, she was as naked as the day she was born.

Keira helped her onto the table and covered her lower body with a sheet. The woman grasped the cloth and pulled it up modestly in front of her.

Jessie rolled up her sleeves and moved to the washbasin, where she proceeded to wash her hands and arms. Then she came to the table and examined the instruments. "Everything seems to be in order. Give her the laudanum."

Keira held the cup to Marjory's lips while she drank it down and stood back when it was done.

Jessie held two fingers against the patient's neck to feel her pulse. After a long moment, she declared "The life signs are strong. I see no reason why we shouldn't proceed." She picked up the cloth strips and spoke in a reassuring voice. "Again, I must ask ye again to be brave."

Marjory's voice was timid. "I shall try."

"Now lie down."

Marjory laid flat on the table and was silent as the women tied her ankles together and fastened her feet to the end of the table. Then they extended her arms over head and tied her wrists to the head bar.

The old woman whimpered. It was clearly something that she hadn't expected.

Jessie stroked her cheek. "Forgive me lass, but we must restrain ye." She directed Keira in a quieter voice. "When we start, cradle her head. She must be still when I cut her." Then she bent over and studied the patient's eyes. "The laudanum is doing its work. We can begin."

***

Jessie prayed silently as she turned to the instrument tray. Today she would use her skill, but the outcome was up to God. She scanned the tray to ensure that the tools were in order. There were: Three sharp surgical knives of various sizes... A small metal clamp... Two threaded needles... A stack of lamb's wool compresses... The cautery iron on coals... Bandages... A leather-wrapped stick.

She picked up the stick and placed it between the patient's teeth. "Keep this here so she won't bite her tongue." Then she uncovered the breast and did a thorough examination, stretching and prodding it in all directions. The ulcerated nipple oozed pus the color of yellow straw. It would have to be removed, as well as the tumorous tissue around it.

Nothing can be saved. She hoped that there would be skin left to close the wound.

Jessie knew that she would inflict pain, but in the end it would ease suffering. It was best to do it quickly, limiting the time that the body was open. She selected a sharp knife and tested it against her thumb. There was no point in delaying any longer. Massaging the breast with the fingers of her left hand, she verified the location of the mass. With this in mind she made a three inch slice, exposing the tumorous flesh. Blood seeped from the wound as she tried to determine the extent of the cancer. Had it gone beyond the breast?

Marjory struggled against her bonds. She was bound and held, but her fingers stretched in agony. The woman cried out in spite of the gag.

Jessie held her breath as she sliced deeper in an arc removing the nipple, tumor, and surrounding flesh. Within minutes, the breast was separated from the body and plopped in a bucket at her feet. Fear rose in her throat. The wound bled freely and there didn't appear to be a vessel to clamp. Sweat beaded on her forehead as she applied compresses to staunch the bleeding. "God help us, daughter."

Keira grimaced. "Did we get it all?"

"The tissue against the chest wall is thick. We should take more, but can go no further." Crimson blood coated her hands and stained the front of her dress. "The bleeding is out of control. We must use the cautery."

Keira looked stricken. "Great Goddess! Should we give her more laudanum?"

"Nay. Too much could stop her heart."

The wound bled profusely as she took the cautery off the coals. In a quick motion, she pressed the hot iron against the bleeding flesh. Two long seconds passed as the iron hissed and the woman shrieked. Then she removed it and examined her work. "I'm going to close the wound."

Keira tried to comfort the patient with words, but the woman's eyes rolled back in her head.

Jessie began to stitch a flap of skin over the open wound. The body flinched with each puncture and pull, but she tried not to notice. As she worked, she counted ten, fifteen, and then twenty stitches. Two more and at last she was done. "Release her and take the stick from her mouth." As Keira obeyed, she went to the basin and scrubbed the blood from her hands and arms.

She returned to the table where Keira was applying a spruce oil dressing. The old woman appeared to be lucid. "Ye're a brave lass," she said, touching her arm gently. "The worst is over."

The patient nodded weakly.

"Daughter... I will send someone to move her to a guest chamber. She must not work for a month. Perhaps we can find her a less strenuous job. Tarrah needs help in the nursery." Jessie rolled down her sleeves and prepared to leave. "May we speak in private?"

Keira followed her into the hall. "Will she be all right?"

Jessie shook her head. "I doubt that we got it on time. We eased her pain, but the cancer is likely to spread to the other breast."

"Oh..."

Jessie took a deep breath. "We must change the dressings daily and watch her for signs of infection."

"I will see to it."

Her head ached, a common occurrence after a difficult surgery. "Tell the other women to come to us at the first sign of this affliction. I hope to never to see such a case again."

With a heavy heart, she headed for her bed chamber to change her clothes and take a nap.

***

LATER THAT EVENING
OUTSIDE THE LIBRARY 7PM

Jenny Geddes approached the library with no small amount of trepidation. She was a simple servant girl at heart. The fact that a Duke had summoned her was wreaking havoc on her nerves.

The past week had been one to remember. She'd risked her life at St Giles to ensure their right to worship. After the riot, some parishioners had been incarcerated to be tortured and tried. She would have shared their fate but for the intervention of a man from a northern estate.

Jamison had whisked her away from the riot to inquire about the will of the people. After a tankard of ale, he'd mentioned that he owned property and served a Duke. These things made him an attractive package to a lady's maid who'd been orphaned at the age of ten. They spent a week together discussing politics, religion, and the future of Scotland. She'd bared body and soul to this handsome man, who seemed to admire her determination. On the sixth night, he'd surprised her by asking for her hand in marriage. With her consent he'd bought the term of her indenture, married her, and taken her north. This was the man that she stood with now, outside the library of his Lord and master.

Jamison seemed nervous. "Remember what is at stake."

Jenny was well aware of what could be lost. True to his word, he owned a farm, a cottage, and thriving vegetable gardens. He had a maid, a gardener, and a barn full of animals, some for food and some for pleasure. She adored his horses and his dogs. The handsome man wanted children. Yet, this wasn't an ideal situation. She'd just learned that the Duke was Catholic, as well as the majority of his subjects. "He's a papist, ye say?"

Jamison reddened. "Aye, but he allows his subjects to worship as they please."

She wrinkled her nose. "That's a rarity. What will he do about the imposition of the false book?" She knew that he couldn't answer this question but asked him nonetheless.

Her husband frowned. "Sometimes these things resolve themselves. The King may back down, given the ferocity of the people's response. He may not interfere with the northern estates."

Jenny's face flushed with anger. "I don't believe it! It's only a matter of time until he looks to the north. What about the rights of the people?"

"I don't know, lass. But if the fervor spreads this far, we will deal with it."

She didn't like his answer, but was unwilling to give up what she'd gained. "So he's a papist! Why does he want to speak to me?"

Jamison took her hands. "The Duke requires my loyalty." His voice was tight. "My choice of mate may have called that into question. To stay in his employ, we need to convince him otherwise."

Jenny felt like she'd been slapped. She wanted to run, but part of her wanted to stay. As this man's wife, she had a chance to be a lady. She swallowed her pride. "I will think as I please, but do as he asks."

He released her hands. "Good enough for now, lass." To seal their pact, he cupped her face and kissed her passionately.

Jenny's body responded to his touch; pushing concern into the background. She reminded herself that he'd saved her life. Surely, he wouldn't expect her to give up her beliefs.

Her husband released her and rapped on the library door. "We must not keep this important man waiting."

***

It was quiet in the library. The windows were closed and the drapes were drawn. No sound entered from the courtyard below. The only exception was the hiss of oil lamps that were placed strategically around the room.

Dughall sat at his rosewood desk, writing in a leather-bound journal. There was much to record, for today he'd attended a funeral and received news that could change his beloved country. In addition, he was worried about his father who could be spending the night in the Tollbooth.

The news that the King was imposing his religion on the Scots was unsettling. How far would he go to make his point? Jamison said that in England, dissenters were hauled before a Star Chamber Court, which could inflict any punishment short of death. Without indictment, due process of the law, or the right to confront witnesses, testimonies were extracted through torture. Was this the future for Scotland?

Dughall sighed. It was an age old question. Why couldn't everyone worship as they wished? As a student of history, he knew that many wars were fought in the name of religion. Since the rebellious acts were sanctioned by Lords, it meant the end of relative peace. To compound matters, Jamison's new wife could cause them considerable trouble. What would she be like? Young or old? Thin or buxom? He'd only seen her from a distance. Would she be quiet or loud? Respectful or defiant? Surely, she'd be aware of the gravity of her situation.

There was a knock on the door, interrupting his thoughts. He was about to find out. Dughall put away his pen and bade them enter. "Come..."

The door opened and the couple entered. They bowed respectfully and waited to be acknowledged.

The Duke motioned for them to take a seat at the desk. He watched the interplay between the two as they sat and was satisfied that they were nervous. At first glance, he could see why Jamison had been stricken with her. Jenny was a beauty with flowing brown hair and a creamy complexion. She had a slightly turned up nose, full lips, and fiery blue eyes.

"My Lord," Jamison said. "I present my wife, Jenny Geddes."

The lass nodded respectfully. "I am at yer service, my Lord."

Dughall wondered if that was true. He started with a benign question. "Welcome, Jenny. I trust that yer new home is comfortable."

She smiled. "Oh, aye. It's a grand cottage and I love the horses."

"Geddes is a common name here. Perhaps ye have relatives among us."

"Nay. I've been an orphan since the age of ten. My only living relative is an uncle."

"His name?"

"Alexander Leslie. He serves in the Swedish army."

Dughall concluded that the man was no threat. "Yer age?"

"Twenty-six."

"Have ye married before?"

"Nay, my Lord." The lass blushed. "Many were interested, but no man could afford to buy my indenture."

Dughall sensed that this was the truth. "So Jamison bought yer freedom."

"Aye."

It was time to test the waters. "Freedom is a precious thing; sometimes more so than life itself." He looked thoughtful. "There are many kinds of freedom; of personal determination, of speech, and religion. But often the road to freedom lay through strife, persecution, and martyrdom."

This seemed to get her attention. The lass leaned slightly forward in her chair. "On this we are in agreement, my Lord. Even so, the quest for freedom is an honorable pursuit. What we have today was paid for by the blood of our ancestors."

"'Tis true…"

She folded her hands in her lap. "Forgive me, but I must ask this. What is yer stance on the rules that are being forced upon the Kirk of Scotland?"

"Jenny!" Jamison cried. "We agreed not to speak of it."

"Let her speak her mind." Dughall's eyes narrowed. "I have not yet decided on a course of action. But I will say this… Catholic, Protestant, whatever their beliefs… My subjects have the right to worship freely, regardless of their choice of religion. I am determined to continue that policy."

Jamison seemed mortified. "I assure ye, m'Lord. My wife will not…"

The Duke made a slight motion, silencing his servant. "It's best to be honest. I know about yer part in the riot, lass."

The young woman flushed. She seemed to be at a loss for words.

Dughall sensed her discomfort. "I see that I've embarrassed ye." He offered an apologetic smile. "How shall I say this? I neither approve nor disapprove of yer actions. Pursue yer beliefs but do not interfere with my subjects. Keep in mind that I will be obliged to punish lawlessness."

For a moment, there was a strained silence between them.

"Ye're not as ye appear," she said.

"Jenny!" Jamison's face was red.

She turned to her husband. "He's a young man, but wise beyond his years. A lord who believes in freedom is a rare thing."

"Wife!"

She stared at him with her blue eyes flashing. "What say ye, Lord Drake? Will ye hear me?"

Her frankness surprised him. She was bold and dangerous, but Dughall admired her spirit. In a way, she reminded him of Aunt Maggie. He decided it was best to keep her close to discover her intentions. "I have much to consider, Jenny Geddes. But I promise that we will talk."

"Soon?"

"Aye, soon."

Alexander Leslie

Chapter 13
Seeds of Rebellion

August 17th 1637
NINE DAYS LATER

EDINBURGH, SCOTLAND

It was hot and dry in the old section of the city, atypical for this time of year. Dust rose from cobblestone streets, choking the hardiest of inhabitants.

Alexander Leslie hiked a sea bag on his shoulder and gazed at the sign on a tavern. The establishment had changed hands since he'd been here last, fifteen years ago. The framed sign featured the innkeeper's name "J. Adams" above a painted image of a man with a gelding. This told him that the inn had stables in addition to beds for travelers.

Alexander placed a hand on the stout wooden door and pushed hard. The portal groaned and opened suddenly into a spacious room with oak plank floors. His first impression was good. Light flooded the chamber from high windows. Rough hewn tables and benches were loosely arranged, occupied by men from a variety of professions.

He felt comfortable here. There were tradesmen, merchants, sailors, and nobles; drinking and talking in small groups. As he walked to the back, he caught fragments of conversation about politics, economics, and the recent unrest. Scruffy dogs lay at their masters' feet, absently scratching fleas. The room reeked of ale, tobacco, and unwashed bodies.

Near the fireplace, a buxom girl in apron and cap rebuffed the advances of a toothless patron. The lass noticed him, her face lighting up with feigned recognition. "What shall it be, good Sir? Ale? Whisky? Or a taste of something more intimate?" She gave him a coy smile, indicating that she was available.

Alexander hesitated. She was bonny enough for a roll in the hay, but he was bound to stay faithful to his wife. His father, Captain George Leslie, had sired four illegitimate children. His mother had been described as a wench from Rannoch. Because of his upbringing, he was unwilling to do that to his children.

"Tankard of ale, lass. That will do for now." He dropped his sea bag on the floor and sat at the nearest table.

As the woman fetched his drink, he thought about his half-siblings. He had a brother in France, another in Spain, and a sister in this fair city. Though she died before they met, he'd learned that she had a daughter. Three years ago, he'd inquired about the lass named Jenny Geddes and learned that she was an indentured servant.

My niece, he thought, *is no better than a common slave. I mean to buy her freedom.*

The lass brought a drink to the table and brushed his shoulder with her bare arm. He mumbled that he was expecting a gentleman and sent her on her way. At fifty-seven, Alexander was an attractive man. A life long soldier in the Swedish army, he had a chiseled look and tight body. He'd earned a reputation as a strategist, been knighted by the Swedish monarch, and had risen to the position of Field Marshal. Now events in his native country compelled him to return. Having amassed a fortune abroad, he could supply an army with cannons and muskets.

The door creaked and opened into the tavern, admitting a well dressed nobleman carrying a gold-topped cane. He stopped and scanned the room, resting his eyes on the seaman.

Alexander guessed that this was the man who had summoned him. The nobleman wore an article of clothing they'd agreed upon; a white silk scarf with gold piping. He signaled discreetly, inviting him to his table.

John Elphinstone, 2nd Lord Balmerino, carefully removed his scarf and crossed the room. He placed the garment on the table and waited to be acknowledged.

"Lord Balmerino?"

"Aye."

"Alexander Leslie, at yer service." He took out a brooch and plunked it on the table. It was a symbol of the Swedish army. "My calling card, as we agreed…" He smiled and extended his hand.

Lord Balmerino shook it. "Glad to have ye on our side." He took a seat opposite him. "The years have been good to ye. Ye don't look a day over forty."

Alexander made a small sound of agreement. "Soldiering is a Spartan existence. Fighting… Guarding… Training the troops… It would be a mistake to go soft."

The man seemed eager to get down to business. "I trust that ye got my letters."

"Aye, as well as those from Sir Thomas Hope. Does this mean that the nobility will back a rebellion?"

Lord Balmerino nodded. "Aye. We're being slowly stripped of our influence and lands, for the sake of his majesty's Bishops and clergy. Most of us will commit men and supplies; some are willing to enlist their sons. There are a few holdouts in Catholic strongholds, but I think that we can bring them to our side."

"Good." Alexander took a sip and rolled the ale across his tongue. It was a bitter variety. He needed specifics. "I heard about the riot and subsequent arrests. What are we in for?"

Lord Balmerino signaled to the serving lass, ordering a round of drinks. He leaned forward and spoke covertly, "After the riot, thousands of men fanned out across the country, spreading the news and carrying petitions. Within weeks we will have them back so that we can face the Privy Council. They will have to inform the King."

Alexander frowned. "He's a stubborn man. What will he do?"

Lord Balmerino was solemn. "The King is not like his father. He will never give in to the will of the people. We're in for a wild ride, my friend."

"Can we raise an army by spring?"

"The people are on fire with religious fervor. The lairds and chieftains should have no trouble gathering troops. But their weapons are primitive."

Alexander was tense. "Leave that to me. I shall return to Sweden to make arrangements. Within weeks, boat loads of cannons and muskets will be on their way."

"Good!" The man smiled. "Of course, we will require yer leadership as well."

"That goes without saying. It is time for this old soldier to serve his country."

"Admirable." Lord Balmerino plunked a bag of gold on the table and pushed it in his direction. "Here is a thousand pounds, a small down payment for yer services."

There was an argument nearby which caused them to take notice. Angry voices rang out as a drink was spilled. There didn't seem to be any immediate danger. They returned to their conversation.

"Did ye inquire about my niece Jenny Geddes?"

Lord Balmerino smiled. "She's a fiery lass; a true asset to the rebellion. She led the riot inside St Giles."

Alexander was surprised. "A woman did this? Did they throw her in the Tollbooth?"

"Nay. I'm told that she left the city to marry a man from a northern estate."

So Jenny had gained her freedom. "Where is she now?"

"Drake Castle; the jurisdiction of the Duke of Seaford. She married his right-hand man." He looked pensive as he fingered the silver brooch. "It's a fortunate thing. We need an organizer in Aberdeenshire."

Leslie nodded in agreement. "What do we know about the Duke?"

"The young man has a reputation. Months ago, he killed his own father in a sword fight to the death. They say that he has the Sight. Some claim that he has supernatural powers."

Leslie smiled. "Ah, the rumor mill… We should all have such things said about us. It gives us an advantage in battle. What are his religious leanings?"

"The man's a Catholic who used to be Protestant, yet seems uncommitted to either."

"How did that happen?"

"He's the long lost son of Robert Gordon, who lost track of him before he was born. Gordon reclaimed him at sixteen from lowly circumstances."

Leslie sipped his ale. "What circumstances would those be?"

"It's said that he was raised by a common fisherman."

"Did Gordon force him to the Catholic faith?"

"Aye."

"It could be useful." Alexander's interest was piqued. "He can't stay neutral in these times. I will visit my niece when I return from Sweden and assess the situation."

The woman brought two tankards and smiled at the soldier as she placed them on the table. She lifted her skirt slightly as she turned and headed for the kitchen.

Lord Balmerino chuckled. "Ye're a lucky man to have influence with bonny young women."

Leslie reddened. "Never mind that. The harlot means nothing to me." He leaned forward to ensure their privacy. "The day grows short. Tell me about the will of the people."

Lord Balmerino smiled. "The people are committed to the cause. What we need is a standard to unite them under." He withdrew a drawing from his cape and unfolded it on the table. "What do ye think?"

Alexander Leslie studied the sketch, which showed a handsome flag bearing the motto 'For Christ's Crown'. He instinctively knew that something was missing. "Can we change this?"

"To what?"

Leslie was pensive as he traced the flag in the sketch. He drew upon his years of military experience. "A standard must portray will and purpose. With yer permission, I would like it to say... For Christ's Crown and Covenant."

"A stroke of brilliance!" the noble remarked as he quickly refolded the paper, "We shall ask them to sign a covenant."

***

DRAKE CASTLE THE COURTYARD

Sweat beaded on the Duke's forehead as he crossed the courtyard. It was a beastly hot day with nary a breeze. Jamison walked at his side, his jaw locked in fierce concentration. They'd been informed that a messenger from Huntly was at the gate.

Dughall had sent a letter to his brother, describing the unrest in Edinburgh. He was eager to see his response.

Jamison approached the guard shack and shouted at the man inside. "Wake up, McBain!"

The burly guard emerged from the shack, bare-chested and sweating. When he saw the Duke, he paled. "Forgive my nakedness, m'Lord. It's ghastly hot out here."

Jamison frowned. "Where is the messenger?"

McBain reached into the shack and grabbed a letter. "The man couldn't stay. But he left this for ye." His chubby fingers held out a parcel.

Dughall accepted it and examined the seal. As expected, it bore the wax mark of the Earl of Huntly, his brother. It was almost noon and getting hotter in the sun. "Thank ye, McBain. That will be all." He turned to Jamison. "Let's find some shade."

They crossed the courtyard to a private garden that featured flowers, trees, and a ring of stone benches. In spite of the oppressive heat, sparrows fluttered and chirped in the canopy. The men selected a bench and sat down.

Dughall opened the envelope with his knife. He removed the single-page letter and unfolded it carefully. Out of respect to Jamison, he read out loud.

"Dear Brother. I am aware of the unrest in Edinburgh. I sent spies to St Giles and Greyfriar's to observe the reading of the book. One of my men returned but the other was swept up in the riot and mistaken for a rebel. He sits in the Tollbooth, awaiting my intervention. Most likely ye are wondering about my position on the matter. Well brother, I am unsure just how far this religious insanity will travel. But know this... If it comes north, we must deal with it accordingly. The Gordons have always been loyal to the King and I intend to continue that policy. We have influence in this area from a religious and economic standpoint. With

the nobles on our side, there are conservative ministers who will listen. Cooler heads shall prevail! Hold yer position and let me know if anything happens. - Gilbert"

Jamison sneered. "I wonder if his spies told him the truth about the riot."

Dughall folded the letter and placed it in the envelope. He was impressed with Gilbert's argument. "Perhaps he's right. With nobles and ministers on our side, we might keep the peace through compromise."

The servant bristled. "The acts I witnessed were not of compromise. I doubt that there will be middle ground." He clenched his teeth. "Damn the King! I wonder if we're headed for war."

Dughall's eyes widened. "War? With our own monarch?"

"Aye, m'Lord. It wouldn't be the first time in Scottish history. Unless the King relents, we'll soon be in the thick of it." The servant sheltered his eyes and gazed across the courtyard. "Well there's a bit of good news. Alex has returned."

"My father?" The young Lord strained to see in the distance. "I don't see him."

"He just crossed the courtyard and entered the castle."

"Was anyone with him?"

"Nay."

The young Lord was relieved. Alex had been gone for more than a month. He'd resisted sending a search party after him, even at the request of his mother.

Jamison stood. "Shall we go after him?"

Dughall joined him. "Nay, allow him some time with my mother. She's been sick with worry." They started towards the castle, taking long strides. "His absence caused me a great deal of trouble."

"Ye could forbid him to go next time."

Dughall stopped. "My father risked all that he loved to rescue me from a terrible fate. The least I can do is to grant him his freedom." His skin crawled. There was that word, *FREEDOM,* which dominated every conversation now that Jenny Geddes was here. He was getting a taste of the trouble it could cause.

***

DRAKE CASTLE A HALLWAY ON THE SECOND FLOOR

Alex was nervous as he walked to his bed chamber. He knew that he owed Jessie an explanation. That morning he'd dressed in common clothes - breeks, a sweater, and a crudely woven shirt. Over one shoulder he carried a sea bag stuffed with soiled garments. Over the other was slung a leather pouch which protected precious documents.

He passed the nursery, a linen closet, and the second floor privy. At last he stood in front of his chamber, thinking about what to say to his wife. A month ago, he'd left Jessie crying at the main gate. She'd been worried that he might not come back. He recalled the tears in her eyes as he promised to return right after the reading of the book.

That hadn't happened. For Alex had been swept up in something larger than himself, fueled by his devotion to God and country. At Greyfriar's, he and Robert had witnessed the birth of a rebellion which spilled into the streets. They'd hidden at an inn to avoid arrest, where they mingled with men willing to risk their lives for the right to worship. They listened to ministers, nobles, and common folk; and took part in heated discussions about church and country. He was convinced that war was imminent.

A nobleman convinced Alex to carry petitions protesting the King's actions. For three weeks he'd traveled tirelessly to Aberdeen and Peterhead and beyond, speaking and gathering signatures. Hay had assumed the mantle of responsibility. Now he was back at Drake, where he planned to gather signatures and return the petitions to Edinburgh.

Bile rose in his throat as he stood at the door. He'd been gone too long without a word to his wife. Hopefully, she would understand. Desperate circumstances threatened to change their very lives.

Beth had informed him that Jessie had taken to her bed, to dispel a terrible headache. She'd scolded him for being gone so long and hinted that he was the cause. He didn't doubt that.

Alex took off his soiled boots and entered the chamber noiselessly. The drapes were drawn to keep out light, but he could make out her slender form. His heart melted when he saw her lying on the bed with a wet compress over her eyes. Was she sleeping? His heart ached at the sight of her. *So bonny... How fortunate I am.*

Alex dropped his sea bag and placed the pouch on a nearby chair. As his eyes adjusted to the light, he saw her touch the compress. He moved to the bed and sat beside her. "Lass..."

Jessie tore the compress from her eyes, looking like she'd seen a ghost. "Alex. Ye came back to me."

He stroked her cheek. "As long as there is breath in this body, I shall return to ye."

She sat up and embraced him. "They said there was trouble in Edinburgh. When ye didn't return, I thought..."

"That I was arrested? Nay, that didn't happen."

She searched his eyes. "Then why have ye been gone so long?" The tips of her ears were turning red, a sign that she was getting angry.

He couldn't lie to her. "It's a long story, wife, which I'll tell after a meal and a bath."

"But what could it be?"

He took her hands and sighed. "I've been called by a higher power to serve God and country."

"Is this about the new prayer book?"

"Aye." He frowned. "That book was sent to us from the depths of hell! I am bound to defend my faith."

She squeezed his hands. "Can it not be left to a younger man?"

He was offended by this, but tried not to show it. "I may not be young, but I command the respect of others. I must carry these petitions protesting the King's actions and get them signed."

Tears flowed down her cheeks. "Will ye leave again?"

"Aye, wife." He decided to bare his soul. "Try to understand. For the first time since we left the sea, I feel like I have a purpose."

"Oh, Alex. We serve the Duke of Seaford. Our children and grandchildren are here. What can ye mean?"

He gathered his thoughts. "This is a comfortable place, I grant ye. But other than the weeks when I'm out to sea, there's nothing for me to do. I've been thinking of returning to our cottage. That way I can serve the cause without involving our son."

Her ears were bright red now. "The cause? Dear God! Why must we defy our King? Think about what Maggie said about winding up on the losing side of a conflict! She lost her grandfather and brothers in battles that we barely remember. How will it end?"

"I don't know, lass." He smiled sadly as he found solace in a bible verse. "But change is already upon us… As Jesus said… 'It will be foul weather:… for the sky is red and lowering.'"

***

DRAKE CASTLE THE LIBRARY THREE HOURS LATER

The Duke relaxed at his desk, sipping ale from a crystal goblet. Murdock had delivered a pitcher of brew with two of his lion-etched glasses. After all, there was something to celebrate, the safe return of his beloved father.

The room was beginning to cool down. They'd opened windows and pulled back the drapes to let in a negligible breeze. Even his sweat-dampened clothes were starting to dry.

Murdock had reported that his father was on his way. According to the servant, Alex looked well, but Lady Jessie had been crying.

Curious, he thought. *My father is alive and whole. Why would my mother cry?* There was a knock on the door, signaling his arrival. "Come…"

Alex entered the room with a leather pouch slung over his shoulder. When he reached the desk, he sat and placed the bag on his lap. His voice was husky from weeks of trail dust. "I have returned, my Lord."

Dughall's heart squeezed painfully. His father seemed cold and distant. "Father… We are alone. Ye don't have to call me my Lord."

Alex took a deep breath. "It's only proper."

"I'm yer son!" The young Lord poured his father a glass of ale and refilled his own to the top. "Now drink with me and tell me where ye've been."

"All right, *son*." Alex lifted his glass and examined the etchings. "This is a fancy thing. He took a long sip and looked at it again. "Almost too fancy for a man like me."

"I will send for another."

"Nay bother." He took another swallow. "I will start from the beginning. After a four day sea voyage, Robert and I docked the boat in Edinburgh harbor. The next morning we attended the service at Greyfriar's Church..."

Dughall was silent as his father described the reading of the book, the reaction of parishioners, and subsequent riots. So far it agreed with what Jamison had said. But Alex's story went further. He paid attention as Alex gave an account of what happened at the inn. He concluded with the fact that he'd been approached by a Lord to carry petitions throughout Aberdeenshire. "What Lord did this?"

Alex stared. "Lord Rothes. Do ye know him?"

"Nay, but I intend to make his acquaintance. So what did ye do?"

Alex looked surprised. "Why, I carried them of course! To Aberdeen and Peterhead and Fraserburgh... That's where I've been the last few weeks."

Dughall's head ached. "Did anyone recognize ye?"

"Some did. I convinced them to sign the petitions and signed them myself at each stop."

Fear rose in his throat. This was a sure way to get targeted by the King. "Father... I don't know what our position will be on this matter. Gilbert wants me to support the monarchy, but I'd like to stay neutral."

Alex reddened. "What! How can ye stay neutral when our right to worship is at stake? The book is an abomination from Satan!"

"These are problems of men, not of God or Satan. We plan to send an envoy to London to ask the King to reconsider. Can we not see if cooler heads prevail?"

"Cooler heads!" He scoffed. "Have ye not listened to what I said? The time for diplomacy has passed. What happened to the lad I raised? Ye've grown soft since ye turned to the papist faith."

Dughall felt wounded to the core. "Nae soft... Catholic... Protestant... It doesn't matter to me."

"Then change back to the true religion."

"I can't. Keira feels comfortable with the Blessed Virgin."

Alex scowled. "Hmmphhh... I've wondered about yer wife."

Dughall felt threatened. "I will not allow ye to speak ill of her. Our choice of religion doesn't matter. What matters is our personal relationship with God."

"Sounds like blasphemy."

The young Lord clenched his teeth to control his anger. He hated arguing with a man he loved more than all others. "Let's not discuss this any more today. Just tell me what ye intend to do."

Alex opened the pouch and showed him the petitions. "I will speak to our people and gather signatures. I planned to visit Huntly as well, but it's clear that I won't be welcome."

"Gilbert will not allow it."

"Then I will work the towns around Huntly. I must deliver these petitions to Edinburgh by late September, where they will be sent to King Charles."

King Charles... The name struck terror in his heart. His father had no idea how bad the man could be. Dughall decided to assert himself. "Present yer arguments to my people, but coerce no one to sign that document. Is that understood?"

"Aye." Alex's eyes narrowed. "I see that my actions have made ye uncomfortable. It won't be for long. I've been thinking of moving back to the sea."

"Nay!" The young Lord could hardly believe it. "Father, do what ye want but don't leave me."

Alex was silent as he packed the documents in the pouch. He took a long sip of ale, finishing the glass. The two men stared, not daring to say another hurtful word.

At last, Alex stood and slung the pouch over his shoulder. "My son. My Lord. The dogs of hell are loose. There will be no middle ground 'til they're caught. I am willing to give my life for it."

"Father, please..."

"Consider what I have said." The man turned sharply and left the room without bothering to say goodbye.

Dughall had a hard time catching his breath. In fact, he felt like vomiting. Hot tears filled his eyes. He knew now why his mother had been weeping.

Chapter 14
Royal Outrage

August 18th 1637
ONE DAY LATER

LONDON ENGLAND

King Charles sat at his desk, fuming over the audacity of his Scottish subjects. For weeks, he'd been seeking a truthful account of the trouble in Edinburgh and today he'd finally got one. The messenger from the Privy Council had cooperated under torture. Charles smiled, even though he thought it inappropriate. Archbishop Laud had supervised it and given him a detailed account.

Laud had been specific about the messenger's fate. They'd suspected that the man was lying to present things in a better light. A week in the Tower and an hour on the rack changed his mind. With feet fastened to one roller and wrists chained to another, they ratcheted the tension on the chains until his joints slowly dislocated. The victim's screams were augmented by popping noises as ligaments and cartilage snapped. Then he confessed.

Charles examined his wrist, tracing the delicate blood vessel at the surface. He wondered what it would be like to stretch the joint until it separated. The pain would be excruciating. *Pain and pleasure are two sides of the same coin,* he mused. *How would we know one without the other?* He understood this sexually as well, and savored the times when his wife was dominant.

From boyhood, he'd been fascinated with torture. At first he experimented with cats, tying them between stakes. Young Charles applied each torture slowly; extending the creature's life. Why kill them quickly? He enjoyed the shrieks and watching their eyes going dead. As a man, he'd studied the history of torture. To the dismay of his subjects, he brought back two of the cruelest devices; the rack and the wheel. Charles expanded the powers of the Star Chamber to examine cases of sedition and suppress opposition to royal policies. Nobles too powerful to be brought to trial in lower courts could be tried in secret with no right of appeal. Torture was applied to extract a confession.

The King hadn't always relied on such measures. As a prince, he was born and bred to the use of Parliaments. During his father's reign, he'd participated in them with his friend, the Duke of Buckingham, treating the process with the utmost respect. After ascending to the throne, he became disillusioned when Parliament failed to provide him with adequate finances for his wars with Spain and France. He blamed them bitterly for the shame and dishonor that the failed campaigns brought upon his country and person. Parliament's disrespect for the deceased Duke of Buckingham had been the last straw. He suspected that they were involved in his assassination and resolved to rule without them.

Charles reddened as he thought about Edinburgh. God's will was not to be denied and he *was* the hand of God. He would force the Privy Council to implement the book and then issue more decrees. From this day forward, no teacher would be allowed to teach children without a bishop's license. No book would be printed without inquisitorial scrutiny. And no preacher would be allowed to preach without signing the canons of belief of the state church. He would send the messenger back in a wagon, bruised and broken and bearing the official letter. There would be no negotiation with these half-clad Scythians! Those who defied him would suffer the consequences.

Chapter 15
The Plot Thickens

September 15th 1637
FOUR WEEKS LATER

MILES FROM DRAKE CASTLE

The weather in the northeast was tolerable. The days were cool and the leaves were beginning to turn. Alexander Leslie galloped through the forest on a magnificent steed named Spirit. The horse was an Arabian, rare for these parts, and had cost him a small fortune. The stallion had a reddish coat, a white facial mask, and a silky mane that could have graced a wig. "Easy, Spirit." He pulled back on reins slightly, slowing the horse to a trot.

Leslie spotted Drake Castle in the distance and found it impressive by any standard. He noted a tower at one end which was attached to a series of tall buildings. His military training prompted him to assess the security. There appeared to be a catwalk along the top, manned by six armed guards. A ten foot outer stone wall was meant to keep intruders out. He located a gate with a guard shack and headed for it.

The business in Sweden had gone well. He'd taken leave from the national army and used his personal wealth to purchase weapons. In the port of Bohus, he'd hired twenty-four mercenaries and sailed the North Sea to Edinburgh. There he'd entrusted the men with the tasks of securing wagons and provisions; and setting up a military camp in the lowlands. After meeting with Lord Balmerino, he purchased the stallion and headed north to visit his niece, Jenny Geddes.

He dismounted at the gate so that he could talk to the guard on an equal level. After all, he was not expected. There was a hitching post nearby, so he tied the animal to it.

"Ho!" An armed guard stepped out of the shack and confronted him. "I dinna recognize ye. What business have ye here?"

Leslie smiled. "I wish to visit my niece, Jenny Geddes. I'm told that she married a man named Jamison."

The guard looked wistful. "Ah... Lady Jenny... Wait here. I shall send a man to fetch her."

Leslie scanned the grounds as he waited. Outside the wall, there were cottages, barns, and hovels for tradesmen. He knew that these were in addition to what lay within the castle walls. This place must have been created with a great deal of wealth. He wondered about the man in charge of this grandeur, the Duke of Seaford. He'd discussed the young man with Balmerino, to determine how to bring him to their side. The old Duke had been a man with a solid reputation, well respected, liked, and strictly Catholic. But the new Duke was an unknown who was plagued by rumors about his character. Perhaps it could work in their favor.

Minutes passed where nothing important happened. White-capped maids with baskets of eggs passed by, giving him long looks of interest. He wished that he knew what Jenny looked like. Soon, he became aware of an attractive girl in her twenties watching him from the top of the wall.

"Alexander Leslie?" Her voice was sweet. "Uncle Alex?"

"Aye, lass!" He gestured for her to come down and watched as she disappeared from the wall.

Jenny burst through the gate and ran to him. "Uncle Alex!" She embraced him and stood back. "Ye don't look old enough to be my uncle."

Leslie appreciated the compliment. "The army keeps us young. Can I impose upon yer hospitality? I would like to spend a few days at Drake."

She linked her arm in his. "Ye are welcome in our home anytime! Ye're my only living relative."

They walked to the gate and untied his horse. Jenny smiled as she stroked the animal's mane. "Oh! He's beautiful. I don't think I've ever seen such a horse."

"He's a rare breed, of Arabian stock. Can I stable him somewhere?"

"Oh, aye. My husband has a cottage with a barn and stables. We would be pleased to have ye stay with us." She led him away from the gate towards one of the outer properties.

"He's a landowner?"

"Aye. The former Duke bequeathed the property to him."

"Yer husband must be an important man."

Her pride was evident. "Jamison is the Duke's right hand man."

Leslie was delighted. Once again, Lord Balmerino had been right. "Can ye introduce me to the Duke?"

"Aye. He's an interesting man."

They walked for a mile until they approached her property. At first glance, Leslie noted a cottage, a barn, and vegetable gardens. He saw an old man tilling a bed with a pitchfork. "Is that yer husband?"

She laughed. "Nay! My husband is a young man. Handsome too. That's the gardener. I have a maid as well."

His niece had done well for herself. They could chat for hours, but it was time to get down to business. He took her hands. "I'm happy for ye, niece. We have much to discuss."

"Why are ye here?"

"It's time for this soldier to serve his country. I've been asked to lead an army against the King."

***

THE BATH CHAMBER

Dughall stepped into the steaming copper tub. He allowed his legs to get accustomed to the warmth and then lowered himself slowly into the water.

The last few days had been difficult. His father returned from the Huntly area, after completing his quest to get petitions signed. He'd informed Dughall that he would be leaving soon to deliver the documents. No amount of cajoling could change his mind. A letter arrived from Gilbert, protesting Alex's actions in his jurisdiction. He owed his brother a response. His own subjects had been mixed about the petition. While some had signed, most abstained, following the lead of their Lord and master. Even Ian refrained, incurring the wrath of his father. His mother had been despondent, leaving the work in the surgery to Keira.

Dughall lay back, allowing the hot water to relax his neck muscles. He didn't know how much more he could take. "Ahhhh..." He thanked God for the warmth and prepared to meet with his father. At breakfast, he'd insisted that Alex join him in the bath chamber.

The door opened and his father entered. Alex stripped silently and stepped into a tub, which had been poured to be at room temperature. Dughall had seen to his father's preference.

The young Lord watched as the man settled in and lathered his chest with a bar of soap. He sensed that his father was brooding over something more than petitions. When he began to rinse, he said, "Thank ye for coming."

"My son. My Lord," Alex began. "I hope that we do not argue today."

Dughall made a small sound of agreement. "This is my hope as well. Nothing should stand between father and son."

"Agreed." Alex lathered his hands and began to wash his feet. "Tomorrow I depart for Edinburgh without my sons. I canna tell ye how long I will be."

Dughall was miserable. The man obviously felt abandoned. "Will ye send word?"

His voice was heavy with emotion. "I shall try. There is one thing that I ask."

"I cannot sign that petition."

"I know what ye said. There is still hope that ye will see our side."

"Aye, there is hope. As a Lord, I must exhaust all possibilities before inciting a war. Then what do ye ask?"

"I've had a premonition. If something happens and I don't come back..." His speech strangled. "Promise me that ye'll care for yer mother."

Dughall's eyes filled with tears. "Of course, Father. But that won't happen. Ye'll leave the petitions and return to us." This is what he'd hoped for. He would allow him to do his part, return home, and that would be the end of it. From Drake, there was a chance that he could protect him from the King's wrath.

Alex didn't answer right away. He poured water over his head and began to wash his hair. "I love yer mother more than life. And my sons have been a source of pride and joy. But I must do what is right."

"Oh, Father."

"Do not hate me."

Dughall's heart ached. "I could never hate ye! Ye're a man of principle, though stubborn to a fault. Do what ye must and come back to us."

Alex sighed. "I shall try, son. I shall try."

***

JAMISON AND JENNY'S COTTAGE

Alexander Leslie sat at a table, watching his niece pour tea. Her slender hands filled their cups to the brim. He hoped that he hadn't told her too much. The lass had provided him with valuable information about the castle, the Duke, and her new husband. She'd told him things about the Earl of Huntly as well, from overheard conversations. Though she seemed naïve, she was committed to the cause and now she was sworn to secrecy.

Jenny returned the kettle to the fire and sat opposite him. "Uncle Alex."

"Aye, lass?"

"Less than a hundred signed the petition. Most are watching the Duke. They will do as he says."

"Hmmphh..." Leslie sipped his tea. "So we must convince this one man. With his lack of commitment to either religion, there has to be a way."

"Agreed."

"Who's carrying the petition to Edinburgh?"

She smiled. "He's a captain in the Duke's fleet and a staunch believer in the rebellion. He also happens to be the young Lord's stepfather."

Leslie slapped the table. "What a stroke of luck! He's the man who raised him?"

"Aye. His name is Alex Hay."

Leslie's mind raced. This opened up a dozen possibilities. He decided upon one.

"Do ye wish to meet with the Duke?" Jenny asked.

"Nay, lass. We'll save that for later. But ye must introduce me to Alex Hay."

"As ye wish."

He needed to know that he could trust her. "There's one more thing. We are kin, are we not?"

"Aye."

"Blood is thicker than water, lass. Promise me that ye'll tell no one of our conversation, especially yer husband."

She nodded her consent.

***

LATER THAT EVENING

Alex Hay put on his coat as he took the stairs to the ground floor of the castle. After an hour with the minister, he was sure of his path. For tomorrow, he would leave on horseback to deliver the petitions to Edinburgh. Alex made peace with his sons, but still had to face his wife. He planned to make love to her tonight, attending to her needs before his own. Oh, how he hoped it wasn't the last time! There was just one more thing he had to do. Earlier, he'd been summoned to the tavern by Jenny Geddes. She had someone who wanted to meet him, a believer in the rebellion. He left the building, crossed the courtyard, and continued through an alley to the establishment.

Alex drew back a black leather flap and entered the tavern with caution. Men tended to drink to excess after nightfall and looked for excuses to get into fights. He needed none of that tonight. Though noisy and poorly-lit, the place had patrons at every table. His nostrils were assaulted with the smell of unwashed bodies.

"Alex Hay!" Jenny shouted to him from across the room.

He'd hoped that she wasn't alone and was relieved to see her with a gentleman. More than a few pairs of eyes followed him as he walked to their table.

She stood and introduced them. "Alex Hay. This is my uncle, Alexander Leslie."

The man extended his hand. "Call me Leslie. I'm pleased to meet ye, Hay. My niece was kind enough to arrange this meeting."

Alex shook it. "I'm pleased to meet ye, but I don't have much time. I leave for Edinburgh tomorrow."

"I must return to my husband," Jenny said with a smile. "On the way out, I'll tell the lass to bring more ale." She turned abruptly and left the table.

Alex took a seat across from the man. He appeared to be in his forties, although he could be older. His body was tight and muscular, that of a military man. But there were crow's feet around his eyes. He wondered if he should be suspicious. "What do ye want, Leslie?"

A lass brought tankards of ale and plunked them down on the table. She turned and went to the kitchen. The two men lifted their mugs and drank.

"I hear that ye're the man in charge of the petitions."

Alex nodded. "I deliver them to Edinburgh tomorrow."

Leslie took another sip of ale. "To Lord Rothes?"

Alex was impressed. It was obvious that the man had connections. "Do ye know him?"

"I'm a long time soldier, a commander of men. Lords Rothes and Lord Balmerino called me back from Sweden to serve my country."

"How so?"

Leslie leaned closer and spoke in low tones. "They say I can trust ye, Hay."

Alex's skin crawled. "Aye."

"He asked me to lead an army against the King. I've gathered mercenaries and weapons, but there's plenty more to do."

Alex was sweating. This was dangerous information, meant for the ears of a few. "Why are ye telling me this?"

"Ye have a reputation, Hay. I'd like ye to be one of my lieutenants."

Alex was stunned. He was a fisherman, not a soldier. Yet here was an opportunity to serve the cause in ways he hadn't imagined. "I have no experience with weapons."

"We will train ye." The man seemed unconcerned with his lack of qualifications. "I leave for Edinburgh tomorrow. Shall we ride together?"

It took him less than a minute to decide. "Aye, Sir."

"Tell no one of our conversation."

Alex swallowed hard. There would be few who would agree with it anyway. "Ye have my word."

Father Ambrose

Chapter 16
Ambrose

September 21st 1637
ONE WEEK LATER ,
THE PAGAN FEAST OF THE EQUINOX

CHURCH OF THE REDEMPTION
ELGINSHIRE, SCOTLAND

The stone chapel was empty on this late September day. A row of pews graced the middle, complete with kneelers and scattered hymnals. Glowing candles cast long shadows, illuminating the altar. A hint of incense lingered in the air.

Father Ambrose knelt at the rail, his bare knees against the cold marble floor. His brown wool robe was stripped to the waist, exposing his back to the mercies of his whip. His bony arm raised and struck again, extracting a grunt and a troubled sigh. Years ago he could bear it for hours, but he wasn't the man he used to be. An inner voice chastised him. *Ye can never suffer what he did. Ten more, sinner.*

The priest clenched his teeth and wielded the strap with determination. Thwack! Thwack! Thwack! Thwack! His hand shook and the instrument dropped, clattering on the floor. He retrieved it quickly and held it to his heart. "Forgive me, Lord. I can't go on." He grasped the rail and tried to stand, but failed miserably. The Almighty wanted him on his knees. *I deserve it,* he thought. *Ten years in this parish and I've failed to purge them of their pagan ways. Beyond these walls, they worship their Gods and the dead in the land of Avalon!* His anguished thoughts turned to self-righteousness. *Sermon upon sermon wasted upon the ignorant. Why can't they see, Lord? Yer way is the only way, not a path among many! Perhaps they need a lesson, more painful than the last.* Ambrose's heart ached. How could it be more painful? The last man to die at the stake was Jock, his dear and trusted friend. Before the accusation they hunted together, traveled afar, and shared many a pint in taverns. His friend was a pious Christian or so he'd thought until a witch named him one of thirteen. After her execution, he had no choice but to put the fire to his feet.

Ambrose, don't do this! Jock's voice echoed in his ears. *For God's sake! Jesus wouldn't want this.* He'd screamed as the fire crawled up his legs. *Ambrose, please!*

The priest glanced furtively over his shoulder. No one was there but the voice was clear. Jock's voice, begging for mercy! "Dinna haunt me, witch! Let me be!"

Nay, friend. Not until ye see it differently.

Perhaps there was hope. "Differently?"

We are sparks of God, both saint and sinner alike. It's God that ye're burning, in spite of yer beliefs.

"Nay!" The priest shrieked, covering his ears. "These are Satan's words! Father in heaven. Why must ye test me this way?" He fell to his hands and retched on the floor. Minutes passed where he clawed the floor, struggling to regain his strength. At last, the chapel was quiet but for the breath of someone behind him. His skin crawled. Was Jock in the flesh?

A man spoke. "Oh, Ambrose. Not again. Are ye all right?"

The priest's heart thumped against his ribs. "Geck?"

"Aye. Supper's on the table. Let me help ye up."

Ambrose wondered how much his simpleton brother had witnessed. He got to his knees, picked up the whip, and handed it to Geck. "Six more strokes. Do it."

"Nay, brother."

"Ye've done it before."

"Aye, but no more."

"It's a holy thing, a matter of repentance. Wield it with honor and we'll go home."

Geck frowned. "It's wrong."

Ambrose reddened. "Idiot! I'm yer priest and confessor! Do what I say or suffer the consequences."

"What will ye do, brother? Harden yer heart and kill me like Jock? Will my spirit haunt ye like his?"

Ambrose felt like he'd been slapped. "Poor Geck. Ye don't have the sense to understand what ye saw. If ye knew what I've done to ye..."

Geck grunted. "I'm not as simple as I look. Ye bedded my wife and gave her a child."

Ambrose's breath caught in his throat. "She told ye that?"

"Lord Gordon said it was true, so I asked her. She admitted it."

He forced the whip into his hands. "Then strike me hard! Six! Seven! Eight! As many times as ye want. For God's sake, ye have reason."

"Nay, brother."

"But I wronged ye!"

Geck's lip trembled. "I forgave ye long ago, for my own peace. Besides, I love the wee bairn."

"Hmmphh..." There would be no redemption tonight.

"Supper's ready. Come with me, brother."

As the man lifted him under the arms, he was reminded of his transgressions against him. *What did she tell ye, brother? I ravaged her in church and gave her a son. We did it in yer own bed. Oh where is my vow of chastity? Woman, thy name is Jezebel!* His mind raced in an attempt to deflect guilty feelings. How did the Duke know about that? And the letter opener he stole as a lad in Edinburgh? His transgressions were nothing compared to this evil warlock who channeled Satan. The attempt on his life failed because the man was well protected. What could he do?

The priest was upright now, though in a fair amount of pain. "Ach! These old bones are not what they used to be." They locked arms, hobbled out of the church, and took the steps to the path. As they walked, Ambrose devised the next lesson. He would find the witch the Duke saved, burn him to death, and kill every man, woman, and child in his village. That would put the fear of God in his people, smoke out Lord Gordon, and make him vulnerable. This time it would be different. The Bishop would reward him with a place in his court, suited to a man of devotion. He would retire and live in a monastery, far from his brother's vixen wife, and repent his sins of the flesh. The voices in his head would stop. His conscience pricked. *I've never killed an infant before.* Ambrose turned to the good book for justification. *Thou shalt not suffer a witch to live.*

All that he needed now was a sign.

Brother Lazarus

Chapter 17
Return to the Forest of Deer

September 30th 1637
NINE DAYS LATER

DRAKE CASTLE

The Duchess stood in the nursery, bundling her daughter for a long journey. After much consideration, her husband had agreed to take them to her forest village. She found it hard to understand his reluctance to travel alone as a family. In addition to the wet nurse, they were to be accompanied by five armed men. Keira sighed. She longed for simpler times and wondered what it would be like to be married to a fisherman. The attempts on his life frightened her.

The little girl cooed as she tucked her dark curls into a red bonnet. Oh how she resembled her father! The first weeks had been difficult, but once the colic passed she'd been a joy.

"Mmm.. ." Wee Maggie waved her arms and smiled.

"That's right, sweetheart. *Momma.* I love ye like my own." She longed to take her to the stones and dedicate her to the Goddess.

Dughall entered the room, dressed in his finest riding clothes. It was apparent that he'd had a bath. She found him hard to resist when he smelled of soap and bayberry, and her face flushed with desire.

His smile told her that he read her intentions. He nibbled her ear, sending shivers down her spine. "Ready, wife?"

Keira blushed furiously. "Oh, aye." He could have her right there on the dressing table.

Dughall drew a finger across her lips. "No time for that, lass. But there is one thing I must do." He reached into his pocket and drew out a pair of gold rings.

Her heart fluttered as he took her left hand and slipped one on her finger. It was an unusual ring with a heart in the center, held by two hands. "It's beautiful. What does it mean?"

The Duke smiled. "Father acquired these for me in Galway. The heart signifies everlasting love and the clasped hands signify friendship. There's a story about them."

"Do tell me."

"A lad was kidnapped by pirates and sold to a Moorish goldsmith, who trained him to be a craftsman. Heartbroken by the loss of his lass, he fashioned a ring to symbolize their enduring love. Years later, he returned to Galway as a free man. She'd waited for him, and they married."

"Oh husband. It's perfect for the way we feel about each other."

"How true." He held up his ring. "There is an inscription inside that says 'I have nothing, for it is given unto ye.'" He slipped the ring on his finger. "Now we are one, in love and friendship."

She smiled as he kissed her hand. Wee Maggie gurgled in her bunting, interrupting the tender moment. They separated and turned their attention to the child.

"My dear wife. The wagon is packed, the nurse is aboard, and the men are waiting. Is our daughter ready?"

She picked up the baby and cuddled her against her shoulder. "Aye. I changed her nappy, so we should be good for a while."

Dughall smiled. "Are ye glad to be going home?"

Her heart swelled with joy. "Oh aye. I've missed my friends. Janet and Allistair.. . Torry and Ailie.. . Dear Michael.. ."

"They're good people. I wish we could convince them to live here."

"Will ye ask them, husband?"

"For all the good it will do. In spite of what happened, Michael insisted he'd die there."

"Oh.. ."

His expression darkened. "Father Ambrose's fight is with me. We must pray that he leaves them alone."

Keira struggled with this new religion. In her village all life was sacred, from the tiniest bee to a pregnant woman. A priest would never destroy it. "Was he the man who hanged Mother?"

"I was a lad of seven, but I remember him well." He stroked her cheek with his fingertips. "When I think that they could have killed ye as well…"

"But ye saved me," she insisted.

"Because our union was meant to be, lass." He stroked the infant's cheek. "Such a precious child. Will they love her like we do?"

"How could they not?"

"Only six months have passed. Ye can't claim her as yer own. Will yer people understand?"

"I hope so." In truth, she'd been thinking about what to tell them. Perhaps a white lie was in order.

"Tell the truth, wife."

Keira blushed. It was impossible to hide things from a man with the Sight. Did he think less of her? His smile reassured her.

"Truth is always the best course of action. Then there's no need to remember the stories ye tell." He took the baby and cradled her against his broad shoulder. "Come along now. We must get underway to reach the abbey by dusk."

With a light heart, Keira followed him out the door and down the corridor.

She was excited about the trip and madly in love with her husband and daughter. What could go wrong on such a fine day?

***

ROAD TRAVERSING A FOREST SOUTHEAST OF DRAKE CASTLE

LATE AFTERNOON

It was a gorgeous fall day in the Highland forest. Oak leaves rustled along the path and the air was ripe with the scent of pine trees. The weather was cool and there wasn't a cloud in sight. Dughall felt at peace as he rode his beloved stallion. His troubles seemed to disappear as he merged with the powerful beast. He was an accomplished horseman and couldn't imagine life without it. Lightning's taut muscles pulsed between his thighs, inviting a response from his master. He leaned forward and caressed his mane. Birds warbled in the canopy and a nearby stream trickled over rocks. This was God's music, superior to any man could create. It reminded him of the times he and Gilbert rode to the moor and beyond to the village where Beathag lived. For a moment, he remembered the old woman who gave her life to protect him. It was something that he regretted to this day.

Overhead, greylag geese honked, reminding him of simpler times.

As a lad he'd traveled the forest on foot, searching for healing plants. It was on such a trip that he met his future wife and asked her to wait for him. *A year ago,* he mused. *I was a fisherman with hardly a care in the world.*

Gilroy and Suttie led the group, riding white stallions with their weapons in plain sight. The two men were skilled warriors and as loyal as his brother. As the horses clopped through leaves, they discussed a servant lass in a manner that disturbed the young Lord. He resolved to speak to them later.

Dughall glanced at his new charge, young Luc Deville. The lad was riding a rust colored pony and carrying the Drake flag. Luc had been more than he'd bargained for. Unable to read, write, or ride a horse, they'd started his lessons within weeks, thinking that he was healed. But Murdock told him that the lad suffered from fits of crying and refused to obey his superiors. He would have preferred to leave the boy at the castle but didn't trust his stepfather, who'd confronted him on more than one occasion. The man would be rotting in irons if not for the lad's intercession.

"My Lord?" Luc wiped his nose on a velvet sleeve.

"Aye?"

The boy tightened his thighs, causing the pony to rear. "I don't understand this horse. What does he want from me?"

"Relax yer thighs, lad. The beast needs to know who is in control. That's better. What do ye want?"

"Are we almost there?"

Dughall smiled. It had been a while since he'd traveled with one so young. "Let's ask an expert woodsman." He looked over his shoulder. The wagon was close, drawn by a team of horses and driven by his faithful servant Murdock. Behind him, Keira and the nurse sat on a bench seat, huddled in blankets and tending to the baby. Further back, Jamison and Ian guarded the rear atop their favorite steeds. He could hear his brother's thoughts as he agonized over leaving Mary and the bairns. "Murdock?"

"Aye, m'Lord."

"The young lad wants to know if we're almost there."

Murdock frowned. "He does, does he?"

"Aye."

"Luc is always full of questions." The servant snaked the reins across the horses' rumps. "Hmmpph.. . If memory serves me, the abbey is another five miles. I could be wrong. This place has bloody few landmarks."

"I've never seen an abbey before." Luc's eyes widened. "That's where monks live! Mother used to call them holy men. Will we stay there, my Lord?"

"Grandfather was their benefactor, so we would be welcome. But we might stay the night with my wife's people."

Gilroy raised a hand and stopped the procession. The heavily bearded man reined in his stallion. "Halt! I smell smoke."

Suttie sniffed. "Forest fire?"

"Nay. It reeks of pine tar and thatch. I'd guess a cottage roof is ablaze."

Dughall dismounted and handed his reins to Luc. Gilroy was right. The air was bitter with the scent of burning straw. As he approached his servants, he sensed people in need. "Let's continue on."

"It might be dangerous," Gilroy said, scratching his wooly head. "The forest could ignite and blanket us in smoke."

Dughall trusted his feelings. "There's no danger here. A woman and child are in trouble."

"It could be a trap."

"Ye know better than to question him!" Murdock snapped. "If the Duke feels that it's safe, then it is."

"Why are we stopped?" Jamison shouted. "And who questions his Lordship?"

"Forgive me Sire," Gilroy replied with downcast eyes. He pulled on the reins and turned his horse.

Dughall mounted his stallion. They followed the path until smoke was visible and saw a cottage throwing sparks up into the dense foliage. A wee lad at the side of the road wailed pitifully as they approached. There was blood on his shirt and a cap in his outstretched hands. "Bring the healer's bag, wife!" Dughall cried. "Get the child! Look, there's a man down by the cottage." He dismounted and ran to the smoldering structure, pursued by Jamison and Gilroy.

Under a tree, a woman in a torn dress kneeled beside a limp body. Her eyes were blackened and her hair was singed. She rocked back and forth in agony. "They murdered my husband."

Dughall crouched by the body of a young male. He was lying face down in a pool of blood and his neck was at an unnatural angle. He turned the body over to get a better look. The lad's tongue was swollen and his eyes were bulging. The young Lord caught a whiff of fecal matter. The woman rolled her eyes and groaned. He was sure she was close to hysteria.

Dughall gagged. Bowels and blood oozed from a belly wound, but the rope around his neck told the story of his last moments. He loosened the cord and took a pulse against his neck. "He's gone, lass."

Jamison's nostrils flared. He drew his sword and signaled for Gilroy to do the same. "Let's head for the wagon. We should return to Drake at once."

"Nay, friend. They've lost their husband and provider. We must help them find safe harbor."

Keira arrived with the healer's bag, carrying the child who greeted them at the road. She shielded his eyes against the sight. "Poor laddie. He says it's his father. Who did this?"

"Three men!" the woman wailed. "They tortured my husband and strangled him."

Keira crouched and placed the child in her arms. "Go to yer mum, wee one." Her voice softened as she touched the woman's forehead. There was a gash over one eye that looked like it came from a blow. "Be still while I seal this wound. Why would they do such a thing?"

"They were looking for witches!" the woman sobbed. "A village among stones. We knew nothing of the place." Tears streamed down her dirty face. "I had a charm of protection above my threshold. They must have thought..."

Dughall's fear blossomed. The murderers seemed to know about the forest village. "What did these men look like?"

"Two were young, but the one in charge was old with white hair."

"Did ye hear any names?"

"Ummm... Ambrose."

"Think, lass! Which way did they go?"

The woman's arm rose slowly. Her bony finger pointed in a southerly direction. "Through the woods."

Dughall helped his wife to stand. He sensed the compassion she had for these people, but it was his duty to protect her. "They've gone in the opposite direction, wife. What shall we do?"

Keira kept her voice low. "Help this woman and her son. Then I must warn my people." She crouched to attend to the injured lass.

How he loved that woman!

Jamison took him aside. "My Lord. This looks like the work of the priest. We should turn back immediately."

"Nay."

"If they're watching us, we could lead them to her people."

Dughall clenched his fists. "Then comb the area. Make sure that we're not followed." He addressed the men. "We will take these people to the abbey. The monks will know what to do for them. Then we will continue to our destination."

Jamison's eyes were full of anxiety. "As ye wish, m'Lord. But from now on, we're armed and ready to fight."

***

The remainder of the journey was fraught with heightened sensibilities. Jamison rode beside his master, sending young Luc to guard the rear. Ian, Gilroy and Suttie scouted ahead and behind and reported back every mile. They agreed on an early warning system, where a man in danger would hoot like an owl. The ladies rode in the wagon behind a nervous Murdock, protecting the young lad and his Lordship's wee daughter. It was quiet except for occasional conversation between Dughall and Jamison.

Dughall was torn between turning back and going on to the forest village. He feared for his wife's people and hoped to convince them to return with him. On the other hand, he felt responsible for his servants and feared for his wife and daughter. Would they be cruel enough to kill women and children? His heart squeezed painfully. "Jamison?"

"Aye?"

"What would ye do if ye were me?"

Jamison's hand tightened around his sword. "I'd turn back and protect the bloodline."

Dughall swallowed hard. The implications were frightening. "What about my wife's people?"

"Send a messenger to the village."

"They won't listen to anyone but my wife." He sighed with resignation. "We must go on."

Jamison made a sound, indicating his displeasure. "Why can't we go another time?"

"When will there be a better time? Scotland is on fire with religious fervor. My father is in Edinburgh awaiting the King's response to the protests. Gilbert expects me to meet with him. And yer wife is causing trouble with my subjects."

Jamison grunted. "Forgive me, m'Lord. I should have never married her."

Dughall nodded. "She's a challenge, my friend. But marriage is a sacred vow; one not to be taken lightly. Motherhood may change her."

"I doubt it."

"Enough about her! We must visit my wife's people. Is there a way that we can keep the children safe?"

Jamison hesitated. "We could obtain lodging at the abbey as a diversion. Suttie and Luc can stay the night, as well as Tarrah with the wee bairn. They'll be safe there. The rest can steal out to the village and return at dawn. It will appear that our purpose was to visit the abbey. Ye can make a contribution to the monk's cause and receive their blessing. Yer grandfather did."

Dughall considered this valuable counsel as they rounded the bend and approached the abbey. "Agreed. We will ask for lodging and base our operations from there. After supper, some will retire to their rooms while we visit the village."

Jamison raised an eyebrow. "My Lord?"

"Aye?"

"They might offer ye confession at the abbey. For God's sake, keep quiet about the witchcraft."

Dughall smiled.

They arrived at the stone steps of the abbey church and stood in awe at the magnificent structure. Cruciform in shape, it spanned one hundred and fifty feet and was adorned with a statue of Saint Drostan. Grand yew trees graced the grounds.

Dughall instructed his party to stay outside while he and Jamison secured lodging. The two men walked up the stone steps and opened a wooden door to the church. Inside, there was a vestibule with a font of holy water and a basket of dried flowers. It was dark except for muted light from stained glass windows and the glow of a single candle.

Jamison removed his cap and held it in his hands. His eyes scanned the church for danger.

Dughall dipped his fingers in the font and made the sign of the cross. "In the name of the Father, Son, and Holy Ghost." It was a ritual that touched his soul.

The men entered the church and walked a long aisle past elaborately carved pews and transepts that housed chapels dedicated to saints. They passed the latticework chancel which provided seating for the choir, and then approached the altar. A monk arranging flowers turned to greet them.

The hairless man stood before them in a white cloak, emanating concern and kindness. "We get few visitors these days. Who are ye, Sir?" His eyes lingered on the lad's royal ring. "Forgive me, my Lord. I did not realize that ye were the Duke of Seaford. I offer condolences on the death of yer grandfather."

Dughall felt a twinge in his heart as he remembered the man who meant so much to him. If Grandfather thought these monks worth supporting, then so would he. How could he deny the holiness of this place and the sense that it protected a great secret? "Thank ye, Brother. Grandfather encouraged me to make a pilgrimage to this place and to contribute to yer cause. So here I am."

The monk smiled. "Then we must offer ye lodging and a meal. We live simple lives, worshipping God and working with our hands. The fare is spartan at best, but that can be good for the soul."

Dughall smiled. "We welcome the hospitality. There are seven men, three women, and two children in our party. A woman and her son require yer charity, as their provider has been cruelly murdered. We found them at the road five miles back."

The monk nodded sympathetically and folded his arms in his long sleeves. "We will keep them until their relatives are found. My name is Brother Luke. Ye are welcome to stay the night." He motioned to a door in the back of the church. "I will take ye to the Abbott."

***

The Abbott's house was a modest stone structure that stood apart from a building housing a parlor, a refectory, and a kitchen. Jamison and Dughall followed the monk through a narrow oak door into the Abbott's study. Barred windows provided light as they seated themselves and waited for the man that Grandfather had spoken of so often.

Soon, a balding monk in a white robe entered the room and sat across from them, fingering a silver crucifix that adorned his neck. He folded his hands in his lap and spoke in a deep voice. "I am Brother Lazarus, Abbott of Deer Abbey. So ye are James' grandson."

"I am," Dughall replied. "Grandfather spoke of ye often, Sir."

The monk smiled. "Perhaps it is I who should call ye Sir, or do ye prefer my Lord?"

The Duke relaxed in the presence of this man. Somehow, he knew he could trust him. "Like ye, Brother, I am a humble servant of God. Ye may call me by my given name, Dughall."

"My Lord!" Jamison objected. "It isn't proper."

"Ask yer servant to wait outside," Brother Lazarus said. "We have business to discuss."

Dughall turned to his manservant. "The Abbott was Grandfather's trusted friend. Go now. I'm safe in this house of God." His expression signaled that he'd be careful.

"Yer rooms are ready," the Abbott offered, "and the horses are being stabled. Brother Luke will take ye to them."

Jamison stood and bowed slightly. "I'll tend to our people and return for ye, m'Lord." He left the study.

Brother Lazarus reached inside a cubbyhole and took out a carafe of wine and two crystal goblets. He filled each glass, handed one to the young Lord, and bowed his head in prayer. "Bless this wine, o' Lord, that we are about to partake of. May we seal our friendship with this bounty." They sipped the dark wine, which had a flavor reminiscent of ripe black cherries. "James said that ye're a moral man with an unshakable belief in God."

He blushed. "I am."

"James said that ye have the gift of the second Sight."

Dughall could hardly believe what he was hearing. The man knew about him and wasn't afraid. "Ye don't want to kill me for it?"

"Nay. Only the ignorant try to destroy it. Others use it for personal gain and corrupt its value. But in the hands of a man such as yerself it is a gift from God. Ye see, in the beginning man had more than five senses. The sixth was what ye call the second Sight. It was taken from us when we fell from grace."

Dughall sipped his wine. "Why do I have it, then?"

Brother Lazarus put down his empty glass. "We don't know why, but it runs in families. Yer mother had the gift, her grandfather before her, and so on. It can also occur in those born on an auspicious day, like the Day of the Dead. I understand that ye were born on that day."

"Aye."

"Ye received a double dose of ability."

Dughall felt naked under his intense gaze, but an inner voice told him to trust. He needed answers. "There have been attempts on my life because of it. Some call me an abomination in the eyes of God."

The Abbott's eyes narrowed. "These men are misguided. Ye are not an aberration, but the next step in spiritual advancement."

The young Lord took a sip of wine and put down his glass. This was quite a responsibility. "Did ye know my mother?"

The monk smiled. "Aye. The last time James brought her here was before her wedding to Lord Gordon. We documented her abilities in a book we keep on the Drake bloodline. Would ye like to see it?"

Dughall had no idea that such a book existed. "Aye. Why did she agree to marry the Earl?"

Lazarus frowned. "Lady Christal opposed it. There were questions about his character, especially in regards to women. From what I know, it was a marriage of convenience to seal an agreement between two clans. She accepted her fate, hoping that love would come later."

His heart ached. "It never did. The Earl hated her gift and beat her relentlessly. She died for me."

"'Tis true. James regretted it. He longed for his own death until he found ye." The man sighed. "He accepted that it was her duty to have a child to inherit her gift, in spite of the consequences."

"Poor Grandfather."

"James was a practical man. In the end, he admitted that it was a blessing ye were raised by a loving family. These gifts need to be nurtured. I understand ye're a healer with a talent for bone setting. Ye wouldn't be the same man if the Earl had raised ye."

He'd come to the same conclusion. "I'd likely be a heartless, angry man, bitter about fatherhood." They were quiet for a moment, basking in the warmth of the wine. "So, it's my duty to have children. I have a daughter named Margaret Christal; born a few months ago."

"The infant ye arrived with?"

"Aye."

The monk smiled. "Excellent! Watch her closely. The gift can manifest at an early age."

"Before birth?"

The monk's eyes widened. "What do ye mean?"

"She appeared in a dream, begging me to save her life. The birthmark on her hand was the same. She also appeared to my wife."

"A gifted child, indeed."

Dughall glanced out a window and noticed his servant approaching. He didn't have much time. Grandfather told him that he could discuss anything with the Abbott. He had a question that had been weighing upon him. "Can I ask a question of a spiritual nature?"

"Of course, my son."

"I am troubled by one of the Ten Commandments. 'Thou shalt not kill.'"

The man folded his hands in his lap and took a deep breath. "Go on..."

"I always thought that it was absolute; that no one should kill under any circumstances. Then I see that we torture and kill each other because we paint different faces on God. To me it's the same thing, whether we see God in nature or the Cross."

"Ye're a deep thinker indeed," Brother Lazarus mumbled.

"That's not all. Men kill to protect me and I am obliged to put men to death for crimes like treason." Dughall thought of the archer. "I feel the axe on their necks! How can I make sense of it?"

The monk appeared to be deep in thought. His answer didn't come for several minutes. "Perhaps if we all felt the pain of our victims, there would be no persecution or crime. Even war would be a thing of the past. I will meditate on yer question."

There was a knock at the door and Jamison entered. He bowed respectfully. "My Lord. Our people are resting in their rooms. Forgive me, but we need to talk before dinner."

Brother Lazarus stood and extended his aged hand. "Ye are a remarkable man, Lord Gordon. I look forward to our conversations. Freshen up and join us for dinner. We are simple men who rise with the sun and retire at dusk."

The young Lord shook his hand. "Thank ye for yer kindness. It seems that we have much to discuss." He released his hand and followed his nervous servant outside.

Jamison's face was full of suspicion as they walked towards their quarters. "Our quarters are in the west range of the abbey, my Lord. What did the Abbott say?"

"I can scarcely believe it."

"What is it?"

"There's no danger here. Let me think on it." He turned his attention to their plans for the night.

***

The refectory was a free-standing stone building near the monk's cloister. The main room was illuminated by narrow windows, as well as torches on inner walls. Two long carved oak tables were graced with matching chairs and pewter dinnerware. The air was moist and filled with the smell of cock-a-leekie soup and fresh bread. The Duke's party sat at one table, partaking of the modest meal. Water and ale flowed freely but talk was subdued, avoiding mention of the night's coming escapades.

Dughall sat at the other table with the Abbott and nine monks. They were an aging order, with no man younger than fifty and several over seventy. Even the cook had been with them more than twenty years. The Duke suspected there was a reason they restricted their ranks, but what could it be?

Brother Lazarus seemed to read his mind. "'Tis true. There's been no new blood here in decades."

Dughall's eyes widened. Again, he sensed that the abbey housed a secret and resolved to ask the Abbott about it later. "When I return to Drake, I will send an emissary with a donation. Do ye have special needs?"

Lazarus smiled. "We would be grateful for supplies to assist us with scroll transcription and preservation. Glasses that magnify… Quill pens and squirrel-hair brushes… Gold and silver foil… Cedar preservation cases and the like... I will provide a list."

Dughall nodded. "Ye shall have it. About the scrolls... Is there a library here?"

"Aye."

"Might I see it sometime? I find myself interested in old manuscripts."

The Abbott smiled. "Ye are welcome to peruse our collection. Do ye read Latin or Gaelic?"

"Nay."

"Then I shall teach ye."

"It will be my pleasure." Dughall stood and bowed his head slightly. "Forgive me, but I must attend to my people. Our trip was fraught with danger, and the ladies are exhausted." He extended a hand to the Abbott. "We will talk again tomorrow." The young Lord left the table, gathered his people, and left the refectory. It was getting close to dusk. They would have to hurry if they were to reach the forest village by nightfall.

Michael

Chapter 18
People of the Stones

DEER ABBEY

The women's quarters were chilly. The Duchess saw their breath in the air. Accommodations were basic. Four rope beds stood in a row, covered with rough wool blankets. Bells rang, calling the monks to the cloister.

Tarrah smiled. "Oh, m'Lady. Angels couldn't make a sweeter sound."

The Duchess nodded, then slipped back into dark thoughts. She was anxious about leaving her daughter in this unheated room. She'd become accustomed to the castle, where cold nights were only a bad memory.

The baby was in the nurse's arms, snuggled against her bare breasts. The child made a sound of contentment as she took a nipple.

Keira felt a pang of jealousy. The babe should be suckling at *her* breast.

"Dinna fret," Tarrah said. "The bairnie will be safe with me."

"But it's cold in here."

Tarrah gathered a blanket around them. "It's nae different than the servants' quarters. I raised two wee ones in a room like this. Nae heat, nor light." She shifted the babe to the other breast. There was a popping sound as the infant took the nipple.

Keira frowned. "What happened to yer children?"

Tarrah looked sad. "The grippe took the wee twins. It broke my heart to pieces."

"Forgive me, lass. I didn't mean to hurt ye."

"Nae bother." She stroked the child's forehead. "Someday I'll have another."

They were silent for a moment, sharing a thought about infant mortality. It was bound to be damp and chilly in the woods. Keira slipped on a pair of wool tights and pulled on her sturdiest boots. "Keep her warm. We'll return at first light."

"God speed, my Lady."

Keira managed a smile. "Bless ye, Tarrah. What would I do without ye? Now, remember what my husband said. If anyone asks, we're indisposed. Don't tell them where we've gone."

"I won't."

"Lives depend on it."

"What about Luc, ma'am?"

"He's staying here with Suttie, though he's none too happy about it."

Tarrah looked up from the nursing. "Best that he stay here. That lad's a pack o' trouble on his best day."

Keira wrapped a plaid around her shoulders. She really had to go. "What do ye mean?"

"He won't obey anyone but m'Lord."

"My husband told him to stay behind."

There was a knock on the door and the Duke entered. "Are ye ready, lass? The sun is going down."

Keira took his outstretched hand. His skin was damp with sweat and he smelled of wood smoke and horses. "I'm ready, but..."

"Dinna fret. She'll be fine."

Keira blushed. Were there no private thoughts? He always knew what she was thinking.

After a backward glance at his daughter, Dughall escorted her into the hallway. They left the abbey via a narrow door and walked to a grove where his protectors waited - Jamison, Ian, and Murdock.

Jamison passed Dughall his ancient sword. "My Lord. Allow me to fetch Gilroy. He's a trained fighter."

"Nay, friend." He tested the weight of the blade in one hand. "I can fight with this if we get into trouble."

Keira was disappointed. "Must ye bring that? My people are unarmed, except for knives and shovels."

Blood rushed to his face as he lifted it higher. "Silence, woman! I will have my sword."

Keira's cheeks burned with indignation. Why did his character change when he wielded the blade? Was the curse real? Gilbert thought so. It would be impossible to convince her people to join them if they appeared as fearsome warriors. She prayed silently. *Great Goddess, give me strength to hold my tongue.*

***

THE FOREST OF DEER

They entered the forest and followed a trail, stopping at a gurgling stream. Dughall kneeled to fill a flask. "It's going to be a long night. We might get thirsty."

Murdock spoke, "I remember this stream. When we came for the lass, we stopped here to get our bearings. The stones can't be far."

Keira pointed. "That deer path will lead us to them. My village is a mile beyond that."

"We need to move on," Jamison said. "It's starting to get dark."

Dughall stood. "I'm ready."

Keira took his arm. "I know it's late. But I must visit the circle, if only for a moment."

It was hard to deny her when she looked so bonny. Dughall brushed a kiss across her forehead. "A promise is a promise. We will stop there first."

They followed the path until they came upon a sign. An arrow made of sticks and twine pointed to a hidden footpath. They lifted a branch, walked underneath, and spotted the stones. Dughall's skin tingled as they approached the ancient monoliths. This place spoke to the core of his being. Ages ago, in another life, he knew that he'd worshipped in circles. He watched as his wife proceeded to the center mound.

Keira stood for a moment in silence and then raised her hands to the sky. "Great Goddess! Mother of all. I am grateful to be in yer presence." She took a deep breath. "Six moons have passed, yet I have not forgotten." She continued her heartfelt prayer, imploring the Goddess to help them.

Dughall was deeply affected. At the castle, she'd found solace in the Blessed Virgin. He'd hoped that she was adjusting to a new religion. Now he realized that he'd kept a caged bird, expecting her to forget her wings. Who was he to deny her? When they returned, he would renew his efforts to find her a stone circle.

***

They pressed on to the village, navigating by the moon and stars. Jamison and Ian fell behind to check out a strange noise. When they reached a clearing, the servant returned, looking worried. Jamison spoke in hushed tones. "We're being followed by one man, not a skilled tracker. I've sent Ian to apprehend him."

There was a rustle of brush indicating a struggle and a sudden shout of surprise. Ian emerged from a row of pine trees, towing Luc DeVille by his ear.

"Ow!"

"Wee bastard!"

"Ye're hurting me."

"I'll do more than that!" They were approaching now.

Jamison took the Duke aside. "Luc was told to stay with Suttie. We can't take him back, but he must be punished."

Dughall didn't want to beat the child. "I can't do it."

"Then I will. Ye must order it or he'll never respect ye."

"But his father..."

"I know what his father did. Perhaps the man had good reason." He drew a leather strap out of his pocket.

The young Lord shuddered. "Are ye sure?"

"I would do this to any man who disobeyed us."

Dughall's heart sank. It had to be done if the lad was to be of use. "Ten strokes, no more. Not on his buttocks." He felt sick. "I don't want to see it."

Jamison nodded and squeezed his shoulder. Ian had arrived with the lad and was holding him in place by his ear. The servant grabbed the boy by the arm and growled a threat in his ear.

"My Lord!" Luc cried, as he struggled against an iron grip. "Don't let him beat me."

The Duke frowned. "Take yer punishment like a man or we'll return ye to yer stepfather."

Luc's expression was grim as he looked up at his captor. It didn't take long to make a decision. "Do it, Sir." The boy's shoulders dropped as Jamison led him into the woods. He wasn't as tough as he appeared to be.

Dughall's nerves were on fire as the beating began. He heard the crack of the strap and felt each stroke on the lad's bare back. One... Two... Three... Four... Five... Oh God. Jamison was no stranger to meting out punishment. Six... Seven... Eight... The child was begging for mercy. How could he know how long it would last? Nine... The tenth was the hardest. Luc cried out, and then it was over.

Dughall suppressed a sob. Keira's hand was on his shoulder, but it gave him no comfort. He spotted them coming out of the woods side by side, the lad walking under his own power. Jamison seemed to be having a talk with him. Surprisingly, he reached out and tousled the boy's hair. A moment later, they reached Dughall and stopped before him.

"Go on," Jamison said.

Luc sniffled. "Forgive me, my Lord. I will obey from now on."

Dughall felt numb. "See that ye do."

***

They reached the outskirts of the village as the last of gray twilight disappeared. Her people lived by the cycles of the sun and had returned to their stone cottages. It was a comforting sight. Wood smoke rose out of squat chimneys and candles glowed behind shuttered windows.

Keira missed this place. Her soul belonged among these kind people. Her sacred forest… her beloved stones... Why did she ever leave them? She'd given up a lot to marry her husband. They'd planned to visit for a few days. But that was before they learned of the danger. Now, all she had was an evening to convince them to come to Drake. Keira decided to rouse Michael, to ask if he could call a meeting.

They stopped at his doorstep and stepped back. Keira knocked on the door. Soon there was a sound of fingers fumbling with a latch and the door opened. Michael's face lit up with recognition.

Keira smiled. His hair was whiter than she remembered it. His expression of pleasure turned to suspicion when he saw her with four armed men. "Michael?" Her voice was soft. "I've come for a visit."

He stepped outside. "Who are these men, lass?"

"Ye remember my husband Dughall?"

He stared. "Aye. He saved my life." He acknowledged Ian and Jamison. "These men helped him."

Keira was eager to get past formalities. "The others are Murdock and Luc. Dughall is the Duke of Seaford. These are his sworn protectors."

"There's no need to come to this place armed."

She hugged him. "I know, dear brother. But there are forces who seek to destroy this village. We came to warn ye."

Dughall spoke, "Can we talk to yer people about a matter of importance?"

Michael frowned. "They're in bed. We will summon a meeting in the morning."

"I'm afraid that we must leave before dawn. Most think that we're staying at the abbey. We made sure that we weren't followed."

"A wise precaution." Michael offered Keira his hand. "Allow me to take yer wife to each cottage. When they see her, they'll be likely to join us. Meet us at the barn."

Dughall nodded.

Michael frowned. "Oh, and sheath those weapons."

***

The people gathered without exception to visit with their former priestess. The barn was unheated, so they sat on the floor bundled in blankets. A crude lantern provided light. Keira started by telling them how much she missed them. She avoided the trouble with the priest, leaving that topic to her husband. The lass looked around at her people. They seemed well given their brush with starvation.

Michael and Torry sat near the door, keeping a watchful eye on the proceedings. Kevin and Morgaine and their son sat next to them, with Craig and Jeannie and the wee twins to their right. The Birnies, Wests, Cummings, and Davies occupied the center, wiping noses and nursing infants. Her friends Alistair and Janet Murray sat to her right holding wee baby Keira. George and Aileana McFay sat across from her, smiling broadly. Aileana looked like a budding young woman. The Duke's men stood guard outside.

Keira began to describe life at the castle. The safety of the fortress... The abundance of food and firewood... The servants... The tradesmen... The chapel... An occasional burp or fart from the wee ones punctuated her lively talk.

Dughall sat beside her, holding her hand for reassurance. When she finished, he cleared his throat. "We come with a warning. On our way here, we encountered a tragic situation. A man was tortured and killed in front of his family. The widow said that the murderers were looking for a village of witches. We think that they're looking for ye." It was quiet until the idea sank in. Women pulled their children close and looked to the men for direction. Dughall continued. "Tonight we entered this village without resistance. If our intent had been evil, ye would be dead."

"What do ye expect us to do?" Michael asked. His voice seemed unfriendly.

Dughall glanced at Keira. "We would like ye to come to Drake Castle. I can protect ye."

There was a flurry of arguments among the men, both pro and con. Women shielded the ears of their little ones. At last, Alistair spoke. "Where would we live?"

Dughall was encouraged. "I'll grant ye a tract of land near the castle. My tradesmen will help ye build cottages and a barn before the snow flies. Until then, the castle will be yer home."

"Can we take the animals?"

"Aye. I'll provide wagons to transport yer belongings."

Michael stood to address his people. "Children of the Stones, listen! There will always be those who seek to destroy us out of ignorance. Shall we leave our ancestral home? Shall we abandon the sacred stones? I think not."

Keira's heart sank. She never expected such opposition after his near execution. "Michael, please. If ye saw what they did to that poor man..."

"I know, lass. They almost burned me to death."

"Then why will ye not consider..."

"I will not live in fear! The Goddess will protect us."

Dughall frowned. "The priest has a grudge against me for saving yer life. He won't rest until..."

Michael held up a hand. "I'm grateful for the offer. But we must stay near the stones." They were quiet for a moment, contemplating their fate. The priest spoke. "This matter is settled. Say goodbye to our sister and return at once to yer hearth fires."

***

Keira was devastated. In spite of their best efforts, they'd failed to convince her people to join them. It was possible that none of them would survive. They left the village and hiked through the woods with moonlight and stars as their guide. Large drops of cold rain fell from the sky, as bitter as their disappointment. Keira consoled herself with a thought. Hopeful that her people would change their mind, Dughall left a map with Torry describing the way to Drake. He only had to appear at the gate.

They reached their quarters before dawn, stripped off their wet clothes, and crawled into bed to get a few hours of sleep.

Doo-ull

Chapter 19
Brother Lazarus

THE NEXT MORNING

It had been a short, cold night. Except for the Abbott's house and cloister, the abbey was unheated. Wool blankets provided warmth; so they slept in spite of the temperature. Dughall rose early, concerned about his daughter. He'd visited the women's quarters and found her sleeping peacefully in the nurse's arms. There was no point in disturbing them. Unable to go back to sleep, he joined the Abbott for a morning walk and was invited to accompany him to the scriptorium.

Dughall was struck with a strange feeling as he followed the monk into the cloister. It was as though he'd been there long ago, surrounded by familiar faces.

Brother Lazarus turned. "Ye've been here before. A soul connection of some kind. It's not unusual for this place."

Dughall was impressed. *Brother Lazarus has abilities of his own.*

"Not like yers, my Lord. My abilities are limited. I have been fooled in the past." They walked a hallway and entered the scriptorium, where monks studied at sturdy tables. A few looked up and greeted them.

"Is my family book here?" Dughall asked.

"Somewhere special. We protect it." The Abbott led him across the room to a wall that was covered with a massive bookcase. He removed a book and touched something. The bookcase rolled to the right, exposing a wall with a doorway that led to a staircase.

"Impressive."

The Abbott smiled. "There have been times when we needed to hide someone. We trust that ye'll keep this secret."

They went down an ancient staircase and arrived at an oak door. Its metal knocker plate was covered with runic seals, which played a part in tripping the lock. "Do ye know what these mean?" the Abbott asked.

"I recognize them," Dughall admitted, as he touched one that looked like a right-facing rake. "Ansuz is my favorite. They say it's the bringer of messages from a higher power, inside and outside of ye."

Brother Lazarus nodded. "I've not heard it put that way. But it fits. The word Ansuz means God, but some scriptures call it 'the Mouth', referring to its association with messages. There's a poem from old Saxony that goes..."

The Mouth is the source of every speech,
The mainstay of wisdom,
And solace of sages,
And the happiness and hope of every nobleman.

Dughall closed his eyes as the monk turned three seals to open the door. *Teiwaz, Uruz, and Kenaz, the symbols for Duty, Energy, and Wisdom.* In his mind's eye, he saw work tables flanked by bookcases and a monk with steel-blue eyes. A name came to mind. *Alpin the fair one.*

"Come now," Lazarus said, holding the door open.

Dughall opened his eyes, entered the chamber, and looked around. The room was as he envisioned it, with rows of tables and massive oak bookcases. "Where is the monk who works here? Alpin?"

Lazarus smiled. "He died a hundred years ago. The fair one found and transcribed our most valuable manuscript."

Dughall got a chill. "Can I see it?"

"In time. Today I will show ye the records we keep on the Drake family." Brother Lazarus opened one of the glass-faced bookcases and retrieved a leather-bound volume. It bore the Drake seal on its spine. He brought it to a table and left it there while he lit candles on nearby tables. "We never light a candle on the table we're working on," he explained. "A spark from the fire could destroy these precious works." They stood at the table and opened the book, being mindful of pages that were stuck together.

Dughall viewed the first page with great interest. Not only were there words describing his history, but each generation started a new page. The first word on a page was larger than the rest. It was inscribed in old script with brilliant colors and gold and silver paint. Such works of art! The word on *this* page was Callum. It was adorned with a silver sword and a familiar red and blue tartan.

The Abbott cleared his throat. "We began recording yer history one hundred and fifty years ago. Callum Drake, yer great, great-grandfather, was our benefactor." He touched the page and pointed out the name. "Lord Drake visited us with his son Tcharloch, demanding that we drive the devil out of him."

"What!? There is no such malady."

Lazarus nodded. "We didn't believe it either. The lad was ten, but he was wise beyond his years. He drove his elders daft with antics. They claimed that he knew what they were thinking and feared that he would be put to death by the townspeople." He turned the page to display the name Tcharloch, beautifully scripted and decorated with a fire-breathing dragon.

"What an interesting creature. What did ye do?"

"We separated the boy from his father and tested his abilities. Not only was he able to read thoughts, but feelings and intentions as well. We explained this to his father, saying that it had nothing to do with the devil. It was a rare gift that needed training and protection. The boy had to be convinced to use it for good instead of mischief."

"What did he do?"

"Those were dangerous times, even more so than now. The chances of that child surviving in open society were close to nil. We offered to take him in, educate him, and send him home when he was twenty-one. Callum agreed."

Dughall stroked the page, avoiding the lavishly painted letters. "So, if Tcharloch was my great-grandfather, he must have had a child."

"'Tis true. We encouraged it so that the gift would be passed on. He married at twenty-four to a woman from a another family we were watching, who gave birth to twin boys. One died within a year. The other, a lad named Ferraghuss, had the gift. But he turned to the dark gate at the age of sixteen."

"The dark gate?"

"Aye, it's another name for evil, but not in the traditional sense. It means that ye consider all else beneath ye and act accordingly."

"So ye fail to see God in all things."

"Aye. Ye do understand. The error is in thinking that ye're separate. James told me that ye studied the Bible."

"Aye."

"Jesus once said, 'Split wood, I am there. Lift up a rock, ye will find me.'"

Dughall frowned. "I don't remember that in the good book."

"It's from the Gospel of Thomas." Lazarus smiled. "He also said, 'If yer leaders say to ye, 'Look! The Kingdom is in the heavens!' Then the birds will be there before ye. If they say that the Kingdom is in the sea, then the fish will be there before ye. Rather, the Kingdom is within ye and it is outside of ye.'"

Dughall was delighted. "It's what I've always believed. I would like to read that gospel. So Ferraghuss turned to the dark gate. I've never heard it called that."

Lazarus took a deep breath. "The term was coined by an Egyptian priest king named Thoth. He left instructions on how to resist it in his Emerald Tablets."

Dughall's eyes widened. Egypt was a place that interested him. "What did he say?"

The monk folded his hands in prayer and took a deep breath. "When unto thee there comes a feeling, drawing thee nearer to the dark gate, examine thine heart and find if the feeling thou hast has come from within. If thou shalt find the darkness thine own thoughts, banish them forth from place in thy mind. Send through thy body a wave of vibration, irregular first and regular second, repeating time after time until free. Start the wave force in thy brain center. Direct it in waves from thine head to thy foot. But if thou findest thine heart is not darkened, be sure that a force is directed to thee. Only by knowing can thou overcome it. Only by wisdom can thou hope to be free."

Dughall could sense when something was true. "How old is that manuscript?"

"It's thought to be over four thousand years old. We have a copy of it here. It is one of our greatest treasures."

He had much to learn from this man. "I would like to study it." He got a strange feeling as he touched the page of his book. "What happened to Ferraghuss?"

Lazarus sighed. "We didn't get to him in time. Tcharloch's wealth and position didn't matter. The boy was identified as a warlock and burned at the stake."

"That's terrible."

"Aye. Tcharloch was heartbroken. His wife died within the year. It was nearly fifteen years before he remarried and had a child."

Dughall turned the page and saw that the child of their union was named James. His name was adorned with silver thread, heather, and a golden lion's head. "Is this my Grandfather?"

"Aye. He didn't have the gift, so we thought that the line was finished. Tcharloch died in peace, convinced that the gift was trouble."

"But it wasn't finished!"

"Nay. When James married and had children, he discovered that his daughter had the gift." He turned the page gently. "She was yer mother, Christal."

Dughall held his breath. The C in her first name was elaborately drawn with flowing symbols that looked like flowers. "Oh…"

"She chose those symbols."

"What can ye tell me about her?"

"We tested her from the age of seven. Lady Christal was clairvoyant, clairaudient, and clairsentient. She was determined to use it for good."

Dughall felt a chill. "Then why did she use it to spy on the Earl and his mistress? It caused a rift in the marriage."

The Abbott seemed uncomfortable with this information. "I don't know. We're human, no matter how good we try to be. They say that marriage can be a trial that tests the soul."

"'Tis true."

Lazarus turned the page again. "That's ye, my Lord."

Dughall was thrilled. The D was a work of art. Scripted with blue and gold thread, the word was adorned with flowing symbols and mythical creatures. There was a name beside it in ornate script that made it look like Doo-ull. "What's this word?"

"That is the old Gaelic for Dughall, my Lord."

"How lyrical. And the next page?"

"Empty. Awaiting yer children. Ye must bring them when the time is right."

Dughall nodded. "I give ye my word."

The monk grew serious. "What I've shown ye today must be kept secret. Tell no one of the scripts, the book, or our conversation."

"Can I write ye about it?"

Lazarus hesitated. "Only after I teach ye a secret code. We monks are known for our skills as cryptographers."

Agreed." The young Lord's practical nature took over. "I must leave today to take care of business. It will take months to locate the supplies ye requested. I shall send them after the new year."

The Abbott bowed his head slightly. "Thank ye, my Lord. If there's anything I can do, just ask."

Dughall thought for a moment. "I'm having a problem with the Church. I saved a man about to be burned as a witch and incurred the wrath of a priest. His name is Father Ambrose. The Bishop and I have been at odds ever since."

Lazarus nodded. "I will speak to the Bishop on yer behalf. I shall tell him that ye're a moral, pious man with a good heart. That much I can do. The priest is beyond my influence."

"Thank ye, brother." The Duke remembered his prior request. "There's one more thing. The commandment 'Thou shalt not kill'. Have ye thought about what I asked? Is it absolute? What am I to do?"

The older man sighed. "I spent the night searching the scriptures to no avail. Do what's in yer heart, lad. There is no absolute. Take each situation on its own merit and ask God what to do."

It made sense, but it didn't relieve his burden. The young Lord nodded and held out his hand in friendship.

Lazarus drew him close, embracing him like a brother. "Take care, my friend. Remember that ye are human. The dark gate calls each of us from time to time. Ye must be strong to resist it."

Dughall swallowed hard. He'd glimpsed the dark gate in a glass of whisky, a sexual obsession, and the cruelty of man to man. Now it was his sacred duty to resist it. "I'll try to be strong." The young Lord kneeled at the Abbott's feet. "I ask for a blessing, brother."

Lazarus laid hands on his head. He offered a prayer of protection and pledged his support.

Dughall focused on the monk's prophecy. Regardless of his gifts, he was only human. The dark gate would tempt him and he would have to resist it. He was married, a father, and a leader of people. War was looming. Challenges lay ahead. He wondered what they would be.

Chapter 20
Hell Breaks Loose

October 18 1637
TWO WEEKS LATER

EDINBURGH

The Privy Council was in an impossible situation. The King blamed them for not putting down the riots and presented them with a list of new regulations. As a body they were weak, divided between clerical and lay representatives. They had no armed force to enforce the King's wishes. They'd passed responsibility for the disorderly mobs to the town council, ordering them to protect readers of the book in churches. No one was brave enough to undertake the reading. Even when the Council offered money to volunteers, they failed to get any takers. A messenger had been sent to London to reason with the King. He returned broken, a victim of the rack.

Within weeks, petitions objecting to the King's policies began to arrive in Edinburgh from most parts of Scotland. They presented a common theme; the forced religious innovations had not been cleared by Parliament or the General Assembly. Sixty-nine petitions arrived, carried by messengers from ministers, nobles, and representatives of boroughs, who remained in the city to reinforce their demands.

In September, the Privy Council suspended the reading of the book. Three petitions with a list of the rest had been sent to King Charles. All of Scotland waited for his reply. They had just received his response. The King refused to consider the petitions until the city was peaceful. He ordered the petitioners out of the capitol within twenty-four hours or they'd be arrested and tried for treason. Worse yet, the Privy Council and law courts were to abandon Edinburgh for a secure location in Linlithgow. A pamphlet published against the service book was called in to be burned.

***

It was a terrible day indeed. Lord Traquair hid in the council chambers, fearing for his very life. With the Lord Chief Justice at his side, he'd just informed the petitioners. Traquair moved to a tall window and looked out upon the town square. More than three hundred men gathered around fires, listening to a speech by Lord Balmerino. He was accompanied by the Lords Loudon, Rothes, and Lindsay.

We are in danger, Traquair thought. A speech ended with shouts of agreement and weapons raised to the sky. *All hell has broken loose in this city. We'll be lucky to escape with our lives.* He couldn't understand why some lords supported it. Only Balmerino had been mistreated by the King; arrested, condemned, and pardoned at the last minute. The others took risks for no apparent reason. Bile rose in his throat as he recalled that it was his vote that condemned Balmerino. But how could he have refused? The King had raised him to Earldom in exchange for complete obedience. Unbeknownst to Balmerino, it was he who advised his majesty to commute his death sentence.

"Traquair! For God's sake! Are ye coming?" Sir William Elphinstone, Lord Chief Justice, stood in the doorway carrying a package of papers. The exquisitely dressed man was sweating and his skin was as pale as a ghost.

Traquair was shocked into movement. "Aye!"

The two men raced toward the back of the building and left through a service exit. With hearts pounding, they hurried through an alley and burst into a cobblestone street. It was too late. They were surrounded by angry petitioners, raising their fists and growling insults. He protested in vain as he was punched, kicked, and knocked to the ground. Before blacking out, he had a morbid thought that this was the way his life would end.

***

The day was cold and clear in Edinburgh, a harbinger of the winter to come. Wood smoke hung in the air as men gathered around barrel fires. Alexander Leslie stood in the crowd, listening to Minister Henderson speak. Dressed in dark clothes, the dour-faced preacher from Leuchars was known for his fiery sermons.

The minister shouted. "The Church of Scotland is free and independent and ought not be dictated to!" His voice was laced with passion. "Follow not the false book. We have a blessed opportunity to rid ourselves of rotten relics, riven rags, and the remainders of popery!"

The people roared in agreement. Judging from their reaction, Leslie would have no trouble raising an army. The King's response had been extreme and had played into their hands. He glanced at his lieutenant, who listened with rapt attention. Alex Hay was a fisherman who had never been called to military service. Yet these words inspired him to take up arms. Leslie had reservations about the man. He'd assigned a mercenary to train him on weapons and teach him military strategy. Hay was strong in body and sharp in mind, but he wondered about his will to kill a man. At this point it didn't matter because he was needed to ensure the cooperation of the northern estates. But in the future his hesitation could get him killed. Yet even his death would serve a purpose, to bring Lord Drake to their side.

"Leslie?" Alex Hay had a pained look on his face.

"Aye, what is it?"

He pointed to a disturbance. "Do they intend to kill those men?"

Leslie squinted. "They're members of the Privy Council. Traquair is a snake! They deserve it."

Hay frowned. "We are bound to defend our faith, not murder innocent men. We're not at war yet. We may need them to negotiate with the King."

The protesters knocked the council members to the ground. They continued to beat them even though one man was unconscious. Leslie's mood darkened. He hated to admit it, but Hay was right. He would discipline him later about questioning his authority. "Let's see if we can pull them off." They headed for the angry mob.

***

LONDON ENGLAND

The King stood at a library table, reading a lengthy petition. He'd received three of these documents last month, with a list of sixty-six others. After a fit of rage and a flurry of edicts, he'd returned to evaluate them for the signatures of men who defied him. His hand shook with anger. *How dare they?* Each inscription came from a particular man in an easily identifiable location. *Did they think him an idiot?*

It was only a matter of time before he taught them about hell on earth. His skin tingled as he devised a suite of suitable punishments. He would deal harshly with all signatories, but his wrath would be reserved for the ringleaders. How could he identify them? *These are three of the petitions. I will obtain the others and make a list of names. We will start with the ones that appear more than once. There's a good chance that these are the organizers.* His finger scanned the longest petition, which came from the city of Aberdeen. As the names appeared, he spoke them, "Alexander Hay... Robert MacNeil... Iain Innes... Malcolm Gibbs..." Would they appear on other petitions?

He wasn't aware of what was happening in Edinburgh. Fresh riots were sweeping the city, damaging property and injuring the men in charge. The city was a powder keg and he had thrown in the match.

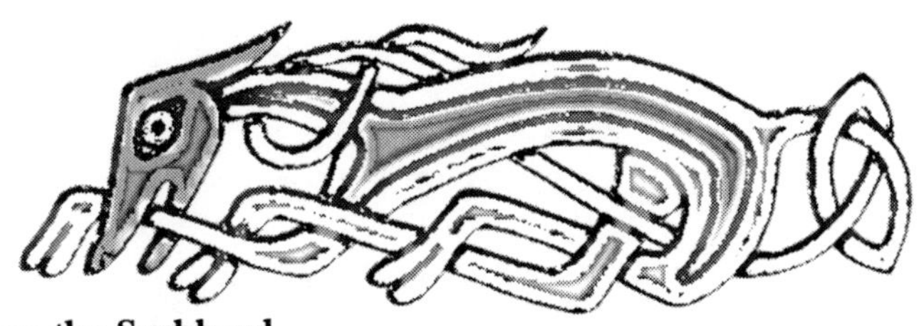
Etching on the Scabbard

Chapter 21
Obsession

December 15 1637
TWO MONTHS LATER

DRAKE CASTLE

Ten weeks had passed since the Duke's party returned from the abbey. The first week was spent attending to local business. An expert trader, Jamison was tasked with finding the Abbott's supplies, a job that involved acquiring goods from Ireland. Near the end of October they received a letter from Alex, stating that he intended to stay in the south. In poor handwriting, he described the riots in Edinburgh and an army being raised against the King. They were stunned to learn that he was a lieutenant in that army. Jessie was devastated by the news. Dughall kept this from Gilbert. They'd already come to an agreement on how to proceed. Gilbert used their vast influence to persuade nobles and ministers to avoid criticizing the book. The strategy worked, bringing a measure of peace to the northeast.

Dughall and Ian celebrated their eighteenth birthday at a private gathering where they gave thanks for their reunion. After all, a year ago Maggie had been murdered, Dughall abducted, and their family torn asunder. But someone was missing from this solemn event. Alex had joined the rebellion. They prayed for their absent father.

In the following weeks, Dughall kept his men busy shoring up defenses and fortifying his army. In spite of Michael's refusal, they began to build cottages for the villagers. Gilroy and Pratt secured supplies, hired tradesmen, and supervised the new construction. With luck, it would be ready by late January. Ian was given an unusual task. He was to scour the area around Drake Castle to locate a stone circle.

But all was not well. The Duke was having marital difficulties. Keira nagged him, asking him to give up the sword. Of course, he couldn't do that. His dreams were plagued with terrifying visions - of war and strife and merciless killing. They always ended the same way. A benevolent Goddess morphed into a raven and devoured his soul. The sword was a key to his survival.

***

THE LIBRARY, LATE MORNING

Dughall sat at his desk, examining the scabbard of the ancient sword. His breath quickened as his fingers traced etched symbols, lingering on a trinity knot. Warriors sketched it on their weapons because it offered protection in battle. He turned over the scabbard and examined it with a magnifying glass. Hidden in the center of a complex design was a picture of a mythical beast. With long snout and open eye, its body formed an interlaced knot. The beast didn't represent anything in nature. What was it? He stared at the dark hair on the back of his hand. In dreams it was red , upon a hand that bore a ring with the same beast. *There's no other explanation. I must be him.* In the past week, he'd developed an attachment to the blade. He carried it constantly and slept with it. People had begun to notice - Keira, Jamison, and even his mother.

Dughall unsheathed the sword and was gripped by a wave of nausea. "Great Goddess, Morrigan!" he cried. "Dinna take me yet!" His heart pounded wildly as he reflected on what the Abbot said. The dark gate was bound to tempt him. Could that be what was lurking? The sword trembled in response.

There was a knock on the door and Jamison entered. His eyes narrowed when he spotted the sword. "My Lord. Murdock is back, reporting for duty. Allow me to take that sword to the weapons room."

"Nay!"

Jamison scowled. "Give it up, lad! Remember what Lord Gilbert said. It's close to the end of the year."

"I won't give it up!" His eyes widened with anxiety. "Ye can't make me!"

The servant grunted. "Perhaps I should summon Lord Gilbert."

"I forbid it!"

"Hmmphh... Can we at least put it in the corner?"

"Aye. But the sword mustn't leave my sight." Dughall watched with suspicion as his servant propped it in the corner. Was the man plotting against him? He'd find out soon enough. "Send Murdock in alone."

Jamison stared and then left the room. Murdock entered and took a seat across from him.

Dughall was pleased to see him. His friend had gone to a clan gathering to meet Sara's relatives. They'd announced that they planned to marry in the summer. Murdock looked good. Having a woman agreed with him. His clothes were clean, his hair was combed, and his eyes were bright and alert. "Murdock!"

"Aye, my Lord?"

"I've missed ye. Luc has a long way to go before he takes yer place."

"Good! Then I won't have to fight him for the job. I'm ready to serve ye."

"How was the journey?"

Murdock smiled. "Sara has kin in Fraserburgh. They put us up and fed us."

"Did ye pass the test? Does she still want to marry ye?"

Murdock chuckled. "She does! Enough about me. Did ye conceive a son?"

Just the thought of it gave him a headache. "Nay. That won't happen. Sometimes I think my wife doesn't like me."

"What!?"

"She's been nagging me to give up my sword. We haven't made love in weeks."

Murdock glanced at the scabbard. "Why don't ye put it away?"

Dughall groaned as the pain intensified. "I can't!"

"Why?"

His voice was anguished. "I'm doomed without my sword."

"How so?"

"I've been having dreams about the Morrigan."

"The Goddess who helped ye defeat the Earl?"

"Aye. Only this time she's not benevolent. The woman appears in three forms. A young lass invites me to father her child. A pregnant lass claims me as husband. Then a crone beckons as she washes my bloody garments. I may be a dead man."

"But it's nay real."

"Real enough, friend. Red Conan lost his life to the crone. So shall I."

"Why?"

"Because I am him."

Murdock paled. "I will fight this apparition with my bare hands!"

"Nay!" Dughall pounded the desk. "This is my responsibility! Mine alone! Only I can change the outcome."

"Ye're not makin' sense."

Dughall stood. "Sense is the last thing I need." He retrieved the weapon from the corner. "I need my sword!"

Murdock joined him. "Why, lad?"

"The dark gate is bound to tempt me. This must never leave my side." He held it high. "Accompany me to my bed chamber and stoke the fire in the hearth."

"As ye wish. Shall I summon yer wife for a tryst?"

"Nay! The answer to my problem lies in dreams."

"Dreams? It's almost time for the mid-day meal."

"I may never eat again."

"Ye're refusing food?"

"Aye! Enough talk! My head hurts from these questions." The weight of the world was on his shoulders. "I must sleep now or die."

The men left the library in silence and headed for the Lord's bed chamber.

Ian Hay

LOWER LEVEL THE WEAPONS CHAMBER

Jamison crouched on the floor, sketching an eight foot circle with a piece of charcoal. His body was present, but his mind was on his master. Was the curse real? What could he do about it?

"We're fighting in this circle?" Ian asked.

"Aye, lad." Jamison stood. "War dictates that we fight in tight spaces."

Ian guided a chain maille vest over his head and down his chest, and slipped on a matching headdress. He fastened on leather cuffs and mounted a shield on his forearm. "This armor is heavy. How can I fight like this?"

The servant was impatient. "Get used to it! Ye're a man! Now, pick up the knife."

Ian picked up a dirk and concealed it under the shield. He appeared to be angry.

The lad will fight better if his blood's a boil, Jamison thought. He picked up his weapon and prepared to spar. "On my mark. One… two… three…" He waited until the lad assumed an attack stance. Then he charged, sweeping his blade in a wide arc toward his ribs.

Ian danced backwards and brought up his shield. Sparks flew as metal struck metal. "Jesus!" He recovered quickly and brought up his blade, nicking the servant's forearm.

"Good! Ye drew first blood." Jamison moved quickly, taking his opponent by surprise. "Ha!" First with a downward thrust; then followed by an upward cut. Ian yelped as the blade scraped his vest, narrowly missing his stomach.

This fighting was serious business, made difficult by the condition that they stay in the circle. The men sparred in earnest using swords and shields and dirks. Metal flashed upon metal and blood splattered from minor wounds. They were breathing heavily and sweating.

"Enough!" Ian cried, as he lowered his sword. The air smelled of dust and fear. "Ye're fighting like a madman! I don't want to kill ye. What's wrong?"

Jamison put down his weapons. "I'm worried about yer brother." He pressed a cloth to a cut on his arm. "He's obsessed with that damned sword. He won't give it up and he's pulling away from me."

Ian frowned. "Is the curse real?"

"Lord Gilbert thinks so. I need to get the story before it's too late. Can ye cover for me while I take a trip to Huntly?"

"How long will ye be gone?"

"Two days."

"I'll cover for ye."

"Tell yer brother that I'm visiting a friend." Jamison examined his wound. "There's one more thing. I need ye to spy on yer brother."

Ian frowned. "What!?"

"Ye're closer to him that any man. Connect to his mind and read his thoughts."

"I don't know."

"Do it, lad! This obsession could kill him. Do ye want to go back to being a fisherman?"

"Nay. This is to help him, right?"

"Aye. He's my Lord and master. I would never do anything to harm him."

Ian agreed reluctantly. "I'll do it."

Jamison smiled. "Good. I'll leave now for Huntly. Watch yer brother and assess his thoughts. I'm counting on ye."

***

THE NURSERY

The nursery was quiet. Mary's twins were absent, as they were suffering from bowel complaints. Tarrah went to the laundry to retrieve a basket of nappies. Wee Maggie had been sleeping, until she woke in a state of terror.

Keira sat in a rocker, comforting her daughter. "Poor child," she crooned. "Yer father will visit soon." The infant sighed, melting her heart. Maggie was a gift from the Goddess. The Duchess struggled with negative emotions. She was upset with her husband, but mustn't show it. Wee Maggie could sense her feelings. She wondered if her father's dreams affected her. Keira rocked her gently. After the child fell asleep, she stood and placed her in the cradle.

Tarrah entered with the basket of nappies. "Poor angel," she whispered. "I don't know what got into her."

"The wee lassie is troubled."

"Where is m'Lord?"

Keira frowned. "I don't know exactly."

"His daughter misses him."

"I know, lass. I promise he'll see her tomorrow." Keira could only hope. "I'm going for a walk in the woods. Then I'll come back to help Mary."

"His Lordship forbade us to leave the castle."

Keira bristled. "I'll die if I stay inside all my life. Send Beth to fetch me if there's a problem." The Duchess left the nursery and took the stairs down to the courtyard. Disguised as a commoner in a simple plaid, she passed the guard and left through the gate. The air was crisp as she entered the woods and took in the sights and sounds of nature. Red squirrels scampered across the path. Wrens and finches twittered in the canopy, announcing the early winter. The scent of pine trees and fallen leaves comforted her very soul. For a moment, it felt like home. Home... The solstice was coming, the shortest day and the celebration of blessed Yule. Her people would gather pine branches and holly. Men would hunt for deer, while women cooked traditional dishes.

Keira left the trail, ducked under some branches, and arrived at a tree that bore the mark of the pentacle. She'd carved it there days ago as an offering to the Goddess. Her heart swelled as she traced the sacred symbol. "Earth, Air, Fire, Water!" Oh, how she missed the circle! She was forbidden to display the sign at the castle, even in her own bed chamber. Her husband's people feared the old religion. He wasn't willing to challenge it. *Dearest Dughall,* she thought. *Where is the lad I married?* How could she defeat the demon that stalked him? Perhaps with a sacred ceremony. The Duchess took a knife and an apple out of her pocket. She cut the fruit in two and noted that the center formed a pentacle. Digging a hole at the base of the tree, she buried the halves of the apple. "Gentle Goddess. Accept this fruit as an offering to my unborn son. Send him forth to rescue his father." She heard someone behind her and turned to face him.

Murdock lowered his eyes. "Forgive me, my Lady. I couldn't help overhearing. The words were bonny."

She was glad to see him. Perhaps he could help her husband. "What are ye doing here?"

The servant smiled. "My master asked me to follow ye."

She stiffened. "Oh... Dughall would fret if he knew that I came here."

"Then we won't tell him. He doesn't need any more problems."

"So ye've seen it too. I try to please him. But each morning he leaves my bed to take up that awful sword." Her eyes filled with tears. "His dreams are strange and violent. Do ye know what's wrong with him?"

"I think so."

Keira took his calloused hands. "What is it?"

Murdock blushed. "Allow me to tell ye about the Morrigan."

***

THE LORD'S BED CHAMBER

Dughall slept with the sword at his side. His dreams were cruel and terrifying. Screams rang in his ears as he applied hot irons to flesh, demanding a confession from a traitor. He threw down the glowing brand in horror. "Show me something good about this life!"

The dream faded, giving rise to another as powerful. Dughall woke in a cold sweat in a bed that was unfamiliar. He detected an insect with a disagreeable smell crawling across his pillow. "Ach! It's a bedbug!"

A female voice giggled. "Red?" She was about to roll over. "Ye paid me for the night. Do ye want to do it again?"

"Red?" He stared at his hand and saw red hair and the ring with the strange beast. "Nay, lass!"

The woman rolled to face him, displaying ponderous breasts and yellow teeth. There was a tattoo on her forehead that resembled a raven. She reached for his manhood. He screamed.

Dughall woke suddenly with a headache, convinced that he was Red Conan.

***

THE DINING ROOM SHORTLY AFTER NOON

Jessie stared at the platters of victuals. Stuffed pheasant with truffles... Beef in blood sauce... Potatoes and turnips... Breads and cakes... There was so much food; more than would feed a dozen peasants. "Where is Dughall?"

"He took to his bed," Ian said.

"Why?"

"Murdock said that he has a headache."

"Hmmm... There's too much food for the two of us. We must share it at the back gate. Where is Mary?"

"Tending the lads." Ian grabbed a piece of brown bread. "They have bowel complaints."

"Poor bairns. We could give them some chamomile tea. I'll see to it after the meal."

"Thank ye, Mother."

"Where is Keira?"

"She's tending to wee Maggie. The child woke with night terrors. Dughall hasn't seen her in days."

"What? He's avoiding his daughter?"

"Aye."

"That's not like him. He missed an appointment in the surgery this morning. I had to treat a difficult case myself. Now, he's missed a meal."

Ian frowned. "Jamison says that he's obsessed with that sword. Do ye think it's cursed?"

Jessie's mood darkened. "That awful sword. I never liked it."

"Jamison asked me to spy on him, to find out what's wrong."

She stared. "Then that's what ye'll do."

Ian reddened. "I will, Mother. But I don't like it. It would help if ye would question him. He respects ye."

She sighed. "There's another he respects more. I wish that Alex was here."

***

THE DINING ROOM THAT EVENING

The Duke sat at the head of the table, studying his family. He had a slight headache and was shaky from the dreams. How could he do such terrible things, even in another lifetime? Interrogation! Torture! And the lass with the tattoo made him feel unfaithful. What would they think if they knew? He studied their faces. They were judging him.

Keira sat to his left. She hadn't mentioned his nap or demanded an explanation for his behavior. Her eyes were kind and compassionate, but that could be a trap. Mary looked thoroughly spent. Children were a blessing, but two at once were a challenge. She turned to Ian and took his hand. Dughall couldn't read his brother, who was blocking him by humming a ditty. He'd never done that before. As his headache flared, so did his suspicions. Jessie sat to his right, unfolding her linen napkin. There was nothing suspicious about that. Murdock sat at the end of the table. The servant had roused him from the bad dreams. Dinner was the least he could offer him.

The table was set with fine china and silver tableware. It was a tribute to the exquisite meal of roast lamb, potatoes, bread, and vegetables.

Ian said grace. "Thank ye, Lord Jesus, for this meal and the company of friends and family. Inspire us to be generous to those who have less. Amen."

"Amen." They picked up their utensils and started eating.

The Duke picked absently at his food, settling on a piece of meat and a crust of bread. It was hard to eat with his stomach in knots.

Keira's voice was timid. "I've missed ye, husband. Are ye feeling any better?"

Dughall offered no answer. Studying her attire, he saw that she wore soiled hiking boots. He took her hand and squeezed it. "Boots, lass? Where have ye been?"

She blushed. "In the forest."

"Tell the truth, wife."

"That is the truth. I went for a walk."

"Ye left the castle grounds?"

"Aye."

"Alone?"

She nodded.

Bile rose in his throat. This was the last thing he needed. "I can't allow that."

Keira reddened but she didn't say a word.

The meal continued in silence. When they were almost done, Jessie put down her fork. "Where were ye this morning, son? We were supposed to meet in the surgery."

Dughall searched his mind for the appointment. "I was sick, Mother. I returned to my bed."

"Are ye better now?"

"I think so."

"Ye haven't visited yer daughter in days," Jessie added.

Dughall disliked these questions. "Why must everyone keep track of me? I wore myself out because I was nervous about something."

"About the sword?" Keira asked.

"Silence, wife!" His eyes flashed with anger. "I told ye never to speak of it."

Keira's eyes filled with tears. "Oh."

Mary gasped.

Jessie paled. "Son, ye shouldn't speak to yer wife that way."

"Mother! This is none of yer business." Dughall was suspicious. Were they all against him or just a few? He sensed that the women had a lot to say. Ian was quiet. Even that bothered him. Tears rolled down Keira's face. She began to sob.

Murdock passed her a handkerchief. "Allow me, m'Lady." He turned to his master. "My Lord. It seems that ye might be suffering from that headache. Shall I accompany ye to yer bed chamber?"

"Aye." Dughall welcomed the opportunity to escape this scrutiny. He stood and threw his napkin on the table. "Forgive me for my strange behavior. Let's go." The servant escorted him out of the dining room. They walked the corridor in silence until Dughall stopped and sobbed into his hands.

Murdock squeezed his shoulder. "What's wrong, lad?"

"I feel it in my bones. They're all against me."

Jamison

Chapter 22
Conspiracy

December 16 1637
6AM THE NEXT MORNING

HUNTLY CASTLE

The servants' quarters reeked of piss and unwashed bodies. The floor was sticky. The air was cold. And there would be no light 'til daybreak. Jamison lay in a hard cot, listening to a chorus of snores and farts. He covered his head with a pillow and prayed that he'd last until morning. After a while, dim light entered through the iron-barred window. Several men abandoned their beds and ran off to start the fireplaces.

Jamison sat up and took stock of his injuries. Scrapes… Bruises… A painful right shoulder… It could affect his ability to fight. The servant was a mess by any standard. His emotions were raw. *Damn that horse! Breaking a leg and leaving me stranded. God, I loved that animal.* The stallion was his favorite. He hated slitting his throat. He'd arrived at the castle on foot at midnight, when it was too late to rouse the Earl. The gate keeper recognized him and provided simple lodging.

The room lightened. Jamison got out of bed and used the chamber pot, noting that it was overflowing. A turd floated on top, adding to the stench in the room.

A boy entered the room, dressed in the clothing of a page. His voice was high but respectful. "Mornin' Sir." He stared as Jamison tucked his member under his kilt. "The Earl asks that ye join him for breakfast."

The servant grunted. "Is there someplace I can wash up?"

The lad pointed to a pitcher and bowl sitting on a rickety nightstand.

Jamison stared into the cloudy water and decided it was better than nothing. He broke some thin ice, washed his hands, and dried them on his sweater. "Let's go."

The boy led him down a hallway towards the Earl's private dining quarters. Not much had changed since he'd been here last to attend the royal wedding. As they walked, he allowed his thoughts to wander. What would he say to the Earl? These were delicate subjects involving powerful men. He didn't wish to alienate him.

"Stop, Sir!" the lad cried, breaking him out of his reverie.

They'd arrived at the dining room and he hadn't even realized it. "Thank ye, lad." Jamison dismissed the page and entered. The dining chamber was a far cry from the servants' meager quarters. The room was warm and comfortable from the heat of a crackling fireplace. Wall sconces and windows provided light. The smell of ham, eggs, and fresh bread made his stomach grumble.

Lord Gilbert turned to face him. "It's good to see ye, Jamison. I'm told that ye had an accident."

The servant nodded. "Aye, m'Lord. My horse stepped in a gully and broke a leg. I had to send him back to his maker."

Gilbert clicked his tongue. "What a shame. That was a fine animal."

"The best."

"I'll provide ye with another horse."

"Thank ye."

"Are ye hurt?"

"Aye. When Blackie fell, I landed on my shoulder. He pinned me to the ground."

"How did ye get free?"

"With a knife." His voice cracked, "Enough about the damned horse! Let's get down to business."

The Earl motioned for them to sit and they did. "Eat first. Ye must be starved."

Jamison's stomach growled like a hungry beast, clouding his judgment. He spooned generous portions of food onto his empty plate. As he devoured the meal, he studied the Earl. The man looked healthy. His manner was calm and there were no signs that he'd been drinking. Perhaps he could accompany him to Drake. "I've come about yer brother."

"Dughall sent ye?"

"Nay."

Gilbert's eyes widened. "Is he all right?"

"Nay. I fear for his sanity."

The Earl paled. "Why?"

"It's that damned sword! He carries it day and night, claiming that it's his salvation. He's forsaken his marital bed and the company of his wee daughter."

Gilbert frowned. "God in heaven."

"The Duchess says he has violent dreams and suffers from crippling headaches. He's getting thin, so I suspect he's avoiding food. I've come to ask about the curse." *Curse...* The word hung between them as the clock on the mantel struck seven. Jamison was losing his patience. "Is the curse real?"

Gilbert sighed. "Oh, it's real all right. Any man who claimed the sword died before the end of the year. Legend tells us that it belonged to a warrior who went by the name of Red Conan."

"Tell me about him."

"The man was six feet tall, a giant by ancient standards. He lived a thousand years ago in the country we now call Ireland. No one could defeat him in battle. Some claimed that he had supernatural powers. He sired more than thirty children, twenty-nine sons and several daughters."

"Was he the original owner of the sword?"

The Earl nodded. "It was cast for him. The sword vanished after his death. It was discovered in Scotland two hundred years ago in the ruins of a monastery. It's been nothing but trouble since."

Jamison frowned. "Tell me about the men who claimed it."

"My Uncle George wasted away. There wasn't a healer in Scotland who could save him. A few died by accident or disease. One man hanged himself from a rafter. Oh. I almost forgot. Another was drawn and quartered by the King. That was later deemed a mistake."

"Poor bastard. Did any of them exhibit signs of madness?"

"Practically all of them. Obsession... Suspicion... Anger... Fear... Friendships were ruined. Families were torn asunder. The legend calls it the madness of the sword."

Jamison grunted. "I've seen my master when he clutches that blade. His eyes flash, his breath quickens; it's like he becomes another. Once he entered a fugue state and couldn't recall his actions. I will tell him about the legend."

"I warned him about the sword."

"He knows?"

"Aye."

"Why would a man cling to a cursed sword that was destined to take his life?"

Gilbert frowned. "I don't know. Uncle George had a daft idea that he was Red Conan in a previous life. So the weapon was his and would not hurt him. It sounds like my brother is in serious trouble. What do ye plan to do?"

"Me?"

"Aye."

"We must destroy the blade! Will ye come to Drake to convince yer brother?"

"Nay." The Earl's voice was anguished, "My wife is due to deliver next week. The midwife says it could be dangerous. I can't go without risking my marriage."

Jamison felt abandoned. He didn't know how to proceed without the Earl. As a servant, he had no right to take the blade from him. There was so much at stake. The Duke's life... The future of Drake... "What am I to do?"

Gilbert looked thoughtful. "Will he listen to his family?"

"Perhaps. Ian promised to read his thoughts."

"That could be insightful."

"We must involve the others. Jessie, the Duchess..."

"What about Alex?"

"He's away at the moment."

"Unfortunate. What about Murdock? He's always been able to talk to my brother."

"Talk won't help!" The servant reddened. "He's shutting us out. Someone must take the blade from him. I will do it if it means my life!"

"I wish I could go." Gilbert's voice was tight, "I love my brother. He's the most decent man I've ever known."

"Many at Drake feel the same way."

"It's up to ye, Jamison! Banish the sword to a remote place where no one will ever find it. Take the secret to yer death."

The servant stood quickly, brooding over his assignment. Without Gilbert's help, it could be construed as treason. "I must go before I'm missed."

The Earl joined him. "When Bridget births, I'll head for Drake to help ye. Is there anything else I can do?"

"Call me friend." The servant smiled. "I left word that I was visiting a friend. My master can smell a falsehood a mile away. He mustn't think that I'm lying."

Gilbert embraced him. "God go with ye, friend. I truly mean it." He smiled. "Now let's go find ye a horse."

***

DRAKE CASTLE, THE GUEST BED CHAMBER 8AM

Keira lay in a guest bed, nursing a broken heart. It had been a long, lonely night. After abandoning her at dinner, Dughall barred the door to their bed chamber, leaving her to find other lodging. Perhaps it was for the best. She needed time to lick her wounds and consider all the options. At first, she regretted leaving her village, where the people were kind and compassionate. There ye never heard talk of war or arguments over weapons. Her marriage was failing. Would Michael take her back as healer? The thought brought her comfort, but at the same time inflicted pain. How could she leave the man she loved and a family she'd been welcomed into? And what about her wee daughter? As the night went on, she resolved to stay and cried herself to sleep.

Keira got out of bed. Dressing in yesterday's clothes, she thought about what Murdock said. Dughall feared the Goddess Morrigan. The crone threatened to take his life if the maiden didn't prevail. There was only one solution. He had to father her child. Her thoughts ran wild. *Regan didn't teach me about this champion of the battlefield. There's no time to ask Michael. Who else can help me?* She felt her daughter reaching out, offering her support and compassion. *Of course! The child knows that her father is in trouble. I'm coming, Maggie! We will face him together.* With hope in her heart, she left the chamber to locate her wee daughter.

***

THE DUKE'S BED CHAMBER 8:15AM

Murdock stoked the fire with apple wood and waited for his master to wake. The man had drifted back to sleep and was having a fitful dream. Thrashing... Grunts... Cries... What was he dreaming about? The servant spotted the sword on the table, unsheathed and ready for action. *God in heaven. Help him to survive this trial.*

Dughall's voice was weak. "Murdock, are ye there?"

"Aye, m'Lord. Don't ye remember? Ye let me in a while ago. The door was barred."

"Oh, aye. I wanted to be sure it wasn't her."

"Her?"

"My wife. She wants to cause trouble."

"Trouble?"

"Aye. About the sword and her need for a child!"

"Ye don't want to bed the lass?"

"Nay!"

Murdock felt his forehead. "Ye don't have a fever."

"There's nothin' wrong with me!"

"Settle down, lad. Would ye like a drink of water?"

Dughall nodded.

Murdock held a glass while he sipped. He noticed dark circles under his eyes and gauntness in his face. "Did ye eat much at dinner?"

"Nay. My stomach was in knots. I tried to eat. Then they all attacked me."

"It's not true, lad. Everyone at that table loves ye."

"Some don't."

"Do ye not remember? They broke into Huntly to save ye. And the lass left her people to be yer wife."

"I guess so." Dughall shuddered. "Oh God. What's wrong with me, Murdock? I suspect everyone of disloyalty, even my own family. Am I going mad?"

"I don't know." Murdock stroked his head. "But on my mother's grave, I will find a way to dispel this terrible curse."

"Thank ye, friend."

"Promise me one thing."

"What?"

"Let yer wife help us."

Dughall sighed. "Oh. The poor lass. Did I hurt her?"

"Aye. But I think she still loves ye."

"I won't hurt her again. I will turn these evil thoughts and feelings inward."

"My Lord!"

"My family is my life. I would rather die than hurt them." He fluffed his pillow and punched it down. "I'm starving. Tell the cook to make me a big breakfast with ham and eggs and cranberry cakes."

Murdock brightened. "I'll fetch ye when it's ready." The servant was hopeful as he left the bed chamber to instruct the kitchen. The morning started badly, but things were starting to look up. He would have to tell the Duchess.

***

THE HALLWAY 8:30AM

Keira found Maggie at her nursemaid's breast and waited until she was finished. Minutes later, she changed a nappy and crooned to the precious infant. "Sweet child. Momma needs yer help." She dressed the baby in a fresh gown and took her to their bed chamber. Now she stood outside, wondering if they should enter. Was the door barred? Was Dughall still angry? Would he send them both away? "Great Goddess," she prayed. "Soften his heart. This child needs her father and I need my husband."

Maggie snuggled, giving her courage.

Keira's eyes misted. "We'll face him together daughter. Are ye ready?" Maggie's little hand clutched her dress. She took it as a silent signal. The Duchess pushed the door. Unlike last night, it opened easily, thrilling her to the core. Her husband lay in bed with his back to them, uncovered to the waist and breathing lightly. She saw the silvery whip marks on his skin. They were a testament to the beatings he'd endured. *Poor lad. I wish that was the cause of yer madness.*

The child whimpered. Dughall reached out to the table to stroke the sword.

Keira stiffened, but she remembered to hold her tongue. *The sword is a sign of his madness, not the cause. I must keep quiet about it.* The child cooed in agreement.

Dughall grabbed the sword and turned. "Oh. I was just…" He put the blade down and waited.

Keira managed a smile. "Wee Maggie misses ye." She brought the child forward and placed her on the bed. "And so do I." The baby gurgled with contentment. Keira watched him closely. The man appeared to be wavering between love and fear. Would he reject his own flesh and blood?

At last he spoke, "Murdock says that I should trust ye."

"Murdock is right!" She touched his cheek. "I love ye so much. Don't send me away."

"Ye won't question me about the sword? Or pester me for a son?"

"Nay! I don't care about the sword. Our son can come when ye're ready."

Dughall stroked the baby's face. "Why do we need a son? We already have a child, as bonny as an angel." Maggie grabbed his beard and wouldn't let go. "Look! She has a grip now."

"Daaaaa…. Da!"

"She knows my name, lass." His eyes misted as he held her tiny hands. "Oh God. My daughter. My wife. I've been awful to ye." He looked up. "Will ye forgive me?"

"We do!" Keira's heart leapt for joy. "We will always love ye, no matter what happens."

"Thank God," he whispered.

Murdock appeared in the doorway. "My Lady. My Lord. Tarrah is waiting in the hallway to take the wee one to the nursery. Let's get ye dressed. A feast awaits in the breakfast room."

Keira smiled. With Murdock's help and Maggie's charms, they had a chance to save her husband.

***

THE FOREST EAST OF DRAKE CASTLE 9AM

The air was crisp and cold and laden with a hint of moisture. The trees were bare and desolate except for pines that towered above him.

Ian was solemn as he rode his stallion into a familiar clearing. He came here when he needed a quiet place to contemplate his problems. The man took his time dismounting and then tied his horse to a tree. He extracted a plaid from his saddle pack and spread it on the ground.

Ian was disturbed. He should have slept like the dead near morning with the twins keeping them up most of the night. Instead, he was plagued with a dream that originated with his brother. He sat and struggled with violent memories. A village on fire... betrayal... execution... It was madness, yet it seemed familiar. He knew this place and these people. Was he losing his sanity? *Nay,* he thought. *Dughall's mind is affecting my own. My brother is in deep trouble.* Last night, he'd connected to his brother and found thoughts that were more than disturbing. Dughall was plagued by unreasonable fears and thought they were out to get him. What would he tell Jamison?

Ian felt abandoned. His father was gone. His mother was fragile. He suspected that Keira had enough of Dughall's abuse. His wife was busy with the children. There was no one left to confide in. He hoped that Jamison convinced the Earl to come here and settle the matter. In the meantime, he'd try to read Dughall's innermost thoughts. He'd have to be careful. The man thought he was spying on him.

A cold wind blew, chilling him to the bone. Ian stood and packed his plaid into the saddle pack. Mary would be expecting him soon. As he mounted the horse, he cocked his head and listened. Miles away in the castle, his brother was eating breakfast. Food was a great healer. Perhaps there was hope after all.

Maggie

Chapter 23
Dreams and Schemes

December 30th 1637
TWO WEEKS LATER

DRAKE CASTLE
THE LORD'S BED CHAMBER

After tending her husband's night terrors, the Duchess drifted into a visionary sleep. She found herself in a glorious meadow, walking through knee-deep grasses. It was dark but for the light of the moon and hundreds of twinkling stars. A gentle breeze brushed her skin and rustled the leaves in the trees. Keira felt renewed. Here she was free from maids and guards and the watchful eye of her husband. She could spend the night communing with nature and worshiping the gentle Goddess. Her heart ached in spite of the freedom. Oh, where was the lad she married? The fisherman who promised her a life by the sea? She closed her eyes and surrendered.

A tree frog croaked his distinctive mating call. "Creck... creck... creck... creck..."

Keira opened her eyes. Moonlight flooded the meadow, illuminating yellow wildflowers. It did her heart good. Crickets buzzed and a hare at her feet hopped away.

A child spoke in a voice that was musical. “All creatures of the Goddess! That’s what my Mother would say.”

Keira recognized a wee lassie sitting beneath a rowan tree. She was adorable at age five. “Wee Maggie?”

She patted the ground beside her. “Aye, Mother. Who else would it be?”

Keira sat and studied her. Her eyes as blue as a cornflower, just like her father’s. “How can this be? We’re dreaming, aren’t we?”

Maggie sighed. “Aye and nay. ‘Tis true that it’s a dream. After all, I can’t speak yet. But the message is real. We need to talk without powder and nappies.”

Keira smiled. “What do ye want?”

Her little nose wrinkled. “There’s something I must tell ye. Father’s dying.”

Keira felt a chill. It supported her own suspicions. “How do ye know?”

“I see what he sees. I feel what he feels. When he dies, I’ll die with him.”

“What! Why?”

“It’s hard to explain We’re intertwined.” Maggie’s lip trembled. “Save us, Mother! Stand up to her.”

“Who?”

“The Morrigan. She is coming to demand that he father her child. If he refuses, she’ll kill him.”

The Duchess wondered about the dream. Maggie seemed wise beyond her years. Was the child real or a reflection of her own suspicions? Somewhere in the meadow a newborn cried, attracting her attention. “Who is that?”

Maggie smiled. “A child who waits to be born. My brother.”

Keira’s heart leapt for joy. Was this the son who would save his father? The apparition was fading. “Maggie, don’t leave! Tell me more.”

“Stand up to her, Mother! Our lives depend on it. Father, me, and my brother.” The child vanished.

Morrigan was the Goddess of the battlefield. Warriors and Kings called upon her. She held magical powers over life and death and was often hostile to women. How could a young priestess stand up to such a powerful force? Keira needed advice. “Oh, Mother. I wish ye were here.”

Elspeth’s spirit appeared, as wispy as a cloud in summer.

Keira hadn’t seen her mother since the day she died on the gallows. “Momma.”

“My child. Yer daughter is delightful. She walks between worlds, consulting with her ancestors."

Keira was proud. "She's good and true, just as ye foretold." She reached out and tried to touch her. "I've missed ye."

The apparition shimmered. "I can't stay. The Morrigan approaches in a golden chariot, swinging her battle armaments. What would ye ask?"

"My husband is the one she comes for. What must I do?"

"Grant him what he needs to stay alive. Allow him to father her child."

Keira frowned. "Dughall is a moral man. He will never bed another."

The spirit looked thoughtful. "Do it within the bounds of yer marriage. Use white magic to channel her presence."

"Are ye saying that I must *become* her?"

"Aye. Become the maiden and seduce him."

Keira was intrigued. "How is it done?"

"Our people call it drawing down the moon. Extract blue dye from the woad plant. Anoint yer body with slashes and circles. Wear a veil to contain her spirit. Then draw a circle and begin the invocation."

"What should I say?"

"Invite her to use yer body to conceive the child. She will demand more, but ye must not let her have it. Demand that she leave when the act is done."

Keira wondered about the child. "What will the fruit of that union be?"

"A son... His... yers... and hers."

Once again, she would share a child with another woman. "What if I fail?"

The image was fading. "Then ye will not survive. I will meet ye at the gates of the Summerland."

"Wait! What if she won't leave my body?"

"The veil will contain her spirit. Ask a trusted friend to snatch it from yer head as soon as the act is done."

It made sense. Her mother's voice was growing faint. "Listen carefully. When we draw down the moon, we never know which aspect will appear - maiden, mother, or crone. Ye must..." She winked out into a beam of light.

"I must what? Oh, Mother. Where are ye?" Keira could only hope that she'd stumble upon the final requirement. In the meantime, she resolved to find a veil and acquire the dye for the channeling.

The dream faded.

***

Keira woke next to her husband, who was coughing. She placed her hand on his forehead. "Ye're feverish again."

Dughall moaned. "Banish the bad thoughts! Oh dear God! My

poor daughter."

"What's wrong?"

He barely got the words out between coughs. "She ... wants... to die... with me."

The child's life was at stake. "I'll look in on her."

He hacked. "Bring her here!"

"I will." She dressed quickly and left the chamber to check on their precious daughter.

***

THE WET NURSE'S CHAMBER

The nursemaid sat on the edge of the bed, comforting the sick infant. Maggie was as limp as a rag doll. "Poor child." Her heart sank as she stroked her forehead, detecting a high fever. "I should fetch yer father." The baby swooned at the mention of his name. Tarrah stood carefully and placed her on the dressing table. She worked quickly, loosening her gown. "Wake, darlin'. Open yer eyes. Dinna die, angel." The door opened but she didn't notice.

Keira came to the dressing table. "So, it's true."

Tarrah breathed a sigh of relief. "My Lady!"

"Is the child sick?"

"Oh, aye."

Keira felt the baby's forehead. Then she opened her gown and saw a rash on her fair skin. The child woke when she touched it. "How long has she been like this?"

The nursemaid paled. "Since dawn. She woke with night terrors and refused the breast. I meant to wake ye."

Keira picked up the baby and cradled her against her shoulder. "Let's bathe her to get the fever down. Fetch some water and a bucket of ice. Send Beth to wake Jessie. I need her here. Oh, and send Murdock to attend to my husband."

"As ye wish, m'Lady." Tarrah bolted for the door with bare feet flying. She was glad that someone else was in charge when it came to the wee one's survival.

***

THE LORD'S BED CHAMBER

As his fever spiked, the Duke drifted between dreams and delirium. His mind became unmoored and he floated in and out of consciousness. He moaned and threw off the blankets. *Why is it so hot? Am I in hell?* His heart pounded. The walls of his chamber were dropping away.

***

Dughall found himself in an emerald green valley. Dressed in a tunic and armed with his sword, he walked towards a shimmering river. *The Land of Eire*, he thought with reverence. *I'm on the banks of the sacred river.* He propped his sword against a tree and kneeled beside the sparkling water. He offered a prayer to the Gods. "Children of Danu! Dagda, Midir, and Angus Og. Guide my steps. Lend me yer magic!"

He studied his reflection. The man who stared at him had long red hair, a ragged beard, and a noble nose. He recognized Conan in his younger days, before the wars of conquest. Up river a siren sang of desire, bidding him to come closer. He stood and followed a narrow bank that was lined with willow and hawthorn.

The woman stood with her back to him, pounding wet garments on river stones. Red plaited braids ran down her back and her skirt was slit from the hem to her womanhood. She bent over and left nothing to the imagination.

His loins stirred as she turned to face him, presenting a handsome face with startling green eyes. A tattoo of a raven spanned her forehead.

She pursed her lips and loosened her blouse. "Father my child, warrior!"

The dream warped, causing him to gaze into the river. Was that bloody laundry she was washing? He remembered that he was spoken for. "I can't bed ye, lass. I'm married."

"I don't care about that!" Her eyes flashed with anger. "Am I not pleasing?"

He couldn't lie. "Oh, aye."

"I am the Morrigan, Goddess of Battle! I choose ye to father my child." The lass grew, towering above him. Soon, she spanned the sides of the riverbank with each foot. The ground trembled as she stepped towards him.

His own body grew suddenly, matching her height and girth. He saw treetops and the wind of the river below. It made him giddy.

"Take me now!" she screeched.

From his mouth came a terrible cry. "Nay, lass!" He picked up his sword and brandished it. "Stay away!"

Her eyes narrowed. "I shall return tomorrow to give ye a choice. Submit to my wish or die!" She opened her mouth and shrieked like a banshee.

Dughall covered his ears. The emerald valley spiraled around him and everything went black.

***

The Duke found himself in his chamber, sweating and clutching the sheets. Staring at his hand, he saw hair that was dark and curly. "Thank God! I'm back." His heart pounded wildly as he tried to get his bearings. Was it day or night? He couldn't tell. There were heavy curtains on the window. Where was Murdock? He desperately needed a drink of water.

Recently, he'd suffered from headaches, fevers, and a terrible cough. How much more could one man bear? His daughter's cries echoed in his mind, fueling his fears for her safety. Would she suffer his fate as well? "Keira! Where are ye?"

The door opened and Murdock entered, carrying a goblet of water. "My Lord. Tarrah asked me to bring this while she gathers supplies." He placed a hand on his back and held the cup to his mouth. "Ach! Ye're burning with fever."

Dughall gulped the water. "Where is my daughter?"

"In the nursery. They're bathing the wee lassie to get her fever down."

The young Lord groaned. "She means to die with me."

"Who?"

"Wee Maggie." His heart was breaking to pieces.

"Jessie won't let her die. She's a bonny healer."

Dughall felt like crying. "Oh, Murdock. I wish ye were right."

"What's wrong, lad?"

"I'm out of time. She wants me to father her child."

"Yer wife?"

"Nay. The Morrigan. She demanded it in a dream and threatened me when I refused her. I'll get one more chance to do her bidding. Then she'll take my life."

Murdock frowned. "Hmmphhh... If it was a dream, why did ye not take her?"

His eyes were wild with fever. "I promised to be faithful to my wife."

"Ye don't want to die! Think about what ye're saying."

Dughall's heartbeat slowed. "Someone's in the hall."

The door opened and the women entered. Jessie toted a pail of ice; while Keira carried wee Maggie against her shoulder.

"Walk with her, daughter," Jessie ordered, as she came to the bedside. "Tread gently so that she doesn't vomit. She mustn't lose any more water." She dumped the ice into a washbowl and handed the bucket to Murdock. "Get more ice, and tell Tarrah that it's not her fault. The lass is hiding in the nursery, terrified that she'll be punished."

"As ye wish." Murdock bowed and left the room.

Dughall's head ached. "Oh God! What about my daughter?"

Jessie examined his neck. "Fever and rash, just like the child." She laid her thumb on his wrist and took a pulse. "Good, it's steady. I'll make some willow bark tea. Murdock can give ye a sponge bath."

"Is it serious?"

"I don't know. Let's see if it gets any worse." She turned to Keira. "Put the child on the bed. That's where we'll examine her." She guided his shoulder. "Now, lay back and rest."

Dughall watched his wife bring wee Maggie to the side of the bed.

They undressed her, leaving her body exposed to the air. The child sucked her hand and wailed.

"Dinna fret," Jessie cooed as she took her temperature under the arms. "Good. That cool bath brought down the fever." She studied the hives. "They have a white pustule in the center. I've never seen anything like this."

Keira watched closely. "It could be from the fever."

"I was thinking the same thing."

Maggie's cries grew insistent. Dughall felt responsible. "Allow me to comfort her." He waited while they swaddled her in a towel and drew the bundle near. "I won't leave ye, child."

Maggie gazed into his eyes. Her hand dropped from her mouth as she snuggled against him. "Da..."

Dughall smiled. With his daughter at his side, he felt grounded to this existence. "I think we should stay together, at least for today."

"Are ye sure, son?"

"Aye."

The woman began to prepare the room to accommodate the child and her nursemaid.

Dughall's daughter meant everything to him. He would find a way to fight this thing, even if it meant his life.

***

Ian entered the castle and took the granite steps to the second floor. He'd spent an hour searching for Jamison, to tell him about his brother's latest dreams. His stomach churned. They seemed like the dreams of a madman or the stuff of a fairy tale. "Jesus, God! Where are ye, Jamison?" Rooms away, his brother burned with fever. He felt the heat in his own body, threatening to spiral out of control. Was that the cause of the madness?

"Ian, wait up!" Jamison caught up from behind. "Where have ye been?"

Ian reddened. "Looking for ye. I must tell ye about his dreams. We may have to act."

Jamison winced. The pain from his injury was getting worse. "We *must* act! Lord Gilbert can't come before the end of the year. A letter just arrived. Lady Bridget hasn't birthed the child."

Ian frowned. Gilbert's involvement would have sanctioned their actions. Now they could be construed as treason. Calm washed over him suddenly, quelling his desperation. Ian knew that something was different with his brother. "Who is with Dughall now?"

"The women just brought his daughter to him. The wee lassie is sick. They may have the same thing."

"Hmmm... I'm not sure what's happening, but she's good for him. Dughall has decided to fight this thing. I've seen them together and always wondered. Do ye suppose they have a connection?"

"It could be true. The child is sensitive and she is his daughter."

"His fever is falling. That buys us time to act."

Jamison groaned. "I told Lady Keira that I'd meet her in the surgery. I'm hoping that she can straighten my shoulder."

Ian gritted his teeth. "I'm going to check on my brother. I'll meet ye in the surgery afterwards." They arrived at a stair case and went in opposite directions, one up and the other down.

***

THE SURGERY

Jamison sat on the examination table, cradling his arm next to his body. It had been two weeks since he'd been thrown from his horse, injuring his right shoulder. He moved his hand out slightly and pretended to grasp a dirk. A bolt of pain shot up his arm. "Damn it!" he groaned. "There couldn't be a worse time for this." When he returned, he'd insisted that he could work through the pain. He endured it for a week, unable to lift a weapon. Then he stopped using his arm to let it rest. That's when things went from bad to worse. *I can barely move it. I can't even grasp a dirk without pain.*

The door opened, admitting Ian Hay. Jamison tensed and was hit with a spasm of pain. "Ach!"

Ian frowned. "It's about time ye had the women look at this."

Jamison's eyes clouded with tears. Was it so obvious? "I'll be all right. Can the lass fix this?"

Ian stared. "My shoulder was out of socket and she put it back. But I'm warning ye, friend. It will hurt like the devil."

"It already does, God damn it! Why are ye here, to torment me?"

"Nay, friend. I'm here to tell ye about his latest dreams. Thirty foot giants… a threat on his life…" Ian sighed. "The only thing missing was dragons. It could be a sign of the madness."

Jamison groaned. "Lord Gilbert will never get here in time. It's up to us to save him."

"What can we do?"

Jamison's voice was laced with pain. "We must steal that sword and throw it in the loch! That's what Lord Gilbert suggested."

They were silent for a moment, each contemplating the meaning. For such an act, they could be accused of treason.

Ian hesitated. "He's not just my brother; he's my lord and master. I hope it doesn't come to that."

"It has come to that," Jamison said, as he grimaced with pain. "After the lass heals me, we'll steal the damned sword."

Ian nodded. "Let me see if I can find it."

The servant watched his friend leave the surgery. When he was gone, he lay down to wait for what would be a painful procedure.

***

Keira left her bed chamber and walked the corridor to the east wing of the castle. Her thoughts wandered, from Dughall's illness to the white magic she needed to save him. She required supplies for the ritual. They would have to visit the wardrobe and the herbalist. But for now it would have to wait. Jamison was waiting for her in the surgery. According to her mother-in-law, he was in desperate need of help for his injured shoulder.

Her husband was in good hands. Jessie and Murdock were providing him with bark tea, a sponge bath, and a breakfast of eggs and bread. Hunger was a good sign. The baby seemed better as well, as long as she slept by her father's side.

Keira arrived at the door of the surgery. As was her custom, she prayed for guidance. *Dear Goddess. Help me to heal this man, who is as loyal and true as a friend can be.* As she entered the surgery, her nose was assaulted with the smell of perspiration. "Jamison?"

"Aye, m'Lady." He grimaced as he sat up and cradled his right arm with his left.

Keira began a silent evaluation. Lank, disheveled hair hung over the forehead of this usually handsome man. His cheeks were pale and his lips seemed thin and bloodless. Dark circles under his eyes meant that he hadn't slept. She touched his injured shoulder and felt him flinch. Her voice was soft as she massaged the joint, searching for broken bones or dislocations. "Jessie said that yer horse threw ye."

"Aye." Jamison's voice was tight, "Ach! Pinned me to the ground. Oh, God. That hurts like the devil." He blushed as she felt under his arm. "Must ye touch me there? It's not proper."

Keira pulled back out of respect. "Of course it's proper. I'm a healer."

"I thought that Lady Jessie would be here as well."

"She's busy with Dughall and our daughter. I'm the only one who can fix yer shoulder, and by the looks of it we have work to do. May I continue?"

Jamison reddened. "Aye. Is it broken?"

"Nay. Take off yer shirt."

"Um. I've been wearing the same shirt for five days. I can't move my arm away from my body. The thought of raising it above my head is painful."

"How did it get this way?"

"I favored my good arm to avoid the pain. I thought that if I stopped using it, it would heal."

Keira frowned. "That's not how it works. An unused joint will lock in place, sometimes after a week. Grandmother used to say that something in there grew together and had to be ripped apart." She took a pair of scissors from the cupboard and began to cut his shirt. "Don't fret. We'll get ye another."

"But, why must ye..."

She completed a cut and slipped the shirt over his head. "There. I have to see both sides of yer body to tell what's normal. Now sit up straight." Keira stood behind him and ran her hands around his left shoulder. When she got a good idea of what his left joint looked like, she massaged the right, detecting a limited range of motion and swelling. His right shoulder was lower than the left by two inches, but that could be from his posture.

He swallowed hard. "How bad is it?"

She came around front. "There's swelling and limited movement."

"I could have told ye that."

"We must find out how far ye can go. It's bound to be painful. Would ye like some whisky?"

"Nay! My mind must be clear to protect my master."

It was a strange thing to say in his condition, but Keira honored it. "Tell me when it's too much. Take a breath." She grasped his wrist and supported the elbow with her other hand. First, she moved the forearm up and down as it stayed by his side. She could see that it was painful, but he wouldn't admit it, choosing instead to breathe deeply. She bent it past the point where it was comfortable, then pressed on until he looked like he would faint. "Is this as far as it will go?"

His teeth clenched. "Aye! Get it over with!"

She leaned in closer and grasped the inside of his arm, supporting his elbow with her other hand. "Now to test the side movement. Cry if ye must. I won't think less of ye." Pushing the arm away from his body, she saw that it moved only a few inches before locking. The pain had to be unbearable, but he didn't say a word. She pushed again and commanded, "Breathe."

His body trembled. "Ach!"

Keira backed off and eased his arm alongside his body. "The joint is locked. This will take weeks to correct if we're lucky."

"Weeks? Can't ye just straighten it?"

"Nay."

"Ye fixed Ian's shoulder."

"That was different. I'll give ye movements to do and bark tea to bring down the swelling. Return every few days to let me stretch it."

Jamison hung his head in disgrace. "I'm as useless as tits on a boar. How can I protect my master like this?"

"Leave that to Ian and Murdock."

"I'd rather be dead than derelict in my duties."

Keira smiled sympathetically. "Accept the Goddess' gift of healing, even if it takes time. My husband will understand. We'll have ye back in shape by the next full moon."

Jamison groaned. "The Duke may be dead by then! The end of the year is tomorrow. I will steal that sword and destroy it, even if it means my life."

She was touched by his loyalty. "It's not up to ye to save him."

"Why, lass?"

"Because I am the one who must save him."

"Ye!"

"Aye. The thing that stalks him is otherworldly. The sword has no power against it."

"How will ye defeat it, then?"

"With white magic," Keira said. "My people call it drawing down the moon. I could use some help. Let me tell ye about it."

Murdock

Chapter 24
Hopes and Fears

December 31st 1637
NEXT MORNING

It was a cold, gray morning at Drake Castle. Heavy snow was falling and the mist was thick on surrounding hilltops. The courtyard was empty, except for an occasional servant hurrying to an assignment.

Young Luc Deville was one of those servants, going to start his day in the smithy. Since Dughall's illness, he'd been temporarily assigned as a helper to the blacksmith.

Luc entered the smithy through a draped hide door and hung his coat on a peg. He slipped on a leather apron, tied it in back, and gazed into the roaring forge. It would be warm in here today.

"Late again, lad?" The blacksmith emerged from the back and gave him an angry look.

Luc played dumb. "Am I, Sir?"

"Aye. Lucky that ye're a favorite of the Duke or I'd tan yer hide. Perhaps I'll do it anyway."

The boy cringed at the thought. "I'll be on time tomorrow."

"Make sure that ye are." He passed a bellows to him. "Fan the fire until that bar turns red. We've got a long day ahead of us, making hardware for the gates."

"Ye won't tell m'Lord that I was late?"

"No one in his right mind would bother him today. Rumor is he's dying."

Luc's breath caught in his throat. How could God take the one man who'd been good to him? He dropped the bellows, untied his apron, and tossed it on the floor. "I must go to him!"

The blacksmith blocked his way. "Nay, lad! Stay here and work like the rest of us."

"But he needs me."

"Ha! Who do ye think ye are?"

"His friend!" The boy saw an opening. "Look, Sir! The fire is dying." As the blacksmith turned and grabbed a poker, Luc ran under his arm and out the door.

***

Murdock stood outside the bed chamber, waiting to see the young Lord. It had been a morning he would never forget. After breakfast, he'd stood by helplessly as his master suffered a convulsive fit. The servant had never witnessed anything like it. There was twitching and thrashing and foaming at the mouth. His skin turned dusky and then... He woke in a state of confusion with weakness in his limbs. Then attended by family and servants; he fell into a deathlike sleep.

Hours had passed since they thought that they'd lost him. Dughall had revived and was receiving his family. His mother had just left his bedside. Murdock was to go in next. The servant was afraid of what he might find.

The door opened and the Duchess emerged wearing a long plaid dress, cradling the baby against her shoulder. She looked calm for a lass who'd been through so much.

Murdock bowed. "My Lady."

"Go in now. But don't tire him out."

"How is he?"

"Weak and pale." Keira's eyes misted with tears. "He's expecting death! He asked me to remarry and raise our child."

"Does he know about the sword?" Ian and Jamison had absconded with the blade to destroy it. Dughall regained consciousness shortly after they left the castle grounds.

"The empty scabbard is on the table, but that won't fool him for long." She shifted the child to her other shoulder. "I'll take my daughter to Tarrah for her nap. Meet me in the wardrobe."

Murdock watched her walk away and entered the chamber. For a moment, he was speechless. His master was sitting up in bed, resting on pillows against the headboard.

Dughall smiled weakly. "Murdock."

"My Lord!" The servant rushed to the bedside and performed the tasks he knew best - arranging his hair and offering him a sip of water. It felt good to touch him. "Do ye need to use the chamber pot?"

"Nay, friend. Just be with me."

"Oh, lad. Ye gave us quite a scare. I thought that..."

The young Lord sighed. "The rumors of my death have been exaggerated." He glanced at the scabbard. "Where is Ian?"

Murdock held his breath. "He left the castle hours ago on horseback with Jamison."

"They took my sword. I can feel it."

"Aye. They meant well and it seemed to help. Ye revived after they left the grounds."

He seemed agitated. "No one understands! Tonight I shall face the Morrigan defenseless. I cannot father her child, so she will take my life."

"Nay, lad! The Duchess has a plan to defeat this thing."

"My wife? I suspected that something was afoot."

"It is, lad! When the time comes, allow her to do what she must."

Dughall sighed. "I'm not afraid to die. When the Earl beat me, I went to a place that was beautiful. I'm a fisherman at heart. The gulls will come for my soul."

"Don't talk like that! We won't let ye die."

The young Lord took a ragged breath. "Mother is worried about my illness. She recalls my friend Jamie who was stricken with convulsions."

"Where is he?"

"Dead. He choked on his own tongue."

"Oh. This affliction..."

"I studied it in the library after my last attack. The Greeks called it the Sacred Disease. Most thought it was a curse or a prophetic power, but Hippocrates proved it was a malady of the brain."

"The brain?" Murdock struggled to understand. "That thing in yer head?"

"Aye."

"Why would ye have this affliction?"

"The Earl beat my mother before I was born. Perhaps I was damaged."

"Blackheart strikes us again."

"What does it matter? I may not survive beyond tomorrow." He took a breath and yawned. "Why am I so tired?"

Murdock felt his forehead. "There's no fever, so get some rest. I'll return to check on ye after I help the Duchess."

Dughall took his hand and squeezed it gently. "Give her what she needs to defeat this."

"I will."

"Murdock..." His eyes were heavy with exhaustion. "If we don't meet again, remember that I loved ye."

The servant's heart was breaking. "Oh... I love ye, too."

"I've bequeathed some land and a cottage to ye. Ask Jamison for the deed when I'm gone."

Murdock choked back tears. "Dinna say such things! I don't want land if it means yer death."

"Love never dies, my friend. Remember that." The young man started to drift. "Forgive me, but I must rest."

There was a knock on the door and Luc entered. He appeared to be crying.

Murdock blocked his way. This disobedient boy was the last thing his master needed in his weakened state. "Go away, lad! No one asked ye to come here."

Luc sniffled. "They said that he's dying! Is it true?"

"Go, lad!"

Dughall's voice was a whisper. "Let him come."

"But m'Lord!"

"Jesus said 'Let the little children come to me… for the kingdom of heaven belongs to such as these.'"

"Hmmphh…" He could hardly argue with the good book.

"Leave us, friend. The boy needs me."

"As ye wish, m'Lord."

Murdock left the chamber and informed Jessie of young Luc's presence. Then summoning his courage, he met the Duchess in the wardrobe. He was determined to do everything in his power to save his best friend.

***

MILES FROM DRAKE CASTLE

Jamison and Ian rode west into the Highlands on roads that were covered with ice and snow. Poorly equipped for bad weather, they were wet and chilled to the bone. They stopped at the inn at Forres, stabled their horses, and went inside to warm up by the fire.

The stone structure was inviting, with dark timbered walls and wrought iron fixtures. Oil lamps provided light and the smell of meat pies hung in the air. They sat at a table next to the fire.

Jamison's arm throbbed to his fingers, in spite of the numbness from the cold. It was by sheer will that he'd gotten this far without stopping. "Seaford Shores is a few miles north on Findhorn Bay."

"Dughall's summer estate?"

"Aye."

Ian kicked off his boots and pointed his feet toward the fire. "God damn this cold! I can barely feel them." He propped the blade against a chair and stared at it. "Why must we go there? Can't we just throw the sword in Loch Ness?"

"I thought better of it, lad. We'll hide the blade at the Duke's estate and wait for Lord Gilbert's instructions. That way we can't be accused of stealing."

Ian snorted. "My brother won't punish me. As long as I'm involved, we're safe."

Jamison frowned. "Well, that's all right for ye. He might pull my ears off or something more vital."

"Dughall would never do that. By the way, my brother's awake and talking."

"I knew it! That sword was making him sick."

"It's more than that. He's still in rough shape."

"Does he know that the blade is gone?"

Ian gazed into the fire. "Oh aye."

"Is he angry?"

"Nay. He's convinced that he's going to die."

Jamison tensed, sending a painful spasm down his arm. "Ach!" He rubbed his shoulder in a circular motion, just like the lass showed him. "The Duchess plans to save him with white magic. Pray that she knows what she's doing."

"It should be easier now that the sword is gone."

"Let's hope so."

The innkeeper came out of a back room and took notice of them. The burly old Scot took out a cloth and wiped the bar.

Ian brightened. "Tonight is the feast of Hogmanay. I bet that he has black buns, shortbread, and plenty of ale."

Jamison groaned. "I need something stronger for this soreness. Ask him for a bottle of whisky."

"Didn't the lass help ye?" Ian said.

"She stretched the joint and showed me some movements. I'm getting better, but it's going to take time."

"So the strength will come back?"

Jamison reddened. "So she says, or I'm done for as a protector." He grimaced. "The snow's coming down hard. Let's ask about lodging for the night."

"I'm for that!"

"Now get up and fetch me that whisky."

***

MILES AWAY IN THE LORD'S BED CHAMBER

Luc approached and knelt at his master's bedside. Tears sprang to his eyes as he kissed his outstretched hand. "Oh, my Lord."

Dughall managed a smile. "Do ye remember when I sat with ye just like this?"

"Aye. It was after my stepfather hurt me."

"What did I do after I treated yer wounds?"

"Ye hugged me."

"I did. So do ye have a hug for me?"

The boy stood and melted into his arms. He sobbed as the Duke whispered in his ear. "Oh, thank ye Sir. I hope it's true. I'll be brave. I promise."

The young Lord held him and stroked his hair. "Shhh... Have faith, lad."

"I do love ye like a father."

Dughall sighed. "I love ye too." He held the boy's shoulders. "Leave me, son, and say a prayer. I must gather my strength for a challenge."

Luc left the bed chamber in good spirits. As he walked, he reflected on what his master said. If the man lived, he would find a way to adopt him as his son.

***

The wardrobe was a windowless room located in the west wing. Illuminated by a single oil lamp, it had no working fireplace. Murdock and Keira saw their breath as they searched through the vast collection of clothing. The chests along a wall were filled with hunting and riding clothes. Wooden boxes contained scores of plaids and other everyday clothing. Formal attire hung on poles in sections for men, women, and children. It was almost too much to look through.

"My Lady," Murdock said, with a shiver in his voice. "What are we looking for?"

Keira held up a red lace veil. "I've found the first item. When the Morrigan appeared to the Daghda, crimson tresses lay upon her head. My hair is as dark as the midnight sky, so this veil will make it look red. I shall wear it on my head to contain her spirit!"

Murdock shuddered. This was a brave lass to be inviting a spirit to possess her. She must really love the young Lord. "How will ye get her to leave?"

"A trusted friend must remove the veil. That's where ye come in."

His heart almost stopped. "What did ye say?"

"Ye must strip off the veil when we're done."

"Lady Jessie would be a better choice."

"Nay. Mother must attend to our daughter."

Murdock reddened. "Ye want me in the chamber? While ye're uhhh..."

"Aye, there's no other way."

"Oh God."

"Will ye help us?"

He remembered his oath to protect his master. "Aye."

"Thank the Goddess." She rummaged through the ladies' clothing. "Help me find a robe that I can drop at will."

"Drop?" His heart pounded like a drum.

She smiled sweetly. "She has to be naked to seduce him."

"Oh God."

"The body is a beautiful thing. Have ye never been with a lass?"

Murdock reddened. "Not yet."

"No matter. Will ye help us?"

The servant searched frantically through the rack in an attempt to allay his fears. "I will do it for my master." He'd never seen a naked lass or encountered a malevolent spirit. No wonder he was a bundle of nerves.

Mairghread

Chapter 25
Apothecary

After finding a suitable robe, they left the castle and walked a mile to a cottage that housed the apothecary. Once inside, they placed a basket on a counter and surveyed the jars behind it.

Murdock didn't like this place or the reputation of the woman who ran it. Mairghread was a disagreeable old hag. In his opinion, she was gruff and vile and a purveyor of substances of questionable value. This was the woman he was staring at now, with no small amount of suspicion.

The Duchess seemed to be at ease with her. The women talked with heads together, going through a list of requirements. What were they saying?

"Why is *he* here?" the hag asked, glancing in his direction.

Keira smiled. "Murdock is a trusted friend."

"He'd better be. What ye plan is dangerous, especially with the Morrigan. Have ye done white magic?"

"Aye."

Murdock strained his ears to hear the rest.

"Brave lass. Don't let them catch ye practicing magic."

"I will call down the moon in the forest. No one will be there to see it."

Mairghread loaded the basket with items. Oil… Lavender… Dried woad…

Keira touched her hand. "Mother said that when we draw down the moon, we never know which aspect will appear. Maiden, mother, or crone… She tried to warn me about something. Do ye know anything about it?"

The woman nodded. "Perhaps. Is it the maiden ye wish to summon?"

"Aye."

Mairghread took a jar off the shelf and held it to Keira's nose. "Cast the circle with this powder."

The scent reminded her of spring flowers. "What is it?"

"The violet of the sorcerers… Blue periwinkle… It will summon the maiden in the Morrigan." She sealed the jar and placed it into the basket. "Good luck, lass."

Murdock cringed as the hag turned to him and demanded payment. He counted three silver coins into her palm and escorted the Duchess out of the hovel. "Forgive me, my Lady. Was it wise to tell her what it was for?"

Keira nodded. "Mairghread is a follower of Brigit, the Goddess of healing. Her intentions are good. She means to help me."

They walked to the castle, went inside, and took the stairs to the second floor.

Keira paused. "I must describe the plan to my husband and check on the condition of my daughter. Meet me in the room next to my chamber at nine. We must prepare my body for the Morrigan."

"My Lady! It's improper."

"Dughall will understand."

Murdock shivered as he watched her walk away. He never liked the spirit world. Torn between hope and fear, he decided to get a meal and pray in the chapel until needed.

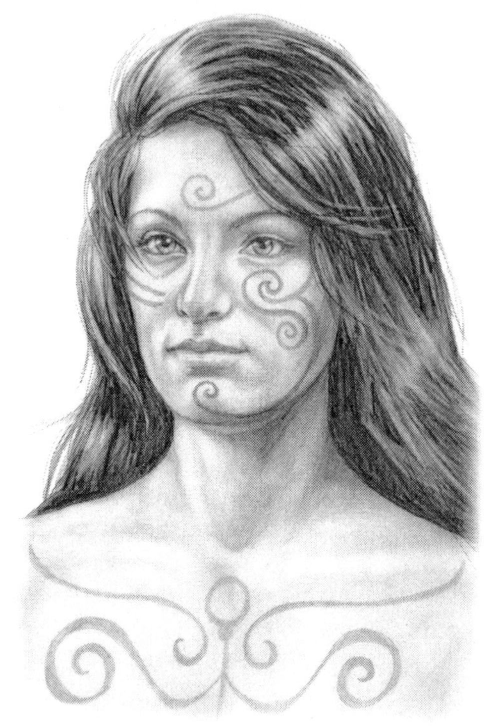

Keira

Chapter 26
Drawing Down the Moon

December 31th 1637
10PM

THE WOODS SURROUNDING DRAKE CASTLE

The forest seemed crystalline in the light of the moon. The trees were coated with ice that sparkled like rare diamonds. Wood smoke hung in the air from Drake's many fireplaces.

Keira's boots crunched through snow as she meditated on the task ahead. *I must not fail. The life of my beloved is at stake, as well as my son and daughter.*

Dughall lay limp and feverish in the castle. Without a miracle, he wouldn't survive. Maggie was burning up as well. Keira expected them to recover when she offered her body to the Morrigan.

The young lass slowed her pace and took in an eerie sight. Cold fog hovered beneath the treetops. It was a sign of a ghostly presence. Her heart fluttered wildly. *I must not fail.*

The Duchess lifted a low branch and arrived at her favorite oak tree.

Her breath froze on her lashes as she traced the symbol that was etched upon it. "Great Mother. I surrender. Come to me in yer fearsome form."

Keira spread a plaid on the ground, opened the basket, and took out the red veil. She wrapped it around her shoulders and opened the jar of periwinkle. It was time to cast a circle and invite the Morrigan. She focused her eyes on the sacred mark. "Earth! Air! Fire and Water! These are the points of the pentacle and the source of strength and protection." She sprinkled powder in each direction, drew a circle, and dabbed some behind her ears. "Oh violet of the sorcerers! Send me the maiden on this winter night."

The wind howled in response.

Keira closed her eyes and imagined herself naked in the moonlight. As the cold air nipped her flesh, she settled into a trancelike state. Until now, she was free to stop the transformation, but what she'd do next would seal her fate. She held her arms to the sky.

"Morrigan Morrigan Three times Three,
Hear the words I ask of Thee.
Grant me vision, Grant me power,
Join me in my darkest hour.
As the night overtakes the day,
Morrigan Morrigan Light my way.

Morrigan Morrigan Raven Queen
Round and round the Hawthorn Green.
Queen of beauty, Queen of Art,
Take my body, Take my heart.
All my trust I place in thee,
Morrigan Morrigan Come to me..."

Lightning flashed, illuminating the landscape. A raven called from a nearby branch with a hoarse "kraaah" and a resonant "prruk", its plumage iridescent in the light of the moon. This was an ominous sign. The raven signified the presence of the crone, the harbinger of death and destruction.

The bird spoke in a gravelly voice. "Do ye know what ye ask, daughter?"

Keira's skin crawled. "Aye."

The raven stretched its wings. "Then prepare to merge with me."

"Wait!" she cried. It was time to negotiate the outcome. "Ye desire my husband?"

"Our coupling is his destiny. Do ye offer yer body to save his life?"

Keira shivered. "Aye. But there are conditions."

"Conditions?!" The voice was angry. "Speak!"

"The son we conceive... We must play equal parts! I must serve as his earthly mother."

"Hmmphh... What else?"

"Ye must leave my body when the veil is removed." The raven gave her a venomous stare. Keira feared that she had gone too far. Was everything lost? It was about to take flight.

The bird left the branch and hovered before her. "Foolish lass," it hissed. "I accept yer terms."

Keira's heart pounded with fear. She was about to draw down the moon.

Its wings vibrated like a hummingbird's, fanning her body. The raven morphed into a voluptuous maiden, surrounded them with light, and the two merged into one.

Keira reached back and drew the veil upon her head to contain the spirit of the Morrigan. Feeling taller and stronger, she saw the world through new eyes. She was the source of life, the wife of the God Dagda, and the Goddess of swelling rivers! No longer innocent; she was a woman of wisdom and power. This body was full of life, young and strong and capable of bearing children. She would birth a son for her beloved.

As the Duchess walked to the castle, her mind surrendered to the entity. The Morrigan grew stronger with every step. She'd been granted the abilities of this mortal, her sight and speech and rare mobility. A man she'd stalked for centuries awaited her, eager to perform the act. She would give him an hour that he'd never forget. Stone walls loomed before her, reminding her of the Land of Eire. She arrived at the gate and pounded on the door.

The guard peeked out a hole and opened the gate. "My Lady! What are ye doing out here?"

"Meditating on the moon." Her voice was as cold as ice. "Allow me to pass."

The guard stepped away. "Yer face is blue! Are ye hurt?"

Keira grasped his hand. With strength beyond her own, she bent back his fingers and brought him to his knees. "Speak of this to no one, mortal."

He gasped as she squeezed harder. "Ach! I will do as ye wish."

She cracked a bone in his hand. "Remember what I said." Ignoring his sobs, she passed through the gate, crossed the courtyard, and entered the side door of the castle.

***

THE NURSERY

Jessie stood in the nursery, drying her granddaughter with a towel. The child's fever had spiked to dangerous levels, prompting them to bathe her in cool water.

Tarrah stood by, chewing her thumbnail. "Will she live?"

Jessie nodded. "Aye, lass. I feared the worst, but her fever has broken." She dressed the baby in a loose gown, working her tiny hands through the arm holes. The infant gurgled. "That's right, sweetheart. Nana's here."

Tarrah sighed. "Thank God. But what of m'Lord? Everyone says that he's dying."

"I sent Beth to check on him." Jessie cast her eyes to heaven. "God brought my son through trials that would defeat most men. He won't desert him." In truth, she was anxious about the outcome, which depended upon magic and a pagan goddess. She put on the infant's socks and cradled her against her shoulder.

"Will ye leave now to tend to m'Lord?"

"Nay. Keira and Murdock will care for him."

"But, m'Lady..."

"I've been ordered to stay away. My duty is to care for the child." She swayed slightly, rocking the infant.

There was a knock on the door. Beth entered in an agitated state, fidgeting with a cross around her neck.

Jessie was afraid. "Wait outside, Tarrah. I must talk to Beth alone."

"Aye, m'am."

She watched the servant leave the room. "The child's fever is gone. How is my son?"

Beth stared. "Alert and talking. Murdock says that his fever broke a short while ago."

"That's good news. What's wrong?"

"I passed the Duchess in the corridor. She looked like a pagan statue! God help us!"

Jessie mustered her courage. "Did she address ye?"

Beth frowned. "Nay. She gave me a vacant stare. Should we stop this?"

Jessie remembered what her daughter-in-law said. She would go into a trance to channel the Goddess. The veil and the marks were part of the ritual. Was this what she saw or something ominous?

The lass cried, "It's not the Christian thing to do!"

So it was the pagan thing that bothered her. She squeezed her shoulder. "Go to the chapel and pray to Jesus for the life of our Lord and master. There's nothing more we can do."

Beth nodded. "I'll stay on my knees until dawn if need be. Call me when it's over."

Jessie sighed. "Say a prayer for me as well."

"I will."

"...and pray that I'm right," she whispered.

***

THE LORD'S BEDCHAMBER

Dughall sat up in bed, marveling at how much better he felt. His fever had broken, the headache was gone, and his strength was coming back. Murdock had bathed him and combed the tangles out of his hair. He'd changed the sheets, fluffed the pillows, and anointed him with bayberry cologne.

Dughall knew what was happening. His wife would appear as the Morrigan. To save their lives, he must obey her and conceive a child. *My poor wife,* he thought. *How can I let her risk this?* If they survived, they would get what they wanted, a son and heir to his estate and title.

Murdock straightened the sheets. "Do ye need to use the chamber pot?"

"Nay, friend." He sensed the man's terror. "Are ye all right?"

"Well enough for a man who's about to see a spirit!" Murdock's hands trembled as he fluffed a pillow for the sixth time.

"Ye don't have to stay."

"I must. I promised to tear the veil from her head when the act is done. Let's hope she knows what she's doing."

Dughall sighed. "So many lives are at stake - mine, my daughter's, and my unborn son."

"She's a brave lass to try this."

Dughall was having misgivings. It was dangerous to invite a spirit to possess ye. Keira could lose her life. Would the Morrigan try to stay? "Do ye suppose that she's done it?"

The servant nodded. "Aye. Look at the change in ye. An hour ago, I thought ye were going to seize."

The young Lord reached out to her, but found that she wasn't there. A fearsome presence walked in her place. "God help us."

Murdock was pale. "Someone is outside the door." He took his hand and squeezed it tightly. "Good luck, lad."

Dughall's nerves were on fire. "Leave me!"

"But, lad..."

He pushed him away. "Stay by the window and don't interfere."

The door opened with sudden force, rattling the window panes. A cold wind blew into the room bearing the aroma of burnt earth.

The young Lord watched with apprehension as the creature that was partly his wife walked into the room. She wore a crimson robe that matched a veil upon her head, partially concealing her face.

"Conan... I am here." She dropped her robe, revealing an athletic body adorned with teal blue paint. "Will ye do the deed?"

Dughall was sure that he'd lived this before. But the last time he didn't survive it. He knew that it was his wife, in body if not in spirit. Yet, she was also a different woman, exuding raw sensual power. His body responded. "Morrigan..." he whispered with tenderness. He threw back the sheets. "Come to me, lass. I surrender."

***

MILES AWAY

Ian struggled to get comfortable on the tavern floor. The innkeeper had allowed them to sleep near the fire using their plaids and saddle packs as bedding.

Jamison rolled onto his good shoulder. "Damned arm! Pour me another whisky."

Ian faced him. "The bottle's gone. Can ye make it to morning?"

Jamison pulled the blanket onto his shoulder. "I guess so."

"We should be grateful we're warm. It was storming like hell when I went for the saddle packs."

"How are the horses?"

"The stables are warm enough."

Jamison groaned. "Have ye sensed yer brother?"

"Aye. He's found the strength to go on."

"So the Duchess' white magic worked."

"Let's hope so. Get some rest. There's nothing more we can do tonight."

Jamison drifted into a fitful sleep.

Ian listened to the sound of the crackling fire. There were other travelers on the floor, four men, a woman, and a child. The air was ripe with the odor of unwashed bodies. His eyes were closed when a vision came, flooding his senses...

Dughall stood at the side of the bed, thrusting his manhood into his wife. His heart raced as he held her thighs apart in response to her animal cries. Her hand rose up and slapped his chest, demanding that he go deeper. Sharp nails raked his skin as she begged him for a son. *Conan, I need ye,* she moaned.

Ian's mind was riveted to their passion. "Do it, brother!" Dughall obeyed and the seed was planted.

Jamison woke with a start. "Is the Duke all right?"

"He's better than all right. Go to sleep."

***

THE LORD'S CHAMBER

Murdock cowered by the window, considering what to do. The act had gone on too long, threatening his master's health. The young Lord was reluctant to go another round. But she was an endless bundle of energy.

Dughall groaned and cried out in pain. Her mouth was busy at his breast. Was she biting him? Surely the child was already conceived.

Murdock was mortified, but it was his job to remove the veil. He summoned his courage and approached the bed. Her head turned suddenly, greeting him with a vicious snarl. This wasn't the Lady Keira he knew. The Morrigan was determined to stay.

Murdock swallowed his fear and tore the veil from her head.

The Morrigan lashed out, knocking him to the floor. The veil went down with him and he lay upon it, refusing to give it up. Terrifying sounds filled the chamber - screeching and wailing and gnashing of teeth. A frigid wind swirled around the room, frosting windows and chilling him to the bone. He gripped the veil. A large raven circled his head and dropped a feather. Then it flew through a window pane.

***

THE NURSERY

Jessie handed her granddaughter to the nursemaid and walked the hallway to her son's chamber. She thought about fetching Beth, but decided to investigate alone. There would be enough trouble keeping things quiet. She entered the chamber and saw Murdock on the floor, staring blankly and clutching a feather.

Jessie's heart was in her throat as she approached the bed. Was her son alive? Keira lay atop him, her naked flesh painted from head to toe. He appeared to be bruised and battered, but she could see that he was breathing. She checked their pulses and found them to be strong. But it was freezing in the room. Like a dutiful servant, she untangled the bedding and drew the blanket to their shoulders.

Just then, the mantle clock struck the hour. Jessie counted the bongs and smiled. For it was midnight, a new year was dawning, and the owner of the sword was alive.

Sara

Chapter 27
The Morning After

January 1st 1638
5AM

DRAKE CASTLE

Dughall slept like the dead on that cold winter night. His body was spent and his mind was stretched to the limit. Near dawn, he was plagued by visionary dreams.

His heart raced as he crossed a moor toward the sound of a woman crying. He came upon the body of a young man lying face down. Dughall stooped and held a finger against his neck to check for a pulse. There was none. Turning the lad, he saw that he resembled Luc. But how could this be? His page was just a boy and this was a bearded young lad. Eyes clouded over, he'd been stabbed in the heart. Dughall roared in anger.

In the distance, the lass cried out in agony. He unsheathed his sword and ran towards the sound, hoping to save her. As he got closer, he saw a young man holding a dark-haired lass against a tree. Her skirt was up and his kilt was raised as he raped her. His blood boiled when he saw that he wore the kilt of his clansmen. "Unhand her!"

The scoundrel decoupled and faced him. The lass dropped to her knees, sobbing piteously.

"Old man!" The lad drew a sword. "Ye can't tell me what to do."

Dughall studied his opponent. He was muscular with long red curls and piercing blue eyes. "Cease and desist! I am the Lord of this clan."

The lad raised his sword. "Not for long, Father."

Father? Dughall's heart sank. *Was this the child they just conceived?* He ducked and parried so the blade missed him. The lad stepped back and prepared to deliver a deadly blow. It was obvious that he meant to kill him.

"Prepare to die!"

The lass cried out. "Nay! He's our father."

As she looked up, Dughall saw a younger version of Kate. She brought a hand to her mouth, revealing the clan birthmark. He faced his son and exploded in anger. "Ye fornicated with yer sister?"

"That's what women are good for." The boy taunted him. "She looks like Kate, doesn't she? Do ye remember her soft lips upon yer member? The patch of hair between her legs? The noise she makes when ye..."

How did he know these things? Dughall could stand no more. He raised his sword in anger. "Stay away from her or I'll..."

The lad assumed a defensive stance. "What, Father? Will ye kill me? Best that ye do it *before* I'm born."

Dughall clenched his teeth. He was angry enough to kill. But what kind of man would kill his son? The world would be better off without him. He dropped his weapon and sank to his knees. "Just kill me now."

The young man sneered. "Weakling! So ye submit to me?"

"Aye. Get it over with!"

Maggie sobbed piteously.

The lad rested the blade on his neck. His voice was cold. "When yer dead, I'll have her again."

***

The Duke woke with a start and threw off the blankets. He prayed that it was a dream, but his sight convinced him otherwise. He glanced at his wife, asleep beside him. Was she pregnant with this wicked child?

Dughall sat up and checked his parts. His chest was tender, his groin was raw, and his leg muscles screamed with exhaustion. He had survived the curse, but at what cost? His thoughts ran wild. Would it matter if he spawned a son who murdered his father? He deserved it for killing his own father. Death didn't scare him and the manner of death was unimportant. But how could he let him destroy his sister? And what about poor Luc? Was there something he could do to prevent it?

His wife lay naked with her raven hair spread upon the pillow. Her breathing was soft and regular. The bed chamber seemed eerie in the light of the dying hearth. The lion's head chair appeared almost as a living creature. He got out of bed, put on a robe, and visited the chamber pot in the corner. His head ached as though he'd consumed too much whisky. He spotted a goblet brimming with water on the bedside table and retrieved it. "Bless ye, Murdock." He recalled the man's pledge to stay at his side and suspected that he'd saved his life. But what did he remember about last night? He pondered this as he sipped the water.

Yesterday was a blur. A raging fever kept him on the edge of consciousness, as friends and family paraded by. Mother... Keira... Ian... Father John... He remembered being given last rites. Servants attended him throughout the day - Anna, Murdock, and young Luc. His headache flared. Luc? He promised to adopt the boy if he survived. How would he accomplish it? Given the dream, was the boy better off without him? Jamison and Ian were away on a mission to destroy the sword. He reached out to his brother to stop him.

His thoughts were scattered. *So many conspired to save my life; but none more than my wife.* She called it drawing down the moon, a risky form of white magic. To save his life and conceive a child, she agreed to merge with the Morrigan. His loins had stirred at the sight of her. Naked, veiled, and painted blue, she'd awakened ancient memories.

He gazed at the sleeping figure. The channeling was powerful. Did any of the Morrigan remain? Just how much of Keira was left? If the dream was true, she carried a fiery son who would inherit his estate and title. He would destroy his adopted brother and rape his innocent sister.

"Forgive me, Maggie," he whispered. "I should have died."

Could he ask Keira to give up the child? It was common knowledge that a pregnancy could be ended with an infusion of mugwort and cohosh. Deeply disturbed by the thought, he decided to get some answers. He brought a washcloth to the bed and began to sponge off her paint.

***

The Duchess drifted in a sea of dreams. Her life passed before her eyes without judgment or emotion. *A child witnessed her mother's execution. She hiked through a forest to find her grandmother, lived in a village, and served the Goddess as a priestess. She married a fisherman who turned out to be a Lord. People, places, and events rolled by like a play, suggesting that Keira was dead. Was this what happened in the Summerland? She tried to wake but she couldn't.*

Stranger dreams followed of a life in a land called Eire. She saw breathtaking waters, rolling green hills, and hundreds of worshippers at her feet. She mated with a God in a sacred river and birthed a blue-eyed son. He grew quickly and sat beside her.

"Máthair." The boy spoke in a lilting tongue, foreign but familiar. "Wake up!"

Her heart overflowed with love. "My son." She was a mother at last. Could she stay here forever?

The boy's angelic face contorted. "Wake up! Father means to cast me away!"

***

"Wake up! Are ye all right, wife?"

Keira woke with a start. "I'm not dead."

Dughall wiped dye from her face. The washcloth was turning blue. "Aye. We survived the night. Do ye remember what happened?"

She couldn't recall anything after merging with the Goddess. Yet she knew that she conceived a son. "Nay."

He seemed disappointed. "Ah, well. Can ye sit up?"

Keira sat up and felt a wave of nausea. She grabbed the bowl from his hands and stared into it. "Dear Goddess."

"What's wrong?"

"I think I might vomit."

"Are ye sick?"

"Nay, husband. It's for the best thing ever. I'm pregnant."

"With the lad of our dreams?"

"Aye." She regarded him with great tenderness. "Our son is here at last."

Dughall's expression was grave. "But at what cost?"

"What do ye mean?"

"I had a dream last night. The child will bring ruin upon us!"

Keira flinched. "Tell me about this dream."

Dughall took her hands and proceeded to tell her about the vision. He left nothing out. He broke into tears when he described the rape of their daughter Maggie.

She squeezed his hands. "Husband, ye were ill. We cannot trust this."

His eyes were wild. "We *cannot* ignore it. It's a prophecy!"

"What would ye have me do?"

He took a ragged breath. "I ask ye to give him up."

Keira was shocked. "Give him up?"

"The apothecary has something to end the pregnancy."

She released his hands and pushed him away. "I won't do it!"

"But my dream…"

She flushed with anger. "Damn yer dream! I would rather die than give him up."

He tried reason. "Is this child more important to ye than the lives of yer husband or wee Maggie?"

Keira got out of bed and dressed quickly. She slipped on her shoes and headed for the door.

"Wait, lass! Listen to me."

"If ye insist on this, I'll go back to my people!"

"Wife!"

She ignored his protest and left the room.

Dughall loved her with all his heart. He could not force her to give up the child. He could only pray that when the time came he would have the courage to defend his family. "God help us! What have we done?"

***

6:30AM THE INN AT FORRES

Ian woke with a cramp in his arm. He'd offered Jamison his plaid and saddle pack and slept on the plank floor. He pushed up into a sitting position and massaged his sore elbow. As the pain lessened, his thoughts ran wild. *I wish I was in bed with Mary; curled against her soft buttocks. I would nibble her neck and take her. How wet she would be!* Yesterday he left without saying goodbye. He loved her more since the twins were born and prayed she would understand.

Ian sniffed the air. The smell of a dying fire mingled with the stench of a common chamber pot. Urine... Excrement... Body odor... A year ago it would not have bothered him, but he'd come to expect better.

Gray light streamed through an iron-barred window. It was going to be an overcast day. Jamison would wake soon and inquire about their master. Did he survive the night? Ian closed his eyes and connected to his brother. Strong emotions flooded his mind, of anguish and regret. He saw a rebellious lad who would destroy his father. Was this Dughall's son? It was the only thing that made sense.

His thoughts were interrupted by a sneeze. The travelers were starting to wake.

Jamison sat up and massaged his upper arm. "My shoulder seems better. Thanks for the bedding. I'm in yer debt."

Ian shrugged. "Nay bother." He ran his tongue across his front teeth. "Yuk. My mouth tastes like an army ran through it."

Jamison attempted a modest stretch and heard a loud pop. "My arm unlocked! The Duchess was right about the movements." He continued to stretch. "How is the Duke?"

"Alive."

"Good!" The servant looked around. "Let's get some breakfast and head for Seaford Shores. We'll hide that blade in a sea cave."

Ian grimaced. "We can't. He just ordered me to return his sword."

Jamison glared. "Can ye act like ye didn't hear him?"

"Nay. It would never work."

***

6:45AM DRAKE CASTLE THE BAKEHOUSE

Murdock hauled a small bucket of yeast from the brewhouse to the bakehouse. It wasn't his usual job. He'd come to see Sara at dawn and offered to give them a hand.

The bakehouse was making bread. Servants busied themselves about the dome-shaped ovens. Hours ago, hot wood was placed into them and the doors tightly sealed. When the right temperature was reached, the ashes were cleared and the dough placed inside.

Widow MacPhee removed the first tray of loaves from an oven. The air grew moist and fragrant with the aroma of fresh bread.

Murdock's stomach growled as he watched them remove the loaves from pans and set them aside to cool. He admired Sara's female form as she bent over to take a pan from an oven.

She glanced at him. "So m'Lord is alive?"

"Aye, lass. The sun's up. I must leave to attend to him."

She handed him a slice of bread. "Will I see ye today?"

Murdock nodded. "Aye, lass. I've neglected ye, and I'm sorry for that."

She wiped her hands on her apron. "Mum keeps asking… Will we set a date to marry?"

It was a question he expected. "Aye." He leaned forward and kissed her on the cheek.

She blushed. "Oh Murdock. I love ye so."

This was the first time she'd said such a thing. It made his heart soar. He patted her behind. "I love ye too. I'll find ye after supper."

Murdock left the bakehouse and hurried across the snow-covered courtyard. The new year was boding well even though he was exhausted. He'd stayed up most of the night, thinking about the raven. An hour ago, he rose and went to the bakehouse to see Sara Beth.

Near the castle he saw tradesmen milling about, awaiting news about their Lord. Everyone thought he was dying. A few had taken to maligning the Duke.

"They said he was close to death. He must be gone."

"What will happen to us now?"

"He left no heir. Who will control us?"

"Not that bastard child."

Murdock approached them. "Fear not. The Duke is alive and well."

They seemed surprised. "Why doesn't he show himself?"

This was a fair question, so he tried to quell their fears. "I suspect that he's sleeping late. It's a Lord's privilege after a long illness."

"He's cured?"

"Aye. I will ask him to address ye today."

They seemed satisfied except for the blacksmith. "MacAdam said that he saw the Duchess in the forest. She said she was praying to the moon."

Murdock lied, "I can attest that she never left her husband's bedside. The woman is an angel from heaven."

"An angel, ye say?" The blacksmith stared. "MacAdam says that she broke his hand. I saw his fingers. Why should we trust ye?"

There were small sounds of agreement.

Murdock swallowed hard. "I am the manservant of the Duke. It would behoove ye to watch what ye say in my presence. MacAdam is a drunkard. He likely fell and broke his hand."

"But…"

"Why…"

Murdock ignored their questions. The servant entered the castle and took the stairs to the floor that housed the Lord's bed chamber. He hoped to find his master awake and willing to address his people. Otherwise, they might have a revolt on their hands. He wished that Ian and Jamison were here.

Conner

Chapter 28
Trouble in Paradise

LATER THAT MORNING 7AM

HUNTLY CASTLE   THE STUDY

Gilbert stood in his study, gazing out the iron-grated window. The courtyard bustled with activity as inhabitants of the castle began their day. A cooper rolled hoops to a hovel, while a boy led a horse out of the stables to be groomed. Small groups of peasants gathered to discuss the news. For earlier that morning, after two days of labor, Bridget had given birth to his son and heir.

The Earl went to the credenza and poured himself a glass of whisky. Normally, he would pause to admire the color, but this was his third in less than an hour. He sipped it slowly, savoring the peaty taste. *Father said that there could be no pleasure without pain,* he thought. *This whisky demonstrates that.* He loved the way that it made him feel, but despised the hold it had on him. Each time he tried to give it up, something happened to drive him back. Threats from enemies... An execution... Even idle gossip... Then there was the pressure to be like his father. Conner suggested that he take the name Blackheart, thinking it was a good thing. But nothing disturbed him more. He even refused to name his son after his father, breaking with family tradition.

"His name is George," he announced in a slightly slurred voice. "After my uncle. He didn't beat his sons." His anger flared at the thought of his father, even though he was cold in the ground. He belted the whisky and poured another. "This one's for my little brother," he said, as he held the glass to the light. "For doing what I don't have the courage to do." He felt a pang of guilt. "That cursed sword! I hope that ye're alive." He vowed to ride to Drake on the morrow and thought of ways to disguise his drinking. "No doubt, ye won't approve of it." There was a knock on the door that drew his attention. He placed the decanter on the credenza and hid the glass behind it. "Come."

Conner entered and bowed respectfully. "My Lord."

Gilbert was impatient. "What is it?"

"Forgive the intrusion. There is a messenger from King Charles at the gate."

He was hardly in any condition to receive a guest. "Are ye sure?"

"Aye. The man displayed a scroll with the royal seal. He comes here with a request."

Gilbert's head throbbed. "Can ye delay him?"

"I can try. He said that he was on an aggressive schedule."

The Earl threw up his hands in despair. "I've been up for two days and had more than a few whiskies. This is the last thing I need."

Connor acted quickly, picking up the decanter and the glass and storing them in the cabinet. "Given the gentleman's disposition, it would be wise to keep these out of sight. I'll tell Marcia to bring ye a glass of water."

"I should thank ye."

"Nay bother. I will take him on a tour and bring him here in an hour."

"Good. Now be off with ye." Gilbert's headache flared as he watched his servant leave the room. He wished that he could have one more drink. "Ah well, I can last a few hours." He sat down in the chair, closed his eyes, and awaited his glass of water.

***

Nearly an hour passed. Marcia brought water laced with peppermint to disguise the liquor on his breath.

Gilbert sat behind his mahogany desk. His expression was grim as he straightened his shirt and tossed his curls over the collar. There was a knock on the door. "Come."

Connor entered with a gentleman who was carrying scrolls. "My Lord," he said, as he seated the man. "I present Sir John Waxman, a messenger from the court of King Charles."

The gentleman cleared his throat. "Leave us now. We must speak alone."

Conner bowed respectfully and left the room.

Gilbert's head throbbed from the lack of whisky. There was no need to question his credentials. The messenger's long grey hair was groomed and his clothing was upper class. He had a nose that seemed to disdain the earth. The scrolls he carried bore the royal seal, which he'd seen on other documents. "Good morning, Sir Waxman. How can I help ye?"

Waxman studied him with beady grey eyes. "Why did you delay me?" His tone was hostile.

Gilbert reddened. "Forgive my servant's behavior. He knew that I'd been awake for two days and gave me a chance to wash up. My wife gave birth to a son this morning."

"Hmmm…" Waxman stared as he considered this information. "I accept your apology. I'm on a mission with little time to complete it. Let's proceed." He unrolled a scroll, pushed wire rim glasses up on his nose, and started to read. "King Charles I requires your presence in London on the fifteenth of February of this year 1638. Be sure to arrive at the Queen's House in Greenwich early in the day…"

Gilbert's mind raced. It was never a good thing to get summoned to the King. Would he wind up in the Tower of London? The severed heads of more than a few Scottish nobles had adorned London Bridge. He wished that he could ask what it was about. "I will be there. Shall I bring anything?"

Waxman nodded. "Yes. The King requests that you bring your brother, the Duke of Seaford."

"My brother has been ill."

The man's voice was as cold as ice. "Then you will bring him on a stretcher if need be."

Gilbert answered quickly. "Of course. I did not mean to imply that he would not come."

"Good." He rolled up the scroll, placing it on the table. "These are your invitations to the royal residence. Do not lose them." He stood. "I shall take my leave now. Oh… Congratulations on the birth of your son."

Gilbert nodded. "Thank ye."

"Was he your first?"

"Aye."

"Another loyal subject for his Majesty the King. Just like his father if he knows what's good for him."

His blood ran cold. "The King can be assured of my loyalty."

"Good." The haughty man headed for the door and turned. "There's no need to call for your servant. I will fare better if I see myself out."

The Earl watched him leave. He stayed seated and clasped his hands in an attempt to control the shaking. After a few minutes he opened the cabinet and took out the decanter and glass. Tomorrow he would stop drinking. He had to be sober when he faced the King. He poured another.

***

9AM DRAKE CASTLE THE BATH CHAMBER

Dughall sat in a steaming tub, attempting to make sense of the morning. He and his wife had their first fight, at the end of which she'd run to his mother. Jessie attempted to mediate but he thought that she'd made it worse. The women tried to convince him that the dream was a result of his illness. He didn't have to act on it. They reminded him of the sanctity of life, which made him feel like the lowest of manly creatures. Perhaps they were right. Was no one glad that he was alive and whole? He was contemplating the mess when Murdock entered. All he wanted was a hot bath to sooth his battered body. "What is it, friend?"

The servant presented him with a towel. "We have an urgent matter to discuss. Are ye ready to get out?"

Dughall sighed. "Nay, not yet."

"What's wrong?"

"I wish I was dead."

"Ye survived the curse. Why are ye not happy?"

"Nothing will ever be the same. Keira and I had a fight this morning. She ran to my mother."

"The lass had a strange night. What's wrong with her?"

"She's with child."

"How do ye know?"

"She woke with morning sickness."

"Poor lass." He hesitated. "Ye must be happy about the pregnancy."

The Duke choked back tears. "Nay."

The servant looked puzzled. "Why, lad? I thought ye wanted a son."

Dughall leaned back until the water covered him to his neck. "I wanted a son, but not this one. I dreamed that he would bring ruin upon us."

"How?"

"He will rape his sister! Then he'll kill me."

Murdock frowned. "Could the dream be wrong? Ye nearly died. Then ye were exhausted by that creature."

"That creature was my wife."

"Forgive my choice of words. But she was something else as well. She tried to kill me when I tore off the veil. Then the winds came. A raven as black as night flew around my head."

Dughall's eyes widened. "That's a bad omen."

"What do ye intend to do?"

"Nothing. When I told her about the dream, she threatened to return to her people. We will never be the same again."

"The Duchess will return to yer bed. She needs protection."

Dughall sat up. "What do ye mean?"

"MacAdam saw her in the forest last night, praying to the moon."

"Painted blue like that?"

"Aye. He spoke to her and she broke his hand. Some think that she saved ye with magic."

"Well, it's true."

"Never say that! It's just what that old priest needs to get ye excommunicated."

"Why would I care about that?"

"Trust me, lad. Ye do."

"No man can separate me from God." He stood up and let the water drip off. "What did ye need to discuss?"

The servant patted him dry. "Some think ye're dead. Some think that ye were saved by magic. We must address yer subjects."

"Ye want me to lie to them?"

Murdock nodded. "A white lie is in order to keep the peace." He held out his kilt to step into.

Dughall proceeded to dress. "What about MacAdam?"

"Gilroy denounced the man as a drunk and a liar and banished him from the castle."

Dughall sensed that this would come back to haunt them. "Has anyone else threatened my wife?"

"Nay. But I wouldn't let her go out by herself."

The Duke put on his shirt. He sat on a chair and allowed his servant to comb his hair. When he was done, he stood and took a breath. It was time to face his subjects. "Let's go to the study to craft a convincing statement." He thought for a moment. "I have an idea. Summon Father John."

***

Hours later, the courtyard was filled with people in spite of frigid weather. A speaking platform had been erected which contained a lectern from the chapel. Light snow fell as Father John took his place to the left of the platform. Gilroy and Suttie took positions to the right.

Dughall stood at a window, looking down on his subjects. Men, women, and children had flocked to the courtyard, bundled in coats and hats. Some had no boots and their feet were wrapped in rags. He resolved to do something about it.

Murdock tapped him on the shoulder. "My Lord. The people have gathered to hear ye speak. Yer family is waiting in the corridor. They will accompany us and stand behind ye."

Dughall felt hopeful. "Is my wife with them?"

"Aye. I told ye that she'd come around."

"Thank God." His heart sank. "Then they will witness my lie."

"*Everyone* agreed to lie. We will testify that Lady Keira was at yer bedside last night. What's wrong?"

He was having misgivings. "I hate lying to my subjects. It's against everything I believe in. For my mother to see it… Oh, the shame."

The servant frowned. "It's for the best. Some would expect ye to divorce yer wife while others would do her harm."

"Would Jamison advise me to do this?"

"Without a doubt."

Dughall saw that his people suffered from the cold. "Let's not keep them waiting."

Murdock helped him into a black woolen cape and adjusted his grandfather's brooch. He arranged his curls and led him to the door, where they stepped into the hallway. Jessie and Keira were waiting, dressed in warm clothes. His wife looked like an angel in a white hooded cape.

For a moment, Dughall regretted the demands he'd made on her. Perhaps he was wrong about his son. They walked in silence down the long corridor to the granite steps that took them to the first floor. As they approached the door, Dughall took his wife's arm and felt her stiffen. "Forgive me," he whispered, and saw that she relaxed. "We will see this through together."

Her voice was soft. "And our son?"

"Shall be born."

Murdock opened the door, admitting a frigid gust of air. "We should limit our time outside today. The Duke's health is at stake."

Dughall walked to the lectern with his wife and then handed her off to Father John. As rehearsed, the priest slipped a chain and crucifix over her head. The symbol that rested over her heart was not lost on the crowd. No doubt they expected her to burst into flames.

A collective gasp went up as he rolled back his hood and showed them that he was alive and well. Some started to cheer as he raised his hands. Then they fell silent.

"These have been difficult days," he started. "I hovered between life and death. My family struggled to find a cure." He gestured to his mother. "With God's help, this lady found a plant that broke my fever." He coughed into his fist. "That being said… I wish to address a rumor. My family and servants will attest that the Duchess was at my bedside throughout the night. Other than her love and devotion, she had nothing to do with my recovery."

There were small sounds of disagreement, but no one dared step forward.

Dughall felt a chill. "There is another possible cause for my cure. When things looked bleak, Jamison and Ian took my sword away."

The blacksmith spoke, "So the curse of the sword has been lifted?"

"Aye."

"Will they bring the sword back?"

"They will. But the curse expired at midnight."

A cold wind whipped across the courtyard, prompting everyone to close their coats. Dughall felt shaky from his illness. "I would like to thank those who saved me. My family, servants, and... " He made the sign of the cross with reverence. "Our Lord Jesus Christ, who granted me another day." He coughed until his face turned red. "I must retire to my quarters and rest." He put up his hood and blew on his hands. "I bid ye farewell."

A few clapped until most joined in.

The Duke smiled. "Some here have no boots. It may take some time, but I will instruct my shoemakers to make footwear for all." A cheer went up. As he left the platform, a nine year old boy burst from the crowd and hugged him tight.

Luc Deville looked up at him. "Father!"

Keira frowned. "What does he mean?"

Murdock looked puzzled. "I don't know. Why did he call ye that?"

The Duke was silent as he took Luc's hand and entered the castle. He had some explaining to do. Looking down at the boy's face, he knew that he truly loved him. He turned to his family and servant. "I intend to adopt him." He faced blank stares and horrified faces. "We will discuss it after dinner."

Dughall ruffled the boy's hair, called him son, and led him down the hallway.

Gilbert

Chapter 29
Brothers

January 2nd 1638
6AM

HUNTLY CASTLE   THE EARL'S BED CHAMBER

Pale light filtered through the curtains, heralding the dawn of a bleak winter day. The Earl of Huntly woke to the sound of rain pelting the window. He snuggled against his wife, whispering that it was a good day to stay under the covers. After a night of interrupted slumber, the storm encouraged them to fall back to sleep.

An hour passed and the room grew colder. Gilbert woke from a sound sleep to the cries of his newborn son. He left the bed and padded to the hearth, wishing that he'd put on a robe. After stoking the fire with apple wood, he went to the cradle, where he swaddled his son and brought him to his mother.

There was a faint odor of talc and ointment as Bridget changed his wet nappy. As she sponged his bottom, she sang a lullaby.

♩♬♩

"Hush ye, my bairnie. Bonny wee laddie. When ye're a man, ye shall follow yer daddie. Lift me a coo, and a goat and a wether. Bringing them home to yer mother together." ♩♬♩

Gilbert was riveted to the sight. This was a side of his wife that he hadn't seen.

Bridget positioned the babe at her breast and encouraged him to take her nipple. He was frantic to begin and flexed his little hands. She smiled and cooed sympathetically.

Gilbert sat on the edge of the bed and watched his wife. She glanced at him, then shifted the child to her other breast, inserting her nipple into his tiny mouth.

She looks like the Madonna, he thought, recalling a painting he'd seen in the Louvre. *I've never seen her happier.* She'd refused to get a wet nurse, insisting on nursing the infant herself. Now, he knew why.

The child's lips made a slight popping sound as he suckled at her breast. He was a small boy, yet he seemed to be in good health. At birth they found no imperfections, except for the clan birthmark on his ankle. The baby took a shallow breath and stopped suckling.

Bridget removed her nipple from his mouth. She smoothed back his curly hair and wiped his lips with a cloth. "Was that good? Momma loves ye, wee one." She kissed his forehead. "Oh husband, I adore him. He's perfect."

Gilbert wished that he shared her feelings. He wanted an heir, but didn't know if he was fit to be a father. He had bad feelings about his own father that he needed to resolve. How could he parent this child when all he knew was discipline and control? The boy would be better off without him.

"Gilbert?" Her voice was soft.

"Aye, lass?"

"Would ye like to hold wee George?"

He would have to do it sooner or later. Yesterday, he had an excuse to stay away because of the royal messenger. Today there were no excuses. She was looking at him expectantly. "Of course, love. Show me what to do."

Bridget smiled. "Sit back on the bed. Aye, that's it. I'll place him in yer arms." She cradled the baby and gave him to his father. "Support his neck like this and *talk* to him."

Gilbert held his breath as the child was placed in his arms. His heart swelled as the tiny infant opened his clear blue eyes. He wondered if his father ever held him like this. "My son." Tears filled his eyes. "He's beautiful, lass."

"That he is."

The Earl examined a tiny hand and was surprised when the child gripped his finger. "He knows me!"

Bridget smiled. "Why would he not? For months, ye whispered to him through my belly. Now he is here."

Gilbert warmed to the wee boy. He vowed to be a good father as he handed him back to his mother. He kissed his wife. "God in heaven. I love ye both."

"I know, Gilbert."

This was too much emotion to bear and he feared he would lose his composure. He left his bed and proceeded to get dressed. "Take care of him, lass. I'm off to Drake to see my brother."

"In this weather?"

"Aye. I will return in three or four days."

***

8AM DRAKE CASTLE
THE SMALL BREAKFAST CHAMBER

The breakfast chamber was nearly empty. In spite of a feast prepared by the kitchen, only Dughall and Luc attended. There was a steaming pot of tea, a pitcher of cream, and plates of ham, bread, and coddled eggs. There was enough for six or more, but only two attended.

Dughall thought that he knew why. At dinner last night, they'd had a heated discussion about his plans to adopt Luc. Jessie opposed it, but relented when he reminded her of his own "adoption". Murdock complained about the boy, but soon gave in to his master. His wife stayed silent, saving her disapproval for a private conversation.

The Duke contemplated the situation. Luc was on his left, wolfing down a hearty breakfast. He was about to snatch another piece of bread. "Luc, ye must leave some for the others."

The boy looked around. "There's no one here, Father."

"'Tis true. But we put what's left on the back stoop for people less fortunate."

Luc looked thoughtful. "We share what we have?"

"Especially in winter when food is scarce. The cook prepares the leftovers with day old bread and cakes. We provide a midday meal."

"Where is Mother?"

So far, his wife was against the adoption. He had to correct the boy without hurting his feelings. "Don't call her that yet. First, I must find a way to adopt ye. Then we'll see if the lass will warm up to ye."

Luc snatched a piece of bread. "Why wouldn't she?"

Dughall remembered her reaction when he'd explained his reasons for adoption. She questioned it in light of their recent argument. Why did he want to adopt a son when he would soon have one of his own? He'd held his ground and insisted. Morning came and she was too ill to discuss it. Pregnancy didn't agree with her. He'd sent a servant to bring her fennel seed tea for the nausea.

"Father?"

"My wife's not feeling well. Woman troubles, I think."

"Oh. Where is everyone else?"

"Mary took breakfast with the twins. My mother ate breakfast in the kitchen on her way to the apothecary."

"Can I call her Gramma?"

"Hmmm..." Dughall had work to do to repair some ruffled feathers. He would start with his mother. "Luc, keep quiet about this until I find a way to adopt ye. No one must know until I settle it with yer stepfather."

The boy looked alarmed. "But he's not my father!"

"I know that, but courtesy dictates that I must speak to him. I'm sure that he will want compensation."

"But I will be yer son?"

"Soon enough." He stood and threw his napkin on the table. "Until that time, ye must call me Sir."

Luc's face fell. "All right, Sir."

Dughall sensed his disappointment. In the meantime, he would acquaint the boy with someone who would accept him. "Come on, lad. Let's go visit wee Maggie."

"The baby who came with us to the monastery?"

"Aye. She's older now."

"Will she be my sister?"

Dughall smiled. The boy was desperate to be part of a family. "Have patience, lad. I promise that someday she will."

***

9AM HUNTLY CASTLE THE STABLES

The Earl of Huntly stood in the stables, preparing his horse for the journey. He placed a blanket over his back, saddled him, and checked the reins. Gilbert stroked the stallion's face. "Easy, Flame. We have a long ride ahead of us."

Connor was in the adjoining stall, saddling a stallion named Demon. He raised his voice. "Spittle and Walters are in the courtyard. Are ye ready, my Lord?"

"Aye." Gilbert led his horse out of the stall and checked his saddle pack. His thoughts were uneasy. "With this weather, it's going to be one hell of a ride. Do we have everything?"

Connor joined him, leading the stallion. "We have the scroll from the King. We're armed and ready for anything that might happen and there's gold in yer saddle pack if we need to stop." He reached into his jacket and took out a silver flask. "We've got whisky to fight the cold."

Gilbert blanched. It took an act of will to leave without his flask and it seemed to have done him no good. For here it was again.

"What's wrong, my Lord?"

"Uh... Are we bringing any water?"

"Aye. Why do ye ask?"

His hands shook. "I've given up whisky as of this morning." His stomach twisted at the mention of it.

Connor frowned. "On a day like today? We're likely to freeze to death without it."

He couldn't stop staring at the flask. "Do what ye like, but keep that away from me."

"I will do as ye wish." Connor slipped the flask into his pocket. He approached his master with a hooded cape and helped him to put in on. "This will keep ye warm. That's if we don't get an ice storm."

Gilbert was grateful. "If only we could predict the weather."

"Ha! That will never happen." The servant took the reins and walked the horses into the courtyard. Spittle and Walters were waiting on two mares. Their hair and beards were rain-soaked.

Flame tossed his head as raindrops landed on his face. Gilbert held him fast. He could feel the icy drops on his hands. "Easy, boy." He mounted the horse and took a deep breath. "Let's go. This is a day not fit for man or beast."

Connor mounted and led the men across the courtyard. His breath hung like a web in the frigid air. Without further ado, they left the castle grounds and crossed the river Deveron. As they headed northeast towards Drake, they witnessed an ominous sign. Lightning flashed in the snow clouds, but they didn't hear any thunder.

***

9AM DRAKE CASTLE THE NURSERY

Dughall and Luc sat on the floor, playing with Maggie and Alexander. Earlier they'd rescued poor Mary, who was at wit's end with a wailing wee Andrew. The Duke sent her away to care for the sick baby. He offered to stay with the infants until one of the servants could relieve him.

Luc was a natural with the babies. He suggested that they put them on the rug to see what they were likely to do. He scattered wooden toys about, as well as a dolly or two.

Dughall sat with Maggie between his legs, supporting her so that she could sit. He was surprised at her strength and declared that she would be sitting on her own soon. The child looked up and offered him a smile. He handed her a rag dolly, which she promptly put in her mouth.

Luc sat with Alexander between his legs, playing with wooden blocks. As the final block was placed, the baby reached out and scattered the pile. "Hey!" the lad exclaimed, as he caught the blocks. The baby laughed out loud, making everyone chuckle.

This was exactly what Dughall needed after a night of conflict.

"I like these babies," Luc said. "They remind me of my sister."

"What happened to her?"

Luc looked sad. "She died of the grippe."

"Oh... I'm sorry."

"Her name was Maggie just like this one. I used to sing her a song." The lad smiled. ♩♬♩

Wha wadna be in love ~ Wi' bonnie Maggie Lauder? ~ A piper met her guan to Fife, ~ And pier'd what was't they ca'd her; ~ Right scornfully she answer'd him, ~ Began ye hall shaker, ~ Jog on yer gate, ~ ye bladderscate, ~ My name is Maggie Lauder. " ♩♬♩

Dughall interrupted. "Does this get bawdy?"

"A bit. But the babies won't know it."

He laughed. "Nonetheless... Perhaps we should stop here."

"Aye, Sir."

"Thank ye, lad. I haven't laughed this hard in months."

The door opened and Mary entered, cradling wee Andrew against her shoulder. Tarrah was with her, toting a basket of nappies.

Mary looked aghast. "Forgive me, my Lord. The wee ones are on the floor?" She handed Andrew to Tarrah and scooped up Alexander.

"Dinna fret, lass. It's warm on the rug. The boy had a wonderful time. He likes to play with blocks." He could tell that she was trying to hold her tongue and he couldn't argue with that. He'd had enough of women's opinions.

Dughall stood with his daughter and kissed her on the forehead. "Da loves ye, wee one." He placed her in a cradle and motioned for Luc to join him. As they entered the hallway, he cocked his head and listened. "Come on, lad. We have a lot of work to do."

"What work, Sir?"

"We need to prepare the guest quarters. My brother Gilbert is on his way."

"Uncle Gilbert?"

Dughall scowled. "Remember what I said. No one must know about the adoption."

***

12 NOON NORTHEAST OF HUNTLY CASTLE
ONE HOUR FROM DRAKE

The men had been riding for three hours. The first two were bearable, as the rain was light and their clothes were dry. Gilbert's hood kept the rain off his head, but the others suffered from lack of a hat. They bore the cold stoically without complaint. The third hour brought misery as they rode in a downpour of freezing rain. Sleet slowed their progress and even the horses suffered. Stallions and men alike looked like mythical beasts with their breath hanging in the air. Tree branches cracked with the weight of the ice and some fell to the ground. They rode out of the storm, cold and wet and physically stressed. The rain refused to let up.

Gilbert coughed hard. The wind had blown off his hood a few miles back. Icy water dripped down his back. He swayed in the saddle and nearly fell.

"My Lord!" Conner cried, jumping from his horse. "Allow me to get ye warm." He grasped the Earl's arm and helped him to the ground. The servant searched a saddle pack for dry clothing and escorted his master to a tree. "Let's get these wet garments off ye."

Gilbert shook from the cold. His lips were blue and he could barely speak. He was on the verge of delirium. "Uh..." His servant's red face loomed in his vision.

Conner stripped off his cloak and tartan and took off his wet shirt. Then he dressed the man in dry clothing. Lastly, he took out a flask and opened it. "Take a swig of this."

Gilbert's lungs ached. "Nay! I must stop drinking."

"Sobriety won't matter if ye catch yer death!" He held the flask to his lips and tipped it. "Just a wee dram, my Lord. I'll help ye to quit tomorrow."

Gilbert surrendered. The first swallow burned his throat and warmed him down to his belly. He grabbed the flask like a mad man and took another. He felt a firm hand on his arm as the servant led him to his horse and helped him to mount.

The servant mounted and the four men rode down a gully that sloped to a mountain stream. In the water lay a maze of gray rocks, interspersed with frozen gorse and heather. As they crossed, the rain let up. They were cold and exhausted, but their spirits were light. They were only an hour from Drake.

***

1PM DRAKE CASTLE THE HALLWAY

The Duke stood at a second floor window, studying the approach to the castle. The old road had been built from stones of every color. Worn smooth by horses and carts, it was a thing of beauty. Dughall turned his attention to the courtyard and watched for his faithful servant. Murdock had gone to the barn to outfit a wagon for a rescue mission.

Minutes ago, his brother's servant had arrived, begging them for assistance. Gilbert and his party were near, but his brother had taken ill.

Dughall wanted to prepare the cart, but Murdock insisted that he stay inside. He was still weak from his illness. Looking down, he saw his servant enter the courtyard leading a horse drawn wagon. The man looked up and waved, sending a signal to join him.

Dughall slung a healer's bag over his shoulder and hurried down the corridor. Slipping on gloves, he took the stairs to the ground floor and burst into the busy courtyard. He ran as fast as he could and reached the cart just as the gate was opened. With a pounding heart, he climbed up on the bench seat and took the reins from Murdock.

"My Lord. Ye ran all this way?"

He struggled to catch his breath. "Aye."

"Ye'll catch yer death."

Walters appeared at the side of the wagon. "I can take ye there, Sire."

Dughall motioned for him to get in the back. He snapped the reins over the horses' backs and prodded them through the gate. The horses' hooves clattered on stone as they traversed the old road. "How far are they?"

Walters hesitated. "Um… Three miles, I'd guess."

Murdock frowned. "They couldn't ride in?"

"Nay. We came through an ice storm soaked to the skin. The Earl fell from his stallion. Connor couldn't wake him."

"He's senseless?"

"Aye."

Dughall urged the horses into a steady trot. There was obviously no time to lose. The wagon entered the woods and followed a well worn path. They rode in silence for miles, with the sounds of the forest to keep them company.

Dughall's mind raced as he considered the situation. Gilbert may have injured his head. He could have frostbite. And there was always the possibility of broken bones.

"There they are!" Murdock shouted. He pointed to a clearing where three horses stood. On the ground was a plaid where the Earl lay, attended by Conner and Spittle.

Dughall frowned. "He's still down." They drew the wagon up beside the injured man.

Conner stood to greet them. "The Earl is as cold as ice. We need to get him someplace warm."

They hopped off the wagon and hurried to the Earl. Dughall did a quick assessment of Gilbert's injuries and found no broken bones, though there were bruises on his side where he hit the ground. One was on his temple. His lips were blue and his skin was cold, even though he'd been covered.

"Get him on the wagon!" Dughall directed the men to lift his brother and place him in the cart on a straw mattress. He covered him with blankets and jumped in the back to watch him.

Conner and his men mounted their horses. Murdock drove the cart as they took the path back to Drake Castle. Upon arrival they called for a stretcher and transported the Earl to a guest bed chamber.

Now, a fire burned brightly in the hearth. Heated bricks had been placed between the sheets to warm them. As they stripped the unconscious Earl and put him to bed, Marsha appeared with a tray of toddies, made of whisky, honey, and hot water. The men were truly grateful.

Dughall directed his servant. "Murdock, take these men to the servants quarters and get them some warm clothes."

Walters and Spittle followed him, but Conner insisted that he stay.

"Conner, go! I will call ye when he wakes."

"I must not leave his side."

Dughall understood loyalty. He reached under the blanket and took Gilbert's foot, warming it between his hands. "They're on the verge of frostbite. How did he get like this?"

"We rode through an ice storm. He insisted on coming in spite of the weather."

"Why?"

"We have a message for ye from King Charles."

Dughall had a bad feeling. He was about to ask about the content of the message when Gilbert groaned, startling them.

The Duke moved to the head of the bed and looked into his brother's face. "I'm glad to see ye."

Gilbert's voice was weak. "Oh God. I must be dead."

"Nay, not yet."

"Where am I?"

"Drake Castle."

His eyes widened. "Ye survived the curse."

"Aye. Thanks to my family and servants." He propped up Gilbert's head and held a flask of whisky to his lips. "Drink this. It will make ye feel better." There was hesitation in his brother's eyes. "What's wrong?"

Gilbert took a ragged breath. "I gave up whisky this morning."

Dughall was torn. "Not today, brother. Ye've been soaked and frozen and tossed from a horse. This is the only way to ward off illness."

Gilbert winced as he touched the bruise on his temple. "That hurts! In fact, I ache all over. Will ye help me to give up whisky tomorrow?"

The Duke smiled. "That's a promise from brother to brother. Now drink this, then lay back and allow me to treat yer wounds."

Chapter 30
An Unlikely Traitor

LATER THAT EVENING

ONE MILE FROM ELGINSHIRE
ALONG A DARK AND TREACHEROUS ROAD

Hamish MacAdam trudged through snow as he approached the hamlet of Elginshire. He'd been walking for more than three hours. With each step he found it harder to put one foot in front of the other. His boots were soaked, his beard was coated with snow, and his nose was leaking like a sieve. Cradling his throbbing hand, he reflected upon his situation. He was a simple man with no wife or children to consider. A warm bed, a full belly, and a tankard of ale were all he needed. Now, he had nary a prospect for that. He hoped that after twenty years absence, his family would take him in. A year ago, he was a tradesman at Drake Castle. As a cooper's apprentice he'd acquired skills which would have led to his own practice. He was hard working and loyal until the Earl of Huntly offered him gold to report on the activities of young Lord Dughall. Shirking his duties, he left the cooperage to serve as a guard, where he could glean more gossip. In a matter of weeks, he'd been rewarded for informing the Earl that his son was going to Peterhead.

His anger flared at the injustice. *I would be a wealthy man if the Earl hadn't met his death!* The servant knew that he was lucky. No one had found him out. He told everyone that he received an inheritance and squandered his reward on drink. Hamish had been drunk when he guarded the castle two nights ago. By the light of the moon, he'd opened the gate to admit the lady of the castle. Veiled and painted like a heathen, she spoke in riddles and broke his hand.

"If only I'd kept quiet!" he cried. "I'd be safe and warm at Drake." Gilroy had banished him from the castle with the clothes on his back and a shilling in his pocket. That coin he'd spent weathering the storm at an inn where he bought drinks for men whose names he couldn't remember.

Hamish stared at the road ahead. In the gloom, there were signs that the hamlet was near. He passed a cottage on the edge of town and saw lights in the distance. As he reached the main street, he decided that the place hadn't changed. Twenty years had passed since he'd left, after the deaths of his mother and father. He never bothered to contact his brothers, but suspected that they were still here. He stopped and coughed uncontrollably, expelling a plug of mucous tinged with blood. "Damn it to hell! How much longer can I go on?"

Hamish reached his parents' cottage and pounded on the weathered oak door. He was about to faint when it opened a crack. His lungs were too frozen to speak.

The face of his idiot brother appeared. "Hamish, my brother!"

His voice was barely a whisper. "Geck?"

"Aye. Come in and get warm by the fire." Geck led him to the hearth, where an attractive woman nursed a toddler. "This is my wife Jenny and our son Rabbie."

Hamish's lungs were starting to warm. He was astounded at his brother's luck. "A lass married ye? Where is Ambrose?"

The simpleton smiled. "He lives at the rectory. Ambrose is our priest." He slapped his brother on the back. "It's been twenty years! Join us for supper and tell us what has happened."

Chapter 31
Triple Jeopardy

January 3rd 1638
THE NEXT MORNING

DRAKE CASTLE THE BREAKFAST CHAMBER

Dughall sat at the head of the table, next to his wife Keira. Beside her was his sister-in-law Mary and beyond her was the boy Luc. To his right sat Gilbert, enjoying a hearty breakfast. Beyond him was Jessie. Compared to yesterday, he was pleased with the attendance. A feast had been prepared in honor of the Earl of Huntly. The table was set with fine linens and china. Platters of eggs, ham, and bread were plentiful and everyone was provided with their own pot of tea. They'd been dining for a half an hour and were running out of conversation.

Dughall needed to talk to his brother about the King, but he knew that it was best to do it in private. He decided to wait until they were the last ones at breakfast. He turned to his wife. "Ye look pale, lass. Are ye feeling better?"

Keira managed a smile. "A bit." She steadied her hand and poured a cup of tea. "Don't worry. Grandmother said that Mother was nauseous early in her pregnancy. It could be a family thing."

Dughall stayed silent. He suspected that it had something to do with the temperament of the child she carried. They'd tried to convince him that the dream was false, but he suspected otherwise.

Jessie interrupted his dark thoughts. "Some women get nausea. There are herbs we can try if it gets worse."

"Bless ye, Mother." Keira stroked her throat. "Oh dear. Here it comes again. I should retire to my room and rest."

Dughall patted her hand. "I will check on ye later."

"Thank ye, husband." Keira stood and placed her napkin on the table. She seemed unsteady.

Mary got up and took her arm. "I'll walk her to her room and make her comfortable." The two women left the room.

Jessie pushed back her chair and stood. "We should leave ye alone to talk to yer brother." She gave Luc a warning glance, which went unheeded. "Shall I take the lad?"

"Nay, Mother. I will see ye at supper."

Jessie nodded. "Lord Gilbert. My son. I must go to the surgery." She left the chamber, leaving Dughall, Gilbert, and Luc alone.

Rain lashed the castle, rattling the narrow windows. It was a day unfit for man or beast. Luc reached for another piece of bread. "Father..." He reddened. "I mean Sir. Have ye seen Artus?"

"Yer dog? I saw him in the courtyard yesterday."

Luc looked worried. "Did he follow ye through the gate?"

"Nay. Pratt held him back as we went through."

"I'm going to look for him."

Dughall didn't like it. But he couldn't keep the boy on a tether. "Artus is a resourceful dog. He likely spent the night at widow MacPhee's hearth. She throws him a bone from time to time. It's nasty out there. Bundle up."

Luc stood, allowing his napkin to drop to the floor. "I will, Sir. He glanced at Gilbert. "It was a pleasure to meet ye, m'Lord."

Gilbert nodded. "Be off with ye, child so that I can talk to my brother."

Luc bounded out of the room, slamming the door behind him. The men shook their heads.

Gilbert put down his fork. "Why did that lad call ye Father?"

Dughall reddened. "He wasn't supposed to tell anyone. I plan to adopt him."

"Yer wife didn't seem friendly towards him."

"She thinks it's a bad idea. All that she cares about is the child that she's carrying."

"That's typical for a woman. Why adopt this lad?" Gilbert smirked. "Is he another child from a previous relationship?"

"The boy is nine! How could I be his real father? Furthermore, I'll never father a child out of wedlock again."

"We'll see about that. Kate seems determined to have ye back in her bed."

Dughall frowned. "Oh, God! How is she?"

Gilbert leaned back in his chair. "She established herself in Paris six weeks after yer daughter was born. A legal firm there sent me an address to transfer funds to. I've received several letters from her asking about ye. If we're lucky, she'll marry a lesser noble and we'll be done with her. It's a small price to pay to get her out of our lives."

"I feel sorry for her."

"Well, don't. She didn't want the child. We offered her adequate compensation. She's done well for a peasant." He changed the subject. "So tell me about Luc."

Dughall hesitated. "His stepfather beat and buggered him, so I took him on as my page. When I was dying, I promised God that I would adopt him."

Gilbert smiled. "Ah… The pitfalls of a deathbed promise. Remind me never to make one."

"He's a good lad," Dughall said, as he poured a cup of tea. "Though he can be mischievous." He noted that his brother's hands were shaking, a sign that his body was missing whisky. "Yer hand are shaking. Are ye all right?"

Gilbert sighed. "Nay. My body aches from the fall. My head feels like it's in a vise. I need a stiff drink." He sipped his tea and frowned. "This would taste better with whisky in it."

Dughall frowned. "No doubt. But it's out of the question today."

"I suppose we should talk about the King." Gilbert winced as he began his story. "On January 1st, I was celebrating the birth of my son. A messenger arrived at the castle who said he was from King Charles. The haughty prick dared to question my loyalty." He placed a scroll on the table. "This bears the royal seal. It's real. I've seen it before on documents. We've been summoned to London."

Dughall's eyes widened. Two years ago he was a fisherman. Now he was invited to the King's palace. "Is it a bad thing?"

"I don't know. One false move and our heads could wind up on pikes on London Bridge."

Dughall swallowed hard. "What does the King want?"

"I don't know. I never thought I'd say it, but I wish that Father was alive. He's dealt with this before."

"When do we have to be there?"

"By February the fourteenth. We meet on the fifteenth."

This was bad news. His wife was pregnant, Luc needed guidance, and some of his subjects doubted his ability to rule. "When must we leave?"

Gilbert unrolled the scroll. "We should leave Huntly by the twenty-third of January. That will give us three full weeks to get there. Here's the formal request." He cleared his throat. "King Charles I requires your presence in London on the fifteenth of February of this year 1638…"

***

CHURCH OF THE REDEMPTION
ELGINSHIRE, SCOTLAND

It was a desolate winter morning in Elginshire. Pale light filtered through the windows of the empty chapel. Ambrose kneeled on the cold marble floor, grousing that no one came to honor God when it was inconvenient. This parish was hopeless. Only he was worthy. The priest had come to pray. "Father in heaven, have mercy on me. Lead me not into temptation with the Jezebel wife of my brother."

For three months he'd tried to avoid her. He renewed his vow of chastity and suffered as God tested his mettle. The woman persisted, taunting him with seductive smiles. She wanted another child. Now he had to see her again. For earlier that morning, Geck had appeared to say that Hamish was in town.

Ambrose needed guidance. He knew he should welcome his long lost brother and offer him hospitality. But the matter of Hamish's inheritance hung in the balance. After ten years, they'd assumed he was dead and split up the property and money. Even if they could hide the fact, there was the matter of another mouth to feed. Ambrose clasped his hands. "Father in heaven; guide my words and deeds. Give me a sign that his return is for the best." He could tarry no longer, so he stood and made the sign of the cross. Wrapping a plaid around him, he left the chapel and walked the snowy road to his brother's cottage. His shoes were soaked by the time he reached the doorstep. Lifting a fist, he knocked and waited for someone to answer. The door opened.

Geck's anxious face appeared. "Thank God!" He escorted him inside and took his wrap. "Hamish is sick."

Ambrose frowned. What strange illness had his brother brought upon them? He passed his sultry sister-in-law and made his way to the sick man.

Geck rattled on. "He came last night, sat on the boy's bed, and fainted. He's running a fever."

Ambrose looked down at his long lost brother. He appeared to be asleep, but was sweating profusely. He hoped that it wasn't the Black Death. "How long has he been asleep?"

"Dunno… He woke at dawn and took some water. Then he vomited it back up."

"Have ye asked him about where he's been?"

"Nay."

Ambrose pulled up a stool and sat. He touched the man's forehead with a single finger and determined that he had a high fever. "This is bad."

Jenny squeezed his shoulder. "Oh, Ambrose. Can I bring ye somethin'?"

The priest brushed her hand off his shoulder. "Nay, lass! Let me be." He reached out and shook his brother's arm. "Wake up, Hamish."

The sick man opened his bleary eyes. He spent a moment focusing and then spoke in a weak voice. "Ambrose?"

"Aye." He was not one to waste words. "Why have ye come back after all these years?"

Hamish coughed. "I lost my job! They banished me from the castle with only the clothes on my back." He hacked until his face was blue.

The priest held his sleeve to his mouth to protect himself from illness. "Which castle?"

"Drake."

He raised his eyebrows. "The estate of Lord Dughall Gordon?"

"Aye. I rue the day when that fool inherited the title."

Ambrose was pleased for God had smiled upon him at last. He would be happy to hear Hamish's story. He kicked off his wet shoes and motioned for the lass to bring him some tea. "Tell us about it. Don't leave anything out." This had to be a sign.

***

OUTSKIRTS OF DRAKE CASTLE
WIDOW MACPHEES COTTAGE

Luc stood in the widow's cottage, warming his backside at the fire. He had a feeling that she was hiding something. He'd asked about the whereabouts of Artus. The widow never answered; instead she welcomed him in and offered him a scone.

She sat and picked up her knitting needles and continued making a scarf. "I thought ye were working for the blacksmith."

"Nay, no more."

"Was the work too hard?"

"No worse than the mill."

"Did the Duke assign ye another job?"

"Nay."

"If ye're not in m'Lord's employ, why are ye not with yer father?"

Luc's skin crawled. "It's a secret. I promised not to talk about it." He bit into the scone. Compared to castle fare, it was as stale as a day old loaf. "Did Artus stay here last night?"

Widow MacPhee slid the stitches to the other end of the needle and pulled yarn across the back of them. "Slept at my hearth he did."

Luc was impatient. "Where is he now?"

She frowned. "I guess we both have secrets that we canna tell."

He knew of no other way to coerce her. "Artus is the Duke's favorite dog. I will tell him ye caused his disappearance." The boy threw the scone in the fire.

"Wait!" the old woman cried. "I will tell ye what I know. Yer stepfather came for him this morning. Said he was claiming what was rightfully his."

"What!" Luc's heart skipped a beat. "Why did ye let him take him?"

There was fear in her aged eyes. "I couldna argue with a man with a flail! He threatened to beat me."

The boy headed for the door. "I'm going after Artus!"

She called after him. "Ye didna hear it from me!"

Luc burst into the courtyard. It was business as usual in the square, with servants and tradesman scurrying about. He considered going for help, then decided there was no time to lose. His stepfather would beat Artus bloody as revenge for what he had done. Fear gripped him like an icy hand as he ran through the gate and left the grounds. Cold rain dripped from branches as he hurried through the forest. Luc stopped at a tree outside the mill and grasped his knees to catch his breath. Bile rose in his throat as he thought about confronting his stepfather. Was it too late to save his friend? He scanned the area around the mill. Duff wasn't outside splitting wood or tending the water wheel. There were no customer wagons and the deerhound was nowhere in sight. The boy summoned his courage and walked the last yards to the millhouse door. It was unlatched so he opened it and went inside. He passed the table where the ledgers were kept and edged his way towards the threshing chamber. There was no sound coming from that room.

"Artus?" he whispered. "Where are ye?" He was greeted with a pitiful whine. Luc rushed into the threshing chamber and was horrified by what he saw. His beloved deerhound lay limp on the floor, unable to raise his head. He hurried to the dog's side, unaware of the footprints in the oat flour. A coppery smell of blood hung in the air. He knelt and stroked the dog as he examined his injuries. "Don't die." The animal had been beaten with a flail and a club. One eye was swollen to the size of an apple and a back leg looked broken. The lad decided to carry him. "I'll get ye to safety."

"Oh, ye will huh?" The voice of his stepfather struck terror in his heart. The man grabbed him by the back of his coat and pulled him to his feet. "I'll kill ye, first."

Luc found himself facing the man. Duff's eyes were bleary from drink and his breath smelled like sour ale. He knew he was in for it. "Let me go! I belong to the Duke."

Duff laughed as he detached a flail from his belt. "Not any more. I heard ye lost yer job as a page. The blacksmith doesn't want ye anymore. It's time ye return to yer father."

"Ye're not my father! The Duke intends to adopt me."

Duff scowled. "Lies! I'll beat the truth into ye. Take off yer clothes!" He struggled with the boy, peeling off his coat and shirt. When the boy was half naked, he raised the flail and struck him hard across the back.

Luc gasped. He knew he should run but couldn't leave Artus. The flail struck him again and again, cutting his back and shoulders. Tears streamed down his face, but he refused to scream. Instead, he called silently to the only father he knew, begging him to rescue him. *Father! Help me!*

The man took off his belt.

***

DRAKE CASTLE THE COURTYARD

Dughall's talk with Gilbert had been productive. They'd planned their trip to London and reviewed what they were going to say. He'd kept his brother away from whisky and convinced him to nap to conserve his strength. Now he was walking in the courtyard with his servant, searching for Luc. "Where can he be?"

Murdock frowned. "That lad is nothin' but trouble. Where did he say he was headed?"

Dughall felt uneasy. "To look for his dog. I wonder if Widow MacPhee knows about it." They crossed the courtyard to her hovel. He was about to knock when he got a bad feeling. In his mind, he heard the lad cry and knew he was being whipped. That could only mean one thing. "Aiken's got him!" Dughall ran across the courtyard with Murdock on his heels. They reached the stables just as a groom brought out two mares. The two men mounted the horses and galloped to the gate.

Murdock drew his sword. "Where are we headed?"

Dughall's heart pounded as he sensed the boy's terror. There was no time to waste. "To the mill!" They left the grounds and headed through the forest, spurring the horses on.

***

Luc grew weaker by the minute. His stepfather wielded a heavy stroke, blistering his skin and drawing blood. His breeks offered some protection, but now even those had been stripped off. No one would come to help him. It was time to beg for his life. He got to his knees and cowered. "Have mercy!"

"I'll teach ye to rat on me!" Duff pushed the lad's head to the ground and unfastened his breeks. He brought out his swollen member and spread the boy's cheeks. "I'll have yer arse whenever I want it."

Luc cried out, but stopped when he realized what was happening. In spite of his injuries, Artus had gotten to his feet and bitten the man in the arse.

Duff roared in pain and indignation. He picked up a belt and began to beat the dog with renewed vigor. Artus yelped and fell to the ground, but the man kept striking him.

The boy hung on his arm. "It's me ye want. Leave him alone!"

Duff grabbed Luc by the hair and dragged him from the threshing chamber. He pulled the struggling child through the front room and out the open door. The man looked around and then dragged him to a trough of icy water.

Luc held his breath when he realized what was going to happen. His head was plunged under the water and held there until his lungs almost burst. He gasped for air and coughed as his head was pulled above water. Another breath and he was plunged under, this time with Duff's sharp elbow in his back. He struggled in vain, kicking and twisting, until he had no strength. The boy could hold his breath no more. He let the air out slowly and then surrendered to impending death. Within minutes he passed out and floated towards a comforting light.

***

Dughall and Murdock burst through the trees into a clearing. They noted a commotion at a water trough by the mill. Dismounting quickly, they ran to it and saw Duff Aiken holding something underwater. It appeared to be a child.

Dughall's anger flared as he grabbed Aiken's shirt and pulled him away from the trough. The angry man turned and punched him square in the face. He was about to strike again when Murdock held a sword to his throat.

Dughall shouted, "Keep him under guard! Tie his hands."

Witnesses gathered; a man and a woman driving a wagonload of barley. They stopped the wagon and gawked.

The Duke pulled the boy from the trough and laid him on the ground. The child wasn't breathing and it was clear that he was drowned. His heart ached as he turned the boy's head to the side and encouraged the water to pour out. He regretted not getting there earlier. Against all hope, he felt the side of his neck and detected a weak pulse. Suddenly, he remembered what he'd done for Jamie McKay when he stopped breathing during a fit. He was desperate enough to give it a try. Dughall inserted a finger into Luc's throat to feel for a blockage. He pushed on the tongue and saw that there was none. The young Lord tilted the boy's head back and dropped his jaw forward. He pinched the child's nose, took a deep breath, and blew into his mouth. The chest rose slightly. He pinched the nose and forced two long, slow breaths into his mouth. Again the chest rose, but the boy didn't respond. Things didn't look good. Dughall wondered if there was trouble with his heart. Instinctively, he placed the heel of his hand on the child's breastbone and pushed downward on the chest, pumping five times. He blew one slow breath into his mouth and watched as the chest rose and fell. Encouraged by the boy's color, he repeated this six times and released his nose.

Luc gasped for air. He coughed for a moment and opened his eyes. "Father."

Dughall's heart swelled. "Don't try to speak, son." He took off his cape and bundled his naked body. "Let's take him home." For the first time he noticed spectators, a farmer and his plump wife. The man looked shocked. But the woman made the sign of the cross as if to ward off evil. He dismissed them with a wave of the hand and watched them turn the wagon away.

Luc shivered. "Artus is hurt. He's in the mill."

Murdock had tied Duff's wrists to a hitching post to prevent escape. He kicked the man in the shins to bring him to his knees. Dughall lifted the boy into his arms and handed him to his servant. He mounted his horse and waited as Murdock placed him in his arms.

Luc whispered. "Where is Artus?"

"Fetch the dog, Murdock. I'll ride on ahead and take him to the surgery. Bind Aiken and drag him behind ye."

"It will be my pleasure!"

Dughall pulled on the reins and trotted towards the forest. Murdock caught up with them when he was almost to the gate. He'd bound Aiken like a beast and was leading him along on a leash. Dughall saw that the dog was not with him. He raised his eyebrows in silent inquiry.

Murdock was solemn. "Forgive me, m'Lord. Yer dog is dead."

Luc sobbed in his arms.

Dughall glared at the bound man. He could think of no good reason that this man should live. "Throw him in the hole! We will send to Huntly for Fang Adams."

Fang

Chapter 32
A Hanging at Drake

January 6th 1638
THREE DAYS LATER 8AM

DRAKE CASTLE THE STUDY

The Duke stood at a window, observing people in the courtyard. Tradesmen worked while ordinary subjects gathered, gossiping in groups of three and four. The weather was cold and clear, augmenting the sound of metal striking wood. There could be no denying it. His carpenters were erecting the gallows.

The scaffold was a crude structure which looked weathered except for a new crossbeam. The platform was eight feet square with a drop area some four feet square. Seven steps led up to the deck where the condemned man would meet his fate. The rope to be used was four-stranded hemp, the strength of which had been tested with a thirteen stone weight. From his vantage point he saw a workman on a ladder, attaching the rope to a ring in the center of the crossbeam. Given the man's weight, this would allow a sudden fall of three feet.

He reviewed the events of the last few days. His brother Gilbert returned to Huntly to summon Fang Adams to Drake. Jamison and Ian returned and held a trial for Duff Aiken, bringing charges of attempted murder, assault on a Lord, and intent to bugger a child. No one dared to speak on his behalf. To the contrary, Widow MacPhee confirmed his evil intentions. The sentence was pronounced without objection. Unfortunately, the trial brought forth sensational facts. Witnesses claimed that the drowned boy had been brought back to life by the ministrations of the Duke. In spite of his explanations, people believed that he breathed life into a dead child. He supposed that it was true. His political stance had gained him enemies who were willing to exploit his indiscretions. He would need to assert himself to gain their respect. *I know what Father would do,* he thought, referring to the late Earl of Huntly. It sickened him to consider it.

Luc was another matter. The boy provided them with needed evidence. But he remained in his chamber with the drapes closed; lost in a state of despair. Dughall visited the lad every few hours. Other than the servants who brought food and water, he was the only one the boy would admit. After numerous lavender poultices, his wounds began to heal and the bruises subsided. There were no broken bones and he hadn't been buggered, but he bore a terrible burden of guilt. The boy felt responsible for the dog's death. The Duke tried to locate a deerhound pup, thinking that it might ease his pain. But it wasn't the season for whelping and none of the bitches had birthed. Gilbert promised to inquire among his breeders, but no word had come as of yet.

Dughall struggled with an unfamiliar feeling. As a man of faith, he held life sacred. Yet, he hated the man who hurt his son and wanted him to die accordingly. Revenge played upon the periphery of his thoughts as he considered how severe the punishment should be. For the first time in his life, he was willing to be ruthless.

There was a knock on the door and Jamison entered. The man had been pressed into service upon return, with no time to bathe or rest. His shirt was sweat-stained and his beard unkempt. "My Lord. The carpenters have completed the gallows. The edict has been posted and Fang Adams just arrived from Huntly."

Dughall breathed a sigh of relief. With Fang here, his men wouldn't need to carry out the sentence. "Thank ye, friend. Provide me with an observation area and we'll hang him this afternoon. I want four of my swordsmen as guards. I'll bring the lad if he's well enough."

"Has the boy left his chamber?"

"Nay. But I feel that this is something he must witness."

"Agreed."

Dughall knew that his family might judge him for what he was bound to do. There was no good reason for them to attend. "Keep the ladies away from the gallows. With Fang involved, it might be gruesome."

"Consider it done. I'll put Murdock on it right away."

Dughall inquired about the servant's injury. "How's yer shoulder?"

Jamison flexed his arm, showing an improved range of motion. He couldn't help but smile. "Good! My arm's normal, though it lacks strength. Stretching and sword practice should bring it back. I have yer wife to thank."

"No doubt."

"People are starting to gather in the courtyard. Shall I escort Fang Adams to the prison?"

Dughall's nerves were on fire. "Aye. Get him situated and then bring him to me for instructions." As he spoke those words, bile rose in his throat like a bitter pill. Today he would be responsible for a man's death and the punishment that led up to it. As if in a macabre play, he watched his servant leave the chamber.

Dughall wondered how he would get through it. His stomach was giving him fits. Could he draw strength from his sword? The sword was a key to many locks, spawning events both wondrous and dreadful. The Duke opened a drawer and retrieved the bronze scabbard. He laid it on the desk and admired the etched designs. The shield knot offered protection in battle. Perhaps it would stand by him today. He turned the scabbard over and studied the trinity knot. It was the symbol of Morrigan, the Goddess who merged with his wife to conceive their son. Would she protect him today or seal his fate? The weapon vibrated slightly.

Dughall unsheathed the sword. It was a work of art. The razor sharp blade was attached to the bone handle with bronze rivets. "Amazing," he whispered. As he tested its balance, his arm muscles twitched. Was he losing his touch? He closed his eyes and raised the sword to an attack stance. "Red Conan, come to this body and give me strength." Within moments, the room grew hot and vibrated with the energy of the warrior. How could he have doubted it? As ancient blood pulsed through his veins, he sheathed the sword and placed it on the credenza.

Though it was early, he took out a decanter of whisky. Pouring a half glass, he sat and savored the smell. It reminded him of the peat bogs he harvested when he was a lad, but that was long ago. He belted it in a single gulp and let the fiery nectar burn him to his belly. There was a tentative knock on the door. "Come."

Fang Adams entered, carrying a deerhound pup. He bowed slightly. "My Lord. Lord Gilbert sends his regards and this young whelp. Just weaned from his mother a month ago… Not a champion, but he was the best we could find."

The Duke was delighted. This could be just the tonic the boy needed. He accepted the pup and signaled for him to sit down. Dughall examined the dog carefully. He was a bit scruffy, but perfect in every way. He didn't look like a deerhound yet, but the harsh wiry coat gave him away. He scratched behind the dog's ears as he stared at the executioner. "Send my brother my gratitude."

Fang nodded. "I will relay the message, my Lord." He changed the subject. "I've brought my tools with me. What would ye have me do?"

Tools... That word carries a heavy significance. My heart is turning to stone. Dughall studied the man, who looked like he hadn't bathed in a decade. Solidly built with a muscled chest, he had a scar that ran along his jaw. He was feared at Huntly and his reputation had spread to Drake. The whisky was starting to have an effect. Duff Aiken's many offences came to mind, fueling his anger. "Let me tell ye about the prisoner. He buggered a child, tortured and drowned my page, and assaulted me personally."

Fang growled.

"That's not all. He killed my dog."

The executioner pounded the table. "He killed a dog?"

"Aye."

"That does it!"

"What would ye do to such a man before ye hanged him?"

Fang's eyes widened. "Are ye asking for my opinion?"

"I'm about to give ye free reign."

The executioner clenched his fists, making his forearms bulge. Excitement danced in his steely eyes. "I have just the thing."

Dughall held up a hand. "I'd rather not know the details. Do what ye must, but don't kill him. He must hang in public." He took another glass out of the credenza and poured them both a whisky. "Drink with me."

The torture master smiled maniacally and accepted the glass. They drank together as friends, bolting dram after dram of the fiery liquid.

The Duke placed a bag of coins on the table and motioned for him to take it. "Forty pieces of silver... Now, be on yer way."

"Verra generous, m'Lord."

Dughall watched the man take his coins and leave the study. As the door closed, the dog jumped up and licked his face, reminding him that he had a job to do. The wee pup melted his heart. "Why, ye can't be more than four months."

The dog barked in agreement.

"Come along, now. It's time to meet yer new master." He stood and with the pup in his arms headed for Luc's chamber. His conscience was starting to bother him and he knew of no better place to block out Duff Aiken's pain. He consoled himself with the fact that the man deserved it.

***

THE BOWELS OF DRAKE CASTLE

Fang Adams stood in a punishment chamber that was situated above the hole. He wiped his nose on his sleeve as he took stock of the layout. There was a work bench to his left where they'd unpacked and displayed his tools. On the wall there were three sets of iron manacles, which corresponded to the prisoner's height and condition. To his right was a chair with leather restraints, a bucket and tongs for hot coals, and a hand vise. Light was provided by a smoking oil lamp that smelled of cooking grease. He approved of the room and was eager to get started. It had been a surprising morning. The Duke treated him with respect and drank with him like a friend. He'd paid him well and given him free reign to punish the prisoner. This man deserved the name of Blackheart more than his weak brother and he would make sure that everyone knew it. He was eager to serve him.

He moved to the bench and inspected his instruments of torture. Ropes and chains sat among thumbscrews, knives, and a board of nails. A chuckle escaped his lips as he unrolled a sheath that contained a leather whip laced with bits of glass. It was stained with the blood of his last victim.

Gilroy entered the chamber. "Is the room suitable?"

The torture master grinned, displaying a mouthful of yellow teeth. "'Tis."

"Good. Will ye need hot coals?"

"Aye, but give me some time alone with him first."

Gilroy nodded. "Shall we bring him up and restrain him?"

Fang could barely contain himself. "Aye." This was the most gratifying part of the job, to look upon the prisoner's face when they brought him in. The servant took the bucket and left. As he waited, Fang reviewed the man's crimes in his head. Killed a dog! Attempted murder… Assault on a Lord... There was also the buggery of the child. Fang grinned as he thought of an appropriate punishment for that.

He stripped off his shirt and oiled his muscles. To appear fearsome, he opened a jar and smeared blue paint on his face. Something tiny crawled along his scalp, breaking his concentration. He rolled the louse between his fingers and crushed it with his teeth.

The oak door opened with a creak and a groan. Gilroy and Pratt entered, dragging Duff Aiken between them. The prisoner started to beg when he saw Fang. "Don't leave me here! Just hang me!" He sobbed. "For God's sake!"

Fang summoned his deepest voice. "There is no God here. Ye've come to the other place. Strip him naked and shackle him facing the wall."

Gilroy and Pratt obeyed, tearing off his clothes and shackling him to the wall. He screamed hysterically when they locked the manacles.

Pratt hissed in his ear. "Rot in hell, Duff! We know what ye did to that lad."

Fang was eager to begin, so he dismissed the servants. His excitement grew as they left the room. It was a moment to savor. He heard the prisoner's frantic breathing, and his sharp body odor was a measure of his fear. The torture master chuckled under his breath. His terror was warranted. For the moment, Fang ignored his instruments. He studied the hairy body like a student of art, memorizing each curve and cranny. Strong muscles… a tapered back… firm cheeks… the body of a laborer… This one would do. It had been a long time since he'd had a piece of arse.

Fang ignored the prisoner's pleas for mercy. The torture master ran his hands down the sides of the prisoner's body and squeezed his trembling cheeks. He growled in his ear. "Buggered a child, did ye? Let's see how ye like it."

The prisoner screamed as he unlaced his breeks and took out his swollen manhood. It was music to his ears.

***

OUTSIDE LUC'S BED CHAMBER

The Duke placed the puppy in a woven basket. He cooed softly as he drew a towel over the dog's head. "Hush, wee one. This must be a surprise." Dughall wanted the boy to attend the hanging, but wasn't sure how to accomplish it. As gruesome as it might be, he believed it could provide closure. He knocked lightly on the door and entered the room. To his surprise, the boy was dressed and standing at the window, observing activities in the courtyard. This was his chance to broach the subject. "Luc…"

The lad turned to face him. "What's happening, Sir?"

Dughall put the basket on the bed and came closer. He placed a hand on the boy's shoulder and pointed to the end of the courtyard. "That structure is a gallows. In a few hours, we'll hang yer stepfather."

Luc flinched at the mention of him. He looked up at Dughall with soulful eyes. "He's going to die?"

"Aye. He'll never beat ye again."

The boy seemed relieved. "Thank God and all the angels." Then his shoulders slumped in despair. "What difference will it make?"

Dughall sensed guilt and shame. He wished he could get to the bottom of it. "I thought ye wanted him dead."

Luc's eyes filled with tears. "I do! But his death won't bring Artus back. He's gone forever."

The Duke considered his next words. "Artus died a noble death defending ye. Must his death be in vain? The dog would want ye to go on."

Tears flowed down the boy's cheeks. "Artus was my friend! How can I live without him?"

There was a sharp yip. Luc rushed to the bed and uncovered the basket. To his surprise, a wee deerhound leaped onto the blanket and into his arms. He laughed as the dog licked his face. "He looks just like Artus when he was a pup! Is he mine, Sir?"

Dughall smiled. "Aye."

"I shall call him wee Artus! No one will ever take him from me."

They sat on the floor with the dog between them, playing with a rag rope. The puppy tugged it out of their hands, delighting them. "He's a fine dog, son. Strong and handsome… a bit scruffy…"

The boy grinned. "He's perfect."

Dughall was glad. With wee Artus in the picture, the child's recovery was a matter of time. As the boy played with the pup, he turned his thoughts to the task at hand. He sensed that the punishment phase had begun. Somewhere in the bowels of Drake, Duff Aiken was receiving his just rewards. As the whisky wore off, he sensed the man's pain and the enthusiasm of his torturer. He felt like he was losing his soul. He struggled in vain to justify the act. *An eye for an eye… A tooth for a tooth… That's what the good book says.* His eyes burned. *What have I done? Soon we will all be blind and toothless.* Dughall buried his face in his hands. *Have courage. This is what Father would have done.*

The boy stopped his play. "What's wrong, Sir? Are ye sick?"

The Duke looked up. "Sick at heart... Sick in my soul… It's hard to take a man's life, even if he deserves it. I don't want to face it alone."

The boy gazed at him with wide eyed innocence. "Let Jamison hang him! Stay away from the gallows."

Dughall shook his head. "I must look upon the man's face as the sentence is carried out. It's the only way to understand the gravity of my decisions. So child, I must go."

Luc winced. "Then I'll face my fear and stand with ye."

Dughall smiled as the child came into his arms. He hugged him close. "My wee warrior… I would be honored to have ye at my side." The time for the hanging was drawing near. He sensed that his men were searching for him. "Stay with wee Artus. I'll send a man for ye when it's time." The Duke stood and left the chamber. He sensed that the torture was out of control, but it was too late to stop it. Wandering the halls in search of his servants, he agonized over the task ahead. How could he do what must be done? He called upon the spirit of Red Conan and hardened his heart.

***

THE COURTYARD 11:30AM

Ian Hay chewed on his thumbnail as he crossed the busy courtyard. Inhabitants of the castle avoided his gaze as he passed them on the way to the gallows. He was no stranger to hangings, having attended a few in Peterhead. But he'd never been involved in a man's death or been viewed as one of his executioners. Worse yet, he'd never witnessed the torture of a man before they brought him to the gallows. He spotted

Jamison near the scaffold and hurried to join him.

The workmen were finishing up a raised platform for the Duke and his party. The air rang with the sounds of hammers hitting wood and nails.

Ian blotted his thumbnail against his breeks. It was bleeding now and sure to get worse before the day was over. He tapped Jamison on the shoulder and saw him turn. "Are we ready to hang him?"

Jamison grunted. "Aye. I sent Gilroy and Pratt to retrieve the prisoner and McGill to fetch the Duke. Where in hell have ye been?"

Ian frowned. "Hell's a good word for it. I've been in the punishment room above the hole. Gilroy asked me to haul a bucket of coals, so I stayed and watched. Jesus! Can't we just hang him?"

Jamison chuckled. "No stomach for it? Be glad that they didn't expect us to do it. We'd be torturing him now if Fang hadn't arrived."

"I can't do that."

"Ye can and ye will, if the Duke orders it. Though I admit that it's good to have an executioner here. I wonder if he'd be willing to stay."

"Fang enjoys it! I'm sure that he buggered the prisoner. His arse was bleeding."

"Ha! An eye for an eye… It's no more than what was done to Luc."

Ian could hardly believe what he'd witnessed. "Did my brother order this?"

Jamison smiled. "He gave Adams free reign to punish the prisoner."

Ian felt a chill. "I can't believe it! A year ago, my brother couldn't kill a pheasant."

"Perhaps he's growing into his role, or the illness changed him. It's about time."

Ian wondered if their own skins were at stake, because they'd absconded with his sword. At least they hadn't destroyed it. He glanced over his shoulder and saw his brother crossing the courtyard. "Looks like McGill found him. He's coming towards us." Ian tried to read his thoughts. Growing up it had been easy. But today Dughall seemed different; agitated, distant, and totally unreadable.

The Duke stopped at the gallows and inspected the handiwork of the carpenters. He took the stairs and stood on the deck where the condemned man would stand. "Seems sturdy. Has the drop been tested?"

Jamison nodded. "The carpenter tested it moments ago."

He came down the stairs with a spring in his step. "Good. I don't want this to drag out any longer than necessary. The noose hasn't been tied."

The servant grunted. "Fang insisted on doing it himself. He says that there's an art to it."

"Well, it's his game." The Duke turned his attention to the platform.

"This is just what I ordered."

The carpenters drove their last nails into the wooden structure. They packed up their tools and scurried away as if to deny their part in the drama.

Jamison examined the platform. "It's sturdy enough. Stand in the middle with Luc. Swordsmen will guard ye from four sides, keeping the spectators at bay. Suttie is fetching a flask of whisky and some plaids to ward against the cold. Is there anything else ye need?"

"Nay. All is well now that my sword is back." He stared at his brother. "I'm glad that it wasn't destroyed."

Ian's heart pounded with fear. "Forgive us, my Lord. Our intent was to protect ye."

Dughall nodded. "There's no need to fear me." He changed the subject. "Pratt told me that Fang's done with the prisoner. He and Gilroy will bring what's left of him to the gallows."

Ian was a wreck. He'd never heard Dughall talk like this and was sure that he didn't like it.

The Duke continued. "Summon the drummer to call my subjects. We shall hang him when everyone is present."

"Consider it done, m'Lord."

"Brother, go to Luc's chamber and escort him here. He must witness this if he's going to be my son."

Ian bowed like a willow in the wind. "Shall I fetch Murdock as well?"

"Nay. Murdock has orders to stay with our women to keep them away from this display. The last thing I want at dinner is a lecture."

Ian was amazed. His brother was handling the situation like he was born to it. Without further ado he hurried across the courtyard and entered the castle. As he took the stairs two at a time, his part in this play was clear. He was to retrieve Luc and bring him to the gallows.

***

PUNISHMENT CHAMBER ABOVE THE HOLE

Fang stood in the corner, relieving himself against the wall. When the urine stream stopped, he examined his manhood for damage. It was raw, but he decided that it had been worth it. After a session with the glass whip, the prisoner had been ready to bargain. He'd offered his body freely. Fang relished the feeling of power that came when a victim surrendered. The torture master snorted as he laced up his breeks. It was time to plan the execution. He went to the prisoner and examined his body.

Duff Aiken was barely able to stand. Manacled to the wall, he teetered on the balls of his feet. His back had been flayed and blood streamed to his ankles. Deep burns marred his arms and legs and a spot on the back of his neck.

Fang smiled. The man had lost consciousness twice, but each time was brought back by dousing with water. He ran a sharp finger nail across the prisoner's back and felt him tremble. The whip marks were impressive, so he decided that they would bring him out half naked. The only thing left to determine was how gruesome the hanging should be. Fang had been an executioner for twenty years. He knew how to prolong death in the case of a disembowelment, where avoidance of major vessels protracted the torture. That left time to show the man his intestines as they were thrown on a crackling fire. He remembered when his fee was based on how long he kept the victim alive. Blackheart had valued these skills and rewarded him for his enthusiasm. His son Gilbert tried to follow in his father's footsteps, but was softened by whisky and marriage. Fang thought that he might transfer to Drake, to serve the Duke of Seaford. Now this was a man who appreciated his talents.

What a Lord needed most was obedience from his subjects. Instilling fear went a long way in accomplishing that. Therefore, he resolved to make the hanging as gruesome as possible. Even with a hanging, there were ways to draw out a condemned man's agony and impress the thrill-seeking crowd. His twisted mind reeled with possibilities.

***

THE COURTYARD

The sun was overhead, but offered no respite from the extreme cold. The wind was raw, but it didn't seem to matter. The courtyard was filled with spectators.

Luc took his place on the platform in front of his Lord and master. They stood in the middle, guarded by four swordsmen; Jamison, Ian, Smith, and Graham. The sound of a large drum echoed, summoning the people to them. Already, scores of men, women, and children stood around the gallows, competing for a front row view.

Luc's heart pounded with fear as he stared at the gallows where his stepfather would die. He wanted to run away, but he needed to support his future father. The boy felt the Duke's strong hands on his shoulders as the drummer struck the bodhran, calling the crowd to order. He hoped that he couldn't tell that he was trembling.

Dughall spoke in a low voice. "There's something ye should know before they bring him up. He's bound to look bad. We punished Duff in the same ways he punished ye."

Luc turned and looked up. "What do ye mean, Sir?"

"He's been whipped and violated."

The boy didn't know what to say. He wanted his stepfather to die, but had no wish to see him suffer. He wished that he could run away.

The Duke seemed to read his thoughts. "It's too late to run, lad. They're bringing him out." He turned the boy forward and placed his hands firmly on his shoulders.

Luc took a deep breath. The drumbeat echoed in the courtyard, vibrating the frosty air. He held a hand to his heart, but all he could feel was the drumbeat.

All eyes were on a door at the end of the courtyard, from which four men emerged. Gilroy and Pratt supported the prisoner under the arms, urging him forward with harsh words. The condemned man was bare-chested with a crude kilt wrapped around his waist. His hands were bound with rope. The executioner followed, garbed in a sweater and blood stained breeks. His face was stained an ominous blue. Luc thought that he looked like the devil. The crowd was silent as the four men crossed the courtyard and stopped in front of the platform. Pratt and Gilroy forced Aiken to his knees, backed away, and took their places as guards.

Fang held the prisoner by the hair and forced him to look at his Lord and master. Then he noticed the boy. "Is this the lad he violated?"

Dughall nodded. "Aye."

Fang's voice was threatening. "Apologize to the boy!"

Duff raised his tied hands. His face was as pale as a flour sack. "Forgive me, Luc!"

Luc flinched. He never expected him to address him personally. "Never!"

The torture master grinned. "The lad won't forgive ye. Should I take ye below and skin ye alive?"

Duff sobbed into his hands. "Tell them to hang me, Luc! Yer a decent lad. For God's sake, don't send me down there with him!"

The boy could bear no more. He turned and buried his face in the Duke's cloak to block out the sight.

Dughall took his chin. "What shall it be Luc? Since he's left it in yer hands, should we hang him or send him below for more?"

Luc's heart pounded. "No more torture. I say that we hang him, Sir."

The Duke nodded. "An admirable choice… Worthy of a Lord's son. We shall continue." He unrolled a scroll and read the sentence. "Duff Aiken. For the crimes of attempted murder, assault on a Lord, and violation of a child; ye are sentenced to hang by the neck until dead. This shall be carried out immediately in the presence of the people of Drake and God. Do ye have anything to say?"

Aiken heaved a sigh when the sentence was complete. He tried to speak, but the words he muttered were confused and meaningless.

In an act of mercy, the Duke passed down the flask of whisky and allowed him to drink as much as he wanted. When he was done, he turned the boy forward and motioned for Fang to begin.

The crowd commented on the prisoner's bearing as he was pulled to his feet and led to the scaffold. Fang and the prisoner started up the wooden stairs, their footsteps ringing in the air.

Luc gasped when he saw his stepfather's back and the burns on his powerful arms. The man looked half dead already.

Fang positioned the prisoner in the center of the drop, under the ring in the center of the crossbeam. He untied his hands and pinioned them behind him and strapped his ankles together with a leather thong. He allowed the condemned to contemplate his situation as he formed the noose. All eyes were on the condemned man, who was wetting his kilt. None kept their eyes on the executioner. As Fang completed the noose, he worked a sharp piece of metal into the rope.

Luc cringed as the executioner slipped the noose over his stepfather's head. The man drew it up under the prisoner's chin and ears and tightened the knot. Duff's face was ghastly pale.

There was a wait of a few moments that tested the nerves of all who had come to see this man die. Then Fang stood back away from the drop and pulled the lever, releasing the door beneath the prisoner. Duff's body plummeted downwards towards sudden death. To everyone's horror, his head was jerked off by the fall and the body fell to the ground. For a moment, the head clung to the noose and then dropped, spattering the crowd with gore, and rolled away from the body. Blood spurted from the neck in a stream. A woman screamed and another fainted. Many in the crowd turned away and there was the frequent sound of vomiting.

Luc turned to the man who would soon be his father and saw that he was in a state of shock. He hugged him tight and buried his face in his cape.

***

Dughall could hardly believe what he'd seen. He had just presided over the bloodiest hanging and now all eyes were fixed on him. He felt like fainting, but a Lord was required to keep his composure. What happened next took him by surprise.

Fang Adams grasped the dead man's hair and raised the head, causing the eyes and mouth to open slightly. Then he sneered as he rolled it into the horrified crowd. He got down on one knee before the Duke. Fang raised his right fist in triumph and shouted "Long live Blackheart!" "Blackheart!" "Blackheart!"

At first it was no more than a whisper. It grew into a murmur and then a chant. One by one, his subjects joined Fang, genuflecting and calling him Blackheart. Dughall was appalled. He allowed the lad to hold him tight as he addressed his people. It was a terrible thing for a child to witness, and he regretted bringing him. He spoke with authority. "Justice was served today, though we never meant to carry it out in such a gruesome way. Some here dare to call me Blackheart, after my late father. While I accept yer criticism, let it be known that I neither deserve nor desire that name."

The crowd grew silent. Dughall turned the boy forward. "I have killed this lad's stepfather in a ghastly manner and left him an orphan. Therefore, from this day forward I take him as my adopted son. Spread the word to the far reaches of my estate. His name shall be Luc Gordon and ye will give him the respect he deserves."

Exhausted, he directed servants to remove the body parts to the burial ground. As they began the gruesome task, he surrounded himself with guards, took the boy's hand, and crossed the courtyard. He was saddened, upset, and ashamed of his part, and his involvement of the child was unforgivable. He could still hear them chanting. "Long live Blackheart!"

Dughall longed to see the one man who could make sense of this debacle, Brother Lazarus of Deer Abbey. He resolved to pay him a visit before his trip to London.

Chapter 33
Dark Lord

January 13th 1638
ONE WEEK LATER LATE MORNING

TWELVE MILES SOUTHEAST OF DRAKE CASTLE

It was a cold winter day. Trees groaned and cracked from icicles hanging on their branches. The road was covered with snow and ice, making it difficult for the horses. Three men rode through the pine-scented forest; a Lord in exquisite riding clothes and two of his loyal servants. They'd been traveling since dawn.

The Duke was a cauldron of emotions as he urged his horse forward. His stallion trudged through the snow, his flared nostrils firing blasts of steam. Dughall bent down to pat its neck and deliver a word of encouragement. "Easy, Lightning. We're almost there."

It had been the worst week of his life. After the hanging, he'd retreated with Luc to observe him for an unfavorable reaction. Instead, the child comforted him when he broke down into tears. Hours later, supper was a disaster. The women heard about the ghastly beheading and offered him plenty of criticism. The next morning, Keira allowed him to make love to her, but followed it with a lecture on the sanctity of life. Worst yet, his subjects regarded him with respect that was driven by horror and fear. He supposed that he deserved it. The Duke sought out with those who would not judge him; his daughter, Luc, and his loyal servants. He avoided everyone else. A letter arrived from Gilbert, congratulating him on being the new Blackheart. Its manner was "tongue in cheek", but it cut him to the quick. He wondered if he'd ever outlive it. Only Ian was quiet about the execution. He'd treated him with the utmost respect and refused to criticize his actions.

He had a decision to make. Fang Adams asked to be transferred to Drake to serve as his official torture master. Gilbert approved of the idea as long as he retained access to him. Jamison was delighted with the prospect. The servant encouraged him to assume Blackheart's name, as it would make it easier to control his subjects.

Dughall hated the name. But what would it mean if he took it? Was it just a name or would he be expected to follow in his footsteps? *It's been a week since the execution. Why must I continue to think about this!*

The Duke glanced at his men. Jamison rode on his right on a black stallion with distinctive marks on its face. He seemed tense as he scanned the forest for threats. On his left, Ian rode a white steed. His face reflected the pain he was in. He'd been suffering all morning from a toothache. Both men were armed to the teeth. Dughall had settled for a modern blade. The old sword affected him and he needed a clear head to speak to the Abbott. His nerves felt like they were on fire. Jamison pressed him to travel with more men, in light of the controversy the hanging caused. But, he'd insisted on these two, to be sure that he'd be among friends. He sensed his protector's apprehension.

Lightning's muscles tensed as he urged him forward. The horse was nervous, a condition shared by his rider. He caressed his damp mane.

Jamison shook the frost off his beard. "My Lord. If memory serves me, the abbey is around that bend."

This was welcome news. The Duke was starting to suffer from the cold. "Are ye sure?"

"Aye. We just passed that burned out cottage." Jamison made a small sound, indicating his displeasure. "We should have traveled with more men. This is dangerous considering the circumstances. If we'd been attacked…"

They rounded the bend. Dughall protested, "But we weren't attacked. And I dare say that we won't be. We haven't passed a soul on this frozen turf."

Ian spoke, "I'm glad we're alone. I've heard enough of malicious tongues. Some have even dared to call ye the Dark Lord."

Dughall flinched. "Why would they say that?"

"They say that ye have the power over life and death. The beheading was bad enough. But most frightening, ye brought that child back from the dead. Unfortunately, there were witnesses."

Dughall was stressed. He dreaded hearing about what his subjects had to say.

Ian squinted. "There's the abbey, brother. We're in luck! Smoke is rising from buildings."

Dughall spotted the tall spire of the church. "Thank God!" He needed the monk's advice more than ever.

They arrived at the steps of the church and gaped at the magnificent structure. Surrounded by barren yew trees, the building was shaped like a giant crucifix. They tied their horses to a hitching post, walked up stone steps, and opened a sturdy door.

The Duke noted that it was cold in the vestibule. It was dim except for muted light from the stained glass windows. They removed their caps and held them in their hands. Dughall dipped his fingers in a font of holy water. Making the sign of the cross, he entered the church, genuflected, and walked past the pews, approaching the altar with his servants close behind.

A bare legged monk kneeled at the rail, wearing nothing but a white tunic. He appeared to be in prayer. It was impossible to recognize him in the hooded garment.

Dughall signaled for his men to be silent. They waited patiently until the monk stood, drew back his hood, and turned to greet them.

The Abbott smiled. "Good morning, Lord Gordon. Or is it afternoon? I've been expecting ye."

Dughall was pleased. He'd been crying out to his mentor since the hanging. It was good to know that he'd been heard. He dropped to his knees and asked for a blessing.

Brother Lazarus placed his hands on his head. "Father in heaven... We give thanks that yer servant was delivered to us safely. We bless his life, his heart, and good intentions. May he always seek his higher self in yer name. Amen."

Tears welled in Dughall's eyes as he stood and thanked the Abbott. There was much that he needed to confess. He hoped for advice to soothe his battered soul.

"Ye've come to the right place, " Lazarus said. "How long can ye stay?"

Dughall sighed. "As long as it takes to feel whole again."

Jamison frowned. "My Lord. Keep in mind that we've been summoned to the King. There are preparations to be made for the trip." He addressed the Abbott. "We're soaked with sweat and tired to the bone. I must get him into dry clothes before he catches his death."

The Abbott nodded. "Where is my sense of hospitality? I will show ye to the guest quarters at once." The monk folded his arms in his long sleeves and motioned to a door. "Will ye join us for supper? The brothers expect ye as well."

***

Dughall and his men were shown to a guest dormitory. The accommodations were austere, consisting of hard narrow beds, a table and a chair, and a single candle. The room had no fireplace, which explained the heavy fur blankets. After unpacking their saddle packs and sheltering the horses, they retired to the dormitory to change into dry clothes. There were a few hours until supper, so the men decided to rest. They drank a dram of whisky and bundled in blankets. Within minutes, the servants were sound asleep.

Dughall had a burning desire to talk to the Abbott. He threw off his blanket and left the chamber, closing the door behind him. In the hallway he found a monk sitting cross-legged on the floor, staring peacefully at the wall. He attempted to pass him.

Brother Luke sensed that he was there. He stood and smoothed his white tunic, speaking in a soothing voice. "The Abbott sent me to bring ye to his study."

Dughall was touched by the gesture. "He knew I would come."

"Aye. Once the man has connected with someone, there is nothing to hide."

The young Lord nodded in agreement.

The monk led him down the hallway past a prayer room and the women's dormitory. They left the building, crossed a courtyard, and entered the Abbott's house. Inside the vestibule, the monk knocked on a narrow oak door and announced their presence. The Abbott's voice responded, telling them to come in.

Brother Luke opened the door and ushered him in. He bowed respectfully and left the building.

The chamber exuded peace and serenity. Light was provided by an array of brightly lit candles. There was a vibration in the room that echoed the beating of his heart.

The Abbott embraced him like a long lost brother. "I'm glad ye came," he said. After a moment, he released him and motioned for them to be seated.

Dughall sat in the overstuffed chair, struggling with his emotions. He felt guilty and ashamed about what had happened. He longed to confess, but was afraid of being judged. Grandfather's words came to mind, reminding him that he could trust the Abbott.

Lazarus waited patiently, fingering a crucifix that hung around his neck. "I see that ye have reservations. Perhaps we should partake in a bit of wine." The monk reached inside a cubbyhole and took out a carafe and two crystal goblets. He filled each glass carefully, handed one to Dughall, and bowed his head in prayer. "Bless this wine, o' Lord, that we are about to partake of. May it help us to bring forth the truth. Amen."

Dughall held the glass to the light. The wine was a golden color, unlike anything that he'd seen. He swirled the liquid and sniffed. "What is this?"

Lazarus smiled. "Mead… Metheglin… Honey wine… Some call it the nectar of the Gods." He took a sip. "Can ye guess what's in it?"

Dughall sniffed. "I detect rosemary, ginger, and something else." He took a swallow and was surprised by the taste, which was spicy to the tongue. "What makes it hot?"

"Cloves, my Lord. A spice imported from islands off the coast of Africa. Years ago, we obtained enough to last us many years."

Dughall tipped the glass and took a swallow. "I must learn how to make this."

The Abbott smiled. "Our beekeeper Brother Adam is starting a batch tomorrow. I will tell him that ye wish to observe." He filled their glasses to the rim and sat back.

Dughall nodded. The wine was a welcome distraction. But not for long. The pain in his heart reminded him that he was here for a good reason.

The monk seemed to sense it. "Ah... But ye have not come here to learn to make mead. Shall we talk about yer trials? The words hang in the air between us like delicate paper birds."

Dughall was amazed. Now he knew how others felt when confronted with evidence of his second sight. It was a slightly uncomfortable feeling. There were many things that troubled him, from the conception of his son to the torture and execution of Aiken. He was a man of faith but had acted like a heathen, driven by desires and emotions. He drank the wine and began with the story of the cursed sword.

The Abbott was silent as he described the events that led up to the conception of his future son. When he got to the part about his dream of a rebellious young man, the monk paled. Was he about to judge him or send him away? The emotions were too much to bear. Dughall hung his head in shame. He was beginning to think that he shouldn't have come when he felt a hand on his forearm.

The monk's voice was comforting. "I'll not judge ye. It's enough that ye must live with what ye've done."

Dughall looked up. "What can I do to make it right? I wanted to end the pregnancy, but my wife and mother convinced me otherwise."

"It's fortunate that they did. It's one thing to kill a man who threatens ye. But ye must never destroy a child, no matter how bad the omen. Keep in mind that nothing is set in stone. Small events beget larger events with the passage of time. We might be able to save this child."

"How?"

The monk put his fingertips together. "Start while he is in the womb. If he has the gift, he is aware of yer hostility. Change yer intentions to love and compassion. After he's born, ye must bring him here for instruction."

Dughall recalled their prior talk. "That didn't work with Ferraghuss. He was burned at the stake as a warlock."

Brother Lazarus looked wounded. "'Tis true. We didn't get to the lad in time, but God has given us another chance. There is a concern, however. I fear that the brothers will be too old to handle yer son as he grows into a man. We shall have to recruit some younger members."

The Duke wanted to be sure about the path to take. "So... I must change my mind about my son before he's born. Love him and be compassionate. What else do ye wish me to do?"

"Give him an honorable name to live up to. James will do, after yer late Grandfather. Raise him with love, but don't spoil him. Make sure that no one else does. Introduce him to religion, morality, and all things spiritual. Stress discipline and responsibility. Then bring him here as soon as he's able to take lessons, around the age of ten. He must stay for at least two years, with no outside influence."

"We won't be able to see him?"

"Only once a year."

Two years… It was a long time. Keira would have to be convinced. "I shall take this advice but as a precaution, I will keep him away from my daughter."

The monk blanched. "Ye must not! Who are we to say why that sweet soul was sent to earth? Perhaps she will be his salvation."

"But, what I saw! He raped his sister."

The monk scolded, "Ye saw one thread of what is possible. There are other threads that he can choose. We can help him, but he needs his father's love and guidance. Are ye willing to give it?"

Dughall reddened. "Aye. I will try to change my thoughts."

"Do not try. Ye must do it." But the man had more to say. "Now about this sword… I am troubled by the influence it has over ye. No object is entirely good or evil and the blade is no exception. But anything ye cling to, be it person, thing, or belief has the power to warp yer soul. Ye should give it up."

"Nay!" His cry surprised him. "The sword is the key to my survival."

The Abbott sighed. "Very well. But I ask that ye consider it."

The young Lord couldn't refuse a reasonable request. "I promise to give it some thought."

"Excellent!" Lazarus poured them another glass of wine. "What else shall we discuss?"

Dughall's heart sank. How could he tell him about the execution? He decided to start at the beginning, with the first assault on Luc. They talked about the lad's recovery, how he took him under his wing, and how he got him away from his stepfather.

The Abbott smiled. "So far, it seems that ye behaved admirably."

"That's not all." Dughall's heart pounded as he told the rest of the story. He painted a picture of the second assault, the drowning, the death of the dog, and the assault on his person.

"It appeared that ye brought the child back from the dead?"

"Aye. I guess in a way it was true."

The monk paled. "What did ye do to the man?"

Dughall felt sick. "We once discussed the commandment 'Thou shalt not kill.' Well, Sir, since then I have killed in the most ghastly manner. I allowed anger to guide me as I meted out his punishment."

Brother Lazarus stared. "Tell me what happened to the smallest detail."

The young Lord described that terrible day, leaving nothing to the imagination. He was simply unable to lie to this kind and gentle man. His eyes brimmed with tears as he described how his subjects now saw him. "They called me Blackheart! I don't deserve it! Will they ever forgive me?"

The Abbott's expression was grim. "Forgiveness is a deep subject.

Do ye understand it?"

"What do ye mean?"

"When the behavior of another bothers us, it is a reflection of our own behavior. Is there someone ye need to forgive?"

Dughall swallowed hard. As a matter of course, he was quick to forgive. But there was one person he'd been unwilling to pardon; his father the Earl of Huntly. He wondered if the Abbott knew. "Some things in life are unforgivable. Ye don't know what happened to me."

"Perhaps I do," Lazarus said. "Let me tell ye a story. When I was young, men from a rival clan captured my father and hung him from a tree in front of our house. They raped my mother and left her for dead. I escaped harm, but not before I got a look at them."

"Were ye in the brotherhood?"

"Nay. As ye can well imagine, I hated these men. How could they do this to my family? How could they do this to me? I vowed to avenge my father's death and spent three years hunting them down one by one."

"Did ye kill them?"

Lazarus sighed. "Oh, aye. Three out of four died at my hand."

"Why not the last?"

"The anger in my heart grew with each killing, along with feelings of grief and guilt. Though they paid with their lives, I couldna forgive them. It was destroying my soul."

Dughall's problems didn't seem so big. "What did ye do?"

"I forgave them and learned a lesson. When I forgive, I set a prisoner free; and that prisoner is myself."

Dughall knew the truth when he heard it. "I must forgive my father."

"Aye. For how can we expect forgiveness if we will not grant it?"

"Nary a day passes without the memory of how he beat me. I have black dreams about it."

"Do ye have a confessor that ye trust?"

"Aye, a man named Father John."

"Ask him to help ye. Write down yer father's transgressions and follow them with a list of yer deepest feelings. The priest can assist ye with a prayer of forgiveness. Then ye must burn the paper as a sign that ye'll obsess no more."

"But how can I forget?"

"Ye will never forget. But once ye forgive, it will be a memory instead of a torture."

This was certainly worth trying. The young Lord nodded his consent and glanced at the window. His men would be waking soon. There were unanswered questions. "About the man I executed…"

Brother Lazarus frowned. "That was a serious matter. Yer grandfather agonized over this very thing. What he decided was that in a civilized society, some actions warrant death. This certainly was such a case. What is disturbing is that ye acted out of revenge."

Dughall hung his head. "'Tis true. I hated the man for what he did to Luc. I wanted him to suffer accordingly. I feel so guilty."

"Guilt can be useful, as long as it points to our behavior and encourages us to change. But ye must not dwell on it beyond that. Remember that greater than the sin itself is the sin of guilt."

"How can guilt be a sin?" This was very confusing. "Why must everything be complicated?"

Brother Lazarus smiled. "The tests of life are not sent to punish us, but to elevate us to a higher level. Chaos provides us with the opportunity to make order. The great sages have said that the road to heaven begins in hell."

He needed advice on how to behave. "So, what should I do?"

"Accept what has happened, even the criticism. In time, with good works ye may outgrow it. Don't torture yerself with bad memories. Resolve to rule with thoughtfulness and compassion, instead of base emotions. Seek out the opinions of advisors."

This he could do. There were many lessons to learn from this man, but their time was growing short. "Sound advice. I shall do my best to follow it. May I ask a question of a personal nature?"

The Abbott raised his eyebrows. "Aye."

"Why did ye take the name Lazarus?"

The monk blushed. "I did not take the name. It was given to me by my mentor, a man far wiser than I will ever be. He said that according to scripture, Lazarus was the disciple whom Jesus loved; the one he raised from the dead, the one who stayed at the crucifixion."

Dughall's skin tingled. There was something about this conversation that seemed familiar. "Impressive."

The brother reddened. "Nay. I don't deserve the name."

"Ye do. In fact, I can feel it in my bones. I wonder what it means." It was time to return to his men. "Thank ye, Sir, for the wise advice. I have much to think about and even more to do."

"We shall talk again tomorrow."

"I'm afraid that we must leave on the morrow. My brother Gilbert and I have been summoned to the King."

Lazarus frowned. "Be careful in the King's presence. Three years ago, I accompanied the Bishop to Edinburgh to meet with him. He is a pompous man who thinks that he is above all others. His word is not to be trusted."

"Oh."

"Allow yer brother to do the talking. That way ye will not get into trouble."

"I will."

"One more thing. Should ye have the occasion to meet Archbishop Laud... Keep yer guard up! Beneath his fancy apparel and smooth manners lies a snake of a man. He is as cold as an iceberg .

Dughall shivered. "I will say nothing to him."

"That's not enough! He has the Sight and can discern yer intentions." He brought his fingertips together. "I will teach ye a trick to block his intrusions." The monk relaxed. "First, we'll do it out loud." He began the instruction. "Take a deep breath. Then sound a continuous note in yer lower vocal register and modulate it with the vowel sounds a, e, i, o, u."

Dughall joined him as he began the intonation. "Aaaaa... Eeeee... Iiiii... Ooooo... Uuuuu..." The sounds created a vibration in his head that seemed to cancel all thought.

"Good. Now take another breath and do it again, lengthening the vowels. Allow the sounds to resonate in yer mouth cavity."

The young Lord complied. After a period of silence, he said, "Remarkable. It seems to block all thought, including my own. But how can I do this in Laud's presence?"

The Abbott smiled. "Practice this fifty times a day, so that the exercise is as familiar as yer own breath. Then one by one, run the vibrations through yer head without using yer voice."

Dughall was excited. He vibrated the letter 'a' through his mind and found that he could do it for a few seconds. "This will work!"

"Aye. But ye must practice."

"I will." He glanced out the window and saw Jamison walking across the courtyard. "It appears that my servant has come for me."

"Ye are welcome to join us for supper. Go with God, my friend."

Dughall stood as his servant knocked. Feeling renewed, he answered the door and accompanied his manservant to their quarters. There would be no point in staying another day. They would spend the night and leave early on the morrow.

Chapter 34
A Fond Farewell

January 23rd 1638
TEN DAYS LATER 8AM

DRAKE CASTLE

The Duke stood before his dresser, quietly rummaging through the drawers. He'd been awake since dawn, preparing for the trip to Huntly. They planned on arriving in early afternoon, spending the night, and then going on to London to see the King. The prospect of a winter journey was not to be taken lightly. Even with overnight stops at inns, the travel could be risky. Ice and snow might impede their progress, as well as bandits and undesirables. There was a sea voyage involved as well and that could be unpredictable. He prayed that Gilbert's health would hold out. According to his letter, he suffered with a cough. He knew that this was complicated by his attempts to give up whisky, and resolved to help him with that. He'd informed Jamison that there would be no imbibing of the fiery drink in his brother's presence.

He found what he was searching for, a butter soft pair of calf-skin gloves, and slipped them into his jacket pocket. Dughall went to the bedside and looked down at his wife. Keira was fast asleep, lying on her back. Even though it was early in her pregnancy, she was exhausted and sleeping late into the morning. He noted how beautiful she was. He reached out and stroked her raven hair, being careful not to wake her. Then remembering the monk's advice, he moved his hand down over her abdomen and made a silent appeal. *Forgive me, my son, for my rash behavior. Fear not, for I shall welcome ye with a loving heart.*

Keira's eyes fluttered open. Her slender hand traveled to her belly. "I just had the strangest sensation. But it's too early for that. How can it be?"

Dughall smiled. "Our son knows his father. He sent me a sign."

She stretched. "Are ye leaving for Huntly?"

"Aye, lass."

"When will ye return?"

Dughall was uncertain. "We meet with the King on the fifteenth of February. He has the right to detain us as long as he wishes."

Her forehead wrinkled. "Oh. Are ye in danger?"

"Nay." He didn't want to upset her in her condition. "Expect us back by the middle of March. I will send word if we are late." He bent down and kissed her tenderly on the mouth. "Take care of the wee ones."

Keira smiled. "Maggie will be fine."

He wanted to ask her to be kind to Luc, but thought better of it. She'd been upset about the adoption and had made her feelings known. Luc needed a mother. Perhaps in time, she could learn to love him. "Get some sleep, lass," he said. "I love ye."

***

Dughall left the chamber and walked the corridor to the central staircase. He'd checked on wee Maggie earlier and said goodbye to his mother. His men were busy preparing the horses and a cart carrying luggage and a gift for the King.

As the Duke took the steps to the ground floor, he chanted a string of vowels, stretching and varying the intonation. "Aaaaa... Eeeee... Iiiii... Ooooo... Uuuuu..." He'd been practicing them a hundred times a day in preparation for a chance meeting with Archbishop Laud. At first, his subjects had found it strange, until they were told that he was taking singing lessons. He ended by running the vibrations through his head without using his voice. It seemed to cancel all thought. The Duke reached the first floor vestibule, which was illuminated by a pair of flaming sconces.

Murdock was waiting with a woolen cape. "My Lord." The faithful servant held it out so that he could slip his arms into it. "Jamison is in the barn. The horses are ready. The cart is loaded."

Dughall slipped on his cape and allowed his servant to adjust it around his shoulders. "I didn't mean to delay us."

"No need to explain, m'Lord. We are at yer beckon call." The servant opened the door and led him outside to the courtyard. The air was crisp and there was a slight breeze. "Did ye find yer gloves?"

"Aye." They crossed the courtyard and headed for the stables. As they walked, they made small talk. "A strange thing happened this morning. I felt my son's presence."

Murdock raised his eyebrows. "Was it a good thing?"

Dughall nodded. "Aye. I told him that I'd welcome him into my heart."

"That should make the lass happy." Murdock led him around the back of the stables where the horse and wagon were waiting. He showed him the trunks strapped to the back. "Yer formal clothes are in this one. The gift for the King is in that one."

"Thank ye." He greeted Jamison as he led Black Lightning out of the barn. The horse nickered when he saw his owner.

Just then, Luc came running across the courtyard, followed by the wee deerhound. The puppy bounded alongside, slipping in the snow. It tripped over its own feet. The Duke laughed out loud.

"Father!" The boy ran to his arms and hugged him.

Dughall got down on one knee to pet the pup and say goodbye to his son. "Murdock will keep ye busy. He promised me that he'd take ye hunting."

"I love hunting."

"The schoolmaster starts tomorrow. Remember yer lessons."

"I shall, Sir. I mean to make ye proud."

"Visit wee Maggie every day. She's bound to be lonely without her father."

Luc's face lit up with joy. "Maggie loves to play with me. After all, she's my sister!"

"That she is."

"And the wee lads are my cousins!"

Dughall stood and ruffled his hair. It did his heart good to see him doing so well after the terrible things that were done to him. What he needed most was a family's love. He said goodbye, mounted his stallion, and waved to his son and Murdock as they departed. His heart was light as they left the grounds and entered the snow-clad forest.

Chapter 35
London

February 14 1638
TWENTY-TWO DAYS LATER

LONDON ENGLAND

It had been a long and arduous journey. Dughall and Jamison had arrived at Huntly on the twenty-third in high spirits. They spent the evening with Gilbert and Connor, eating well and planning the expedition. The Duke had been pleased to find his brother healthy. His cough was gone, except for hoarseness in his voice. Even that could work to their advantage. It made him appear older.

The four men set off at dawn, heading southeast towards the city of Aberdeen. Stopping overnight in Inverurie, a burgh on the bank of the River Don, Dughall learned of a nearby stone circle and resolved to explore it later.

The next day they continued southeast, taking their mid-day meal in the burgh of Kintore, where they saw an ancient stone in a church yard bearing a carving of what looked like a cooking pot and a salmon. On the other side, there was an inscription of a broken arrow, a crescent moon, and a beast which reminded Dughall of a dolphin. They were told that the stone was left by the Picts, a tribe that inhabited those parts in the early 600's.

They reached the city of Aberdeen by nightfall and obtained lodging at an inn on the harbor. This was a mercantile center and port, consisting of massive granite structures and timber and wattle houses. There were scores of churches and two universities. It was the largest city that Dughall had ever seen.

They followed the coast for three days, traveling from Aberdeen to Dundee. Dughall loved it, as it was more than a year since he'd been by the sea. Dundee was a town of fisher folk. The wool export industry was flourishing there. In their nightly foray into town, they found imported goods from Scandinavia and the Baltic. Dughall had never seen so many mariners in one place. There had to be more than three thousand.

The next four days were spent traveling from Dundee to the capital city of Edinburgh. The Duke's idea of a large city was challenged when they approached the city of granite. They had reservations on a ship leaving Edinburgh for London in three days, so they had time to explore the city. There was a long road that connected Holyrood Abbey to the castle, hundreds of narrow alleyways, and buildings that were twelve floors tall. They learned to avoid these alleys when those living higher up threw human waste out the windows, yelling 'Garde Loo'.

In taverns, they heard about the recent unrest and the stripping of the city's courts and power. There were remnants of bonfires and damaged buildings left over from the riots. Dughall's concern for his father grew. He knew that Alex had been here and was nearby, serving under General Leslie. But this was not the time to find him.

Gilbert instructed him in what they would say to the King. Their behavior in the presence of this powerful monarch was of the utmost importance.

Finally, the ship took them all; men and horses, on a windy voyage on the North Sea. Dughall felt right at home, while Gilbert and the servants suffered from varying degrees of sea sickness. With several stops and an overnight repair, they arrived in London on the fourteenth of February.

Dughall smelled the Thames before he saw it. In Scotland he could drink from any river and see almost clear to the bottom. But this tidal river was dark and stank like the waste of cattle. "Better not let the horses drink that."

Jamison snorted. "Ha! The horses aren't the only ones. Better stick to whisky and ale in this city. Look! That tanner is dumping hide wash in the river."

Dughall frowned. "I know it. I saw a butcher dumping viscera and trimmings too. I hope we can buy fresh water."

They decided to take rooms at an inn. Looking up, Gilbert saw a wooden placard hanging from a multistory building which identified it as the 'Drunken Duck'. The weathered sign had a picture of two plucked ducks standing around a leaking barrel of ale.

Dughall chuckled. "What a strange name for an inn. I'll be sure to ask its meaning."

Gilbert dismounted. "This is as good a place as any for a night." He handed his reins to Connor and told the men to stable the horses around back.

Dughall and Gilbert entered the inn. A vestibule led to a sprawling chamber with oak beamed ceilings and a fireplace. Their eyes adjusted to the low light that was provided by strategically placed oil lamps and a roaring log fire. This was the warmest they'd been in a week.

They spotted the innkeeper and engaged him in conversation. Gilbert removed his gloves. "I am Lord Gordon, Earl of Huntly. We'd like two rooms. One for my brother and I and one for two man servants… We might need the rooms for as long as a week. I don't know how long we'll be at the Queen's House."

The innkeeper raised his eyebrows. He was clearly looking them over. "The Queen's House?"

"Aye. We've been summoned to the King's presence."

The man seemed suspicious. "Ye'll pay for the rooms in advance?"

Gilbert seemed displeased. "We will if we have to."

"Pardon my sayin' so. But ye don't seem the type that the King has to supper. Where are ye from?"

Dughall stared. "Scotland."

The innkeeper flashed a mouthful of yellow teeth. "Ha! Where all the trouble is? Run like hell. He's likely to throw ye in the Tower."

"We are loyal subjects of the King," Gilbert insisted.

The man mumbled. "Then ye're among the few left."

Dughall was perplexed. "Why do ye say that we're not the type to be called before the King?"

"Yer clothes, Sir. Proper English gentlemen don't dress that way. Neither do foreign dignitaries." He escorted them up a narrow staircase and showed them two rooms that looked comfortable. Each room had beds, but lacked the usual trappings like dressers and chairs. Then he went from room to room lighting each fireplace. "Pay when ye come down to supper."

Dughall remembered the sign. "Why do they call this place the Drunken Duck?"

The innkeeper smiled. "The landlady one day found all of her ducks dead in the yard. Unaccustomed to waste, she plucked them ready for cooking. As she finished, the ducks began to revive. A search of the yard revealed a leaking ale barrel surrounded by webbed footprints. She was so sorry that she knitted little jackets for them until their feathers grew back."

"Ha! What a great story!"

The innkeeper left them alone.

Dughall sat on a bed, testing its hardness. "Not bad. What did he mean about our clothes?"

Gilbert frowned. "I don't know. We'll wear our best kilts tomorrow. Surely, that will impress the King."

"The King called us here. Why would he throw us in the Tower?"

"Because he can. That's why it's important that ye let me do the talking. No matter what he says, don't disagree, even if it offends ye."

Dughall sighed. "I will keep my mouth shut."

"Good. We will have to present an excuse for yer silence."

"Tell him that I'm a fisherman who lacks social graces. That's what some think."

Gilbert nodded. "That's not what I think of ye. But nevertheless, that's what I'll tell him. There's no need for the both of us to be in mortal danger."

"Let's keep our eyes and ears open in the tavern. Perhaps we can get an idea of what Londoners think of the unrest in our country."

"Good idea." Gilbert looked up as Jamison and Connor entered the room hauling a trunk of clothes. "Over there. Don't bring too much up. We leave tomorrow for the Queen's House."

***

THAT EVENING

The 'Drunken Duck' was a popular place as the daylight started to wane. Fifty-two patrons crowded the tables, partaking in supper and drinking ale. The air was smoky from pipes and cigars. Conversation was lively, punctuated by an occasional burp or curse. Shouts emanated from a back room, where a cock fight was going on. The Gordon party decided to take a peek. From the door they could see two roosters, circling each other in a ritualized dance. As spectators urged them on, each rooster lowered a wing and circled nearer the other, neck feathers flaring. Suddenly, one attacked and the other leaped to meet the challenge. They exchanged kicks in midair, slashing with razor-sharp cock spurs attached to their legs. Birds screeched and feathers flew while they pecked and sliced each other to pieces. In a few minutes it was over. One bird lay lifeless while the other struggled, maimed on the floor. Men settled their bets, while two more birds were brought out.

Dughall felt nauseous. "That's enough for me!" He turned and led them towards the fireplace in the main room, where they sat at two tables. Within minutes, they were descended upon by a serving lass and ordered supper and tankards of ale.

The Duke sat across from his brother, eating a meat pie. Their servants were at a nearby table, drinking and planning the next day. Ale was the drink of choice. They hadn't located a source of fresh water.

Two men entered the tavern and sat at a table across from Dughall and Gilbert. They were strangely dressed in leather breeks, wool jerseys, and long fur coats. From their knit caps, they appeared to be mariners, but there was something wild about them. Tankards of ale and a plate of bread and cheese were delivered to the table.

Dughall listened as they talked, catching bits and pieces of their conversation.

"Shepherding another group to the colonies... Terrible religious persecution... Works in our favor though..." The burly man with bad teeth crushed out his cigar in a dinner plate.

His companion nodded. "Before long, we'll be transportin' Scots."

Dughall couldn't hold his tongue. "Did ye mention the colonies?"

The older man glared. "Aye. Virginia and Massachusetts... Who might ye be?"

Gilbert signaled Connor. The tension in the room was palpable.

Dughall offered his hand to the man as a sign of good will. "Dughall Gordon, Duke of Seaford. I'm looking for a sea captain who can trade with the colonies. Do ye know one?"

The man shook his hand. "Ye've found one. Captain Woodget's my name. A Duke ye say? Where do ye hail from?"

Dughall deepened his voice. "Northeast Scotland. I have a fleet that runs out of Moray Firth."

"Never heard of it. Ye look young."

"I am, Sir. I was the only heir to my late grandfather's estate. What do ye transport?"

"Ah…" He shook his head as he sized up the brothers. "Tobacco, cotton, and ginger… Sometimes sundries and tools… The last few years, it's been people."

This got Dughall's attention. "People?"

Gilbert had relaxed and was listening to the conversation.

The man's eyes flashed with excitement. "Aye! I'm not talkin' slaves, though there's been some of that. Those Africans are as dark as the midnight sky. There's been a brisk trade in transportin' Puritans to Massachusetts to escape the King's wrath."

"Why?"

"The King won't let 'em worship as they wish. Imposed his rules on their church and whipped and imprisoned some. That Prynne man had his nose split and his ears chopped off. Now he sits in prison; what's left of the poor fellow. That was the last straw for some."

Dughall frowned. Was this what was in store for the Scots? "Why do they go to Massachusetts?"

The man wrinkled his nose. "Pardon me. I think I need another cigar. The governor of that colony promised religious freedom to all. Don't know much about it. I'm not a religious man."

"But ye're saving people."

Captain Woodget sneered. "They're just cargo to me. Nothin' more… Do ye need a captain? I dare say that the exodus will start when the King sets his sights north."

Dughall knew he was right. They had a short time to stand up for their rights and prevent a similar catastrophe. He wondered how he would do it. He took a calling card out of his pocket and handed it to the man. "Contact me, Sir. We will discuss a mutually beneficial arrangement."

The captain placed the card in his pocket. The two mariners stood, threw some coins on the table, and left the tavern.

Gilbert was quiet as he sipped his ale. When it was gone, he stared at his brother. "Don't get any daft ideas. These Protestant problems are none of our business. Remember what Father used to say. Through thick and thin, the Gordons are loyal to the King."

Dughall didn't know what to think of that.

Queen Henrietta Maria

Chapter 36
Command Performance

February 15th 1638
NEXT DAY

APPROACHING THE QUEENS HOUSE
LONDON BOROUGH OF GREENWICH ENGLAND

Snow fell like ashes as the Gordon brothers approached the Queen's House on horseback. They were traveling unarmed without their servants, per the specific request of the King. Jamison and Connor had been told to stay at the inn and wait for their return. If that didn't happen in three days, they were to make inquiries about their welfare.

Dughall and Gilbert had arisen before dawn and spent a goodly amount of time on their appearance. They washed in a common basin, combed out their long black locks, and donned their best clothes. They completed their outfits with solid gold kilt pins and sporrans made of fine leather. Surely, they were appropriately dressed.

The saddle felt cold against Dughall's arse. Up until now, they'd been wearing breeks. The kilt was too thin to offer him protection. His lower legs were warmed by long wool socks and boots, but his thighs were feeling the cold.

Gilbert shivered. He absently stroked the place where his dirk would be. "I feel naked without a weapon."

"I was thinking the same thing."

The Queen's House straddled the main Deptford to Woolrich road. It was possible to pass from the Palace Gardens into the Royal Park without being seen crossing the road. It was this street that the Gordon brothers followed as they approached the royal residence.

They urged their horses off the cobblestone road towards the impressive white structure. To Scottish eyes, it was nothing less than revolutionary.

Dughall stared. "It's magnificent!"

Gilbert agreed. "Like something from the Greeks."

The two story building had high rectangular windows and a graceful balustrade that ran along the top. There was a rounded entrance at ground level and a pair of curved staircases on each side that led to a first floor terrace.

Six armed guards stood at attention, three on each side of the entrance. They stared into space with frozen expressions, without a flicker of recognition of the approaching men.

As the brothers reached the entrance, the door opened and a servant emerged. The middle-age man was clad in blue velvet breeks, a tunic, and a shirt with a white ruff collar. His silver hair was long and tied back in a leather thong. The servant bowed stiffly. "Good day, Sirs. Might I inquire as to who you are?"

"I am Gilbert Gordon, the Earl of Huntly." He pointed to his brother. "This man is Dughall Gordon, the Duke of Seaford." He extracted the invitations from a pocket and handed them over. "We are here at the request of the King."

The servant looked them over them with a critical eye, lingering upon their clothing. Then he opened the folded parchment and began to read. He looked up. "You are expected, my Lords. His Majesty is away on business, but is due to arrive in several hours. In the meantime, I shall give you a tour and provide refreshments."

Gilbert coughed. "We would be grateful for the hospitality. I'm afraid that we came unprepared for the bitter cold."

The man nodded. "It has been an unusual winter. Dismount and follow me. The guards will attend to your horses." Upon these words, two guards put down their weapons and walked to their location. They stood by in silence, ready to take the horses.

Dughall and Gilbert dismounted, removed their saddle packs, and handed the reins to the guards. Anxious to get out of the cold, they followed the servant through the door. They found themselves in an elegant vestibule, where their outer coats and packs were taken and stored in a small room. The servant, who introduced himself as Afton, respectfully checked them for weapons. Passing this test, they were allowed to continue to the next room. They entered the Great Hall and looked around in stunned silence. This room was a perfect forty foot cube that stretched skyward through the center of the house's north side. It featured tall windows and a geometrically patterned black and white marble floor, the center of which was a circle containing concentric circles of diamond shapes. Flaming sconces added to natural light streaming in through the windows. There were stone benches placed about the perimeter of the room, pillars supporting busts of royalty, and a wooden balcony that ran around the Hall at the first floor level.

"What a magnificent place!" Gilbert said.

Afton nodded. "The Queen's House was recently completed by the architect Inigo Jones. It is a rare example of Renaissance architecture."

Dughall walked to the center of the room and stared up at the high ceiling. Nine Italian paintings adorned it, showing a female figure surrounded by twenty three women holding objects alluding to astronomy, victory, reason, music, and arithmetic. He looked down and studied the black and white patterns that seemed to swirl about his feet. Like a stone circle, this was a place of vibration. His disorientation grew. He covered his eyes and nearly lost consciousness.

"Brother?" Gilbert touched him on the shoulder. "Are ye all right?"

His voice was weak. "Just a bit dizzy. I'm better now."

Afton cleared his throat. "Come away from the center, Sir. It has an affect on some individuals. Even the Queen has experienced faintness."

Dughall felt his brother's hand on his elbow as he was led away from the center. He was inclined to describe his experience, but remembered his pledge to hold his tongue. It was important that he appear to be uneducated. "Forgive me. I don't understand these things."

The servant was sympathetic. "Would you like to lie down?"

"Nay, Sir. But I accept yer offer of a tour."

Afton nodded and led the way. They were told that the next room was a 'retiring room', where the King and Queen and honored guests retreated to after a long day. Brocade couches, stuffed chairs, and side tables were tastefully arranged around a large fireplace that was carved from Italian marble. Wood paneled walls and polished floors gave it a warm look. From there, they were escorted through several rooms to the library.

Dughall had never seen so many book cases, not even in the Abbey of Deer. He was impressed with the number of manuscripts and maps that graced this chamber. The furniture was massive and hewn from the finest oak. This was truly the domicile of a King. They lingered there for half an hour, luxuriating in the warmth of the fireplace and examining a world globe. Afton left to fetch them refreshments, so Dughall opened a book case.

"Don't touch that, brother." Gilbert's voice was full of concern. "The King will be angry if we damage his personal collection."

"I don't mean to damage it."

"We can't take the chance."

Dughall closed the case gently. "We don't want to wind up in the Tower of London."

"So far, we've been treated with respect."

Afton appeared with a tray of tea and biscuits. He encouraged them to sit at a library table and partake in the offerings. As they ate and drank, he informed them of the King's arrival. "His Majesty has arrived and is freshening up. He will meet with you within the hour."

Gilbert asked a question. "Have the other Scottish Lords arrived?"

Afton seemed confused. "There is no one here but yourselves. It seems that you have his full attention."

Dughall felt his brother's apprehension. This could be a different meeting if they were the only participants. He watched as the servant took his leave and left the room. "What does it mean?"

Gilbert was pale. "I don't know. Just remember what I told ye. Keep quiet and plead ignorance. There's no sense in risking us both."

"I will."

He raved on, quoting their father and emphasizing the danger. When finished, there were tears in his eyes. "I have a request. If something happens to me, ye must be guardian to my son George."

"Brother! Let's not think about that."

Gilbert gripped his hand. "Promise me that ye will."

Dughall tried to be brave. "I promise, brother. Ye have my word."

The door opened and Afton appeared. He bowed slightly, in a stiff manner unique to the English. "My Lords... The King is ready to see you."

***

The brothers had their hearts in their throats as they were escorted to the King's private study. Gilbert's hand traveled to his neck, while Dughall sympathetically experienced his fear of being beheaded. They were both over their heads, politically speaking.

Afton knocked on the chamber door and was greeted by a voice.

"Come."

The servant turned the ornate twenty-four carat gold knob, opened the door, and escorted the brothers in. Afton bowed deeply before his King. "Your Majesty... I present to you Lord Gilbert Gordon, the Earl of Huntly, and Lord Dughall Gordon, the Duke of Seaford."

King Charles walked away from his desk. "That will be all, Afton. You are excused."

The servant made a hasty retreat.

Dughall was humbled by the King's appearance. Though short in stature, he projected an amazing presence. The monarch was neatly dressed in a rich brown doublet and velvet breeches. A white lace collar fanned to his shoulders, emphasizing his perfectly groomed face and hair.

The King spoke with a slight stammer, "Which one of you is the Earl of Huntly?"

Gilbert bowed slightly. "I am, yer Majesty." He couldn't hide his nervousness.

The King turned. "And you, Sir, are the Duke of Seaford?"

Dughall bowed. "I am, yer Majesty."

The man studied them for a moment. "The country of my birth certainly provides me with interesting styles of dress." He moved gracefully to his desk, sat down, and motioned for them to take a seat. "There is something to be said for tradition."

Gilbert and Dughall sat. Their red faces were a testament to their confusion about his comment.

King Charles offered a slight smile. "I did not mean to insult." He folded his well groomed hands on the desk. "You are welcome to wear what you wish."

"No offence taken," Gilbert said. "We are yer loyal subjects."

The monarch smiled. "You are wondering why I called you here today. As you are aware, there is unrest in Scotland, some of it bordering on treason. God has given me the task of uniting three countries under one spiritual philosophy..." He droned on, describing his belief in the divine right of kings... His respect for Catholicism... His commitment to the Anglican style of Protestantism... His willingness to eradicate dissenters... His eyes flashed as he mentioned the men who carried the petitions... God was not to be denied!

Dughall could barely breathe. The man thought that he was the hand of God and was willing to exercise his power to support it. He could feel Gilbert's discomfort, although he couldn't see it by studying his face.

The King was growing agitated. "There are protests and petitions and riots across your land!"

"Forgive us, yer Majesty!" Gilbert cried. "We used our economic and political influence to keep Aberdeenshire under control. We are succeeding at the task."

The King smiled.

Dughall sensed that they were being manipulated.

"I am aware of your efforts, Lord Gordon. Aberdeenshire and the Highlands are bright spots in this mess, as well as the primarily Catholic boroughs." He drummed his fingertips on the table in an attempt to unnerve them. "I called you here today to ask for your support."

Gilbert flushed. "Of course ye have it..."

"Let me finish. What you have done so far is admirable. But forces have arisen that threaten to turn the port city of Aberdeen against me. I ask that you help me root them out."

Dughall knew that he was talking about his father, his uncle, Jenny Geddes, and scores of other Scots he knew. Would he be able to protect them?

The monarch ranted, demanding that they hunt down the ringleaders, turn them over to the crown, and provide military support should he require it.

Gilbert pandered to his desires. In return, he was offered the expansion of his lands from the estates of those who opposed them. It appeared to be an equitable trade.

The King stared at Dughall. "You've had little to say."

Gilbert spoke in his stead. "Forgive him, yer Majesty. My brother recently claimed his birthright without the benefit of a proper education. He is inexperienced in the ways of politics."

He regarded the Earl with an eye of scrutiny. "An intriguing story… You must tell me about it later. Are you his guardian?"

Gilbert took a breath. "Aye. Whatever I agree to stands for us both. Is it not true, brother?"

Dughall responded in a dull voice. "'Tis true." He was glad that the monarch didn't have the Sight.

The King stared at the brothers, in an attempt to see who would blink first. They eventually gave in out of fear. The monarch seemed satisfied. "The midday meal is being prepared. I ask that you join the Queen and me for a light repast."

They thanked him profusely and followed him to the formal dining room.

***

THE QUEEN'S BED CHAMBER

Queen Henrietta Maria sat at her ornate dressing table, brushing her high cheek bones with rouge. Her furniture had been brought from France and was nothing less than a work of art. The bed set had been carved from ebony and featured characters from mythology, nymphs, satyrs, and allegories of the season. The chairs were padded with the finest brocade.

Normally, this would be the time that she would nap or visit her children, but not today. She'd been commanded to attend the midday meal, to offer hospitality to two foreign dignitaries. Mon Dieu! The last one was fat and bald and unable to carry on a conversation. He'd stared at her breasts, drawing the ire of the King.

The woman yawned. This year had been the most tedious since her husband's dismissal of her French staff, an event that caused her consternation. They'd been replaced with English servants and companions, stiff in presence and unwilling to gossip. None would tolerate criticism of the King.

Henrietta stared in the mirror and flashed a smile. Even at twenty-nine, she was pleased with what she saw. The woman who stared at her had a long, heart shaped face, dark eyes, and well shaped lips. Radiant brown hair framed her face in ringlets and flowed to bare shoulders. Her skin was soft and supple, the product of exotic creams and years of care. She couldn't understand why other women grew old.

She was wearing an exquisite floor length gown. Made from orange silk taffeta, it reflected the natural light. The dress was trimmed with the finest lace produced by nunneries in France.

The Queen used a small brush to apply color to her lips, a final step; and fastened a string of pearls around her neck. She stood and stared in a full length mirror, first at her front and then the back. She had to look good for the King.

She sighed. *I am so bored.* Her melancholy mind longed for a diversion. *I would do a thousand penances to meet someone interesting.*

***

THE DINING ROOM

The Dining chamber was light and airy, drawing its illumination from a series of six tall windows. Two walls displayed portraits of the royal family, painted by the Dutch artist Anthonis van Dyck. The fourth wall contained the door, which opened into the Great Hall and its magnificent geometric floor.

The dining table was sixteen feet long, made of highly polished walnut, and featured elaborately turned legs. The chairs had armrests, which were padded and upholstered with the finest pastel silk. Four place settings graced the table at one end. Highly polished silver tableware sat next to delicate china and leaded wine glasses.

The King sat at the head of the table, with his wife to his right. The Gordon brothers sat to his left, with Gilbert closest to the monarch.

The meal that was served was fit for royalty, consisting of roast pheasant, tiny onions and potatoes, and a variety of unusual vegetables. Warm breads and a rich dessert complimented the repast. Red wine was served that came from the finest vineyards in France. They ended with an after meal liquor that tasted like anise.

Dughall studied the interaction between the King and the Queen. He was clearly fond of her and treated her with respect. She responded to his compliments with grace, but Dughall sensed something else. She was bored and resentful of her Protestant prince.

The young Lord thought that she was exotic. Petite in stature, she had eyes that were as black as night and glittered like precious gemstones. There was radiance about her that exuded her indomitable spirit. He knew that she had to be in her late twenties, but looked no older than his wife.

The King started a private conversation with Gilbert, so the Queen focused on Dughall. "Tell me something interesting about yourself, Lord Gordon."

The Duke reddened. "Forgive me, my Queen. I am a simple man who only recently claimed my birthright. I have little to say."

Her eyes widened. "But you're a Duke! What did you do before?"

He kept his voice low. "I was a fisherman."

She giggled. "Such tall tales! Do you tell them to all the women?"

Dughall wasn't used to being challenged, but he found her laugh intoxicating. He knew that it could be the effects of the liquor. "I don't get to speak to many women. I'm married."

She smiled, but continued to tease him. "So your wife has you on a leash. Any offspring?"

"I have two children and one on the way."

"Such a fertile wife."

Dughall cleared his throat. "Well… Only the last belongs to her."

This piqued her interest. "You seem young. Are the other two bastards? Or from a previous marriage?"

The young Lord thought that this was none of her business, but she was the Queen after all. He had to answer. "My daughter was born to a mistress, my son to another woman who…"

Henrietta giggled. "So you have three women? How do you manage it?"

Dughall reddened. He was growing angry, but he remembered his promise to play dumb. "I attend only to my wife now. She agreed to accept my children." He looked to his brother for help, but he seemed to be deep in conversation with the King.

The Queen sighed deeply, indicating her boredom.

King Charles looked up. "My dear wife. Are we boring you?"

"Oui mon amour. Je suis ennuyé."

"I have important business to discuss with the Earl. I would be *in your debt* if you would take the Duke on a tour."

Dughall noted that she shivered with delight when he spoke the words 'in your debt'. It was a secret code that had consequences in their lovemaking.

"Henrietta… Show the Duke the Tulip Staircase and the Observatory."

The Queen stood and fanned herself with the grace of a lady. "Avec plaisir." She turned to the Duke. "Come along, Lord Gordon."

***

They left the dining room and walked a long hallway that was decorated with Italian landscape paintings. The floor boards were made of the finest oak and polished until they threw a reflection.

Dughall walked slightly behind her, guessing about the etiquette of the situation. He didn't like being alone with her, considering her prying questions. It would be a challenge to stay in his role. He could hear the swish of her silk petticoats, a sound that was arousing.

The Queen stopped at the foot of an elegant staircase and turned. "This, Sir, is the Tulip staircase."

Dughall had never seen anything like it. Located in a vestibule that featured tall windows and natural light, a spiral staircase twisted around and around as it flowed to the top floor. Looking up, it reminded him of the inside of a sea conch. The iron hand rails were curved and the balusters were crafted in the shape of tulips. "This is magnificent!" He followed her up the stairs, winding round and around until they reached the second floor. It was enough to make one dizzy. He laughed out loud. Perhaps it was an effect of the liquor.

Henrietta smiled. "You're tipsy, Sir."

"Nay, my Queen. These stairs make me dizzy."

Henrietta led him down a short corridor to an exquisitely paneled oak door. Then she turned a solid gold knob and escorted him into an octagonal chamber.

Dughall was delighted. This palace was full of optical illusions! The eight sided room was illuminated by seven narrow windows that ran nearly the length of ceiling to floor. The plaster walls were adorned with beautiful wood panels, housing a fireplace, a clock, and astronomy equipment. He got excited when he saw the large telescope. Over six feet in length, it was mounted on a wood tripod to make it easier to use. The top section was supported on the rung of a ladder. "May I use it?"

The Queen evaluated him with a critical eye. "Oui. Do you know how?"

"Aye." Dughall walked across the polished wood floor to the telescope and adjusted its height for his use.

"Ah… But you are tall, Sir."

He sat upon a stool and looked through the eyepiece. At first he couldn't see anything, so he tried to make an adjustment using the focuser. "I can almost see now. Just a few more turns. I have an interest in the moon and stars."

Suddenly her fingers were upon his, helping him to turn the focuser. "Is this better?"

His heart was in his throat. "Aye, but…" Dughall gently disengaged and stepped away from the telescope. He was stammering and it wasn't an act. His sight told him that she found him attractive. "I don't think I should be touching ye."

The Queen stared. "You're not as dull as you claim to be." She walked away to the window. "You may continue with the telescope."

He sat on the stool again, looked in the eyepiece, and made adjustments as to its direction. The instrument was exquisite and afforded him views that were far away. Buildings and church spires that were many miles away appeared close. He wished that he could use it on the midnight sky. "Astonishing."

"Breathtaking, isn't it?" she said. "At night, we can see the moon, some planets, and the configuration of the stars. We have charts that we use to identify them."

He turned to her. "Who invented such a wonder?"

"An Italian scientist named Galileo invented the instrument. The first thing he noticed was craters on the moon."

"Craters?"

"Yes, deep holes in the ground from an impact of some kind."

"Is Galileo alive?"

"Yes, but unfortunately he is in trouble with the Church. His beliefs do not support our view of Heaven."

"Where is he now?"

She shrugged. "He's been called to Rome to answer to the Inquisition. I would imagine that he's under arrest."

Dughall was outraged. "Are they torturing him?"

"Most likely."

"Can't someone stop it?"

"Who wants to take on the Holy See? It would be suicide for a Catholic like you. This is one room that even I do not show my priest."

This matter was more complicated than he thought. "Oh…" He jumped off the stool and smoothed his kilt. "What shall we do now?"

She led him to a table to show him the star charts. They unrolled a tube and spread one flat. It seemed that the night sky unfolded before him.

He used a finger to trace the stars in the Big Dipper. "See the bucket? I've wondered about this many times."

She placed a delicate hand over his. "There's one thing that I've wondered about."

His heart pounded in his ears. "What is that, my Queen?"

She giggled. "What *do* Scotsmen wear under those kilts?" Her hand traveled to his groin. "I see…"

There was a sudden noise. The woman drew back her hand just as the door opened.

Afton appeared with a message. "My Queen. Lord Gordon. The King has completed his meeting with the Earl. He asks that you join him in the retiring room for drinks."

Her voice was cold. "That will be all, Afton. We shall follow in a few minutes." The servant bowed and left the room.

She turned to Dughall. "He's a spy, you know. I cannot trust him." Her delicate neck was turning red. "Tell no one of what happened here today. If it gets back to the King, I will say that you forced me."

Dughall's stomach was in knots. "I will tell no one."

"Good. I would hate to see a virile man like you languishing in the Tower of London." She rewarded him with a sly smile. "We will continue this tryst at another time. Promise me."

Dughall could barely think. "As ye wish, my Queen."

Henrietta spoke in a husky voice. "You won't regret it. French women can be passionate in bed. I will tell you how to contact me." She walked to the door in silence, leaving him to contemplate his fate.

***

LATER THAT DAY THE CARRIAGEWAY

They'd met for drinks in the retiring room, lingering for more than an hour. Once again, they were served fine French wines and delicately flavored liquors.

Dughall was an emotional mess. He felt like he'd dodged a bullet, but it seemed that it was only for the meantime. The Queen's intentions were clear. If they returned to the palace, he was in for trouble. The young Lord deadened his fears with a spiced liquor called Benedictine. In his weakened state, he was grateful that Archbishop Laud had declined to meet them.

As a final gesture, they presented the King with a gift from their country, an exquisitely crafted gold brooch featuring the crest of arms of Scotland. He was pleased, but no invitation was extended to stay the night.

With a measure of relief, Gilbert and Dughall said their goodbyes, retrieved their coats, and left the Queen's House through the Great Hall. As instructed, they walked a short distance and stood in a cobblestone carriageway, to wait for their horses.

Gilbert rubbed his hands together. "That went well."

"Did it?"

"Aye, brother. There are details we have to address, but not right now."

Two royal guards approached with their horses. They handed over the reins and took their leave.

The brothers mounted, with Dughall swaying a bit at the end. "My head hurts."

Gilbert scolded him as they guided the horses out of the carriageway onto the path. "Don't drink so much in a risky situation. It's fortunate that ye had no one to impress."

"Ye have no idea."

"What do ye mean?"

"Nay bother. Thank God that we're going back to the inn."

They turned off the path onto Woolrich road. It was growing dark and snow was lightly falling. Dughall's head started to clear. "What details do we have to address?

Gilbert took a deep breath. "It's about yer stepfather. Alex Hay is on the King's list of traitors."

Chapter 37
Covenant

February 28th 1638
THIRTEEN DAYS LATER

EDINBURGH SCOTLAND

The morning was cold and dry in the city. There had been little snow or rain that month, causing fresh water shortages. The sun had just risen, casting rays through low clouds. The streets were bustling with activity. Women swept their doorsteps and hung out damp bedding to dry. Children ran with dogs, shouting and spinning hoops. Tradesmen and mariners left their homes to go to their daily jobs. These things were happening and more. For more than fifty thousand men had descended upon Edinburgh to sign the National Covenant. They came from all parts of Scotland; the Highlands, Lowlands, and even the islands.

***

Back in October, the King had stripped the capitol city of purpose and influence. He'd ordered the petitioners to leave or be arrested and tried for treason. Worse yet, the Privy Council and law courts were advised to desert Edinburgh for a secure location. The King had promised to consider the petitions when the city was peaceful, but that hadn't happened. Instead, he seemed content to let them stew in their own juice. Dozens of petitioners were arrested and transferred to London to await their fate in the Tower of London. Many of the Lords involved withdrew to safe locations to raise money and support for Leslie's army. There was no doubt as to how this would go down.

Word of the rebellion traveled to the far reaches of Scotland via letters, posters, and personal accounts. The protest grew into a campaign of petitions and supplications denouncing the Laudian prayer book and criticising the power of bishops.

Led by the lords Loudoun, Rothes, Balmerino, and Lindsay, the supplicants organised four elected "Tables" or committees to represent the nobility, gentry, burgesses and clergy. A fifth Table was to act as an executive body. In the face of the Privy Council's impotence, they acted as an alternative government.

The well-respected clergyman Alexander Henderson and the lawyer Archibald Johnstone were tasked with drawing up a National Covenant. It was to unite the supplicants and clarify aims, the main one being a rejection of untried "innovations" in religion.

Favors were called in and loyalties tested. By early December, the specter of religious persecution was the basis for fiery sermons, town hall meetings, and supper table conversation. Money was raised; weapons and supplies gathered, and men committed themselves to the cause. They awaited marching orders.

Word came in mid-January, asking them to report to Edinburgh by the end of the third week of February. There they would be given the opportunity to sign a covenant and pledge their support for the rebellion. In vague terms, they were told about Leslie's army and encouraged to join the ranks.

Lord Traquair, after his brush with death in the Edinburgh riot, obtained permission to come to the King. He told Charles frankly that he must either abandon the new Liturgy requirements or come to Scotland with 40,000 armed men. Instead of an army, Traquair was given a proclamation to deliver. The King made it clear that it was he not the bishops who was responsible for the new service book. Anyone who dared to oppose it directly challenged the King's authority. The proclamation was read on the twenty-second of February to a hostile crowd who greeted it with hoots and jeers. A rival protestation was read in the presence of his Majesty's heralds, who could not escape the crowd. They were bound to report to the King.

This created a need for a signed Covenant. Henderson and Johnstone were encouraged to complete it in a manner that would leave little open to debate. Not all ministers were convinced that Episcopacy was against divine law, so no mention was to be made of bishops. They were to ask all signatories to pledge themselves to defend the reformed religion and resist innovations, unless accepted by free assemblies and Parliaments.

***

It was now the twenty-eighth of February. According to posters and the word on the street, the National Covenant would be presented today. Supporters were to attend a ceremony in Greyfriars Kirk to commit to preserving the purity of the church.

***

Alex Hay was one such man. He'd spent five months in Leslie's army, with only sporadic contact with his family. The militia had grown rapidly after the riot, from a private army of mercenaries to a loosely organized force of thousands. They'd made him a lieutenant and put him in charge of a band of plough boys no older than his sons. Camped out within twenty miles of Edinburgh, they were supported by a group of farmers. Hay and his lads had entered the city this morning and sought shelter in an inn near Greyfriars. Leslie told him that they would not be needed until noon, after the nobility had their say. That gave him time to seek out his contact to see if he'd received any letters.

Walking the cobblestone street, he agonized over his personal affairs. Five long months had passed since he left his family. He was starting to have strange dreams. Jessie begging him to return… Ian asking for fatherly advice… and Dughall, his lord; warning him of imminent danger. What could it be? Was his family all right? Perhaps there would be a letter. His boots clacked as he approached his contact's row house. Standing on the stoop, he straightened his rumpled clothes and rapped on the door.

The portal creaked open and a man's face appeared in the crack. George Adams was a sturdy gent with green eyes and red hair. He was a blacksmith by trade, married, and the father of three adult sons. A staunch Presbyterian, he supported the rebellion. The man's eyes widened. "Alex Hay!" He glanced up and down the street. "Come in. I have something for ye."

Alex entered the house. It hadn't changed much in two months. There was a fireplace on one wall that was burning faggots of wood. An iron pot was suspended over the fire. Steam was rising from it; a sign that something was cooking. The aroma of soup made his stomach growl. There was an unmade bed, a small table, and two rickety chairs. "How have ye been, George?"

The man smiled, revealing rotting front teeth. "Good! Wife's gone to the country to care for her sick mother. Sit down! I'll bring ye some of her soup."

Alex thanked God for the man's hospitality as he took a seat at the table.

George spent a few minutes at the hearth and came back with a bowl. He placed it in front of Alex and brought him a dirty spoon. "Eat! Ye look half-starved."

Alex wolfed the cloudy soup, which was a concoction of chicken broth and stringy leeks. It was just what he needed to keep hunger at bay. "Thank ye, friend."

"Aren't they feedin' ye?"

"Oh, aye. It's been tough these last months, lodged at that farm house. My men and I stay in the barn with the animals. As to the food… Can't expect anything better than what the farmer eats."

George made a small sound of agreement. "That'll change. I hear that more than fifty thousand pounds arrived in the city, as well as men, weapons, and supplies. We'll find out more today."

This was good news. It had been a challenge living with Leslie's army, which lacked stable quarters and a reliable source of supplies. Sometimes, they didn't know where they would stay the night. Alex had been one of the lucky ones. Upon leaving Drake, his son had given him a bag of gold coins and the name of this man as a contact. Help was only a month away if he needed to ask for it. "Things are bound to get better. Will ye go to Greyfriars with me?"

"Aye, for sure." George stood and walked to his bed. The big man got down on his knees and reached underneath, extracting a small wooden box. He stood and brought it to the table. "This was hand delivered here a week ago. It's a fancy piece of work."

Alex stroked the top of the box. Crafted of black walnut, it bore the sign of a lion's head. "It's from my son,' he said under his breath.

"Yer son sent this?"

"Aye."

"Does he have a crest on his jacket that looks like this lion?"

Alex's heart squeezed. "Aye. Did he deliver it?"

"Seems so. Gave me a fair reward for taking it." He sat opposite him. "Will ye open it?"

Alex nodded. He took out his dirk and worked the lock, managing to pry it open. As he'd hoped, there was an envelope on top that bore the wax seal of the Duke of Seaford. Dughall had been here days ago! Beneath it was a layer of gold and silver coins and a sprig of rosemary. His heartstrings tugged when he realized that it was from Jessie.

George's eyes widened. "Yer son must be a man of means."

Leslie had told him not to mention his connection to the Duke. Still, he didn't want to lie. "He owns a fleet of ships that sail out of Moray Firth."

"Explains it. What about the letter?"

Alex unfolded the parchment. It was a one page note written in his son's hand. He read silently...

Dearest Father... I hope that this letter finds ye well. Mother is in good health but poor in spirit as she misses ye terribly. As ye can see, I survived the advent of the new year in spite of the curse of the sword. There is a story to tell when I see ye next. Ian, our wives, and children are well and I have adopted a lad. Perhaps ye remember him, the miller's step son. My duties have taken me to London to appear before the King with my brother G. (Forgive me for speaking in code.) Our visit was an eye-opener and I am beginning to understand yer position. Which brings me to the purpose of this letter. In the course of our meeting, I learned something that raised concern for yer safety. The King is determined to squash the rebellion by rounding up and executing the ring leaders. He has poured over sixty nine petitions and compiled a list of names that appeared frequently. Father, I am sorry to say that ye are on his list of traitors.

Alex felt like he'd been kicked. How could anyone call him a traitor? He loved his country so much that he was willing to give his life for it! Fear replaced anger as he recalled the prescription for a traitor's death. Hanging 'til near dead... drawing... and quartering... He swallowed hard.

Uncle Robert is on the list as well. Oh, the shame of it! My brother G and I are expected to participate in this roundup of traitors. G is commited to his Majesty's wishes, but I am struggling with my conscience. How I wish ye were here! In any case, we have agreed to protect ye, but ye must stay away until I send word that it's safe. I will send a letter to Uncle Robert. I have to go as a ship is waiting for us. My heart is heavy and my thoughts confused. I will find a way to resolve this, even if it means my life. Stay well, write, and ask Commander Leslie to contact me. I may have to make an unpopular stand. Goodbye for now. Yer loving son, D.

Alex's heart ached. Dughall needed him desperately. He'd placed him in an unbearable situation. If anything happened to him on his account...

"Are ye all right?" George's voice was insistent. "Ye look like ye've seen a ghost."

Alex folded the letter and put it in his jacket pocket. "Bad news, I'm afraid."

"About yer family?"

"That and more. I can't talk about it." He stood, closed the box, and placed it under his arm. "Come along, my friend. With these coins, we'll have a good meal at the inn. God knows my lads need it."

George smiled. "Family problems, ye say? A couple of whiskies will fix ye up."

"Ye could be right. Then we'll head over to Greyfriars Kirk."

His thoughts were dark as they left the house. Would the Covenant result in negotiation or an all out war with the Crown? He longed for a quick resolution.

***

GREYFRIARS KIRK LATER THAT MORNING

The place chosen for the presentation and acceptance of the Covenant by the gentrie was Greyfriars church. It was located in the upper yard of the monastery of the Franciscans, or Greyfriars as they were called. It was a plain building, but large enough to accommodate large throngs of men. Around the church was a vast cemetery, containing hundreds of burial stones. There was a grassy slope at the bottom of which was the Grassmarket, a market square of sorts and a place of public executions. This was surrounded by lofty tenements which looked down upon the gibbet, a gallows-style structure which was used to execute and display criminals. On the northern skyline lay the castle, a reminder of ancient heroes who shed their blood in pursuit of liberty.

On this day, calls for freedom could be heard throughout city streets, from the lowliest man to the loftiest lord. It started early on this chilly morning. Through streets, alleyways, and closes; from comfortable mansions and apartments, the nobility traveled to this spot to fast, pray, and sign their names to the National Covenant. Along the way they encountered crowds of citizens, many of them strangers, ready to join and do their part. They gathered in the church yard and cemetery, praying, singing, and pledging support. The sound of their entreaties could be heard for a mile. As noon approached, they were joined by the men of Leslie's army.

***

Hay and his men arrived at the church at noon after consuming a good meal and a fair amount of ale. They hooked up with Leslie's army and joined in the praying and singing. Their intentions were heartfelt and after a while, there was nary a dry eye in the battalion.

Alex had recovered from the shock of the letter. Convinced that he was on the right path, he agreed with those who wanted a free Scotland. Radical as that was, it would achieve what everyone wanted. The right to worship the true religion… the right to rule by governing bodies… only then would he be free of the label placed upon him, that of a traitor. He stood with General Leslie, awaiting the arrival of the Covenant. "There's something I must tell ye."

Leslie seemed irritated. "What is it, Hay?"

Alex felt humbled. "I received a letter from my son, the Duke." He proceeded to tell him about the note, except for the personal details.

Leslie's eyes flashed. "So we've been marked as traitors!"

"He didn't mention yer name."

"Ye can damn well believe that I'm on that list too. I guess it's expected."

"I didn't expect it."

"So, the Duke wants to talk to me?"

"He does. After meeting with the King, he's gained an understanding of our position."

The commander rubbed his hands together. "Good. He's willing to go against his brother?"

Alex reddened. "It seems so. The letter was no more than a note."

"Then we'll welcome him to our side." He paced. "We need supplies. Bandages, scalpels, and medicines… Not to mention horses, wagons, and weapons... Can he contribute men?"

Hay shrugged. "Most of his subjects are Catholic. But some of the others may join us."

"What will he do about the roundup of traitors?"

The word caused his stomach to flop. "I have no idea. We must contact him."

Leslie seemed pensive. "I will use my niece Jenny as a go-between. When the Covenant is signed, I'll ask Lord Balmerino to deliver a copy to her and request an audience with yer son. It's time that they met."

Alex agreed in principal. As they shook hands, he noticed a

procession arriving at the church. A cheer went up. "They're here with the Covenant."

Leslie smiled. "I can take one man into the church for the reading of the National Covenant. I choose ye, Hay."

His heart swelled with pride. "Me?"

"Aye. It's important that ye witness this."

***

It was two o'clock in the afternoon. The procession was led by the lords Rothes and Loudoun, the Ministers Henderson and Dickson, and the lawyer Johnstone, who carried on high a ram's skin parchment, four feet long and over three and a half feet wide. Everyone could see that upon it was inscribed the National Covenant of Scotland. They entered the church with great flourish, to emphasize the importance of the occasion.

Because of the size of the crowds, only a select few were allowed to follow; nobles, burgesses, barons, ministers, and General Leslie's representatives. The church was packed to capacity. The seats were full and behind them men stood shoulder to shoulder. The heat generated by thousands of bodies served as an incentive to begin.

Alex Hay stood in the crowd next to Commander Leslie. He was familiar with the church as he'd been here in July, to attend the reading of the book. That day and those that followed had completely changed his life.

The crowd grew quiet as Minister Henderson took the pulpit. Dressed for the occasion, he wore a dark suit with a ruff collar. Stately and erect, he had neatly trimmed facial hair and bushy eyebrows. His dark eyes shone as he opened the proceedings with a prayer that was urgent and decisive.

Alex's nerves were on fire. Surely this was the message that God meant them to hear!

They barely caught their breath when Lord Loudoun walked back and forth across the front of the church, eloquently stating the righteous cause of the Covenanters. A seasoned politician, the man with sunken eyes and long nose presented the case for rebellion. When done, he was greeted with grunts of agreement and a round of heartfelt applause. Amidst the clamor, Archibald Johnstone took the pulpit. The round-faced man waited for the crowd to calm. Then taking the parchment in hand, began to read the National Covenant slowly and clearly for all to hear.

Alex listened intently. He was an intelligent man, but some of this was beyond his understanding. The first part was a repetition of the King's Confession of 1580, and its rejection of 'all kinds of Papistrie.' Growing up on the seacoast during a period of peace, he'd had no exposure to it. The second part specified the Acts of Parliament that suppressed Popery and established the Protestant religion. He glanced at Leslie and saw that he was attentive.

Johnstone took a moment to catch his breath. He scanned the crowd to heighten the drama and began to read the third part, which consisted of an elaborate oath to maintain the true reformed religion. "Finally, being convinced in our minds and confessing with our mouths, that the present and succeeding generations in this Land, are bound to keep the foresaid national oath and subscription inviolable, we Noblemen, Barons, Gentlemen, Burgesses, Ministers, and Commons under subscribing, considering diverse times before and especially at this time, the danger of the true reformed Religion, of the King's honor, and of the public peace of the Kingdom... By the manifold innovations and evils generally contained, and particularly mentioned in our late supplications, complaints, and protestations, do hereby profess and before God, his angels, and the world solemnly declare that with our whole hearts we agree and resolve all the days of our life, constantly to adhere unto and to defend the foresaid true Religion..."

This, Alex understood. Having made the case, they were asking them to take a solemn oath.

Johnstone continued on. At last, he came to the beginning of the conclusion. "...And therefore from the knowledge and conscience of our duty to God, to our King, and country, without any worldly respect or inducement, as far as human infirmity will suffer, wishing a further measure of the Grace of God for this effect... We promise and swear by the great name of the Lord our God to continue in the profession and obedience of said religion, and that we shall defend the same and resist all those contrary errors and corruptions, according to our vocation, and to the utmost power which God hath put in our hands all the days of our life..."

Alex wondered how the King could object. The document stated that there was no intent to diminish the monarch's greatness or authority. He would ask General Leslie about it later.

"...Most humbly beseeching the Lord to strengthen us by his Holy Spirit for this end, and to bless our desires and proceedings with a happy success, that Religion and Righteousness may flourish in the land, in the glory of God, the honor of the king, and peace and comfort of all of us. In witness thereof we have subscribed with our hands all the premises."

Alex saw a tear running down Leslie's cheek. What did it mean when this great man showed such raw emotion? He turned away and watched as noblemen and ministers were invited to come forward.

James Graham, the Marquess of Montrose, was the first to affix his signature. Sir Andrew Moray was next. They were followed by the lords Rothes, Cassillis, and Eglinton.

Alex couldn't help thinking that he'd been identified as a traitor for signing petitions. Would this be another nail in his coffin?

The gentry were done and the rest were invited to sign the oath. They streamed to the pulpit and signed willingly, some with their own blood. There were many wet eyes, as they knew of the sorrows to follow.

Alex Hay followed his commander to the pulpit. When it was his turn, he took the quill and inscribed his name as clear as could be, adding the phrase 'until death' after it. He had no doubt that he would be called upon to prove it.

Chapter 38
Home Again

March 21st 1638
THREE WEEKS LATER 6AM

DRAKE CASTLE THE BREAKFAST CHAMBER

The breakfast room was nearly empty. The sun was beginning to rise, casting rays of light through the tall windows. Because of the early hour, only a few had been inclined to leave their beds. Dughall had risen early to meet Ian for a private conversation. After breakfast, the brothers planned to ride their horses to the moor.

Breakfast had been a hearty affair consisting of poached eggs, ham, and a variety of breads and pastries. This was accompanied by a tray of butters, preserves, and pots of steaming hot tea. There was far too much food for two men.

Dughall watched with amusement as Ian snatched four pieces of brown bread and stuffed them into a pouch. His brother had an endless capacity for eating. "How far are we going?"

Ian smiled. "Three miles." He rolled the remaining strips of ham in a napkin and stuffed it in the bag. "I have something to show ye."

"That's enough food to last us to sundown. Will we miss the mid-day meal?"

Ian reddened. "Nay." He closed his hand around an imaginary handle and flexed his muscles. "Since I started practicing with the throwing axe, I can't seem to get enough food."

Dughall thought that this might be a good time to talk. "I need a favor. Fang Adams is willing to do what he does best, but he'd like to serve as my protector. Can ye train him?"

Ian's nose wrinkled. "Fang?"

"What's wrong?"

"He's an animal! I saw what he did to the prisoner. Duff deserved to be punished, but..."

"I ordered that."

Ian's eyes widened. "Specifically?"

Dughall sighed. "Nay, but I gave Fang free reign to punish him. That makes me responsible for what ye witnessed."

"Two years ago ye couldn't kill a hare!"

"'Tis true. I acted out of anger for what he did to Luc. I could blame the sword, but it's not the only thing that's changed me. My days as an innocent are gone." He felt sad. "I had to grow up. Soon we will be embroiled in a conflict that will test our mettle."

Ian frowned. "What conflict?"

"I've been quiet about my London trip because I was deciding what to do. The King gave the Gordons the task of keeping peace in Aberdeenshire. We are expected to use our influence to suppress protests to the liturgy book."

"But some of yer subjects are involved."

"I know. That's not the worst part. The King identified the ringleaders of the rebellion and compiled a list of traitors. Gilbert and I are expected to round them up and turn them over to the Crown."

Ian let out a low whistle. "Do ye know what they do to a traitor?"

"Oh, aye." Dughall felt compelled to tell him the rest. "Father's name is on that list."

Ian's voice was anxious. "How did that happen?"

"He carried petitions throughout the northeast and signed them at every stop. The name of Alexander Hay appears prominently on seven of them."

"Does Mother know?"

Dughall shook his head. "Nay, but we will have to tell her. When she begged me for news, I told her we hadn't seen him. She knows that I left a letter for him."

"What did ye tell him?"

"That he's been marked as a traitor. I asked him to stay away until I send word that it's safe. Gilbert has agreed to let him be as long as he doesn't set foot in the county."

"Poor Father." Ian looked miserable. "So we are expected to round up our own people?"

Dughall kept his voice low. "I thought about this long and hard, brother. Executing men for the sake of their religion goes against my beliefs. I plan to oppose the King."

"Does Gilbert know?"

"Nay. I shall tell him when it becomes an issue."

"How long will it be before we're on that list?"

Dughall swallowed hard. "Not long. I would understand if ye decided to leave me. Go back to Peterhead where it's safe."

"Nay!" Ian stood and grabbed his pouch. "I'm with ye brother. Let's ride to the moor before all hell breaks loose. We can talk along the way."

Dughall joined him. "So, will ye train Fang to fight alongside us?"

Ian winced. "Aye. We'll need every able bodied man we can get."

***

THE FOREST WEST OF DRAKE CASTLE 7:30AM

The mist made for slow progress as the brothers rode through the thickening forest. After a harsh winter, the trees and shrubs were coming to life. The path narrowed, so Ian took the lead. Dughall loosened the reins and encouraged his stallion to follow. As they merged with the sights and sounds of the forest, he took time for private reflection. The events of the last few weeks weighed on his mind.

***

They'd taken a ship from Edinburgh to Peterhead to shorten the journey. This was a good move because the weather turned, blanketing the northeast with snow. After staying a night at 'The Crack', they'd started on horseback towards Huntly. A trip that would have taken a day in good weather took two on snow covered roads. They arrived at Huntly exhausted. There, Dughall faced an unpleasant reception. Gilbert's subjects were afraid of him. They'd heard about the gory execution, as well as his efforts to save Luc's life. Fang had given him the title of Blackheart, and no one was willing to dispute it. Gilbert wanted the torture master gone. So the next morning, Dughall, Jamison, and Fang left Huntly to return to the safety of Drake.

Once home, the Duke had been reminded of life's simple pleasures. Keira had welcomed him with open arms. She'd been feeling better since the morning sickness passed. She'd even made an effort to be kind to Luc. His loving wife was back, untouched by her brush with the Morrigan. She allowed him to make love to her.

Luc was overjoyed to see him. Since the adoption, he'd become the perfect child, obeying his elders and attending to his studies. The puppy had given him a reason to live and the adoption gave him a family. Wee Maggie melted into his arms. She'd changed so much! Now eight and a half months old, she could sit alone, crawl across the room, and say "momma" and "dada".

Ian had been tasked with keeping order at the castle. He'd performed his duties well and deserved a rest. Dughall decided not to burden him with his troubles, masking his feelings for a while.

***

Now, the cat was out of the bag. As they trotted through the mist, he knew he made the right decision. His brother was eager to support him.

Ian slowed his horse. "We're nearing the moor."

The path widened as they rode into a clearing that bordered the moorlands. From there they traveled a hundred feet and merged with a rare scene. An eerie landscape lay before them, higher than its surroundings but not quite mountainous. Heather, gorse, and rough grassland was interspersed with bare rock. The moor was wet and windy and haunted by the calls of birds.

Dughall put aside his troubles and basked in the beauty. There were peat bogs too, reminding him of his childhood. His nose wrinkled from the pungent smell. "Remember when we used to cut peat?"

Ian nodded. "Aye. We'll never have to do that again."

"I didn't mind it. Life was simple then." Lightning was getting restless, stamping his feet. Dughall tapped the reins and guided him next to his brother. "What did ye want to show me?"

Ian smiled. "Months ago, ye assigned me a task. Follow me." He turned his horse and galloped to the other side of the moor.

Dughall loved surprises. He urged his horse on, following his brother into the forest and up a narrow deer path. Soon, they came to a clearing where he took in the majesty of the moment. An ancient circle of stones lay before them with a remarkably intact altar. One of the flankers was down as well as two of the standing stones. It was knee deep in docks and nettles.

Dughall thought of what he would say to his wife. Who could describe this scene which required the pen of a poet? He smiled inwardly. They were three miles from Drake Castle. Surely her people would come to him now.

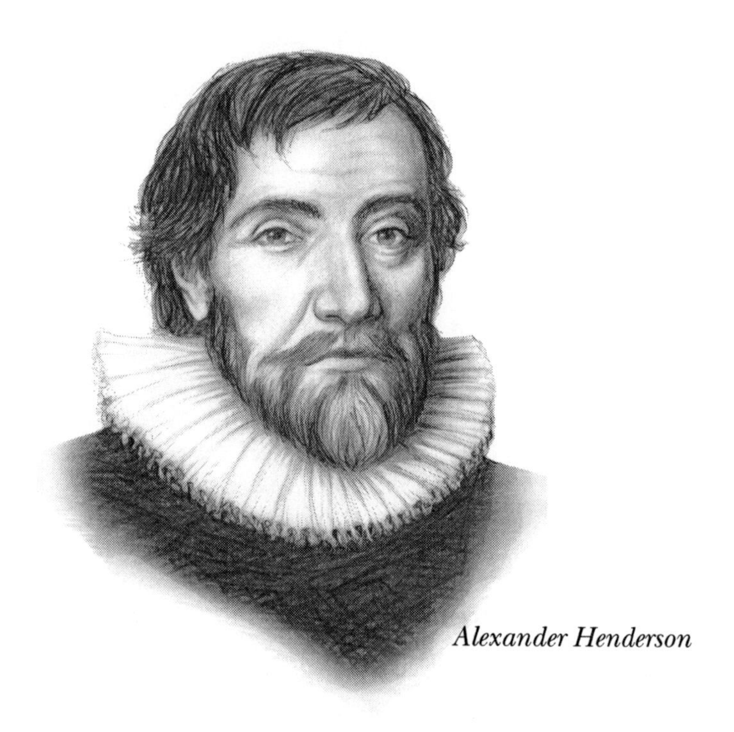

Alexander Henderson

Chapter 39
A Minister from Fife

April 30th 1638
FIVE WEEKS LATER

EDINBURGH

Spring had come early to the city of Edinburgh. The weather was unseasonably warm, encouraging trees and vegetation to flourish. Rain fell almost daily, filling collection barrels and providing fresh water for the city. The inhabitants went about their lives as usual. Mariners went to sea, tradesman plied their trades, and merchants hawked wares. Taverns prospered while children roamed the streets, running errands and begging. One would never suspect that the city was the breeding ground of the rebellion. Since the signing of the Covenant, it was a hub for military and religious men involved in the mobilization.

Alexander Henderson was one such man. The Presbyterian minister from Fife was known as an eloquent and powerful debater. A firm believer in the power of the pen, this was his second brush with an unreasonable monarchy.

***

Twenty years prior, he'd courageously opposed the Five Articles of Perth. King James introduced these dictates to impose Episcopalian principles on his Scottish subjects. Like other objectors, Henderson was threatened with banishment and the loss of his stipends and office. Not to be intimidated by threats, Henderson opposed the innovations, refused to comply, and composed a book questioning the validity of the Perth assembly. Summoned before the court of High Commission, the minister prepared to accept the King's wrath. But when he debated the charges against him with talent and force of reason, his judges could gain no advantage over him. They released him with a warning, promising to deal with him harshly if he re-offended. King James eventually retreated from his demands. The minister from Fife retired to his parish and stayed out of the public eye. Twenty years later, the struggle ignited again.

***

GREYFRIARS CHURCH AN OFFICE IN THE RECTORY

Henderson was now in his mid-fifties. His joints were stiff and sore and hardly a day passed without pain in his chest. He'd hoped to spend the rest of his days in his rural parish, but that wasn't likely to happen. Not since King Charles revived his father's quest to impose Episcopalian principles on the Scots. As a minister, he'd been ordered to purchase the new liturgy book for use in his parish or face a charge of rebellion. It was a demand that coaxed him out of semi-retirement to write protests, craft petitions, and direct the proceedings of nonconformists. Taking up residence in Edinburgh, he gave impassioned sermons condemning the proposed religious innovations. When the King refused to reconsider, he drew up the National Covenant.

Henderson sat at a desk, massaging his aching fingers. He longed to return to his parish, but knew that there was no hope of a quick resolution. It seemed that they were headed for war. The weight of the world rested on his shoulders as he waited for Lord Balmerino. *This time we are committed until death. The Church of Scotland must be free!*

There was a knock at the door, accompanied by a cough. The minister checked the knife in his sock. "Who is it?"

"Lord Balmerino."

He relaxed. "Come in."

Lord Balmerino entered the room and took a seat. He carefully removed his gloves and waited to be acknowledged.

"John."

"Alexander, my good friend. How is yer arthritis?"

Henderson winced. "I have a flare up, but it means nothing." There was no sense trying to hide his condition. His swollen finger joints betrayed him.

Balmerino smiled sympathetically. "Ah, the perils of growing older. But consider the alternative."

The meaning wasn't lost on the minister. He'd been identified as a traitor, the penalty for which was a horrible death. "Hmmphh... What do ye want?"

"I've received communications from a contact in Aberdeen. The Covenant is being resisted. Few have signed the document."

The minister was anxious to have the voice of all Scotland on their side. The city of Aberdeen was too important of an exception. "What's causing the resistance?"

Balmerino took out three coins and placed them on the desk in a narrow triangle. "Forgive my poor illustration. Three cities are giving us trouble." He pointed to the two lower coins as he spoke. "Glasgow and St. Andrews seem indifferent to the Covenant. We think that they will be forced to support us once the southern border is threatened." His finger traveled to the third coin, in the upper right. "Aberdeen is another story. Two things are at play there. Throughout the county there are remnants and symbols of the Catholic and pagan religions. Church art, abandoned monasteries, stone circles, and Pictish monuments. There seems to be a tolerance for their existence."

"So the innovations might be seen as another sign of diversity?"

"Perhaps. Or not something to risk yer skin over."

"Hmmphh.. What else?"

Balmerino coughed. "Pardon me. The Highlands are home to a fair number of Catholics who would naturally be indifferent to our cause. They are led by Lord Gilbert Gordon, the Earl of Huntly."

Henderson frowned. "Most of the northeast accepted the Reformation."

"True. But many Protestants in Aberdeenshire are indebted to the house of Gordon. Their economic and religious influence is impressive. The Earl convinced most conservative ministers to reserve judgment on the new book. Their congregations followed suit."

Henderson's blood boiled. "How dare they interfere with ministers of the Church of Scotland? This is an outrage! What should we do?"

"Accompany me to Aberdeen, my friend. Speak, debate, and cajole. It's what ye do best. Bring those wayward congregations to our side!"

"I will *make* them sign the Covenant!" the minister said forcefully. "What will ye do?"

"I will talk to local nobles. With a bit of luck, they might come to our side. Then we will ride northwest to pay a visit to an important man."

Henderson was sure that he knew the answer. "The Earl of Huntly?"

"Nay. I've sent Colonel Munro to Huntly to make him an offer that will be hard to refuse."

"Who shall we see if not the Earl?"

"I have a way of circumventing his influence. We shall enlist the help of Lord Dughall Gordon, the Duke of Seaford."

He was surprised. "The Earl's brother? Why would he help us?"

Balmerino smiled. "Someone dear to him serves as a lieutenant in our army."

"Who?"

"Alexander Hay, the man who raised him. The Duke considers him a stepfather. Hay's name is on the King's list of traitors."

It was starting to make sense. "Does the Duke know?"

He stifled a cough. "Aye. According to Leslie, he's offered to help the cause."

The minister smiled. "What do we know about this man?"

Lord John coughed. "Quite a lot, actually. Some of it is disturbing. He is not a man to be trifled with. We will talk about it along the way."

"When do we leave?"

Balmerino stood. "Tomorrow, my friend. Gather yer bible and scrolls and meet me in the alley at dawn."

Chapter 40
Fathers Brothers and Sons

May 19th 1638
TWO AND A HALF WEEKS LATER

HUNTLY CASTLE

Gilbert Gordon stood in his study, looking out the window. It was late morning and the courtyard bustled with activity. Servants hurried across the flagstones, lugging water buckets and baskets of food. Others toted wood for bakehouse fires and carried yeast from the brewhouse to the bakehouse. A few men and women wielded brooms and shovels. Per his instructions, the courtyard and outbuildings were to be swept clean, removing debris from the winter. Spring had arrived. The river Deveron was swollen to its banks from frequent rains, which had infused life into the bleak landscape. Trees and plants blossomed, attracting a myriad of butterflies and bumblebees.

Gilbert's heart was light. It was hard to believe that he was master of it all. He'd awakened that morning to the sound of birds twittering in the trees. Rolling over in bed, he'd been blessed with the sight of his lovely wife, sleeping with their son at her breast. Wee George had given him more joy than he could have imagined. He loved being a father. Gilbert smiled as he thought of the child. The boy had spoken his first real 'word' yesterday, calling him 'Dada'. He sniffed his silk shirt for signs of the wee one's scent.

There was a knock at the door, breaking his reverie. "Come."

Connor entered the room and bowed slightly. "Forgive the intrusion, my Lord. Sir Robert Munro is at the gate. He desires an audience with ye."

Gilbert's brow wrinkled. "Munro? Father spoke of him once or twice. He's an officer who served in the German wars."

The servant agreed. "We've had dealings with the Munro clan, some good and some disastrous. I wonder what he wants."

"Has he come a long way?"

"He said that he came from Edinburgh."

The Earl was suspicious. During the last few months, he'd been approached by royalists and rebels, hoping to gain his support. He had a feeling that this was more than a social call. "Tend to his horse and offer him lodging for the night. When he gets settled, bring him to me."

"Will that be all?"

"Ask Marcia to bring us tea and scones."

"As ye wish." The servant left the room, shutting the door quietly behind him.

Gilbert sat down at his desk to think. It had been two months since they'd returned from London and a week since he'd received a letter from the King. The monarch knew about the unrest in Scotland. In his letter, he condemned the Covenant and promised to bring the rebels to justice. He praised the Gordons for their actions in the northeast, which had kept the city of Aberdeen in the royalist camp. They could expect to be rewarded after taking care of one outstanding issue. The Earl opened the desk drawer and saw the letter, along with a scroll that contained a specific directive. Two days ago, he'd dispatched a courier to Drake with a letter summoning his brother.

The door opened and Marcia entered, carrying a tray of tea and scones. She set it on the sideboard. "My Lord. Shall I pour ye a cup?"

He closed the drawer. "Aye, Marcia."

The woman placed two tea cups on the desk, one for Gilbert and one for his intended guest. She arranged a plate of scones between them, along with pots of jelly and butter. Pouring his tea, she asked, "How is the wee one today?"

Gilbert smiled. His subjects were enthralled with the baby. "Wee George is doing well. He can hold his head up for quite a while and creep along the floor."

"A prodigy! I remember when ye were a babe. Such great blue eyes just like the wee one."

The Earl knew that his mother had died at birth. He was raised by a nursemaid. "Marcia, did ye know the lass who raised me?"

The servant smiled. "Aye. She was Jenny Craig, a mother of two. She had just finished nursing a babe and was honored to take the Earl's son."

"I don't remember her."

"The lass was forbidden to see ye after the weaning. She tried to get a glimpse of ye, but stayed her distance."

"Is she alive?"

"Nay, my Lord. She died ten years ago."

He was saddened by the news. She was the closest thing he had to a mother. "What about my father? Did he ever hold me?"

Marcia hesitated. "A few times, perhaps. Once at the baptism." She blushed as she began to make excuses. "It's hard for a man when he loses his wife."

"Tell the truth."

She sighed. "Ah, well. Blackheart was a cold one. He was proud that he'd sired a son, but that was as far as it went."

Could his opinion of his father sink any lower? "Thank ye, Marcia. That will be all."

The servant gathered her tray and left the room.

Gilbert's thoughts were full of ire. *I'll never forgive him for what he did.*

***

DRAKE CASTLE

The Duke's library was a comfortable place. The windows were open, admitting the sounds and scents of a fine spring day. Dughall savored it. Breathing deeply, he identified the smell of wet earth mingling with the fragrance of wood smoke. Standing at the window, his senses heightened. He heard dew dripping from trees, the trill of a robin, and the laughter of children in the courtyard. For a moment, he felt one with everything around him. It was a feeling that he had often as a lad, standing on the sea cliffs at Whinnyfold. As a man, he missed it terribly. Nature was a wonder to behold. It was sacred, strong, and resilient. Men played a role in this magnificent equation. Surely they could learn to get along. If they could see God in all things, the symbols that divided them would melt away.

Dughall kept this in mind as he sat down at the desk. His trusted advisor Jamison was expected. They had a number of things to discuss. He'd received a letter from his father at the beginning of April, thanking him for the warning. Deeply wounded by the accusation of treason, Alex agreed to follow his advice. He would stay and fight with the army until it was safe to return. He sent his love and respect and begged him to keep Jessie safe. Yesterday, he'd received a second letter from Alex, which he planned to read to Jamison. He'd also received a letter from Gilbert, summoning him to Huntly.

The situation in Scotland was reaching a critical point. Copies of the Covenant were circulating, gathering signatures and inspiring common men to leave their homes to fight in the army. His subjects were split on the matter. Supporters of the Covenant, led by Jenny Geddes and Minister Keith, held fiery meetings and prayer events. They'd met with Dughall to force his hand, but so far had been unsuccessful. The Duke had managed to play both sides. He'd avoided signing the Covenant and participated in an effort to make cooler heads prevail. This involved traveling with Gilbert to Aberdeen to discuss the matter with conservative ministers. Much to his relief, the King hadn't yet provided them with a list of traitors. When that happened, he would be forced to make a decision.

There was a knock on the door and Jamison entered, carrying a leather-bound ledger and a quill pen. He bowed slightly and sat at the desk. "My Lord. I have taken the liberty of reviewing the requests. It seems that everything is in order. All that it requires is yer mark." He presented the open ledger to him, along with the pen.

Dughall scanned the list. He trusted this man implicitly, so he affixed his signature to the end. There was simply too much to cover today. "How is yer wife?"

The servant reddened. "Jenny and Minister Keith left for Aberdeen yesterday with a group of supporters. Word has it that Minister Henderson intends to speak there."

"Are ye concerned for her safety?"

Jamison clenched his teeth. "Aye! There's nothin' I can do. The lass has a mind of her own."

"I remember ye saying that's why ye married her."

"It's different now. She's carrying my child!"

Dughall saw his point. "A babe at her breast will slow her down. Would ye like me to order her back?"

The man looked miserable. "Nay. I tried to stop her. She threw a plate at my head."

Dughall suppressed a chuckle. The image it invoked was funny. "Ah, well. We can deal with her later. In the meantime, we have two important matters to discuss."

Jamison seemed willing to get off the subject. "What are they?"

Dughall took a letter out of his jacket pocket. The outside was frayed and soiled. "This is from my father." He unfolded it and began to read out loud. *"My beloved sons. I write this by the light of a camp fire. My men and I are stationed far from Edinburgh (I can't say where), so I haven't been able to relay a letter. A military courier promised to get this into the right hands. Ye would be surprised to see me now. As old as I am, this body is strong and can handle a weapon like a young man. Many thousands have joined us, bringing horses and provisions, and yet we are lacking in both. We are preparing for a war that must be won if I am to come home as a free man."* Dughall sighed.

Jamison spoke, "My Lord. Ye don't have to continue if it's personal."

"I must." He continued reading. *"I've caused ye trouble and for that I'm sorry. But I beg ye to support the rebellion. As I write, our forces amass at the southern border. Either the King shall relent, or fight we will. Scotland must be free."*

Jamison let out a low whistle.

Dughall was solemn. "He goes on to express his love for my mother and the family. There are burial requests as well."

Jamison frowned. "Perhaps we've been misinformed. Many thousands have amassed?"

"That's what he said."

"So the lords and clergy of Aberdeenshire have the dissenting opinion. I wonder if Lord Gilbert knows."

Dughall frowned. "There's one more thing we need to talk about. I think it's related." He closed the ledger. "Gilbert has summoned us to a meeting. He received a directive from the King."

Both men were quiet for a moment, each contemplating the meaning of it.

"What are yer feelings about this, my Lord?"

Dughall sighed. "Sometimes I wish I didn't have the Sight. Our days of neutrality are gone, my friend. We have to make a stand."

Jamison's expression darkened. "When is the meeting?"

"Tomorrow. We must leave in the morning."

"What about my Lady's trip to the stones?"

Dughall sighed. "I will ask her to put it off. If she objects, Ian and Gilroy can take her."

***

HUNTLY CASTLE

Gilbert was pouring cream into his third cup of tea when Sir Robert Munro was escorted into the room. Months ago he would have added whisky or foregone the tea for a dram, but watching his wee son grow changed all that. He now had a steadfast rule. No whisky ever. And no ale or wine until the midday meal. The Earl stood to greet his visitor. "Colonel Munro." He extended his hand in friendship.

"Lord Gordon." The trim, neatly bearded man was dressed in a military uniform. He shook his hand and released it. "I'm a General now. Thank ye for seeing me at short notice."

Gilbert took a seat and motioned for Munro to join him. The military man moved carefully, pulling out the chair and sitting down. Gilbert poured him a cup of tea, topped off his own, and invited him to partake in the scones. He studied the man's demeanor as he slathered jelly on a pastry. "I am unfamiliar with yer pursuits. As ye know, I only recently succeeded my late father."

"I'm sorry for yer loss."

Gilbert almost said 'Don't be.' But there was no need to reveal the hatred he had for his father. "Thank ye, Sir. My father died over a year ago. His death was unexpected, but warranted."

Munro raised his eyebrows.

Gilbert continued, "Father spoke of ye several times. According to him, ye served in the German wars."

He took a sip of tea. "I served decades in the Swedish army under Gustavus Adolphus, the Lion of the North. Clan Munro fought valiantly as part of the MacKay Highlanders regiment, laying siege to cities and securing victories. We are fierce fighters, highly skilled with the sword and half-pike."

"Impressive. Ye appear to be in uniform. What are ye doing in Scotland?"

Robert Munro cleared his throat. "We have a vast amount of military skill. More than seven hundred of us have returned to Scotland to liberate her from the demands of an unjust King."

Gilbert was shocked by his frankness. "Why are ye telling me this?"

"I assume that ye know about the National Covenant."

"Aye."

"The Covenant has been well received in all but three places. Glasgow... St. Andrews... and Aberdeenshire... The Covenanters would like to speak and act with the support of all Scotland."

"Hmmphhh..."

"Glasgow and St. Andrews will comply when hostilities break out on our southern border. The city of Aberdeen is openly opposing it."

Gilbert was doing a slow burn. "What do ye want from me?"

"Lord Gordon. I was sent here by a consortium of lords and nobles who support the Covenant. We are aware of yer family's influence in the northeast. We are desirous that ye join us in this great cause."

"I don't think that I can."

"Hear me out." General Munro presented a number of convincing arguments. But he'd saved the best one for last. "If ye join us and sign the Covenant, we would make ye a leader of our forces. Furthermore, we would make yer state and fortunes greater than ever before. We would pay off and discharge yer debts, which as far as can be told are one hundred thousand pounds sterling."

This got Gilbert's attention. He wasn't struggling by any means, but there was an attraction to being debt-free. Still, only a fool opposed a powerful King. "What will happen if I don't join ye?"

Munro's face hardened. "Our forces and associates stand one hundred to one against the King's. Without a parliament, he is unlikely to get the funding to raise a decent army. There is no purpose to taking up arms against us." He took a breath. "In that case, we would find a way to ruin ye."

Gilbert didn't like being threatened. Yet such was the way of war. The offer was tempting to an ambitious man like himself. His head ached as he thought about the King's directives.

"Yer answer?"

This was insane! He thought of what his father would do and then made an ill-fated statement. "The Gordons have risen and stood by the kings of Scotland. Even if this proves the ruin of the King, I will lay my life, honors, and estate under the rubbish of his ruins."

General Munro stood. "An unfortunate choice, seeing as it may come to that."

Gilbert joined him. "I have nothing against ye, Sir, or yer clan. Thank ye for bringing the offer."

Munro nodded. “I will relay yer message to my colleagues in Edinburgh. Many have had a long and profitable past with yer family. That will soon change. Our hope is that ye’ll reconsider.”

Gilbert didn’t reply.

“Goodbye, Lord Gordon.” The soldier turned and left the room abruptly, leaving the Earl alone with his thoughts.

Gilbert was shaken. He resisted the urge to get lost in a bottle and headed for the nursery. His son’s future was at stake as well. His thoughts were dark. No matter which way they turned, they were in deep trouble. The Gordon clan needed to make a united stand. Perhaps his brother would have an answer.

Chapter 41
Meeting of Minds

May 20th 1638

ONE DAY LATER EARLY AFTERNOON

TWO MILES FROM HUNTLY CASTLE

The highland forest was teeming with life. Pine trees stretched to the sky, sporting orange-brown bark and green foliage. Oak leaves burst from bud scales, providing meals for hungry caterpillars. Birds flitted in the canopy, gathering beetles and aphids for their chicks.

Dughall and Jamison rode two abreast on the trail to Huntly. The Duke's senses heightened as the narrowing path forced them to single file. He became aware of his horse's earthy smell and the supple reins between his hands. He gazed upward into the pines; where redpolls and bullfinches trilled. It reminded him of the times he and Gilbert rode their stallions to the moor. A sparrow hawk appeared in a flash, striking down a spotted thrush. Its loud screech was followed by the warning calls of other birds. It was a reminder of the fleetingness of life.

Dughall forced himself to look away and concentrate on the path ahead. He was feeling anxious. Two things weighed on his mind. The meeting with Gilbert promised to be a sticky one. His brother was a royalist and there was little chance he would change his mind. The other thing was the way that he was perceived there. Even his friends saw him as a force to be reckoned with.

Dughall studied Jamison's backside. Due to the injury, one of the servant's shoulders was slightly lower than the other. He sensed the man's tension as they neared Huntly. They were traveling alone against his advice.

Lightning neighed nervously as they approached a fork in the trail. The horse was restless, reflecting the mood of his rider. Dughall patted his neck. He recognized the signs of a worried horse; ears flicking back and forth and roving eyes. Before long the animal would be breaking a sweat. He took a breath and released it slowly. Perhaps if he lowered his energy, the horse would calm as well. It worked. Lightning took a sympathetic breath and let it out audibly through his nostrils. It sounded like a sigh. After the split, the trail widened.

Dughall guided his horse along side his servant. "Lightning is too sensitive to my moods. We must work with him before I take him into battle."

Jamison grunted. "Rider and beast must act as one in a skirmish. We'll start the training when we get back."

They broke the deep forest and came upon a medieval road made of cobbled stones. The horses' hooves clopped noisily as they traversed it. The sound reminded him of a road near Drake and caused him to think about his wife. Keira was visiting the circle for the first time today. They'd taken two months to clean up the site, removing debris and straightening stones. Because of its pagan roots, the location was a closely held secret. It worried him that he couldn't be with her. He spurred on Lightning and galloped ahead of Jamison. It gave him a sense of freedom.

"My Lord, wait!" Jamison whipped his horse to keep pace. "What's wrong?"

"I'm worried about my wife."

"She's in good hands."

"I know it." He'd intended to take her to the stones himself until duty made it impossible. He'd ordered Ian and Gilroy to accompany her, giving them specific instructions. The men were to arm themselves and take a winding route that would end at the moor. From there, they would go on foot through the woods to the circle. This part bothered him, because of her delicate condition. The men were prepared to carry her if she tired.

Jamison seemed to read his mind. "They won't let any harm come to her. She's carrying our future master."

The Duke allowed himself to smile. Fatherhood gave him great joy. In spite of earlier misgivings, he was looking forward to the birth of his son. The dream seemed false in the midst of so many urgent realities.

"No one would dare to hurt her after what ye did to Aiken."

Dughall hated being reminded. Everyday, he heard whispers of 'Blackheart' and gossip about the 'Dark Lord'. Sometimes he imagined that Fang encouraged it. He was worried about his wife. "Will they be safe from outlaws?"

Jamison chuckled. "Aye. The Dark Lord's reputation spread far and wide. Pratt heard talk in an Inverness tavern."

"Oh God."

The servant snickered. "I think ye should play the part. Wear a black cape and carry a scepter."

"Jamison!"

"I'm serious. Carry the blade as well. We'll need every advantage if we go to war."

"I've been practicing with it every day." He heard the rush of the river Deveron and the sound of water slapping the banks. The bridge to Huntly was ahead. Dughall felt uneasy. Normally he would be overjoyed to see his brother, but this time was different. Gilbert's letter had been short and insistent. It was a sign of the trouble they were in.

Jamison squinted. "I see the tower."

Dughall gritted his teeth. "I hope we get a better reception than last time."

"Get used to it. Revel in it. This is how they treat a Dark Lord."

***

MILES FROM DRAKE CASTLE

Three riders followed a road through the highland forest. Stallions bore two muscular men, armed with swords and dirks. They rode on either side of a young lady of stature, who guided an exquisite red mare. Five and a half months pregnant, she was clad in a loose fitting dress and a hooded cape.

The lady could barely contain her excitement. They were nearing the stone circle. Keira's heart fluttered with anticipation. The description of the site awakened her fantasies. More than a year had passed since she'd stood in a circle and served as Priestess. So many things had happened since. The Goddess had granted her requests. She'd married the man she loved and was carrying his son. They were well cared for and had enough to eat. Dare she ask for more? The lady marveled at the changes in her body. She'd gained weight and had womanly breasts. She'd examined herself in a full length mirror that morning. Her skin was radiant and her belly swelled. She loved being pregnant.

There was only one thing that overshadowed her happiness. Except for Mary and Jessie, she was friendless here. This month had been particularly lonely. Mary was occupied with the twins while Jessie grew despondent over her husband's absence. The truth couldn't be denied. She'd left her friends in the woodland village.

A whinny escaped from her mare's nostrils. The animal was dear to her heart. Keira turned to her brother-in-law, riding beside her. "Are we almost there?"

Ian smiled. "Aye, my Lady. The circle is in a forest beyond the moor. Are ye tired?"

"Nay. Dughall protects me too much. I'm stronger than he thinks."

Ian nodded. "Just like my wife." He turned to the other man. "We're coming upon the moor. Make sure that we're alone."

Gilroy rode on ahead at a fast clip, kicking up dirt in the road.

Keira frowned. "The trail was deserted. Why must we be so cautious?"

"Perhaps ye should ask yer husband."

"I'm asking ye."

Ian reddened. "There are men who seek to destroy my brother. They will stop at nothing to gain advantage over him."

"Would they hurt us?"

"Perhaps... or abduct us for ransom."

She feared for her child. "Why do they want to destroy him?"

"My brother is an important man. They expect him to commit to one religion and defend it to his death."

"Dughall will never do that."

"Exactly. My brother defends each man's right to worship as he pleases. This includes some misunderstood religions."

Her heart sank. "Oh. Mine. So I am responsible for the danger he faces."

Ian seemed frustrated. "I wish it were only that."

"Then what is it?"

"A struggle is taking place between groups of Christians. Powerful people are involved, including our King. My father joined an army. It's likely we'll go to war."

She found this bewildering. "They would fight a war over religion?"

"I'm afraid so. We'll know soon enough."

Her heart was troubled. "Why did my husband seek a stone circle in the midst of this madness?"

"None of us know. But it's important that we keep it secret."

"I shall."

Gilroy galloped towards them. "It's clear ahead. We're the only ones on the road."

They guided their horses until they came to a split in the road. There was a break in the canopy, allowing sunlight to stream through. Wildflowers painted the ground red, white, and blue with poppies, mayweed, and cornflower. They were as plentiful as ragwort in Spring. Gilroy led them onto a path that they followed for several hundred yards. Progress was slow as the servant stopped to clear overhanging branches. Finally, they emerged from the forest into a wondrous scene.

Keira was breathless. The moorlands were a stark and unfriendly place. To the untrained eye, it seemed a mass of scrub and boulder. Yet it had a strange beauty. She listened to the cacophony of nature. This place was home to thousands of nesting birds. They were all creatures of the Goddess. "Where is the circle?"

Ian pointed. "The path lies beyond that stand of trees. The rest of the journey is on foot."

The three dismounted and secured their horses. They crossed the moor on foot, entered the forest, and started up a narrow deer path. After a hundred yards, they came to a clearing.

Keira's heart soared as she took in the sight. A magnificent circle of stones stood before her, complete with an altar and two flankers. "Great

Goddess!" She walked to the center of the circle and stood in silence. Time stood still as she basked in the power of the place. Energy pooled in the center and radiated to the stones. The altar held the highest charge. The lass was overcome with emotion. Tears streamed down her face as she held her hands to the sky. "Great Goddess. I stand here in love and humility, soon to be a mother. Grant me a healthy child." Energy coursed through her body and awakened the child within her. She felt him move! Oh joy! She spoke softly, "My son shall know ye. I promise it."

Keira closed her eyes, seeking a prophetic vision. In her mind, her friends appeared among the stones, performing a ritual. The Goddess knew what she needed. She felt herself lifting off the ground and soaring above the circle as a bird. Her friends joined her one by one, until they were a flock circling the stones. A sparrow hawk dived from above, striking down one of their males! More attacked in the midst of shrieks, preying on the strongest. Nature didn't work this way. The females and young were next. Keira opened her eyes. She was hot, shaky, and her heart was beating like a drum. What was the Goddess telling her?

Ian took her arm. "Ye seem unsteady. What's wrong?"

She leaned on him. "We must go back. I had a disturbing vision."

***

HUNTLY CASTLE THE STUDY

They'd shared a cigar and reviewed the King's request without involving their man servants. Dughall expressed a flurry of moral objections. He was unwilling to roundup the rebels. The Duke had never seen his brother so agitated. Gilbert paced the floor and threw up his hands in exasperation. The man seemed close to a breakdown. Even so, Dughall felt compelled to make his case. "Brother, listen to me. We must do what's right."

Gilbert reddened. "I cannot do this! How can we oppose our King?"

"He's wrong! Men should have the right to worship as they please."

Gilbert clenched his teeth. "The King is not threatening *our* right to worship. He assured me that we will be allowed to maintain our churches. He's married to a Catholic!"

Dughall hadn't thought about the Queen in a while. The woman had made her intentions clear, offering him an open invitation to her bed. "We can't trust this King's word. How long will it be before he targets us?"

Gilbert frowned. "I don't know. Obviously, ye won't support me. What do ye intend to do?"

Dughall took a breath. "I plan to support the rebels, covertly. Armies are forming south of Edinburgh, preparing to fight the King's forces. I've lost a hundred men to the cause."

"I know about the armies! General Munro paid me a visit representing lords and nobles who support the Covenant. They offered to pay off and discharge my debts if I agreed to lead their forces."

"That's a generous offer. Was it tempting?"

Gilbert reddened. "Of course, but I had to turn him down. The meeting didn't end there. Munro promised to ruin me if I didn't comply."

Dughall was surprised. "He threatened ye?"

"Aye." Gilbert sat down and wiped the sweat from his brow. "I hate to admit it, but I wish that Father was alive. As head of this clan, I'm in a dangerous position. Supporting either side could bring me ruin."

"I see what ye mean."

Gilbert sighed. "I must stay loyal to the crown. I could be drawn and quartered if I oppose the King. So could ye."

"Even so, I must risk it."

"Do ye know what's involved in drawing and quartering?"

"Aye."

"The Gordons must present a united front!" Gilbert clenched his fists. "Why would ye do this? Is it because of yer stepfather?"

Dughall couldn't lie. "Partly. The King said that we're to deliver him to London."

"I told ye that we would protect him. My men won't capture him as long as he stays out of the county."

"He will eventually return home to my mother."

Gilbert scowled. "Don't be naïve! He can never come home. The man made his bed and now he must lie in it. If the King insists on his capture, we'll send yer step parents to the colonies."

Dughall didn't want to lose his parents to a foreign shore. "Sending them away is a last resort. In the meantime, I intend to support the rebels."

"Why, brother?"

"I believe that their cause is just. More importantly, I think that it would be safer if we were on opposite sides of the issue. One of us may come to ruin, to be saved and supported by the other."

The Earl's face was grim. "As long as we avoid the hangman's rope… or worse… Our heads could wind up on London Bridge."

"I know it." They were silent for a moment, contemplating that reality.

Gilbert was pale. "Ye propose that we stay on opposite sides of the issue. I daresay that ye chose the more dangerous path." He sighed deeply. "The idea has merit. What will we do if we meet on a battlefield?"

Dughall loved this man. "We'll cross that bridge when we come to it."

***

LONDON, ENGLAND PALACE OF WHITEHALL

Sunlight streamed through windows in the King's office, raising the temperature to an uncomfortable level. The King seemed unaffected by the heat, while his guest struggled to keep his composure.

James Hamilton had been summoned that morning. The 3rd Marquess of Hamilton had no time to prepare his thoughts. The man had attended to his cascading brown locks, but had neglected his long fingernails. These he tried to hide as the monarch ranted. My God, it was warm! The last thing that James wanted was for the King to see him sweat. Sitting across from the angry monarch, he'd endured attacks on the character of his fellow Scotsmen.

He hadn't been a true Scotsman in decades. After moving to London at age eleven with his father, the 2nd Marquess of Hamilton, he'd spent time at court and was educated in Oxford. Influenced by the Duke of Buckingham, he'd been trapped into a marriage with his low-born niece. When his father died suddenly at Whitehall, he received his annuity from the court and became the 3rd Marquess of Hamilton. King James passed three weeks later, leading to the coronation of Charles I, at which the young James Hamilton bore the Sword of State. How had he fallen so far from grace?

James pulled out a lace handkerchief and patted the sweat from his forehead. How could the King say that he was a Scot? Oh, it was true that he was born in Scotland. He'd been designated the Earl of Arran after the death of his insane great uncle. At one time, he was in line to the throne of Scotland, if the House of Stewart failed to produce an heir. *Perhaps that's it. He considers me a rival.*

"Are you listening to me?!" Charles gripped the desk in frustration. "What's wrong with you, Hamilton? I feel like I'm talking to a wall."

His heart almost stopped. "I *am* listening, my King! Forgive me if I seem distant. I was thinking that my countrymen must be possessed by the devil to oppose you."

The monarch nodded. "Possessed they are! Laud and I came to this conclusion last night. Perhaps it's just the ringleaders."

James was emboldened by the King's response. "Your Majesty. As you have astutely observed, the common man may not be at fault. Perhaps something can be done to appease their discontent."

"Hmmm…"

James added quickly. "Of course, your interests are non-negotiable."

The King's eyes narrowed. "That goes without saying. You are my chief advisor in Scottish affairs. I am appointing you commissioner for Scotland so you can investigate and recommend a way to appease the discontents."

"From London?"

"Of course not! I will update you on the situation in your homeland. We have powerful allies in the northeast, Glasgow, and St Andrews who have been willing to share information with us. We are awaiting one more report from Lord Huntly. Once apprised, you will leave for Edinburgh as my commissioner with the specific task of resolving the crisis."

Hamilton had no desire to leave England, even though it would mean getting away from his nagging wife. The last time he'd left was seven years ago, to lead a force of six thousand men to assist Gustavus Adolphus. After four years in Germany they'd returned from the failed expedition, having lost many to disease and starvation. He swore that his military days were over.

The King's face was red. "Well?"

James swallowed hard. "I will do what you wish, my King." He wanted to say more but didn't trust his mind to find the right words. Ever since he'd suffered a head injury in the war, he had occasional trouble assigning words to objects. Few knew of his disability, but those who did attributed it to family madness.

The King seemed satisfied. "I chose you because of your military experience."

Military experience? James thought. *My army was destroyed by poor leadership, disease, and starvation.* He experienced a sudden sensitivity to light and shaded his right eye. It was the start of a crippling headache. "Forgive me, your Majesty. Do we anticipate an armed conflict?"

Charles I stroked his neatly trimmed beard. "It's possible. I've been told that Alexander Leslie and Robert Munro have been engaged to lead the Covenanter forces."

Hamilton winced. The names struck fear in his heart. Leslie and Munro had impressive records. They commanded fierce fighters who were loyal to the death. Would these men follow them? "Are they forming an army?"

The King looked grim. "It would seem so. There are reports of troops amassing south of Edinburgh."

Hamilton's world was falling apart. He broke out in a full body sweat. "This is madness!"

"Possession by the devil, as you said."

He made a small sound of agreement. "I will do everything in my power to appease the discontents. This conflict will tear this nation asunder, pitting brother against brother and father against son. It must be avoided."

The King stood. "Those are strong words, worthy of the King's commissioner. Use them to convince your countrymen of the futility of this revolt."

James stood and joined him. "I shall, your Majesty."

The King's tone was threatening. "I'm depending on you."

Chapter 42
Vengeance

June 15th 1638
THREE AND A HALF WEEKS LATER

THE FOREST OF DEER

Vengeance is mine, saith the Lord. These were the words that were foremost in his mind as he searched for the pagan village. The priest's joints ached in spite of his holy purpose. Uneven ground was a challenge for a man with arthritis. The trails seemed to punish his knees. Unyielding rock slabs, plummeting descents, and thudding drops over boulders compressed his joints and caused considerable pain.

***

The last few months had been difficult. The church wouldn't sanction this mission. With religious strife plaguing the land, no one cared to listen. People turned a blind eye to his fiery sermons. Even his brother refused to support him. Some days it seemed that even God was against him. Out of desperation, he'd recruited three mercenaries, paying them secretly from church coffers.

Father Ambrose justified it. First there had been Hamish's account of the events at Drake. He'd witnessed a pagan act and was banished from the castle because of it. The journey home had caused his demise. His brother had died of the grippe. News arrived of a gruesome execution and proof of the Duke's power over life and death. Witnesses saw him bring a drowned child back to life. At last, Ambrose's accusations had been vindicated. Gordon's own people feared his supernatural powers. Finally, news came that a child had been conceived, the spawn of a witch and this warlock. To prevent the birth of this abomination, he would attack their pagan roots.

***

They'd been hiking since dawn. It wasn't a problem for the mercenaries. The soldiers moved through the forest in tight formation, armed with long swords, bows, and throwing axes. The priest relied on his walking stick. His bones creaked, but he didn't complain. It would be a mistake to show weakness. The soldiers entered a clearing and declared it a place to rest. They sat on the ground and passed a flask of water.

Gibb handed out strips of salted meat. "Eat this, Father. Ye'll need strength to face their men."

The priest chewed the strip, wondering if he'd be able to get up.

Rourke was a giant of a man with a tattooed face. "Are we close, Father?"

Ambrose nodded. "This is the place where we captured the witch."

"Should we kill all the villagers?"

"We will allow a few women to escape to carry the story to Lord Gordon."

Rourke seemed pleased. "So the children die too?"

"Aye."

Gibb snorted. "Can we take them as slaves?"

The priest's eyes narrowed. "Nay. They're the spawn of the devil. It's best that we be done with it."

One soldier sat apart, listening to the callous discussion. Cameron Hunter was an archer known for accuracy at great distances. He was an exotic looking man with long dark hair and high cheekbones. "I didn't agree to kill children."

The priest scowled. "Ye agreed to follow my orders."

The archer stared. "Only cowards kill children."

"They're pagans!" Ambrose cried. "The root of the trouble between Christians. Eliminate them and we can go forward as brothers."

"Killing children is wrong!"

Ambrose reddened. "Are ye not a Christian?"

"Aye."

"I am a priest. Allow me to determine right and wrong."

Cameron made the sign of the cross. "God forgive us."

Ambrose wondered if he could trust him. He struggled to stand, leaning on his walking stick. When he got his balance, he urged them on. "Rise and find the village!"

***

THE FOREST VILLAGE

The barn had a familiar warmth to it. The sweet aroma of hay mingled with the scent of dung from a cow, her calf, and two baby lambs. Aileana felt blessed. The calf and lambs would provide them with milk and wool for many seasons to come. She'd grown up in the past year, serving her people as healer, bonesetter, and occasional midwife. She'd moved into Keira's cottage and taken responsibility for the barn. She still took care of her brothers Torry and George, sewing and cooking meals. Now that they lived in separate cottages, she'd come to love and appreciate them. The cow bellowed, acknowledging her presence.

"Ye're spoiled," she said, placing a handful of oat straw in the trough. "I fed ye this morning." The animal munched lazily. Aileana smiled as she looked into the lamb pen. Two adorable black faces stared up at her and began their plaintive baaaa's. There was one male and one female, named Mungan and Morna. She reached down and stroked Morna's coat. The wool was white and wiry, yet soft to the touch. It would make a wonderful sweater. "Hush. I'll feed ye now. Or perhaps we should wait for George." She'd sent her brother to fetch a ball of twine.

The male nuzzled her hand, searching for food. The lambs were growing insistent now, crying loudly in unison. Aileana grabbed a handful of oat straw. Feeding the twins, she wondered, "Where is that lad?"

***

George McFay ran through the woods with his red hair flying behind him. The ten year old was feeling guilty and more than a little afraid. His sister had sent him to fetch twine, but he had gotten distracted. The warm day tempted him into the woods. It was a fortunate thing. He'd spied on a band of men who appeared to be armed and dangerous. He couldn't hear their words, but their gestures were threatening. They were heading towards his village.

The lad sprinted, jumping over logs and low boulders. When he reached the village, he could barely breathe. He saw Michael and Torry at the wood pile and ran to them. The sound of an axe splitting wood rang in the air. "Stop!" George cried. He knew that the sound would bring the men to them.

Michael put down the axe and wiped his brow. "What's wrong?"

George's heart pounded. "There are men in the woods! Armed with swords and axes! One had a bow."

Michael's eyes widened. "How many?"

"Four. They're coming this way."

"From which direction?"

George pointed to the path he'd emerged from. "There."

Torry sucked in his breath. "Great Goddess! How far away are they?"

"I ran like the wind. One man has a cane, so that will slow them up. They'll be here in the time it takes to walk to the circle."

Michael picked up his axe. "Gather the women and children and take them out of the village. Torry. Tell Kevin and Morgaine to alert Craig and Jeanne and the Birnies, the Wests, and the Davies." He turned to George. "Tell Alistair and Janet, the Cummings, and fetch yer sister. The women and children must leave immediately and take nothing."

The boy frowned. "What about the animals?"

"Take my horse and leave the rest."

"What? My lambs..."

"Forget them!" Michael roared. He turned to Torry in a panic. "I will gather picks and knives. The axes can serve as weapons. Tell the men to meet me at the barn to defend the village."

"I'll fight with ye!" George cried.

Michael squeezed his shoulder. "Nay, lad. Ye must lead the women and children to safety."

George was disappointed. "Where will I take them?"

Torry tucked a knife in his belt. "Remember the map?"

"The one from Lord Dughall?"

"Aye. Use it to get to Drake Castle." The sixteen year old embraced his brother. "I'll come for ye when it's safe. Be brave."

George stared. "I will."

Torry had a strange look in his eyes. "Ask Lord Dughall to send help."

"But, brother..."

"Tell my sister that I love her."

George struggled to hold back tears. Something told him that if they made it to Drake, his brother and Michael would be dead. He watched the two men he admired most run in opposite directions. With a sense of dread, he hurried to the barn to fetch his sister.

***

NEAR THE VILLAGE A HALF HOUR LATER

The archer was a bundle of nervous energy. They'd located the village and were observing it from a distance. The priest identified the witch, wielding an axe at a wood pile. Two men worked nearby, splitting and stacking logs. They appeared to be unarmed and unaware of their presence. The raiding party spread out in two directions. Cameron was sent with Gibb to rouse the women and children from the cottages. They were ordered to hold them at knifepoint, bind them, and lead them to the square. They'd searched nine cottages and found no one.

Cameron was having misgivings. He didn't like these soldiers and was starting to wonder about the priest. Father Ambrose had recruited him in a tavern for a military mission. The archer had killed plenty of men in his day, but never a child or a woman. He'd managed to avoid blood feuds and religious crusades. How could this be what God wanted?

***

Cameron had no wife or children. As a lad, he'd fallen in love with a red-haired lass and suffered terrible consequences. Gráinne... Sweet Gráinne ... Her name meant 'Goddess of Grain'. He'd loved her so much that his heart ached to think of it. He was the only who knew she was carrying his child. His family objected when they planned to marry because of religious differences. They cajoled, argued, and threatened to disown him if he went forward with the ceremony. He told them that he intended to marry her nonetheless and take her to a neighboring county. Then tragedy struck. Cameron returned from a day in the fields to find that Gráinne had been murdered. The girl he loved had been burned at the stake for following the old religion. His heart was racked with poisonous emotions: anger, rage, revenge, and guilt. When he learned that his father was responsible for her death, he left his family to begin a new life.

***

Cameron froze as they approached the last cottage. How could he take part in the same acts of madness that killed his beloved Gráinne? This priest seemed far from Godly - conceited, judgmental, and self-righteous. This was wrong!

Gibb whispered, "They must be huddled together in there."

Cameron thought he heard a baby cry. He swallowed hard and announced his decision. "I won't kill these people."

"Ye can't back out now."

"I can."

Gibb grabbed his shirt. "We trust each other because we're equally guilty. The priest will order us to kill ye."

"Then so be it."

The soldier released him. "Fool! I'll deal with ye later." He ducked into the remaining cottage and returned empty handed. "There's no one inside. Where are they hiding?"

They heard shouts and saw a group of men resisting Rourke and the priest. Crudely armed, they were trying to defend their homesteads. Gibb drew his sword and ran off to fight them. The archer watched from a distance. The villagers fought valiantly, but were no match for soldiers with swords and axes. They were falling quickly. Five men lay motionless on the ground, their bodies hacked and bloody.

Father Ambrose taunted a lad who was cradling a broken arm. He drove him out of the village with his cane, commanding him to run to Lord Gordon. It was about to get worse. The soldiers tied the remaining three men to a tree and surrounded it with fire wood.

They're going to burn those men alive! Cameron smelled smoke and heard the villagers' pleas for mercy. The priest laughed hysterically. The archer's blood boiled with anger. This was no holy man! What could he do? He was fifty feet away so it would take them a few seconds to get to him. He reached back, drew an arrow out of his quiver, and loaded his bow. He stilled his breath, took careful aim, and released the deadly dart. "Shooop….." The arrow flew and made its mark, straight into the priest's heart. Quick as a jackrabbit, he drew another.

***

HOURS LATER NINE MILES FROM THE VILLAGE ON A ROAD GOING WEST TOWARDS DRAKE CASTLE

They walked for miles under a cloudless sky. The weather was mild with a faint breeze, making it easy to travel. So far, the Goddess was with them. The women and children had been walking for five hours. They were tired, worried, and terribly thirsty. They'd fled the village with the clothes on their backs.

George felt important leading his people to safety. But the little boy in him was frightened. It was dangerous to walk these woods without men. Unscrupulous people could prey upon them. He looked back at the somber procession. The women walked slowly, carrying babies and shepherding the young. Morgaine led the horse, allowing women with infants to take turns riding. Aileana was busy, offering words of encouragement and bandaging scratches.

George noted that the sun was getting lower. If Torry didn't find them soon, they would need a place to stay the night. His thoughts darkened. Torry should have caught up with them. He was beginning to think that his brother was dead. He counted his people to relieve his anxiety. Ten… Fifteen… Twenty… Twenty-five… Twenty-nine… That meant they left nine men in the village to face the intruders. That was nine against four; good odds if they'd been armed. Did any of them survive?

Aileana appeared at his side, speaking softly to keep the conversation private. "Georgie?"

The term of endearment warmed his heart. "Aye, sister?"

"Dear brother. We must find water. The children are parched and starting to complain. Michael once told me that a stream runs along this road a hundred yards to the north."

George had an idea, "Do we have anything to carry water in?"

"Nessia brought a water bag and Janet has a flask. It's not much for this many."

The boy agreed. "Let's find the stream and stay there for the night. If Torry doesn't find us, we'll go to Drake tomorrow."

Her eyes misted. "The men would have found us by now. I fear that our brother is dead."

It hurt to see her forlorn. "Don't give up, sister! They might be wounded and unable to travel."

She lowered her eyes. "I'm their healer. I should have stayed with them."

His voice cracked. "Nay. Torry wanted ye safe. He told me to say that he loves ye."

Tears rolled down her cheeks. She quickly brushed them away. "I mustn't let them see me cry. I won't give up. I will pray to the Goddess to keep him safe."

George spotted a path between a stand of trees. He pointed to the right and whistled. "Follow this trail! It leads to a stream where we'll spend the night." He allowed his people to pass and found a sapling near the side of the road. "Give me yer hair ribbon, sister."

Aileana let down her hair and handed him the wool strip. She gave him a puzzled look.

George tied it to a branch. "This will help Torry to find us." He forced a smile, hoping to lift her spirits. The lad didn't reveal his true feelings. He'd seen the weapons the soldiers were carrying. Torry and the others were dead.

George didn't want to be important. He was ten years old, in charge, and his world was falling apart.

Chapter 43
Aftermath

June 16th 1638
EARLY NEXT MORNING

HALFWAY BETWEEN THE VILLAGE AND DRAKE CASTLE
CAMPED ALONG A STREAM

George McFay had been up half the night. He'd slept like a wolf protecting his pack, sometimes with one eye open.

They'd found the stream just as Michael described it. It was more of a babbling brook, calf deep; with slow moving water and tiny fishes. Thanking the Goddess, they'd quenched their thirst and set up camp for the night. A few women gathered berries and nuts, while Aileana and Morgaine searched for wild turnips and onions. George built a small fire to cook with and keep warm, but not so big as to give away their location. They shared a meal, gathered their children, and bedded down in pine boughs for the night. No one dared to mention the unthinkable. They talked about the men catching up with them and making a new life at Drake.

George didn't have the heart to discourage them. When the moon reached the highest point in the sky, he walked to the road to wait for his brother. But hours passed without a sign of him. With a heavy heart, he'd returned to the group and laid down beside Aileana.

Now George stood in the clearing, watching the sun rise in the eastern sky. It penetrated the woods, casting gold and purple hues upon his people. In spite of their trials, it was peaceful here. He remembered what Michael taught him. Peace was not something that others gave ye. It lived in yer heart and was expressed in yer life. It was the same with love.

Aileana touched his shoulder. "Brother?"

He turned. "Aye, sister?"

"Nessia and Morgaine are filling the water carriers. We must leave to make Drake by nightfall."

There was something unspoken between them. He sniffled. "I waited for Torry at the road last night. He never came."

Her voice was soft. "So have we lost him?"

The sunrise inspired him. "I don't know, sister. We can only hope for the best."

Aileana smiled. "Then ye understand the way the women feel. Our brave men stayed behind. Until we know that they've passed to the Summerland, we will speak of them as alive and well."

He took her hands. "I love ye, sister. Let's pray to the Goddess for the best."

***

THREE MILES AWAY ON THE MAIN ROAD

Two middle-aged farmers drove a horse drawn cart, carrying their goods to Drake Castle. Fergus and Farlan Keir had a long standing contract to deliver honey and bees wax. They'd just entered the road and were hoping to make Drake by supper. The Duke had a custom of offering hospitality to those who supplied the castle. They rounded the bend and took notice. A lad staggered in the road, cradling his arm in a makeshift sling. Farmers tended to look out for each other.

Fergus snorted. "Will ye look at that?"

Farlan never spoke more than three words at a time. "Know him?"

"Nay, but it looks like he's hurt."

"Pick him up?"

"Aye." They pulled alongside and yelled to the red-haired lad. "Need a ride?"

***

Torry could hardly believe his eyes. He'd been walking all night to catch up to his people. His arm was broken and he'd been stabbed, but he managed to stay alive.

Fergus offered a friendly smile. "Cat got yer tongue?"

"Uh…" His lips were so parched that it hurt to speak. "I would be grateful for a ride."

"What happened to ye?"

Torry thought it wise to hide the truth. "Broke my arm chopping wood."

Farlan winced. "Ouch! Done that."

"Well, come on up." Fergus climbed down and boosted him up onto the bench.

The pain was enough to make him cry. "Oh!"

"We should get that arm properly set. Where ye headed, lad?"

"Drake Castle."

Fergus got back into the wagon and sat beside him. "Ye're in luck. That's where we're headed."

Farlan whipped the horses and the wagon lurched forward.

Torry clenched his teeth. Each sharp movement caused him excruciating pain.

"What's yer name?"

"Torry."

"Got a brother-in-law named that. Where's yer people?"

The truth hurt. "Headed for Drake. Have ye passed a troupe of women and children?"

Farlan grunted. "Nay."

"Women and children only? Where are the men?" Fergus asked.

Torry's heart ached. "Mostly dead."

"Too bad," Fergus said. "Good men are hard to come by in these parts. Know anyone at Drake?"

"Lord Dughall Gordon."

"Ah! The Lord of the castle himself. Then ye'll be sure to find food and shelter." He smiled. "And help for yer arm."

The horses got into a rhythm and the wagon moved along at a fair clip. The farmers grew silent and fixed their eyes on the road. This allowed the lad time to think. Torry was grateful to be alive, but he wasn't ready to face his people. There was a heart-breaking story to be told, and he didn't know if he could tell it. Last night, wandering the dark road, he'd wondered why he'd been spared. He closed his eyes and prayed silently. *Oh great Goddess. My heart aches for the loss of my brave friends. I know not why I was spared.*

"Hey, lad! Are ye asleep?" Fergus shook his knee to get his attention.

Torry opened his eyes to a welcome sight.

Fergus smiled. "Know these people?"

Almost thirty women and children were emerging from the woods, led by his brother George. Torry's spirits soared. "They're my people."

"Will ye join them?"

"Aye. Thank ye for yer kindness."

"We're Fergus and Farlan Keir. Put in a good word for us with Lord Gordon."

Torry was grateful. "I will."

The wagon stopped. Fergus helped him down, being mindful of his injury. The landing caused him considerable pain and he almost dropped to his knees.

Aileana and George held him up. "Brother!"

"See ye." Farlan tapped the reins and the wagon lurched forward. Soon, they were out of earshot.

The women and children gathered around. Torry gazed into their faces and experienced the emotions there. Hope, love, and a touch of gratitude. As their priest, he owed them an explanation.

"His arm is broken," George said.

Aileana peeked inside his bloody shirt. "Ye've been stabbed! Lie down, brother."

Torry was weak, in pain, and suffering from a lack of water. “Nay. Allow me to speak to them.” He shook off his siblings and stood on his own. “Dear friends,” he started. But it was not to be. The forest seemed to spin and the ground rose to meet him as he fainted into his brother’s arms.

Chapter 44
State of Shock

June 17th 1638
NEXT DAY LATE AFTERNOON

DRAKE CASTLE THE LIBRARY

Dughall sat slumped at his desk, suffering from a frightening headache. It felt like he was being stabbed with an ice pick. The pain was sharp and radiated to his temples. "Aghhhhh... Oh, dear God!" The young man was in a state of shock. He hadn't slept in over thirty-six hours. He and his wife had been up all night, trying to make things right.

***

Yesterday had been a day from hell. News arrived of an injured lad traveling with a band of women and children. The lad's name was Torry and he claimed to know the Duke. This had been welcome news - his wife's people were coming to Drake. The odd thing was that only women and children were mentioned. If the messengers were right, where were the men?

Dughall packed a healer's bag and took a team of wagons to pick them up. What they found had torn their world asunder. Torry was delirious with fever and suffering from breaks and wounds. He'd been in a skirmish that only he could describe. He'd have to recover for that. Dughall dressed his wounds, which had been inflicted with a sharp blade. He coaxed him to swallow a potion and stabilized his arm in a brace.

The injured lad raved like a madman, begging for death. What had he witnessed? Dughall saw that the men were missing. Torry and George were the only ones left. He'd grilled George and learned about a possible attack. Dughall decided to return to Drake, to treat Torry in the surgery. He sent Jamison, Ian, and Gilroy to the village to retrieve the men and their possessions. They were accompanied by several wagons.

Dughall and Murdock led the procession to Drake, arriving before nightfall. They'd put up the visitors in the guest wing and instructed the staff to provide for them. Torry was rushed to the surgery, where

Dughall and Jessie worked on him until midnight. The lad raved until his fever broke. Then he became lucid.

Keira asked him about the missing men.

"All dead," Torry said.

Dughall thought she would lose the child. She'd collapsed to the floor and had to be lifted to a chair. When she recovered, Jessie took her to the women's quarters to inform them about their men. They'd stayed until morning, caring for infants and comforting friends.

Dughall remained with the injured lad. When they were alone, Torry delivered a message meant for his ears. It came from the old priest. *This is on yer head, Lord Gordon.*

It wounded him - causing more pain and guilt than he'd known in his lifetime. He begged for details. Eight men had been slaughtered on his account, three of them burned to death. The Duke was engulfed with rage, a feeling that was physically crushing. He promised the boy that he'd grant the priest an equally painful death.

Torry broke his fury. "Forgive him," he said. "That's what Michael would have wanted."

He'd fled the room in a sea of shame.

***

It had been a sleepless night that was followed by a day of conflict. His subjects were asking questions about the guests and spreading ugly rumors. His staff had been stretched to their limits, with so many more mouths to feed. Jamison usually handled these matters, assisted by his brother Ian. With both men away, the task fell to Murdock, who had trouble dealing with his subjects.

Dughall was sick at heart. Jamison was expected soon, bearing details of the carnage. He recalled that he'd been arrogant with the priest. He'd used his Sight to question his morality, naming his bastard son and calling him a thief. The memory caused intense throbbing on the side of his head. Flashes of light streaked his vision, causing sweating and nausea. *What is happening? Where is Murdock?* The door opened with a creaking sound that grated his nerves to a frazzle.

Murdock entered and brought forth a goblet. "Are ye all right, lad?"

Dughall accepted the cup. "Nay. This headache is frightening." He took a sip and frowned. "What is this?"

"Lady Jessie brewed a tea of feverfew."

The Duke gulped the bitter liquid. "Thank ye, Murdock." He felt his heart pounding in his temples.

"She said that it works on a stubborn headache."

He took a breath. "I hope it's true." He remembered the task he'd assigned to Murdock. "How are my subjects?"

The servant hesitated. "I met with Robson and Dobbie."

"Troublemakers."

"Aye. I told them ye were ill. We can't hold them off for long. They want to know about the visitors."

Why couldn't they understand charity? "We'll tell them soon enough. Is there word from Jamison?"

"He just arrived at the gate."

Dughall flinched. "Oh God."

Murdock smiled. "There's a bit of good news."

He was desperate for a good report. "What is it?"

"Jamison wants to show ye."

Dughall stood and nearly lost his balance. "I'm dizzy."

Murdock took his arm. "Allow me to guide ye."

The pain in his head was lessening. "All right, friend. But I must see Jamison."

The servant was steadfast. "Let's walk together." They took a few steps towards the door. "Ye seem steadier now."

They entered the hallway, where Dughall insisted that they separate. It was unwise to let the staff see him in such a state. They walked past the Lord's study, the retiring room, and a wall of family portraits. As they turned a corner to the next wing, they saw Luc coming towards them.

The boy's face lit up with recognition. "Father!" He ran to him and hugged him tight.

Murdock stiffened. "Master Luc. The Duke is suffering from a headache. It would be best if ye would amuse yerself elsewhere."

Dughall stroked the child's hair. Tiny flecks of hay dotted the straight brown strands. "Let him stay. This may be just what I need." He got down on Luc's level and rested his hands on his shoulders. "Have ye been playing in the barn?"

"Oh, aye!" The boy was excited. "With a new friend! His name is George."

"One of my wife's people?"

"Aye. He loves to hunt and he likes my dog!"

Dughall managed a smile. "Everyone loves Artus."

"For true. Will George be staying here?"

"I think so." Dughall loved being a father. "Have ye seen Maggie today?"

"Nay. I was just going there."

"I have business to attend to, so I won't see her until tonight. Give her a kiss for me."

"I will, Father. I love my sister."

Dughall stood. " I will see ye at supper."

Luc smiled. He glanced at Murdock and ran down the hallway.

The servant cleared his throat. "The boy has changed for the better, my Lord. When I think of how he used to behave…"

"There's good in everyone. All it takes is someone to love and respect ye."

Murdock nodded. "Let's see what Jamison has for us." They took the steps to the ground floor and stopped to get their breath. Murdock nodded to a guard and opened the door to the courtyard. "Shield yer eyes, my Lord. Bright sun always bothers ye when ye have a headache."

Dughall shaded his eyes as they went through the door. "I wonder why?"

Their boots clacked on cobblestones as they crossed the courtyard to a staging area on the side of the barn. On a usual day, vendors unloaded hay and livestock there. Murdock spoke, "Jamison is around back."

They rounded the corner and saw a cart loaded with livestock: a cow, a calf, and two baby lambs. Several cats slinked about, stalking crates of ducks and chickens. A second wagon was piled high with the villagers' belongings. Jamison stood talking to three familiar men.

Dughall could hardly believe his eyes. "Alistair! Kevin! David!" He approached the men. "Ye're alive and whole." He scanned the yard for the others.

Jamison spoke, "There's no more, my Lord. These three were lucky to escape with their lives. They were saved by an archer."

Dughall was intrigued. "Where is he?"

"Ian and Gilroy took him to the hole."

"Why?"

"There's a story to be told and a judgment to make."

Alistair spoke, "The archer refused to help the priest. Without his help, we would all be dead."

"I will take that under consideration." Dughall turned to his servant. "Murdock, take these men to their families; then bring back help to unload the wagons."

The servant nodded. "Shall we move everything to the cottages we built?"

"Aye."

"I'll be back." Murdock bowed slightly and led the villagers away.

Dughall's headache was almost gone. "This is the work of the old priest. After we deal with the archer, we must bring him to justice."

Jamison smiled. "That won't be necessary." He led him to the back of a wagon. "I have something to show ye." He pulled back a blanket with a grand gesture, exposing the priest's body.

Dughall sucked in his breath. Strong emotions flooded his senses - anger, misery, and relief. They were so intense that he couldn't speak.

"He won't bother us again, my Lord."

The Duke managed to find his voice. "How did this happen?"

"The archer killed him as he was about to set fire to those men."

This was unexpected. "What was he doing there?"

"He was one of three mercenaries hired by the priest."

It was a puzzle. "What happened to the other soldiers?"

"The man's an accomplished archer. He shot them from a distance of fifty feet."

Dughall was impressed. "We need this man on our side. Why did he stay in the village?"

"Kevin said that he helped them bury their dead."

"There *is* hope for this world, my friend. This is a man I need to meet."

***

DRAKE CASTLE THE CHAPEL

The Chapel was a small gathering room by castle standards, only twenty by forty feet. Stained glass windows spanned floor to ceiling, providing rainbows of colored light. The granite walls were decorated with tapestries, depicting the Immaculate Conception. The chamber was furnished with a marble altar, kneeling rail, and six carved pews. Its centerpiece was a life size statue of the Blessed Virgin, clad in a blue robe and white hood. She pointed to her heart, which was prominently displayed on her chest. Fresh lilies decorated the altar, signifying purity, sweetness, and everlasting life. Their sweet fragrance permeated the air.

Janet was grateful for this place. After a night of mourning her husband, she needed a place to pray. Jessie had escorted her here, after seeing to her daughter-in-law's comfort. They were concerned that Keira would lose the child.

Janet approached the sculpture with a sense of wonder. In her world, the Goddess had three guises; maiden, mother, and wise crone. Surely this was the Goddess in her mother state. She felt light-headed as she kneeled before the statue. "Oh, great Goddess. Alistair was a good husband, gentle father, and brave protector. He gave his life so that we could live." Her voice choked with emotion. "He worshipped ye with a faith that was strong and true. Take his hand and guide him to the Summerland." Janet looked up at the statue. The heart appeared to be glowing. "I know not why this happened. But I surrender to yer wisdom. Bless the Duke for providing this place of refuge." Janet was in the early stages of pregnancy, almost to her third moon cycle. Alistair had been hoping for a boy. She touched her belly. "I carry his child. A son, I'd hoped, for my husband." She heard rustling behind her. Jessie must have returned to fetch her. Footsteps sounded and came closer. The woman was compassionate. Perhaps she would help her get up.

A familiar male hand rested on her shoulder, causing her to tremble with delight. Magic was at work here. The Goddess had granted her a last tender touch. Her heart filled with gratitude. "Oh, Alistair. I wish ye were truly here."

"I am, lass," he said, offering her a weathered hand.

Janet took his hand and allowed him to pull her to her feet. As he drew her close, she smelled his body, musty from a day of work. Surely, this was a dream.

Alistair cupped her face and kissed her tenderly. "Life is so precious."

The trek, no sleep, and this blessed apparition - left her light headed and unable to stand. The room seemed to spin as she smiled sweetly and fainted in his loving arms.

***

DRAKE CASTLE THE HOLE

The holding cell was infested with mice. Rusty chains hung from the walls, encrusted with dried blood. An evil chair sat in the center, equipped with leather restraints. It smelled like a week old chamber pot.

Cameron Hunter was an unhappy man. Upon arrival at the castle, he'd been disarmed, bound, and led to this cell. Here he'd been searched, shackled, and assigned to a man who threatened him with torture. The archer sat on the floor, staring at his fettered wrists. *How could this be?* After saving the men, he'd expected a hero's welcome. *It's true what they say. Let no good deed go unpunished.*

Cameron knew that he was at the mercy of a man known as the Dark Lord. He'd heard tales about a gory execution and the man's supernatural powers. But he knew that rumors could be tainted by the teller, according to their fears or agenda. He decided to judge for himself. Would he be granted an audience with the notorious man? Had he stolen his pleasure by killing the priest?

The cell door creaked open, admitting the prison keeper. The fearsome man had a whip on his belt, but was carrying a ring of keys.

Cameron tried to read his intentions. Which would it be - the whip or his freedom?

The keeper seemed disappointed. "The Duke will see ye now." Lice jumped from his hair as he stooped to unlock Cameron's shackles.

The archer stood and massaged his wrists. The shackles had rubbed him raw in places.

"Gilroy is coming for ye," the keeper said.

His heart pounded. "Am I being released?"

"Dinna ask me. I'm the prison keeper. Fang Adams."

"How long have ye served the Duke?"

Fang stared. "Since the first of this year."

"Is he a fair man?"

"Aye. He's the only man who gave me respect."

Gilroy entered the cell. "Yer imprisonment was a mistake. The

Duke wishes to see ye."

Cameron was relieved. The meeting was no more than a formality. "Can I have my weapons back?"

"After the meeting." Gilroy led him down a hallway. They took the steps to the first floor and entered the castle proper.

"Why does he want to see me?" They continued up a second staircase.

"He wants ye to stay."

Cameron's thoughts darkened. Why should he stay? The Duke had a bad reputation. The hallway was well lit with sconces at regular intervals. There were paintings, sculptures, and glass windows. They passed people, the last being a young woman with flaming red hair. Cameron could hardly believe his eyes! Had the woman he loved come back to haunt him? His heart was breaking. He turned and shouted to the vision. "Gráinne!"

The girl looked back and smiled innocently, then continued on her way.

Cameron was dumbstruck. She had flowing red hair, clear blue eyes, and a face of endearing freckles. It had to be her. "Come back to me, Gráinne!"

Gilroy chuckled. "Her name is Aileana. She comes from the village whose men ye saved."

His heart skipped a beat. "Is she married?"

"Nay." They arrived at the study and knocked. "The Duke is within."

Cameron watched the girl disappear around a corner. His heart was waking from a long sleep. "She's enchanting."

Gilroy held the door open. "The lass can wait! Are ye coming?"

The archer nodded. What did it matter if he served the Dark Lord? She was reason enough to stay at this place.

***

The Duke sat at his desk, contemplating a course of action. He'd been informed that the archer was on his way.

Jamison stood by to provide protection. "We shouldn't have thrown him in the hole."

Dughall agreed. They would have to apologize and make him a generous offer. After discussing it with Jamison, he'd agreed to use a bit of dark influence. The Duke was willing to exploit his reputation. He was dressed in an outfit befitting a Dark Lord; a kilt, silk shirt, and a black velvet doublet. On one end of the desk lay a bone handled dirk. "I'm starting to like these clothes."

"Ye look powerful in them," Jamison said. There was a knock on the door. "Come."

Gilroy escorted the archer into the chamber. He bowed slightly and left. Jamison motioned for Cameron to take a seat.

The archer sat and looked around. His eyes settled on the Duke and then lingered on the unusual weapon. He took a breath. "My Lord."

Dughall's eyes narrowed. "Am I?"

Cameron reddened. "For now."

"Who do ye serve?"

The archer hesitated. "No one. I issue from Ayrshire, though I haven't been back in years. I've made my home in cities and seaports, looking for work."

Dughall knew, but he had to ask. "What is yer line of work?"

"I'm a mercenary."

"An archer, I hear, and a damn good one."

"Aye. I'm a soldier too, skilled in hand-to-hand combat."

"Yer name?"

"Cameron Hunter."

Dughall picked up the dirk and ran his thumb along the edge of the blade. His voice was cold. "It seems we have a score to settle. I hear that ye killed a priest."

The archer was shaken.

Dughall pressed until the blade broke his skin. "My father used to say that there can be no pleasure without pain."

Cameron paled. "Forgive me! I killed the priest, but it was the only way to save those men."

The Duke put down the blade and blotted his bleeding finger. "Why did ye save them?"

Cameron frowned. "The priest hired me for a military mission. When we reached the village, he expected me to kill women and children. I refused."

"Commendable."

The archer was surprised. "The others obeyed his orders, while I stayed out of the fray. At first it seemed a fair fight. But when he tied those men to a tree to burn them…" His face reddened. "I had to act."

Jamison said, "They say that ye shot the priest from a distance of fifty feet."

"That's a short distance for me."

"What happened to the other mercenaries?"

"I took three shots in a row. They're dead."

Dughall sensed that there was more to the story. "Why did the burning bother ye? Tell the truth. I've been known to read men's souls."

Cameron stammered. "She… My beloved Gráinne… was burned at the stake."

"Yer wife?"

His eyes misted. "My intended. She was carrying my child."

The Duke stroked the ivory handle of the dirk. "So ye've been subjected to persecution."

"A long time ago." Cameron was transfixed. "It's a rare knife."

"It's a gift from my late grandfather." Dughall offered a smile. "Some call me the Dark Lord. Those who serve me know me as a fair man. I'm glad that the priest is dead. The man was my mortal enemy."

"I did what was right."

Dughall nodded. "I apologize for yer rough treatment and ask that ye join us."

"Join ye?"

"I would like to hire ye for protection and military missions."

Cameron considered the offer. "What do these missions involve?"

"Rest assured that we will not wreak havoc upon women and children. It involves the trouble with the King."

"I've heard of it."

Dughall rubbed his hands together. "Good. We can discuss the details after supper."

Cameron's stomach growled. "I would be grateful for a meal and a pint of ale." He felt bold enough to ask for a favor. "I'm willing to stay. But there's one condition."

"What's that?"

"I want to meet the woman Aileana."

Dughall smiled. This was going to be easier than he thought. "I can arrange that. But ye must give me time."

Chapter 45
Heating Up

June 21st 1638
FOUR DAYS LATER

EDINBURGH COUNCIL CHAMBERS

The King's chief advisor in Scottish affairs was pessimistic about a quick resolution. Awaiting representatives of the Council, James Hamilton concentrated on the words he wanted to say. His spontaneity was getting worse, so much so that he'd consulted a physician.

"Concussive blows to the head can cause memory lapses," the doctor said. "We have no medicine for that."

Hamilton considered telling the King about his malady, but couldn't find the words. Just thinking about it made him sweat. James lifted his long locks and tossed them over his shoulders. He was mopping his forehead when Lord Traquair arrived with Sir William Elphinstone, the Lord Chief Justice. They took a seat opposite him at the table. Hamilton was grim. "Gentlemen."

Traquair seemed nervous. "We came from Linlithgow with the intent to take yer report to the Council. We must meet quickly. It's dangerous in this city."

"I've encountered hostilities myself."

"No doubt. What do ye intend to tell the King?"

James looked to the Lord Chief Justice. Did he have something to ask as well? It was confusing to converse with two people.

Sir William fingered a silver watch fob. "This is madness! The last time we were in Edinburgh, we were nearly killed. They've formed their own government and a lawless one at that!"

Traquair grew insistent. "I ask again. What will ye tell the King?"

Hamilton glanced at notes to jog his memory. "Hmmm... The King appreciates the risks you've taken. These are trying times." He tried to focus with all his might. "When I arrived twelve days ago, I thought my fellow Scots possessed by the devil. I wondered how they could resist the dictates of one as powerful as our King."

Lord Traquair scowled. "Go on."

Sweat trickled down his neck. "I thought they would be ignorant of the danger of their stance, poorly organized, and willing to negotiate rather than face a painful death."

"Hardly!" Sir William scoffed.

James searched for words. "Forgive me." He glanced at his notes. "I met with the leaders of the rebellion - Lords Loudon, Rothes, and Lindsay, as well as ministers and common folk. Each man was willing to die horribly for the cause, as well as incur the loss of status and property."

Sir William pounded the table. "This is what we've been trying to tell the King! Our letters go unanswered."

Traquair scowled. "He ignores us as armies form south of the city! These are not rag tag militias. They are led by distinguished military men. Leslie! Munro! And a host of mercenaries."

James nodded. "I see the gravity of the situation. I shall return to the King and urge him to reconsider."

Traquair's eyes widened. "At last, the truth shall come out. Ye're a brave man or a complete fool. I haven't figured out which."

"I don't envy yer position," Sir William said. "Tell the King that the rebellion will lose support if he foregoes the new liturgy book. If he continues on this path, we are headed for civil war. When will ye leave?"

A lump settled in the pit of his stomach. Hamilton swallowed hard. "Tomorrow."

"Then go with God. Ye're going to need it."

***

DRAKE CASTLE THE LORD'S PRIVATE STUDY

The Duke rolled a quill pen between his fingers and regarded the scroll in front of him. The time for hesitation was gone. With a flourish, he dipped the nib in an inkwell and affixed his signature to the document. "There, I've done it."

Jamison sucked in his breath. "Shall I send for refreshments, my Lord?"

Dughall looked up. "Tell the kitchen to prepare a meal for these gentlemen. They deserve our hospitality."

Jamison left the room, allowing them to contemplate the enormity of the act. Several long minutes passed where no one dared to speak.

Minister Henderson broke the silence. "We appreciate yer support, Lord Gordon. Yer signature on the Covenant will mean a lot to the resistance."

Dughall feigned irritation. "Ye realize that I'm doing this because of my stepfather, Alex Hay? He's been named a traitor by the King."

Lord Balmerino nodded. "As we all have. I'm at the top of his list."

Henderson massaged his swollen fingers. "Surely, ye have other reasons for signing."

"I do." Dughall chose his words carefully. "I believe that the cause is just. Men should have the right to worship as they please."

"All men?"

This was a rare chance to get his point across. "Aye. Christians, Jews, *and* everyone else. No matter how strange the faith seems. I believe that God comes in many flavors."

The minister stared in disbelief. "Ye're a Catholic?"

The Duke nodded. "Aye. But it wasn't always so. Perhaps ye've heard of my humble beginnings, growing up in a fishing village. I was baptized a Protestant at birth."

"How did ye become Catholic?"

"When my clan reclaimed me, I was baptized anew."

Henderson stared. "Then why not come back?"

Lord Balmerino interrupted. "We are not here to convert him to our church. It is enough that he's agreed to help us." He leaned forward slightly. "How will ye handle yer brother?"

Dughall looked thoughtful. "Lord Huntly is free to speak for himself and make his own alliances. Gilbert knows that I'm of a different opinion. As long as we're not pitted brother against brother, everything should work out."

Balmerino seemed satisfied. "We won't put ye in that position. For now, we need yer support. Money, horses, and a hundred strong men..."

"I will not force any man to serve. But as Minister Keith told ye, there are many who are eager to follow."

"Good. When can we expect the first shipment?"

"I'll put my men on it right away." The Duke stared. "There is one condition. In return, I expect ye to keep me informed about my stepfather."

"We shall make it a priority."

"Good." Dughall glanced at the Covenant. "The deed is done. Is there anything else?"

Minister Henderson was unwilling to let the matter drop. "Pray hard, Lord Gordon. Search yer soul for what is proper and right. When ye're ready to come back to the true faith, I will be here to act as yer guide."

Dughall smiled. "I'm sure ye will."

***

DRAKE CASTLE THE NURSERY AFTER SUPPER

The Duke stood in the nursery, holding his daughter. He loved it when she rested her head on his shoulder. Maggie Christal was almost one year old. Today she'd taken her first steps, on tiptoe with feet slightly outward. His mother assured him this was normal. Evening playtime had been delightful. The children stacked wooden blocks and giggled as they knocked them to the floor. Luc brought wee Artus to join in the fun. The dog allowed the children to maul him, without the smallest objection.

Dughall held the baby against his shoulder, supporting her bottom. The wee angel sighed and fell asleep. His heart was filled with love.

Keira entered, dressed in a white pregnancy gown and an emerald green robe. He thought that she looked lovely. She'd gained weight in all the right places, her breasts, thighs, and lower belly. The lass snuggled against him. "Is she asleep?"

"Aye. The wee lassie was tired."

"I heard that she took her first steps."

"She toddled into my arms." They lingered in a three way embrace. "We are so blessed." They separated so he could put the child in the cradle. He covered her to the waist with a blanket. "She's so precious."

Keira took his hand and placed it on her belly. "Feel him kick? I wonder how they'll get along."

Dughall grinned. "They'll be the best of friends." Long ago, he'd dismissed his dream as a symptom of his illness.

She guided his hand lower. "He's a hardy lad, like his father. He kicks like this every day."

Dughall was ecstatic. "Our daughter is asleep at last. Let's go to our bed chamber."

There was a knock on the door and Murdock entered. He bowed slightly. "My Lord. My Lady. Forgive the interruption."

The couple separated. "What is it?" Dughall asked.

"There's a visitor at the gate. I told him to come back, but the man seems desperate. He claims that he's a friend of yers, Hugh MacNeil."

The Duke frowned. "He comes from Whinnyfold. Perhaps he has news of my father. Show him to the library."

"As ye wish." The servant left.

Dughall kissed his wife. "I will join ye in our bed chamber within the hour." The pregnancy hadn't hindered their lovemaking.

Keira smiled. "I'll be ready."

***

THE LIBRARY

The library was illuminated by wall sconces. Windows were closed and drapes were drawn, blocking sound from the courtyard. The Duke sat at his desk, dressed in casual clothes. To appear less threatening, he'd changed into breeks, a sweater, and a plain linen shirt. He looked across the desk and studied the face of his friend.

Hugh looked like he was on the verge of exhaustion - frazzled, disheveled, and pale. His voice was strained. "Forgive the late hour, my Lord."

Dughall smiled. "There's no need to be formal, my friend." Reading the man, he sensed anger, fear, and desperation. He hoped it didn't involve his father. "To what do I owe this visit?"

Hugh's eyes were wild. "My brother Robert's been taken."

"Taken? What do ye mean?"

The man coughed. "Robert was arrested along with several men from Peterhead."

"Arrested by whom?"

"Lord Huntly's men."

"What are the charges?"

He practically spat the word. "Treason! They said that he led a rebellion against the King."

"Is it true?"

Hugh shook his head. "There was no rebellion. They arrested him because he carried the Covenant."

The Duke's heart sank. "Did he not get my warning? He and my father are on the King's list of traitors. They carried the Covenant across Aberdeenshire and signed it at every stop."

Hugh sighed. "Robert refused to read the letter. He's angry with ye for leaving the Church."

Dughall shook his head. "I advised him to go into hiding or to come to me for protection. Where did they take him?"

"To London to be tried."

So Gilbert had begun to fulfill his promise. The King must have insisted on the action. What was he to do? The brothers had agreed to not interfere in each other's jurisdictions. "Have ye talked to the Earl of Erroll?"

"Aye. He's unwilling to oppose Lord Huntly and fears the reprisal of the King."

"I can hardly blame him." Dughall was frustrated. "Lord Huntly is acting on behalf of the King. There's nothing I can do."

Hugh looked crushed. "Robert was like an Uncle to ye! He's stubborn and foolish, but still yer friend. Do ye wish to see him tortured and executed?"

Dughall relented. "Of course not. I will talk to Lord Huntly, but I can't promise anything."

"Thank ye, my friend."

"How long ago did they pick him up?"

"Seven days ago."

Dughall stared. Why did the man wait so long? It would be impossible to stop it now. He contemplated his options.

Murdock returned with news that a bed had been prepared for the guest. He escorted the man to the kitchen to get him a late meal.

Dughall's thoughts were grim as he headed for his chamber. He had to be true to himself. Robert's predicament dwarfed the fear that he had for his own father. This wasn't just about Robert and Alex. Signing the Covenant was akin to signing yer own death warrant. As he placed his hand on the door of his chamber, it occurred to him that he had done just that.

Chapter 46
Preparing for War

June 28th 1638
ONE WEEK LATER

THE WEAPONS RANGE

The Duke turned his attention to the weapons range. Unused for over a decade, it had fallen into disrepair. Each day brought news of impending war, emphasizing the need for an army. Horses and men had grown soft from a generation of relative peace. They required intensive training. The range was located south of the castle on a horse farm. It included rolling hills, meadows, and dense woods, as well as a cook house and barracks for soldiers. It was home to more than two hundred men who served the Lord of the castle. The property had lodging for citizen militias as well and stables and a blacksmith for horses. There was a sizeable weapons cache.

Clear skies and warm weather provided the perfect setting for the Duke's visit. The Lord had come to inspect troops and practice with the men on the range. To the lads stationed here, it was an honor. Now, the inspection was over. Soldiers gathered on the field, watching the Duke's new archer.

***

Ian was riveted to the sight. They'd propped up a straw man a hundred feet away and asked the archer to demonstrate. Cameron surprised them by hitting the target four times in a row. Then he moved back twenty feet.

Ian was amazed. *One hundred and twenty feet! Some men can't see that far.*

The archer took the next shot was from a kneeling position. He raised the bow, took aim, and let the arrow fly. "Shooop….." The deadly dart made its mark, straight into the straw man's heart. Cameron stood and took a bow. He tried to speak but was interrupted by clapping.

Ian whooped. "Great shot, Hunter!" Then he thought about a battle, where men would be on the run. "What if the target is moving?"

Cameron smirked. "I have one arrow left. Toss the target into the air in any direction."

Ian walked to the target and removed the arrows, noting that each struck in a vital area. Without warning, he lifted the straw man and tossed him to one side. The figure was speared within seconds.

Soldiers gathered around the archer. "Well done!" "What skill!"

Ian crossed the field and joined them. "Will ye teach me how to do that?"

The archer grinned. "Aye. But I expect lessons on the axe in return."

Ian was flattered. He had a fondness for medieval weapons. He'd acquired a ninth century Francisca throwing axe and practiced until he was accurate. The head of the weapon was thick, sharp on both sides, and rested on a short handle; requiring powerful arm muscles.

The Duke stood apart, outfitted in official battle regalia. He broke into a smile. "Impressive, Hunter. I'd like ye to train a dozen archers for battle conditions. We will stage a competition to see who has ability."

Scores of men came forward to express interest in the contest. This included the Duke's personal servants. Ian sized up the competition. To his right were his friends; Jamison, Murdock, Gilroy, and Pratt. To his left was the infamous Fang. The rest had been left to guard the castle. Fang seemed an unlikely choice. He was here at the request of the Duke, who was determined to give him a noble occupation. Ian was dubious about the idea. But true to his word, he'd befriended the man and offered to teach him about weapons. Ian glanced across the field where Cameron was removing the target. His heart pounded with anticipation. It was his turn now. He'd been asked to demonstrate the axe.

***

DRAKE CASTLE THE SURGERY

Jessie stood in the surgery, washing her hands in a porcelain bowl. She'd just treated a rash on a wee girl who came from the forest village. Ailsa Cummings was three years old. She had just lost her father.

The mother watched as she applied a salve and thanked her in a heartfelt manner. The woman had lost her husband, yet she centered herself in gratitude.

Jessie's heart ached for her. These widows were brave. The vicious attack that took their husbands left fifteen children fatherless. They'd never gone beyond their village. Castle life had to be a frightening prospect. Their bravery caused her shame. Jessie's husband lived, yet she'd fallen into a state of hopelessness.

She forced her thoughts to better days, when they lived by the sea. Their cottage was small by castle standards. Daily life was a struggle to keep up with fishing, hauling, and preparing the lines. They barely scraped a living from the shore. Domestic duties were difficult, hindered by the scarcity of fresh water. Then there were the trips to surrounding farms to trade fish for eggs and cheese. She'd carried a hundred weight creel on her back. Was she daft to yearn for those days? Nay. Jessie knew they'd been happy there. Alex was strong, hard working, and a good provider. They had two healthy sons. What more could a woman ask for?

Her thoughts darkened. Why were men so eager to go to war? She longed for the days when family came first, before religion, politics, and country. Would they ever be a family again? She'd been told that Alex had been named a traitor, making it next to impossible to return. At first, she'd been furious. Why would her husband take such chances? Then fear set in. The punishment for treason was drawing and quartering.

Dughall assured her that he would protect his father. But that seemed unlikely now that Robert had been arrested. Where was his influence there? She couldn't imagine what Colleen was going through, with her husband in the Tower of London.

Jessie surrendered to God's will. She loved Alex more than life, in spite of his stubbornness. "Does he miss me?" she wondered. His letters had been few and far between, filled with talk of religious injustice. Addressed to Dughall, they usually ended with the words "Give my love to yer mother."

She gazed into a small round mirror on the wall. It had been months since she'd paid attention to her appearance. Her face was lined with worry marks and her hair was streaked with white. "I'm starting to look like old Maggie. If he walked through that door, would he find me attractive?" Suddenly, she felt ashamed. How could she be so vain in the face of these brave widows? "My husband is alive and whole," she said. "Until he returns, I will dedicate my life to helping these women and children." She wondered if he was thinking about her.

***

SOUTH OF EDINBURGH

The rebel army was camped south of Edinburgh, on an estate belonging to a sympathetic Lord. The site had advantages. To start with, it was halfway between the city and the English border. Should the King attempt to invade, they could intercept his forces. The property had outbuildings, stables, and a reliable source of fresh water. Situated in a wooded area, there were few neighbors. The location was a closely held secret. They'd established false camps throughout the south to confuse spies and make their numbers appear larger.

Alex and his men were assigned quarters near the captains. They lived in open face wall tents with overhanging eaves, propped up with poles and wedges. The tents were easy to transport, quick to pitch, and provided a dry, comfortable camp. Eaves served to shed water away from the walls and overlapping doors discouraged rain from entering. The captains' tents were easy to identify. Each flew a standard bearing the Scottish coat of arms and the golden motto 'For Christ's Crown and Covenant'.

The soldiers were a devout bunch. From the tents one could hear the sound of men praying, reading scripture, and singing psalms.

♩♬♩ *And blessed be His glorious name,*
Long as the ages shall endure.
O'er all the earth extend His fame:
Amen, amen, for evermore. ♩♬♩

A man gave a speech, "We are not traitors! We would shed our last drop of blood for the King if he gave us the right to worship. We will make him listen."

Lieutenant Hay sat on stump, whittling a walking cane. *The King will never change his mind. There are other things afoot here.* Alex was privy to sensitive information. As a lieutenant, he was a sounding board for Commander Leslie.

His sharp knife traveled the length of the stick, stripping off the last of the bark. He felt useful when he worked with his hands. He turned the stick and began to shape the head. Scrape… Dig… Chip… Scrape… *Cut away from yerself,* he reminded. *Wounds can be fatal without a healer.* For a moment, he allowed himself to consider his wife. Could he ask her to serve at his side? *Nay! The lass would follow me into battle.*

He returned to his whittling. Chip… Shape… Chip… Smooth… He had to finish it. Tomorrow, he was sending one of his men home to attend the birth of a child. The ploughboy from Ayrshire twisted an ankle and was having trouble walking.

Alex was grateful that his head was bowed because it hid the tears in his eyes. Counseling the lad on family matters, he'd been obliged to ponder his own. Nine months had passed since he left his family. He'd missed Christmas, Easter, and a clan gathering. Dughall was about to sign the Covenant. Ian would be expected to fight. His sons needed their father. But most of all he missed his wife; her grace, kindness, and gentle ministrations. He stifled a sob. *I wish I could hold her for a night!* It was a desperate thought. The King's men were looking for him. He couldn't go home.

He forced his thoughts to better days. Christmas by the sea… several years ago… a snow storm prevented them from walking to church. They'd fetched Maggie and gathered at the hearth to pray. The peat fire glowed, giving the room a slight haze. He remembered their faces; Jessie, the lads, and dear old Maggie. That woman was like a mother to him. When prayers were done, Jessie got up to brew tea. *My bonny wife. My heart, my soul, and my life.*

Army life was taking a toll on him. His straggly hair was streaked with white and his beard was turning grey. *I look like an old man! Would she welcome me to her bed tomorrow?* He closed his eyes and fantasized. There was something about separation that intensified the union. They'd retreat to their chamber, strip off their clothes, and drop them to the floor in a heap. Jessie would have that look in her eyes. *Come to me, husband.*

His pleasant fantasy was interrupted. A bare foot boy stood before him, waiting to be acknowledged. "Ah, hem... Lieutenant Hay?"

Alex opened his eyes. "What is it?"

"General Leslie needs ye."

The lieutenant stood and put aside his whittling. *Duty calls. I can't go home.*

***

DRAKE CASTLE THE LADIES' RETIRING ROOM

Keira stood at a table, solemnly regarding her handiwork. Spread out before her lay charcoal portraits of the men who'd been slaughtered. The lass had been deeply affected by their deaths. She'd lost her father, mother, and now these dear friends to religious persecution. It was foolish to think that Dughall could protect them. She'd mourned in seclusion, until Janet came to counsel her.

Keira had poured her heart out. "How can I go on? Their faces haunt me."

Janet had embraced her. "Then draw them. Ye have the skill. Immortalize them for us."

She'd begun at once, directing servants to bring supplies. For the last five days, she'd done little else except sketch the faces of the fallen. The married men were first. Donald Cummings was a handsome man, with long dark hair and kind grey eyes. Drawn with a sparse beard, he was the father of six children. His cousin Brice Davies had strong features; high cheekbones, flaming red hair, and fair skin. He was the father of three boys and two girls. Craig Ross was a burly man with curly locks and a heavy beard. He was the father of infant twins. John Birnie's sketch tugged at her heartstrings. She recalled birthing his son Duncan in the circle. The father of two boys was a man of few words.

The last sketch evoked bitter-sweet feelings. She'd been betrothed to Michael. It had been painful to draw his wrinkled face and expressive eyes. She recalled the love in those eyes when he asked her to marry. "Oh, Michael. I begged ye to come to Drake. None of this needed to happen." She'd heard about his sacrifice. Michael had been the first to die, offering his life for his people. The black robe told him to kneel on the ground. When he dropped to his knees to pray, a soldier beheaded him. That hadn't stopped the killing. Michael's men fought for their lives, resulting in the death of four of them.

Beheaded! I don't care what Dughall says. These black robes are not to be trusted. There was a knock on the door. The widows had been invited to see the sketches. "Come in."

Nessia Birnie entered the room. "I've come, lass. May I see my husband?"

Keira showed her the portrait. She managed a smile. "Here he is."

Nessia stroked the paper with reverence. "Bless ye, lass. Now, I will always be able to look upon his face. My sons will remember their father."

Keira had a story to tell. "John was a good man. Remember when we birthed wee Duncan in the circle? He was worried about ye. Michael and I sent him to fetch blankets…"

***

THE WEAPONS RANGE

They'd lashed the straw man to a tree to prepare for the axe demonstration. Expectations were high. Ian hadn't disappointed them. First, he told them about the origins of the weapon, the warlike clan of the Franks. These fearsome warriors threw their axes before hand to hand combat to break shields and disrupt enemy lines. A strong man could throw the axe up to forty feet, wounding or killing an enemy. Just the weight of the head caused serious injury. The axe had a tendency to bounce unpredictably when it hit the ground, making it difficult for an enemy to block. It rebounded up legs, broke knee caps, and took out shields. Thrown in a volley, it scattered enemy ranks.

The story set the scene for the demonstration. Ian threw the axe at the target from varying distances, each time striking a vital area. Once, the axe was so imbedded that it took two men to dislodge it. He'd planned a grand climax. Ian paced off thirty feet from the tree and then ran yelling towards it. Approaching the target, he hurled the axe to the ground, causing it to bounce and strike the dummy's legs. There was an intense round of clapping.

The Duke showered him with praise. It wasn't necessary. Ian knew that his brother was pleased. The link between them had grown stronger. He didn't know why this was happening. Perhaps it was the challenges of fatherhood or Alex's dire predicament.

***

The Duke's visit was deemed a success. They shared a meal and a cask of ale. Murdock distributed two wagon loads of clothing, footwear, and protective gear; and took letters for the soldiers' families. It was time to return to the safety of Drake. The Duke and his men prepared their horses and headed out in formation. Jamison rode ahead, scouting for potential danger. Ten yards behind, Dughall and Ian rode abreast. Then came two wagons; with Murdock and Pratt in one and Hunter and Fang in the other. Gilroy rode alone, guarding the rear from attack. As they traveled, the sound of hooves on the gravel road lulled them into complacency.

Ian was looking forward to a good night's sleep. He usually slept like a rock, but last night he'd been plagued by a nightmare. He decided to ask Dughall about it. "Ye've always been a believer in dreams."

Dughall nodded. "Ah, dreams. They depict our hopes and ambitions, sometimes times our greatest fears. The ones to watch out for warn and foretell."

"Do they always come true?"

"Not always. Why do ye ask?"

"I had a nightmare about Father."

Dughall flinched. "Tell me about it."

Ian took a breath. "I'm in Whinnyfold. It's a gloomy day with an overcast sky. I'm wearing my sea jacket. There's a quarter moon hanging in the sky. It reminds me of the saying 'When ye can hang yer jacket on the moon, look out for squalls!'"

"Ha! Maggie used to say that."

Ian nodded. "She's not there. The stone cottages are deserted. A fierce wind howls through the rows. I raise my collar."

"I remember those days."

"I walk down the cliff side path to the harbor. The sea is wild. There I find Father at the edge of the water staring out to sea. I greet him."

"Did he speak to ye?"

Ian sniffled. "Father never takes his eyes off the sea. He says 'Do ye know what this is, my son? This is the ocean of tears to be shed when we fight for our freedom. I promised God to stay in this place until all of the tears are gone.'"

Dughall frowned. "So now we know how he feels. He thinks he can never come home."

Ian's heart ached. It was more than he cared to think about.

Chapter 47
Love is in the Air

June 30th 1638
TWO DAYS LATER 7AM

DRAKE CASTLE THE LORD'S BED CHAMBER

Dughall stretched, luxuriating in the feel of silk sheets against his bare skin. He snuggled up to his wife, who was sleeping with her back to him. She'd taken a bath and smelled like lavender. He traced the curve of her hip and smiled. The pregnancy had given her womanly curves. Dughall moved closer until they fit together like hand and glove. What joy! When he stilled his breath, he could feel her heart beat. She was pregnant with his child. What more could a man ask for?

His member stiffened, preparing for the act. But it wasn't to be. The last time she'd spotted blood, raising concerns about the pregnancy. Jessie told them to avoid sex until after the baby was born. His member didn't understand. When *would* he be able to make love to her? He counted the days. His son was due at the end of September. She would need time to heal after that. They had to abstain for four months. One hundred and twenty days! He sniffed her hair and his member grew larger.

Keira shivered. "We can't. Mother said that it's dangerous."

"I know, lass."

She turned to face him. "I'm sorry."

Dughall stroked her cheek. The look in her eyes took his breath away. "I can wait." He kissed her lips, which were as silky as a rose petal. How could he resist? His tongue found hers and made a swirling motion.

She grasped his chest hair and moaned. Her thighs opened slightly and closed. "We mustn't."

They moved apart a few inches, but their minds were locked in desire. For a moment it seemed that they might ignore Jessie's warning. Dughall's heart throbbed as he tried to calm his swollen member. She would never forgive him if they lost the child. Could he teach her about the French practice? Nay. He closed his eyes and turned his thoughts to his son.

Keira spoke softly, "Are ye all right?"

He opened his eyes and saw that his erection was gone. "Oh, aye. I was thinking about our son."

She patted her belly. "Just three more months. I'm going to miss having him inside me." She threw back the covers. "Let's get dressed. Today is the wedding of Murdock and Sara."

Dughall reddened. There was something he had to ask her. He should have done it before now. "I have a favor to ask." His wife waited. "We will attend their wedding of course. But at the end of the ceremony, I've arranged a surprise. We will renew our wedding vows in the presence of Father John and the wedding party."

Keira looked confused. "Why is that necessary?"

He took her hand and fondled her ring. "Some say that our marriage wasn't sanctioned by the church. In their minds, it's illegitimate."

"How can a marriage be illegitimate?"

"I don't know, lass. But it's best that we retake the vows. Then there will be no question about our son's inheritance."

She looked troubled. "They would deny him that?"

He nodded. "Aye. They consider my daughter a bastard."

"So Maggie has no rights?"

"None, but what I grant her during my lifetime."

"Then, Luc has no rights either?"

"'Tis true. Adoption is not the same as being born into the bloodline."

Keira frowned. "I don't understand these things. Among my people, a marriage or a child is always legitimate."

Dughall looked sheepish. "Do ye not want to marry me?"

She managed a smile. "Of course."

He kissed her hand. "Good. Today, I shall marry the woman I love."

"For the second time," she added.

"Oh, aye."

***

THE COURTYARD GARDENS 9AM

Aileana sat on a warm stone bench, waiting for Cameron Hunter. She'd been told that he wanted to meet her and agreed to give him a chance.

Their new home was nothing like the forest village. She'd never seen so many buildings, animals, and people living together in one place. Her people had been moved from the castle proper to a group of cottages a mile away. Their animals had been moved as well, along with their meager belongings. Torry had been restricted to bed rest to encourage his wounds to heal. He'd joined them only once, to lead a memorial service for their men. George was having the time of his life. He'd befriended the Duke's adopted son and spent hours with him role playing and hunting.

She took in familiar fragrances - wood smoke, pine, and flowering trees. She heard sparrows and robins twittering in the canopy. Aileana was happy. Her brother's life had been spared and they'd been guided to this place of refuge. They were fed, clothed, and looking forward to a new life. She offered a prayer of gratitude. "Thank the Goddess for all that is good." The girl allowed herself to think about her future. Weeks ago, she had no prospects for marriage. The men in her village were either too old, related, or already spoken for. It hadn't bothered her until recently, when changes in her body brought on her first moon cycle.

Torry advised her against seeing the archer. But some of the villagers were sympathetic to the man, who seemingly had acted out of conscience.

Curiosity was getting the best of her. *What does he want with me?* She'd passed him in the courtyard, encountering his desperate stares. He was a good looking man. Cameron had thick locks of hair that fell to his broad shoulders. He had high cheekbones, a well-trimmed beard, and startling green eyes. The lass smoothed her saffron-dyed skirt and waited. Minutes later, footsteps sounded on a path to her right.

The archer appeared, carrying a nosegay of posies. He approached the bench, dropped to one knee, and handed her the bouquet. "Miss Aileana?"

She felt a shiver go up her spine. Her graceful hand rose and touched his arm. "Cameron? Would ye like to sit with me?"

"Oh, aye." He stood and sat beside her on the bench, suddenly at a loss for words.

She blushed, making the freckles on her face stand out. "Ye asked to see me?"

"Aye, lass. Ummm... Oh." His eyes misted. "Forgive my loss for words. Ye're so like her that I can hardly stand it."

"Her?"

He stammered. "Gráinne... My intended. She was carrying my child when she died."

Many men lost wives in childbirth. "What happened to her?"

His voice cracked, "She was burned at the stake for worshipping the old religion."

"How did it happen?"

He gripped the bench with both hands. "I returned from a trip to find her murdered. My father had a hand in it!" He began to sob.

Her voice was soft. "Ye loved her."

"I did. Oh God. I was heartbroken, angry, and out for revenge. My heart turned to stone."

She felt sorry for this man. "This is why ye saved our men."

"Aye. I couldn't bear to see it happen again."

Aileana took his hand. "Cameron, why are ye here?"

He sounded practical. "I'm a man of means, an archer by trade. The Duke hired me for a long engagement and provided me with food and lodging. Over the last five years, I've amassed a small fortune."

No man had ever tried to win her hand; so she didn't understand his argument. "What does it mean?"

He sighed deeply. "Gráinne is dead. She will never come between us. I want ye to be my wife."

Aileana was stunned. "I hardly know ye."

He gripped her hand. "Please, lass! Our union is meant to be."

"Do ye know what I am? I worship the Goddess."

"Aye, lass." He gave her a kiss that sent quivers through her belly. "Say that ye'll give me a chance."

She was surprised by her response. "I will."

***

THE GREAT HALL 2PM

The Great Hall had been modestly decorated for Murdock and Sara's wedding. Three tables were draped with tartan cloth and adorned with bowls of fresh flowers. They were arranged in a U-shape so that the twenty-one guests could face each other. Murdock and Sara sat at the head table, with Sara's elderly mother. They were joined by Jamison and Jenny, their witnesses, and three ladies from the bakehouse. Gilroy and Pratt sat at the second table, accompanied by their wives. They were joined by Hunter, McGill, and the infamous Fang Adams. He'd been persuaded to take a bath.

The third table was reserved for the Duke and his family, with a place of honor for the clergy. From left to right, it was occupied by Jessie, Ian, Mary, Dughall, Keira, and Father John.

The wedding ceremony was simple. Murdock and Sara were now man and wife. They were holding hands like two young people. Wine and ale flowed freely and a light meal was provided.

The tables were abuzz with laughter and conversation when Dughall rose to make a toast. The room grew quiet as he raised a goblet. "Here's to my loyal friend, Murdock, and his lovely bride."

"Here! Here!" They joined him in the toast. "May they live long and prosper!" "Have many children…" "Or have fun trying…" There was laughter.

Dughall sat down and squeezed Keira's hand.

She whispered, "Will Murdock and Sara mind?"

"Nay. I spoke to them. They're honored to share the day with us."

Father John stood and cleared his throat. "My Lord, my Lady, and honored friends. We gathered here today to witness the joining of Murdock and Sara. There is another purpose as well." He motioned to Dughall and Keira. "Our Lord and Lady wish to renew their wedding vows in yer presence."

The people were all smiles. Sara spoke to her elderly mother, who was having trouble hearing. The woman's eyes grew wide.

Dughall stood and took Keira's hand. He helped her up and led her to the oak podium where the ceremony would be performed. Father John followed, carrying his prayer book.

Dughall had been married for more than a year, yet this ceremony meant a lot to him. He was about to pledge his love and loyalty in front of his friends and family. The only one missing was his father. The Duke gazed at his wife. She was wearing a cream silk gown, embroidered with tiny pearls. The tight fitting bodice displayed her ample breasts. Dughall was clad in his finest kilt, a white shirt, and a royal blue dinner jacket. He wore a leather sporran and his ivory handled dirk was in his sock. They were a magnificent couple. Dughall nodded to the priest. He'd asked him to change the ceremony slightly to accommodate his wife.

Father John began, "Dear friends. I am honored to preside over such a prominent joining." He opened his book. "Dearly beloved, ye have come together in this place so that the Lord may seal and strengthen yer love in the presence of the Church's minister. Christ and the Blessed Virgin sanctify this love. They enrich and strengthen ye by special sacrament so that ye may assume the duties of marriage in mutual and lasting fidelity. And so, in the presence of Christ, the Church, and the Blessed Virgin, I ask ye to state yer intentions." He turned the page. "Have ye come here freely and without reservation to give yerself to each other in marriage?"

Dughall watched her eyes. "Aye."

Keira smiled. "Oh, aye."

"Will ye love and honor each other as man and wife for the rest of yer lives?"

They answered together. "Aye."

"Will ye accept children lovingly from God and bring them up according to the law of Christ and his Church?"

They reddened. "Aye."

"Join yer right hands, and declare yer consent before God and his Church."

They held hands.

"Lord Dughall Gordon, will ye take Keira MacPherson here present, for yer lawful wife according to the rite of our Holy Mother, the Church?"

His heart swelled. "I will."

Father John turned. " Keira MacPherson, will ye take Lord Gordon here present, for yer lawful husband according to the rite of our Holy Mother, the Church?"

She smiled like an angel. "I will."

"It's time to recite the promise, my Lord."

They faced each other and held hands. "I, Dughall Gordon, take ye Keira, for my wife, to have and to hold, from this day forward, for better, for worse, for richer, for poorer, in sickness and in health, until death do us part."

It was her turn. "I, Keira MacPherson, take ye Dughall, for my husband, to have and to hold, from this day forward, for better, for worse, for richer, for poorer, in sickness and in health, until death do us part."

The priest smiled. "Since the rings are already upon yer fingers, I now pronounce ye man and wife. Ye may kiss the bride."

Dughall kissed her tenderly, being mindful of those who were present. "Now we are man and wife in everyone's eyes. Are ye happy?"

"Deliriously," she whispered.

They returned to their table amidst a storm of clapping. Fine French wine flowed as toasts were offered.

Dughall let them have their say and then turned his attention to Murdock and Sara. He made a surprise announcement granting them permanent quarters in a cottage reserved for visiting noblemen. It was the least he could do for the man who saved his life.

With the spotlight elsewhere, he turned to his wife. "Let us not forget the love we shared here. Thank ye for consenting to renew our vows. Now no one can question our son's birthright."

The Juggler

Chapter 48
Happy Birthday

July 3rd 1638
Three Days Later

Drake Castle

It was a special day. Wee Maggie Gordon and Andrew and Alexander Hay were celebrating their first birthday. Keira and Mary had gone to great lengths. The Great Hall was whimsically decorated. Three tables were covered with cloth embroidered with scenes from fairy tales. Upon the head table was an elaborately carved box filled with toy horns, stuffed animals, and rag dollies. The second table had gifts, wrapped in dyed paper and brightly colored ribbons.

The floors were covered with rugs to accommodate crawling infants. The third table was loaded with goodies - a large cake and several plates of sweet biscuits. There were jams and honey and an assortment of fruit. Serving girls arranged pitchers of milk and water, surrounding them with children's cups and glasses.

On the stage, an old woman played a dulcimer, while her daughter sang a nursery rhyme.

♩♬♩

Here we gae roon the jing-a-ring,
The jing-a-ring, the jing-a-ring;
Here we gae roon the jing-a-ring,
Aboot the merry-matanzie.

Twice aboot, an than we fa,
Than we fa, than we fa,
Twice aboot, an than we fa,
Aboot the merry-matanzie.

Guess ye wha the guidman is,
The guidman is, the guidman is;
Guess ye wha the guidman is,
Aboot the merry-matanzie.

Honey is sweet, an so is he,
So is he, so is he;
Honey is sweet, an so is he,
Aboot the merry-matanzie.

He's merried wi a gay gowd ring,
A gay gowd ring, a gay gowd ring;
He's merried wi a gay gowd ring,
Aboot the merry-matanzie.

A gay gowd ring's a cankerous thing,
A cankerous thing, a cankerous thing;
A gay gowd ring's a cankerous thing,
Aboot the merry-matanzie.

Noo they're merried, we'll wish them joy,
Wish them joy, wish them joy,
Noo they're merried, we'll wish them joy,
Aboot the merry-matanzie.

Faither an mither they maun obey,
Maun obey, maun obey,
Faither an mither they maun obey,
Aboot the merry-matanzie.

Lovin ilk ither like sister an brither,
Sister an brither, sister an brither;

Lovin ilk ither like sister an brither,
Aboot the merry-matanzie.
We pray the couple tae kiss thegither,
Kiss thegither, kiss thegither;
We pray the couple tae kiss thegither,
Aboot the merry-matanzie.

The honored guests were starting to arrive. Mary and Ian walked in, carrying the red-haired twins. The boys' eyes lit up with surprise when they spied the fancy tables. Andrew clapped. Alexander pointed. They prepared a plate of goodies and took their places at the head table.

Dughall arrived, carrying Wee Maggie. Keira and Tarrah were close behind, escorting the juggler. The man had been found wandering the halls, looking for the birthday party. They left the juggler near the stage to unpack and took their places at the head table.

Jessie arrived, having been delayed by a case in the surgery. She helped herself to food and drink and brought it to the head table.

In the background, the old woman struck up a tune. Her daughter encouraged them to sing along.

Clap, clap handies,
Mammie's wee, wee ain;
Clap, clap handies,
Daddie's comin' hame,
Hame till his bonny wee bit laddie;
Clap, clap handies,
My wee, wee ain.

Clap, clap handies,
Mammie's wee, wee ain;
Clap, clap handies,
Daddie's comin' hame,
Hame till his bonny wee bit laddie;
Clap, clap handies,
My wee, wee ain.

Dughall held his daughter on his lap. He was delighted by her reaction. The lassie giggled and clapped her hands to the music. He was sorry that he hadn't introduced her to music. Keira and Tarrah laughed out loud. It certainly was contagious.

The boys wriggled out of their parents' arms and reached into the toy box for the tin horns, managing to grab two of them.

Ian put a horn up to his lips and blew. The sound was smooth and pleasing. Andrew snatched the horn and sucked on it, causing it to sputter.

The woman on stage began to sing.

♩♬♩ *Ring around the rosy*
A pocketful of posies
"Ashes, Ashes"
We all fall down!
Ring around the rosy
A pocketful of posies
"Ashes, Ashes"
We all fall down! ♩♬♩

Dughall paled. "Tarrah! Tell her not to sing that." The servant stood and hurried to the stage.

"Why not?" Keira asked. "It seems harmless."

"That song is about the plague that hit England in the 1300's. One symptom was a rosy skin rash in the shape of a ring. People carried pockets of posies because they believed it was spread by bad smells."

Keira frowned. "What about the ashes?"

"That refers to the cremation of bodies! The death rate was six in ten."

"I've never seen such an illness."

"It rears its head from time to time, usually in crowded cities. We don't know what causes it."

The dulcimer player began a different tune.

♩♬♩ *Yokie pokie,*
Yankie, fun,
How do ye like
Yer tatties done?

First in brandy,
Then in rum,
That's how I like
My tatties done.

Yokie pokie,
Yankie, fun,
How do ye like
Yer tatties done?

First in brandy,
Then in rum,
That's how I like ♩♬♩
My tatties done.

"That's better," Dughall said.

Luc arrived with his new friend George. Artus bounded at his side, excited by the commotion. They sat on a bench across from Dughall. They were soon having the time of their lives. The lads clapped their hands and sang along to the nursery rhymes. When a song stopped, they ate sweet cakes.

Dughall smiled. "Are ye having a good time, son?"

Luc grinned. "Oh, aye! I've never been to a birthday party."

"When is yer birthday?"

"I don't know."

"We'll find out about yer birthday. Where were ye born?"

"France, I think. Mother said we came from Calais."

Dughall knew that could pose a problem. Nevertheless, he owed it to his son. "I will make inquiries. If we're unsuccessful, we'll choose a birthday."

Luc was excited. "Oh thank ye, Father. Can I have a party like this?"

Dughall chuckled. "Well, not exactly like this. Ye're a grown lad, not a wee baby. We would arrange things appropriate for yer age."

The boy smiled. "George likes it here. He told me."

"Do ye, George?"

The lad blushed. "Aye. It's different from the village."

"I grew up in a small village too. It took me a while to get used to the castle."

Keira accepted the baby from her husband. "Luc. Go see if the juggler is ready to start. Take George and the dog with ye."

The boys ran off to pester the juggler.

Dughall didn't like the tone of her voice. "Why did ye send them away?"

She stroked the infant's hair. "It's Maggie's birthday. We should pay attention to her."

"There is enough of me to go around. Luc is my son. Yers as well."

She reddened. "I'm sorry."

"Try to warm up to him, lass. He's had one hell of a life."

The boys ran back with the deerhound on their heels. "Father! The juggler is ready to begin. He's coming over."

The juggler appeared at the table, ready to give a performance. He was a middle-aged man of short stature, thin and pale. He was clad in a kilt, vest, and white blousy shirt, accented by long socks and lattice laced shoes. His hat was silly, a wool cap with a tuft on one side. It accentuated his large ears.

He took off his hat and bowed. "My Lord… My ladies…. Beloved children!"

The old woman struck up a silly tune.

The juggler pulled out a chair and placed all of his props upon it.

He smiled like a child as he took four wooden rings and placed them around his neck. He counted, "One... Two... Three... Four..." and then took the rings off his neck one by one, tossing them into the air.

"They're not dropping!" Luc squealed.

The juggler threw the rings up the midline of his body in a rotating outside circle, catching them as they fell. Each hand controlled two rings in perfect sequence. He tossed them high and low and then stopped juggling to take a bow.

Everyone clapped, even the babies.

The juggler put aside the rings. He brought a horn to his lips to announce the next trick. "Dah... Dah... Dah..." Then he picked up a three foot polished stick. "Now I will balance a dish on this stick. My Lord. Could I please have one of those fine china plates?"

Ian snorted. "He's going to break it."

Dughall chuckled. "It can be replaced." He cleared off one of the plates and handed it to the juggler.

He held the stick and placed the plate upon it. Watching intently, he balanced the dish and walked around the room.

"How does he do that?" George cried.

"Shhh... Don't distract him," Jessie said.

The juggler returned to the table and lowered the plate. Still balancing it on the stick, he gave it a gentle spin. Round and round the plate went as he repeated the spin. When it was going at a fair clip, he raised the stick and walked around the room.

Everyone held their breath. Surely, he would drop it now.

The juggler returned to the table and took a bow, catching the plate in one hand. He pretended to inspect it for damage and handed it back to Dughall. "It's in one piece, my Lord."

"Do it again!" Luc cried.

The juggler put away his stick and approached the boy. "What a fine lad. He must be a prince!" He fooled the crowd with a twirl of one hand, while extracting an egg from Luc's ear with the other. "My goodness! Ye should wash yer ears more often."

Luc laughed. Then he accepted the egg as a gift. He showed it to George with excitement.

"Shall I continue, my Lord?"

Dughall smiled. "Aye!" He was enjoying this.

The juggler picked up two drum sticks and a three-foot striped pole. Holding the sticks in one hand, he tossed the pole slightly into the air. Quickly transferring a drumstick to the empty hand, he tapped the pole back and forth, suspending it in the air.

Maggie shrieked. "Dada!

"Ah, the wee baby likes it." Tap... Tap... Tap... Tap... The juggler hopped back and forth and gave the pole a sudden spin. He lifted and tapped and lifted and tapped until the rod was almost a blur. "Now, for my grand finale…" He used the sticks to guide the pole around the back of his knees and spin it around his waist. In a quick motion, the sticks were captured in one hand as the pole appeared in the other.

"Wonderful!" Ian stood and clapped.

The juggler bowed. "Thank ye for the chance to serve, my Lord. I love performing for children. Send the wee ones to me if ye wish. I will entertain them in the corner." He picked up his props and headed towards the stage.

Dughall looked around. "Well? We can open gifts after he's gone. Does anyone care to join him?"

Luc's eyes shone. "May I go, Father?"

"Of course. I wonder how many more eggs he'll find."

"Oh, Father!" Luc and George stood and ran to the stage, followed by the deerhound.

Tarrah stood and opened her arms to Maggie. "Come, precious. Let's go see the juggler. Is it all right, m'Lady?"

Keira nodded. "Aye, lass."

Tarrah lifted the child and headed for the stage. Keira stood and followed.

Ian handed Andrew to his mother. "Mother… Mary… Take the twins. They shouldn't miss this."

The women took the babies to the stage, where the demonstration was in progress.

Dughall and Ian stayed at the table, eating cake and drinking water.

"Yech," Ian said. "It's water."

"Aye, well it's a child's party."

Ian gazed at the second table, which was laden with gifts for the children. "We never had this much. Are we spoiling them?"

"Nay, not yet."

He grunted. "The juggler was amusing."

"He has talent."

Ian looked thoughtful. "We could use that agility on the battlefield."

Dughall sighed. "This is a happy occasion. Can we not talk about war for once?"

Ian grunted. "I know what ye mean."

Chapter 49
A Calculating Mind

July 10th 1638
A WEEK LATER

PALACE OF WHITEHALL   LONDON, ENGLAND

King Charles sat at his desk, awaiting the arrival of the Marquis of Hamilton. His chief advisor in Scottish affairs tended to make him furious. Normally, he would dispense with such a man. But he had to be careful with this one.

Two months ago, James Hamilton had been sent to Edinburgh with alternate sets of instructions - one to demand the disbandment of the Covenant, the other a vague mandate for obedience. Not certain of the mood in Edinburgh, he'd been trusted to gauge it upon arrival. When he returned in June, Hamilton painted a grim picture. Unless the King made concessions, civil war was inevitable. The Covenanters were threatening to summon a parliament and assembly on their own authority. In addition to the abolition of the Prayer Book and canons, they demanded the suspension of the articles of Perth and weakening of the authority of Bishops. Hamilton reported that some of the King's own council members supported the cause. Only force could break this Covenant.

The King scowled. His advisor wasn't much of a diplomat. In fact, he'd accomplished nothing. They'd interrogated, cajoled, and threatened Hamilton, until he begged to be released from his duties.

Charles couldn't allow that. To change horses now would be a sign of weakness. No matter that the man fell ill after the interrogation and took to his bed for a week. The physician said that he suffered from a mild heart ailment, aggravated by nervous tension.

Charles fumed. *Nervous tension! I can do far worse to him! Strip him of rank. Subject him to the boot! If it was up to Laud, we'd do it now.*

The King took a pinch of snuff between his thumb and forefinger and sniffed it sharply into one nostril. Then the other... It helped to clear his head. *We shall see what this meeting brings.*

Charles knew that he had to make concessions, at least temporarily. He was prepared to lay aside the Prayer Book and canons and modify the role of the High Commission. But he would not negotiate until the Covenanters dismantled their alternative government. The Marquis' report wasn't a total surprise. The issue at hand was what he suspected; that of obedience to authority. *How dare they cloak their true intentions in religious fervor!*

In June, Hamilton had advised him that nothing could reduce those people to obedience but force. Since that day, the King adopted two plans. He would continue diplomatic missions, but prepare covertly for war. They were commissioning artillery, ordering arms from Holland, and organizing a sailing fleet. Hamilton didn't need to know. His job would be to play for time.

The King was devious. He hoped to drive the Covenanters to illegal measures that would reveal them as traitors. This would erode their support. On June 28th, he'd issued a declaration proclaiming his commitment to the Protestant religion and his willingness to consider proposals by an assembly or parliament. It had been scheduled to be read in Edinburgh on the fourth of July, with Hamilton in attendance. Today he would learn the outcome.

There was a knock at the door. "Come!"

A servant entered, escorting a guest. "Your Majesty. The Marquis of Hamilton." The white haired man bowed slightly, then turned on his heels and left the room.

James Hamilton sat opposite the monarch.

Charles regarded him with a careful eye. Hamilton looked well-rested, an improvement over the last time he saw him. Perhaps he would be of use after all. He inquired after his health. "Feeling better?"

James reddened. "Yes, your Majesty. Thank you for inquiring."

The King forced himself to smile. "Good. How did the reading fare?"

Hamilton lifted his brown locks and tossed them back on his shoulders. "Forgive me, Sire. I have trouble with the heat in London."

Charles scowled. "Perhaps you'd rather be stationed in Scotland."

"Nay, Sire! I meant nothing by it."

"Well?"

He fidgeted. "I attended the reading in disguise, along with Lord Traquair and Lord William Elphinstone. The crowd seemed to consider it at first. Then one of the Covenanters protested, stating that the bishops could have no place in such an assembly. Rather, they were to be tried for their crimes."

"Utter madness!"

Sweat beaded on his forehead, which he promptly mopped with a handkerchief. "These are the lawless acts you predicted. They clearly smack of treason."

"What was the mood of the common people?"

James swallowed hard. "They will follow the Covenanters at any cost. Oh, how I wish it wasn't so! Confusion and ruin threatens my homeland. They intend to invade England."

"What!" He pounded the desk. "I'm not ready to staunch an attack. How can we buy time?"

Hamilton paled. "Withdraw the Prayer Book and canons."

Charles fumed. How dare they? He was willing to back off by his own decision, but he wouldn't be forced to comply. "Never!"

James flinched. "It's the only way to avoid invasion. You can reintroduce them later."

The King felt like striking him and it must have shown in his eyes. The man was cowering. "You will spend a week under my tutelage, learning what is and is not negotiable. Then you shall return to Edinburgh as an *Englishman* to lay down the law and assess the situation. Am I clear?"

His voice was weak. "Yes."

"Is there anything else?"

He was starting to stutter. "I... was... asked about the prisoners."

Charles was thrilled. "Ah, the prisoners. So they do care about something. I haven't tortured them yet, though I have a mind to after this conversation. They're being kept in the Tower, under conditions suitable for traitors. I've located more than half of the men on my list. When the rest are found, we will begin the executions."

"Hanging, drawing, and quartering?"

Charles stared. "That's what we do to traitors."

"I will tell the common people in Edinburgh. Perhaps it will change their minds."

The King scowled. "I hope you're right. Otherwise, we're headed for war."

Chapter 50
Robert

July 24th 1638
TWO WEEKS LATER

SOUTH OF EDINBURGH

Alex Hay walked through the camp, searching for the courier. Months had passed since he'd gotten a letter and he was worried that his contact had been compromised. Only a few knew the address. What could have happened? He stopped in front of the General's tent, where men were gathering to retrieve their mail.

The courier was getting to the bottom of his sack. "Two for Alex Hay!"

Alex's heart leapt. Were they from his family? He accepted the letters gratefully and retreated to his tent. Lying on his cot, he examined the envelopes. One was made of fine stationery and had likely come from Dughall. The other was addressed in poor handwriting on paper that could be obtained by a commoner. He decided to read that first. Alex opened the envelope with his knife. He pulled out a one page note and started to read.

Dear Alex. I hope that this letter finds ye safe and in good health. Unfortunately, I can't say the same for my brother. Robert has been arrested and taken to London. He's been accused of being a traitor for carrying and signing the Covenant. Rumor is he was taken to the Tower to await execution. Colleen is heartbroken. The family is devastated. The Bonnie Fay struggles without a proper captain. There were tear stains on the paper. *I don't know what to do. Perhaps ye can find out the truth and tell us in a letter. Not knowing whether he's alive or dead is torture. Good luck. - Yer friend, Hugh MacNeil.*

Alex's heart sank. His best friend was in the Tower of London. Did he dare open the second letter? He sliced the envelope open and began to read.

Dearest Father. I hope that this reaches ye. The family is well. Ian's boys and my daughter turned one a few days ago. I am soon to become a father again, for my wife is due in September. My subjects are praying for a son to succeed me. Politics have forced me to make a decision. I've signed the Covenant and offered my support, to the dismay of my brother G who remains a Royalist. So far I haven't had any trouble over it. I'm afraid that there's bad news. I once said that ye and Uncle Robert were on the King's list of traitors. Robert ignored my warning and was taken by the English a month ago. By the time I heard, he was on the way to London. Inquiries tell me that he's locked in the bowels of the Tower, awaiting execution.

Alex felt sick but he continued reading. *Oh, Father. My power does not extend to the Tower of London. I fear that he is doomed. Even so, I have engaged a London agent to bribe his warden so that he is fed and given water. I will also offer support to Colleen and his family as a way of consolation. I am sorry to have to deliver this news. Please stay safe and out of harm's way! Write Mother soon. She really misses ye. - Yer loving son, D.*

Alex tucked the letters into a pocket. He decided to visit General Leslie to see if he could shed light on this.

***

LONDON

The Tower wasn't a single building. Rather, it was a complex of towers and outbuildings located on the north bank of the River Thames. Surrounded by a moat and high walls, it served as a fortress, royal residence, and prison. It was also a place of torture and execution, an armory, and a menagerie of rare animals. The complex was separated from the eastern edge of the city by an open space known as 'Tower Hill'. Prisoners were given accommodations according to their status in life. A peasant found circumstances quite deplorable.

Robert MacNeil had been brought to this place over a month ago. He'd arrived through the water entrance to the Tower, referred to as 'Traitor's Gate', named so because prisoners accused of treason such as Sir Thomas More passed through it. After traversing St. Thomas' Tower, he was taken to the bowels of the Salt Tower, where he was manacled and locked away. So far, he hadn't been tortured. It was a frightening prospect for a fisherman.

Robert stared at his hands. The iron cuffs were tight, on the verge of cutting off circulation. The cell was dirty and infested with a variety of vermin. The chamber pot overflowed in the corner. His belly ached from the scarcity of food. For the first few weeks he'd existed on a thin gruel, the color of sickly vomit. Then for some reason the food got better. A crust of bread and a piece of cheese certainly made a difference. Even so, Robert was growing thin and weak. His cellmate had fared no better. Robert's lips were cracked and dry. "How are ye, Gibbs?"

The middle-aged man sat on the floor, propped against a wall. "What does it matter? We're dead men."

Bile rose in his throat. "We must not give up. My family has friends in high places. Someone will rescue us."

Gibbs snorted. "Those walls are fifteen feet thick. The place is surrounded by moats."

"God will not abandon us."

"He already has, my friend. Do ye know what they do to traitors?"

Robert swallowed hard. "Aye."

"Best that we refuse food and water. It would be a merciful death compared to hanging, drawing, and quartering."

His cell mate was fixated on the gruesome death. "Let's not talk about it." Robert slumped against the wall. *Could he be right? Should I deny myself food and water? It would be over with in a few weeks.*

Gibbs was snoring.

Robert grieved for what he had lost. *I shall never see my wife and children again. My home, my boat, my best friend. God is all that I have left.* He prayed silently. *The Lord is my shepherd, I shall not want. He makes me lie down in green pastures. He leads me beside quiet waters. He restores my soul. He guides me in the paths of righteousness for His name's sake. Even though I walk through the valley of the shadow of death, I fear no evil, for Ye are with me. Yer rod and Yer staff, they comfort me. Ye prepare a table before me in the presence of my enemies. Ye have anointed my head with oil. My cup overflows. Surely goodness and loving kindness will follow me all the days of my life, and I will dwell in the house of the Lord forever.*

Robert sighed. He would leave it in God's hands, at least for the time being. He prayed that Alex would escape this fate. *Stay safe, my friend. Remember me to our children.* There was nothing else to do. Like Gibbs, he fell into a restless sleep.

Chapter 51
Between a Rock and a Hard Place

September 24th 1638
TWO MONTHS LATER

LONDON

James Hamilton rose at dawn, to prepare for his meeting with the King. He took a tepid bath, washed his hair, and anointed himself with cologne. He hadn't found a solution for his excessive sweating.

He'd arrived in London after midnight, having traveled by coach from Edinburgh. There was news to report. He wanted to present it in the best light.

The last two months had been harrowing, so much so that a cowardly man might have taken his own life. Per the King's instructions, he'd returned to Edinburgh on the tenth of August to divide and rule; and if not conduct a holding operation. None of this was realized.

The situation worsened. The Covenanters insisted that the Bishops be deprived of their votes and were beginning to tax men. So grave were these developments that he decided to confer with the King again. Back to London he went to incur the wrath of the monarch. To his surprise, Charles heard him out without resorting to scathing criticism. Together with Archbishop Laud, they crafted a thoughtful response.

Hamilton returned to Edinburgh on the seventeenth of September to announce substantial royal concessions. The King offered to withdraw the Prayer Book, the canons, the High Commission, and the articles of Perth. In addition, he agreed to limit the power of the bishops to make them more responsible to the assembly. To undermine the Covenanters, the King proposed a bond of faith to replace the National Covenant. Signatories would swear to stand by the King for the promotion of the true religion.

James believed that these concessions were real, in spite of rumors that they might be a play for time. Military supplies were on their way from the Tower to the town of Hull, traveling under the cover of night. He observed quarrels about the upcoming Assembly and spread the word that refusal of the offer would expose the Covenanters' disobedience of authority.

The Councillors signed the King's bond, praised the royal concessions, and scheduled an assembly and parliament for November. But the Covenanters entered a protest, rejecting the bond of faith and proposed limitations of episcopacy. They reserved their arguments for the upcoming Assembly.

James Hamilton knew what this meant. His primary job was to preserve episcopacy, a thankless task at best. Too many of his country men embraced the puritanical way and would accept nothing less than the abolition of episcopacy. The specter of war loomed before them. He planned to advise the fortification of Berwick, Carlisle, and Newcastle.

His thoughts were grim as he arranged his hair. What would the King do when he told him about the protest? Which Charles would he encounter today? Would he honor his chief advisor or send him to languish in the Tower? He was truly between a rock and a hard place.

Chapter 52
A Child is Born

September 25th 1638
NEXT DAY 7:30AM

DRAKE CASTLE THE STUDY

There comes a time in the midst of conflict and confusion to reflect upon a ray of hope. Men can be stretched to their limits, yet they pause when a child is born. For in that instant, the world appears through rose colored glasses. This is especially true when the first male child is born to an important man. Expectations are high. Will he grow up to turn hate to love, and war to peace? Will he avoid the faults of his forefathers that caused misery and suffering?

These were the Duke's private thoughts as he awaited the birth of his son. He'd long ago dismissed the dream that came on the night of the child's conception.

Keira had gone into labor at midnight. Six long hours passed before the pains became regular. The nervous father stayed at her side until she insisted he go to breakfast. Jessie was summoned and relieved him at dawn. Now the two women kept him from the birthing room, suggesting that he go about his business.

The Duke sat at his desk and poured himself a cup of tea. He was shaky from the lack of sleep and needed to conserve his strength. No matter how long it took, he intended to be present at the birth. Dughall drank the tea and then stood to look out the window. It was a typical fall morning in the Highlands. Light frost blanketed the ground and glistened in the trees. The sky was dark with thunder clouds which could easily bring a rainstorm. At best, they could look forward to a day of drizzle. Peasants crossed the courtyard with collars raised and coats buttoned.

Dughall moved to the fireplace. Apple wood burned brightly, emitting a fruity odor. It reminded him of the first time he'd smelled it, in his bed chamber at Huntly. It seemed so long ago! Now he was Lord of a large estate with more than a thousand men to command. A man of his stature needed a son, for no one else could succeed him. He was desperate to attend the birth to ensure that the child would survive.

Why were they excluding him? *How strange. Keira banished me from the room. When Kate was in labor, she begged me to stay.* The lass had been like clay in his hands, helpless and open to suggestion. *Oh God. Why am I obsessed with Kate Gunn?* He thought about her regularly since he'd been denied the comforts of his wife. It made him feel disloyal. *This must stop!*

There was a knock on the door. He'd sent Murdock to his chamber to check on the condition of his wife. Did they need him? "Come in."

The servant entered. "My Lord."

Strong winds buffeted the windows. "The weather is worsening. How is my wife?"

Murdock smiled. "She's well, but the birth is progressing slowly. They want ye to get some sleep."

Dughall stared. "Sleep?! My son is about to be born. I should be with her."

"Lady Jessie asks that ye stay away. She's a fine midwife. Perhaps we should leave this to the women folk."

The Duke paced the room. "I stayed in the room when Kate was birthing."

Murdock frowned. "We're lucky to be rid of that shrew. Why must we talk about her?"

Dughall stopped pacing. "I can't stop thinking about her. What's wrong with me?"

"Nothing's wrong." The servant chuckled. "Ye're a man! I might have a different opinion if she visited my bed. This frustration will pass."

"I've gone three months without the comforts of my wife. I'm going mad!"

Murdock appeared to be in thought. "Let's go to the indoor range and spar for a bit. It will take yer mind off women."

"But what if my wife needs me?"

"We will leave word so they know where to find us."

Dughall agreed. An hour or two of sparring might do him good. "Let's go, my friend." He might as well hone his fighting skills. He felt as useless as tits on a boar.

***

THE LORD'S BED CHAMBER 8:30AM

Jessie stood at a bedside table, washing her hands in a bowl. She was preparing to examine her daughter-in-law, who was struggling through a strong contraction. They were coming ten minutes apart. "Tell me what ye feel."

Keira winced. "There's a tightening in my belly. Oh! It's worse than before." She squirmed. "I can't get in a comfortable position."

This sounded normal. "Breathe like I taught ye."

"But it's been so long! I started contractions at midnight."

"Breathe, daughter." Jessie tried to allay her fears. "First labor can take a day. It doesn't mean that something's wrong. Let me time the next contraction."

The contraction ended. They talked about their plans for a second nursery as they waited. One nursery would be for infants, the other would be for toddlers.

Keira took a sharp breath. "It's starting."

Jessie began to count, "One tattie… Two tattie… Three tattie… "

Keira gripped the sheets. "It's building like a wave; higher and higher. I can bear the pain but it's getting worse. Dear Goddess!"

"Hang on, lass. Twenty-one tattie… Twenty-two tattie…" She counted to sixty as the lass panted.

"Thank goodness!" Keira announced. "It's going back down." Her silk nightshirt was stained with sweat. "It's done."

They were going to be there for a while. "That contraction lasted only a minute. Let me examine ye."

Keira threw off the sheet and lay back on a pillow. As a midwife, she knew what to do. The lass raised her knees, opened her legs, and took shallow breaths. "Go ahead."

Jessie had to work fast. She inserted her fingers between her folds and gently into the vagina. It was slippery so she pulled back her hand and examined a glob of pink mucous. "Ye've lost the plug, daughter. That's a good sign."

"Oh."

Jessie inserted her fingers and felt for the cervix. The knob at the top of the vagina was softer, shorter, and thinner than usual, and allowed her to insert two fingers. She removed her hand and washed it. "Two fingers, lass. This is the beginning of the middle stage. I'd guess another six hours."

Keira seemed disappointed. "I thought I was further along than that! I've birthed a dozen babies, but I never understood the pain."

Jessie helped her sit up and covered her with a sheet. "Every woman is different. Some can bear a wee bit of pain and some can bear a lot. It's hard to tell when it's not yer pain. Shall I summon Dughall?"

Keira frowned. "Nay. There's no sense making him worry."

"He wants to witness the birth."

"We'll call him when we get near the end."

Jessie felt uneasy. Her son left instructions to summon him when the middle stage started. "He's our Lord and master. We can't keep him away."

Keira stiffened. "Then help me, Mother! Promise me that when he comes, ye will stay with me and my baby."

She heard fear in her voice. "I will, daughter."

***

THE INDOOR WEAPONS RANGE 9:30AM

Thunder rolled and rain fell in torrents. The stormy weather encouraged men to practice their trades inside. The Duke's protectors were no exception. The indoor weapons range was busy. Ian and Cameron were situated on the north side of the eighty foot chamber. They'd been there since first light, hurling axes into a wooden wall. Dughall and Murdock sparred on the south side, using shields adorned with the head of a lion. The Duke had ordered a hundred of these made for his growing army.

Ian took off his chain maille tunic, slipping it over his head. "It's hard to believe ye've never thrown an axe. It must come naturally to ye."

Cam smiled. "I'd like to get better at it. How did ye get such big arm muscles?"

Ian wiped sweat from his brow. "I'll show ye. Let's do pushups." He dropped to the ground and assumed the position.

Cam joined him and they proceeded to do fifty pushups. He was red in the face when they were done.

"Had enough?" Ian taunted.

"Nay! What's next?"

"One-armed pushups." He held his left arm behind his back, transferring all of his weight to the right. "Let's start with ten."

Cam joined him and grunted as he lifted his body for the first time. "Daft!"

"One... Two... Three... Four... Five..." Ian counted as he pressed up and down. "Six... Seven..." He made it look easy.

Cam groaned and fell to the floor.

"Eight... Nine... Ten..." Ian lowered himself to the floor and sat up. "Are ye all right?"

Cam sat massaging the underside of his forearm. "My elbow aches like a bad tooth. It doesn't seem that different from a regular pushup. Why does it hurt so much?"

"Ha! Ye're working a different set of muscles. With a bit of practice the pain goes away."

"How many do ye usually do?"

"Three sets of twenty."

Cam's eyes widened. "Sixty? Will it help me to throw the axe?"

"Aye."

"Hmmphhh." They stood and looked south.

Ian was surprised to see his brother sparring. "I wonder why he's not with his wife. She's giving birth."

"Ah... Childbirth... Isn't that up to the women folk?"

"Ye don't know my brother."

Cam stared at the Lord of the castle. "Ye don't look like brothers. Ye're as different as night and day."

Ian grunted. "It's a long story, which we can talk about it over a tankard of ale. Meet me at the tavern for the midday meal?"

"I will," Cam said. "I'm glad that I agreed to stay. This place gets more interesting by the day."

"The food's good, too. How's the lass?"

"Aileana? Oh, she's sweet! I mean to make her my wife."

"Ye'll have to convince her brother Torry. I hear that he's against the match."

"I know it. Perhaps ye can help me with that."

"We can't take him to the tavern. He won't touch whisky."

Cam frowned. "We'll think of something."

They left the chamber by the north door to avoid disturbing their master.

***

Dughall and Murdock were done sparring. They stored the swords and shields in a specially made cabinet. They'd worked up a sweat practicing close combat forms.

Dughall wiped his face on a towel. "That was just what I needed. Phew! Do I stink?"

Murdock wrinkled his nose. "It could be me."

Dughall sniffed his armpit. "Ach! I think it's both of us."

"Would ye like a bath?"

Dughall smiled. "What about my wife?"

"We'll inquire about her on the way to the bath chamber."

"All right." They started for the door. "I saw Ian practicing with the archer."

Murdock opened the door. "They've become good friends." They stepped into the hallway and shivered. "The temperature dropped. It's feels like winter."

Dughall smiled. "Murdock. Will ye join me for a bath?"

"It wouldn't be proper, my Lord."

"Not to worry. This isn't Huntly. I get to say what's proper."

"Then I will."

***

THE LORD'S BED CHAMBER 1PM

Keira was discouraged. She'd made almost no progress in the last three and a half hours. The contractions were ten minutes apart and her water hadn't broken. The pain was exhausting.

Jessie massaged her back and rubbed her cramping thighs. The midwife offered words of encouragement and told her not to worry. Then she left the room to visit the privy.

Keira *was* worried. Her mother-in-law would need to rest if the labor went on much longer. Dughall could take her place, but each time she considered it the baby kicked fiercely. Did her son suspect something?

Nine months had passed since Dughall's prophetic dream. That morning, he'd been so upset that he suggested ending the pregnancy. Jessie had convinced him that it was only a dream, the result of a high fever. They never spoke of it again. Now the man was looking forward to the birth of his son. Or was he? Her fears blossomed. Did he mean to hurt the child after it was born? What if her son needed protection?

She recalled the pact she made with the Morrigan on the night of his conception. This child would have two mothers. Could she call upon this fearsome force? Keira held her hands out, "Great Goddess Morrigan! Protect our son from harm!"

There was a blinding flash, followed by a crack of thunder. The window blew open, admitting a blast of cold air. A raven black as night sat on the window sill.

Keira shrieked. "Nay! Ye can't have him!" She covered her eyes to block out the sight.

Jessie rushed in. "What's wrong, daughter?" She looked around. "Oh, the window blew open." She proceeded to close it. "I heard the thunder, too. There's a terrible storm outside."

Keira stared. "Did ye not see a raven on the sill?"

"Nay." Jessie placed a hand on her forehead. "Ye don't have a fever."

She felt a chill. "I'm not sick. The raven was there."

Jessie seemed unconvinced. "Well, it's not there now. I can't imagine any bird being out in this weather. They're all tucked away in the pine trees."

A contraction started. "Oh, dear..."

Jessie helped her get comfortable. "Breathe deeply... That's it. Focus on the breathing. I've brought ye something." She placed a rag doll at the foot of the bed. "When the pains come, concentrate on this figure."

Keira rode the waves of pain as she gazed upon the doll. "Oh! I swear that the pain is getting worse."

Jessie washed her hands. "I'll examine ye when the contraction is done. Perhaps there's been some progress."

Keira winced. "It's starting to go down." She waited and sighed. "There, it's ended."

Jessie worked quickly, helping her to sit up against the headboard. "Let's do this differently. Press yer back against the board. Hold yer knees and take small breaths."

Keira buried her fingers in her thighs. "The pains were strong. I wanted to push."

"Don't push! I need to see how far ye are. Hold yer knees and take small breaths."

Keira panted. She felt an odd sensation as the woman examined her. "What is it?"

"Wait." Jessie tried again and pulled out her hand. "There has been a slight bit of progress. I was able to insert three fingers."

Keira whimpered. "Three fingers? Oh, dear Goddess. Is something wrong?"

Jessie washed her hands. "Nay. The child's being stubborn. Perhaps it has a big head." She ran her fingers across Keira's belly, feeling for the baby's position. "The bottom is up here. The head is down and the size seems normal. It isn't breech."

Keira's thoughts were desperate. *It's only one day. I can bear it for the sake of my son. Think of what Janet went through, or Nessia, or Mary, or yer own mother!*

Jessie stared. "I'll get Dughall."

The child within kicked. "Nay!"

"What's going on between ye two?"

Keira reddened. "Nothing."

"Then we must call him. He's been hanging around, asking after yer welfare. I think he's getting offended."

There were no more excuses. "Will ye stay in the room with us?"

"I will stay as long as ye both want me."

A contraction started suddenly. "Oh! It's starting again!"

Jessie frowned. "Dughall has a pocket watch. We can use it to time the contractions."

"Don't send for him yet!"

Jessie left the room.

***

The Duke waited in the hallway outside of his bed chamber. He'd been there for nearly an hour. Murdock had supplied him with a small table and chair and brought him a pitcher of water. Jessie kept him informed of his wife's progress, but suggested he stay outside.

Dughall was a bundle of emotions. His first concern was for his wife. Keira was having trouble bearing the pain and there were signs she was getting discouraged. The birth was taking too long. He worried about his son as well, and prayed for a normal presentation. Some of his feelings were bad. He was angry that they were leaving him out and embarrassed that others knew about it. The news would be grist for the rumor mill.

The door opened suddenly, startling him. Jessie emerged into the hallway and came to him.

Dughall stood. "Mother. Why did she shriek when the thunder clapped?"

Jessie looked flustered. "The window blew open, making an awful sound. She claimed that she saw a raven on the sill."

He felt a chill. “Was it there?”

“Nay. I shut the window.”

“Her people consider the raven a bad sign. Is she any further along?”

“A wee bit. But it’s only three fingers. I can see why she’s discouraged.”

“Can I go in?”

“Aye.”

“Thank God! She needs me at last.”

Jessie frowned. “It’s not like that. I insisted that we summon ye against her wishes. Tell the truth. Has there been trouble between ye?”

Dughall gritted his teeth. “Nay! Why do ye ask?”

“She seems to fear ye. She begged me to stay in the room, especially when the child is born.”

“Why would she fear me?”

Jessie spoke softly. “The dream ye had when the child was conceived…. Did ye bring it up again?”

Dughall reddened. “Nay. My fever caused it. Ye said so yerself.”

She kept her voice low as a servant passed. “Then I can’t say why she’s afraid. It could be hysteria.”

“I’ll ask her myself.”

“I wouldn’t do that. She has too much to bear.”

They heard a voice. “Mother, come quickly! I need ye.”

Jessie blanched. “Let me handle this.”

Dughall bristled. “Nay, Mother! This has gone on long enough. I must talk to her alone.”

“But, I promised…”

“Don’t make promises ye canna keep! Stay here until I send for ye. I mean to get to the bottom of this.”

***

Dughall stood before the door, trying to gain his composure. He’d never seen a woman suffering from hysteria. What would she do? He remembered that Kate threw a plate at him. Keira’s cry spurred him to action. He shoved the door open and hurried inside.

She flinched when she saw him and covered her nakedness. “Stay out! Where is Mother?”

Dughall walked to the bed and sat down beside her. He forced her to take his hands. “Mother is outside.” Dark circles under her eyes made her look like she’d been in a fight.

“Call her!”

“Nay. We have to talk.” He could feel the terror building within her. “Settle down, lass. I won’t hurt ye.”

She started to cry. “I’m afraid.”

He longed to take her in his arms. "Of the birth?"

"Nay, of ye."

His heart was breaking. "Why?"

She spoke between sobs. "Our son. Ye wanted to get rid of him. Don't hurt him!"

He embraced her. "Shhhhh... I had a bad dream, but it was only a dream. Mother said that the fever caused it. I promised ye our son would be born."

She looked up with tears in her eyes. "And afterwards?"

Dughall opened his mind. Could he trust his second sight? His senses told him something terrible. She thought him capable of killing his own son. For a moment, he wavered between anger and compassion. Then love prevailed. He sighed deeply. "Remember when we met in the meadow?"

"Aye."

"Ye said that ye'd dreamed of me and our newborn son."

"'Tis true."

"Then that is what shall be." He kissed the top of her head. "I will not hurt him."

She seemed to be waiting for a sign. Finally, she smiled. "We trust ye."

He was about to ask who the "we" was when she started a contraction. Her body stiffened against the pain.

"Oh! It's starting again. My back feels like it's going to break."

He sprang into action, massaging her lower back. Then he propped up pillows to make her comfortable. "Sit back against these." "Breathe slowly." "That's right." "Use the pain. Think of our son!"

Keira rode the wave of pain until it subsided. Then she nearly collapsed in his arms. "I can't do this alone. Tell me what to do."

Dughall's heart melted. She was helpless and open to suggestion. There could be no doubt. Together, they would birth their son.

***

THE STUDY TEN HOURS LATER CLOSE TO MIDNIGHT

Dughall relaxed in an overstuffed chair, enjoying a fine cigar. While the women attended to his wife, he and Ian had retired to the study to celebrate the birth of his son.

An hour ago, he held the newborn and decided that his dream was false. How could a child with such an innocent face commit such terrible atrocities?

The Duke leaned back and blew out a ring of smoke. He was accustomed to fine tobacco and welcomed any occasion to use it. "We should do this more often, brother."

Ian smiled. "I'm for that. So now ye have a son. Yer subjects will be happy."

His heart swelled with pride. "Aye. They expected me to produce a male heir. Now my property and title are safe."

"He's a robust lad. I heard him screaming down the hall."

Dughall nodded. "The only thing that pleases him is the breast. Not like my daughter."

The clock on the mantle struck twelve. Ian crushed his cigar in a large brass ashtray. "I have to go. There's only one thing that bothers me. Where did he get that red hair?"

"Hmmphh..." The Duke frowned. That worried him too. There was a strip of red fur down his back as well. He recalled that the Morrigan had crimson hair.

"Dinna fret," Ian said. "It will likely change within days. I just don't want anyone to think that I had a part in it."

"Ha! They wouldn't dare say such a thing." He knew beyond a shadow of a doubt that the child was his. The boy bore the clan birthmark on his left shoulder.

Ian stood. "Congratulations, brother. Things will get back to normal before ye know it. It took Mary and me a month."

Dughall sighed. "I hope so. Three months is a long time without the comfort of my wife. I almost went mad."

"Ha! Are ye coming to bed?"

"Nay. I want to stay here a while and think."

Ian left the room and closed the door behind him. Dughall crushed out his cigar and sank into the soft chair, closing his eyes. He'd been up for twenty-four hours. Before long, a pervasive cold sent chills through his body. He opened his eyes, saw his breath, and wondered what was going on. *How strange.*

"Hello, son."

The voice struck terror in his heart. Dughall's skin crawled. The Earl was sitting in the opposite chair, pouring a glass of whisky. He was dressed in his best kilt, a velvet dinner jacket, and a fine shirt. "Father!"

"Who else would it be?" He lifted the glass to his lips and belted the contents. "Ah. I see that ye're drinking the good stuff." His eyes narrowed in mock anger.

He can't hurt me now, Dughall thought. *He's dead.*

"Ha!" The Earl poured another glass. "'Tis true that I'm dead. Killed by yer own hand as legend tells it."

Dughall's heart pounded with fear. The man was reading his thoughts. His body stiffened as he planned an escape.

"Settle down, lad. I won't hurt ye."

"Then why are ye here?"

"To give ye some fatherly advice."

"Advice?" The young Lord leaned forward in the chair. "What is it, Father?"

Blackheart smiled. "So now ye've got a son…"

"Aye."

"Named him after the old bastard I see. Not a bad move, considering that ye inherited his title and property."

Dughall didn't like where this was going. "What do ye want?"

"This child of yers is the talk of the spirit world. It's a risky thing ye've done, playing with pagan magic. The boy has the temperament of his mother, and I don't mean yer wife. Ye'll have one hell of a time keeping him under control."

"But he's just a baby!"

The Earl sipped his whisky and smiled. "Ah. I would give anything to be in the flesh again and enjoy its pleasures. How is Kate, anyway?"

"Father!"

"Got her all to yerself, now? A wife, children, and a beautiful mistress… It's finally happened. Ye're the mirror image of me."

"I'm *not* sleeping with Kate."

"Ye will soon enough. She'll do things to ye that yer wife would never do. Perhaps I can watch."

Dughall reddened. It had been a long time since he'd had sex and in truth he had thoughts about Kate. But how could he know about that? "Father, please!"

"See! Ye *have* been thinking about her. When I think about how it felt to have her soft lips on my cock…"

"Stop it! This is torture."

"Can I watch?"

"Nay!"

Blackheart chuckled. "Well, it's not like I need yer permission. I liked ye from the start, lad. Ye took a whipping without complaint and stood up to me when things got tough. Not like yer weak-willed lily-livered brother."

"Gilbert?"

"Aye. I'm grateful that ye took me down. If it had been him, my reputation would be ruined."

He raised his eyebrows. "Ye don't hate me for killing ye?"

"Nay." The Earl raised his eyebrows. "Do ye hate me for beating ye?"

Dughall reddened. "Sometimes."

Blackheart grinned. "Oh come on! I beat ye and ye killed me. Can't we say that we're even?"

It made sense in a strange way. "All right. I'll *try* not to hate ye."

The Earl slapped his thigh. "I'm glad that we settled that. Now to the matter of the child! From what they say, he'll be nothing but trouble. Strong willed, hotheaded, and fast with the ladies, though I can't fault him for that. Ye'll need what I brought ye."

"What's that?"

Blackheart reached in his pocket, took out the three tailed strap, and threw it on the table between them.

Dughall's head pounded as he stared at the bloodstained whip. "Ye never change, do ye?"

"Ha! That's the beauty of being dead."

"I threw that in the North Sea."

The Earl chuckled. "We have no such boundaries here."

"Take it back!"

"Nay, son. Ye're going to need it and a good set of bindings as well."

"Oh God!" he cried. "Tell me that it's a dream."

"I have to go now." Blackheart stood and smiled. "We'll talk again soon, perhaps after ye bed Kate."

"Nay!" Dughall held his head in his hands and groaned. "Stay away!" He heard a window open and slam shut. He held his breath and listened to his heartbeat until the room grew warmer. When at last he looked up, the spirit of his Father was gone. Was it a bad dream?

The truth was hard to deny. On the table before him lay the three tailed strap.

Jessie

Chapter 53
Letters from the Front

October 9th 1638
TWO WEEKS LATER

DRAKE CASTLE   THE SURGERY

The Duke stood at the medicine cabinet, checking on the progress of his healing vinegars. The works of the ancient Greek physician Galen emphasized the value of these infusions. At first he'd questioned the premise, being accustomed to administering herbs in tea. As he experimented, he found that water did a poor job of extracting essence from plants, but vinegar dissolved them easily. Medicines made in this way proved to be ten times stronger. Vinegar had healing properties of its own. According to Galen, it improved skin tone, strengthened bones, and balanced the four bodily humors. Adding herbs and wild roots made it more powerful. He checked the clear bottles of tonic one by one, noting their healing properties.

Garlic calmed spasms, killed parasites, and fought infections. Alfalfa treated digestive weakness and restored lost vitality. Burdock was good for skin eruptions. It induced sweating and urination. Blackberry relieved diarrhea. The roots were the strongest. Catnip calmed nerves and reduced fever. Dandelion root and flower stimulated digestion. Borage was good for rheumatism.

Dughall checked the bottle containing his latest experiment, an infusion of mugwort. Slightly grey and fuzzy, it could restore a woman's moon cycle. It was also good for digestive ailments, frayed nerves, and bouts of sleeplessness. The color indicated that the medicine was ready.

There was a knock on the door and Jessie entered. She came to the cabinet and looked at the tonic. "It looks good, son."

"Aye, Mother. The wine maker will save us the purest vinegar. With a bit of effort, we can put up enough tonics to last the winter."

She smiled. "Perhaps we can send some to the men in the camps. I hear that they lack medicines."

He closed the cabinet. "'Tis true. Infections are rampant. It's said that even a cut can be fatal."

Jessie looked hopeful. "Has there been any news?"

Dughall nodded. That morning, he'd received four letters from his contact in Edinburgh. One was a report from Lord Balmerino. He acknowledged the receipt of supplies and men and thanked him. He reported that Alex Hay was well and not in immediate danger. The man was being true to his word. The second letter was from a mole in the Tower. He reported that Robert was alive, though his condition was rapidly deteriorating. The last two letters were from his father and these he would share with Jessie. One was for her. He could barely contain his excitement. "Father sent two letters. They were sent in late August."

She blushed. "*Two* letters?"

"Aye." He extracted them from his jacket. "The first is addressed to me, but mentions the family." He unfolded it and began to read out loud. "*My dear son, I was grateful to receive yer letter. The camp moves from place to place and mail delivery is unreliable. I am well. Due to the support of lords like yerself, we are fed, clothed, and armed for battle. I appreciate the support and know full well what a dangerous position it puts ye in.*"

Jessie paled. "Is that true?"

Dughall nodded. "Oh, aye. There is no safe place anymore." He continued reading. "*So, ye are to be a father once more! Perhaps it has already happened. I, too, hope that ye have son to succeed ye. Someday, I shall hold the wee lad on my knee and tell him what a brave father he has. I miss the wee ones, Maggie, Andrew, and Alexander. How they must have grown! Nary a day passes when I don't think of my family; my sons, my wife, and my grandchildren.*"

Jessie sighed. "At last, he writes about his feelings."

"There's more. But it's not pleasant."

"Go on."

He cleared his throat and continued reading. "*I know about Robert.*

My heart breaks when I think of him locked away in prison, awaiting a terrible fate. General Leslie assures me that we will do what we can to free him."

"Is that possible?"

Dughall frowned. "Nay. The Tower is a fortress. Leslie is trying to pacify him."

"Oh. Is there more?"

"He ends the letter by sending his love."

She looked hopeful. "There are two letters?"

Dughall smiled. At last, his father had showed some sense! She'd been waiting months for a personal letter. He placed it in her hands. "This one's for ye."

She seemed shocked. "Shall I read it out loud?"

"Ye don't have to."

"I want to." Her hand trembled as she began. "*My dear wife, forgive me for being such a fool. When I arrived here, there was so much to do. I missed ye terribly but hardened my heart to get me through difficult days. No more! My thoughts are with ye constantly. Oh, how I wish I had ye at my side!*" Jessie suppressed a sob. "*Oh, Jessie. God willing, we will be together again, at Drake or at our cottage by the sea. My only wish is to die in yer arms at the end of my natural life.*" Tears rolled down her face. She couldn't continue. "Oh dear..."

Dughall's heart was breaking. "Don't cry, Mother. I can't bear it."

She held the letter to her heart. "They're tears of joy, son. For a year I've wondered if he loved me. Now I know."

He embraced her. "Of course, he loves ye."

"Will he come home?"

Dughall couldn't lie. "I don't know. Gilbert's men will be obliged to capture him if he shows his face in this county."

"When will the madness end?"

He'd received hopeful news that morning. "Jamison just returned from Edinburgh. He tells me that the King is willing to make concessions. The Council called an assembly for November. The people are deeply divided, but there is a chance we can settle this peacefully."

She gazed into his eyes. "Then, he could come home?"

"I think so."

"And Robert?"

"We shall see."

Chapter 54
Dedication

October 31st 1638
TWENTY-TWO DAYS LATER

MILES FROM DRAKE CASTLE
APPROACHING THE LOCATION OF THE STANDING STONES

It was a glorious fall day. Stately pine trees stretched to the sky, bristling with fragrant needles. The oaks were ablaze with gold and red leaves which blanketed the ground below them. It was a bright, clear day that awakened your senses.

Keira was solemn as they approached the stone circle. Her son was five weeks old. Even though he'd been baptized in his father's religion, it was time to dedicate him to the Goddess. There were things about the baptism that shocked her. They had to promise to raise the child in only that faith. She'd said the words to please her husband, but her heart did not comply. She'd been surprised to learn that Dughall named him James *Conan*, in honor of the owner of the troublesome sword.

Now, it was her turn. She'd chosen this date to take advantage of the circle's power. Intentions set forth on the feast of Samhain had a chance of being realized.

Dughall was away on official business, but would return tonight to celebrate his birthday. In his absence, she'd seized the opportunity to introduce her son to the Goddess. She'd left Drake on horseback with Torry, George, Aileana, and a contingent of protectors. As the Duchess, she was forbidden to travel alone. Therefore, she'd chosen three sympathetic men, Gilroy, Suttie, and Murdock.

Keira was dressed in warm woolen clothes - a long dress, heavy socks, and a cape with a generous hood. She wore a sturdy pair of boots, a necessity for uneven ground. She carried her son in her arms, swaddled in a wool blanket. The scent of fallen leaves filled her nostrils, reminding her of her childhood home.

They were silent as they entered the circle. They walked to the center mound, where she turned to her protectors. "Wait for us in that stand of trees."

Gilroy objected, but Murdock silenced him with a stare. The three men left the circle and walked to the trees, staying in line of sight.

Torry smiled. "It's a fine circle. I must thank the Duke for finding us a place to worship." He opened his rucksack and took out a copper bowl, a measure of salt, and a bottle of anointing oil. He accepted a water flask from George and handed the oil to Aileana. The priest poured water into the bowl and then sprinkled it with sea salt. "We're ready to begin."

Keira's heart swelled with pride as she uncovered the baby's head. James looked innocent when he was asleep. Awake, he was a force to contend with. Demanding, colicky, and prone to rashes, he'd driven her to the brink of exhaustion. His red hair shimmered in the sunlight. Where on earth did he get that from? He opened his green eyes. Did he know what she was thinking? She held out the child. "He's awake. Let's begin."

Torry washed his fingers. "As rain washes the mountains, as oceans wash the beaches, I cleanse this body with water and salt. May it please the Goddess."

They answered in unison. "So mote it be."

He dipped again and brought his fingers to the child's forehead. With a gentle touch he drew the sacred sign, pausing at each position. "East is element Air. The source of light, wisdom and thought." "South is element Fire. The source of energy, will, and blood." He drew a breath. "West is element Water. The source of purification, emotions, and love." The child began to wail. "North is element Earth. The source of knowledge, speech, and silence." Torry sounded nervous. "Center is Spirit, universal energy. The source of life, death, and rebirth." He cleared his throat. "The oil, please."

Aileana opened the bottle and poured a drop on his finger.

Torry drew the sign of the pentacle on the infant's forehead. "We dedicate this child to the Goddess. May he always enter this circle in perfect love and perfect trust."

James wailed in his mother's arms.

"We are done, lass. State yer intentions."

Keira's heart pounded. She could feel the energy building in the circle, supporting their invocation. She uncovered the boy and held him naked to the sky. "Great Goddess! I dedicate my son to ye. May he thrive, prosper, and grow to be a good man."

They answered in unison. "So mote it be."

The baby arched his back and screamed. Keira gasped. Was he objecting to the ceremony or did he simply need to nurse? The boy was hungry most of the time. He nursed around the clock, each time taking a little.

Aileana frowned. "What's wrong with him?"

The Duchess felt like crying as she swaddled him in a blanket. His screams were ear-piercing. "I don't know what's wrong. I never do. I'm so tired."

"Ye need a rest." Aileana took the infant from her arms. "Be still, child! His face is as red as an apple. Oh, whatever is the matter?"

Keira motioned to her protectors. "He's being difficult again. We should go."

Aileana stroked his belly. "His stomach's so tight! Do we have medicine for it?"

Keira sighed. "Nay. Colic is a terrible thing. Everything I tried made it worse. I'm hoping he'll grow out of it."

The three men arrived. Murdock spoke, "Are we ready to leave?"

The Duchess managed a smile. "Aye, friend. Can ye help me back to the horses? I'm suddenly very tired."

Gilroy eyed Aileana. "Can we trust this lass to carry the wee master?"

"Aye."

Gilroy was a burly man, known for his strength. "Then I shall carry ye." Without waiting for permission, he lifted the Duchess into his arms and headed for the woods. The others followed.

Chapter 55
The Glasgow Assembly

November 22nd 1638
TWENTY-TWO DAYS LATER 8AM

PALACE OF WHITEHALL LONDON ENGLAND

King Charles was in a terrible mood. He woke this morning with a feeling of foreboding that escalated to a pounding headache. His wife had been no help. She'd insisted upon coupling to conceive a child. Why should he care? He had two strong sons to succeed him. This headache was intolerable. Why on earth did he marry a French woman? Henrietta was spoiled, fiery, and impossible to please. As he aged, her sexual appetites exceeded his, leaving both of them dissatisfied.

"French whore!" There, he'd said it. Why couldn't she understand that he was under pressure? A man under duress couldn't be expected to perform.

Perhaps she had a problem with boredom. After their marriage, she'd arrived at the castle with a contingent of haughty French servants. He'd tolerated them for quite a while, until he learned that they were undermining him. How dare they come between him and his wife? He'd sent them back to their homeland and surrounded her with English servants. She'd screamed, cried, and begged, but he didn't change his mind. That's when she became focused on having children.

Her cycle! Her cycle! Why was it always her cycle? His genitals were sore. "Damn her!" The woman didn't know when to stop. He too, wished that she was pregnant. At least then, he could relax and keep to separate bedrooms. They'd been married for fourteen years! How could he be expected to be passionate about the same woman? His headache flared. "She drives me mad! I must not think of her." He slumped at the desk, massaging his temples. "Breathe, Charles... Imagine a garden... Roses... Lilies... Your beloved dogs are there... It's a perfect painting." He continued this fantasy until the headache subsided.

Charles took a sip of tea and followed it with a swig of laudanum. He sighed deeply and turned his attention to matters of State. His minister of Scottish affairs was in Glasgow, presiding over the Assembly. Charles didn't trust Hamilton, even though he was a kinsman. The man had too much of a stake in Scotland to be a selfless agent of the King. He was a compromiser who changed his mind with bewildering rapidity. Archbishop Laud said that he had an incoherent mind.

The King wondered if that was true. Hamilton was no diplomat, but he had a military record. This would be vital if they went to war. Unbeknownst to his minister, he'd been making preparations. So far, he'd been able to raise money for weapons and soldiers by selling crown lands and levying taxes. Swords and pikes were starting to arrive from Belgium and the Netherlands. He'd engaged a mathematician to advise him on fortifications. The expense was mind boggling. Unfortunately, the prospect of full scale war would force him to summon a Parliament. *A parliament is a risky enterprise,* he thought. *I've ruled without one for more than ten years.* Yet, it had to be done. Opposition to one of his taxes called Ship Money had caused widespread discontent.

The King needed time to prepare for war. A successful assembly would accomplish that. The initial signs were good. The Councillors had signed the King's bond of faith and invited his bishops to attend. Glasgow had been chosen as the venue due to the nearness of Hamilton's tenants and kinsmen. It was a sympathetic place to hold the Assembly.

Charles opened a fancy bottle and took another swig of laudanum. It had a strong alcoholic taste with a touch of cinnamon. He sighed deeply. "Laudanum is the nectar of the angels. To hell with my doctor's warning!"

***

GLASGOW CATHEDRAL 1PM

Glasgow Cathedral was a severe-looking structure reminiscent of the medieval period. Built during the 13th - 15th centuries on the site of St. Mungo's church, it had been a place of Christian worship for hundreds of years. The interior was breathtaking, featuring richly vaulted ceilings and fluted stone pillars. This was the site selected by James Hamilton for the Assembly of the Scottish Kirk.

Hamilton was a bundle of nerves. Entering the congregational area, he sensed the spirits of thousands of men who walked this path before him. He'd been given an awesome responsibility, made difficult by a changing political situation. In his absence, events had once again marched ahead of him. In the opening session, Lord Rothes and other Covenanters made it clear that the bishops would only be allowed to appear as criminals before the bench. Leading laymen intended to be present as elders of the church. It was a cunning move on the part of the Covenanters. The elections would be managed so that no opponent of the Covenant had a chance to appear before the Assembly.

James grumbled under his breath. Glasgow had turned out to be a hostile venue. His tenants and kinsmen were under the control of his mother, Lady Cunningham, who recently announced that she was a Covenanter. *My own mother is against me!*

His worst fears had been realized. None of the King's bishops attended, because they followed Bishop Spottiswood into exile. The bishop had been falsely accused of debauchery - profaning the Sabbath, carding and dicing, adultery, incest, and drinking in taverns. He'd narrowly escaped with his skin. Leading lay Covenanters attended the Assembly as elders, many of them armed for conflict.

That morning, James had written a note to the King. *Your Majesty. Truly Sir, my soul was never sadder than to see such a sight; not one gown amongst the whole company, many swords but many more daggers. The commissioners, some illiterate, many rigid and seditious Puritans, fill me with despair. What then can be expected but disobedience to authority, if not rebellion?*

Things got worse. Archibald Campbell, one of the most powerful Scots, attended as the eighth Earl of Argyll because of the recent death of his father. A member of the Privy Council, he now had few reasons to prevent him from signing the Covenant. He'd confronted Hamilton about the King's plot to use his father's influence against him, which made him a ready opponent.

The King's commissioner was sweating. This afternoon, he had to read a protest on behalf of the truant bishops. The participants were taking their seats in the meeting area surrounding the pulpit. As the day wore on, he tried to have the protest read and failed. Hamilton was ignored as the Assembly elected Alexander Henderson as Moderator and Archibald Johnstone as clerk. It was an ominous start to the Assembly.

Six days later, after a long and bitter argument with the Lords Rothes and Loudoun over election, membership, and powers of Assembly, James Hamilton declared its dissolution. He pronounced the gathering illegal in the eyes of the King and commanded all present to depart on pain of treason. The commissioner and other royal officers withdrew, leaving Scotland in the hands of the Covenanters.

***

AFTERWORD

The Assembly continued to meet until December 20th. Radical feelings prevailed. Acts were passed that nullified all that Kings Charles and James worked for in the church: the Liturgy, Canons, Five Articles of Perth, and the Court of High Commission. The Covenanters abolished Episcopacy and condemned the Bishops. After a fiery speech by Minister Henderson, they excommunicated them one by one. Lastly, Presbyterianism was restored as the true religion of the Kirk of Scotland. In the end, the General Assembly defied the King and officially launched the revolution. Everyone knew that war was imminent.

Chapter 56
An Uneasy Christmas

December 25th 1638
9AM

HUNTLY CASTLE

The Earl woke for the second time that morning to the sound of wind rattling the windows. As the gale subsided, he heard a noise - a click as the baby broke suction. Gilbert sighed. *The child is eating solid food. How long does she intend to nurse?* He rolled and faced them.

Bridget adjusted her breast. "Oh, ye're awake. It's Christmas, love."

Her long blonde hair was ruffled from sleep. He found this incredibly attractive. "Ah, Christmas." His heart softened. "How is the wee lad?"

She regarded him with soulful eyes. "George is well. I have to be careful. He has two teeth."

"Ouch!" Gilbert said, because he knew it would make her smile.

Bridget rewarded him with a grin. "He hasn't bitten me yet! The teeth are too far apart." Her nipple popped out with a wet sound. For once, the baby seemed content to rest.

He presented the idea. "George is starting to eat solid food. For the rest, we could get a wet nurse."

Bridget gazed at the boy with a look that reminded him of the Madonna. "Not yet. My baby deserves his mother's milk."

Gilbert tried logic. "If ye stopped nursing, ye could get pregnant. A brother for George or a sister…"

She smiled. "I want more children. Is there any hurry?"

"Nay." They had plenty of time to have another child. Gilbert was feeling left out because they hadn't made love in weeks. "Ye're a good mother," he said, and then pointed to his chest, "But *this* lad needs attention too."

A coy smile crept over her face. "I'll take him to the nursery." Bridget stood and laid the infant on the bed. She tied her robe at the waist, slipped on her shoes, and picked up her year-old son. "Wait, my Lord," she teased. "Don't get started without me." She left the room.

Gilbert knew that she wouldn't be gone long. The nursery was three doors away, though it often went days without use. Bridget was determined to be a good mother. He prepared the bed, fluffing the pillows and tearing off blankets. The room was warm, so all they needed was sheets. "Maybe not even those," he said hopefully. Gilbert longed to see her naked and would settle for nothing less. He removed his nightshirt and sat on the bed.

Bridget entered and latched the door. Her blue eyes swept the room, noting his preparations. "Oh, Gilbert. Don't feel neglected. I need ye so." The lass knew what he wanted. She slipped off her shoes and then turning her back, dropped her robe to the floor.

His loins swelled. Her alabaster skin was pink with the flush of arousal. Since the pregnancy she'd become voluptuous, with curves in all the right places. He decided to play a game. "Turn around wench and come here."

She turned. "Command me, my Lord." Her breasts were brazenly exposed. She crawled on the bed and sat beside him. "Do with me what ye will."

Gilbert could wait no longer. He cupped her face, kissed her deeply, and then laid her back on the bed.

"Oh!" Bridget gasped when his mouth found her breast. She reached up and slid her fingers through his hair, encouraging him to continue.

He suckled her nipples until they were stiff and sensitive. Then he whispered in her ear. "Ye taste so good. No wonder the wee lad likes it." He fondled her breasts until her thighs clenched.

Bridget moaned. "Take me, now!"

The Earl's heart pounded in his temples. "Nay, lass." He wanted to taste all of her. Gilbert started at the small of her neck and moved down, running his tongue between her breasts. He lingered at her navel for a long moment and then continued on to her belly.

She arched her hips. "Oh, dear God!"

His manhood felt like it was going to explode. Gilbert parted her thighs and entered her, experiencing a hot silkiness. Her hips rose to meet him as they rutted like young lovers. Bridget dug her nails into his back, a sign that she was ready.

There was a moment or two of wild abandon. Then he arched his back and cried her name as his seed spilled into her. The lass gripped him tightly and shuddered as she came to climax.

Sweat dripped off Gilbert's forehead. He took a breath and crawled off her. "Are ye all right?"

Her lips were red. "Oh, Gilbert. It was just like it was when we were lovers."

He ran his fingers through her hair. "Woman… We must play this game more often."

She snuggled against him. "Tomorrow, we will take George to the nursery again. Then I will serve ye."

Gilbert held her until she fell into a light sleep. He considered himself a lucky man for having a willing wife.

His thoughts darkened. His wife... His son... His title and property... There was so much at stake. He'd received a letter from the King, outlining his responsibilities. Civil war was imminent and he was expected to be a good soldier. He'd also heard from Sir Robert Munro, who repeated his earlier offer. What should he do? Defy the King and join his countrymen? What would be best for his family? Would he prosper or lose his head?

He watched his wife sleep. She was truly a gift from the angels. "Help me, lass. Tell me what to do."

***

DRAKE CASTLE 11AM

Dughall stood outside the Great Hall, preparing to greet his family. He needed to clear his mind. He'd just come from a meeting with Jamison and Jenny, who'd attended the Assembly with the minister. Jenny was heavy with child; due any day. *That lass is tougher than nails. How did she travel like that?*

Why didn't he wait until tomorrow to be updated? What he learned cast a grim shadow over the Christmas celebration. The Covenanters had seized Scotland and excommunicated the King's bishops. It was likely they were headed for war. He wondered if Gilbert knew and resolved to visit him in January.

Dughall put aside these concerns so that he could be fully present with his family. He diverted his thoughts to the morning service. Father John delivered an inspiring sermon, telling the story of the birth of the Savior. They'd taken Keira to the Chapel afterwards, to pray before the statue of the Virgin. Servants had taken the children off their hands, to wash and dress them for the party.

Dughall placed his hand on the door and entered the Great Hall. He hadn't been involved in the preparations, so the arrangements were a surprise. In one corner stood a pine tree adorned with candles, ribbons, and intricately carved animal figures. There were dozens of gifts underneath, wrapped in colored paper. A minstrel troupe performed on stage, playing carols on a harp and dulcimer.

People greeted him with smiles. The first table was laden with food - sweet breads, cakes, and a variety of biscuits. A second table held drinks - milk for the children, mulled wine, and grog for the adults. Two tables were reserved for family and friends and another for invited servants. Kitchen lasses scurried about, serving food and cleaning up messes.

Dughall took a seat next to his wife, who was holding their infant son. Tarrah sat beside her, balancing wee Maggie on her knee. He kissed his wife and son, and then turned to the servant. "Pass my daughter to me."

Tarrah held the child out and placed her in his arms.

"Dada!" The wee girl's face lit up with joy.

Dughall was convinced that Maggie was a prodigy. At fifteen months, she could walk independently, recognize items by name, and follow simple commands. "Give Dada a kiss."

The dark haired child grabbed his face with her little hands. Puckering up, she kissed him on the lips and drew back to see his reaction.

Dughall's heart melted. "I love ye, wee Maggie. It's hard not to spoil ye, as bonny as ye are." He held her close to James. "See? He's yer brother."

Maggie touched the baby's head. Her wee fingers explored his face, his cheeks, and at last his mouth. She looked at Keira. "Momma!"

Keira smiled. "Aye, darling."

"Father?" Luc stood before them, dressed in his finest clothes. "Can I hold him?"

Dughall was glad. Keira had kept everyone away from the infant, because of his trouble with colic. After three months, the baby was calming down. "Aye."

Keira gave him a worried look.

"They're brothers, lass."

Luc sat down and prepared to hold the child.

Keira stood and placed the infant in his arms. "Be sure to support his head and neck."

Luc seemed at home holding a baby. "I will. I've held many babies, Mother. Maggie, the twins, and my own wee sister." There was sadness in his voice. He stroked the baby's cheek. "James, my brother. I promise that we will be great friends."

Dughall smiled. "That ye will. Speaking of friends, where is George?"

"With his sister and brother."

"Ye may invite them to the evening gathering."

Luc's face lit up. "Oh, thank ye, Father! I will." He stood and placed the infant in Keira's arms.

Dughall smiled. "Where is Artus?"

Luc blushed. "Mother said not to bring him to the party. I left him with George and Aileana." He gazed at the tree with eyes of wonder. "There must be a hundred candles! When will we open the gifts?"

Dughall pretended to stall. "Gifts? Have ye been a good boy this year?"

"Father!"

The Duke laughed. He stood with his daughter in his arms, took Luc's hand, and approached the tree. It amazed him that he was the father of a ten year old boy, even if it was by adoption. Babies were fun, but a child was interesting. "Let's see how many of them are for ye." Dughall motioned to the second table, where Ian, Mary, and Jessie sat with the twins. "Bring the children! It's time to open the gifts."

As the children approached the tree, they were barely able to contain their excitement. Jessie began to hand out the gifts.

Dughall watched their shining eyes. *Such precious children... How many mornings will we have like this?*

Thoughts of war could wait 'til tomorrow.

***

CITY OF EDINBURGH GREYFRIAR'S KIRK 2PM

Greyfriars church was filled to capacity. For the first time in years, Scots were free to worship without the interference of the bishops. After the assembly, they'd been sent into exile. Many royalists had gone into hiding. Some prominent families changed sides.

There was no news from London and the silence was deafening. Everyone knew it was temporary. King Charles was known for two things - an unwillingness to compromise and the inability to keep his word. No matter what he said, signed, or promised, he was likely to punish his Scottish subjects.

But today they were free. The birthplace of the Covenant teemed with Scots; soldiers, clergy, gentry, and commoners. Worshippers filled the pews and aisles as well as the church yard and cemetery. They'd come to celebrate the birth of Jesus Christ and to hear Minister Henderson.

Alex Hay sat in a place of honor. General Leslie had been invited to occupy the front pew with six of his loyal soldiers. To his surprise, Hay had been chosen to sit with the commander. The fisherman from Whinnyfold felt like he had a front row seat to an important moment in history.

The Christmas service concluded and Henderson began a fiery sermon. "The LORD said unto my LORD, sit thou at my right hand, until I make thine enemies thy footstool." He stared at the congregation. "What meaning can we take from this?" The crowd hung on his every word. "The WORD was made flesh. Jesus set up his tent and tabernacle amongst us. It was said that amongst the children of men, he should drink of the brook; that is stiff bitter things. Having done so, he would be exalted above all creatures in heaven, and in the fullness of his glory and majesty sit down at the right hand of the Father, and should from thence rule and dispose upon the affairs of his church magnificently and mightily, according to the worthiness and excellence of so great a King and so glorious a Majesty. Until at last all his enemies, both foreign and domestic, should be brought low, and made his footstool; and as they had trodden upon the holy blood of the SON of GOD, he should tread upon them, and poor shame and confusion upon them, and utter banishment from his face forever!"

Alex's heart pounded in his chest. Sitting this close to the fiery minister was having an effect on him.

"The LORD said. This hath an eye to the time to come. There is a time coming when all the enemies of GOD, the most proud and insolent of them, shall be made the footstool of GOD, shall be brought low, and made base and contemptible. And it helps us to lift up our eyes from things on earth to things above, especially to CHRIST himself, who is in the highest heavens, at the top of glory and majesty, the right hand of the FATHER."

"Amen!" the crowd shouted.

"Right honorable and well beloved, we are but short-sighted naturally. We look upon persons and things that are present, and cannot look afar off to things that are past, neither have we a very great prospect to look forward to things that are to come. And as our sight is short, so it is weak also: if we but look upon things here below, our eyes are soon dazzled with the splendor of them, although, when all is done, their luster be not great; we cannot get in with our sight to things that are above. But if we will take the right view, it would help us both in the one and in the other; for ye see it leads from that which is past, to that which is to come." Henderson took a sip of water from a goblet. "My friends; the time has come. We are faced with the enemies of GOD, the most proud and insolent of them. They tread upon the holy blood of the SON of GOD. What shall we do?"

There were shouts. "Crush them!"

"Are ye willing to be the hand of GOD?"

The response was deafening. "Aye!"

The minister mopped his forehead. "The Assembly liberated us. We continued to sit when the King's minister dissolved it. We excommunicated their bishops and cowed their supporters. What does this mean? The future is in our hands. There will be challenges!"

"Long live the Covenant!"

His face was ashen. "In truth; there is only one Kingdom, that of our Lord Jesus Christ. Earthly kingdoms may exist, but they must answer to the ultimate kingdom." He cleared his throat. "King Charles violated that principal. His words and deeds cannot be trusted! Civil war is imminent."

There was silence as the congregation absorbed his words.

Henderson's eyes swept the room and rested on a man in the first pew. "I shall leave the pulpit to allow General Leslie to speak of it."

Alex Hay had conflicting emotions. He took stock of them as his commander entered the pulpit. He was proud to be amongst these men, serving in God's army. He was a devout Christian and a staunch

Presbyterian. But unlike some in the audience, he knew the risks they were taking. The stakes were high. How many would lose everything they cherished - their property, their families, and their very lives? He recalled a Bible verse. Peter told Jesus, "Lord, thy grace enabling me, I will lay down my life for thy sake." The Lord warned him, "It was an easy thing to leave thy boats and nets to follow me, but not so easy to lay down thy life."

Alex's heart ached. He was willing to lay down *his* life for the Lord. That decision came easily. But he feared that his faith might waiver if it meant the destruction of his family. He closed his eyes and saw their faces - Jessie, Ian, Dughall, and the grandchildren. Even his friend, Robert... Oh, Robert... He would be the first casualty.

Henderson was right. There would be challenges.

Chapter 57
Specter of War

January 26 1639
ONE MONTH LATER

LONDON WHITEHALL PALACE

Sunlight streamed through windows in the King's office, casting squares of light on the opposite wall. London was getting a respite, after weeks of punishing rain and snow.

The King sat at his desk, facing one of his advisors. They were discussing the trouble in Scotland. "I refuse to believe it! The average man cannot support this rebellion. The Assembly was a gathering of traitors!"

Archbishop Laud's face was colorless. "The Scots are presenting a united front, from the loftiest Lord to the lowest man. Your Majesty. This Scottish business must be opposed with force. My misgiving soul is apprehensive of great evils coming on. I see no cure without a miracle or war."

Charles gripped the desk. Laud was known for his second sight. "You say that you sense things. Could this be a conspiracy engineered by the Puritans and Cardinal Richelieu?"

Laud sighed. "No, my King. Inquiries have been made. Spies have been planted. There is no conspiracy. In matters of faith, the Scots will not bow to royal authority."

His face reddened. "How dare they? This is not a question about whether a Service book is to be received or not, nor whether Episcopal government should be replaced. The question is simple. Am I their King or not?"

Laud frowned. "They dismissed your bishops. I doubt that they mean to remove their King."

He pounded the desk. "No bishop! No King! It's as simple as that. This situation is intolerable! The answer is war."

The advisor took a conciliatory tack. "What shall we call this war?"

"My bishops were driven out of Scotland. We will call it the Bishops' War."

Laud recorded it in a leather bound journal. "It's a fitting name." He took a breath and began a new page. "The fortifications are underway, but there are problems. The border defenses at Carlisle and Berwick are in desperate need of repair."

"I'll need to garrison two thousand soldiers at Berwick and five hundred at Carlisle."

Laud took notes. "Our citizen's militias are poorly armed with only longbows and scythes. We have no professional army."

Charles trembled with rage. "What are you saying?"

"Substantial funds must be raised to wage war. Are you willing to summon a Parliament?"

The King didn't trust his subjects. During his early reign, he had a contentious relationship with Parliament, taking heavy criticism for his wars with France and Spain. The body refused to provide him with adequate finances, which caused the campaigns to be miserable failures. From that point forward, he resolved to rule without them. He rebuked his advisor. "I've been ruling for ten years without Parliament."

Laud grew even paler. He laid the quill down. "My King. I say this at great risk to my person. We cannot impose enough taxes and fees on the people to wage this war. The majority of crown lands have been sold or leased. We must call a Parliament."

Charles gritted his teeth. The man *was* overstepping his bounds. "I shall deal with that later!" He balled his fists to control his temper. "We are not destitute. The Lord Treasurer assures me that two hundred thousand pounds can be spared from the Exchequer."

Laud seemed properly chastised. "That would be enough to get started."

"That should be enough to resolve the matter! The Foreign Council Committee advised me to raise men and supplies and go to York at the head of an army of thirty thousand. We can launch the campaign from there. They assure me that no common man will be so mad as to hazard their lives and estates with the King's army in the fields."

"Let's hope that they're right. Who else can we depend on?"

King Charles stared. "The High Clergy will make the case to our people. There are a substantial number of wealthy Catholics willing to support the conflict in hopes that I'll bring back the Catholic Church. Ha!"

Laud flushed. "Any military support, my King?"

"I sent a courier to Lord Huntly, instructing him to raise an army and secure the northeast."

"Good. What do you wish me to do?"

"Craft a declaration. Tomorrow we will proclaim my intention to raise an army against the Scots."

"As you wish, my King."

Charles knew how to manipulate people. "This Sunday, announce in every church that the Scots have risen in arms to invade us."

Laud cleared his throat. "Our last report said that their forces were gathered around Edinburgh for defensive purposes."

"Defensive! How long will that last? Summon the northern barons and their vassals. We'll tell them that they intend to invade the Shires. They must meet me at York on April the first."

"As you wish, my King."

"With invasion imminent; if I call a Parliament, they will be forced to grant me the funds."

Laud picked up his pen. "I bow to your infinite wisdom. Where shall we begin?"

"Let us craft the declaration. But before it's released... Arrest all Scottish ships lying in English harbors and stop all commerce between the two countries. Intercept all posts and passengers bound from England to Scotland. The Covenanters must not learn the extent of our preparations."

***

EDINBURGH J ADAMS TAVERN

General Leslie sat at a table in the J. Adams Tavern, nursing a tankard of ale. Since the signing of the Covenant, the establishment had served as a meeting place for its supporters. The owner was determined to keep their business. A false wall had been erected to provide privacy for five tables.

Today, Leslie was alone in the private section. He was waiting for Lord Balmerino, who was coming to give him an update. There'd been a meeting of prominent Covenanters that he was anxious to hear about. The oak door groaned, signaling that someone entered the tavern. Footsteps sounded across the hard plank floors. Moments later, Lord Balmerino came around the partition. The nobleman appeared no worse for wear. He wore a tailored woolen cape and carried his gold-topped signature cane.

"Good day, Alex." Balmerino bowed his head slightly and took a seat opposite him.

"John." Leslie signaled to the tavern lass to bring another tankard of ale. "I have an hour before my men return. How goes it?"

"We met at Greyfriar's this morning to finalize preparations. Our guess is that we have until spring before the King leads a land army upon Louthian and Edinburgh. It is likely that one part of his navy will go to Aberdeen to join with Lord Huntly, another to the coast of Fyfe. A third may launch from Ireland and land in the west."

Leslie nodded. "We've had similar discussions. Did the Tables agree to raise a larger army?"

"Aye."

"Good We must prepare for these invasions. Should we move our forces to the southern border?"

"That's the plan. We're working on the details."

He sipped his ale. "We will have to rely on others to protect the ports. Who met with ye?"

Balmerino smiled. "Lords Rothes, Montrose, and other prominent Covenanters. The eighth Earl of Argyll attended."

Leslie raised his eyebrows. "Archibald Campbell? Has he signed the Covenant?"

Balmerino accepted a tankard of ale from a lass and waited until she was out of earshot. "Not yet. But we expect him to soon. We convinced him of the threat of an invasion from Ireland. What a boon! Campbell commands twenty thousand men. The man is respected in the Highlands and Lowlands."

"It's good to have him on our side. Does he have any military experience?"

"Nay, but he's a skilled politician. We could use such a man at the head of our movement. It's being discussed."

Leslie's eyes widened. "Won't that anger Montrose?"

"He'll get over it."

He scowled. "It's too bad that Lord Huntly refused our second offer."

Balmerino nodded. "Rumor is that he's been appointed as the King's lieutenant. Expect trouble from the northeast, especially the port of Aberdeen."

The General sipped his ale. "Yet, we have his brother on our side. How strange."

Balmerino made a small sound of agreement. "The man who raised him is a Covenanter."

"Alex Hay."

"Aye. But I think that there's more to it than that. Henderson and I met with him last June. Lord Drake is a Catholic who used to be a Protestant. He was forced to convert when he was claimed by the Gordons. He says he believes in freedom of religion."

"Hmmphh… It's an interesting concept. Perhaps someday, it will be worth fighting for."

"Lord Drake signed the Covenant."

"Impressive… What did Henderson think of him?"

Balmerino smiled. "Henderson pressed him to return to the true religion. He sees everything as a battle for souls."

Leslie chuckled. "So the Gordon brothers are on opposite sides. What will happen if they face each other?"

Balmerino sipped his ale. "It wouldn't be the first time that brothers met on a battlefield." He put down the tankard. "How is Alex Hay? I must give Lord Drake an update."

Leslie thought for a moment. How could he put this in a good light? "Lieutenant Hay is strong in body and devout in faith. He's not a man I would choose as a lieutenant because he lacks battlefield experience. I did it solely to attract Lord Drake to our side. That's not the disturbing part."

"What else?"

"He cares for people too much. I wonder how he'll act in a desperate situation."

"I hear that his friend is imprisoned in the Tower."

Leslie frowned. "Aye. Now that war is imminent, the man is as good as dead."

"How is Hay handling it?"

"Badly. He asked permission to go to London to see if he could free him."

Balmerino stared. "Fool! It's not like the Tollbooth in Peterhead. What did ye tell him?"

"I denied his request. I said that we would try to negotiate his freedom."

"That won't happen. We have more pressing matters."

Leslie nodded. "Agreed. Perhaps we should send Hay back to his family. The Duke can hide him from Huntly's men."

"Nay, keep him here. It will assure us of Lord Drake's support."

"Enough about Hay! What will the English think when we gather at their border?"

"Our peddlers have been busy, my friend. They distributed a manifesto across England, addressed to all good Christians. It makes the case that our cause is nothing more than an opposition to Popery; that we are not just rebels aimed at subverting royal authority. It disavows the thought that we mean to invade the Shires."

"Brilliant!"

Balmerino stood and straightened his coat. "Let's meet again in a week, unless I summon ye sooner. By that time, ye should have marching orders." He offered his hand.

Leslie stood and shook it. "Goodbye, my friend. We will win this war one way or another."

They left the tavern ten minutes apart so that no one would connect them.

***

HUNTLY CASTLE

Dughall sat in the study, waiting for his brother Gilbert. When he arrived at Huntly with Jamison, they'd been told that the Earl was occupied. The two men had been offered drink and a chance to freshen up in the guest quarters. In a way, it was divine order. Over several drams of whisky, Jamison expressed a deep sadness. He'd been devastated when his son died at birth. The young Lord didn't know what to say. All he could do was squeeze the man's hand.

Dughall thought it strange that his brother hadn't greeted them, until one of the serving lasses let it slip. Gilbert was meeting with local nobles to raise an army against the rebellion.

It was well after four o'clock when he was informed that Gilbert had returned. Dughall had been escorted to the study and told to get comfortable. That was an impossible task, short of drinking himself silly. He was nervous and needed to talk to his brother.

The door opened and Gilbert entered. Dughall stood to greet him, but the man went straight for his bottle.

"Forgive me, brother," Gilbert said, as he poured a glass of whisky. "I've had an abominable day." He brought out another glass and proceeded to fill it. "Ye look like ye need one too."

They sat in the oversized chairs. Dughall sipped the amber liquid, allowing it to wind slowly to his stomach. Soon, things didn't seem so bad. He owed his brother an apology. "I'm sorry that I didn't get here sooner. I had to mediate a conflict between my subjects. Then my adopted son got sick with the grippe."

"Is he all right?"

"Luc is better." He looked around. "Are there any cigars?"

Gilbert smiled. "Forgive my bad manners." He handed him a mahogany humidor. "These are from the Caribbean islands."

The Duke opened the humidor and extracted two cigars. He held one under his nose to sniff the aroma and gave the other to his brother. "Smoke with me."

Gilbert accepted it and trimmed the end. They passed a lit taper.

Dughall held the cigar level in contact with the flame. He rotated the fire around the open end and then puffed lightly. The flavor reminded him of spicy black pepper. "Father was right. There's nothing like a good cigar."

Gilbert seemed surprised. "I thought ye hated him."

"Aye, but no more. I decided to forgive him."

"How did that happen?"

Dughall took a draw and then blew out smoke. "On the night my son was born, Father appeared to me."

Gilbert's eyes widened. "In a dream?"

"Let's call it that. He came to give me fatherly advice about raising my son."

"He's the last man I would take advice from."

"That's what I thought! At first, I was angry that he'd come. My mind reeled with the things he'd done to me."

"Just out of curiosity... What did he say?"

Dughall put down the cigar. "He asked me if I was still angry at him. I said 'aye'."

"And..."

"Then Father said, 'Oh come on! I beat ye and ye killed me. Can't we say that we're even?'"

Gilbert chuckled. Then he broke into a resounding laugh. "Sounds like him."

Dughall smiled. "It does. But the logic is good. I think we *are* even."

"So ye've forgiven him."

"Aye. It was good to get rid of those poisonous feelings."

Gilbert sighed. "I've been thinking about him lately, wishing that he was alive. Not that I liked being under his thumb. It's a wonder that *I* didn't kill him."

"We both had reason."

"Father was cruel and arrogant, but he knew how handle politics. I don't have the knack. There are so many viewpoints to each situation. Some of my subjects refuse to compromise. This rebellion will be the death of me."

They were silent for a minute, contemplating their circumstances.

Dughall sipped his whisky. "The Covenanters banished the King's bishops and took over the Assembly. They passed articles excommunicating the bishops and abolishing Episcopacy."

Gilbert sat back in the chair. "I know. A mole in the cathedral provided me with a transcript. It doesn't matter what they passed. The King declared the proceedings illegal. He called it an Assembly of traitors."

"Have we heard from the King since the Assembly?"

Gilbert reddened. "Heard from him? The King is about to declare war. He expects me to raise an army under the royal standard. Then I must secure the northeast."

Dughall swallowed hard. "Has he mentioned me?"

"Nay. Ye should be grateful. We must have put on a convincing show. He thinks ye're an ignorant peasant."

So the Queen hasn't told him, Dughall thought. *She has other plans for me.* "What will ye do?"

Gilbert bolted his whisky and then poured another glass. "I don't know, brother. Go through the motions. I'll have to raise an army. Arrest a few men. Claim the port of Aberdeen in the name of the King. I'm not a military man. Hopefully, it won't go beyond that."

His heart sank. "And if it does? Will ye come to the other side?"

"Nay." Gilbert sipped his drink. "The Gordons have always been loyal to the King. I will do what he asks."

Dughall's voice was soft. "Even if it comes to me?"

Gilbert sniffled. "Ye're the only man I care about, brother. I will see ye safe, even if it means my life." There were tears in his eyes as he lifted his glass. "Here's to a speedy end to the conflict. Let's pray that it never comes to that."

James Graham, Earl of Montrose

Chapter 58
Montrose

February 6th 1639
ELEVEN DAYS LATER

THE EARL OF MONTROSE'S WINTER ESTATE IN THE COUNTY OF ANGUS

James Graham, Earl of Montrose, relaxed in a comfortable chair in front of a roaring fireplace. He was taking a rest at his estate before setting out on an assignment. He was a zealous Covenanter who'd spent more than a year in Edinburgh, serving on the Table of the Nobility. The twenty-seven-year old hadn't always been at odds with the King. After an early marriage he'd spent time abroad, becoming proficient in Latin and Greek and acquiring a reputation as an accomplished gentleman. Returning to Scotland with large expectations, he met with the royal court and received a less than desirable reception. As a result, in November of 1637, James Graham joined the Tables at Edinburgh along with Lords Rothes, Lindsay, and Loudon, becoming an efficient and outspoken member. When Traquair published the King's proclamation approving of the service book, Graham was outraged. He stood bravely on the scaffold beside Archibald Johnstone as he read the protest in the name of the Tables.

Rothes had dared to declare, "James, ye will never be at rest 'til ye be lifted up there - above yer fellows on a rope."

Graham had scoffed. "That will never happen."

The Glasgow Assembly had increased his reputation and brought him to the forefront of the rebellion. With war imminent, he'd been given a commission. His assignment was to visit the Aberdonians to secure support for the covenanting cause. The truth was, they'd tried this before. Last July, he'd traveled to Aberdeen with sympathetic lairds and clergy to persuade the 'Aberdeen Doctors' of the university to sign the covenant. They'd been unsuccessful. "They will listen to me this time," he stated with determination, "or I shall resort to the point of a sword."

There was a knock at the door and a servant entered. The elderly man bowed slightly and handed him a sealed envelope. "My Lord. This was just delivered."

Graham recognized the wax seal of a friend. "Is the gentleman here?"

"Nay, my Lord. The man was a courier. He dropped the letter and headed for Glasgow."

"That will be all."

The servant bowed slightly and left the room.

Graham picked up a silver letter opener from the side table and sliced opened the envelope. The one page letter appeared to be hastily written.

James, my friend. I received yer letter with interest. I too am sympathetic to the cause, though it puts me at risk in my surroundings. As ye may know, there is to be a meeting of Covenanters in this quarter at Turriff on the fourteenth of February. By intercepting letters, we have learned that Lord Huntly intends to assemble friends and followers to prevent said meeting from occurring. Huntly has vast influence in Aberdeenshire and is likely to arrive with hundreds of well armed men. He is in league with the King and has arrested and sent dozens of us to the Tower. I hope this reaches ye in time. We need yer help and protection so that we can proceed with this important convocation. Go with God. Yer friend, Donald Grant of Clan Grant

Graham stood and crushed the letter in his hand. "By God! The fourteenth is only a week away. To protect them, I must arrive before Lord Huntly." He paced the room in front of the fireplace. James Graham had been weaned on tales of knights and battles. This was his chance to make a name for himself as a warrior. "I shall gather my surest friends and lead them against these royalists!" He left the room in a rush, eager to get started.

***

CITY OF ABERDEEN

Lord Huntly was beginning to understand his predicament. As Gilbert gathered an army under the royal standard, nearby lords undermined him. The Earl of Sutherland, accompanied by Lord Reay and the Master of Berridale, scoured Inverness and Elgin persuading people to sign the covenant. Gilbert wrote Sutherland confidentially, rebuking him and advising him to declare for the King. He'd just received the man's terse reply, stating that he was against the bishops and their innovations but not against the King. Sutherland then had the nerve to advise Gilbert to join the covenanters for the good of his native country. Until that time, he was unwilling to aid him in his present affair.

Gilbert felt nauseous. "This is a disaster! What would Father have done?"

Lord Sutherland had provided him with a list of others on his side; the Earl of Seaforth, The Master of Berridale, the Lord Lovat, The Lord Reay, the laird of Balnagown, the Rosses, the Monroes, the laird of Grant, Mackintosh, the laird of Innes, and the sheriff of Moray. He even had the gall to mention the politics of Lord Drake, his beloved brother.

Gilbert was outnumbered. At the same time, the King demanded that he march an army upon the city of Aberdeen to possess it in the name of the crown. He'd assembled his forces at Turriff, and afterwards at Kintore, whence he marched upon the city with slightly more than five hundred men. They'd encountered few hostilities. Aberdonians by nature supported Episcopacy and were unwilling to break with the King. Lord Huntly was welcomed by most inhabitants, led by those associated with the university. In a public display, he'd claimed the city for the King and then taken advantage of their hospitality. That was when he was informed that a meeting of covenanters residing in his district was to be held at Turriff on the fourteenth of February.

Emboldened by success, Gilbert resolved to disperse them. He wrote letters to his allies and chief dependents, requiring them to meet him at Turriff on that morning. He considered writing to his brother, but thought better of it. There was merit in what they were trying to do - stay on both sides of the issue. When Dughall proposed the idea, he'd thought that he'd have the easier path by remaining a royalist. Now he was the one who was facing obstacles.

The meeting was a week away. In the meantime, he'd been afforded private quarters at the best inn, complete with a cabinet stocked with fine spirits. This was certainly no time to limit his drinking. He sat at an elaborately carved round table and poured himself a tall glass of whisky.

There was a knock at the door. "Come..."

Connor entered, bearing a tray with their evening meal. The food smelled good, like a prime cut of roasted beef. "They're treating us like royalty, my Lord. Should I serve ye at this table?"

Gilbert stared. "Aye. But dine with me."

Connor's eyes widened. He put down two plates, extracted silverware from a pocket, and arranged it at each setting. Lastly, he took a seat.

The Earl poured him a generous glass of whisky. "First, join me in a drink."

Connor picked up the glass and took a long swallow. "Ye seem preoccupied, my Lord. Are ye all right?"

Gilbert managed a smile. "Aye. Connor, ye've been with the Gordons a long time."

The servant nodded. "More than twenty years. I came to Huntly when ye were a child."

"My father faced situations like this."

"Oh, aye. Politics! Negotiations! Betrayal! I followed him into battle often."

"Did he always know what to do?"

Connor took another sip. "Nay. But he always *acted* like he knew what to do. That's what inspired confidence in the men. We would have followed him through the gates of hell."

Gilbert finished his whisky. "Tell me about one of the battles."

The servant smiled. "My Lord, ye never talk about yer father. I thought ye hated him."

"I did."

"Has something changed?"

His answer surprised him. "I've forgiven him."

Conner picked up his fork. "Good! Now ye can draw on his vast experience as told by his loyal servant." He stabbed a piece of meat and watched juice drip off it. "Ah… Blood… I'll start with the skirmish we had with the Camerons. Back then, they called yer father the 'Cock of the North". He was about yer age…"

Lord Aboyne

Chapter 59
Decision Points

February 14th 1639
EIGHT DAYS LATER 6AM

DRAKE CASTLE THE LORDS BED CHAMBER

The Duke stood at a long oval mirror, smoothing a wrinkle in his kilt. He tucked in his silk shirt and adjusted his best sporran. The top of the leather pouch was trimmed with silver and decorated with a precious stone.

Keira called from the bed. "Ye look handsome in those clothes. Where are ye going today?"

Dughall slipped on a formal jacket and came to the bed. "I have a meeting with Jamison to discuss the troops. Then we're expected at a meeting."

"With who?"

"Some local nobles." He stopped, entranced with the scene. His wife was nursing their infant son. "James seems better this morning." The baby had gone from three months of colic to weeks of angry skin rashes.

Keira moved him to the other nipple. "Mother gave me an ointment for his pimples. It seems to have done some good."

"Thank God!" Dughall didn't hide his frustration. "The child has so many problems. I long for the morning when we can couple in peace."

Keira stiffened.

He didn't mean to hurt her. "Forgive me, lass. I meant nothing by it."

She sighed. "It *has* been a while since we've made love. I'll ask Tarrah to take the morning feeding."

The baby abandoned her nipple and screamed. James screwed up his angelic face and drew up his legs to his stomach. He shrieked as he passed gas.

Keira was close to tears. "Not this again! Every time I consider help, he takes a turn for the worse."

Dughall wondered if the child sensed her intentions. Early on, he'd learned to block such thoughts when in the baby's presence. But his wife held nothing back. *Oh, no. She's starting to cry. I should take a more active role in his care.*

James shrieked at this thought.

Dughall stroked his hair. "There, there, my son. Have mercy on yer poor mother."

Tears streamed down her face. "Go to yer meeting. I'll be all right."

Dughall knew that staying would make it worse. They could always talk later, when the child was asleep. He bent down and kissed her on the forehead. "I love ye both. We'll be gone most of the day. I'll see ye after supper."

The child shrieked as he left the room, fraying his nerves. He dreaded the meeting, but it was better than staying here. The boy was driving him to distraction. Oh, he loved his son. It wasn't that. He had just one wish - to see his wife back to her lighthearted self.

He walked to the infant nursery, but hesitated at the door. *Keira needs to ask Tarrah for help, not me. She must be willing to let the boy out of her sight.*

For Keira loved and protected James with a rare fierceness. She hadn't been as concerned about their daughter, who'd stayed with the wet nurse from the start.

This has gone too far! James' cradle must be moved to the nursery. We need the peace and privacy of our bedroom.

The Duke walked to the top of the staircase and looked back. He sensed that the boy was asleep at her nipple, and they were both resting comfortably. His guilt subsided. Perhaps they would be all right. He took the stairs to the west wing, hurried down the corridor, and entered his favorite room, the library. Dughall smiled as he looked around. Tall windows allowed sunlight in on good days and kept out the cold on others. The rosewood furniture was polished, enhancing its pinkish hues. Glass-faced bookcases housed thousands of books, maps, and scrolls. He hadn't read all of them. To top it off, there was a world globe and a fine telescope. Jamison had been here. There was a provisions ledger on the desk, along with an ink well and several quills. There was also an unopened letter from his father.

Dughall suppressed his feelings of dread as he sat at the desk and handled the letter. It had been months since he'd received word from Alex. Lord Balmerino had kept him informed of his status, although he wouldn't disclose his location. Oh, how he wished that Father was here to advise him on family matters! He sliced open the envelope, removed the letter, and began to read.

My beloved son. This must be short because we are on the move. Words cannot express how much I miss my family. When we retire to our cots at night, I remember our days by the sea. My wife, my sons, and dear old Maggie. Those were the best times of my life. I attended the Christmas service at Greyfriars and heard Minister Henderson speak. It was awesome to be in his presence. Many more thousands have joined the army, swelling our ranks to beyond capacity. We will soon be expected to protect our southern border. There is no word on Robert as yet. Last I heard he was weak and discouraged from the long incarceration. Pray for him. And pray for me, because if they do not release him, I will be obliged to go to London. Leslie says that they are trying to secure his release, but I do not trust him.

Dughall clutched the letter. "Nay, Father!"

Jamison entered with a breakfast tray and set it upon the desk. "What's wrong, my Lord?"

"My father's letter," he sputtered. "He means to try to rescue Robert!"

Jamison sat at the desk. "What did he say?"

He says, "Pray for me, because if they do not release him, I will be obliged to go to London."

Jamison let out a low whistle. "The King's men will capture him when he sets foot on the Tower grounds. Can we contact Lord Balmerino?"

Dughall was having trouble thinking. Fear washed over him like an ocean wave. "I don't know where he is. My last letter took a month to reach him. Everything's moving so fast. There's a race to protect the sea ports and borders."

Jamison poured him a cup of tea. "Here. Drink this."

Dughall sipped it. "What would ye do?"

"Ask Lord Balmerino to recall Alex. It's for the best. He shouldn't be commanding men if he's considering desertion."

"I'm sure that my father doesn't see it that way."

Jamison chewed a biscuit. "It *is* desertion. The General would have the right to execute him if he left his men."

Dughall's head ached. "I'll write Balmerino. But we must show this to Ian."

"Agreed."

"For God's sake, don't tell my mother. Could we go after Father?"

"We don't know where he is."

The Duke frowned. "I'll send that letter today." He looked at the ledger. "Let's talk about the troops. Why do they need so many supplies?"

Jamison smiled. "The ranks have swollen to eighteen hundred. Men arrive daily from other jurisdictions to join the Dark Lord's regiment."

The name wounded him. "Fang is responsible for the Dark Lord name."

Jamison looked thoughtful. "It's a good thing, my Lord. Men who don't know ye are willing to follow ye through the gates of hell. Not only do they fear ye, they think ye have the power over life and death."

"Because of Luc..."

"Aye. That story spread far and wide. Ye brought him back from the dead."

"I guess so." Dughall sighed. "It's an unnatural thing but I don't regret doing it."

Jamison offered him a scone. "Eat some breakfast. In the meantime, embrace the name and act the part. We should call ye Blackheart. There's nothing fair about war. It will give us an advantage on the battlefield."

Dughall bristled. "All right." He signed the bottom of the ledger with a scrawl. "Send the provisions. But talk to our suppliers. We'll need more if the ranks continue to swell."

"Thank ye, Blackheart."

Dughall cringed. "Few of these men are soldiers by trade. What about training?"

"I've stationed Ian, Suttie, Fang, and Cam at the range to oversee training."

"Do we have enough weapons?"

The servant folded the list and tucked it into his jacket. "One of our ships just returned from Holland with a cache of weapons. Swords and pikes... Dirks... Pistols and ammunition for officers... I inspected it yesterday. The quality is good."

"Hmmm... What about bows and arrows?"

"We're making them at the weapons range. Cam is overseeing it."

Dughall wolfed down the biscuit. "Station Gilroy and Pratt at the weapons range until further notice. Send Ian home for a few days. I need to talk to my brother."

"As ye wish." Jamison stood. "Alex might be valuable here. We could use him at the range or captaining a ship."

Dughall joined him. "It's a good idea."

"My Lord. We must leave now or we'll be late for the meeting."

"Ah, the nobles... What else can go wrong today?"

"I don't know, my Lord."

"I wonder what Gilbert is facing."

"Can we talk about that later? We have enough to worry about."

***

TURRIFF 7:30AM

The village of Turriff was fifteen miles northeast of Huntly Castle. It had an ancient church, established in the seventh century. A hundred twenty feet long by eighteen feet wide, it was surrounded by stone walls. The gateway to the courtyard was protected by iron bars and there was an ornate belfry with a bell. Turriff was a center of trade. The town was comprised of red sandstone houses and the workshops of craftsmen and artisans.

James Graham, Earl of Montrose, stood proudly in the old churchyard. The young man had accomplished the impossible in seven days. He'd collected his friends in Angus, his own and their dependents, and crossed the range of hills between Angus and Aberdeenshire called the Grangebean. That morning, his company of eight hundred took possession of the village to protect the covenanters. Graham was feeling smug. Now, the meeting could take place without interference from Lord Huntly. According to the intercepted letter, Gordon and his army were expected soon to arrest men and breakup the gathering.

James scoffed. *He'll get a surprise! We're armed and ready to fight for freedom.*

Donald Grant stood at his side. The stocky man was armed with a sword and a dirk. "We appreciate this, James. Lord Huntly has been persistent. Good men have been taken to the Tower."

"Huntly is that determined?"

"Oh, aye. He's worse than his late father. Blackheart was willing to negotiate for hostages. Lord Gordon turns them over to the English."

"Once in the Tower they're as good as dead."

Donald paled. "My brother is one of them."

James grunted. "Poor bastard."

Grant mumbled, "If we win this war, we can get him back."

Graham didn't answer. The King would leave a bloody trail before he released any prisoners. "Hmmphhh... What is that?"

The church bell was ringing frantically. They heard a skirmish outside the churchyard and went to investigate.

***

George Gordon, known as Lord Aboyne, was a cousin of Gilbert Gordon. Unmarried at nineteen, he'd had minimal contact with his cousin. They'd been reacquainted at the funeral of his uncle, where he'd offered his support.

Weeks ago, he received a letter from Lord Huntly, requesting help with a situation. He was to gather his supporters and dependents, and ask them to meet him at Turriff on the fourteenth day of February. They were to bring with them their usual arms. Acting under the royal standard, his cousin intended to break up a meeting of covenanters. George expected this to be easy. For decades, his uncle had enjoyed the support of the northeast. Surely this had been extended to his successor. Perched on his favorite steed, he led more than four hundred armed men on the approach to Turriff.

It was late morning when Lord Aboyne's men entered the town. To their surprise, it was filled with hostile armed soldiers, some who leveled firearms at them across the walls of the churchyard. The church bell rang frantically, calling men to arms, and his cousin Gilbert was no where to be seen. Not knowing how to act without Lord Huntly, George retreated to a place two miles south called the Broad Ford of Towie, where he was joined by other lords, as well as Gilbert and his large army. Here a debate ensued, about whether they should advance and attack the place or withdraw.

Lord Aboyne was frustrated. He knew what his uncle would have done. His cousin seemed a weaker version of his father. "Let us attack! We have almost two thousand men."

Gilbert reddened. "Did ye count their men?"

George stared. "Nay, but their numbers are far less than ours. We should teach them a lesson while we have the advantage."

Gilbert appeared to be considering this. "Who is commanding them?"

"The Earl of Montrose... I saw his standard."

"Did they attack ye?"

"Nay, but that doesn't matter. They are testing our resolve, cousin. We must show force."

Lord Huntly paled. "We expected no fighting forces. My commission authorizes me to act only on the defensive."

"What?"

"That's what the King's letter said."

George threw up his hands. "This is a disaster! What will we do?"

"Perhaps we can provoke them."

After a heated discussion, Gilbert and George came to an agreement. They left Towie and led their men in battle formation along the northwest side of the village of Turriff.

Lord Aboyne was livid. *If even one man fires at us, I will lead the charge to destroy them.*

***

James Graham was as tense as a bowstring as they joined the lookout in the belfry. He could hardly believe his eyes. The churchyard was secure. But thousands of armed men marched in battle formation along the northwest side of the village. With his spyglass, he located Lord Huntly and Lord Aboyne, leading the long procession. "Damn them! Why do they not attack?"

The lookout was silent. Donald Grant dared to answer. "They're cowards."

Graham growled. "Nay. It can't be. They have twice as many men as we do. Something must be stopping them."

"Well, it won't for long. Shall we attack?"

"Nay. Everyone must hold their fire." Graham's resolve hardened as he watched them march out of sight. "They're leaving. By God's grace, we averted a battle. But tomorrow is another story. Their numbers are impressive."

"Aye. What will we do?"

"I must collect a large force to serve the covenanters and take back the city of Aberdeen."

Chapter 60
Retreat

March 30th 1639
SIX WEEKS LATER

APPROACHING THE CITY OF ABERDEEN

The Earl of Montrose was in fine form. Upon returning to his county, he'd proceeded to assemble troops, according to a commission he'd received from the Tables. Two things aided him - his enthusiasm and the willingness of men to enlist. Within a month, he'd drawn three thousand horse and foot soldiers from the counties of Fife, Forfar, and Perth.

The troops were divided into regiments with officers presiding over companies. They had five colors or banners. Montrose's banner was blue and bore the motto 'For Religion, the Covenant, and the Country'. The Earl of Kinghorne had one, the Earl of Marischall had another, and the town of Dundee had two. They were well armed with quality weapons. Every footman had a sword and pike. Each musketeer had a musket, sword, and a belt with pouches for powder, balls, and matches. Every horseman had a rifle and two pistols in his belt. Officers wore buff coats, thick leather jerkins that protected them from swords and balls.

This is what James Graham was wearing. The Earl smiled. The King's men wore red ribbons. He'd insisted that each footman wear a bunch of blue ribbons on his bonnet as a distinguishing badge.

Trumpeters accompanied the horsemen, drummers marched with the footmen, and others trailed behind, carrying meat, drink, and necessary provisions.

The Earl of Montrose glanced at the man riding at his side. General Leslie was a striking figure whose presence commanded respect. The fact that he'd come north to join forces with them was to his credit. He'd recently heard that Archibald Campbell joined the movement and was rising to power. He'd never liked the man and intended to surpass him.

Graham hadn't been totally honest with Leslie. He didn't tell him that Lord Huntly and the city of Aberdeen attempted to enter into a peace agreement with him. He'd rejected their proposals, thinking that they wished to stall for time until the King's forces relieved them.

Trumpeters sounded as they approached the Kirkgate port of the city. General Leslie stroked his stallion's mane. "Not much longer. The gates are ahead." He turned to Graham. "I don't see any troops guarding the city. A military man wouldn't recall his army without attempting to negotiate a truce."

Graham reddened. "It appears that Lord Huntly has."

Leslie raised his eyebrows. "There's been no contact between ye and Huntly?"

He grew redder still. "Nay."

"Then he is a fool."

A bearded messenger rode towards them at a fast clip. He stopped in front of Leslie. "Sir. I have news."

General Leslie nodded. "What did ye find?"

"Lord Huntly abandoned the city yesterday upon hearing of our approach. Some troops remained, but they are now retreating via a northern gate. The Episcopalian doctors are nowhere to be found. Some think that they left for London to volunteer their services to the King."

"Hmmphhh… So we appear to have won for the moment." He turned to Graham. "I will help secure the city. Then my troops and I must be on our way. The southern border needs protection."

"Understood."

"Once Aberdeen surrenders, I trust that ye will treat the citizens with respect."

Graham nodded in agreement, but he intended to do the opposite. *These Aberdonians must be taught a lesson. I won't stop there. I will cow the son of the Cock of the North as soon as I get a chance.*

***

INVERURIE

Gilbert Gordon felt the weight of the world on his shoulders. After months securing the city of Aberdeen, he'd retreated to avoid a bloody conflict. His thoughts were bleak as he stood on a bridge overlooking the River Urie. *How can I fight my own countrymen? Yet, how can I betray my King?*

Connor interrupted his self-deprecation. "My Lord. The horses are ready. If we leave now, we should make Huntly by nightfall."

Gilbert's heart was heavy. "Tell me, friend. Have I done the right thing?"

"That's not for me to say. History will judge us. Let's hope that she's kind."

He disapproves, Gilbert thought, *and with good reason. My father would never retreat from a battle.*

They'd left the city under cover of darkness and traveled sixteen miles northwest, stopping at the town of Inverurie which straddled the rivers Don and Urie. He and his officers stayed the night in the inn, while the troops camped in the woods. He wondered what they were thinking. *Am I a coward? Or a diplomat? I tried to negotiate with that young hothead Graham. My messenger was lucky to return with his head.*

Connor didn't dare to criticize him, but his cousin George gave him an earful. Lord Aboyne had been ready to stand and fight in spite of their lesser numbers. He considered the retreat a disgrace and continued to bring up his handling of Turriff.

In retrospect, we should have broken their forces at Turriff. George is right. We had the advantage.

Connor cleared his throat. "My Lord, we must go. The troops have gone on ahead. It's not safe to stay here."

Gilbert agreed. "All right. Where is Flame?"

The servant pointed. "The horses are beyond that stand of trees."

Lord Huntly took one last look at the River Urie. It seemed so peaceful here. Thoughts of Bridget and wee George came to mind. "It will be good to go home."

***

SOUTH OF EDINBURGH NEAR THE ENGLISH BORDER

Alex Hay was depressed. He woke this morning with stiff joints, reminding him that he was getting old. General Leslie was gone, on a mission to help the Earl of Montrose liberate Aberdeen. He'd been left behind. For two days they'd moved their encampment south, positioning themselves near the English border. Once they'd chosen a site, the men got busy pitching tents, hauling water and wood, and locating sources of food. The new site was not as hospitable as the old one. Alex was tired, in pain, and longed for the comfort of his family. He wanted the war to end so that he could return to his cottage by the sea. But how could he abandon Robert to suffer a horrific death?

They'd just finished a meager evening meal. Men from several companies were gathered around a large campfire. One of them brought out a Gaelic hand harp and began to play. Another man sang.

♩♬♩

I wandered today to the hill, Maggie
To watch the scene below
The creek and the rusty old mill, Maggie
Where we sat in the long, long ago.
The green grove is gone from the hill, Maggie
Where first the daisies sprung

The old rusty mill is still, Maggie
Since ye and I were young.

A city so silent and lone, Maggie
Where the young and the gay and the best
In polished white mansion of stone, Maggie
Have each found a place of rest
Is built where the birds used to play, Maggie
And join in the songs that were sung
For we sang just as gay as they, Maggie
When ye and I were young.

They say I am feeble with age, Maggie
My steps are less sprightly than then
My face is a well written page, Maggie
But time alone was the pen.
They say we are aged and grey, Maggie
As spray by the white breakers flung
But to me ye're as fair as ye were, Maggie
When ye and I were young.

And now we are aged and grey, Maggie
The trials of life nearly done
Let us sing of the days that are gone, Maggie
When ye and I were young. ♩♬♩

Alex's cheeks were wet with tears. His heart was breaking for the loss of his family - Jessie, the lads, and dear old Maggie. He'd never see her again. It was too much for one man to bear. He was having an epiphany. This war could be fought without him. He needed to return to what was important in life; his wife, his sons, and his friends. Why did he ever desert them?

Alex went to his tent and packed a traveling sack. Taking care to not appear suspicious, he filled a water flask and sneaked out of camp through a densely wooded area. Nearly an hour later, he found himself at a road that headed north and south. He stood transfixed staring to the north, imagining himself in Jessie's arms. He wanted nothing more than to grow old with her. All he had to do was take a step in that direction.

"Forgive me, lass," he whispered. Alex turned and headed south to London. His family was safe. Their reunion would have to wait until he rescued Robert.

Chapter 61
Confrontation

April 1st 1639
TWO DAYS LATER

ON THE MOVE

The Earl of Montrose used his triumph with discretion. There was a slight chance that the King would compromise. In that case, it would be foolish to alienate the Aberdonians.

They'd taken Aberdeen that Saturday with no resistance and banned the display of the red royal ribbon. There his army was joined by the forces of Lord Fraser, the master of Forbes, the laird of Dalgettie, the Earl of Marischal, and others, swelling his army to nine thousand.

That afternoon, Graham left a garrison in Aberdeen under the Earl of Kinghorn and set out across country with seven thousand men to confront Lord Huntly. They camped at Kintore, rose in the morning, and proceeded to Inverurie where they set camp again. They were now less than twenty miles from Lord Huntly's domain. Graham knew that this news would travel fast to the son of the 'Cock of the North'.

The town was a pleasant enough place to stay. There was one street extending along the green bank of the Urie, having a tollbooth with grated windows, and a lovely church. He inspected the troops, questioned the populace, and decided to stay put for a few days.

***

HUNTLY CASTLE

Gilbert had unknowingly spent the last few days in the eye of a storm. Upon arriving at Huntly, he'd dismissed his troops, sending them home to local lords. He thought that he had a month to regroup and decide upon a plan of action.

Bridget had been glad to see him, and he'd spent much of his time in her arms. His son George was now thirteen months old and had changed a great deal in his absence.

Connor had objected when he dismissed the troops. He'd been

pressing him to reorganize and contact his brother. Gilbert tried to alleviate his fears by agreeing to an evening meeting.

The Earl sat at his desk, waiting for his servant. He'd spent a peaceful day with his family and wasn't looking forward to the meeting.

There was a knock at the door and Connor entered. The servant looked drawn and pale. He took a seat at the desk and waited to be acknowledged.

Gilbert was getting a bad feeling. "What is it?"

Connor reddened. "My Lord. I just spoke with a messenger at the gate. He came all the way from Inverurie. It seems that the Earl of Montrose won't leave us alone. He is camped there with his army and intends to descend upon us."

Gilbert gripped the desk. "My God! How many men did he bring?"

"The messenger wasn't sure. But he thinks there's at least five thousand."

Raw fear gripped him. "Five thousand! A force that large could overrun the castle."

"Aye. We must act fast."

"What would Father have done?"

Connor's eyes were wild. "Blackheart would never have dismissed the troops. We must reassemble them! Will ye listen to me?"

"Aye."

"I've sent men southeast to make sure that they're not descending upon us. I stationed lookouts and armed guards at each gate. We must send messengers to our supporters, especially Lord Aboyne and Lord Oliphant. Ask them to recall their men. We should also contact yer brother."

"Make it so." Gilbert felt nauseous. "We're in dangerous straits. I fear for my wife and son."

Connor seemed irritated. "Then remove them from the castle. We'll send them to Drake tonight under heavy guard. They can accompany the messenger to yer brother."

"That's a good idea. What else?"

"We should try to head off the conflict by requesting a meeting with Montrose."

"Won't that be dangerous?"

Connor scowled. "Aye. Someone else should make the initial contact. I've summoned Robert Gordon of Straloch. We will send him to Montrose with a proposition. Let's craft it now."

Gilbert opened his desk drawer and took out a piece of writing paper. He dipped a quill in a crystal inkwell and poised his pen to write. "I'm ready."

Connor took a deep breath and began to dictate. "To James Graham, Earl of Montrose. From Gilbert Gordon, Earl of Huntly." He cleared his throat. “Lord Montrose. It’s been brought to my attention that ye are encamped with a large force of men not far from my doorstep. The time has come for us to meet and work out our differences. I’m sure that we can come to a mutually acceptable settlement. It is not necessary to advance upon my domicile when it is my person that ye desire.”

Gilbert swallowed hard. “Continue.”

“I propose that we meet on Blackhall moor several miles from yer encampment. Each of us must bring only eleven attendants with no arms but a single sword at their sides....”

***

APRIL 2ND DRAKE CASTLE
EARLY THE NEXT MORNING

Dughall woke shortly after five with a deep sense of foreboding. Something was terribly wrong, but he couldn’t put his finger on it. Who or what did it involve? He got out of bed quietly, being careful not to disturb his wife and son. Against his advice, she’d taken him into their bed after a long fit of crying.

The Duke relieved himself in the chamber pot and then dressed quickly in breeks and a jersey. He slipped his feet into sturdy shoes and armed himself with a dirk. When he opened the door, he got a surprise.

Murdock was poised to knock on the door. “My Lord!”

Dughall’s intuition had been right. The servant looked like he’d been roused from bed. “What’s wrong?”

Murdock stammered, “There’s been some trouble involving yer brother Gilbert. He sent his wife and child here for protection. Anna is seeing them to a guest bedroom as we speak.”

Dughall was anxious. “I thought that Gilbert was in Aberdeen. What happened?”

Murdock frowned. “I’m not sure, my Lord. Lady Bridget was hysterical and the child was wailing. A messenger escorted her here with four armed guards. The men are waiting for ye in the breakfast room.”

“Where is Jamison?”

“He stayed last night at the weapons range. I sent a man to fetch him.”

Dughall and Murdock walked the long hallway. Their footsteps echoed in the empty passageways as they made their way to the breakfast room.

Dughall hesitated before going in. “Ask the kitchen to bring us tea, scones, and a tray of breads.”

Murdock turned and headed for the kitchen.

The Duke opened the door and entered the breakfast room. The fire had been stoked and the wall sconces were lit. Five men were standing about the room, looking out windows and warming themselves by the fire. He recognized two of them. "I ordered refreshments. Please take a seat."

The five men pulled out chairs and sat down.

Dughall joined them. "Can someone tell me what's going on?"

The messenger produced a sealed letter and handed it to him. "This is from Lord Huntly. Ye are to read it in private. He needs yer help."

Dughall addressed a man he knew. "Alan. What happened?"

Alan Troup reddened. "My master returned from Aberdeen several days ago to avoid conflict with a large army."

"Who commands this army?"

"Lord Montrose."

"How many men?"

"More than five thousand."

Dughall frowned. "Is my brother safe?"

Troup shook his head. "Nay. After they took Aberdeen, the army advanced to Inverurie. Lord Gilbert believes that they intend to take the castle. That's why he sent ye his wife and child."

The messenger spoke, "He sent a messenger to negotiate with Montrose. In the meantime, he asks that ye ready yer army."

"How does he intend to negotiate with him?"

"We don't know. The answer might be in the letter. He wants us to return to guard the castle."

Murdock entered with a serving lass. They placed trays of scones and bread on the table, along with several pots of tea. The woman left in a hurry.

Dughall stood and the men joined him. They drank tea and stuffed their pockets with bread and scones.

Murdock looked puzzled. "Where are they going?"

Dughall answered him. "They have to return to Huntly. The castle is in danger." He watched as the men bowed slightly and took their leave. "How is my sister-in-law?"

Murdock was pale. "Anna says that she's resting comfortably. She asked Lady Jessie to look after her and the child."

They pulled back chairs and sat down. "What's going on, my Lord?"

Dughall sliced open the sealed letter with his dirk. "Gilbert sent this." He began to read out loud.

"My dear brother. The hostilities have commenced. Aberdeen has been occupied by an army of covenanters, which has driven me back to my castle. Their commander is the Earl of Montrose, an impulsive young man who rejected my previous bids for an armistice. I am trying once again, and have sent a messenger to his campsite at Inverurie to arrange a meeting. Oh, how I wish that

ye were at my side! Ye have more common sense than me and twice the bravery."

Dughall took a breath. "Dear God. I must help him."

Murdock was tense. "What else does he say?"

"I've asked Lord Aboyne and Lord Oliphant to accompany me to the meeting, along with nine others. What I need from ye is this - ready yer army in case I am captured. If that happens, use yer influence to secure my release. And most importantly, take care of my beloved wife and son. I will contact ye soon with the outcome of this affair. If ye don't hear from me in a week, assume the worst and make some inquiries. I must go now. Yer brother, Gilbert

Dughall put the letter down. "I knew that something was wrong. I woke with a feeling of foreboding."

"The Sight again," Murdock mumbled.

"I'm not so sure. If so, it's becoming unreliable. I could have sworn that it was about my father."

"Alex?"

"Aye"

The servant winced. "Let's hope not. We have enough trouble."

***

APRIL 3RD HUNTLY CASTLE THE NEXT DAY

Gilbert paced the room to dissipate some nervous energy. Robert Gordon of Straloch had just left his office, after describing the terms of the meeting. Montrose had objected to the location, so Robert arranged a new one. They were to meet on the fourth at Lowess, a secluded hamlet midway between Aberdeen and Huntly Castle. There were specific terms for the engagement. Each party was to bring eleven men armed only with swords. To be fair, each could send an advanced guard to search the other for concealed arms and offensive weapons.

Connor approved of the plan and was preparing the horses for the trip. Lord Aboyne and Lord Oliphant had just arrived.

Gilbert suspected that it might be a trap. That's why he'd insisted that Gordon of Straloch go with them. The elderly man hadn't balked. He was an eminent historical and geographical writer, known for his ability to mediate. Gilbert's thoughts were bleak. *He said that Montrose has the welfare of this country at heart. I certainly hope that it's true. If not, I may be a dead man. At least Bridget and wee George are safe.*

That morning, the Earl had confessed his sins. He didn't want to walk into a firestorm with stains on his soul. The priest had been unusually kind. He bowed his head and prayed. *Lord, God. Father in heaven. Protect us from those who would do us harm.*

Feeling at peace, he straightened his clothes and went to join his traveling party.

***

APRIL 4TH LOWESS EARLY THE NEXT DAY

Lord Huntly's party rose early and ate a hearty breakfast. They'd traveled all evening and stayed the night at an inn near Pitcaple Castle.

They set out and arrived at the meeting place first. One of Montrose's guards met them and searched them for concealed weapons. Connor followed him back to subject the other party to the same.

Gilbert and his men settled themselves at a long table in the only tavern in Lowess. The place was in need of serious repair. The roof was full of holes and the door was off its hinges. Chickens ran in and out of the establishment. They didn't mind. The meeting was to take place outside, in a grove of apple trees.

Connor returned and announced that Montrose's party was a mile away. The men bolted their drinks and left the premises.

Gilbert queried the servant as they walked their horses to the grove. "How many were they?"

Connor was tense. "Twelve, including Montrose."

"Good. Did they have any unexpected weapons?"

"Nay."

"Does it look like a trap?"

Connor reddened. "It's impossible to tell. Keep in mind that they have an army five miles away."

Gilbert had a sick feeling in the pit of his stomach. "I wish my brother was here."

"So do I. They say that he's raised an army of two thousand."

"In favor of the very thing we oppose." They stopped and tied their horses to a tree. Gilbert picked an apple and fed it to Flame. "Don't fret. They won't hurt such a magnificent steed. They'll see yer value and give ye a home."

"My Lord! Ye must not talk that way!"

Gilbert saw Montrose's party entering the far end of the grove. Lord Aboyne and Lord Oliphant were greeting them. He recognized Lord Coupar and Lord Echo. They were flanking a young Lord that he assumed was the Earl of Montrose. They were accompanied by eight other gentlemen and their swords were clearly in sight.

Gilbert swallowed hard. It was time to join his men. He grasped his sword and addressed his servant. "Forgive my lack of bravery. I will try to act like my father."

Connor grunted. Without a word, they left their horses and crossed the grove to greet their adversaries.

***

Gordon of Straloch introduced Huntly and Montrose. They saluted each other with utmost respect and then the conference began.

Gilbert was willing to negotiate, but his adversary wouldn't give him a chance. James Graham was proud, fiery, and resentful and insisted upon their surrender. Gilbert lost his temper and high words passed between the two. Soon, swords were grasped and defiances exchanged.

Gilbert gripped his sword. "Piss-ant!"

James raised his weapon. "How dare ye!"

For the first time in his life, Gilbert felt his blood a' boil. He was blind to the danger he was in.

"My Lords!" Robert Gordon stepped between them to prevent bloodshed. The sixty-two year old man was a mediator. "Cooler heads must prevail. Both of ye have Scotland's interest at stake. Surely ye can come to an agreement." Both men reddened, but they lowered their swords.

Robert continued, "Heartfelt discussion is required. Perhaps it would be best to retire beyond the hearing of yer followers."

Gilbert and James agreed.

"Now, lay down yer swords."

The two Lords marched to the far side of the grove and spent some time in earnest conversation.

Gilbert was shocked to learn that the covenanter army was eleven thousand strong. They were to be augmented soon by twenty thousand more, under the command of the Earl of Argyll. *Archbald Campbell has joined them. I would be a fool to resist them. My life and fortune hang in the balance.* He kept his voice low. "I cannot sign the covenant. I am a Catholic."

James seemed willing to negotiate. "I have a proposal whereby we can both save face."

"Go on..."

"Ye will sign a bond, obliging yerself to maintain the King's authority so far as it is consistent with the religion now established by law."

"Hmmphhh..."

Montrose's eyes narrowed. "In return, I will march my army back to Aberdeen, leaving the Gordons and the Keiths unmolested."

"That's it?"

"Aye."

It was an acceptable plan. Gilbert thought that he could live with this. "I agree."

"Then let's return to our men and draw up the bond."

They marched to the other side of the grove and explained their positions in detail. Gordon of Straloch prepared the bond and witnessed Gilbert signing it.

The Earl of Montrose was cocky. "Accompany me to my camp at Inverurie. Now that we have an agreement, we would like to extend our hospitality."

Gilbert's hair stood up on his neck. He was getting a bad feeling.

Connor was giving him a desperate look. "We are grateful for the invitation. But we must take our leave."

James' nostrils flared. "As ye wish."

The sun was setting in the western sky. They stared each other down, said half-hearted farewells, and went their separate ways.

That night, Gilbert and his party retired to the house of Pitcaple on the south bank of the Urie in Chapel-of-the-Garioch. The Earl was humbled, tired, and grateful to be alive. He kneeled at the bedside, said his prayers, and pondered the future. *It may be time to change sides. I will discuss the matter with my brother.*

Chapter 62
Treachery

April 9th 1639
FIVE DAYS LATER

ABERDEEN

The Earl of Montrose had been busy. He marched his troops to Aberdeen, entering the city on a Saturday. The next day, church pulpits were besieged by covenanting preachers who gave abusive sermons against excommunicated bishops. Most Aberdonians stayed in their pews and bore the tirade stoically. Those who tried to leave were confronted by armed soldiers.

Montrose resorted to intimidation. On Tuesday, he demanded a tax from all citizens; most of whom claimed an inability to pay. When complaints proved false, their property was seized at twice the rate. Wednesday was observed as a day of solemn fast when everyone was urged to sign a modified bond.

Catholics couldn't be expected to make a pledge that abjured their own faith. So Graham issued an order that all who signed the modified bond should be protected. This applied even though it contained no confession of faith.

Anger and fear were rampant. Some holdouts were persuaded by the presence of Lord Huntly's signature on the document. As noxious as it was to Episcopalians and Catholics, the reversal of the son of the 'Cock of the North' convinced many to sign it.

Graham needed unity to meet the coming invasion. The port of Aberdeen was vital to his plans. He spoke throughout the city, portraying Gilbert's turnabout as a victory for the rebellion.

It was now April 9th. The Earl's breast swelled with pride as General Leslie and his infantry disappeared into the distance. The man had left him in charge of the cavalry with the task of maintaining the city. But how would he accomplish that? His thoughts darkened. Some intended to seek out Lord Huntly to verify his signature on the document. Graham bristled at the thought of this man who'd dared to call him a piss-ant. It wasn't just personal. He'd heard terrible things about the Gordon clan from the Forbeses and the Frasers. "Leslie asked me to respect Lord

Huntly," he thought aloud. "But now I am in charge."

A soldier to his left straightened, "What was that, Sir?"

Graham scowled. It irked him that he'd spoken aloud. "Make yerself useful. Fetch me a scribe!"

***

HUNTLY CASTLE ONE DAY LATER APRIL 10TH

Gilbert sat at his desk, absently stroking the polished surface. The activity tended to calm his nerves. It was different sitting on this side of the desk. In one way he felt superior, in another he felt exposed.

This morning he was awaiting the arrival of his brother. Since he'd returned from Lowess, he'd seen him only once. Dughall had been kind enough to bring Bridget and the baby home flanked by twenty of his soldiers.

Gilbert hadn't told his brother about his reversal. He'd needed time to evaluate his options. Lord Aboyne had been angry with him for signing the bond. They'd had an unpleasant exchange at Pitcaple, followed by the man's hasty departure. No matter what he did, he couldn't please everyone. And what would he do about the King? He hadn't exactly signed the Covenant, but what he'd endorsed was akin to it. How could he remain his lieutenant?

Gilbert's hand trembled as he touched an envelope bearing his Majesty's seal. It had arrived that morning and he hadn't the courage to open it. "I hope that the King hasn't heard about the bond." He couldn't put it off any longer. He open the letter and scanned the page.

Lord Huntly. Perhaps there has been a misunderstanding. I authorize you to use force to secure the northeast for the crown. You may defend yourself and act offensively against rebel forces. Let me be clear. They are enemies of the monarchy and therefore your enemy.

Gilbert groaned. "Now he tells me."

I promise that when this sordid affair is over, you will retain a prominent position in Scotland and share in the wealth seized from our adversaries. I regret that this letter must be short. I am busy amassing troops to invade Scotland's southern border. My foot soldiers and infantry are almost ready. Ships are being prepared to take the ports. Irish troops are training to take the west. I'm relying on you to secure the northeast until I take Aberdeen in the spring. Farewell for now. I will contact you again soon. King Charles

Gilbert's heart sank as he saw the date. The letter was written a day before his meeting with Montrose. The King might feel differently now.

Connor entered the room and waited to be acknowledged.

"What is it?"

"My Lord. The Duke of Seaford is at the gate. He is accompanied by his manservant."

"See my brother in."

"Shall I stay for the meeting?"

"Nay." Gilbert's eyes narrowed. "My brother and I need to speak in private."

The servant bowed. "I will inform Jamison." He turned on his heels and left the room.

The Earl grabbed a decanter and two glasses from the credenza. Without a thought, he opened the bottle and poured three fingers of whisky into each glass. He poured again, carefully filling his own to the brim. "I'll have one before Dughall gets here." Gilbert sipped the amber liquid. As it traveled to his gut like a fiery thread, he had a thought that he shouldn't drink so much. He turned and placed the glasses on the desk.

Dughall entered the room. The man was dressed in fine highland garb, a kilt, a sporran, and a woolen jacket. He took a seat. "I'll have one of those. Perhaps two."

Gilbert chuckled. "I thought ye'd criticize me for pouring us a stiff one."

"Not today, brother. I had a shock inspecting the troops. Jamison convinced me to take the title of Dark Lord to give us an advantage. The men gave me an ovation, shouting 'Blackheart! Blackheart!' I felt like vomiting."

Gilbert laughed out loud. "Forgive me, brother; but it is amusing. Ye of all people."

Dughall lifted his glass to his lips. "No wonder Father drank so much."

Gilbert nodded. "He had reasons. There was no love in his life. Not even from his sons."

"That was his fault."

"Aye." They were silent for a moment. Gilbert spoke first. "Father knew how to lead men." He took another sip. "I wish that he was alive. Then *his* head would be at stake."

Dughall waited for him to put down his drink. "That leads me to a question. I heard that ye signed a bond similar to the Covenant. Is that true?"

Gilbert reddened. "I was coerced into it. Montrose met me with eleven men, but told me that we were surrounded by seven thousand. I signed to avoid being slaughtered."

"What about yer religion?"

"The bond did not contain a confession of faith."

"I see. Do ye intend to honor it?"

Gilbert's stomach burned. "We're vastly outnumbered. I'm afraid that I must."

Dughall brightened. "So we're on the same side?"

Gilbert poured a tall one. "For the moment. But I don't know what to do about the King." He handed over the letter. "Read this."

Dughall read the letter and let out a low whistle. "This declares the King's intentions. We should give it to the rebellion."

Gilbert was miserable. "The King will put a price on my head when he learns that I betrayed him."

"Ye're in good company, brother. I've been advised to stay away from London."

Gilbert opened a drawer and took out a piece of paper. He inked a quill and poised it to write. "Let's tally our forces. I have eighteen hundred men under my command. With effort, I can raise three hundred more. Lord Aboyne is angry, but as my cousin he'll have to support me. He can muster seven hundred. Lord Oliphant will supply three hundred."

Dughall smiled. "Good. Take heart, brother! This morning we counted thirty four hundred men in my camp."

The Earl brightened. "Trained?"

"Aye. Foot soldiers… infantry… at least five dozen archers…"

"Yer Dark Lord strategy is working." He sighed. "The time has come. We must join with Montrose and commit our forces."

Connor entered the room. "My Lord."

The Earl stared. "I asked not to be disturbed. What is it?"

The servant approached the desk and handed him an envelope. "A messenger left this at the gate. It's from the Earl of Montrose."

"That will be all." The servant left the room. Gilbert opened the letter and read aloud. *"Lord Huntly. I require yer presence at once in Aberdeen. On the 12th of April, we intend to hold a council to determine the settlement of the northeast. Due to yer support, the bond was accepted by the magistrates of Aberdeen, as well as most of the nobility and gentry. I assure ye that whatever the resolution of the committee, ye will be allowed to return home safely. As before, ye are welcome to come with a small party of escorts. - James Graham, Earl of Montrose"*

"He sounds sincere."

Gilbert had a sinking feeling. "Graham is ambitious. I don't trust him."

Dughall frowned. "Then allow me accompany ye."

"Why, brother?"

"I supported the rebellion from the start. Montrose won't harm ye with me at yer side."

Gilbert wasn't convinced. "Ye're a brave man, brother. We'll leave at dawn."

***

ABERDEEN APRIL 12

The council took place on the 12th of April, with Lord Huntly and Lord Drake in attendance. The Covenanting lords welcomed the information they'd brought. That day, the Gordons supped in a house occupied by the chief Covenanters. The meal was social and friendly, where ale flowed and food was plentiful. There was no indication of the treacherous plot that was hatching.

James Graham *was* ambitious. It wasn't enough that Aberdeen had been pried from the royalists. Lord Huntly appeared to be on their side, but Graham didn't trust him. To enhance his reputation, he intended to take this man captive. He would lead him to Edinburgh and present him to the Tables as proof of victory over the royalists.

Graham smiled. Surely, they would praise him and grant him the title of General. He was tired of living in Leslie's shadow.

The Covenanting lords agreed with this action. The Frasers and Forbeses presented convincing arguments, urging him to clip the wings of the new 'Cock of the North'. The presence of Lord Drake was an unexpected problem. The Duke supported the rebellion and couldn't be taken prisoner. He would have to deal with him separately. He'd also heard that the man had the Sight, so he'd been careful to mask his intentions.

Graham decided to test Gilbert's loyalty. "Lord Huntly."

Gilbert glanced in his direction. "Aye."

"Given the present state of affairs, ye should resign yer commission of lieutenancy." He signaled to a man, who brought a quill and a sheet of paper. These were laid in front of the Earl.

Gilbert reddened, but he picked up the quill and began to craft a resignation. When it was done, he signed it and pushed it across the table.

Graham reviewed it and pushed it back across the table. "Good. Now, write a letter to the King in favor of the Covenanters, describing us as good and loyal subjects."

Gilbert stared at the faces around the table. Vastly outnumbered, he wrote the recommendation. His face was grim. "Will that be all?"

Montrose grinned as he grabbed the paper. "Aye. Tomorrow we shall dispatch the laird of Cluny to London with the letter and resignation." He rubbed his hands together. "Gentlemen. We accomplished much today and it is time to retire to our respective quarters. Lord Huntly and Lord Drake. We arranged lodging for ye close by."

Gilbert stood to leave. "We appreciate the hospitality."

"My men will take ye there."

Dughall joined him. "We will take our leave now as we intend to leave in the morning."

Graham masked his thoughts. "Have a safe and pleasant journey."

***

THE NEXT MORNING

Dughall woke as the first rays of sunlight came through the window. He'd had a hard time falling asleep. The bed's mattress was thin and lumpy, reminding him of his humble beginnings. He'd laid awake obsessing about the meeting and was having serious misgivings. The Earl of Montrose was impossible to read. Every time he sensed danger, the man successfully changed subjects. Dughall had relayed his concerns to his brother. Before retiring, they'd posted guards to ensure their privacy and safety.

The Duke got up, stretched his arms, and approached his sleeping brother. He shook the man slightly. "Wake up, Gilbert! We must leave to make Huntly by nightfall."

Gilbert sat up and massaged his shoulder. "Ach! This bed is as hard as the ground."

"Aye."

"Where are Conner and Jamison?"

Dughall began to dress. "I haven't seen them." He slipped on his outer jacket. "I don't sense them either. Perhaps they're asleep."

"I'll have their hides!" The Earl got out of bed and relieved himself in the chamber pot. He straightened his shirt and put on his kilt and socks.

Dughall frowned. "There must be an explanation."

They put on their boots and slipped dirks into their socks. Gilbert scowled. "Where the hell are they?"

The Duke sensed trouble as they walked to the front of the house. "I'll go out first." He placed a hand on his dirk as he opened the door. At first glance, it looked safe. Across the street, there was a row of houses and a post for hitching horses. But Conner and Jamison were no where in sight. As he stepped through the door, he prayed that they went to fetch breakfast.

A deep voice commanded, "Step aside, Lord Drake."

Dughall's heart pounded as sentinels appeared to his left and right, armed with swords and pistols. "Gilbert, it's a trap! Go back!"

But it was too late. Several men secured the door and escorted the Earl from his lodgings.

Gilbert was angry. "Who are ye?"

The burly guard narrowed his eyes. "Duncan Forbes."

"What is the meaning of this?"

"Lord Montrose requests yer presence at a meeting. We were sent to escort ye."

Dughall's eyes widened. "We concluded our business last night."

Forbes smirked. "Not all of it."

"Where are our servants?"

"They will be returned to ye after the meeting."

Gilbert paled. "Let's accompany them. There must be a misunderstanding."

Forbes stared. "Lord Drake is free to go."

Dughall tasted fear in his throat. "I will not leave my brother!"

"As ye wish."

They walked to the lodge with the sentinels forming a ring around Gilbert. They didn't seem concerned about Dughall.

The Duke's thoughts ran wild. *What do they intend to do to us? Are they rogue soldiers? Or has Montrose lost his mind?*

They entered the lodge and were seated across from Graham. Gilbert spoke first. "What is the meaning of this?"

Graham smiled. "There's no need for alarm. We have a few more things to settle."

Dughall frowned. He sensed that the man was up to no good.

Graham put his fingertips together. "While ye were doing the King's business, the Covenanters incurred a large debt. Two hundred thousand merks were borrowed from a merchant named Sir William Dick. We demand that ye pay half of this."

Gilbert flushed with anger. "I will pay no debt that I had no share in incurring! I have been at great expense because of this business, as any nobleman in this country."

Graham narrowed his eyes. "So ye refuse us. Then I ask that ye order yer vassals to suppress a band of Highland robbers who have given trouble to the friends of the Covenant."

"Of whom do ye speak?"

"James Grant, John Dugar, and their accomplices."

Gilbert clenched his teeth. "James Grant obtained a remission from the King. I must cooperate with a neighbor to apprehend John Dugar. I have no commission to that effect!"

"Brother, be careful. This is a trap!"

Graham continued. "Yet another refusal. Then lastly, I ask that ye become reconciled to Crichton, Laird of Frendraught. He is a loyal supporter of the Covenant."

Gilbert pounded the table. "Never! He set fire to my kinsmen's house. Our clans have been feuding for years."

Dughall blurted, "Ye have no intention of allowing us to leave!"

Graham's stare was cold. "On the contrary, Lord Drake... Ye may leave, along with yer servants. Yer brother is another matter." He turned to Gilbert. "My Lord, seeing as we are all friends under the same covenant, will ye go south with us?"

Gilbert paled. "Nay. I must return to Huntly."

Graham's voice was threatening. "Methinks, my lord, ye will do well to go with us willingly."

Gilbert took a deep breath. "I came to this town upon assurance that I should come and go at my pleasure, without molestation. Now I see, by the condition of my lodging and yer mysterious discourse that ye mean to take me against my will to Edinburgh. This is not fair or honorable."

"Brother! Let me speak."

"Nay." Gilbert took a deep breath. "Lord Montrose… If ye give me back the bond I signed at our first meeting, ye shall have an answer to yer request."

Graham stared as he reached in a jacket pocket and took out the bond. This he handed to Lord Huntly. "Ye mean to deny this?"

Gilbert tore it in half. "Aye. I will deny the letter of resignation as well. If I'm to be taken prisoner, I shall remain the King's lieutenant."

Dughall felt nauseous. Why had he not foreseen this? It was exactly what Graham wanted.

Gilbert handed the bond to Dughall. "Destroy this with fire. Tell Lord Aboyne that I reconsidered." He turned to the Earl of Montrose. "Will ye take me by force or of my own accord?"

"Make yer choice."

"I will not go as a prisoner, but as a volunteer."

Dughall pounded the table. "How can ye do this? I supported the rebellion from the beginning!"

Graham stood. "That is why ye are free to go. Leave us, Lord Drake."

"Gilbert! This is treachery."

"Go, brother. Take our servants home and protect my family." He swallowed visibly. "Use yer influence to ensure my safety."

The Duke stood. Gilbert was right. There was no point in them both being imprisoned. He squeezed his brother's shoulder with affection. "I will."

Graham smiled. "Yer servants and horses are on the outskirts of the city. Forbes will take ye to them."

Dughall wanted to fight these men and free his brother, but he knew he was outnumbered. This was exactly what he and Gilbert had discussed. They would remain on both sides of the issue, so that one could help the other. Without a fight, he allowed himself to be escorted out of the lodge.

As he followed the guard to the city gate, the Duke blamed himself for not seeing this coming.

***

BEYOND THE GATES OF THE CITY

Jamison and Conner were remanded to Dughall's custody, along with three of their horses. Forbes and his sentries headed back to the city.

The Duke comforted his horse by running a hand down his neck. The stallion had been abused by a sentry after he'd nipped him in the rear. Lightning had whip marks across his flanks. "Calm down, boy. They can't hurt ye anymore."

Lightning snorted.

Jamison's forearms bulged as he gripped the reins. "We should leave before they change their minds. They might come back."

Dughall mounted his horse. "Agreed. At least they left us our horses."

Connor reddened. "The Earl is my lord! I cannot leave him."

Dughall felt his anguish. "We must. My brother insisted that we leave. He asked me to do three things - destroy the bond, protect his family, and use my influence to guarantee his safety. We can't help him if we're in prison."

Connor gritted his teeth. "What shall we do?"

"We've burned the bond. Now we must tell my cousin that Gilbert reconsidered." Dughall took charge. "Connor. Ride to Lord Aboyne's castle and tell him about this turn of events. Then return to Huntly to protect our interests. Alert yer troops, secure the castle, and then escort Bridget and the wee one to Drake under guard."

Connor nodded. "What will ye do?"

"Jamison and I will follow the procession. When we get to Edinburgh, I will confront the Tables. We came to Lord Montrose in good faith. This was betrayal."

Jamison stared. "What do we hope to accomplish?"

"Lord Balmerino may release my brother to stay in my good graces."

"I doubt it. He has Alex's fate to keep ye in line."

Dughall frowned. "I intend to bring my father home. If he balks, I'll tell him that Mother is dying."

Jamison grunted. "He hates being lied to."

"I know. But I can no longer have this over my head."

Connor snapped his reins. "We have a plan."

"When ye get to Drake, tell Ian to take responsibility for the castle. He must move a hundred soldiers inside and post guards at the gates. Tell him that I went to Edinburgh to fetch Gilbert and Father. With luck, we should return in a month."

Connor nodded. "I'd best get underway." He pulled on the reins, turned his horse, and galloped down the path.

Jamison waited until he was out of sight. "He's a good man."

"He is loyal to my brother."

Jamison stiffened. "I see a procession of riders in the distance. We should hide and observe them. Hurry! They're crossing the city gate."

They turned their horses and headed for the forest. When the animals were hidden, they climbed a tree and waited. So far everything was going according to plan. Soon, Montrose's party passed by, escorting the captive Lord Huntly. Gilbert wasn't bound, but he was surrounded by armed sentinels. He would die if he tried to escape.

"Be brave, brother," Dughall whispered. "I'll do my best to get ye released."

Lord Balmerino

Chapter 63
Complications

April 26th 1639
TWO WEEKS LATER

EDINBURGH

The Adams tavern was bustling. Serving lasses scurried about, carrying trays and waiting on customers. Strong odors permeated the air - of cooking, stale ale, and body odor. Dughall and Jamison sat at a table, awaiting the arrival of Lord Balmerino. After several inquiries, the man agreed to a meeting.

It had taken nine days to reach Edinburgh. Following Montrose at a distance, they'd endured heavy rain, washed out roads, and a storm of biting insects. Arriving in the city, they watched with dismay as Gilbert was escorted into Edinburgh Castle. There was nothing that could be done that night. They'd acquired a room at an inn and schemed into the wee hours of the morning. Days later, the Duke was granted access to his brother. Lord Huntly was imprisoned in quarters befitting his stature, attended upon by guards at his own expense. Gilbert had been surprised to see Dughall and begged him to negotiate his release.

The Duke had high hopes for this meeting. When he approached the Tables, they'd insisted that he meet with Lord Balmerino. It took several days and a few greased palms to arrange today's meeting.

Dughall and Jamison occupied a table in the private section. The men had arrived early to secure a place. There they'd supped on standard tavern fare - mutton stew, coarse bread, and a soggy root vegetable.

Dughall pushed aside his bowl. "Yech. What *was* that?"

Jamison grunted. "I don't know, my Lord. They must have boiled it for a week." He scratched his arm from wrist to elbow.

"Stop that! Those bites will fester."

The servant frowned. "They already have."

Behind the wall, men engaged in a heated argument. Obscenities flew, a table overturned, and plates clattered on the floor. Jamison's nostrils flared. "These seamen are a rough bunch."

Footsteps sounded across the plank floor. Moments later, Lord Balmerino came around the partition, looking dapper in a grey woolen jacket. His face lit up with recognition. "Good day, Lord Drake." He took a seat and put down his gold topped cane. "Who might this be?"

"Thank ye for seeing us." Dughall introduced his companion. "This is my manservant, Jamison."

Lord Balmerino stared. "Can he wait outside?"

The servant reddened.

Dughall stood fast. "Nay. Jamison is present at all my negotiations."

"Ah, a diplomat of sorts."

"Aye."

A woman appeared with three tankards of ale. She placed them on the table and carted soiled dishes away.

Balmerino smiled. "I've taken the liberty of paying for yer meal." He sipped his ale. "Drink up."

The ale was much appreciated.

Balmerino set down his tankard. "Let's get down to business. I suppose that ye are inquiring about yer brother, Lord Huntly?"

Dughall got a chill. "Aye. Might I speak freely?"

"Go on."

"The circumstances of his arrest deserve discussion. Weeks ago, my brother signed a bond that endorsed the Covenant. Because he is Catholic, this was done without a declaration of faith."

Balmerino nodded. "I know about this. His signature was used to convince Aberdonians to sign the Covenant."

"I met with my brother afterwards. He was prepared to change sides and support the rebellion."

Balmerino frowned. "Now he denies the bond. Why did he change his mind?"

Dughall kept his voice low. "Lord Montrose insisted that he come to Aberdeen to participate in a council. I was present when he opened the letter. Montrose assured him that whatever the resolution of the committee, he would be allowed to return home safely."

"Hmmphhh..."

"I accompanied him to Aberdeen, along with our man servants."

Balmerino stroked his beard. "What happened?"

"The meeting was cordial. Gilbert presented Lord Montrose with a letter from the King that described his military plans."

"I have seen it."

"Lord Montrose insisted that Gilbert write the King to resign his commission of lieutenancy. My brother complied with his wish."

Lord Balmerino stroked his beard. "I have not seen this resignation."

Dughall's stomach knotted. "That's because treachery arose! We supped with them and returned to our lodgings, intending to leave the next morning. But it was not to be. We woke to find our quarters surrounded by armed sentries, who took us to Lord Montrose for a meeting."

Balmerino cleared his throat. "Did they disrespect ye personally?"

"Nay. But they threatened my brother."

"I see. What was the purpose of the meeting?"

Dughall slapped the table. "Lord Montrose made unreasonable demands upon my brother. He insisted that he cover a two hundred thousand merk debt that he had no part in incurring."

"Hmmphhh."

"Then he demanded that he suppress a band of Highland robbers and reconcile with a man who wronged our clan."

Balmerino seemed troubled. "Lord Huntly refused these requests?"

"Aye. That's when Montrose took him prisoner. Facing that prospect, Gilbert recalled his bond and asked me to destroy it."

They were quiet for a moment.

Balmerino spoke first. "Lord Montrose's actions were regrettable. The man tends to be misguided by zeal. I assure ye that he'll be disciplined."

"My brother is free to go?"

The older lord stared. "Nay. Unfortunately the die is cast. Days ago, Lord Huntly denied the bond and declared his loyalty to the King."

Dughall panicked. "He will sign the bond again."

Balmerino was solemn. "Lord Drake. The Tables gave him that opportunity. He told us 'They may take my head from my body, but they should not take my heart from my sovereign.'"

"I don't believe it!"

"I witnessed it. We cannot trust him so he must remain a prisoner."

Dughall was livid. "How can ye do this to me? I supported the rebellion from the beginning."

"That is why ye are free to go."

"I've supplied yer armies and raised a regiment for the cause!"

Balmerino stared. "Lord Huntly will be safe as long as that continues."

"This is blackmail!"

Jamison grabbed his arm. "Be careful, my Lord. Yer brother is safe. We can negotiate for his release later. Ask him about Alex."

Dughall felt defeated. "I wish to recall my stepfather Alex Hay from his position in the army. My mother is dying."

Lord Balmerino clasped his hands. "I'm afraid that I have bad news. Lieutenant Hay deserted the army over a month ago. At first we thought he was abducted, but then he turned up in London as a free agent."

Dughall's heart pounded. "London?"

"Aye. According to sources, he inquired about a prisoner and then tried to break *into* the Tower." He rolled his eyes. "Only God knows why. The man's been arrested."

Jamison frowned. "What's he charged with?"

"Treason. They identified him from a letter he carried."

Dughall could barely think. At last, he spoke. "Has he been tortured?"

"We don't know. General Leslie changed his plans so that he can't betray us."

"Are ye trying to free him?"

"Lord Drake. Yer stepfather deserted his post. General Leslie has the right to execute him. We cannot negotiate for a man who acts foolishly."

Dughall blurted, "I must get him out!"

Jamison tensed. "My Lord!"

Balmerino scoffed. "No one gets out of the Tower without a royal pardon. Lieutenant Hay knew the risks."

Dughall stood. "This is a serious matter, Sir. My stepfather is in danger. I must rescue him."

Jamison rose. "My Lord, wait! We must discuss this."

Balmerino raised his eyebrows. "Listen to yer servant. Stay away from London! The Archbishop is aware of yer loyalties."

The Duke bolted out of the tavern. He walked aimlessly for miles in an attempt to clear his head. Dughall was furious at his father for putting him in this position, but he feared for his very life. How could he free him? Balmerino said that he would need a royal pardon.

Jamison walked at his heels. "My Lord! For God's sake, talk to me!"

Dughall stopped and faced him. "My father risked his life to rescue me from Huntly Castle."

"This isn't Huntly."

"I must save him."

Jamison paled. "No one has escaped from the Tower in decades. This is daft!"

The Duke swallowed hard. "I have a plan. There is an ally I can call upon."

Jamison reddened. "Who?"

Dughall's heart pounded like a drum. "The Queen. She left me with an invitation."

The servant grabbed his arm. "To do what?"

His world was crumbling. "Oh, Jamison. I'm ashamed to say."

They turned and walked towards the inn.

Dughall's thoughts were desperate. Alex faced torture and execution. The Queen wanted him in her bed. How could he rescue his father without being unfaithful to his wife? There was simply no way to avoid it.

***

DRAKE CASTLE

It was early evening. The lace curtains in the retiring room were drawn for privacy. Apple wood burned steadily in the hearth, emitting a pleasant odor. Four overstuffed chairs were arranged in a circle to accommodate the ladies of the castle.

Jessie Hay sat talking with the young women. To her right was Dughall's wife, Keira. The dark-haired lass sat in a comfortable chair, nursing her infant son. Ian's wife Mary sat beside her, enjoying her childless state. The twin boys were with their father. Jessie looked to her left. Lady Bridget relaxed in a brocade chair, nursing wee George. The women were concerned about their men, but so far no one had mentioned it.

Jessie allowed herself a measure of hope. Ian said that Dughall meant to recall Alex. Would her husband agree to come home? She tried to send him a silent message. *Come home, Alex. I need ye at my side.*

There was a pop as Keira switched the baby to her other nipple. "How long have the men been gone?"

Bridget looked up. "Gilbert and Dughall left Huntly over two weeks ago." Her fair face darkened. "I'm worried about my husband. Connor says that he's been taken to Edinburgh."

Jessie touched her arm. "Dughall won't let anyone harm him. He'll bring him home and Alex as well."

Mary stretched. "Ian says that it may take time."

Keira smoothed the baby's hair. "This wee lad misses his father. I'll never understand it. Why must men fight about religion?"

Jessie sighed. "These problems wouldn't exist if women ran the world."

The women clucked their agreement.

LONDON THE BOWELS OF THE SALT TOWER

The prisoner could tell that the sun was setting. A barred window near the ceiling admitted waning light. Commoners weren't allowed to have candles. Too much of an expense, he'd been told, and there was the prospect of fire. He hated sunset.

Alex Hay sat at a rickety table, flexing the fingers in his right hand. Each movement caused him a sharp pain that radiated from hand to elbow. He clenched his teeth and began again. "I must regain the use of my hands."

The chamber was darkening. He took a breath and worked on his left hand. The fingers could barely move. "God help me!" But even these small steps represented an improvement.

He'd lost track of time in prison. After his capture, they'd searched his belongings. Though he'd been careful to discard things that identified him, it seemed that he'd missed one. An envelope addressed to 'Alex Hay' served as a liner for a boot. They threw him in a rat infested cell and passed the paper to the Archbishop. Three days later, he was identified as a traitor. Alex was given a chance to redeem himself before they put him to the torture. He was asked to betray the men who sent him by supplying their names and locations. As a Christian, soldier, and devoted father, he heartily refused to tell them.

The next morning he was awakened by guards who brought him to a punishment room. Again they asked him to betray his companions and again he vigorously refused them. They wrapped his wrists in iron chains and suspended him from the ceiling. The pain had been excruciating. Left alone, he'd gasped and cried and turned his pleas to heaven. For two days, rusty chains chafed his skin and restricted his circulation. Ignoring offers to confess and live, he'd prayed for death and lost consciousness. Waking in his cell, he was appalled at the damage. The pain was constant and his hands were useless. His flesh was dark with bruises and wrist wounds hindered any progress.

Warden Steere had been kind, bringing him a leather ball to strengthen his grip. The jailor provided wood and a whittling knife and encouraged him to use his fingers. This same warden gave him a report on Robert. His friend was locked in the same tower. Frail from a year of imprisonment, he was scheduled to be tried next week.

"Has anyone been found innocent?" he'd asked.

"Not by this King," was the answer. "Shall I tell MacNeil that you're here?"

"Aye, and tell him that I love him like a brother."

There was more bad news. Alex had to confess soon. Otherwise, the Archbishop would oversee his torture.

Alex was terrified. *The man is the spawn of the devil himself!*

It was pitch-dark. Alex felt his way from the table to the floor and crawled to his filthy straw bed. He knelt and folded his hands to pray.

Words would not come, so he recited a hymn:

When peace like a river attendeth my way
When sorrows like sea billows roll
Whatever my lot, thou hast taught me to say
It is well, it is well with my soul

Though Satan should buffet, though trials should come
Let this blessed assurance control
That Christ hath regarded my helpless estate
And hath shed His own blood for my soul

My sin, O the bliss of this glorious thought
My sin, not in part but in whole
Is nailed to the cross, and I bear it no more
Praise the Lord, praise the Lord, O my soul!

And Lord, haste the day when my faith shall be sight
The clouds be rolled back as a scroll
The trump shall resound and the Lord shall descend
Even so, it is well with my soul

Alex was at peace, but his trials were far from over. They intended to torture him again. He would need divine strength to resist their demands. He prayed from the depths of his soul. *Heaven help me. May they cut out my tongue before I betray my people.*

The prisoner lay down, but sleep eluded him. He was plagued by images of dear ones. Robert... Dughall... Ian... and Jessie....

Oh, God. Poor Jessie... He sobbed himself to sleep.

***

EDINBURGH

Dughall lay in bed, listening to his servant snore. He considered getting up and shaking the man, but thought better of it.

The evening had been exhausting. After a heated discussion, they'd agreed on a plan and posted letters to Drake and Huntly. Tomorrow they would board their horses on a farm and reserve passage on a ship to London. There were many details. He needed to sleep, but his mind was on fire. Could his brother help?

He relaxed each muscle one by one and invited his brother to contact him. To his surprise, Ian never responded. Instead he saw his father - injured, in pain, and in deep despair, lying in a rat infested chamber. Alex was praying for death.

Dughall sat up in bed. "Don't give up, Father," he whispered. "I'm coming."

Chapter 64
Commencement of Hostilities

April 27th 1639
NEXT DAY

YORK ENGLAND

York was a walled city at the confluence of the Ouse and Foss rivers in northern England, located halfway between London and Edinburgh. It was known for its medieval streets and houses. The city had gone through hard times during the reign of James I because the citizens opposed religious reform. Now, they were being given a second chance.

King Charles had come to York to prepare his army to invade Scotland. Just that morning, he published a proclamation at the market-cross that offered an Act of Oblivion to his insurgent subjects. It had two conditions - the Scots had to lay down arms and restore his forts. If they refused to comply, the entire nation would be denounced as traitors. The proclamation was intended to enlighten the misguided peasants and tradesmen of Scotland. Nineteen of their leaders - Argyle, Rothes, Montrose, Leslie, and others - were excepted from the pardon; though a promise was added that if they submitted within twenty-four hours their cases should get favorable consideration. After that time, a price would be put on their heads. A free pardon would be granted to all others who participated in the rebellion. To attract the common man, he promised that all vassals and tenants of lords in rebellion would keep their rents, one-half to be paid to the King. Tenants taking the King's side would receive long favorable leases. Disloyal tenants of a loyal lord would be expelled from their holdings. All rebels not laying down arms within eight days would be named traitors and as such would forfeit their goods and estates. How could they not comply?

The King was feeling self assured. The Marquis of Hamilton had been dispatched with a fleet of twenty-eight war ships to invade the Firth of Forth. Bearing five-thousand foot soldiers and a cache of arms, they were due to cast anchor opposite Edinburgh in a few days. How could the Scots resist the King's army when it landed in their midst?

Charles stroked his beard as he surveyed the troops. Weeks ago, he'd despaired at the condition of the troops, who were unready and undisciplined. Now they were progressing, in fitness, speed, and accuracy with weapons.

To his left, a messenger bearing the royal standard arrived on horseback. The soldier had been sent to the border to glean the news from Edinburgh. He dismounted and tied off his horse, approached the monarch, and bowed deeply. "Your Majesty."

Charles interrupted his fawning with a wave. "Enough. What is the news from Edinburgh?"

The messenger straightened. "Our fleet has not been spotted. But there is news. Lord Huntly has been taken prisoner in Edinburgh Castle."

Charles felt the anger rise in him. "How dare they detain my lieutenant? Who is responsible?"

The man paled. "Lord Montrose captured him in Aberdeen."

"So Gilbert Gordon has been incarcerated. Is his brother Lord Drake with him?"

"Nay. They say that he supports the Covenant."

Charles seethed. "Laud was right! The man has returned to his Presbyterian roots. When I get my hands on him…"

"Do you have further orders for me, Sire?"

The King didn't like being interrupted. "Get out of my sight! I will send for you later."

The soldier bent like a sapling in the wind and then fled his presence.

Charles trudged across the field towards a structure that housed his field command. With attendants in tow, he entered the building and looked around. "Lord Astley!"

Major General Jacob Astley emerged from a back room. The sixty-year old man commanded the army and was responsible for drawing up men in battle formation. He was an honest, brave, and plain man, fit for the office he exercised. His sharp grey-haired features reminded the King of a terrier. "Your Majesty."

The King scowled. "Lord Huntly has been taken prisoner! They have him in Edinburgh Castle."

Lord Astley frowned. "I will send Prince Rupert to intercept Hamilton. When Edinburgh surrenders, we will free him."

"Good." The monarch snapped his fingers. "Bring me my writing implements and the royal seal." The King sat at a table as attendants fulfilled his request. He selected a sheet of paper, dipped his quill in ink, and began to write a letter to the Archbishop.

William,

I'm afraid that treachery is afoot. Lord Huntly has been taken prisoner by the rebels. As you predicted, his brother Lord Drake has joined the rebellion. We gave the peasant a chance and he sank to his plebeian roots. Just let him set foot in London again! I will display his head on London Bridge! Never before have I witnessed such betrayal. I offered the insurgents an Act of Oblivion and they chose to spit in my face! Therefore, I have decided to execute our prisoners, starting with the ones who have been there longest. This task I leave in your capable hands. Kill three per day on Tower Hill in a fashion befitting a traitor. Make a spectacle of them so that the Scots will fear us. Display their heads on pikes around London!

Hamilton's forces will land at Edinburgh within days. They will free Lord Huntly and secure the city. Upon his victory, I will take my forces north. In the meantime, be steadfast my friend. The Scots are weak. This war will be over before you know it.

The King signed and folded the letter, poured wax on the joint, and impressed it with the royal seal. The monarch took a moment to admire his handiwork and then gave it to Lord Astley. "Arrange for a courier to deliver this to London. He must put it directly into the hand of Archbishop Laud."

Astley accepted the letter. "Consider it done, my King."

"Step up the army's training. They must be ready in three weeks to leave for the Borders."

"I shall. Do you require anything else?"

Charles gave a cunning smile. "Find out what you can about Lord Drake. Specifically the peasant stock he came from. We will use it to our advantage."

***

EDINBURGH SCOTLAND MAY 1ST 4 DAYS LATER

The Marquis of Hamilton stood upon the bow of a ship with wind spitting gusts of spray against his face. He gripped the gunwale and took a ragged breath. James had never led a naval campaign before. Eight years prior, he'd commanded six thousand ground troops to fight for Gustavus Adolphus against the German Hapsburgs. Most of his army died from sickness before taking part in the fighting. He'd requested more troops, but was ordered back to England. To say the least, it was a source of embarrassment. Would this campaign end the same way?

The Marquis was in a terrible state. He should have been cold from the sea spray. Instead, he was profusely sweating. This was a regular occurrence since he'd assumed command of the Navy. Now there was a stabbing pain in his right temple. *Dear God!*

The lookout lowered a telescope. "My Lord. We are entering the Firth of Forth. Edinburgh lies within our grasp."

James extracted a journal from his jacket and opened it to a dog-eared page. *What did the King say to do?* "Tell the captain to cast anchor opposite Edinburgh."

The seaman blinked. "We're not going to attack?"

"Nay. Unless provoked, we must wait until the royal army approaches the Borders."

"But, Sir. We have the advantage of surprise."

"Obey my orders!" Hamilton watched the man scurry below. He knew that his soldiers were miserably raw - scarcely two hundred of them were able to fire a musket. Many were English peasants sickened by the turbulent sea voyage. This was worse than Germany! Who could expect them to fight? He would be better advised to resort to diplomacy.

Soon the King's fleet entered the inner harbor and dropped anchor opposite Edinburgh. People gathered on the shore, but they didn't seem organized.

Hamilton took this as a good sign. He ordered a party to take a dinghy ashore and proceed to the city market-cross. There they were to nail up the King's Act of Oblivion to give his countrymen a chance to surrender. Then they were to identify themselves to the Tables as messengers from the fleet of the Marquis of Hamilton. James watched the dinghy land. His men were kept from the market-cross, but sent back to the fleet unmolested. How would he post the King's proclamation? More trouble was brewing. Over the next two hours, thousands of Scots flocked from the city to the shore.

The Marquis peered through the telescope. They appeared to be of all ranks, ranging from gentry to peasant. Wielding weapons, they seemed prepared to resist the invasion. The King never expected this. What was he to do now? He adjusted the eyepiece and looked again. "God help me. Is that Mother?"

***

Among the multitude which flocked from the city to the shore, there was one person whose appearance excited surprise and inspiration. The dowager Marchioness of Hamilton, mother of the fleet commander, was a stern old dame and a staunch Presbyterian. Mounted on horseback with two pistols at her saddle-bow, this respected lady declared to the crowd that she would be the first to fire upon her son if he dared to set foot upon his native country. One could tell from the state of her hair that she'd been roused from bed. "Let him land!" she cried. "He will have to face his mother."

The crowd went wild.

***

Hamilton was torn, but his path was clear. Unless provoked, he had orders to wait until the royal army approached the Borders. His soldiers needed refreshment, so he placed some upon the islands of Inch Colm and Inch Keith, which the rebels neglected to fortify. As a tactic, the men set off explosions on the islands to try the nerves of the peasants. The Master of Artillery pled anxiously with Hamilton for permission to use his new cannon. He was one of many who argued that a show of force was needed.

That week, correspondence took place between Hamilton and the chief Covenanters. Some came aboard to talk, but it seemed impossible to resolve the differences between them and their sovereign. Hamilton could only offer them the terms of the late proclamation, which amounted to throwing themselves upon the King's mercy.

They gave him sound reasons not to surrender. Their army was superior. Their cause was just. The north was under their control. The Irish forces were known to be delayed. And the worst yet - Because he had not attacked, Hamilton's fleet seemed harmless.

In the meantime, the Marquis was paid a visit by Prince Rupert, who told him about the fate of Lord Huntly. None of this seemed to matter to Hamilton. He continued to beat a dead horse, relying on diplomacy and negotiation.

***

YORK ENGLAND MAY 7TH

The King was convinced that the campaign would be short. The news from Edinburgh was encouraging. According to Prince Rupert, Hamilton's fleet had secured the harbor. In the face of this awesome presence, the Marquis was pressing the citizens to accept the Act of Oblivion. Soon, Charles would complete the deal by arriving in their midst with his army.

In addition, the King had just made arrangements to secure the northeast. After the capture of his cousin, Lord Aboyne arrived in York to take up the royalist cause. Charles had been struck with the spirit of the man and believed he could raise his clan's dependents. He'd given him the commission of lieutenancy previously bestowed on Lord Huntly. In addition, he entrusted him with a letter to Hamilton, ordering him to provide assistance to raise an army.

Lord Aboyne had been cooperative. Flattery caused him to be forthcoming with information about his new found cousin. According to him, Lord Drake had been raised in a fishing village by a man named Alex Hay.

The King frowned. *That name seemed familiar. Ah, yes. It appeared frequently on petitions and on a copy of the hated Covenant.* Charles smiled. *The man was imprisoned in the Salt Tower.*

The King trudged across wet ground to the field command house. Once inside, he sat at a table and snapped his fingers. "Fetch my writing implements and the royal seal." Servants scrambled to fulfill his request, placing them on the table before him. Charles selected a sheet of parchment, inked a quill, and began to write Archbishop Laud.

William,

I discovered a way to punish that traitor, Lord Drake. Information has surfaced naming the man who raised him, a fisherman named Alex Hay. If memory serves me, this man was captured before my departure and locked in the Salt Tower. Torture him as you please, but do not kill him. When I return, I shall use his execution to lure Lord Drake into our clutches. The Gordons are a strange clan. Lord Huntly is a loyal supporter. Lord Aboyne has agreed to be my lieutenant in the north. How can Lord Drake support the rebels? It is beyond my comprehension. As always, I leave this matter in your capable hands. Keep me informed.

He signed and folded it, then sent it on its way.

***

EDINBURGH HARBOR   SAME DAY

James Hamilton bit down on his thumbnail, drawing blood. He was terribly nervous. Days ago, he'd painted a rosy picture for the King's messenger, telling him that negotiations with the Covenanters were progressing. Well, that had been *his* impression.

This morning's meeting had been discouraging. In no uncertain terms, he was told that they rejected the Act of Oblivion. Worse yet, they were unwilling to meet again until he had something new to offer.

The Marquis took out a handkerchief and blotted his bleeding digit. His heart sank as he sat at a table and took out his writing implements. He selected a piece of paper, inked a quill, and began to write in his best hand.

My beloved King.

As I write this letter, the royal fleet remains in Edinburgh harbor. We have restricted access to the port, blockading commercial traffic. Never before has this city experienced such a show of majesty and force. Even so, I have bad news. Unable to land troops or publish your proclamation, I negotiated with the chief Covenanters. At first, the outcome looked hopeful. This was the sentiment I expressed to Prince Rupert. But now I am informed that my insurgent countrymen will never submit peacefully. Indeed, there are reports that the Covenanter army has positioned itself on the border.

Forgive me, for I have failed. Negotiations are over. Not only do they reject the Act of Oblivion, they refuse to meet again until something new is offered. Your Majesty's affairs are in desperate condition. The enraged citizens run to the height of rebellion and walk with a blind obedience to their traitorous leaders. They are resolved to die rather than accept your last most gracious proclamation. You will find it difficult and expensive to curb them by force, their power being greater than can be imagined.

In closing, my troops grow restless as rationing looms. I've sent men to search the islands for sources of fresh water. Our supplies will last a month, but no more. We must attack or sail away. What do you wish me to do? Sincerely - James Hamilton, Marquis of Hamilton

LONDON ENGLAND MAY 14TH ONE WEEK LATER

The citizens of London were suffering. The day was unusually hot, bringing thunderstorms, rain, and pea-sized hail. Tornadoes were reported across England, particularly in Suffolk and Norfolk. There was a bright side to this. Because of the erratic weather, they'd called off the executions.

Days after meeting with Balmerino, Dughall and Jamison sailed for England on a cargo ship. The North Sea was rough and traffic was heavy. Dughall had never seen so many sailing ships. One time they passed almost thirty! Arriving in London, they'd secured a room at the Drunken Duck under the pseudo name of Lord Keith. The next day, they made inquiries about the King, the Queen, and the condition of Alex and Robert.

Two weeks had passed since they landed. During that time, Archbishop Laud began executing rebel prisoners as traitors. At three per day, it wouldn't be long before he got to Alex and Robert. They had to make a move. The men sat in their room eating their evening meal. They joked that it could be their 'last supper'.

Dughall lay down his fork. "Let's go over the details."

Jamison's nostrils flared. "The King is away on business. He's not expected for weeks."

"Good thing for us."

"The Queen is in residence at the Queen's House."

"I am prepared to write her a letter. I expect that she'll accept my proposal."

Jamison reddened. "Alex and Robert are imprisoned in the Salt Tower. At least that was true a week ago. I haven't witnessed their executions."

Dughall agreed. "Their heads are not on pikes around the city."

The servant cleared the dishes. When he was done, he brought forth paper, a quill, and an inkwell and set them before his master. "Write her."

Dughall inked the quill and poised it over the paper. "She asked me to sign it with a secret moniker." He began to write.

My beloved Queen. Ye once gave me the name Lord K and left me with a tantalizing offer. I accept with one condition. I ask that ye grant the release of two prisoners in the Salt Tower; Alex Hay and Robert MacNeil. In return, I shall serve ye with total obedience in a location of yer choosing.

Jamison reddened. "Must ye humble yerself?"

"It's a small price to pay for their lives." He poised the quill and continued.

Leave me a letter at the Drunken Duck, addressed to our secret moniker. Make haste as the prisoners are awaiting execution. I am in London, ready, and at yer service. Affectionately, Lord K.

"What does the 'K' stands for?"

Dughall blushed. "Kilt. She's always wondered what we wear under our kilts."

Jamison chuckled. "She's wondering about nothing. Shall I deliver the letter to the Queen's House?"

Dughall nodded. "Ye're the only one we can trust. She said to bribe the guards with a coin wrapped in a piece of red silk."

"She's done this before."

"It doesn't matter." Dughall folded the letter and sealed it with wax. As it dried, he fashioned an elaborate 'K' into it. "Take this to her. I'm ready."

The servant accepted the letter and left the room. The door creaked shut, emphasizing the inevitability of their undertaking.

Dughall was running on nerves. In truth, he feared what any man would - a traitor's execution. It could be worse. What would the King do to a man who made him a cuckold?

Jamison had warned him. They would need to keep this secret forever to protect the lady's integrity. No one must be told - not Gilbert, not Alex, or even Keira. His future was in the Queen's hands. He mustn't violate her trust.

Dughall sank to his knees and prayed. "Father in heaven... Protect my servant, myself, and Queen Henrietta." He sighed. "And forgive me for what I must do."

Chapter 65
A Traitors Death

May 15th
ONE DAY LATER

LONDON
THE QUEEN'S HOUSE   EARLY MORNING

Queen Henrietta sat in the breakfast room, sipping a cup of raspberry tea. It was exactly as she liked it. The twenty-nine year old mother of five was accustomed to getting her way. Like many Frenchwomen, she enjoyed sex and liked being pregnant. Children were delightful when their needs were met by servants. Her latest pregnancy ended in stillbirth. She'd given birth to a girl who they buried at Westminster Abbey. This was the second stillborn child her husband had given her. Could it be that his seed had soured? Lately, he had no time for her. They hadn't made love since late November. Then he'd gone to war.

The Queen put down her cup and read the letter that had arrived last night. That interesting Scot, that magnificent specimen, was ready to come to her bed! True, there were conditions, but they were nothing she couldn't arrange. Her eyes lingered on a phrase that made her tingle. *In return, I shall serve ye with total obedience.*

She whispered, "That you will, Lord Gordon."

Her servant entered the room. Pierre LaRouche was a French physician who had recently joined her staff. Sent by her family after the stillbirth, he was the only one she trusted. They spoke in French so that no one could listen.

Pierre bowed. "My Queen."

Henrietta smiled. "I have several tasks for you. But you must be discreet."

He straightened. "As always, my Queen."

She gave him an envelope addressed to 'Lord K'. "Take this to the Drunken Duck. Find 'Lord K' and give him this letter."

He placed it in his jacket. "As you wish."

"There's more." She handed him an envelope impressed with the Queen's seal. "Take this to the warden of the Salt Tower. By this order, he must release two prisoners to you - Alex Hay and Robert MacNeil.

Transport them here under guard and lock them in the cellar."

"Are they dangerous?"

"Non, mon ami. I intend to pardon them. You must hurry as they are executing prisoners."

"What if they've been taken to Tower Hill?"

She thought for a moment. "Then their fate is beyond my intervention."

Pierre accepted the letter. "Which should I deliver first?"

"Leave the one at the Drunken Duck. It's important that I see the recipient."

The Frenchman nodded. "I will go there now." He bowed gracefully and left the room.

Henrietta sipped her tea. The King couldn't object to this act of mercy. The Gordons were their allies. She read the letter again and stuffed it in the bodice of her gown. The clock on the mantel struck seven melodious tones. "There's time for a bath and a warm oil rubdown. Then Margaret can arrange my hair. I must look good for my lover."

***

EIGHT O'CLOCK THE DRUNKEN DUCK

The Drunken Duck was quiet. Because of the hour, the only patrons were residents requiring breakfast. The innkeeper worked alone; cooking and waiting on tables.

Pierre LaRouche entered the tavern and shook the rain off his plumed hat. Surveying the room, he saw two tables occupied - one by a seaman and another by a pair of Scots. One man looked like he might be a Lord. But he had to be sure. The Frenchman introduced himself to the innkeeper and asked him to identify 'Lord K'.

The man snorted. "Ye represent Her Majesty?"

Pierre was surprised by his tone. "Herself."

"Then I'm the King's brother." He pointed to a table with two men. "Take no offense. Lord Keith is on the left."

Pierre approached the table. "Forgive the intrusion, my Lord. I carry a letter from the Queen. I believe you are the recipient."

Dughall's eyes widened. "I am."

"Can you identify yourself?"

"She knows me as 'Lord K'."

Pierre took a letter out of his jacket and laid it on the table. "Read this in private after I am gone. If all goes well, I will see you later."

***

The Duke watched him walk out of the tavern. His clothes were fancy and his accent was French. Was this man going to free his father?

He suppressed an urge to follow. “I wonder if he’s headed for the Tower.”

Jamison scowled. “I hope that the Queen can trust him.”

Dughall stood and snatched the letter. “Let’s go to our chamber.” They paid for the meal and took the stairs to their room. Once inside, they read the letter:

Dear Lord K.

I read your letter with interest and am willing to accept your proposal. As to my part of the bargain; my agent is headed to the Tower to order the release of the two men. It is the least I can do for one of our allies. In return, I expect you to come to the Queen’s House at noon for a two hour tryst to fulfill your promise.

Jamison snorted. “Two hours? How long does she expect a man to last?”

Dughall reddened. “A long time. Kate was like that.”

“Did ye last?”

“Aye. There’s more than one way to revive yer manhood.” He stared at the paper.

The prisoners will be turned over to you after our rendezvous. In closing, the Drunken Duck is a filthy place. I ask that you bathe before coming to my quarters. Anxiously awaiting your arrival, H

Jamison chuckled. “She expects ye to bathe?”

“Aye.”

“Women!”

“I’d better get started.”

The servant stood. “I’ll haul the water.”

***

NINE O’CLOCK ST JOHNS CHAPEL

Archbishop Laud kneeled at the altar, asking God to purge a stain from his soul. He hadn’t committed a sin - either venial or mortal. He’d simply been involved in an act of ugliness. That morning he’d ordered the slaughter of three traitors to be enacted on Tower Hill. William despised public executions. The crowd’s reaction was uncivilized and the agonized screams were disturbing. After weeks of presiding over them, he’d had enough. That morning he’d given orders and retired to St. John’s Chapel in the White Tower.

The 11th century chapel was built from imported stone. Thick, round piers supported arches adorned with scallop and leaf designs. The Romanesque chamber had a solemn history. Royal families worshipped here. The knights of the Order of the Bath spent their vigil in this chamber the night before a coronation. He was honored to join their ranks. The chapel was a place of sanctuary. No enemy could hurt him here - either mortal or immortal. No man… No woman… No frightening apparition…

He reached in the pocket of his robe and withdrew a letter that appeared to be from the King. The messenger had apologized profusely because he'd been delayed. Laud opened it with a long fingernail. His eyes scanned the parchment, searching for items of importance. The King wanted him to torture a prisoner named Alex Hay. *The idiot who tried to break into the tower... So Hay is important to Lord Drake. I will reserve something special for him.* His mind searched for possibilities. On the first day, he would flog him with a glass whip with no opportunity for confession.

The bell rang, signally the start of the executions. William sighed. Hay was locked in the Salt Tower. His torture could wait until tomorrow.

***

Pierre LaRouche crossed the moat and arrived at the entrance to the Lion Tower. After displaying the Queen's credentials, a guard escorted him inside. The cocky lad took him past a wall of lion cages, dragging a baton against the bars. The beasts went wild.

The Queen's agent masked his fear. He'd been told that it was best to ignore the felines.

They left the tower and crossed a courtyard, arriving at a raised drawbridge. The guard lowered the apparatus and took him across into the Middle Tower. Pierre was glad that he had an escort. The man led the way through towers, gardens, bridges, and courtyards until they arrived at the infamous Salt Tower. Traitors were kept in this place.

The Queen's agent shivered. Six ravens watched from a tree, making a low throaty rattle. "What are they doing here?"

The guard stiffened. "Legend has it that if the ravens ever leave the Tower of London, the White Tower, the monarchy and the kingdom will fall. Our Ravenmaster knows the story."

"In France, we see them as evil things."

The guard frowned. "Warden Steere is in his personal quarters."

Pierre nodded. "Will you wait while I conclude my business?"

"I shall, Sir." He snapped to attention.

Pierre entered the building and knocked on an inner door. He was familiar with the system. Wardens lived in the same tower where their prisoners were held. They were often accompanied by wives and sometimes even their children.

The door partly opened and a ruddy face appeared in the crack. "Who are you?"

Pierre waved his credentials. "Pierre LaRouche. I am an agent from the Queen, come with a request about two prisoners."

The man opened the door and motioned him inside. He put on his official jacket before he spoke. "Forgive the poor state of these quarters. My wife is away, tending to her sick mother." He offered a hand. "My name is John Steere. What do you have for me?"

Pierre shook it. "I come to retrieve two of your prisoners. Her Majesty wants them released to her custody. She intends to pardon them." He took out the letter with the Queen's seal and laid it flat on the table.

Warden Steere read the document with maddening slowness. "Hmmphhh... I can release Alex Hay." He scratched his head. "But MacNeil was taken to Tower Hill this morning."

Pierre feigned irritation. "The Queen will be displeased. Can you call him back?"

The warden glanced at a clock. "I'll try." He summoned a boy from within his quarters and handed him a hastily scribbled note. "William. Take this to the Hill and give it to the executioner. He's to spare a man if he's not dead." The boy took the letter. "Don't tarry, son! A man's life is at stake."

The lad ran out the door.

Warden Steere slipped on a pair of leather boots. "Come along, now. I'll take you below to Hay."

They left the Salt Tower and entered a door on the far side of the building. Steere led them down narrow stone steps that took them to the lower level. This was where the poorest of traitors were kept. When they reached one of the cells, the warden took out a ring of keys and inserted one in a keyhole. He unlocked the door and pushed it open. The prisoner sat at a table, flexing the fingers of his left hand. His wrists were raw with weeping abrasions. He regarded them with anxiety.

Pierre approached the prisoner and examined his wrists. "What happened to him?"

Steere shrugged. "He was tortured in the usual fashion."

"How?"

"Suspended by chains." He tapped the prisoner's shoulder. "It's time to go."

Prisoner Hay flinched. "To my death?"

"Nay. You're being moved."

"Where?"

That's not for me to say. Collect your belongings."

Pierre watched the man gather a few articles of clothing. It was hard to gauge his condition. He was dirty, injured, and justifiably frightened.

The warden produced a pair of manacles. "I'll put these on."

Hay held out his wrists.

Pierre reached out and stopped him. "They'll aggravate those wounds. Are they necessary?"

The warden scratched his beard. "Hay has been a good prisoner. I think that you can trust him."

"I won't run," Alex said.

Warden Steere made it official. "Alex Hay. I hereby remand you to the custody of Pierre LaRouche, Her Majesty's agent." He smiled and squeezed his shoulder. "May God go with you, my friend."

The three men left the cell in silence and took the steps to the ground floor.

***

NINE THIRTY TOWER HILL

The Tower fortress was separated from the city by an open space known as 'Tower Hill'. The area served as a place of execution for high profile prisoners. The public was encouraged to attend. Here, various methods of execution were employed. Beheading was reserved for nobles who committed treason. The prisoner would be forced to kneel and rest his neck on a shaped wooden block, while the axe man delivered a deadly blow. Those not of noble birth faced a gorier execution. Men convicted of treason were hung, drawn, and quartered. Women were burned at the stake. To accommodate this, the Hill featured a block, a scaffold, and a large stone surface for disemboweling and quartering. There was a cache of butchering tools, a pen to hold prisoners, and an open area for spectators.

Robert's heart thumped in his chest. Two of his fellow prisoners were being brutally tortured. Oh, why did he have to watch it? He wished that he had been taken first.

A week ago, he'd been transported by boat to Westminster Palace. Twelve men had endured a bewildering trial where the case against them was presented. There was no rebuttal and no escape. By the end of the day, they'd been convicted of treason and scheduled to be executed.

Iain Innes was on the scaffold, being hung by the neck until near dead. Malcolm Gibbs had survived this process. Now he was stretched on a stone slab, screaming as they disemboweled him. The crowd cheered with approval as they displayed his entrails.

Robert sank to his knees and prayed. "Let him die! Oh God. Let him die!" As the screaming continued, his prayers became frantic. "The Lord is my shepherd. I shall not want. He makes me to lie down in green pastures. He leads me beside quiet waters. He restores my soul." Tears streamed down Robert's cheeks. "Dear Jesus… I'm so afraid." They were coming for him now. Two soldiers were crossing the green accompanied by a lad. They approached the prisoners' pen and unlocked the gate.

Robert paled. "God help me."

A soldier gave him an order. "Stand up and put out your hands."

Robert obeyed and watched them snap on a pair of manacles. Blood roared in his ears as he saw them quarter Gibbs' dead body. "Am I next?" he asked.

The soldier smiled. "Nay. We're taking you back to the Tower."

Robert fainted.

Chapter 66
Homage to the Queen

May 15th 1639

SAME DAY HOURS LATER 12:30 PM

LONDON THE QUEENS HOUSE

She had the darkest eyes he'd ever seen, deep pools of brown that searched his soul. Dughall's heart raced as he watched her remove her frilly underclothes. The woman was bonny, petite, and ten years his senior. She was also the Queen of England, Ireland, and Scotland.

He'd arrived at the Queen's House at noon accompanied by his faithful servant. After kneeling at her feet, they got down to business. Alex and Robert were in her custody. She would release them to him afterwards.

Afterwards... The word hung between them like a tantalizing promise.

Dughall sensed that she was telling the truth. Now it was up to him to fulfill their bargain. He'd sent Jamison to the docks to secure passage for four on the next ship leaving for Scotland.

His eyes panned her personal chamber. The headboard was a work of art, decorated with scenes of gods and goddesses. He'd asked about their origins, but she would have none of it.

Chestnut hair framed her face in ringlets. They flowed to her bare shoulders. "Lord Gordon." She was naked.

Dughall reddened. "Aye."

"You're blushing."

He knew that it was true. "Women say that it's part of my charm."

Henrietta smiled. "I see. You promised to serve me with total obedience."

He swallowed hard. "I did."

"Then remove your clothes. I expect you to be my slave."

Slave... The word invoked memories of a tryst with his father's mistress. He'd already removed his boots and socks. Now he pulled his shirt over his head and tossed it on the floor. His kilt was all that remained. *Slowly... This is part of the game.*

Henrietta stared. "You must not spill your seed in me. My husband is away. I can not get pregnant."

That was fine with him. "As ye wish, my Queen. Then what shall we do?"

The woman moved closer and fondled him through the wool garment. "There are other ways to make love. So… What do Scots wear under those kilts?"

Dughall's manhood responded in spite of his morals. He unpinned his kilt and let it drop to the floor. "We wear nothing, lass."

This pleased her. She nestled her naked body against his, causing his heart to pound in his ears. Her skin was white and fragrant and as soft as a rose petal.

She ran her slender fingers through his chest hair. "Très masculin. What's the other part of your charm?"

He couldn't lie. "I know what women want before they ask for it."

Henrietta stood back and smiled. "Then give me what I want. If you guess, I shall give you what men want most."

She had just given him permission to invade her private thoughts. Dughall opened his mind and was besieged by her desires. She was inviting him to enact her fantasy; and what a fantasy it was! Without a word, he picked her up and laid her on the exotic bed. There was a nightstand nearby. He opened a drawer, extracted four silk scarves, and tied her spread-eagle to the posters.

"Oh, mon Dieu!" she cried.

"Is this what ye want?"

"Oui!"

"Do ye want me to stop?"

"Non!"

Dughall crawled on the bed and examined her from head to toe. He'd never seen such a woman. Except for a patch around her privates, she was practically hairless. Did she shave? He didn't have the nerve to ask. He stroked her arm from wrist to armpit. "So soft," he whispered. "So perfect."

She tested him. "We must hurry."

Dughall sensed that she wanted to be teased. "Nay, my Queen. I can make this last a long time." He straddled her and cradled his throbbing member between her thighs. She squirmed slightly and then surrendered. He ran his fingers up her sides and lingered on her breasts. "I know what ye want, lass."

"Mon Dieu!"

She was silently begging him to use his tongue. He started at her graceful neck and traveled to her erect nipples. It wasn't an unpleasant task. Her skin was soft and supple. The lass wanted him to linger there, so he did. She liked being teased.

The Queen strained against her bonds as he suckled her like a newborn. He could tell that she was close to climax. He paused and took a breath.

She whimpered. "Ne s'arrêtent pas!"

Dughall teased her. "I don't understand. Do ye want me to stop?"

"Non!"

Her thoughts were changing now, becoming serious. He moved his body lower and raked his hands down her form, making their way to her slender hips. His tongue entered her navel and traveled lower, causing her to whimper with desire. Dare he invade her private place? He heard a silent plea. Oh, aye. His heart raced as he lowered his head to her mound.

He spread her petals and blew on them. "Do ye want this?"

"Oui! But untie me."

He unfastened the scarves one by one as though it was part of a ceremony. When he was done, they met in a passionate kiss.

She lay back and spread her legs. "Get on top and face my feet. We shall do this together."

"What do ye call this?" he asked, as he got into position.

"In France, we call this soixante-neuf."

***

ELSEWHERE IN THE QUEEN'S HOUSE

The prisoners were locked in a dimly lit room that served as the food cellar. Shelves were stocked with bags of grain and crocks of vinegar and honey. The bins contained last year's root crops - onions, turnips, and purple beets. There was a table and chairs, used for preparation. The prisoners were warm enough. Searching the bins they found food, but they were desperately in need of water.

The Queen's agent entered the room, carrying a medical satchel. He plunked the open bag on the table and offered them each a silver flask of water. They accepted gratefully.

Alex's hands shook as he struggled to open the flask. He succeeded after several tries and managed to get a drink of water.

Pierre frowned. "I'm a physician. Allow me to examine your hands."

Alex was surprised. "Thank ye, Sir." He sat at the table and held out his wrists.

Robert gasped. "Dear God! What did they do to ye?"

"I don't want to talk about it."

The physician took a seat across from him. He handled his wrists gently, turning them over to assess the damage. "The wounds are weeping. It could be a sign of infection. I should remove the dead flesh." He reached in his bag and took out pincers and a thin scalpel. "Are you up to it?"

Alex winced. "Aye."

"I don't have any whisky."

"Go ahead."

Alex clenched his teeth as the man worked on him. After being hung by chains for days, the pain seemed bearable.

Pierre pulled off a strip of dead skin and discarded it. "This wrist is done." He applied a waxy salve to the raw spots. "That should stop the infection. I'll cover it now." The physician removed a strip of cloth from his bag, wrapped the wrist, and secured it with a silver clip.

Alex asked, "Will I regain the use of my hands?"

Pierre began to work on the other wrist. "You're doing remarkably well, considering that the blood was restricted. I saw you making attempts to move your fingers. Keep that up. Perhaps in time, you will be normal."

Alex inhaled sharply. A long strip of skin was removed, leaving a bloody patch.

"Forgive me. We're done here." Pierre applied salve and wrapped the wrist.

"Thank ye, Sir. Why were we released?"

The physician stared. "The Queen ordered your release. I don't know the details." He stood to leave.

"What will happen to us?"

"I will return soon. At that time, you will be released to a gentleman named Lord Keith." He packed his bag and left the room, locking the door behind him.

Alex spoke, "Do we know a Lord Keith?"

"Nay."

"Then let's pray that he's Dughall."

***

THE QUEEN'S BED CHAMBER

Dughall lay naked beside the Queen, recalling their intense encounter. There was more to this woman than met the eye. He stroked her cheek with affection. "Are ye satisfied, lass?"

She gazed at him with soulful eyes. "Oui."

The Duke sensed that it was true. Their lovemaking had gone on for more than an hour. He'd held up his part of the bargain, serving her with total obedience. In return, he'd been taken to new heights by a woman ten years his senior. "I shall never forget this, my Queen."

She smiled. "Nor I. No wonder you have children by three women."

He didn't bother to correct her. "I must go."

"Our lives are at stake. You must be discreet."

"I will."

She sighed. "If you ever need another favor…"

He touched a finger to her lips. "Shhhh…"

Dughall got up and dressed quickly, noting the lateness of the hour. As he slipped on his boots, he inquired, "Where are my men?"

Henrietta stood at his side, clad in a yellow silk robe. "My agent is waiting in the hall. He will take you to them." She stole a final kiss. "Stay safe, Lord Gordon. Come back to my bed."

He kneeled before her and kissed her hand. "My Queen."

***

The Duke left the chamber and found her agent waiting in the hall. He followed the man until they came to a doorway that led to the cellar.

Pierre took him down a flight of stairs and stopped at a windowless door. "I warn you, Sir. They're weak and vulnerable. One was saved from the clutches of the hangman. The other was tortured. I'm a physician. I treated his wounds."

"I am in yer debt, Sir."

Pierre unlocked the door and ushered him inside.

Dughall's heart filled with gratitude. In the dim light, he made out the figures of two men leaning against the far wall. They were familiar. "Father! Robert!" He hurried to them.

Father and son embraced, but there was no time for a proper reunion. They had to leave London before the Archbishop discovered the missing prisoners. They hurried out of the cellar, thanked Pierre, and left the Queen's House to search for Jamison.

***

ESCAPING LONDON

The men followed the Thames in search of the large boat harbor. They were careful not to attract attention. The former prisoners looked like ruffians. Their clothes were ragged and their feet were bare. They were hardly the type that would accompany a Lord, so Dughall walked ten paces behind them.

The Duke was worried. Robert was emaciated. His eyes were unaccustomed to sunlight and his sanity was in question. The man mumbled constantly, repeating the same phrases. Alex's mind was sound but his body had been weakened by torture. He struggled to lace up his breeks and grasp a simple object. Dughall wanted to examine his wounds, but knew that it would draw suspicion. For now, they had just one priority - to reach the docks and flee London.

Soon they came to a narrow bridge that crossed the river to the shipyard. They spotted Jamison waiting for them on the other side. So far, their plan was flawless. The servant started towards them.

Robert and Alex stepped onto the bridge first. It was a rickety affair with holes in the planks that had to be avoided. They were half way across when Robert stopped in his tracks and wailed. On a tall spike attached to the rail was the bloody head of a prisoner.

Dughall ran to the pair. "Be quiet! Ye'll get us killed."

Robert shrieked. "His eyes are open! He's judging me!"

Jamison arrived. "For God's sake. We have to get out of here."

Dughall's stomach turned. The sight of the head with hanging flesh was enough to make him vomit. He tried reason. "Did ye know him, Uncle Robert?"

"Oh, aye! Gibbs."

"The man is dead. He can't judge ye. We must go."

Robert wailed. "It should have been me!"

People were gathering on the docks, pointing in their direction. Jamison cold-cocked Robert and caught him as he slumped to the ground. In a quick move, he slung him over his shoulder and led them off the bridge.

Alex scowled. "Why did he hit him?"

Dughall reddened. "We're in grave danger. Robert would have gotten us killed."

"I thought we were pardoned."

Dughall gritted his teeth. "Not for long! We must flee London before the Archbishop misses ye."

Jamison led them along the dock until they reached a cargo vessel. He grunted. "This is our ship." Robert was starting to recover. The servant sat him down and talked to him.

Alex confronted his son. "I don't understand. The Queen got us out. What did ye have to give her?"

"Remember what we agreed upon," Jamison growled. "Leave him alone, Alex!"

Dughall started up the gangplank to avoid his father's questions. How could he explain his immoral behavior?

Alex followed. "What did ye give her?"

He turned and faced him. "My body... My integrity... My soul..."

"What do ye mean?"

"I can't tell ye, Father."

"Ye should have left me there!"

"Nay. Now, go help Robert. We must never speak of this again."

Chapter 67
Aftermath

May 16th 1639
ONE DAY LATER

TOWER OF LONDON PRISON

It was early morning. Guards supervised inmates as they emptied chamber pots and supplied the towers. Prisoners of lofty stature walked in gardens, conversing and communing with nature.

Archbishop Laud ignored them. Once again, he was on his way to the infamous Salt Tower. This morning he would order the execution of three more Scots and oversee the torture of another. *Ten more days of this,* he thought. *Then we will run out of traitors.* Laud entered the tower and knocked on an inner door. Soon, a ruddy faced man admitted him. He acknowledged Warden Steere with a nod and spread his orders on a table.

The warden stared at the document. "Three more for the Hill?"

"Aye."

"Who are they?"

Laud ran a finger down the page. "Adams, Grant, and Ian MacVey." Sometimes, he wondered if the man could read.

Steere frowned. "At this rate, you'll put me out of business."

The Archbishop handed him the document. "Not a chance. The King will return with a hundred political prisoners."

"Hmmphhh... Will that be all?"

"Nay." The archbishop wiped sweat from his upper lip. "I require a punishment room, a torture master, and one of your prisoners."

"Which prisoner would that be?"

"Alex Hay."

The warden gawked. "I don't have him. The Queen took possession of him yesterday."

Laud inhaled sharply. "Her Majesty was here?"

Steere searched through a stack of papers. "Nay. She sent her agent." He handed him a letter with the Queen's seal. "Here is the order."

Laud's anger grew as he scanned the document. "It says to release *two* men. I sent Robert MacNeil to his death yesterday."

The warden stared. “Beggin’ your pardon, Archbishop. But the Queen’s orders trump yours.”

“Both men are gone?”

“As of yesterday morning.”

“Idiot! Assemble the guard and search the city! Start with ships in the harbor.” As the warden fled his presence, Laud pondered a course of action. What if they didn’t find them? What would he tell the King? He would allow them to do their search. In the meantime, he would visit the Queen.

***

THE QUEEN’S HOUSE ONE HOUR LATER

The Queen sat at her husband’s desk, across from the Archbishop. The vile man had barged in to her quarters, demanding an urgent meeting. *The nerve! What did her husband see in him?* She sipped her tea to annoy him. “You interrupted my morning massage. What do you want?”

His voice was harsh. “Did *you* release…”

She didn’t like his tone. “How dare you! You will address me as ‘my Queen’.”

Laud reddened. “My Queen.” He trembled with anger. “The warden of the Salt Tower said that you ordered the release of two prisoners.”

She didn’t expect this to come up. “I did.”

“Do you have them in your custody?”

“Non.”

His left eye twitched. “This is a serious breach of justice. Why did you release them?”

Henrietta studied her manicured nails. “I released them to one of our allies.”

“Who?”

“Lord Drake.”

A vein bulged on his forehead. “Lord Drake! Why would you do such a thing?”

“Mind your tone with me! As Queen, it is my duty to entertain the requests of nobles when my husband is absent. Lord Gordon is our ally.” The man looked like he was about to suffer an apoplexy. She sincerely hoped that he would.

Laud gritted his teeth. “Lord Gilbert Gordon is our ally. His brother is a traitor.”

Henrietta sipped her tea. “Last year, we entertained both Gordon brothers in this very house. To my knowledge, we obtained their support for the crown. If one brother strayed, then I was not informed. My husband should speak to me more often.”

The Archbishop balled his fists. “These were important prisoners.

Did Lord Drake say where he was taking them?"

She smiled sweetly to irritate him. "Non."

"Surely, you heard something."

Henrietta was determined to protect her lover. She knew that they boarded a ship to Scotland. "Lord Drake mentioned horses."

Laud stood suddenly. "Horses! I will direct the guards to search the roads. We must find them for *your* sake."

Her voice was as cold as ice. "You will find them for *both* our sakes. I warn you. Do not blame me or you will suffer the consequences."

He bowed slightly. "I will take my leave now, my Queen."

Henrietta dismissed him with a wave. "Be off with you."

The angry man turned and left the room. The door slammed shut behind him.

As usual, Henrietta had the last word. "Imbécile."

***

EDINBURGH

The commissioners of parliament assembled to discuss the King's offer. Not that any of them took it seriously. The Act of Oblivion demanded that they abandon the cause and surrender. The debate was short but heated. The King had made no concessions. If they accepted his offer, it wouldn't be long before he imposed the hated book upon them. They scoffed at the idea that he meant to brand an entire nation of people as traitors.

Regardless, they resolved to pay the idea deference to pacify the sovereign's feelings. An official reply was diplomatically crafted and sent to the Marquis of Hamilton.

The commissioners moved on to state business. They ratified Leslie's appointment as army General and gave Lord Balmerino command of Edinburgh Castle. They discussed Montrose's transgressions and refused his request for a promotion.

Balmerino brought up the subject of Lord Huntly, suggesting that he remain in prison. He didn't mention his brother Lord Drake. The impetuous man was beyond comprehension.

General Leslie spoke eloquently about some of their recent victories. The nobles and gentry of Inverness had agreed to support the Covenanters. Arms and ammunition sent by Lord Huntly had been seized from Inverness Castle. The royalist Earl of Douglas had abandoned his castle to the rebels. Lord Rothes seized Dalkeith Castle, containing the King's main Scottish arsenal and the crown jewels, which were transferred to Edinburgh Castle. Dumbarton Castle was captured by the rebels, denying Royalists the use of the western seaport for the landing of reinforcements from Ireland. And as of late, the city of

Aberdeen was occupied by Covenanting forces.

These victories were overshadowed by a few stubborn facts. The royal army was at York, preparing for an invasion. Close by, a fleet of warships was anchored in Edinburgh harbor. No one dared to venture a guess at what would happen next.

***

NEWCASTLE, ENGLAND

Newcastle was founded at the lowest place the river Tyne could be crossed. On this site in 1080, the Normans built a bridge and fort to safeguard the vital crossing. This in essence was the first castle on the site. The 'new castle' was rebuilt in stone in the 12th century, giving rise to the name of the town that grew up in its shadow.

Now, Newcastle was a busy seaport with a population of ten thousand. A major exporter of coal and wool, it was close to the border of Scotland. For this reason, Charles had come to Newcastle with his army. But all was not well with the King. The monarch was on a rampage, after receiving a series of unfavorable reports.

Hamilton's letter had left him speechless. Not only had the rebels refused to surrender, they'd positioned their army at the border. Rumor had it that General Leslie was prepared to confront the sovereign with a force of 30,000 men. Unrest was reported near Aberdeen as well, but they hadn't been able to verify it. The news from Ireland was devastating. Charles had depended upon the Earl of Antrim to land 10,000 men in the western Highlands to overpower the Earl of Argyle. Now he learned that that Antrim had neither 10,000 men at his disposal nor the capacity to guide such a force if entrusted to him.

To make things worse, he'd received a letter from the Lord Treasurer, describing the state of the Exchequer. The effort to raise money by asking citizens to freely contribute had been an abysmal failure. Ship money was coming in more slowly than ever. If this campaign was to continue, he'd have to call a parliament to raise taxes.

The King paced in his field headquarters. "I will never call a parliament!"

A letter had fallen into his hands, written by one official of the court to another. It said: *The tales they told at London, that the Scots would disband and run away at our approach, are every day disproved more than other, for they are 40,000 strong at least. I think that no man, who loves the honor of his prince and safety of his country, but must be sensible of the loss and danger of both by this fatal business, wherein all men are losers, but the King the most.*

Charles balled his fists. "How dare he expose our position? I will see that he rots in the Tower."

The printer entered the room, carrying a stack of papers. The man had come from London to print copies of a proclamation. He laid them on a table and bowed respectfully. "Your Majesty."

Charles glared. "Why did these take so long?"

The man paled. "I had trouble with the press. Forgive me, Sire."

"Get out of my sight!"

The printer fled the room.

Charles picked up the top copy and read it. You couldn't trust these printers. Most of them could barely spell.

Days ago, the King decided to regroup in the face of unexpected opposition. The document proclaimed that he would settle all Scottish grievances only when order was restored. He promised that the Royal army would not invade Scotland as long as the Covenanter army remained ten miles north of the border.

The King smiled. On the surface this looked like a victory for the rebels. But was it? Of course not! He never intended to keep his word. God was on his side. He was free to strike when he wanted.

Chapter 68
A Guilty Reunion

May 25th 1639
NINE DAYS LATER

MILES FROM DRAKE CASTLE

The forest was soggy after a week of rain. The roads were wet and muddy, making travel difficult. Miles from Drake, two black stallions struggled to pull a cart uphill. After a week of hauling men, the beasts were near exhaustion.

The Duke frowned as he urged the wagon forward. The horses were clearly in distress. White foam coated their sides and shoulders. Pressing on could cause their death. "Everyone out of the cart!"

Three men jumped off the back and the wagon lurched forward. Dughall drove the cart to the top of the hill and got out to tend to the horses. He tapped a cask of water and offered them a pail. Diamond drank greedily, but Lightning nudged it away. This was a bad sign. "What's wrong with ye?"

The stallion reared and came stomping down. Dughall worked the harness to regain control. "Easy, my friend."

Jamison, Alex, and Robert appeared over the rise. The servant frowned. "What's wrong?"

"Lightning is in trouble. We should walk them the rest of the way."

Jamison grunted. "Let's unhitch the wagon. We're only a few miles from Drake."

Dughall saw his father cradling his right arm in his left. "Can ye walk?"

Alex sniffled. "Aye. My hand is throbbing like a toothache, but there's nothing wrong with my legs."

They all had aches and pains. It had been a long and arduous journey.

***

The sea voyage had been short. Warships dominated the port of Edinburgh, discouraging merchant vessels. The captain decided to divert to Denmark, where he could sell his precious cargo. Jamison argued to stay onboard, but Dughall opted to retrieve the horses. The men put ashore in a dinghy at the mouth of the blocked harbor. Under cover of night, they walked to the farm where Lightning and Diamond were boarded. After purchasing a wagon of questionable value, they began the long trip northward.

***

Dughall helped his servant unhitch the wagon. They began to walk, leading the horses behind them.

Robert coughed. "I want to go home."

"Ye can't. The King's agents will recapture ye. Do ye want to go back to prison?"

Robert flinched. "Nay. What about my wife?"

Dughall gritted his teeth. He'd answered these questions before and it was beginning to grate on his nerves. "We'll send for Colleen when we get to Drake."

The man coughed again. "But my boat…"

"For God's sake!" Alex cried. "No boat is worth yer life!"

Jamison scowled. "Why does he ask the same questions?"

The Duke whispered, "Something happened to his mind in prison."

"What about my son and his family?"

Dughall lost patience. "Stop worrying, Robert! We'll send for them."

They settled into an uncomfortable silence. The only sounds were the rustling of leaves and the clip-clop of hooves on gravel. Soon, they passed a familiar stone formation. In another mile, they'd see Drake Castle.

Dughall felt guilty about his tryst with the Queen. *How can I face my wife knowing that I've been unfaithful?* He wasn't worried about her reaction. Keira would never know because he'd been sworn to secrecy. But God knew. How would it affect his soul? Even more shameful was the fact that he'd enjoyed it. The Queen was ten years his senior, yet he couldn't stop thinking about her. Her skin, her mouth, her willingness to surrender… The woman was unforgettable. *I must stop this!*

Dughall forced himself to focus on the reunion. Keira and the children would welcome him with open arms. His mother would be glad to see Alex and Robert. But what of poor Bridget? It could be years before they freed his brother.

They rounded a bend and spotted the castle in the distance. Jamison whooped. "We made it, my Lord."

"Thank God for a safe journey." Dughall waved to a sentry on the tower, who sent up a piercing whistle. "They see us! Let's pick up the pace."

They pressed forward and arrived at the gate just as it opened. Twenty armed sentries spilled out, shouting. "Welcome home, my Lord!"

Dughall handed the reins to a stable boy. "The horses have been pushed to their limits. Water them. Feed them. Allow them to rest. See that they get good care."

The lad snapped to attention. "As ye wish, my Lord."

"There is a wagon several miles back. Retrieve it."

The men drew attention as they crossed the busy courtyard. Tradesmen and artisans emerged from their shops to get a glimpse of the returning Lord. Children ran along side, spinning hoops and shouting. The Duke acknowledged them all. One by one, they began to clap until a sharp sound echoed in the courtyard.

Dughall spotted Ian, crossing the square to meet them. His brother looked tan and fit and was clad in his best clothing.

Ian's grin widened. He sprinted to them and embraced his father. "Ye're free."

Alex was close to tears. "My son."

Ian slapped his brother on the back. "Ye did it." Then he spotted Robert. "Uncle!"

The Duke was pleased. "I saw the sentries."

Ian nodded. "We moved a regiment inside. Gilroy and I tended to business, though I confess we struggled with the ledgers. Murdock, Cam, Pratt, and Fang took charge of the men at the range."

They started moving towards the castle. "How is the range?"

"Busy. We're forging weapons, chopping wood, and building barracks. There's been a confrontation. Sir George Ogilvy attacked the rebels at Turriff."

This was disturbing news. So the northeast was in turmoil as well. Dughall frowned. "We'll discuss it after supper. How are the women and children?"

"The women are anxious. The children miss ye, especially yer daughter."

"Do they know we're here?"

Ian nodded. "I sent messengers to tell them to gather in the Great Hall. Where is Lord Gilbert?"

Dughall's heart sank. "Imprisoned in Edinburgh Castle." He sighed. "Gilbert sealed his fate by declaring his loyalty to the King."

Ian let out a low whistle. "It's an ugly war that pits brother against brother."

"Aye, at least *we're* on the same side." Dughall looked up as they approached the entrance. The second floor windows were filled with people. One of them looked like Luc. "I want to see my family."

Jamison cleared his throat. "My boots and breeks are covered with mud. I must go to my cottage to change clothes and tell my wife that I'm home."

Dughall nodded. "Join us in the Great Hall later."

The procession entered the castle.

***

THE GREAT HALL

Their Lord and master had returned! The servants were inspired by the news of his homecoming. They scurried about, laying tablecloths and bringing refreshments. One stoked the hearth, while another used a taper to light tall candles.

The women had been summoned - Keira, Jessie, Mary, and Bridget - and were starting to arrive with their children. Luc was invited as well.

The Duchess stood near the hearth, cradling her baby against her shoulder. James had awakened from his nap in a foul mood. She'd retrieved Maggie from the nursery and was trying to care for both of them. The toddler was sitting at her feet. *Oh dear. Where is Mother?*

Maggie clapped her hands in delight. "Da!"

Keira's heart melted. "Aye, wee one. Ye know that he's back."

Luc approached with a grin on his face. "Where is Father?"

She shifted the baby to her other shoulder. "Ian went to fetch him."

"Um… Mother… Would ye like me to watch wee Maggie?"

Keira smiled. She'd grown to admire this lad, in spite of her early opinion. "Aye, Luc. That's very thoughtful."

Luc helped the toddler to her feet and took her tiny hand. The four made their way across the room and sat at a table. Maggie seemed contented to be with her adopted brother.

Keira was nervous. "Hold her firmly."

Luc smiled. "I know how to hold her, Mother. I play with her every day."

The Duchess knew that it was true. Since the birth of her son, she'd had little time for her precious daughter. Luc had been a gift. She would have to tell her husband. Keira's heart swelled with gratitude. *My husband is home! Thank the Goddess!*

The last of the women had arrived with their children. Mary and Tarrah stood near the hearth, holding wee Andrew and Alexander. Bridget sat in a rocking chair, nursing her son George. Only Jessie was missing.

Time seemed to stand still as they waited for their men.

***

THE SURGERY

Jessie stood at the examination table, finishing the last stitch in a boy's hand. Angus Smith had come to the surgery after cutting himself on a scythe. She tied a knot and straightened. "There, now."

The boy sniffled. "Are ye done?"

Jessie nodded. "Aye, lad. No more stitches." She applied a salve of garlic paste and wrapped it in a strip of cloth. "See me in three days or earlier if something happens to the bandage."

Angus stared at his hand. "It's good as new. Thank ye, ma'am."

Jessie helped the boy off the table and sent him on his way. She brushed off the bench and washed her hands in a bowl. There was a bit of work to do. To prepare for the next case, the instruments must be washed and stored.

Beth entered the room in a hurry. "My Lady! The Duke has returned. Ye must join the ladies in the Great Hall."

Jessie's heart skipped a beat. "Did he bring anyone back with him?"

"Jamison and two others."

"My husband?"

"I don't know." Beth reddened. "I must go. I'm needed in the kitchen." The servant fled the room.

Jessie was hopeful. Her son had returned with three men. *Jamison. Gilbert? Could it be Alex?* "I'll clean the instruments later." She whipped off her apron, hung it on a peg, and bolted through the open door.

***

THE GREAT HALL

News of the homecoming spread throughout the castle. It was common knowledge that the Duke had gone to London. Some had feared that he would never return. Servants gathered in hallways, shouting "Welcome home, my Lord!"

Dughall greeted them as he walked. It didn't matter that he was only nineteen. He was a father figure to these people. He reached the entrance to Great Hall and looked inside. "Where is Mother?"

Ian shrugged. "I sent Beth to the surgery to retrieve her. Let's go in."

The men brushed the mud off their boots and entered the Great Hall. The room fell silent but for the squeal of a little girl. Everyone stood and waited their turn to greet the returning Lord.

Dughall's spirits soared as he spotted his wife and children. Keira looked beautiful in a simple tartan dress. She was cradling their son against her shoulder. Luc stood by with a grin on his face, holding his precious daughter.

Maggie cried out, "Da!"

Dughall was glad. The mission had been dangerous. There were times when he thought he might never see them again. He approached his family and picked up his daughter. "Da's home, wee one."

Maggie squealed with delight. The little girl tugged his beard and laughed when he protested.

Dughall kissed her forehead and placed her in Luc's arms. "Watch her, son." He kissed his wife tenderly and held his infant son. "Have ye been a good lad?"

Keira smiled. "He's getting better."

The Duke wondered if that was true. Luc waited respectfully, never taking his eyes off his father. Dughall handed the baby back to his wife. He sat down, picked up Maggie, and encouraged Luc to come into his arms. "My oldest son. But where is wee Artus?"

"He's nae wee any more." Luc hugged him tight. "Oh, Father. I'm glad ye're back!"

Keira blushed. "Luc has been a great help caring for wee Maggie."

Dughall was glad that she'd warmed to the boy. He desperately needed a mother. That reminded him. "Where is Mother?"

Keira's eyes rested on Alex and Robert. "Ye got yer father back!"

"Aye."

"Thank the Goddess! Mother was in the surgery. We sent Beth to retrieve her."

***

Alex was feeling guilty. Jessie wasn't there to greet him, but he didn't know if it meant anything. He couldn't blame her for being distant. He'd barely written to her since he joined the army. Now he'd returned a broken man, expecting her to greet him. He spotted Ian, standing with Mary and the twins. Robert had just joined them. Should he? Nay. He had to find Jessie and hear her out, no matter what the outcome. He walked into the empty corridor, leaned against a wall, and waited.

***

Jessie was out of breath. She'd taken the stairs two at a time and run along the corridor. Near the entrance to the Great Hall, she held her knees and panted. "I'm too old for this."

"Yer not too old for me."

Jessie froze. That sounded like her husband. She straightened slowly and looked behind her. "Oh."

Alex stood a few feet away. "I'm home for good."

Jessie's eyes filled with tears. Her husband was alive and whole and now he was home to stay. She approached him. "Oh, Alex. Why did ye not write me more often?"

He reddened. "Forgive me, lass. It was too painful to think of what I left behind."

Jessie felt his arms encircle her. "How can ye say that?" She hugged him tight, expecting a firm response. But something was amiss. Had he lost his strength? She stood back. "What's wrong?"

Alex pushed back his sleeves, revealing the bandages. "My hands are weak, almost useless." He flexed the fingers on his right hand. "But Dughall thinks it will improve with time."

She peeled back a bandage. "How did it happen?"

"Did they not tell ye I was imprisoned?"

Her heart squeezed painfully. "Nay."

"I was tortured. Our son rescued me from the Tower of London."

Jessie felt like crying. Tortured! She needed to know what happened. She reached out and grasped his shoulders. "Does this hurt?"

"Nay."

She moved to his upper arms. "Here?"

"Nay. The problem lies with my wrists and hands."

"What did they do?"

Alex reddened. "I want to see my family. We'll talk about it later."

Jessie hugged him. "We have all the time in the world. Ye say that ye're here to stay?"

His voice was heavy with emotion. "Aye, lass."

"Then, that's all that matters."

***

Bridget was sick with fear. The Duke had returned with three men, and Gilbert was not among them. She waited respectfully as he reunited with his wife and children. Then she passed wee George to Tarrah and got up the courage to ask the question.

Bridget approached him with her heart in her throat. "Where is my husband?"

Dughall took her hands. "I'm sorry, lass. They imprisoned him in Edinburgh Castle. He's alive and well, but they won't release him."

Her worst fears had been realized. "Dear God."

He continued, "I saw him. Gilbert asked me to care for ye and to serve as George's guardian."

Tears rolled down her cheeks. "When will they free him?"

Dughall hesitated. "I don't know. He has declared his loyalty to the King."

Bridget nearly swooned.

Dughall took her slender arm and helped her to the rocking chair. "Gilbert is alive and well. This war won't last forever. I promise we will get him back."

Bridget stared through tears. "Thank ye, brother. Please ask Tarrah to bring me my son."

"Of course." Dughall signaled for the servant and soon wee George was back with his mother. He squeezed her shoulder and walked away.

Bridget stared into the face of her son. "Poor laddie. We must get yer father back. Ye're too young to be an Earl."

***

The Duke spotted his parents talking in the corridor. He hoped that they could put aside the past and remember the love between them.

Perhaps a reminder of the old days would help.

Dughall approached Robert, who was having a drink with Ian. “Uncle.”

Robert raised his tankard. “Aye.”

“Come with me. There’s someone who needs to see ye.”

Robert stood and put down the tankard. “Who?”

“My mother.”

They walked to the exit and entered the corridor. Jessie’s back was to them as Dughall placed a hand on her shoulder. “Mother.”

She turned and smiled. “My beloved son.” Then her face lit up. “Oh, Robert.”

Chapter 69
Strategy

May 25th 1639
LATER THAT EVENING

DRAKE CASTLE   THE LIBRARY

After the party, a late supper was served in the dining room. When the last dish was cleared, those without duties retired to their chambers. The Duke was not among them. He and his brother went to the library to discuss political matters.

Dughall stood at a tall table, reviewing a map of northeast Scotland. He pointed to a spot southeast of Turriff. "What happened at Towie Castle?"

Ian stood to his left. "Rebel forces seized a cache of arms from Inverness Castle. They stored them at Towie."

"Hmmphhh... Gilbert supplied those arms."

Ian nodded. "Aye. Things get stranger by the day. Did yer brother ever mention Sir George Ogilvy?"

Dughall thought hard. "From Banff. He's loyal to the King."

"Aye. Two weeks ago he led an attempt to recover those weapons."

"Was it successful?"

"Nay. There was one casualty. A servant was killed."

Dughall frowned. "Ye mentioned Turriff. What happened there?"

Ian pointed to a spot on the map and dragged his finger northwest. "Four days later, Ogilvy, the Gordons, and their knights and barons drove the rebel forces out of Turriff. I'm told that they brought 2,000 horse and foot soldiers and enough cannons to surround the town. Ogilvy forced the inhabitants to sign the King's Covenant."

This was disturbing news. "Was there bloodshed?"

Ian was grim. "Oh, aye. There were scores of casualties. Some of them were ours. Two hundred of our men were there, guarding an Assembly. We lost forty nine soldiers in the battle. Twenty more were wounded."

Dughall bit down on his thumbnail. "Did we care for them?"

"Aye. Mother and Aileana patched them up so that they could return to duty."

"Did Ogilvy remain at Turriff?"

"Nay." Once again, Ian drew his finger along the map. "We

heard that he went on to occupy Aberdeen and plunder the houses of Covenanters. There's been no word since."

Dughall frowned. "The King's warships are blocking the port of Edinburgh. His army is gathering on the southern border. Leslie and his army are preparing to meet them. We can't let Aberdeen fall to the Royalists!"

Ian smiled. "We were hoping that ye'd say that."

"What else can I say? We must go to war if we value our heads." Dughall folded the map. "Tell Gilroy to ride out immediately. He must notify our commanders at the range. I will inspect the troops tomorrow. We'll move out on the following day."

***

NEWCASTLE

The King sat in his room at the inn, going through a stack of correspondence. So far, the news was bad. He planned to advance his army north to Berwick but his military commanders opposed it. It was rumored that General Leslie led 40,000 men. The King could muster no more than 15,000. So gloomy did the situation appear that days ago Charles wrote Hamilton ordering him to be ready to bring his forces to the Borders. The reply was in his hand and he couldn't be more disappointed. Hamilton had penned a dispatch even more despondent than his others.

Your Majesty - The Scots have refused your generous offer. My countrymen made no peace but ratified their mad acts in their General Assembly. They are resolved to force a battle. As to your request, I can send two out of three of my regiments to reinforce the army, but I should hold one back to police the harbor. The rebels seem pinched by the stoppage of trade. Take care as you advance. They are stronger in infantry. They may try to cut off your army from its base of supplies at Newcastle. In closing, I am ready to begin hostilities as soon as I am ordered to. There is no longer any hope of a treaty. - Your servant, James Hamilton

Charles crafted a stiff reply, ordering Hamilton to send two regiments to Holy Island. That would increase his forces by 3,000 men. He would request 4,000 more from London and put out false word that 14,000 reinforcements were coming.

A second letter brought good news from the north. Lord Huntly's friends had risen against their Covenanting neighbors and driven them out of Turriff. Then they'd pushed on to occupy Aberdeen.

Charles was frustrated. "I wish I had larger forces to give to Aboyne and Hamilton." He opened the last letter, which bore the seal of Archbishop Laud.

Your Majesty, I write to give you a status on that which you have entrusted to me. As per your order, the executions proceeded at three per day. The Scots traitors are dead. Unfortunately, I have bad news as well. The traitor named

Alex Hay was released to Lord Drake the day before I got your letter. We searched the harbor and outgoing roads, but did not find the prisoner. I initiated an investigation and found that the truth was shocking. It seems that Lord Drake petitioned the Queen and secured a pardon.

Charles crushed the letter in his fist. "My wife? Why did *she* interfere in this?" He unfolded the crinkled paper.

My Lord, I do know what is in Her Majesty's mind and heart. But something is amiss. The Queen claimed that she simply granted a request from one of your allies. She was hostile to my questions, and threatened my person.

"One of my allies!" Charles cried. "Drake is a traitor! My wife isn't fit to handle state business." She hated Laud, so he wasn't concerned about her attitude. But he sensed that there was more to the story. "Gordon is a virile young man. They spent time alone in the Observatory. Could there be something between them?"

His wife had unusual sexual appetites. He hadn't touched her in almost a year. Had she taken a lover? *I will press her on this when I get back. She'd better not be pregnant.*

***

OUTSIDE OF DUNGLASS CASTLE

General Leslie took long strides as he walked through the camp with his lieutenants. Two days of pitching tents and forming entrenchments had made a big difference. As they passed, they were greeted by soldiers - ploughmen, rustics, and city dwellers - their bodies muscular from exercise and minds exalted by patriotism and religion. There were more than 17,000 men - all Scots but for one German trumpeter. They'd come from hearths and altars to be defended, with nary a selfish motive.

The army had covered a lot of ground. On May 20th, upon hearing that the King was preparing to advance, the Tables ordered the army to meet him at the Borders. Final muster took place that day on Leith Links, where they were read articles of war compiled by Leslie. Each soldier was given a printed copy. Leslie publicly took an oath of fidelity to the Covenanting government and the army marched for the Borders. At 16,000 strong, they were but a piece of the rebel force. Most available men beyond Tay were serving under the Earl of Montrose. In the west, Argyle's Highlanders gathered at Stirling to defend the coast from Irish invaders. Some men from Ayrshire, Galloway, Lothian, and Fife remained at home, prepared to defend the coast against Hamilton's navy. General Leslie marched from Leith Links on May 21st with half of his army, giving orders for the rest to follow the next day. As they marched, they implored country people to contribute supplies and asked those who intended to join to bring arms and provisions. Their forces swelled by 1,000. The first night, they rested at Haddington. The second night at Dunbar... And the third at Dunglass Castle, where they halted and built entrenchments.

They were now less than a day's march from the Borders. General Leslie was encouraged by what he saw. His soldiers were organized, obedient, and devoted to the cause. That couldn't be said about the English soldiers. He turned and addressed his lieutenants. "I am well pleased. We would win if the battle were held today."

***

EDINBURGH

James Hamilton was in a quandary. He'd spent days preparing two regiments to join the King's army at the Borders. Now, Lord Aboyne had arrived by ship, expecting him to fill a royal order.

The royalist sat across from him. "Lord Hamilton." His voice was respectful. "The King's orders state the ye are to give me the support I need."

James stared at the King's letter. Did the monarch have a change of heart? Would he be allowed to keep his three regiments? He mopped his forehead with a handkerchief. "I'm not sure about this."

Aboyne bristled. "With all due respect, how else can I secure the northeast?"

Hamilton reviewed the letter. It was the monarch's handwriting to be sure. But he hadn't been specific about what kind of support to provide. Troops? Officers? Weapons? Could he possibly mean ships? "The King needs my troops at the Borders. In light of this, I can provide you with a small contingent."

Aboyne flushed with anger. "A small contingent! Aberdeen is a vital port. Our forces occupy the city, but it won't be long before the rebels retake it! I need at least one ship, some troops, and artillery."

James hesitated. He could spare these things if the King allowed him to keep his regiments. "When must you leave?"

The man lost patience. "Tomorrow at the latest!"

The Marquis saw strange auras around the candle flames. From past experience he knew that he could collapse from weakness within minutes. Some of his men had fallen ill with smallpox. Was he next? The order lay before him, written in the King's own hand. How could he deny it? "All right! Two ships, the crews, and two experienced officers. Each ship carries a working cannon and four field pieces. That's all I can spare."

Lord Aboyne smiled. "Thank ye, Sir. Should we visit the harbor now?"

Hamilton rubbed his temples in an attempt to quell the pain. "Forgive me, but I seem to be ill." Whatever enthusiasm he had for this enterprise was long since gone. "Have patience. We will provision your ships tomorrow."

***

ABERDEEN

The Earl of Montrose was furious. Weeks ago, he'd left Aberdeen in the hands of the Frasers and Forbeses. He'd returned today with his cavalry, pike men, and cannoneers to find that the city had been occupied by royalists. The intruders, led by Gordons, fled to the mountains upon hearing of his approach. The Earl of Marischal then retook the city with a force of 800 troops.

Graham's blood boiled. Surely this would vindicate his capture of Lord Huntly. The Gordons had shown their true colors. That morning, he led his forces into the city via the Upper-kirkgate port to the sounding of trumpets and the beat of drums. They'd marched down Broadgate, where the Earls Marischal, Kinghorne, Murray and minor lords joined them. With these nobles, Graham held a council of war about marching against the enemies of the Covenant. They hadn't come to any decisions.

Graham looked around his quarters. The place had been ransacked and the furniture burned. He'd been told that no Covenanter dared to show their face in the streets when the royalists were around. "Cowards!" he cried. "Damn them to hell!" He left the building to get some fresh air. Walking aimlessly, he wondered how the city was taken. Lying on the sloping bank of the Dee, the town nestled within strong walls and gates. Why were they not defended? Could there be sympathizers amongst the townspeople?

Aberdeen was an impressive city. The streets were narrow. Houses were generally four stories high with stairs of stone and galleries of carved timber. Many houses were thatched and the wynds and closes were paved with flint-stones. The city had a marketplace big enough to garrison two regiments, but it was known for its colleges and cathedrals. Celtic garb was banned. The citizenry disliked their Highland neighbors.

After a long walk, the Earl of Montrose returned to his quarters. He had no desire to harm this city. He'd decided to call another council of war to deliberate upon measures to be taken with anti-Covenanters. This time he would invite the clergy as well.

***

ENCAMPED IN THE MOUNTAINS

The Gordons and their followers were regrouping. With pipes sounding and banners unfurled, they'd marched up the banks of the Dee in Highland garb. They met up with Donald Farquharson of Monaltrie who joined them with all the claymores of Strathdee, Braemar, Strathavon, and Glenlivat. They went up into the mountains and made camp, where they would be better able to withstand an attack from Montrose. It was the calm before the storm.

Chapter 70
The Day After

May 26th 1639
NEXT MORNING 6AM

DRAKE CASTLE

Jessie lay in bed, cuddling against her husband's warm backside. Like the times when he returned from the sea, his skin was rough and salty. When she closed her eyes, she could almost believe that they were back in Whinnyfold. Jessie was grateful. Somehow, they'd defeated the grim reaper. Alex was home to stay. There was one major difference however. For the first time in their lives, he needed her more than she needed him.

She'd pressed him about his wounds upon retiring to their bed chamber. He'd been exhausted and refused to talk about it. She needed to know about the torture if she was going to help him. They hadn't made love. She doubted that he could raise himself up on his hands. They'd have to find a new way, before he lost faith in his manhood.

Jessie sighed. *Maggie said that time heals all wounds or makes them less important.* What mattered was that he was home to stay. Was it selfish to have questions? *Why did he not write more often? Why did he not come home sooner?*

Alex murmured in his sleep. "Have mercy!"

Jessie's heart ached. Was he reliving the torture? She snuggled closer.

Soon his breath became more regular. "Are ye awake, lass?"

She melted at the sound of his voice. "Aye, husband."

Alex turned to face her with tears in his eyes. "My bonny lass." He stroked her curls. "With hair the color of copper."

Jessie reddened. "With white streaks! I've been mad with worry."

He smiled. "Have ye seen my hair? We're growing old together."

"Oh, Alex. I love ye."

"I love ye, too." He withdrew his hand. "But I don't deserve ye. I've done things that are unforgivable."

"Don't say them!" Had he been unfaithful?

"I must confess," he said. "Ye asked me why I didn't write. It broke my heart to think of ye. I should have returned long ago." Alex frowned. "Even after I deserted..."

"Ye deserted the army?"

Alex nodded. "I ran away like a coward. Oh, Jessie. I stood at a crossroads looking north and south. I wanted to go home but I couldn't abandon Robert."

"Ye went to London?"

"Aye. It was the act of a fool. When I tried to save him, I got arrested."

She took his wrist and unwrapped it. There were signs that he'd been bound. Red wounds ringed the wrist in a pattern. "How did this happen?"

Alex winced. "I don't want to think about it."

He was shutting her out again. "I must know if I'm to help ye!"

His body tensed. "They questioned me for days, pressing me to betray the army. They wrapped my wrists in chains and hung me from the ceiling."

Jessie took a sharp breath. "For how long?"

"Two days. The pain was unbearable. I cried. I prayed. I begged for death. Then by God's mercy, I fell senseless. I woke up in my cell unable to move my fingers."

"What did yer hands look like?"

"Black and blue and swollen."

Jessie's heart ached. They'd cut off the flow of blood. "Oh."

"They weren't done with me. Dughall rescued me just in time."

"How did he do it?"

"Our son risked too much to free me." His voice cracked, "He should have let me die."

"Dughall loves ye!"

"Oh, aye. But I fear that he made a deal with the Devil."

Jessie wondered if his mind had been affected. Dughall often said that he didn't believe in a devil. "Our son would never..."

"I tell ye he did."

She stroked his cheek. "Shhh... What's done is done. Pray for him. But promise me that ye'll not dwell on it."

Alex reddened. "All right."

"Now, flex the fingers of this hand." She watched carefully. "Hmmm... Show me the other. Good! There seems to be a difference between them."

"Will they improve?"

"I think so." To tell the truth, she wasn't sure. The damage could be permanent. "I'll give ye exercises to work the fingers." She placed his hand on her breast. "We'll start now. Squeeze them like ye used to."

Alex frowned. "My wrists can't support my weight. How can I make love to ye?"

"We'll find a new way to do it."

He squeezed her breast gently. "If this is one of exercises, I think I'm going to like it."

Jessie smiled. It seemed that there was hope after all. He still had a sense of humor.

***

THE LORD'S BEDCHAMBER

Dughall's heart pounded as he lay naked in bed. His arm muscles cramped and started to spasm. In the dim light, he recognized the Queen's bed chamber and sensed her presence. The young Lord struggled in his bonds. He was tied to the bedposts.

"Nay, my Queen!" he cried. "This is not what we agreed to."

Henrietta dropped her robe. "You promised to be my slave. It's my turn to dominate." She kissed him roughly on the mouth. "Be honest. Not an hour passes when you don't think of this." Her soft lips touched his neck and started downward.

"Oh God," he groaned. "I must be dreaming." Her lips were insistent now, attending to his erect nipples. "I can't bear it. Let me wake!"

She crawled on the bed and positioned herself above him, facing his manhood. The patch between her legs was inches from his face, releasing a musty perfume. "Soixante-neuf?" she teased. "Shall we begin?"

"Aye!" he blurted. "I mean nay! Oh God, please stop. I'm married." His heart pounded desperately.

She giggled. "Your wife will never do this."

***

Dughall woke with a start and examined his wrists with trembling hands. *It was a dream!* His bonny wife lay next to him, her innocent face a reminder of his guilt. *The Queen is right. I think of it all the time.*

The Duke got out of bed and put on a robe and slippers. If he stayed, Keira might wake and ask him what was wrong. He had to find a place where he could avoid her questions. He left his chamber and walked to an alcove where two brocade chairs sat by a window. Dughall sat and rested his head in his hands. Guilt racked his body as he thought of his wife and children. "Oh God," he groaned. "Take this from me! I want to be a good man." He sobbed until his head ached.

A familiar hand rested on his shoulder. "My Lord?"

Dughall looked up. "Murdock!"

"Aye. I heard that ye returned." The servant pulled up a chair and sat opposite him. "I thought ye might need me, so I started out before dawn." He reached out and brushed back his hair. "Ye're crying like yer heart's broke in two. What's troubling ye?"

Dughall sniffled. "I had the most awful dream."

"About what?"

"I'm ashamed to tell ye."

"Go on, lad."

He wiped his eyes. "There's a story to tell. I went to London."

"I know. Ye freed Alex and Robert from the Tower. How did ye do it?"

The Duke clasped his hands. "Can ye keep a secret?"

"Aye."

"I offered my body to the Queen."

Murdock looked puzzled. "Yer life? Yer loyalty? What do ye mean?"

Dughall reddened. "My body. She wanted to be my lover. I wanted my Father and Uncle."

"She accepted the offer?"

"Aye."

His eyes widened. "Ye *fornicated* with the Queen?"

Dughall rubbed his temples. "Aye!"

Murdock frowned. "Who knows about this?"

"Only Jamison."

"See that it stays that way."

"I won't tell anyone."

"Ye just told *me*! So this is what ye dreamed about?"

Dughall blushed. "Worse! In my dream, she tied me to the bedposts and teased me until I was mad with pleasure. I begged her to stop, but she wouldn't."

"My Lord."

"The Queen expects me to be her lover. I don't know what to do!"

Murdock paled. "Do ye want to see her again?"

Dughall panicked. "Nay!"

"Thank God." The servant changed to a soothing tone. "My Lord. I'm a simple man. These things are beyond my experience. What can I do to help?"

The Duke took a ragged breath. "Allow me to talk about it."

"Only to me?"

"Aye."

Murdock smiled. "Oh, lad. I promised to serve ye and I will." The servant stood. "The troops expect ye in a few hours. Would ye like a hot bath?"

It was just what he needed. "Aye."

***

THE LORD'S BEDCHAMBER

The Duchess woke to the sound of rain pelting the window. Normally, her son would wake her as he was used to sleeping in their bed. But not this morning. After midnight, Dughall had insisted on taking the child to the nursery.

Keira frowned. She couldn't object to the nursery. Tarrah and Marjory staffed it day and night. Wee Maggie slept there, though it was time to move her to a bedroom. James was the problem. In his father's absence, he was used to getting his way.

Keira sat up and stretched. They'd made love last night in spite of the late hour. Her husband had been unusually tender. She noticed a change in him, though she couldn't put her finger on it. "Dughall is home at last. Thank the Goddess." Now she would get some help with their son. "The wee lad needs his father."

Screaming… The Duchess heard screaming coming down the hall. The voice was unmistakable. *Goddess, help me!* Tarrah was having trouble with James. She got out of bed and slipped on a robe.

There was a frantic knock on the door. "My Lady!"

Keira composed herself. "Come in."

Tarrah entered with the wailing infant in her arms. His face was red. "I tried to nurse the young master but he wanted to bite. I walked and rocked him for more than an hour. The child won't stop crying! I don't know what's wrong with him."

The Duchess accepted the child into her arms. "It's not yer fault. My son is difficult to say the least. I'm glad that his father is home for a while."

The nursemaid frowned. "Have ye not heard the news? M'Lord is going to the weapons range. There's terrible trouble in Aberdeen. The army must leave tomorrow."

Keira's heart sank. *He's going away again?* She groaned. "Oh, why must men engage in war?"

The servant didn't answer.

***

THE WEAPONS RANGE 2PM

The rain had stopped by the time they arrived at the weapons range. But there were puddles of water in the fields. Dughall saw that the encampment had been expanded. It was almost a town unto itself. There were quite a few rough hewn buildings - a carpentry shack, a forge, a weapons cache, provision sheds, and a score of barracks. There were a sea of tents, an apothecary, and a healer's station. All around, there were fire pits and stacks of split wood. Where months ago only a practice range had existed, there was now an encampment supporting over three thousand soldiers.

The practice field had been expanded to two acres. It featured areas for training, sparring, artillery, and archery. Because of the large expanse, this is where the Duke chose to address his men.

Dughall's stomach tightened as he approached the platform.

Carpenters had erected it that morning so that he could be seen and heard by everyone. He was accompanied by his lieutenants - Jamison, Ian, Cam, Gilroy, Murdock, and Fang; who remained at the foot of the structure as he climbed the stairs.

The Duke was dressed in his best Highland garb; a kilt, sporran, and fine linen shirt. He'd topped it off with a black cape and accented it with his grandfather's lion head cane. To appear older, he'd tied back his hair in a tail. Dughall had never addressed this many men and decided to speak from the heart. As he scanned the sea of soldiers, he sensed a myriad of emotions - admiration, curiosity, determination, and fear. But under them all, there was a common feeling. They held him in great esteem. He hoped he could live up to their expectations. Their faces regarded him intently.

"Gentlemen." Dughall cleared his throat. "I know about the raid on Turriff. I'm told that some of our brave men lost their lives in the skirmish. Others were wounded." He took a breath. "My heart goes out to these men and their families. We will do our best to support them." He paused. "Unfortunately, we cannot rest. Aberdeen has been captured by the Royalists. We must reclaim the city."

There were sounds of agreement.

"These are desperate times indeed. I just returned from the south, where the King's warships are blocking the port of Edinburgh. His army is gathering on the southern border. General Leslie and his army are preparing to meet them. Our brethren in the west are gathered at Stirling to defend the coast from Irish invaders."

The men grasped the weapons at their side.

"This is a critical time for the rebellion. We must do our part. We can't let Aberdeen remain in the hands of the Royalists."

There were shouts. "Aye!" "We must fight!" "Let's march!"

The Duke waited until they were quiet. "We must go to Aberdeen to assist the Earls Marischal, Kinghorne, and Montrose in retaking the city." This last name galled him because of Gilbert's predicament. But war made strange bedfellows.

The shout was unanimous. "Aye, my Lord!"

Dughall was humbled by their support. "In closing, I stand before ye as an ordinary man."

But they would have none of it. "Nay! He saved two men from the Tower of London!" The crowd murmured agreement.

The Duke interrupted, "That's true. But..."

"He breathed life into a dead child! He has the power over life and death."

"I can explain." Dughall's eyes met Jamison's. The man was warning him against it. He shrugged his shoulders. "The boy was drowned. I helped him to breathe."

"He admits it!"

Fang Adams raised his sword. “Blackheart! Blackheart! Long live the Dark Lord!”

Dughall felt like he’d been punched in the gut. Yet, there was Jamison nodding in agreement. He held out his hands to quell the enthusiasm.

“Blackheart!” “Blackheart!” “Hail to the Dark Lord!”

“Silence!” he cried, and waited for them to cease. “Five hundred men will be stationed around the castle to ensure the safety of my property and progeny. The rest will accompany me to Aberdeen tomorrow.”

Jamison mounted the stairs and faced the soldiers. “Gilroy and Murdock will choose the five hundred. Everyone else prepare to move out. Dismissed!”

Dughall was solemn as he watched the men disperse. He turned to his lieutenant and spoke softly. “I might be leading them to their death. Am I doing the right thing?”

Jamison grinned. “Aye, Blackheart.”

Dughall stared. It was the first time that his friend had called him that in public.

Chapter 71
Face to Face

May 30th 1639
FOUR DAYS LATER

ABERDEEN

James Graham, Earl of Montrose, was glad to be leaving Aberdeen. The Council of War had been a mistake. He thought that the clergy would bring forgiveness to the table. Instead they caused angst and confusion with their incitements to shed blood. In bitterness and zeal, these fiery ministers demanded that the villages of Aberdeenshire be given up to military execution by fire and sword. Montrose balked at such severity to his countrymen. He was not adverse to meeting them on a battlefield, but he shrank from the horrors of military execution. He gave strict orders that life and property were to respected by his soldiers.

This hadn't gone well with the nobles. Enraged that he would not allow the country to be ravaged, some disbanded their vassals and retired to their homes. Others sanctioned public complaints. The chaplain of Lord Eglinton's regiment complained bitterly about Montrose's mercy in sparing the 'unnatural' city of Aberdeen.

Montrose's men were affected by these tirades. A few committed atrocities in the countryside, but the chief outrages were inflicted upon Aberdeen. Salmon-nets were robbed of their catch and all the dogs in the city were slaughtered. To protect the fishermen of the Dee and the Don, the Earl posted sentinels along the banks of both rivers to free the watermen from further oppression.

The citizenry was on the verge of a revolt. To regain control, Montrose took measures. The Earl levied a fine upon the city, took twelve of its cannons, and by beat of drum summoned everyone to surrender their personal weapons. Under the threat of death - swords, pikes, muskets, and pistols were reluctantly delivered. One man was executed for concealing his firearms. This last act caused Montrose to become very unpopular. When the day was done, he opted to march against Royalists elsewhere to reduce their numerous castles.

Now, James sat upon his steed, leading 8,000 men and a long train of artillery. The infantry were in front for show, marching with bagpipes sounding and drums beating. Their burnished weapons shone in the sun. The clansmen wore tartans and carried claymores, dirks, and axes. Lowland musketeers were clad in buff coats, over which they wore sword belts and bandoliers.

Graham felt self-assured. Clad in half-armor with gorget, breast and back plates, arm pieces and tassels; he started the march at the head of the cavalry with baton in hand. Dragged by horses, the brass field pieces followed, their wheels clattering over the pavement of the Broadgate. He was glad to leave the city and suspected that they were glad to see him go.

***

Dughall's army was a few miles from Aberdeen. They intended to arrive a day ago, but their efforts were needed elsewhere. After posting soldiers at Drake, they'd sent a small contingent to defend Huntly. Gilroy departed with three hundred men with a letter to inform Connor. The rest of the army, nearly twenty-eight hundred, headed south towards Aberdeen.

Ten miles out, they were informed that the situation in Turriff was desperate. The citizens suffered under Royalist control. They diverted to the village at once and engaged in a battle to reclaim it. Their opponents fought fiercely. Sadly, some of them were Gordons. Dughall insisted on joining the fray, and was stabbed in the arm in the process. It was only a flesh wound, but he wore it like a badge of honor. The outcome could have been worse. With Jamison and Ian engaged in taking a building, Fang stepped forward to defend him. The man everyone despised fought like a madman, slaying three men to save his master.

Now, Dughall was flanked by Jamison and Ian. Yet his thoughts were with his junior lieutenant. *I owe my life to Fang. I can't send him back to Huntly.*

They rounded a bend and saw the city in the distance. To their surprise, an army was leaving via the main gate.

Jamison scowled. "Stay alert! We know not if they are friend or foe."

Dughall strained his eyes. "I see Montrose's banner."

Ian grunted. "Then the city was retaken."

Fang brought his horse alongside. "Blackheart! Should we proceed or fall back to a safe position?"

Dughall's spirits lifted as he spied the blue and white flag of the Covenant. For the moment, Scotland was free of English oppression. "Proceed. They appear to be Montrose's men. Send our standard bearers forward so that they shall know us."

Fang straightened in the saddle. "As ye wish, my Lord."

"Oh, and Fang..."

"Aye."

"Thank ye for saving my life."

"It was my duty, my Lord." The man headed for the standard bearers.

The armies met at a point about a mile from the city gate. Dughall rode to the front of the line. He was surrounded by his protectors.

The Earl of Montrose advanced on his steed. "Ye!"

The Duke stared. "We bear the flag of the Covenant, Sir. We're on the same side."

"Ye're a Gordon! Yer kinsmen oppose us."

"'Tis true. But here I stand, ready to fight for the freedom of Scotland!"

"Yer brother is in prison."

Dughall gritted his teeth. "An unfortunate turn of events, considering that he was willing to support us. If ye had not taken him prisoner..."

Montrose reddened. "He never meant to support us!"

Dughall masked his anger. "On that, Sir, we shall never agree. Nevertheless, we are at yer service. My army just liberated Turriff."

Montrose sneered. "Why should I believe ye?"

A soldier ran to them. "Because he was raised a Hay!"

Dughall brightened. "Hugh MacNeil! Yer brother is safe at Drake. We rescued him from the Tower."

"Glory be to God!"

Montrose growled. "Impossible! How is it that ye were raised a Hay?"

Dughall pointed to Hugh. "This man will attest to what I say. Lost as an infant, I was raised by a fisherman named Hay. When I turned sixteen, the Gordons reclaimed me."

"Is this true?"

Hugh nodded. "Aye, my Lord."

Montrose hesitated. "Then I will allow ye to help us. The Royalists have been driven out of Aberdeen, but the place is in a state of confusion. Enter the main gate. Yer army can assist the Earl of Marischal in securing the city for the Covenanters."

The Duke sensed that something bad was afoot. "What will *ye* do?"

"We shall march against the Royalists to take possession of their castles."

Dughall frowned. "Ye must not touch Huntly!"

"Why not?"

"I am the guardian of my nephew George, the acting Earl since his father's imprisonment. Huntly is under my protection."

Montrose bristled. "This had better be the truth, Gordon!"

"Ye have my word, Graham!"

His voice was as cold as ice. "Then I shall spare it for now." The Earl guided his steed to the right. "Move yer army to the side. We must be on our way."

Dughall signaled to his men. "Let them pass!"

As the armies came side by side, Hugh MacNeil came forward. "Bless ye for saving my brother! How is he?"

Dughall hesitated. "Alive and whole." He had to tell the truth. "But his mind was affected."

Hugh paled. "I see… Can ye give him a message?"

"What shall I tell him?"

Hugh beamed with pride. "That I fight for the cause. For us. For our children. I follow in his footsteps. Scotland shall be free!"

Dughall felt vindicated. The man was a messenger from God. They were doing the right thing.

Chapter 72
Paranoia

June 3nd 1639
FOUR DAYS LATER

BIRKS, NEAR BERWICK

Faced with strategic failures and a shortage of money to pay troops, paranoia gripped the King and his advisors. It wasn't entirely unfounded. After advancing to Berwick, they learned that Aberdeen and Turiff had surrendered to rebel forces.

An officer expressed his despair. "So now all Scotland is gone. It will take a great time and cost much blood to reduce them again."

The King refused to give up. Too much of his prestige was invested in this enterprise for him to step down without concessions. How could this happen to him? He'd been given this task by God.

They joined his army camped at Birks, three miles west of Berwick on the English side of the Tweed. Initially, the soldiers' morale was boosted by his arrival, but all was not well. The troops were disorganized, food was scarce, and fever had broken out. Most believed that the Scots outnumbered them.

Charles ignored these facts. Two days ago, he'd sent a small party across the Tweed to the town of Dunse, to publish his Newcastle proclamation. To his surprise, General Leslie reacted by sending part of his force to the border town of Kelso. General Munro sent troops as well, stationing them at Jedburgh.

The King was livid. "How dare they break the ten mile limit!" He paced before the Earl of Holland, ranting like a madman. "Take 3,000 foot soldiers and 300 horsemen. Leave immediately for Kelso! Drive them out!"

Holland snapped to attention. "As you wish, Sire."

***

ABERDEENSHIRE
THE HOWE OF FYVIE EARLY MORNING

The Earl of Montrose's army had marched northwest towards the territories of the Gordons. They passed the castle of Kellie, which was the seat of Sir John Gordon of Haddo. The structure was unfinished and not worth their effort. Montrose had another target in mind. They marched on with enthusiasm until they approached the residence of Sir George Gordon of Gicht.

Situated on the fertile banks of the Ythan, the fortress of Gicht overhung the north bank of the river, projecting battlements above thick foliage. Sir Gordon was ready for him. He'd assembled a garrison of men, mostly Gordons, who occupied and strengthened the castle.

Montrose posted his musketeers in the woods. He set up ten cannons on the south bank of the river and battered the castle for two days and nights. To his dismay, the castle could not be breached. The walls were impossibly thick and his cannons threw shot too light for the purpose. From the shelter of the woods on his side and high ramparts on the other, the musketeers shot at each other.

Graham had a problem, but it was about to be usurped by another. Bad news had just arrived. Hostile ships were spotted off the coast, heading for the city of Aberdeen. He dropped the assault and drove his troops towards the city, hoping that Lord Drake could hold it.

***

ABERDEEN

Dughall was in good spirits as he walked along the harbor with Ian and Jamison. His troops had maintained order in the city for almost four days.

The Earl of Marischal had welcomed his support. With only 800 troops of his own, he'd been at a disadvantage. He hadn't been suspicious of Dughall. He'd heard good things about him from Ian's father-in-law Andrew McFarlein.

Dughall looked out upon the water. "I miss the sea. There are times that I wish that I was a fisherman."

Ian snorted. "Not me, brother. But this is a good place to be stationed."

Jamison agreed. "Aye. But I feel sorry for the people. One day they're occupied by Royalists, the next by rebel forces. They don't know who to trust. Who can blame them?"

"Aye," Dughall said. "Montrose's men caused a lot of trouble. They shouldn't have killed the dogs."

"Just because a few wore red ribbons on their collars," Ian added.

Dughall strained his eyes. "What is that on the horizon? Ships?"

Ian lifted his telescope and gazed at the sea. "They're ships all right! Three of them. They bear the standard of the King!" He handed his brother the telescope.

Dughall took a peek. "They cannot be allowed to come ashore. We must fortify the waterfront." He thanked God that they'd brought cannons and positioned them along the harbor.

***

MILES FROM KELSO

The day was sweltering. The Earl of Holland was miserable as he struggled to keep up with his cavalry. The armor he wore was oppressive. *Why was I chosen?* he wondered. *The Earl of Essex has far more military experience.* Indeed, this had been a cause of resentment among the other noblemen.

His foot soldiers and infantry were miles behind, led by experienced officers. They rounded a bend and were met with a surprise. Covering a rolling brae and throughout the thick woods were thousands of Scots soldiers. Pipes sounded, weapons flashed, and they were confronted by a hoard of screaming kilted warriors.

Holland wasn't ready to die. Vastly outnumbered, he gave the order to make a hasty withdrawal. They barely made an escape. They didn't return with their army.

***

LATER THAT DAY

The King stood in his quarters, chastising the Earl of Holland. The man was sitting on a chair while the monarch walked around him. "Coward! You turned tail and ran."

Holland reddened. "Forgive me, your Majesty. Their forces outnumbered ours."

Charles whacked him on the back with a riding crop. "How large?"

The man flinched. "Five thousand. They covered the brae and the surrounding forest like ants on a hill. They were armed and in formation. They knew we were coming."

The King scowled. "Are you saying we have a spy among us?"

"There's no other explanation."

Charles whacked him again. "Next time, you will fight to the death. I don't care if it's a thousand to one. Do you hear me?"

The Earl paled. "Yes, your Majesty. Forgive me."

"Be silent!" His voice was cold. "Leave my presence before I give you to the hangman!"

Holland fled the room.

Charles paced. "Why did God give me an idiot for a commander? The coward lacks a spine." He recalled that the man had no military experience. He'd appointed him at the request of the Queen. "The

French whore wants me to fail!"

Someone cleared his throat behind him. He whirled to see a messenger, grasping his hat and staring at the floor. "What in hell do *you* want?"

The soldier trembled. "Forgive me, Sire. I didn't mean to interrupt." He glanced around the room furtively. "There's a message from one of our spies."

The King stared. "What is it?"

"Ummm... Oh, God... General Leslie has broken camp at Dunglass. He's marching on Dunse Law."

"Dunse Law!" he roared. "We could strike them with a stone from here." That would allow his enemy to intercept any move on Edinburgh, from Kelso or Berwick. "Leave me!"

The lad ran from the room, knocking over a chair.

Charles righted the chair and sat down. His head was pounding and his stomach was sour. He took out his telescope, left the tent, and walked to the river side. Adjusting the lens, he saw a terrible sight. Across the river, the Scottish army was settled upon the top of Dunse Law, with a force of at least 18,000. There were high large tents adorned with large blue flags with the motto "For Christ's Crown and Covenant." He seethed with anger. "What intelligence is this, when the rebels can march with their army and encamp within sight of mine, and I never hear of it 'til their appearance gives alarm?"

The game was over. All that was left was to send a message to Hamilton. The man must abandon his efforts in the bay of Edinburgh and join him immediately at Birks.

***

ABERDEEN LATER THAT NIGHT

Dughall stood at one of the cannons guarding the harbor. The city was safe. Lord Montrose had just arrived with his cavalry. His army and infantry were a day behind. The two men stood talking to each other.

Dughall was giving him a summary. "The ships bear the King's standard. They sailed up the Dee, but no one dared to come ashore. Some say that they're led by Lord Aboyne and his brother James."

Montrose sneered. "Yer cousins."

"War makes for strange opponents and even stranger alliances."

"Hmmphh... How many cannons did ye bring?"

This sounded like criticism. Dughall gritted his teeth. "Eleven. That's everything in my traveling arsenal."

Graham stared. "No offence meant. I'm in yer debt, Gordon. But I am curious about something. Why did ye lie to Hugh MacNeil?"

"I didn't."

"No one escapes the Tower."

"His brother did and my stepfather."

Montrose stroked his beard. "How did ye do it?"

Dughall was solemn. "It's a closely guarded secret. Let's just say that I had a mole in the Tower."

"Is he still there?"

"Nay."

"Too bad. Two of my men are imprisoned there." They gazed out into the harbor at the hostile ships. "The gall of them! We should get some sleep. They may reveal their purpose tomorrow."

Dughall smiled. "We'll be waiting for them. With yer army and mine they can't get past us."

Montrose offered a hand in friendship. "Aye."

***

DUNSE LAW

Morale at the rebel camp was high. Many noblemen maintained military fervor among the troops. They often shared the watch and slept on bare ground in boots and cloaks like common soldiers. Ministers roamed the camp in great numbers, giving sermons and holding services. There was a perpetual sound of prayer, psalm-singing, and reading of scripture. One minister said that they felt the favor of God shining upon them, and a sweet, meek, humble, yet strong and vehement spirit leading them along.

The soldiers were well-fed on wheaten bread and mutton and compensated at six pence per day. Their numbers were increasing by the hour.

***

BIRKS

Morale at the English camp slumped to a new low at the news of Holland's retreat. There were rumors that the enemy was being informed of every move the royal army made. With the prospect of an advancing Scottish army, the English soldiers grew increasingly miserable. Most were tormented by lice. Few had shelter. And smallpox was an ever present hazard. They were disorganized, dirty, and underfed. The enemy seemed almost supernatural. Desertions were a daily occurrence.

Chapter 73
End Game

June 6th 1639
THREE DAYS LATER

ABERDEEN

Lord Drake went to great lengths to secure the city. He camped his troops along the Dee and the Don to simulate greater numbers. To prevent a raid, he ordered his gunners to point cannons at the ships in the harbor. The strategy worked. For a week, no one came ashore. The troops stayed vigilant and waited for reinforcements. They didn't have long to wait. Soon, Lord Montrose's army appeared over the hills and arrived under cover of darkness. Now his soldiers, infantry, and artillery occupied the marketplace and every square.

The two commanders met at headquarters. After a debate, they concluded that there was no need to stay in a defensive position. Their combined forces numbered more than six thousand. Montrose was ready to give the order to attack the ships when a messenger arrived from the Borders. The man bore a report from General Leslie about a stalemate that might lead to a peace treaty. Leslie's note was short. The King was vastly outnumbered. The Scots had sent him a request to open negotiations. They should cease hostilities and wait for instructions.

An hour later, a man disembarked from one of the English ships. He rowed ashore and was escorted to headquarters by a band of rebel soldiers. Dughall was eager to hear his story.

Lord Montrose was more cautious. "Yer name?"

The grizzled man wore an English uniform. "Lieutenant William Gunn."

"Yer purpose?"

"I bring news from Lord Aboyne."

"My cousin," Dughall remarked.

Gunn's eyes widened. "Who might ye be?"

Dughall straightened. "Lord Drake, Duke of Seaford."

"Ye serve the Covenant?"

"Aye."

Traitor! The man never spoke the word, but Dughall heard it clearly.

He swallowed his anger. "What does my cousin want?"

Gunn stared. "Lord Aboyne bears a commission written in the King's own hand. He has been named the royal lieutenant."

They were silent for a moment. Montrose continued the questioning. "So he has taken Lord Huntly's place. What are his intentions?"

"To post a royal proclamation in the market-cross."

Dughall sensed that he was telling the truth. He turned to a guard. "Escort Lieutenant Gunn outside. We must discuss this in private."

The sentry took the messenger's arm and escorted him out of the building.

Dughall gazed out a window. "My cousin comes in an official capacity, bearing a royal proclamation. Could it involve the treaty?"

Montrose frowned. "How could it? Those ships sailed over a week ago."

"Perhaps the King informed his navy first. With a treaty in the works, it might be dangerous to resist."

"Point taken." Montrose stroked his beard. "Hostilities could retard pacification with the King."

"Agreed." Dughall brightened. "It would be a shame to kill our countrymen in the final hours of the conflict."

"Let us move our troops towards Angus and make camp at Dunnottar Castle. There might be news of a treaty."

"What's the risk?"

"Negligible. We can always retake the city." Montrose walked to the door. "Let's tell Gunn that we'll move out at noon."

Dughall joined him. "I feel sorry for the citizens. This will be the fourth occupation in a month."

***

LATER THAT DAY

Lord Aboyne's party landed after the rebel troops evacuated. They got a frosty reception. The citizens were wary after so many occupations. Would these men pillage the town or save them from destruction?

Aboyne had no knowledge of a treaty, so he judged his opponents harshly. "They ran like cowards when confronted with the King's banner!" He publicly announced his commission and issued a proclamation at the market-cross summoning citizens to the royal standard. Much to his surprise, the people were slow to respond to his offer.

The next few days brought more surprises. He'd expected three thousand reinforcements from Hamilton's navy. In their stead came several cannons, a train of gunners, and a note stating that this was all he could offer. Disgusted with the lack of support, the Earls of Tullybardine and Glencairn abandoned him.

Lord Aboyne was undaunted by these desertions. He scoured the city for recruits, convincing two hundred citizens to join him. Late in the day, his brother Lewis arrived. Barely thirteen, he'd mustered a thousand horse and foot soldiers and four brass field pieces from their vassals. When the citizens saw that they were brave and noble men, they contributed money towards the war against the Covenant. Lord Aboyne was encouraged. In a fiery speech, he vowed to march against Montrose and his traitorous cousin.

***

JUNE 11TH 1639
BERWICK

The King stood before a full length mirror, preparing to meet with the Scottish representatives. He'd spent days arguing with his advisors about the futility of the mission. He had to admit that their reasons were sound. The treasury was out of money. The royal army was outnumbered. He could expect no help from Ireland. The Marquis of Hamilton had been present at these talks. Even he argued that the strategy had failed. They should accept the Scots' request to open negotiations.

Charles was resentful. Had these men opposed him in London, he would have banished them to the Tower. Instead, he'd been obliged to consider their opinions. Therefore, two days prior, he'd summoned the Scots to negotiations. This morning their contingent arrived - the lords Rothes, Henderson, Warriston, and three others.

The King fussed as he arranged his lace collar. "Calm yourself, Charles. God is on your side. You will achieve your goal eventually."

The Marquis of Hamilton entered. "Forgive me, Sire. The Scots are in The Earl of Arundel's tent. They are ready to meet with us."

Charles gritted his teeth. *I would rather die than yield to their impertinent and damnable demands.*

"Your Majesty?"

He had his pride. *I will offer them what they want, and break my promises later.*

"Are you ill, My King?"

"Nay." He brushed a hair off his shoulder. "Don't worry. I plan to be charming."

***

JUNE 14TH 1639 THREE DAYS LATER
FROM ABERDEEN TO STONEHAVEN

The citizens of Aberdeen plied Lord Aboyne with stories about the Covenanters. Some joined his ranks when he announced his intention to march against Montrose. He now commanded more than four thousand men. Eager for action, they marched south to take revenge on the rebels. He directed his ships to follow the coast, hauling their cannons, artillery, and ammunition.

Lord Montrose and Lord Drake were camped near Dunnottar Castle. They never expected Lord Aboyne to follow. Anticipating a truce, they'd sent home most of their troops - Montrose's to Angus and Drake's to the Highlands. They were now a force of eight hundred.

When they learned that Lord Aboyne was marching against them, they positioned their troops near Stonehaven. Guarding their rear was Dunnottar Castle, an impregnable cliff-side castle. The owner provided them with artillery - two brass nine-pounder cannons and six field culverins. The gates of his fortress were left open to receive them.

Lord Aboyne halted for a night at Muchalls and sent forth a party to investigate. Upon return, they devised a plan to plunder a Covenanter's mansion. They didn't expect trouble because the house was relatively unguarded. Lord Aboyne didn't wait for their ships to land to claim their artillery. He led the raid the next morning, flanked by his brothers and Sir John Gordon.

***

Lord Montrose was outraged when he heard about the attack. "They molested our allies! Now we *must* face them." He crafted a letter and handed it to Dughall. "Send a man to intercept their army. He must present this to Lord Aboyne and wait for a response. I expect that he'll accept my offer."

"I will take it," Fang said.

Dughall had come to appreciate this man. He was as loyal as a dog and fearless in battle. He placed the letter in his hand. "Give this to my cousin and wait for his answer."

Fang grunted and was on his way.

There were shouts and squeals as men and horses moved artillery, positioning the pieces around Megray Hill. The canons were unwieldy, even though they were on wheels. Field culverins were brought forth on wagons because of their excessive weight. The twenty-nine caliber guns included a swivel for support and aiming. It was an awesome display of power.

Dughall was curious about the strategy. "Why are we moving the artillery here?"

Montrose smiled. "Lord Aboyne will accept my challenge to a duel. His army must pass through here. I told him to meet me at Dunnottar Castle."

"Ye plan to fight him one on one?"

"Nay. Let him think that." Montrose chuckled. "Megray Hill offers no cover. It's a perfect place for an ambush."

Dughall bristled. "So it's a trap."

"We have to do it. We're outnumbered."

The young Lord didn't like it.

***

With artillery in place, they proceeded to create piles of shot and ammunition. Gunpowder barrels were cracked, torches were lit, and musketeers checked their ball and powder. Pikers gathered in phalanx formation, ready to defend the musketeers as they reloaded. Standard bearers waved the Covenant flag. Drummers stood by, ready to relay orders. Fang returned, carrying a message for Montrose. His challenge was accepted. The royal army was just over the rise.

Montrose shouted, "Hide the artillery! Stand in front of it!"

Dughall watched as soldiers formed human walls in front of the deadly guns. Everyone waited.

Fang appeared with an eight-foot pike in hand. "My Lord. I must help the musketeers."

"Go with God, my friend," Dughall said. As he ran away, the young Lord unsheathed his sword.

Jamison grasped his weapon. "We've been ordered to stay on the sidelines. But if anyone attacks, I will defend ye to the death."

Soon, Lord Aboyne's army appeared over the rise. They advanced in orderly fashion, displaying the royal standard. First, Sir John Haddo led the guard onto Megray Hill. They were a hundred gentlemen on horseback, armed with swords and pistols. Scores of musketeers followed with match cords lit and bandoliers open. The brave Highland companies marched behind them, brandishing swords. Wisely, Lord Aboyne and his brother rode at the end of the procession. They flaunted their weapons, eager for battle.

Montrose tensed. "That's all of them. Open fire!" The drummers relayed his command.

The rebel soldiers moved aside, revealing the heavy artillery. Gunners scrambled to load powder and shot and apply fire to the fuses. Musketeers and pikers moved to the sides and assumed offensive positions. Montrose ran off to oversee a line of cannons.

Jamison whooped. "It's a perfect trap!"

Dughall frowned. "I don't like it."

"Why?"

"It's not fair. We got them here under false pretenses."

"War isn't fair."

"Make way!" a man shouted.

The cannons fired in a volley, launching nine-pound shot into center of the advance guard. The ground shook and the sound was deafening. Dozens of men fell along with their horses, missing limbs and other parts. The surviving guardsmen shifted to the sides but couldn't avoid the carnage. As gunner crews swabbed and reloaded the canons, the culverins opened fire, hurling three inch shot into the advance guard. Limbs were severed. Bones were cracked. Men and horses screamed in agony. The injuries were horrific.

***

Fang's eyes gleamed as he watched the carnage. They were outnumbered three to one, but the artillery gave them the advantage. Clouds of white smoke drifted across the battlefield in a deadly haze. He stayed with the rebel musketeers as they assumed a firing position.

Forced to the front, the enemy musketeers took aim and fired. The sound was sharp and loud. The smell of burning sulfur permeated the air as they exchanged fire with the rebels. Bodies dropped on both sides. Drums sounded over the screams of the wounded and dying.

The rebel musketeers started to reload. There were quite a few steps to this process. They had to put a small amount of powder into the pan, a lot into the barrel, then insert the lead ball. A bit of grass wadding and a scouring stick was used to push it down the barrel. The enemy musketeers advanced on them, using the butt of their guns as weapons.

Fang sprang forth with the pikers to defend his musketeers as they reloaded. He fought like a madman, speared a man through the heart, and could barely dislodge his weapon. Now, the drums were beating a different code, telling him to get out of the way. With his heart in his throat, he ran back to the cannons.

The gunners stood back and covered their ears. "Make way!" The mighty guns roared. Once again, the enemy line was breached, shattering men to pieces. One musketeer was a monstrous thing, gushing blood. A cannon ball had smashed off his head. Men near him found bits of flesh clinging to their dusty, sweat-stained clothes. As the body fell, they turned and ran, slipping and sliding on blood.

The Highland companies gave their battle cries as they advanced through the gore with their claymores gleaming. There were shouts, screams, and loud pops as the field culverins fired into their midst. For the men under fire, moments became hours. The royalist army was in chaos.

***

Bile rose in Dughall's throat. He'd witnessed action at Turriff, but nothing of this caliber. The devastation was immense. There were bodies lying everywhere. He took stock of the injuries. Without tourniquets, most of them would be fatal. An enemy soldier lay writhing on the ground with his leg beside him, a piece of smashed, bloody flesh. He gripped his sword and advanced on the battlefield.

"My Lord!" Jamison cried, as he ran alongside.

"I must help him!"

Jamison grabbed him arm. "There's nothing ye can do! He's a dead man."

Little Lewis Gordon ran towards them, brandishing a short sword. "Fight to the death!"

Montrose shouted. "Kill him!"

"Nay!" Dughall cried. "He's just a child." But no one heard him.

Before his eyes, Lord Aboyne braved musket fire to rescue his brother. Dughall's heart raced as their gazes met. His cousin's eyes glittered with hate. Then he dragged off his little brother.

Jamison led his master to a safe position. "I cannot let ye risk yerself. Stay here!"

The drums sounded again. "Make way!" The cannons fired in a volley. The clansmen who were accustomed to fighting with swords were unable to endure the barrage. They wheeled about in confusion and fled to the rear of the company.

The pikers moved to the side, making way for a torrent of musket fire. Men wailed. Casualties mounted. Within minutes, what was left of the royal army fell back in confusion. Raising a white flag, they were allowed to retrieve their wounded and retreat from the hill unmolested.

Dughall agonized over the battle. His cousins had been spared. But so many men had been killed or wounded. Valuable horses had been slaughtered. How could this be what God wanted?

Jamison seemed to read his mind. "It's the price of freedom, my Lord."

Montrose slapped him on the back. "We won, Gordon! Even though we were outnumbered."

Dughall caught his breath. He longed to tend to the wounded, but knew that Montrose would consider it improper. He didn't have his healer's bag or cloth strips for a tourniquet. "What will we do now?"

"We shall proceed at once to Edinburgh. Perhaps there is news of a treaty."

***

JUNE 18TH 1639
BERWICK

The negotiations had gone on for a week. The first day was the ugliest. In the face of six wary Scottish Commissioners, the King failed to make progress. Charles was partly to blame. At first, he'd been positively frosty. Deep down, he'd expected them to fall to their knees and beg him for mercy and forgiveness. Of course, none of that happened.

Negotiations were failing, so Charles tried a different tactic. On the second day, he forced himself to relax and turned on his famous charm. The Scots responded favorably except for Lord Warriston, who was as stiff and passionate as ever.

Then, there were the details. Charles refused to recognize the dictates of the Edinburgh Assembly. But he promised a new Assembly and Parliament to settle the Church question. He vowed that he would personally preside over this important gathering.

The next five days were challenging, but they managed to come to an agreement. Both sides would disband their armies within forty eight hours of the declaration. Charles agreed to summon a new Assembly to meet in Edinburgh on August 20th to be followed by a Parliament. All matters ecclesiastical should be determined by the Assembly, and matters civil by the Parliament. Impounded royal castles, forts, and stores should be immediately turned over to his Majesty's agents. There were other details as well, involving logistics and political prisoners.

The King's scribes had been hard at work drawing up seven articles of pacification. Both sides would gather today to affix their signatures to the document.

The King was satisfied with the outcome. The monarch had no intention of keeping his word. The document was simply a play for time. He would fortify his castles, obtain funding, and come back at them with a vengeance.

Chapter 74
Welcome News

June 22nd 1639
FOUR DAYS LATER

EDINBURGH THE J ADAMS INN

The Duke woke at the crack of dawn to the sound of his servant snoring. He rose and dressed quietly, grabbed a pitcher, and left the room to order breakfast. The young Lord was exhausted. They'd spent seven days on the open road, traveling to Edinburgh from Stonehaven. Parting with Montrose near Dunfermline, Dughall and Jamison camped their army and rode into the city. Arriving last night, they heard of a treaty and hoped that it wasn't a rumor.

Dughall walked down the narrow staircase and proceeded to the kitchen. He ordered breakfast from the innkeeper's wife, a stout middle-aged woman. "Breakfast for two. Eggs. Ham. Bread. Tea."

She smiled, revealing rotten teeth. "As ye wish. Would ye like me to fill that for ye?"

Dughall handed her the pitcher and watched her fill it from a large wooden tub. "Thank ye kindly." He accepted it from her hands and took it upstairs to his room. He desperately needed a bath.

Jamison woke as he began to wash. "My Lord?"

"Aye?"

"I would have hauled that for ye."

"I know, friend. I wanted to let ye sleep."

Jamison sat up and stretched. "I feel better. But my mouth tastes awful."

Dughall ran his tongue across his front teeth. "Now that ye mention it." He wiped his hands on a towel. "The innkeeper said that a copy of the treaty is posted at the market-cross."

Jamison got up and started to get dressed. "We will go there this morning."

The Duke ran a comb through his hair. "Ouch! It's tangled like a bird's nest."

"Would ye like me to comb it?"

"Not now."

"Will we try to see Lord Gilbert?"

Dughall smiled. "Aye. I hope to convince Balmerino to release him."

The men went downstairs, had breakfast, and left the inn to visit the market-cross. When they arrived at the market square, they had to wait their turn to see the document. Hundreds of men stood in line to read the important announcement. They approached the post in groups of six.

When it was their turn, they stood in front of the cross-shaped monument. The Duke began to read a long scroll that was nailed to the post. "This is it."

"Can ye read?" an old man asked.

"Aye."

"Tell us what it says."

It was written in legal language, so Dughall decided to explain it. "Let's see. The treaty was signed on the 18th of June, 1639 at Berwick by King Charles I and Scottish representatives. It talks about avoiding war. Then it describes the benefits of a treaty."

Jamison interrupted. "Ha! What are the terms?"

Dughall ran a finger down the scroll. "There are seven articles of pacification. Hmmm…" The men waited as he read silently. "Both sides must disband their armies within forty-eight hours of the declaration."

A man said, "So they must be disbanded now."

"Aye. Royal castles, forts, and stores seized in the conflict must be turned over to His Majesty's agents."

Jamison scowled. "Everything for the King. What do we get out of this?"

"Wait." Dughall skipped some fancy language. "Several articles describe it. The King will not respect the results of the recently held Edinburgh Assembly. But he agrees to summon a new Assembly to meet in Edinburgh on August 20th to be followed by a Parliament. Ecclesiastical matters will be determined by the Assembly, and civil matters by the Parliament."

There were small sounds of agreement. Jamison grunted. "So we are free to determine our own affairs. Can we trust him?"

The Duke frowned. "That's a good question."

The old man spoke. "What else does it say?"

Dughall read the final article. "It talks about the reestablishment of royal rule in Scotland. The logistics and such… Ah… Then it pardons all rebels, including the leaders."

A man shouted. "Did ye hear that? We can't be named as traitors!"

"Aye." A few of the men walked away. Dughall continued. "The last paragraph talks about political prisoners. According to this, they must be freed within a week of the agreement." Several men thanked him.

Dughall and Jamison walked away so that they could talk in private. The Duke's heart swelled with gratitude. "Oh, Jamison."

"What is it, my Lord?"

"It specifically mentioned Lord Huntly."

"Yer brother is free to go?"

"Aye. Let's get our horses and go to the castle."

***

EDINBURGH CASTLE

Gilbert's heart was light as he gathered his belongings for the journey. That morning, he'd been told that a peace treaty had been signed that freed all political prisoners. Lord Huntly had been specifically named in the document. He was free to go.

The Earl took a last look around his chamber. Other than the loss of his freedom, it hadn't been a bad place to stay. They'd treated him in a manner consistent with his title and provided him with amenities.

Gilbert ran his hand across a section of the wall. He'd kept track of the days with tiny scratch marks on the stone. "Two and a half months!" he said aloud. "Too long to be away from my family."

A guard arrived with a saddle pack. "Yer pack, my Lord."

He wondered about Flame. "What about my horse?"

"The stallion has been prepared for the journey."

"Thank ye. Am I to ride alone?"

The guard seemed surprised. "Nay, two gentlemen are waiting for ye."

"Good." Gilbert packed his bag with his belongings. Was it Dughall? His cousin George? Connor? He handed the guard a silver coin. "For yer kindness."

The man smiled. "Thank ye, Sir! Follow me."

Gilbert shouldered his bag. They left the chamber and walked a long corridor until they came to a granite stairway. Their footsteps echoed as they took the steps to a lower floor. This part of the castle was unfamiliar to him. He'd spent most of his time between his chamber and a hall used for interrogation.

They arrived at a door that led to a courtyard. Passing through, they crossed the square and encountered a gate that was protected by a portcullis. The guard worked chains to raise the grille and then removed a bar from the gate.

Gilbert noticed arrow slits in the sides of the walls. He knew that they enabled archers and crossbowmen to attack trapped invaders. Rescue was impossible. The castle was a fortress.

The guard pushed open the gate.

Gilbert shaded his eyes. The sky was clear. The sun was strong. It had been months since he'd seen daylight. *Praise God! I'm free.*

The guard pointed. "Yer horse is over there. Good luck, Sir." He turned on his heels and walked away.

Gilbert squinted. Coming towards him were two men on horses, leading his beloved stallion. His heart leapt for joy. "Brother!"

Chapter 75
A Fragile Peace

September 25th 1639
THREE MONTHS LATER

DRAKE CASTLE

The Duke stood in the Great Hall, watching his wee son open birthday gifts. The entire family was present. The children sat in a circle on the floor as the one-year-old ripped up colored paper.

Wee Maggie shrieked with delight. "Ah!"

Red-haired James broke into a smile. Then he balled up the paper and gave it to her. Dughall was encouraged by this behavior. His son rarely shared anything. But he had a special affinity for his sister.

James opened the package and pulled out a wooden horse. He placed the head in his mouth and bit down.

"Nay, James!" Luc cried. "Ye can't eat it."

The infant glared at his adopted brother. Andrew and Alexander kept quiet. They'd had too many brawls with their cousin.

Dughall handed him another package. "Put it down, James. Open this one." He wasn't about to take the toy away. The child tended to bite and this wasn't the place to discipline him. "Now!"

Keira stood by nervously. "I'll take it from his mouth." She knelt down and stroked the child's hair until he released the miniature Black Lightning.

Dughall wished that she wouldn't rescue him. The child expected her to resolve his problems. He'd had family problems since he returned from the war. In his absence, Keira had taken the infant to their bed. The child was accustomed to sleeping with her. His first act was to give Maggie a bedroom and place the boy in the nursery. James screamed, cried, and bit Tarrah when she tried to comfort him. Keira begged to intervene, but Dughall stood his ground and imposed his wishes. James eventually settled down, but he sensed that the boy resented him.

The Duke adored his wife, but he couldn't understand her obsession. She'd spoiled their son rotten, leaving him the role of disciplinarian. That only left him one choice. He would give her more children, so that she had less time to dote on this one. He'd insisted on making love each day, in an effort to get her pregnant.

Now James held up his last gift, a finely stitched leather ball. The children clapped and squealed with delight. The party was almost over.

Mary picked up one of the twins. "Ian. It's late. Help me bed them down."

Ian lifted a boy into his arms. "I will, lass." He turned to his brother. "Shall we meet for a cigar afterwards?"

"That sounds good." Dughall picked up wee Maggie. "I must tuck the children in first. Meet me in an hour in the study." He touched Luc's shoulder. "Come along, lad."

Keira held their son. "It's past his bedtime."

They took wee James to the nursery and placed him in the cradle. The child screamed when they left him. They took Maggie to the bedroom that she shared with her friend and nursemaid Marjory. Luc was dropped off at the door to his chamber.

Finally, Dughall took his wife's hand. "We're alone, at last." He squeezed her slender fingers and led her into their bed chamber.

She seemed nervous. "Will we try again, tonight?"

He kissed her gently. "Perhaps later. I need to talk to my brother."

"Then can I?"

He knew what she wanted to say. "Nay, lass. The child stays in the nursery."

***

THE STUDY

The Duke sat at his rosewood desk, sipping a glass of whisky. His brother hadn't arrived yet. He pondered the events of the past few months as he studied the amber liquid.

***

It had taken three weeks to travel from Edinburgh to Drake Castle. They stayed in decent inns along the way. He took a proper bath, the first in a month, and untangled his greasy hair. At first he'd been worried about his brother, but Gilbert seemed unscathed by his incarceration. He was hungry for news of his wife and son, the Highlands, his estate, and any battles. They arrived home in mid-July, to grateful wives and heartfelt celebrations. By then, everyone knew that the war was over.

Dughall knew that it was a fragile peace. Facts and rumors supported it. Neither side entirely honored the treaty. The Covenanters did not dissolve their whole army, but kept many troops throughout the country. They did not raze the fortifications at Leith as agreed, but destroyed as much as they could rebuild in a few hours. The King was at fault as well. He strengthened his forts at Berwick and Carlisle and fortified

Edinburgh Castle.

Some Covenanters persecuted royalists who dared to appear in public. The Earl of Traquair was hauled from his coach and beaten by a mob of devout women. On the other hand, some royalists sought revenge on their Covenanting neighbors. Even Lord Aboyne challenged Dughall to a duel. The event was avoided, due to Gilbert's skillful intervention.

Having no success with commoners, the King tried to win over influential individuals. He sent fifteen letters to Scots who distinguished themselves in the late troubles, commanding them to attend him in London. Alarmed, only three responded - the lords Montrose, Loudon, and Lothian, bearing an apology for the rest. Dughall was one of the non-responders. He believed that the monarch would imprison him.

Snubbed, the King broke his promise to preside over the General Assembly. He appointed Lord Traquair in his place with instructions to abandon the cause of Episcopacy. The Assembly met on the 6th of August and proceeded to the business of determining the professed religion of Scotland. Showing delicacy to the King, no expressions were used that could cause contempt among the English. Within these parameters, they abolished the Articles of Perth, the Book of Canons, and the Liturgy along with powers granted to certain clergy. They ended on August 30th by establishing Presbytery as the official sanctioned religion. Dughall attended the Parliament that convened the next day. With church affairs settled, they got down to civil business. They supplanted the former role of the bishops with a tier of lesser barons.

They'd heard that the King was displeased.

***

Dughall sipped his whisky. He was in possession of information that proved that the peace was temporary. It involved a secret, so he didn't know what to do about it. Perhaps Ian could give him some advice.

There was a knock on the door and his brother entered. Ian looked self-satisfied. At the party, he'd announced that Mary was pregnant.

Dughall poured a glass for his brother. "I'm glad ye came." He pointed to the humidor. "Let's have a smoke."

Ian lit a taper in the fireplace and brought it to the desk. He opened the humidor, extracted two cigars, and proceeded to light them. The man sat down and passed one to his brother. "They smell good."

Dughall took a drag. "Aye. They're one of the constant pleasures in life."

Ian raised his eyebrows. "Trouble, brother?"

"It's no secret. Keira has spoiled our son. She gets angry when I discipline him."

Ian frowned. "We were wondering when ye would take matters in yer hands. The boy can be overbearing."

"He's only a year old."

"May I speak freely?"

Dughall was apprehensive. "Aye, of course. Ye're my brother."

"James is a terror. Andrew and Alex won't play with him. They've been bitten too many times."

Dughall appreciated his honesty. "This is partly my fault. I was gone so much this year. Meetings... Skirmishes... Occupations... James barely knows his father. I think he resents me."

"Why?"

"I banished him from his mother's bed."

Ian sipped his whisky. "Keira was sleeping with him?"

"Aye."

"That's a bad thing, brother."

Dughall nodded. "Now that things have settled down, I'm thinking of taking Maggie and James to see Brother Lazarus. He wants to test them."

"To see if they have the Sight?"

"That, and more. The monks will document their abilities. Perhaps he can give me some advice about the boy."

"I know what he'll say. Spare the rod and spoil the child."

Dughall frowned. "Father never beat us."

"'Tis true. But Mother and Father set the rules and we were expected to obey. They always stood together."

"That's the difference. I have to work on my wife. I've been trying to get her pregnant."

Ian smiled. "More children will keep her busy. She'll have less time to dote on the boy."

Dughall sat back and blew out smoke. "I'll plan a trip to the abbey and ask Mother to talk to Keira. A bit of friendly womanly advice. She'll know what to do." He was ready for another conversation. "We need to discuss one more thing. But it involves a secret."

Ian leaned forward, his eyes full of interest. "What?"

Dughall promised that he would never speak of it again. But this was his brother. "The King is planning to resume the war."

Ian's eyes widened. "How do ye know?"

"Ye must never repeat what I'm about to say."

"I won't."

Dughall sighed. "Remember when I went to London to free Father from the Tower?"

"Aye. I've always meant to ask how ye did it."

"I called upon an ally to release him. The ally was the Queen."

Ian stared. "That was dangerous, considering ye'd been named a traitor. What were ye thinking?"

Dughall reddened. "It's a strange story. When Gilbert and I were summoned to the King, she and I were left alone to visit the Observatory.

That's where she propositioned me."

Ian let out a low whistle. "Did she know ye were married?"

"Oh, aye. I guess it didn't matter. At the time I didn't promise anything. But when Father was captured and scheduled to be executed... Well... I offered her my body."

"Dear God."

"It had nothing to do with God. Quite the contrary. I sold my integrity to rescue Father."

Ian frowned. "Who else knows about this?"

"Only Jamison and Murdock."

"Good. Let's keep it that way. Have ye heard from her?"

"Yesterday." Dughall bolted his whisky. "I received a letter from her saying that her husband is planning to renew the war. She has details but wants something for them. Another tryst on my terms. We'd have to be discreet. She suspects that he knows about us."

"Jesus!"

"What should I do?"

"I don't know, brother." They sat for a moment in an uncomfortable silence. Finally, Ian grinned. "Few men get to fornicate with the Queen. What's she like?"

"Brother!"

"I'd like to know."

Dughall blushed. "She's a remarkable woman. Bonny and petite, with skin like silk. She taught me things that I'll never forget. "

"Tell me about them."

He did just that.

***

LATER THAT NIGHT THE LORD'S BED CHAMBER

Dughall's heart was pounding like a drum. He'd just made love for more than an hour. After describing the tryst to his brother, he went to his chamber and woke his wife. Her bonny face and willing body was a recipe for an intense encounter.

Keira cried out with pleasure and begged him to continue. She allowed him to take her from behind, like a forceful stallion. Now, they lay in an erotic tangle.

My dear wife, he thought. *Let them fight their war. Never again will I be unfaithful.* His heartbeat slowed and he came to a realization. There were three people in the bed. He reached out and touched her belly.

Dughall smiled. *Praise God. We conceived a daughter.*

Epilogue

The people of Scotland found only intermittent peace. After the treaty, the King vowed to subdue the rebels by force. He convinced the Irish government to fund a foreign army against the Scots and then summoned a Parliament to raise funds. When this failed, he appealed to Spain for a loan.

Dughall rebuffed the Queen's offer, incurring her anger. She supported her husband's effort, appealing to her brother the King of France and even to the Pope. Her inquiries failed, leaving the King to his own devices.

Charles moved forward without funding, raising an army in the south. By August 1640, he'd mustered forces in Northumberland and Yorkshire. They were unpaid, underfed, and poorly armed, and desertions were common. The Irish army was not ready.

The Scottish Parliament reacted by creating a Committee of Estates to facilitate the defense of the nation. The Covenanter armies rose once again to subdue the Scottish royalists. The Earl of Marischal occupied Aberdeen, while General Munro invaded the estates of royalist Gordons. Huntly Castle was seized and occupied by rebels, who destroyed the interior and defaced religious stonework. Gilbert, his family, and a few servants escaped capture and fled to Drake to live with his brother. There wasn't much that Dughall could do about Huntly's occupation. He and Gilbert had cast their lots and had to live with it. Then things got worse. The Earl of Argyll led five thousand Campbells on a quest to burn and pillage the estates of royalist clans in the Highlands.

By August 1640, the Covenanter army had reassembled on the border with England. This included a contingent from Drake Castle, led by Ian, Fang, and the archer Cameron Hunter. Dughall and Jamison stayed in the north, to protect their families and property.

The rebel army invaded England. In a surprise move, General Leslie avoided the fortifications at Berwick and marched for Newcastle to secure the coalfields that supplied London. As the King raced north, his field commander Viscount Conway sent 4,500 troops to guard the ford with four hundred musketeers and four light artillery pieces. But Leslie's response was superior. With sixty pieces of artillery mounted on a church tower, they dominated the enemy position. A bloody battle ensued, but in the end the rebels were able to cross the ford and possess the river bank. Viscount Conway decided that Newcastle could not be defended and withdrew his forces to Durham. Leslie and his army took Newcastle on the 30th of August.

Once again, King Charles was forced to negotiate. A treaty was signed at Ripon agreeing to the cessation of hostilities. A permanent settlement was to be ratified as soon as a Parliament could assemble in London. In the meantime, the Scottish army was to occupy Northumberland and Durham at the English's expense.

The King summoned a Parliament in November, which was attended by Scottish commissioners. It was at this gathering that the English representatives took the opportunity to express their displeasure. Against a backdrop of civil unrest, Parliament impeached the King's ministers Laud and Strafford and scheduled them to be executed. Then Parliament forced the monarch to sign a bill which enabled them to sit as long as they liked, not liable to royal dissolution. Oliver Cromwell delivered a blow to his authority by criticizing the King's taxes and corruption in the Church of England. He proposed demolishing the concept of the Established Church of England.

King Charles was livid. Anxious to conclude Parliament, he moved on to the treaty and agreed to concessions. He ratified a resolution by the General Assembly that banished Episcopacy from the Scottish Church. No Scots would be persecuted for signing the Covenant. All proclamations and publications against the Covenanters would be suppressed. And England would recompense them 300,000 pounds for the cost of the war. The treaty was signed in August of 1641.

The King was now caught between the Scots, his people, and his own Parliament. The monarch initially showed respect to his Scottish subjects, visiting Edinburgh and granting titles. While the King bestowed favors on his former enemies, he was not permitted to help the loyalists. He could only ask that they not be given up to popular vengeance. Thus, Gilbert and his family remained at Drake Castle. The Earl of Montrose, to Dughall's surprise, was now squarely in the camp of the monarch. Perhaps it was because of his hatred for the Earl of Argyle.

The King returned to London to trouble with the House of Commons. Public criticism of the monarch had reached a feverish pitch and the mob rendered it impossible for him to stay in London. When an attempt to arrest five members of the House failed, he retired to York and set up his standard at Nottingham among royalist supporters. England slipped into a civil war with the Scots as interested bystanders. Parliament took control of the militia and the war began. For almost two years, Charles' forces fought relentlessly, regaining authority over the west and north of England.

The Scots loyalties were torn by fear, self-interest, and religious fervor. Some believed that Puritans in the English Parliament meant to reestablish their religion. Others believed that the King meant to break their treaty. Finally after much debate, in summer of 1643 they turned their back on the King and committed 21,000 horse and foot soldiers to assist the English Parliament. This tipped the scale against the monarch and contributed to the overthrow of his forces. After a series of bloody battles, Charles I surrendered in May of 1646 to a Scottish regiment and was handed over to the English Parliament. He was imprisoned in Holdenby House, Northamptonshire to await trial for treason. The English government held debates to decide on a new constitution.

***

Now, back to our hero... Dughall was unable to shake his reputation as the Dark Lord. Even his own men called him 'Blackheart'. He vowed to change their minds someday. The sword continued to cause him problems, inducing blackouts and strange behavior. After repeated advice from Brother Lazarus, he allowed Jamison to hide it at Seaford Shores. He should have destroyed it. Some saw this as a lost opportunity to rid the world of its evil influence. Dughall disagreed. Now in his late twenties, he had more pressing problems.

This story continues in book three of the Dark Birthright Saga. "Dark Destiny" is a work in progress. For a sneak peek and release updates, visit: www.darkdestinythenovel.com

AUTHOR'S NOTES

The state of medicine and healing

If you lived in a major city like Edinburgh and had money and stature, you could have engaged a trained physician. Healers, midwives, and bonesetters would have been available for common folk. This was a trade passed down from mother to daughter, or in rare cases from mother to son. They were skilled in the use of herbs and other natural materials such as tar or honey to cure disease or treat wounds. In the book, I tried to make the healing and midwifery scenes authentic, given the time and place and resources available. However, my advice to the reader is to not try them at home without formal training.

The struggle between religions that precipitated the first Bishop's War

Dark Lord was not meant to be an endorsement or criticism of any religion.

The religious and political upheaval in "Dark Lord" was true to that period. It couldn't be ignored. The ideas that pervaded the culture would have effected every Scot, from the loftiest lord to the lowliest peasant. The Reformation was fresh in their minds as it had occurred in the previous century. There was a great struggle between Catholicism and the various sects of Protestantism. Some may think it strange that Christians would seek to destroy each other. Others may find the speeches of Minister Henderson or the text of the Covenant confusing. They were based on historical records, listed in the bibliography.

From another perspective, it was the story of an arrogant King who was convinced that he was the hand of God. Charles I was willing to go to any lengths to impose his religious beliefs on his subjects.

The Geography

"Dark Lord" is a work of historical fiction. It takes place during 1637-1639 (with the epilogue advancing to 1646), and is set in Scotland and England. See the maps in the beginning of the book. Most locations in the book exist today or existed in the 17th century. Here are a few exceptions. Drake Castle is a fabrication of the author's mind. (Sorry...) The Abbey of Deer's life as a religious institution came to an end with the Reformation in 1560, before the time frame of this book.

HISTORICAL CHARACTERS

"Dark Lord" is a work of fiction. Names, characters, places, and incidents are either the product of the author's imagination or are used fictitiously. Any resemblance to actual events or persons, living or dead, is entirely coincidental.

Some characters' names and the events depicted in this novel have been extracted from historical records; however, neither these characters nor the descriptions of events are held to accurately represent real people or their conduct. Every effort has been made to present readers with an exciting, interesting story set in a reasonably authentic environment. No other purpose than entertainment was intended or should be implied.

That being said:

Historically, from 1562-1636, George Gordon served as the 1st Marquess of Huntly. The novel portrays an alternate reality for the Gordon clan if George had succumbed to the madness of the sword of Red Conan, to be succeeded by a mythical brother Robert. Robert then spawned a son named Robert, who became the cruel and powerful Earl of Huntly in Dark Birthright. His son Gilbert, who succeeded him after death, is the Earl of Huntly in Dark Lord. Even though Gilbert Gordon is a mythical character, I tried to portray what happened to the real Lord Huntly as a commander during the first Bishop's war.

Jenny Geddes was a real woman who started the riot at St. Giles by throwing her three-legged stool at the Dean. However, she was a thirty seven year old vegetable seller, not a young servant girl as I have portrayed.

NOTE ON THE USE OF THE SCOTS DIALECT

Some may wonder why I used only a bit of the Scots dialect in this book. I decided to lightly salt the manuscript with Scots to make it authentic, but easy for the reader. In this novel, you will find a lot of ye's, scores of lads and lassies, and a few self-explanatory words. Forgive me if it's not more widespread. I will leave that to Sir Walter Scott.

HONORABLE MENTION

There are many songs referenced in this book, taken from traditional Scottish and English folk music. These beautiful compositions are over 100 years old and in the public domain. I have also included some traditional poems and nursery rhymes.

Here is a translation of one of them.

'Burnie Bouzle'

Gin ye'll mairy me lass, at the kirk o Burnie Bouzle
till the day ye dee lassie, ye will ne'er repent it
Ye will weir whan ye are wad, a kirtle an a Hieland plaid
An sleep upon a heather bed, sae couthy an sae canty

Ye will gang sae braw, lassie, tae the kirk o Burnie Bouzle
Little brogues an aw, lassie, vou, but you'll be canty
Yer wee bit tocher is but smaw, but hodden gray will weir for aw
A'll sauf ma siller for tae mak ye braw an ye will ne'er repent it

We'll hae bonny bairns an aw, some lassies fair an laddies braw
Juist like thair mither ane an aw, an yer faither he's consentit
A'll hunt the otter an the broch, the hart, the hare an heather cock
A'll pou ye limpets frae the rock, tae mak ye dishes denty.

TRANSLATION COURTESY OF CECILIA PENNY

If you marry me my lass at the church of Burnie Boozle, 'til the day that you die you will never regret it. You will wear when we are wed, a kirtle (a piece of cloth, usually tartan, over her skirt) with a plaid around you to keep you warm. And you will sleep upon a bed of heather, comfortable and neat ("canty" has several shades of meaning all good like - lively, pleasant, small, neat).

And you will go looking so fine to the church of Burnie Boozle with brogues (leather shoes) on your feet as well and my goodness you will look great. You don't have a lot of money ("tocher" can mean bride's "dowry") but hodden gray (coarse home spun material) will last well. I shall save the money (siller) I have to make you look fine, and you will never regret it.

We shall have some bonnie bairns as well, some lassies fair and handsome ladies, all like their mother, one and all, and your father has consented (given his blessing on our marriage). I'll hunt the otter and the brock (the badger), the hart (deer), the hare, and the heather cock (grouse or partridge). I shall pull the limpets (whelks, buckies, snails) from the rocks, to make you dishes dainty.

*The title 'Burnie Bouzle' means a thicket or clump of trees beside a small burn or stream.

Bibliography

Books

Carlton, Charles, *Charles I the Personal Monarch.* Routledge, London and New York, 1995

Chambers, Robert, *History of the Rebellions in Scotland, Volume I.* Constable & Co., Edinburgh,1828

Grant, James, *Memoirs of James, Marquis of Montrose.* George Routledge & Co., New York, 1858

Leloup, Jean-Yves, *The Gospel of Thomas, the Gnostic Wisdom of Jesus.* Inner Traditions, 1986

Lowe, Harry, *Scottish Heroes, Tales of the Covenanters.* Pacific Press Publishing Association, USA, 1950

Mackay, Charles, *Songs of Scotland.* 1877

Melville, Mary, *Deer Abbey.*

Mencken, August, *By the Neck.* Hastings House, New York 1942

Nichols, John, *The Progresses, Processions, and Magnificent Festivities of King James, Volume 1.* London, 1828

Paterson, Raymond Campbell, *A Land Afflicted, Scotland and the Covenanter Wars 1638-1690.* John Donald Publishers LTD, Edinburgh, 1998

Reformed Presbyterian Church Of North America, *The Book of Psalms For Singing.* Pittsburgh, 1987

Sharpe, Kevin, *The Personal Rule of Charles I.* Yale University Press, New Haven and London, 1992

The Emerald Tablets of Thoth, various texts

The Holy Bible – old and new testaments, various texts

Wardwell, Joyce, *Healing Herbal Wines, Vinegars, & Syrups.* A Storey County Wisdom Bulletin

Williams, Guy, *The Age of Agony, the Art of Healing.* Academy Chicago Publishers, 1986

Whyte, Henry, *The Celtic Lyre.* Bibliolife, 2009

Online Resources

Contemplator.com/scotland/, *Traditional songs in the public domain, Hush Ye My Bairnie, Maggie Lauder*

Magicspells.in and others, *Invocation of Morrigan.* Origination unknown.

Mamalisa.com, *Traditional English and Scottish nursery rhymes in the public domain*

Rampantscotland.com/songs, *Traditional songs in the public domain, When You and I Were Young, Maggie*

Scots-online.org/reader/trad.htm, *Traditional songs in the public domain, Burnie Bouzle*

The Covenanter 2005, the hymn *'It is well with my Soul'*, written by Horatio Spafford in the 1870's

TrueCovenanter.com, *The Bishop's Doom.* A sermon preached before the General Assembly which sat at Glasgow *anno* 1638, by Mr. Alexander Henderson, Printed by John Gray and Gavin Alston, Edinburgh

Various sources - Traditional and ancient wedding and baptism ceremonies